I0763246

E M Forster Collected Works

By

E M Forster

Cover Photograph: David Talley

ISBN: 978-1-78139-373-4

Contents

A ROOM WITH A VIEW

PART ONE

PART TWO

HOWARDS END

THE LONGEST JOURNEY

PART 1 — CAMBRIDGE

PART 2 — SAWSTON

WHERE ANGELS FEAR TO TREAD

THE CELESTIAL OMNIBUS AND OTHER STORIES

A ROOM WITH A VIEW

PART ONE

Chapter I: The Bertolini

"The Signora had no business to do it," said Miss Bartlett, "no business at all. She promised us south rooms with a view close together, instead of which here are north rooms, looking into a courtyard, and a long way apart. Oh, Lucy!"

"And a Cockney, besides!" said Lucy, who had been further saddened by the Signora's unexpected accent. "It might be London." She looked at the two rows of English people who were sitting at the table; at the row of white bottles of water and red bottles of wine that ran between the English people; at the portraits of the late Queen and the late Poet Laureate that hung behind the English people, heavily framed; at the notice of the English church (Rev. Cuthbert Eager, M. A. Oxon.), that was the only other decoration of the wall. "Charlotte, don't you feel, too, that we might be in London? I can hardly believe that all kinds of other things are just outside. I suppose it is one's being so tired."

"This meat has surely been used for soup," said Miss Bartlett, laying down her fork.

"I want so to see the Arno. The rooms the Signora promised us in her letter would have looked over the Arno. The Signora had no business to do it at all. Oh, it is a shame!"

"Any nook does for me," Miss Bartlett continued; "but it does seem hard that you shouldn't have a view."

Lucy felt that she had been selfish. "Charlotte, you mustn't spoil me: of course, you must look over the Arno, too. I meant that. The first vacant room in the front—" "You must have it," said Miss Bartlett, part of whose travelling expenses were paid by Lucy's mother—a piece of generosity to which she made many a tactful allusion.

"No, no. You must have it."

"I insist on it. Your mother would never forgive me, Lucy."

"She would never forgive me."

The ladies' voices grew animated, and—if the sad truth be owned—a little peevish. They were tired, and under the guise of unselfishness they wrangled. Some of their neighbours interchanged glances, and one of them—one of the ill-bred people whom one does meet abroad—leant forward over the table and actually intruded into their argument. He said:

"I have a view, I have a view."

Miss Bartlett was startled. Generally at a pension people looked them over for a day or two before speaking, and often did not find out that they would "do" till they had gone. She knew that the intruder was ill-bred, even before she glanced at him. He was an old man, of heavy build, with a fair, shaven face and large eyes. There was something childish in those eyes, though it was not the childishness of senility. What exactly it was Miss Bartlett did not stop to consider, for her glance passed on to his clothes. These did not attract her. He was probably trying to become acquainted with them before they got into the swim. So she assumed a dazed expression when he spoke to her, and then said: "A view? Oh, a view! How delightful a view is!"

"This is my son," said the old man; "his name's George. He has a view too."

"Ah," said Miss Bartlett, repressing Lucy, who was about to speak.

"What I mean," he continued, "is that you can have our rooms, and we'll have yours. We'll change."

The better class of tourist was shocked at this, and sympathized with the newcomers. Miss Bartlett, in reply, opened her mouth as little as possible, and said "Thank you very much indeed; that is out of the question."

"Why?" said the old man, with both fists on the table.

"Because it is quite out of the question, thank you."

"You see, we don't like to take—" began Lucy. Her cousin again repressed her.

"But why?" he persisted. "Women like looking at a view; men don't." And he thumped with his fists like a naughty child, and turned to his son, saying, "George, persuade them!"

"It's so obvious they should have the rooms," said the son. "There's nothing else to say."

He did not look at the ladies as he spoke, but his voice was perplexed and sorrowful. Lucy, too, was perplexed; but she saw that they were in for what is known as "quite a scene," and she had an odd feeling that whenever these ill-bred tourists spoke the contest widened and deepened till it dealt, not with rooms and views, but with—well, with something quite different, whose existence she had not realized before. Now the old man attacked Miss Bartlett almost violently: Why should she not change? What possible objection had she? They would clear out in half an hour.

Miss Bartlett, though skilled in the delicacies of conversation, was powerless in the presence of brutality. It was impossible to snub any one so gross. Her face reddened with displeasure. She looked around as much as to say, "Are you all like this?" And two little old ladies, who were sitting further up the table, with shawls hanging over the backs of the chairs, looked back, clearly indicating "We are not; we are genteel."

"Eat your dinner, dear," she said to Lucy, and began to toy again with the meat that she had once censured.

Lucy mumbled that those seemed very odd people opposite.

"Eat your dinner, dear. This pension is a failure. To-morrow we will make a change."

Hardly had she announced this fell decision when she reversed it. The curtains at the end of the room parted, and revealed a clergyman, stout but attractive, who hurried forward to take his place at the table, cheerfully apologizing for his lateness. Lucy, who had not yet acquired decency, at once rose to her feet, exclaiming: "Oh, oh! Why, it's Mr. Beebe! Oh, how perfectly lovely! Oh, Charlotte, we must stop now, however bad the rooms are. Oh!"

Miss Bartlett said, with more restraint:

"How do you do, Mr. Beebe? I expect that you have forgotten us: Miss Bartlett and Miss Honeychurch, who were at Tunbridge Wells when you helped the Vicar of St. Peter's that very cold Easter."

The clergyman, who had the air of one on a holiday, did not remember the ladies quite as clearly as they remembered him. But he came forward pleasantly enough and accepted the chair into which he was beckoned by Lucy.

"I AM so glad to see you," said the girl, who was in a state of spiritual starvation, and would have been glad to see the waiter if her cousin had permitted it. "Just fancy how small the world is. Summer Street, too, makes it so specially funny."

"Miss Honeychurch lives in the parish of Summer Street," said Miss Bartlett, filling up the gap, "and she happened to tell me in the course of conversation that you have just accepted the living—"

"Yes, I heard from mother so last week. She didn't know that I knew you at Tunbridge Wells; but I wrote back at once, and I said: 'Mr. Beebe is—'"

"Quite right," said the clergyman. "I move into the Rectory at Summer Street next June. I am lucky to be appointed to such a charming neighbourhood."

"Oh, how glad I am! The name of our house is Windy Corner." Mr. Beebe bowed.

"There is mother and me generally, and my brother, though it's not often we get him to ch—— The church is rather far off, I mean."

"Lucy, dearest, let Mr. Beebe eat his dinner."

"I am eating it, thank you, and enjoying it."

He preferred to talk to Lucy, whose playing he remembered, rather than to Miss Bartlett, who probably remembered his sermons. He asked the girl whether she knew Florence well, and was informed at some length that she had never been there before. It is delightful to advise a newcomer, and he was first in the field. "Don't neglect the country round," his advice concluded. "The first fine afternoon drive up to Fiesole, and round by Settignano, or something of that sort."

"No!" cried a voice from the top of the table. "Mr. Beebe, you are wrong. The first fine afternoon your ladies must go to Prato."

"That lady looks so clever," whispered Miss Bartlett to her cousin. "We are in luck."

And, indeed, a perfect torrent of information burst on them. People told them what to see, when to see it, how to stop the electric trams, how to get rid of the beggars, how much to give for a vellum blotter, how much the place would grow upon them. The Pension Bertolini had decided, almost enthusiastically, that they would do. Whichever way they looked, kind ladies smiled and shouted at them. And above all rose the voice of the clever lady, crying: "Prato! They must go to Prato. That place is too sweetly squalid for words. I love it; I revel in shaking off the trammels of respectability, as you know."

The young man named George glanced at the clever lady, and then returned moodily to his plate. Obviously he and his father did not do. Lucy, in the midst of her success, found time to wish they did. It gave her no extra pleasure that any one should be left in the cold; and when she rose to go, she turned back and gave the two outsiders a nervous little bow.

The father did not see it; the son acknowledged it, not by another bow, but by raising his eyebrows and smiling; he seemed to be smiling across something.

She hastened after her cousin, who had already disappeared through the curtains—curtains which smote one in the face, and seemed heavy with more than cloth. Beyond them stood the unreliable Signora, bowing good-evening to her guests, and supported by 'Enery, her little boy, and Victorier, her daughter. It made a curious little scene, this attempt of the Cockney to convey the grace and geniality of the South. And even more curious was the drawing-room, which attempted to rival the solid comfort of a Bloomsbury boarding-house. Was this really Italy?

Miss Bartlett was already seated on a tightly stuffed arm-chair, which had the colour and the contours of a tomato. She was talking to Mr. Beebe, and as she spoke, her long narrow head drove backwards and forwards, slowly, regularly, as though she were demolishing some invisible obstacle. "We are most grateful to you," she was saying. "The first evening means so much. When you arrived we were in for a peculiarly mauvais quart d'heure."

He expressed his regret.

"Do you, by any chance, know the name of an old man who sat opposite us at dinner?"

"Emerson."

"Is he a friend of yours?"

"We are friendly—as one is in pensions."

"Then I will say no more."

He pressed her very slightly, and she said more.

"I am, as it were," she concluded, "the chaperon of my young cousin, Lucy, and it would be a serious thing if I put her under an obligation to people of whom we know nothing. His manner was somewhat unfortunate. I hope I acted for the best."

"You acted very naturally," said he. He seemed thoughtful, and after a few moments added: "All the same, I don't think much harm would have come of accepting."

"No harm, of course. But we could not be under an obligation."

"He is rather a peculiar man." Again he hesitated, and then said gently: "I think he would not take advantage of your acceptance, nor expect you to show gratitude. He has the merit—if it is one—of saying exactly what he means. He has rooms he does not value, and he thinks you would value them. He no more thought of putting you under an obligation than he thought of being polite. It is so difficult—at least, I find it difficult—to understand people who speak the truth."

Lucy was pleased, and said: "I was hoping that he was nice; I do so always hope that people will be nice."

"I think he is; nice and tiresome. I differ from him on almost every point of any importance, and so, I expect—I may say I hope—you will differ. But his is a type one disagrees with rather than deplores. When he first came here he not unnaturally put people's backs up. He has no tact and no manners—I don't mean by that that he has bad manners—and he will not keep his opinions to himself. We nearly complained about him to our depressing Signora, but I am glad to say we thought better of it."

"Am I to conclude," said Miss Bartlett, "that he is a Socialist?"

Mr. Beebe accepted the convenient word, not without a slight twitching of the lips.

"And presumably he has brought up his son to be a Socialist, too?"

"I hardly know George, for he hasn't learnt to talk yet. He seems a nice creature, and I think he has brains. Of course, he has all his father's mannerisms, and it is quite possible that he, too, may be a Socialist."

"Oh, you relieve me," said Miss Bartlett. "So you think I ought to have accepted their offer? You feel I have been narrow-minded and suspicious?"

"Not at all," he answered; "I never suggested that."

"But ought I not to apologize, at all events, for my apparent rudeness?"

He replied, with some irritation, that it would be quite unnecessary, and got up from his seat to go to the smoking-room.

"Was I a bore?" said Miss Bartlett, as soon as he had disappeared. "Why didn't you talk, Lucy? He prefers young people, I'm sure. I do hope I haven't monopolized him. I hoped you would have him all the evening, as well as all dinner-time."

"He is nice," exclaimed Lucy. "Just what I remember. He seems to see good in every one. No one would take him for a clergyman."

"My dear Lucia—"

"Well, you know what I mean. And you know how clergymen generally laugh; Mr. Beebe laughs just like an ordinary man."

"Funny girl! How you do remind me of your mother. I wonder if she will approve of Mr. Beebe."

"I'm sure she will; and so will Freddy."

"I think every one at Windy Corner will approve; it is the fashionable world. I am used to Tunbridge Wells, where we are all hopelessly behind the times."

"Yes," said Lucy despondently.

There was a haze of disapproval in the air, but whether the disapproval was of herself, or of Mr. Beebe, or of the fashionable world at Windy Corner, or of the narrow world at Tunbridge Wells, she could not determine. She tried to locate it, but as usual she blundered. Miss Bartlett sedulously denied disapproving of any one, and added "I am afraid you are finding me a very depressing companion."

And the girl again thought: "I must have been selfish or unkind; I must be more careful. It is so dreadful for Charlotte, being poor."

Fortunately one of the little old ladies, who for some time had been smiling very benignly, now approached and asked if she might be allowed to sit where Mr. Beebe had sat. Permission granted, she began to chatter gently about Italy, the plunge it had been to come there, the gratifying success of the plunge, the improvement in her sister's health, the necessity of closing the bed-room windows at night, and of thoroughly emptying the water-bottles in the morning. She handled her subjects agreeably, and they were, perhaps, more worthy of attention than the high discourse upon Guelfs and Ghibellines which was proceeding tempestuously at the other end of the room. It was a real catastrophe, not a mere episode, that evening of hers at Venice, when she had found in her bedroom something that is one worse than a flea, though one better than something else.

"But here you are as safe as in England. Signora Bertolini is so English."

"Yet our rooms smell," said poor Lucy. "We dread going to bed."

"Ah, then you look into the court." She sighed. "If only Mr. Emerson was more tactful! We were so sorry for you at dinner."

"I think he was meaning to be kind."

"Undoubtedly he was," said Miss Bartlett.

"Mr. Beebe has just been scolding me for my suspicious nature. Of course, I was holding back on my cousin's account."

"Of course," said the little old lady; and they murmured that one could not be too careful with a young girl.

Lucy tried to look demure, but could not help feeling a great fool. No one was careful with her at home; or, at all events, she had not noticed it.

"About old Mr. Emerson—I hardly know. No, he is not tactful; yet, have you ever noticed that there are people who do things which are most indelicate, and yet at the same time—beautiful?"

"Beautiful?" said Miss Bartlett, puzzled at the word. "Are not beauty and delicacy the same?"

"So one would have thought," said the other helplessly. "But things are so difficult, I sometimes think."

She proceeded no further into things, for Mr. Beebe reappeared, looking extremely pleasant.

"Miss Bartlett," he cried, "it's all right about the rooms. I'm so glad. Mr. Emerson was talking about it in the smoking-room, and knowing what I did, I encouraged him to make the offer again. He has let me come and ask you. He would be so pleased."

"Oh, Charlotte," cried Lucy to her cousin, "we must have the rooms now. The old man is just as nice and kind as he can be."

Miss Bartlett was silent.

"I fear," said Mr. Beebe, after a pause, "that I have been officious. I must apologize for my interference."

Gravely displeased, he turned to go. Not till then did Miss Bartlett reply: "My own wishes, dearest Lucy, are unimportant in comparison with yours. It would be hard indeed if I stopped you doing as you liked at Florence, when I am only here through your kindness. If you wish me to turn these gentlemen out of their rooms, I will do it. Would you then, Mr. Beebe, kindly tell Mr. Emerson that I accept his kind offer, and then conduct him to me, in order that I may thank him personally?"

She raised her voice as she spoke; it was heard all over the drawing-room, and silenced the Guelfs and the Ghibellines. The clergyman, inwardly cursing the female sex, bowed, and departed with her message.

"Remember, Lucy, I alone am implicated in this. I do not wish the acceptance to come from you. Grant me that, at all events."

Mr. Beebe was back, saying rather nervously:

"Mr. Emerson is engaged, but here is his son instead."

The young man gazed down on the three ladies, who felt seated on the floor, so low were their chairs.

"My father," he said, "is in his bath, so you cannot thank him personally. But any message given by you to me will be given by me to him as soon as he comes out."

Miss Bartlett was unequal to the bath. All her barbed civilities came forth wrong end first. Young Mr. Emerson scored a notable triumph to the delight of Mr. Beebe and to the secret delight of Lucy.

"Poor young man!" said Miss Bartlett, as soon as he had gone.

"How angry he is with his father about the rooms! It is all he can do to keep polite."

"In half an hour or so your rooms will be ready," said Mr. Beebe. Then looking rather thoughtfully at the two cousins, he retired to his own rooms, to write up his philosophic diary.

"Oh, dear!" breathed the little old lady, and shuddered as if all the winds of heaven had entered the apartment. "Gentlemen sometimes do not realize—" Her voice faded away, but Miss Bartlett seemed to understand and a conversation developed, in which gentlemen who did not thoroughly realize played a principal part. Lucy, not realizing either, was reduced to literature. Taking up Baedeker's Handbook to Northern Italy, she committed to memory the most important dates of Florentine History. For she was determined to enjoy herself on the morrow. Thus the half-hour crept profitably away, and at last Miss Bartlett rose with a sigh, and said:

"I think one might venture now. No, Lucy, do not stir. I will superintend the move."

"How you do do everything," said Lucy.

"Naturally, dear. It is my affair."

"But I would like to help you."

"No, dear."

Charlotte's energy! And her unselfishness! She had been thus all her life, but really, on this Italian tour, she was surpassing herself. So Lucy felt, or strove to feel. And yet—there was a rebellious spirit in her which wondered whether the acceptance might not have been less delicate and more beautiful. At all events, she entered her own room without any feeling of joy.

"I want to explain," said Miss Bartlett, "why it is that I have taken the largest room. Naturally, of course, I should have given it to you; but I happen to know that it belongs to the young man, and I was sure your mother would not like it."

Lucy was bewildered.

"If you are to accept a favour it is more suitable you should be under an obligation to his father than to him. I am a woman of the world, in my small way, and I know where things lead to. However, Mr. Beebe is a guarantee of a sort that they will not presume on this."

"Mother wouldn't mind I'm sure," said Lucy, but again had the sense of larger and unsuspected issues.

Miss Bartlett only sighed, and enveloped her in a protecting embrace as she wished her good-night. It gave Lucy the sensation of a fog, and when she reached her own room she opened the window and breathed the clean night air, thinking of the kind old man who had enabled her to see the lights dancing in the Arno and the cypresses of San Miniato, and the foot-hills of the Apennines, black against the rising moon.

Miss Bartlett, in her room, fastened the window-shutters and locked the door, and then made a tour of the apartment to see where the cupboards led, and whether there were any oubliettes or secret entrances. It was then that she saw, pinned up over the washstand, a sheet of paper on which was scrawled an enormous note of interrogation. Nothing more.

"What does it mean?" she thought, and she examined it carefully by the light of a candle. Meaningless at first, it gradually became menacing, obnoxious, portentous with evil. She was seized with an impulse to destroy it, but fortunately remembered that she had no right to do so, since it must be the property of young Mr. Emerson. So she unpinned it carefully, and put it between two pieces of blotting-paper to keep it clean for him. Then she completed her inspection of the room, sighed heavily according to her habit, and went to bed.

Chapter II: In Santa Croce with No Baedeker

It was pleasant to wake up in Florence, to open the eyes upon a bright bare room, with a floor of red tiles which look clean though they are not; with a painted ceiling whereon pink griffins and blue amorini sport in a forest of yellow violins and bassoons. It was pleasant, too, to fling wide the windows, pinching the fingers in unfamiliar fastenings, to lean out into sunshine with beautiful hills and trees and marble churches opposite, and close below, the Arno, gurgling against the embankment of the road.

Over the river men were at work with spades and sieves on the sandy foreshore, and on the river was a boat, also diligently employed for some mysterious end. An electric tram came rushing underneath the window. No one was inside it, except one tourist; but its platforms were overflowing with Italians, who preferred to stand. Children tried to hang on behind, and the conductor, with no malice, spat in their faces to make them let go. Then soldiers appeared—good-looking, undersized men—wearing each a knapsack covered with mangy fur, and a great-coat which had been cut for some larger soldier. Beside them walked officers, looking foolish and fierce, and before them went little boys, turning somersaults in time with the band. The tramcar became entangled in their ranks, and moved on painfully, like a caterpillar in a swarm of ants. One of the little boys fell down, and some white bullocks came out of an archway. Indeed, if it had not been for the good advice of an old man who was selling button-hooks, the road might never have got clear.

Over such trivialities as these many a valuable hour may slip away, and the traveller who has gone to Italy to study the tactile values of Giotto, or the corruption of the Papacy, may return remembering nothing but the blue sky and the men and women who live under it. So it was as well that Miss Bartlett should tap and come in, and having commented on Lucy's leaving the door unlocked, and on her leaning out of the window before she was fully dressed, should urge her to hasten herself, or the best of the day would be gone. By the time Lucy was ready her cousin had done her breakfast, and was listening to the clever lady among the crumbs.

A conversation then ensued, on not unfamiliar lines. Miss Bartlett was, after all, a wee bit tired, and thought they had better spend the morning settling in; unless Lucy would at all like to go out? Lucy would rather like to go out, as it was her first day in Florence, but, of course, she could go alone. Miss Bartlett could not allow this. Of course she would accompany Lucy everywhere. Oh, certainly not; Lucy would stop with her cousin. Oh, no! that would never do. Oh, yes!

At this point the clever lady broke in.

"If it is Mrs. Grundy who is troubling you, I do assure you that you can neglect the good person. Being English, Miss Honeychurch will be perfectly safe. Italians understand. A dear friend of mine, Contessa Baroncelli, has two daughters, and when she cannot send a maid to school with them, she lets them go in sailor-hats instead. Every one takes them for English, you see, especially if their hair is strained tightly behind."

Miss Bartlett was unconvinced by the safety of Contessa Baroncelli's daughters. She was determined to take Lucy herself, her head not being so very bad. The clever lady then said that she was going to spend a long morning in Santa Croce, and if Lucy would come too, she would be delighted.

"I will take you by a dear dirty back way, Miss Honeychurch, and if you bring me luck, we shall have an adventure."

Lucy said that this was most kind, and at once opened the Baedeker, to see where Santa Croce was.

"Tut, tut! Miss Lucy! I hope we shall soon emancipate you from Baedeker. He does but touch the surface of things. As to the true Italy—he does not even dream of it. The true Italy is only to be found by patient observation."

This sounded very interesting, and Lucy hurried over her breakfast, and started with her new friend in high spirits. Italy was coming at last. The Cockney Signora and her works had vanished like a bad dream.

Miss Lavish—for that was the clever lady's name—turned to the right along the sunny Lung' Arno. How delightfully warm! But a wind down the side streets cut like a knife, didn't it? Ponte alle Grazie—particularly interesting, mentioned by Dante. San Miniato—beautiful as well as interesting; the crucifix that kissed a murderer—Miss Honeychurch would remember the story. The men on the river were fishing. (Untrue; but then, so is most information.) Then Miss Lavish darted under the archway of the white bullocks, and she stopped, and she cried:

"A smell! a true Florentine smell! Every city, let me teach you, has its own smell."

"Is it a very nice smell?" said Lucy, who had inherited from her mother a distaste to dirt.

"One doesn't come to Italy for niceness," was the retort; "one comes for life. Buon giorno! Buon giorno!" bowing right and left. "Look at that adorable winecart! How the driver stares at us, dear, simple soul!"

So Miss Lavish proceeded through the streets of the city of Florence, short, fidgety, and playful as a kitten, though without a kitten's grace. It was a treat for the girl to be with any one so clever and so cheerful; and a blue military cloak, such as an Italian officer wears, only increased the sense of festivity.

"Buon giorno! Take the word of an old woman, Miss Lucy: you will never repent of a little civility to your inferiors. That is the true democracy. Though I am a real Radical as well. There, now you're shocked."

"Indeed, I'm not!" exclaimed Lucy. "We are Radicals, too, out and out. My father always voted for Mr. Gladstone, until he was so dreadful about Ireland."

"I see, I see. And now you have gone over to the enemy."

"Oh, please—! If my father was alive, I am sure he would vote Radical again now that Ireland is all right. And as it is, the glass over our front door was broken last election, and Freddy is sure it was the Tories; but mother says nonsense, a tramp."

"Shameful! A manufacturing district, I suppose?"

"No—in the Surrey hills. About five miles from Dorking, looking over the Weald."

Miss Lavish seemed interested, and slackened her trot.

"What a delightful part; I know it so well. It is full of the very nicest people. Do you know Sir Harry Otway—a Radical if ever there was?"

"Very well indeed."

"And old Mrs. Butterworth the philanthropist?" "Why, she rents a field of us! How funny!"

Miss Lavish looked at the narrow ribbon of sky, and murmured: "Oh, you have property in Surrey?"

"Hardly any," said Lucy, fearful of being thought a snob. "Only thirty acres—just the garden, all downhill, and some fields."

Miss Lavish was not disgusted, and said it was just the size of her aunt's Suffolk estate. Italy receded. They tried to remember the last name of Lady Louisa some one, who had taken a house near Summer Street the other year, but she had not liked it, which was odd of her. And just as Miss Lavish had got the name, she broke off and exclaimed:

"Bless us! Bless us and save us! We've lost the way."

Certainly they had seemed a long time in reaching Santa Croce, the tower of which had been plainly visible from the landing window. But Miss Lavish had said so much about knowing her Florence by heart, that Lucy had followed her with no misgivings.

"Lost! lost! My dear Miss Lucy, during our political diatribes we have taken a wrong turning. How those horrid Conservatives would jeer at us! What are we to do? Two lone females in an unknown town. Now, this is what I call an adventure."

Lucy, who wanted to see Santa Croce, suggested, as a possible solution, that they should ask the way there.

"Oh, but that is the word of a craven! And no, you are not, not, NOT to look at your Baedeker. Give it to me; I shan't let you carry it. We will simply drift."

Accordingly they drifted through a series of those grey-brown streets, neither commodious nor picturesque, in which the eastern quarter of the city abounds. Lucy soon lost interest in the discontent of Lady Louisa, and became discontented herself. For one ravishing moment Italy appeared. She stood in the Square of the Annunziata and saw in the living terra-cotta those divine babies whom no cheap reproduction can ever stale. There they stood, with their shining limbs bursting from the garments of charity, and their strong white arms extended against circlets of heaven. Lucy thought she had never seen anything more beautiful; but Miss Lavish, with a shriek of dismay, dragged her forward, declaring that they were out of their path now by at least a mile.

The hour was approaching at which the continental breakfast begins, or rather ceases, to tell, and the ladies bought some hot chestnut paste out of a little shop, because it looked so typical. It tasted partly of the paper in which it was wrapped, partly of hair oil, partly of the great unknown. But it gave them strength to drift into another Piazza, large and dusty, on the farther side of which rose a black-and-white facade of surpassing ugliness. Miss Lavish spoke to it dramatically. It was Santa Croce. The adventure was over.

"Stop a minute; let those two people go on, or I shall have to speak to them. I do detest conventional intercourse. Nasty! they are going into the church, too. Oh, the Britisher abroad!"

"We sat opposite them at dinner last night. They have given us their rooms. They were so very kind."

"Look at their figures!" laughed Miss Lavish. "They walk through my Italy like a pair of cows. It's very naughty of me, but I would like to set an examination paper at Dover, and turn back every tourist who couldn't pass it."

"What would you ask us?"

Miss Lavish laid her hand pleasantly on Lucy's arm, as if to suggest that she, at all events, would get full marks. In this exalted mood they reached the steps of the great church, and were about to enter it when Miss Lavish stopped, squeaked, flung up her arms, and cried:

"There goes my local-colour box! I must have a word with him!"

And in a moment she was away over the Piazza, her military cloak flapping in the wind; nor did she slacken speed till she caught up an old man with white whiskers, and nipped him playfully upon the arm.

Lucy waited for nearly ten minutes. Then she began to get tired. The beggars worried her, the dust blew in her eyes, and she remembered that a young girl ought not to loiter in public places. She descended slowly into the Piazza with the intention of rejoining Miss Lavish, who was really almost too original. But at that moment Miss Lavish and her local-colour box moved also, and disappeared down a side street, both gesticulating largely. Tears of indignation came to Lucy's eyes partly because Miss Lavish had jilted her, partly because she had taken her Baedeker. How could she find her way home? How could she find her way about in Santa Croce? Her first morning was ruined, and she might never be in Florence again. A few minutes ago she had been all high spirits, talking as a woman of culture, and half persuading herself that she was full of originality. Now she entered the church depressed and humiliated, not even able to remember whether it was built by the Franciscans or the Dominicans. Of course, it must be a wonderful building. But how like a barn! And how very cold! Of course, it contained frescoes by Giotto, in the presence of whose tactile values she was capable of feeling what was proper. But who was to tell her which they were? She walked about disdainfully, unwilling to be enthusiastic over monuments of uncertain authorship or date. There was no one even to tell her which, of all the sepulchral slabs that paved the nave and transepts, was the one that was really beautiful, the one that had been most praised by Mr. Ruskin.

Then the pernicious charm of Italy worked on her, and, instead of acquiring information, she began to be happy. She puzzled out the Italian notices—the notices that forbade people to introduce dogs into the church—the notice that prayed people, in the interest of health and out of respect to the sacred edifice in which they found themselves, not to spit. She watched the tourists; their noses were as red as their Baedekers, so cold was Santa Croce. She beheld the horrible fate that overtook three Papists—two he-babies and a she-baby—who began their career by sousing each other with the Holy Water, and then proceeded to the Machiavelli memorial, dripping but hallowed. Advancing towards it very slowly and from immense distances, they touched the stone with their fingers, with their handkerchiefs, with their heads, and then retreated. What could this mean? They did it again and again. Then Lucy realized that they had mistaken Machiavelli for some saint, hoping to acquire virtue. Punishment followed quickly. The smallest he-baby stumbled over one of the sepulchral slabs so much admired by Mr. Ruskin, and entangled his feet in the features of a recumbent bishop. Protestant as she was, Lucy darted forward. She was too late. He fell heavily upon the prelate's up-turned toes.

"Hateful bishop!" exclaimed the voice of old Mr. Emerson, who had darted forward also. "Hard in life, hard in death. Go out into the sunshine, little boy, and kiss your hand to the sun, for that is where you ought to be. Intolerable bishop!"

The child screamed frantically at these words, and at these dreadful people who picked him up, dusted him, rubbed his bruises, and told him not to be superstitious.

"Look at him!" said Mr. Emerson to Lucy. "Here's a mess: a baby hurt, cold, and frightened! But what else can you expect from a church?"

The child's legs had become as melting wax. Each time that old Mr. Emerson and Lucy set it erect it collapsed with a roar. Fortunately an Italian lady, who ought to have been saying her prayers, came to the rescue. By some mysterious virtue, which mothers alone possess, she stiffened the little boy's back-bone and imparted strength to his knees. He stood. Still gibbering with agitation, he walked away.

"You are a clever woman," said Mr. Emerson. "You have done more than all the relics in the world. I am not of your creed, but I do believe in those who make their fellow-creatures happy. There is no scheme of the universe—"

He paused for a phrase.

"Niente," said the Italian lady, and returned to her prayers.

"I'm not sure she understands English," suggested Lucy.

In her chastened mood she no longer despised the Emersons. She was determined to be gracious to them, beautiful rather than delicate, and, if possible, to erase Miss Bartlett's civility by some gracious reference to the pleasant rooms.

"That woman understands everything," was Mr. Emerson's reply. "But what are you doing here? Are you doing the church? Are you through with the church?"

"No," cried Lucy, remembering her grievance. "I came here with Miss Lavish, who was to explain everything; and just by the door—it is too bad!—she simply ran away, and after waiting quite a time, I had to come in by myself."

"Why shouldn't you?" said Mr. Emerson.

"Yes, why shouldn't you come by yourself?" said the son, addressing the young lady for the first time.

"But Miss Lavish has even taken away Baedeker."

"Baedeker?" said Mr. Emerson. "I'm glad it's THAT you minded. It's worth minding, the loss of a Baedeker. THAT'S worth minding."

Lucy was puzzled. She was again conscious of some new idea, and was not sure whither it would lead her.

"If you've no Baedeker," said the son, "you'd better join us." Was this where the idea would lead? She took refuge in her dignity.

"Thank you very much, but I could not think of that. I hope you do not suppose that I came to join on to you. I really came to help with the child, and to thank you for so kindly giving us your rooms last night. I hope that you have not been put to any great inconvenience."

"My dear," said the old man gently, "I think that you are repeating what you have heard older people say. You are pretending to be touchy; but you are not really. Stop being so tiresome, and tell me instead what part of the church you want to see. To take you to it will be a real pleasure."

Now, this was abominably impertinent, and she ought to have been furious. But it is sometimes as difficult to lose one's temper as it is difficult at other times to keep it. Lucy could not get cross. Mr. Emerson was an old man, and surely a girl might humour him. On the other hand, his son was a young man, and she felt that a girl ought to be offended with him, or at all events be offended before him. It was at him that she gazed before replying.

"I am not touchy, I hope. It is the Giottos that I want to see, if you will kindly tell me which they are."

The son nodded. With a look of sombre satisfaction, he led the way to the Peruzzi Chapel. There was a hint of the teacher about him. She felt like a child in school who had answered a question rightly.

The chapel was already filled with an earnest congregation, and out of them rose the voice of a lecturer, directing them how to worship Giotto, not by tactful valuations, but by the standards of the spirit.

"Remember," he was saying, "the facts about this church of Santa Croce; how it was built by faith in the full fervour of medievalism, before any taint of the Renaissance had appeared. Observe how Giotto in these frescoes—now, unhappily, ruined by restoration—is untroubled by the snares of anatomy and perspective. Could anything be more majestic, more pathetic, beautiful, true? How little, we feel, avails knowledge and technical cleverness against a man who truly feels!"

"No!" exclaimed Mr. Emerson, in much too loud a voice for church. "Remember nothing of the sort! Built by faith indeed! That simply means the workmen weren't paid properly. And as for the frescoes, I see no truth in them. Look at that fat man in blue! He must weigh as much as I do, and he is shooting into the sky like an air balloon."

He was referring to the fresco of the "Ascension of St. John." Inside, the lecturer's voice faltered, as well it might. The audience shifted uneasily, and so did Lucy. She was sure that she ought not to be with these men; but they had cast a spell over her. They were so serious and so strange that she could not remember how to behave.

"Now, did this happen, or didn't it? Yes or no?"

George replied:

"It happened like this, if it happened at all. I would rather go up to heaven by myself than be pushed by cherubs; and if I got there I should like my friends to lean out of it, just as they do here."

"You will never go up," said his father. "You and I, dear boy, will lie at peace in the earth that bore us, and our names will disappear as surely as our work survives."

"Some of the people can only see the empty grave, not the saint, whoever he is, going up. It did happen like that, if it happened at all."

"Pardon me," said a frigid voice. "The chapel is somewhat small for two parties. We will incommode you no longer."

The lecturer was a clergyman, and his audience must be also his flock, for they held prayer-books as well as guide-books in their hands. They filed out of the chapel in silence. Amongst them were the two little old ladies of the Pension Bertolini—Miss Teresa and Miss Catherine Alan.

"Stop!" cried Mr. Emerson. "There's plenty of room for us all. Stop!"

The procession disappeared without a word.

Soon the lecturer could be heard in the next chapel, describing the life of St. Francis.

"George, I do believe that clergyman is the Brixton curate."

George went into the next chapel and returned, saying "Perhaps he is. I don't remember."

"Then I had better speak to him and remind him who I am. It's that Mr. Eager. Why did he go? Did we talk too loud? How vexatious. I shall go and say we are sorry. Hadn't I better? Then perhaps he will come back."

"He will not come back," said George.

But Mr. Emerson, contrite and unhappy, hurried away to apologize to the Rev. Cuthbert Eager. Lucy, apparently absorbed in a lunette, could hear the lecture again interrupted, the anxious, aggressive voice of the old man, the curt, injured replies of his opponent. The son, who took every little contretemps as if it were a tragedy, was listening also.

"My father has that effect on nearly every one," he informed her. "He will try to be kind."

"I hope we all try," said she, smiling nervously.

"Because we think it improves our characters. But he is kind to people because he loves them; and they find him out, and are offended, or frightened."

"How silly of them!" said Lucy, though in her heart she sympathized; "I think that a kind action done tactfully—"

"Tact!"

He threw up his head in disdain. Apparently she had given the wrong answer. She watched the singular creature pace up and down the chapel. For a young man his face was rugged, and—until the shadows fell upon it—hard. Enshadowed, it sprang into tenderness. She saw him once again at Rome, on the ceiling of the Sistine Chapel, carrying a burden of acorns. Healthy and muscular, he yet gave her the feeling of greyness, of tragedy that might only find solution in the night. The feeling soon passed; it was unlike her to have entertained anything so subtle. Born of silence and of unknown emotion, it passed when Mr. Emerson returned, and she could re-enter the world of rapid talk, which was alone familiar to her.

"Were you snubbed?" asked his son tranquilly.

"But we have spoilt the pleasure of I don't know how many people. They won't come back."

"...full of innate sympathy...quickness to perceive good in others...vision of the brotherhood of man..." Scraps of the lecture on St. Francis came floating round the partition wall.

"Don't let us spoil yours," he continued to Lucy. "Have you looked at those saints?"

"Yes," said Lucy. "They are lovely. Do you know which is the tombstone that is praised in Ruskin?"

He did not know, and suggested that they should try to guess it. George, rather to her relief, refused to move, and she and the old man wandered not unpleasantly about Santa Croce, which, though it is like a barn, has harvested many beautiful things inside its walls. There were also beggars to avoid and guides to dodge round the pillars, and an old lady with her dog, and here and there a priest modestly edging to his Mass through the groups of tourists. But Mr. Emerson was only half interested. He watched the lecturer, whose success he believed he had impaired, and then he anxiously watched his son.

"Why will he look at that fresco?" he said uneasily. "I saw nothing in it."

"I like Giotto," she replied. "It is so wonderful what they say about his tactile values. Though I like things like the Della Robbia babies better."

"So you ought. A baby is worth a dozen saints. And my baby's worth the whole of Paradise, and as far as I can see he lives in Hell."

Lucy again felt that this did not do.

"In Hell," he repeated. "He's unhappy."

"Oh, dear!" said Lucy.

"How can he be unhappy when he is strong and alive? What more is one to give him? And think how he has been brought up—free from all the superstition and ignorance that lead men to hate one another in the name of God. With such an education as that, I thought he was bound to grow up happy."

She was no theologian, but she felt that here was a very foolish old man, as well as a very irreligious one. She also felt that her mother might not like her talking to that kind of person, and that Charlotte would object most strongly.

"What are we to do with him?" he asked. "He comes out for his holiday to Italy, and behaves—like that; like the little child who ought to have been playing, and who hurt himself upon the tombstone. Eh? What did you say?"

Lucy had made no suggestion. Suddenly he said:

"Now don't be stupid over this. I don't require you to fall in love with my boy, but I do think you might try and understand him. You are nearer his age, and if you let yourself go I am sure you are sensible. You might help me. He has known so few women, and you have the time. You stop here several weeks, I suppose? But let yourself go. You are inclined to get muddled, if I may judge from last night. Let yourself go. Pull out from the depths those thoughts that you do not understand, and spread them out in the sunlight and know the meaning of them. By understanding George you may learn to understand yourself. It will be good for both of you."

To this extraordinary speech Lucy found no answer.

"I only know what it is that's wrong with him; not why it is."

"And what is it?" asked Lucy fearfully, expecting some harrowing tale.

"The old trouble; things won't fit."

"What things?"

"The things of the universe. It is quite true. They don't."

"Oh, Mr. Emerson, whatever do you mean?"

In his ordinary voice, so that she scarcely realized he was quoting poetry, he said:

"'From far, from eve and morning,
And yon twelve-winded sky,
The stuff of life to knit me
Blew hither: here am I'

George and I both know this, but why does it distress him? We know that we come from the winds, and that we shall return to them; that all life is perhaps a knot, a tangle, a blemish in the eternal smoothness. But why should this make us unhappy? Let us rather love one another, and work and rejoice. I don't believe in this world sorrow."

Miss Honeychurch assented.

"Then make my boy think like us. Make him realize that by the side of the everlasting Why there is a Yes—a transitory Yes if you like, but a Yes."

Suddenly she laughed; surely one ought to laugh. A young man melancholy because the universe wouldn't fit, because life was a tangle or a wind, or a Yes, or something!

"I'm very sorry," she cried. "You'll think me unfeeling, but—but—" Then she became matronly. "Oh, but your son wants employment. Has he no particular hobby? Why, I myself have worries, but I can generally forget them at the piano; and collecting stamps did no end of good for my brother. Perhaps Italy bores him; you ought to try the Alps or the Lakes."

The old man's face saddened, and he touched her gently with his hand. This did not alarm her; she thought that her advice had impressed him and that he was thanking her for it. Indeed, he no longer alarmed her at all; she regarded him as a kind thing, but quite silly. Her feelings were as inflated spiritually as they had been an hour ago esthetically, before she lost Baedeker. The dear George, now striding towards them over the tombstones, seemed both pitiable and absurd. He approached, his face in the shadow. He said:

"Miss Bartlett."

"Oh, good gracious me!" said Lucy, suddenly collapsing and again seeing the whole of life in a new perspective. "Where? Where?"

"In the nave."

"I see. Those gossiping little Miss Alans must have—" She checked herself.

"Poor girl!" exploded Mr. Emerson. "Poor girl!"

She could not let this pass, for it was just what she was feeling herself.

"Poor girl? I fail to understand the point of that remark. I think myself a very fortunate girl, I assure you. I'm thoroughly happy, and having a splendid time. Pray don't waste time mourning over me. There's enough sorrow in the world, isn't there, without trying to invent it. Good-bye. Thank you both so much for all your kindness. Ah, yes! there does come my cousin. A delightful morning! Santa Croce is a wonderful church."

She joined her cousin.

Chapter III: Music, Violets, and the Letter "S"

It so happened that Lucy, who found daily life rather chaotic, entered a more solid world when she opened the piano. She was then no longer either deferential or patronizing; no longer either a rebel or a slave. The kingdom of music is not the kingdom of this world; it will accept those whom breeding and intellect and culture have alike rejected. The commonplace person begins to play, and shoots into the empyrean without effort, whilst we look up, marvelling how he has escaped us, and thinking how we could worship him and love him, would he but translate his visions into human words, and his experiences into human actions. Perhaps he cannot; certainly he does not, or does so very seldom. Lucy had done so never.

She was no dazzling executante; her runs were not at all like strings of pearls, and she struck no more right notes than was suitable for one of her age and situation. Nor was she the passionate young lady, who performs so tragically on a summer's evening with the window open. Passion was there, but it could not be easily labelled; it slipped between love and hatred and jealousy, and all the furniture of the pictorial style. And she was tragical only in the sense that she was great, for she loved to play on the side of Victory. Victory of what and over what—that is more than the words of daily life can tell us. But that some sonatas of Beethoven are written tragic no one can gainsay; yet they can triumph or despair as the player decides, and Lucy had decided that they should triumph.

A very wet afternoon at the Bertolini permitted her to do the thing she really liked, and after lunch she opened the little draped piano. A few people lingered round and praised her playing, but finding that she made no reply, dispersed to their rooms to write up their diaries or to sleep. She took no notice of Mr. Emerson looking for his son, nor of Miss Bartlett looking for Miss Lavish, nor of Miss Lavish looking for her cigarette-case. Like every true performer, she was intoxicated by the mere feel of the notes: they were fingers caressing her own; and by touch, not by sound alone, did she come to her desire.

Mr. Beebe, sitting unnoticed in the window, pondered this illogical element in Miss Honeychurch, and recalled the occasion at Tunbridge Wells when he had discovered it. It was at one of those entertainments where the upper classes entertain the lower. The seats were filled with a respectful audience, and the ladies and gentlemen of the parish, under the auspices of their vicar, sang, or recited, or imitated the drawing of a champagne cork. Among the promised items was "Miss Honeychurch. Piano. Beethoven," and Mr. Beebe was wondering whether it would be Adelaida, or the march of The Ruins of Athens, when his composure was disturbed by the opening bars of Opus III. He was in suspense all through the introduction, for not until the pace quickens does one know what the performer intends. With the roar of the opening theme he knew that things were going extraordinarily; in the chords that herald the conclusion he heard the hammer strokes of victory. He was glad that she only played the first movement, for he could have paid no attention to the winding intricacies of the measures of nine-sixteen. The audience clapped, no less respectful. It was Mr. Beebe who started the stamping; it was all that one could do.

"Who is she?" he asked the vicar afterwards.

"Cousin of one of my parishioners. I do not consider her choice of a piece happy. Beethoven is so usually simple and direct in his appeal that it is sheer perversity to choose a thing like that, which, if anything, disturbs."

"Introduce me."

"She will be delighted. She and Miss Bartlett are full of the praises of your sermon."

"My sermon?" cried Mr. Beebe. "Why ever did she listen to it?"

When he was introduced he understood why, for Miss Honeychurch, disjoined from her music stool, was only a young lady with a quantity of dark hair and a very pretty, pale, undeveloped face. She loved going to concerts, she loved stopping with her cousin, she loved iced coffee and meringues. He did not doubt that she loved his sermon also. But before he left Tunbridge Wells he made a remark to the vicar, which he now made to Lucy herself when she closed the little piano and moved dreamily towards him:

"If Miss Honeychurch ever takes to live as she plays, it will be very exciting both for us and for her."

Lucy at once re-entered daily life.

"Oh, what a funny thing! Some one said just the same to mother, and she said she trusted I should never live a duet."

"Doesn't Mrs. Honeychurch like music?"

"She doesn't mind it. But she doesn't like one to get excited over anything; she thinks I am silly about it. She thinks—I can't make out. Once, you know, I said that I liked my own playing better than any one's. She has never got over it. Of course, I didn't mean that I played well; I only meant—"

"Of course," said he, wondering why she bothered to explain.

"Music—" said Lucy, as if attempting some generality. She could not complete it, and looked out absently upon Italy in the wet. The whole life of the South was disorganized, and the most graceful nation in Europe had turned into formless lumps of clothes.

The street and the river were dirty yellow, the bridge was dirty grey, and the hills were dirty purple. Somewhere in their folds were concealed Miss Lavish and Miss Bartlett, who had chosen this afternoon to visit the Torre del Gallo.

"What about music?" said Mr. Beebe.

"Poor Charlotte will be sopped," was Lucy's reply.

The expedition was typical of Miss Bartlett, who would return cold, tired, hungry, and angelic, with a ruined skirt, a pulpy Baedeker, and a tickling cough in her throat. On another day, when the whole world was singing and the air ran into the mouth, like wine, she would refuse to stir from the drawing-room, saying that she was an old thing, and no fit companion for a hearty girl.

"Miss Lavish has led your cousin astray. She hopes to find the true Italy in the wet I believe."

"Miss Lavish is so original," murmured Lucy. This was a stock remark, the supreme achievement of the Pension Bertolini in the way of definition. Miss Lavish was so original. Mr. Beebe had his doubts, but they would have been put down to clerical narrowness. For that, and for other reasons, he held his peace.

"Is it true," continued Lucy in awe-struck tone, "that Miss Lavish is writing a book?"

"They do say so."

"What is it about?"

"It will be a novel," replied Mr. Beebe, "dealing with modern Italy. Let me refer you for an account to Miss Catharine Alan, who uses words herself more admirably than any one I know."

"I wish Miss Lavish would tell me herself. We started such friends. But I don't think she ought to have run away with Baedeker that morning in Santa Croce. Charlotte was most annoyed at finding me practically alone, and so I couldn't help being a little annoyed with Miss Lavish."

"The two ladies, at all events, have made it up."

He was interested in the sudden friendship between women so apparently dissimilar as Miss Bartlett and Miss Lavish. They were always in each other's company, with Lucy a slighted third. Miss Lavish he believed he understood, but Miss Bartlett might reveal unknown depths of strangeness, though not perhaps, of meaning. Was Italy deflecting her from the path of prim chaperon, which he had assigned to her at Tunbridge Wells? All his life he had loved to study maiden ladies; they were his specialty, and his profession had provided him with ample opportunities for the work. Girls like Lucy were charming to look at, but Mr. Beebe was, from rather profound reasons, somewhat chilly in his attitude towards the other sex, and preferred to be interested rather than enthralled.

Lucy, for the third time, said that poor Charlotte would be sopped. The Arno was rising in flood, washing away the traces of the little carts upon the foreshore. But in the south-west there had appeared a dull haze of yellow, which might mean better weather if it did not mean worse. She opened the window to inspect, and a cold blast entered the room, drawing a plaintive cry from Miss Catharine Alan, who entered at the same moment by the door.

"Oh, dear Miss Honeychurch, you will catch a chill! And Mr. Beebe here besides. Who would suppose this is Italy? There is my sister actually nursing the hot-water can; no comforts or proper provisions."

She sidled towards them and sat down, self-conscious as she always was on entering a room which contained one man, or a man and one woman.

"I could hear your beautiful playing, Miss Honeychurch, though I was in my room with the door shut. Doors shut; indeed, most necessary. No one has the least idea of privacy in this country. And one person catches it from another."

Lucy answered suitably. Mr. Beebe was not able to tell the ladies of his adventure at Modena, where the chambermaid burst in upon him in his bath, exclaiming cheerfully, "Fa niente, sono vecchia." He contented himself with saying: "I quite agree with you, Miss Alan. The Italians are a most unpleasant people. They pry everywhere, they see everything, and they know what we want before we know it ourselves. We are at their mercy. They read our thoughts, they foretell our desires. From the cab-driver down to—to Giotto, they turn us inside out, and I resent it. Yet in their heart of hearts they are—how superficial! They have no conception of the intellectual life. How right is Signora Bertolini, who exclaimed to me the other day: 'Ho, Mr. Beebe, if you knew what I suffer over the children's edjucaishion. HI won't 'ave my little Victorier taught by a hignorant Italian what can't explain nothink!'"

Miss Alan did not follow, but gathered that she was being mocked in an agreeable way. Her sister was a little disappointed in Mr. Beebe, having expected better things from a clergyman whose head was bald and who wore a pair of russet whiskers. Indeed, who would have supposed that tolerance, sympathy, and a sense of humour would inhabit that militant form?

In the midst of her satisfaction she continued to sidle, and at last the cause was disclosed. From the chair beneath her she extracted a gun-metal cigarette-case, on which were powdered in turquoise the initials "E. L."

"That belongs to Lavish." said the clergyman. "A good fellow, Lavish, but I wish she'd start a pipe."

"Oh, Mr. Beebe," said Miss Alan, divided between awe and mirth. "Indeed, though it is dreadful for her to smoke, it is not quite as dreadful as you suppose. She took to it, practically in despair, after her life's work was carried away in a landslip. Surely that makes it more excusable."

"What was that?" asked Lucy.

Mr. Beebe sat back complacently, and Miss Alan began as follows: "It was a novel—and I am afraid, from what I can gather, not a very nice novel. It is so sad when people who have abilities misuse them, and I must say they nearly always do. Anyhow, she left it almost finished in the Grotto of the Calvary at the Capuccini Hotel at Amalfi while she went for a little ink. She said: 'Can I have a little ink, please?' But you know what Italians are, and meanwhile the Grotto fell roaring on to the beach, and the saddest thing of all is that she cannot remember what she has written. The poor thing was very ill after it, and so got tempted into cigarettes. It is a great secret, but I am glad to say that she is writing another novel. She told Teresa and Miss Pole the other day that she had got up all the local colour—this novel is to be about modern Italy; the other was historical—but that she could not start till she had an idea. First she tried Perugia for an inspiration, then she came here—this must on no account get round. And so cheerful through it all! I cannot help thinking that there is something to admire in every one, even if you do not approve of them."

Miss Alan was always thus being charitable against her better judgment. A delicate pathos perfumed her disconnected remarks, giving them unexpected beauty, just as in the decaying autumn woods there sometimes rise odours reminiscent of spring. She felt she had made almost too many allowances, and apologized hurriedly for her toleration.

"All the same, she is a little too—I hardly like to say unwomanly, but she behaved most strangely when the Emersons arrived."

Mr. Beebe smiled as Miss Alan plunged into an anecdote which he knew she would be unable to finish in the presence of a gentleman.

"I don't know, Miss Honeychurch, if you have noticed that Miss Pole, the lady who has so much yellow hair, takes lemonade. That old Mr. Emerson, who puts things very strangely—"

Her jaw dropped. She was silent. Mr. Beebe, whose social resources were endless, went out to order some tea, and she continued to Lucy in a hasty whisper:

"Stomach. He warned Miss Pole of her stomach-acidity, he called it—and he may have meant to be kind. I must say I forgot myself and laughed; it was so sudden. As Teresa truly said, it was no laughing matter. But the point is that Miss Lavish was positively ATTRACTED by his mentioning S., and said she liked plain speaking, and meeting different grades of thought. She thought they were commercial travellers—'drummers' was the word she used—and all through dinner she tried to prove that England, our great and beloved country, rests on nothing but commerce. Teresa was very much annoyed, and left the table before the cheese, saying as she did so: 'There, Miss Lavish, is one who can confute you better than I,' and pointed to that beautiful picture of Lord Tennyson. Then Miss Lavish said: 'Tut! The early Victorians.' Just imagine! 'Tut! The early Victorians.' My sister had gone, and I felt bound to speak. I said: 'Miss Lavish, I am an early Victorian; at least, that is to say, I will hear no breath of censure against our dear Queen.' It was horrible speaking. I reminded her how the Queen had been to Ireland when she did not want to go, and I must say she was dumbfounded, and made no reply. But, unluckily, Mr. Emerson overheard this part, and called in his deep voice: 'Quite so, quite so! I honour the woman for her Irish visit.' The woman! I tell things so badly; but you see what a tangle we were in by this time, all on account of S. having been mentioned in the first place. But that was not all. After dinner Miss Lavish actually came up and said: 'Miss Alan, I am going into the smoking-room to talk to those two nice men. Come, too.' Needless to say, I refused such an unsuitable invitation, and she had the impertinence to tell me that it would broaden my ideas, and said that she had four brothers, all University men, except one who was in the army, who always made a point of talking to commercial travellers."

"Let me finish the story," said Mr. Beebe, who had returned.

"Miss Lavish tried Miss Pole, myself, every one, and finally said: 'I shall go alone.' She went. At the end of five minutes she returned unobtrusively with a green baize board, and began playing patience."

"Whatever happened?" cried Lucy.

"No one knows. No one will ever know. Miss Lavish will never dare to tell, and Mr. Emerson does not think it worth telling."

"Mr. Beebe—old Mr. Emerson, is he nice or not nice? I do so want to know."

Mr. Beebe laughed and suggested that she should settle the question for herself.

"No; but it is so difficult. Sometimes he is so silly, and then I do not mind him. Miss Alan, what do you think? Is he nice?"

The little old lady shook her head, and sighed disapprovingly. Mr. Beebe, whom the conversation amused, stirred her up by saying:

"I consider that you are bound to class him as nice, Miss Alan, after that business of the violets."

"Violets? Oh, dear! Who told you about the violets? How do things get round? A pension is a bad place for gossips. No, I cannot forget how they behaved at Mr. Eager's lecture at Santa Croce. Oh, poor Miss Honeychurch! It really was too bad. No, I have quite changed. I do NOT like the Emersons. They are not nice."

Mr. Beebe smiled nonchalantly. He had made a gentle effort to introduce the Emersons into Bertolini society, and the effort had failed. He was almost the only person who remained friendly to them. Miss Lavish, who represented intellect, was avowedly hostile, and now the Miss Alans, who stood for good breeding, were following her. Miss Bartlett, smarting under an obligation, would scarcely be civil. The case of Lucy was different. She had given him a hazy account of her adventures in Santa Croce, and he gathered that the two men had made a curious and possibly concerted attempt to annex her, to show her the world from their own strange standpoint, to interest her in their private sorrows and joys. This was impertinent; he did not wish their cause to be championed by a young girl: he would rather it should fail. After all, he knew nothing about them, and pension joys, pension sorrows, are flimsy things; whereas Lucy would be his parishioner.

Lucy, with one eye upon the weather, finally said that she thought the Emersons were nice; not that she saw anything of them now. Even their seats at dinner had been moved.

"But aren't they always waylaying you to go out with them, dear?" said the little lady inquisitively.

"Only once. Charlotte didn't like it, and said something—quite politely, of course."

"Most right of her. They don't understand our ways. They must find their level."

Mr. Beebe rather felt that they had gone under. They had given up their attempt—if it was one—to conquer society, and now the father was almost as silent as the son. He wondered whether he would not plan a pleasant day for these folk before they left—some expedition, perhaps, with Lucy well chaperoned to be nice to them. It was one of Mr. Beebe's chief pleasures to provide people with happy memories.

Evening approached while they chatted; the air became brighter; the colours on the trees and hills were purified, and the Arno lost its muddy solidity and began to twinkle. There were a few streaks of bluish-green among the clouds, a few patches of watery light upon the earth, and then the dripping facade of San Miniato shone brilliantly in the declining sun.

"Too late to go out," said Miss Alan in a voice of relief. "All the galleries are shut."

"I think I shall go out," said Lucy. "I want to go round the town in the circular tram—on the platform by the driver."

Her two companions looked grave. Mr. Beebe, who felt responsible for her in the absence of Miss Bartlett, ventured to say:

"I wish we could. Unluckily I have letters. If you do want to go out alone, won't you be better on your feet?"

"Italians, dear, you know," said Miss Alan.

"Perhaps I shall meet some one who reads me through and through!"

But they still looked disapproval, and she so far conceded to Mr. Beebe as to say that she would only go for a little walk, and keep to the street frequented by tourists.

"She oughtn't really to go at all," said Mr. Beebe, as they watched her from the window, "and she knows it. I put it down to too much Beethoven."

Chapter IV: Fourth Chapter

Mr. Beebe was right. Lucy never knew her desires so clearly as after music. She had not really appreciated the clergyman's wit, nor the suggestive twitterings of Miss Alan. Conversation was tedious; she wanted something big, and she believed that it would have come to her on the wind-swept platform of an electric tram. This she might not attempt. It was unladylike. Why? Why were most big things unladylike? Charlotte had once explained to her why. It was not that ladies were inferior to men; it was that they were different. Their mission was to inspire others to achievement rather than to achieve themselves. Indirectly, by means of tact and a spotless name, a lady could accomplish much. But if she rushed into the fray herself she would be first censured, then despised, and finally ignored. Poems had been written to illustrate this point.

There is much that is immortal in this medieval lady. The dragons have gone, and so have the knights, but still she lingers in our midst. She reigned in many an early Victorian castle, and was Queen of much early Victorian song. It is sweet to protect her in the intervals of business, sweet to pay her honour when she has cooked our dinner well. But alas! the creature grows degenerate. In her heart also there are springing up strange desires. She too is enamoured of heavy winds, and vast panoramas, and green expanses of the sea. She has marked the kingdom of this world, how full it is of wealth, and beauty, and war—a radiant crust, built around the central fires, spinning towards the receding heavens. Men, declaring that she inspires them to it, move joyfully over the surface, having the most delightful meetings with other men, happy, not because they are masculine, but because they are alive. Before the show breaks up she would like to drop the august title of the Eternal Woman, and go there as her transitory self.

Lucy does not stand for the medieval lady, who was rather an ideal to which she was bidden to lift her eyes when feeling serious. Nor has she any system of revolt. Here and there a restriction annoyed her particularly, and she would transgress it, and perhaps be sorry that she had done so. This afternoon she was peculiarly restive. She would really like to do something of which her well-wishers disapproved. As she might not go on the electric tram, she went to Alinari's shop.

There she bought a photograph of Botticelli's "Birth of Venus." Venus, being a pity, spoilt the picture, otherwise so charming, and Miss Bartlett had persuaded her to do without it. (A pity in art of course signified the nude.) Giorgione's "Tempesta," the "Idolino," some of the Sistine frescoes and the Apoxyomenos, were added to it. She felt a little calmer then, and bought Fra Angelico's "Coronation," Giotto's "Ascension of St. John," some Della Robbia babies, and some Guido Reni Madonnas. For her taste was catholic, and she extended uncritical approval to every well-known name.

But though she spent nearly seven lire, the gates of liberty seemed still unopened. She was conscious of her discontent; it was new to her to be conscious of it. "The world," she thought, "is certainly full of beautiful things, if only I could come across them." It was not surprising that Mrs. Honeychurch disapproved of music, declaring that it always left her daughter peevish, unpractical, and touchy.

"Nothing ever happens to me," she reflected, as she entered the Piazza Signoria and looked nonchalantly at its marvels, now fairly familiar to her. The great square was in shadow; the sunshine had come too late to strike it. Neptune was already unsubstantial in the twilight, half god, half ghost, and his fountain plashed dreamily to the men and satyrs who idled together on its marge. The Loggia showed as the triple entrance of a cave, wherein many a deity, shadowy, but immortal, looking forth upon the arrivals and departures of mankind. It was the hour of unreality—the hour, that is, when unfamiliar things are real. An older person at such an hour and in such a place might think that sufficient was happening to him, and rest content. Lucy desired more.

She fixed her eyes wistfully on the tower of the palace, which rose out of the lower darkness like a pillar of roughened gold. It seemed no longer a tower, no longer supported by earth, but some unattainable treasure throbbing in the tranquil sky. Its brightness mesmerized her, still dancing before her eyes when she bent them to the ground and started towards home.

Then something did happen.

Two Italians by the Loggia had been bickering about a debt. "Cinque lire," they had cried, "cinque lire!" They sparred at each other, and one of them was hit lightly upon the chest. He frowned; he bent towards Lucy with a look of interest, as if he had an important message for her. He opened his lips to deliver it, and a stream of red came out between them and trickled down his unshaven chin.

That was all. A crowd rose out of the dusk. It hid this extraordinary man from her, and bore him away to the fountain. Mr. George Emerson happened to be a few paces away, looking at her across the spot where the man had been. How very odd! Across something. Even as she caught sight of him he grew dim; the palace itself grew dim, swayed above her, fell on to her softly, slowly, noiselessly, and the sky fell with it.

She thought: "Oh, what have I done?"

"Oh, what have I done?" she murmured, and opened her eyes.

George Emerson still looked at her, but not across anything. She had complained of dullness, and lo! one man was stabbed, and another held her in his arms.

They were sitting on some steps in the Uffizi Arcade. He must have carried her. He rose when she spoke, and began to dust his knees. She repeated:

"Oh, what have I done?"

"You fainted."

"I—I am very sorry."

"How are you now?"

"Perfectly well—absolutely well." And she began to nod and smile.

"Then let us come home. There's no point in our stopping."

He held out his hand to pull her up. She pretended not to see it. The cries from the fountain—they had never ceased—rang emptily. The whole world seemed pale and void of its original meaning.

"How very kind you have been! I might have hurt myself falling. But now I am well. I can go alone, thank you."

His hand was still extended.

"Oh, my photographs!" she exclaimed suddenly.

"What photographs?"

"I bought some photographs at Alinari's. I must have dropped them out there in the square." She looked at him cautiously. "Would you add to your kindness by fetching them?"

He added to his kindness. As soon as he had turned his back, Lucy arose with the running of a maniac and stole down the arcade towards the Arno.

"Miss Honeychurch!"

She stopped with her hand on her heart.

"You sit still; you aren't fit to go home alone."

"Yes, I am, thank you so very much."

"No, you aren't. You'd go openly if you were."

"But I had rather—"

"Then I don't fetch your photographs."

"I had rather be alone."

He said imperiously: "The man is dead—the man is probably dead; sit down till you are rested." She was bewildered, and obeyed him. "And don't move till I come back."

In the distance she saw creatures with black hoods, such as appear in dreams. The palace tower had lost the reflection of the declining day, and joined itself to earth. How should she talk to Mr. Emerson when he returned from the shadowy square? Again the thought occurred to her, "Oh, what have I done?"—the thought that she, as well as the dying man, had crossed some spiritual boundary.

He returned, and she talked of the murder. Oddly enough, it was an easy topic. She spoke of the Italian character; she became almost garrulous over the incident that had made her faint five minutes before. Being strong physically, she soon overcame the horror of blood. She rose without his assistance, and though wings seemed to flutter inside her, she walked firmly enough towards the Arno. There a cabman signalled to them; they refused him.

"And the murderer tried to kiss him, you say—how very odd Italians are!—and gave himself up to the police! Mr. Beebe was saying that Italians know everything, but I think they are rather childish. When my cousin and I were at the Pitti yesterday—What was that?"

He had thrown something into the stream.

"What did you throw in?"

"Things I didn't want," he said crossly.

"Mr. Emerson!"

"Well?"

"Where are the photographs?"

He was silent.

"I believe it was my photographs that you threw away."

"I didn't know what to do with them," he cried, and his voice was that of an anxious boy. Her heart warmed towards him for the first time. "They were covered with blood. There! I'm glad I've told you; and all the time we were making conversation I was wondering what to do with them." He pointed down-stream. "They've gone." The river swirled under the bridge, "I did mind them so, and one is so foolish, it seemed better that they should go out to the sea—I don't know; I may just mean that they frightened me." Then the boy verged into a man. "For something tremendous has happened; I must face it without getting muddled. It isn't exactly that a man has died."

Something warned Lucy that she must stop him.

"It has happened," he repeated, "and I mean to find out what it is."

"Mr. Emerson—"

He turned towards her frowning, as if she had disturbed him in some abstract quest.

"I want to ask you something before we go in."

They were close to their pension. She stopped and leant her elbows against the parapet of the embankment. He did likewise. There is at times a magic in identity of position; it is one of the things that have suggested to us eternal comradeship. She moved her elbows before saying:

"I have behaved ridiculously."

He was following his own thoughts.

"I was never so much ashamed of myself in my life; I cannot think what came over me."

"I nearly fainted myself," he said; but she felt that her attitude repelled him.

"Well, I owe you a thousand apologies."

"Oh, all right."

"And—this is the real point—you know how silly people are gossiping—ladies especially, I am afraid—you understand what I mean?"

"I'm afraid I don't."

"I mean, would you not mention it to any one, my foolish behaviour?"

"Your behaviour? Oh, yes, all right—all right."

"Thank you so much. And would you—"

She could not carry her request any further. The river was rushing below them, almost black in the advancing night. He had thrown her photographs into it, and then he had told her the reason. It struck her that it was hopeless to look for chivalry in such a man. He would do her no harm by idle gossip; he was trustworthy, intelligent, and even kind; he might even have a high opinion of her. But he lacked chivalry; his thoughts, like his behaviour, would not be modified by awe. It was useless to say to him, "And would you—" and hope that he would complete the sentence for himself, averting his eyes from her nakedness like the knight in that beautiful picture. She had been in his arms, and he remembered it, just as he remembered the blood on the photographs that she had bought in Alinari's shop. It was not exactly that a man had died; something had happened to the living: they had come to a situation where character tells, and where childhood enters upon the branching paths of Youth.

"Well, thank you so much," she repeated, "How quickly these accidents do happen, and then one returns to the old life!"

"I don't."

Anxiety moved her to question him.

His answer was puzzling: "I shall probably want to live."

"But why, Mr. Emerson? What do you mean?"

"I shall want to live, I say."

Leaning her elbows on the parapet, she contemplated the River Arno, whose roar was suggesting some unexpected melody to her ears.

Chapter V: Possibilities of a Pleasant Outing

It was a family saying that "you never knew which way Charlotte Bartlett would turn." She was perfectly pleasant and sensible over Lucy's adventure, found the abridged account of it quite adequate, and paid suitable tribute to the courtesy of Mr. George Emerson. She and Miss Lavish had had an adventure also. They had been stopped at the Dazio coming back, and the young officials there, who seemed impudent and desoeuvre, had tried to search their reticules for provisions. It might have been most unpleasant. Fortunately Miss Lavish was a match for any one.

For good or for evil, Lucy was left to face her problem alone. None of her friends had seen her, either in the Piazza or, later on, by the embankment. Mr. Beebe, indeed, noticing her startled eyes at dinner-time, had again passed to himself the remark of "Too much Beethoven." But he only supposed that she was ready for an adventure, not that she had encountered it. This solitude oppressed her; she was accustomed to have her thoughts confirmed by others or, at all events, contradicted; it was too dreadful not to know whether she was thinking right or wrong.

At breakfast next morning she took decisive action. There were two plans between which she had to choose. Mr. Beebe was walking up to the Torre del Gallo with the Emersons and some American ladies. Would Miss Bartlett and Miss Honeychurch join the party? Charlotte declined for herself; she had been there in the rain the previous afternoon. But she thought it an admirable idea for Lucy, who hated shopping, changing money, fetching letters, and other irksome duties—all of which Miss Bartlett must accomplish this morning and could easily accomplish alone.

"No, Charlotte!" cried the girl, with real warmth. "It's very kind of Mr. Beebe, but I am certainly coming with you. I had much rather."

"Very well, dear," said Miss Bartlett, with a faint flush of pleasure that called forth a deep flush of shame on the cheeks of Lucy. How abominably she behaved to Charlotte, now as always! But now she should alter. All morning she would be really nice to her.

She slipped her arm into her cousin's, and they started off along the Lung' Arno. The river was a lion that morning in strength, voice, and colour. Miss Bartlett insisted on leaning over the parapet to look at it. She then made her usual remark, which was "How I do wish Freddy and your mother could see this, too!"

Lucy fidgeted; it was tiresome of Charlotte to have stopped exactly where she did.

"Look, Lucia! Oh, you are watching for the Torre del Gallo party. I feared you would repent you of your choice."

Serious as the choice had been, Lucy did not repent. Yesterday had been a muddle—queer and odd, the kind of thing one could not write down easily on paper—but she had a feeling that Charlotte and her shopping were preferable to George Emerson and the summit of the Torre del Gallo. Since she could not unravel the tangle, she must take care not to re-enter it. She could protest sincerely against Miss Bartlett's insinuations.

But though she had avoided the chief actor, the scenery unfortunately remained. Charlotte, with the complacency of fate, led her from the river to the Piazza Signoria. She could not have believed that stones, a Loggia, a fountain, a palace tower, would have such significance. For a moment she understood the nature of ghosts.

The exact site of the murder was occupied, not by a ghost, but by Miss Lavish, who had the morning newspaper in her hand. She hailed them briskly. The dreadful catastrophe of the previous day had given her an idea which she thought would work up into a book.

"Oh, let me congratulate you!" said Miss Bartlett. "After your despair of yesterday! What a fortunate thing!"

"Aha! Miss Honeychurch, come you here I am in luck. Now, you are to tell me absolutely everything that you saw from the beginning." Lucy poked at the ground with her parasol.

"But perhaps you would rather not?"

"I'm sorry—if you could manage without it, I think I would rather not."

The elder ladies exchanged glances, not of disapproval; it is suitable that a girl should feel deeply.

"It is I who am sorry," said Miss Lavish "literary hacks are shameless creatures. I believe there's no secret of the human heart into which we wouldn't pry."

She marched cheerfully to the fountain and back, and did a few calculations in realism. Then she said that she had been in the Piazza since eight o'clock collecting material. A good deal of it was unsuitable, but of course one always had to adapt. The two men had quarrelled over a five-franc note. For the five-franc note she should substitute a young lady, which would raise the tone of the tragedy, and at the same time furnish an excellent plot.

"What is the heroine's name?" asked Miss Bartlett.

"Leonora," said Miss Lavish; her own name was Eleanor.

"I do hope she's nice."

That desideratum would not be omitted.

"And what is the plot?"

Love, murder, abduction, revenge, was the plot. But it all came while the fountain plashed to the satyrs in the morning sun.

"I hope you will excuse me for boring on like this," Miss Lavish concluded. "It is so tempting to talk to really sympathetic people. Of course, this is the barest outline. There will be a deal of local colouring, descriptions of Florence and the neighbourhood, and I shall also introduce some humorous characters. And let me give you all fair warning: I intend to be unmerciful to the British tourist."

"Oh, you wicked woman," cried Miss Bartlett. "I am sure you are thinking of the Emersons."

Miss Lavish gave a Machiavellian smile.

"I confess that in Italy my sympathies are not with my own countrymen. It is the neglected Italians who attract me, and whose lives I am going to paint so far as I can. For I repeat and I insist, and I have always held most strongly, that a tragedy such as yesterday's is not the less tragic because it happened in humble life."

There was a fitting silence when Miss Lavish had concluded. Then the cousins wished success to her labours, and walked slowly away across the square.

"She is my idea of a really clever woman," said Miss Bartlett. "That last remark struck me as so particularly true. It should be a most pathetic novel."

Lucy assented. At present her great aim was not to get put into it. Her perceptions this morning were curiously keen, and she believed that Miss Lavish had her on trial for an ingenue.

"She is emancipated, but only in the very best sense of the word," continued Miss Bartlett slowly. "None but the superficial would be shocked at her. We had a long talk yesterday. She believes in justice and truth and human interest. She told me also that she has a high opinion of the destiny of woman—Mr. Eager! Why, how nice! What a pleasant surprise!"

"Ah, not for me," said the chaplain blandly, "for I have been watching you and Miss Honeychurch for quite a little time."

"We were chatting to Miss Lavish."

His brow contracted.

"So I saw. Were you indeed? Andate via! sono occupato!" The last remark was made to a vender of panoramic photographs who was approaching with a courteous smile. "I am about to venture a suggestion. Would you and Miss Honeychurch be disposed to join me in a drive some day this week—a drive in the hills? We might go up by Fiesole and back by Settignano. There is a point on that road where we could get down and have an hour's ramble on the hillside. The view thence of Florence is most beautiful—far better than the hackneyed view of Fiesole. It is the view that Alessio Baldovinetti is fond of introducing into his pictures. That man had a decided feeling for landscape. Decidedly. But who looks at it to-day? Ah, the world is too much for us."

Miss Bartlett had not heard of Alessio Baldovinetti, but she knew that Mr. Eager was no commonplace chaplain. He was a member of the residential colony who had made Florence their home. He knew the people who never walked about with Baedekers, who had learnt to take a siesta after lunch, who took drives the pension tourists had never heard of, and saw by private influence galleries which were closed to them. Living in delicate seclusion, some in furnished flats, others in Renaissance villas on Fiesole's slope, they read, wrote, studied, and exchanged ideas, thus attaining to that intimate knowledge, or rather perception, of Florence which is denied to all who carry in their pockets the coupons of Cook.

Therefore an invitation from the chaplain was something to be proud of. Between the two sections of his flock he was often the only link, and it was his avowed custom to select those of his migratory sheep who seemed worthy, and give them a few hours in the pastures of the permanent. Tea at a Renaissance villa? Nothing had been said about it yet. But if it did come to that—how Lucy would enjoy it!

A few days ago and Lucy would have felt the same. But the joys of life were grouping themselves anew. A drive in the hills with Mr. Eager and Miss Bartlett—even if culminating in a residential tea-party—was no longer the greatest of them. She echoed the raptures of Charlotte somewhat faintly. Only when she heard that Mr. Beebe was also coming did her thanks become more sincere.

"So we shall be a partie carree," said the chaplain. "In these days of toil and tumult one has great needs of the country and its message of purity. Andate via! andate presto, presto! Ah, the town! Beautiful as it is, it is the town."

They assented.

"This very square—so I am told—witnessed yesterday the most sordid of tragedies. To one who loves the Florence of Dante and Savonarola there is something portentous in such desecration—portentous and humiliating."

"Humiliating indeed," said Miss Bartlett. "Miss Honeychurch happened to be passing through as it happened. She can hardly bear to speak of it." She glanced at Lucy proudly.

"And how came we to have you here?" asked the chaplain paternally.

Miss Bartlett's recent liberalism oozed away at the question. "Do not blame her, please, Mr. Eager. The fault is mine: I left her unchaperoned."

"So you were here alone, Miss Honeychurch?" His voice suggested sympathetic reproof but at the same time indicated that a few harrowing details would not be unacceptable. His dark, handsome face drooped mournfully towards her to catch her reply.

"Practically."

"One of our pension acquaintances kindly brought her home," said Miss Bartlett, adroitly concealing the sex of the preserver.

"For her also it must have been a terrible experience. I trust that neither of you was at all—that it was not in your immediate proximity?"

Of the many things Lucy was noticing to-day, not the least remarkable was this: the ghoulish fashion in which respectable people will nibble after blood. George Emerson had kept the subject strangely pure.

"He died by the fountain, I believe," was her reply.

"And you and your friend—"

"Were over at the Loggia."

"That must have saved you much. You have not, of course, seen the disgraceful illustrations which the gutter Press—This man is a public nuisance; he knows that I am a resident perfectly well, and yet he goes on worrying me to buy his vulgar views."

Surely the vendor of photographs was in league with Lucy—in the eternal league of Italy with youth. He had suddenly extended his book before Miss Bartlett and Mr. Eager, binding their hands together by a long glossy ribbon of churches, pictures, and views.

"This is too much!" cried the chaplain, striking petulantly at one of Fra Angelico's angels. She tore. A shrill cry rose from the vendor. The book it seemed, was more valuable than one would have supposed.

"Willingly would I purchase—" began Miss Bartlett.

"Ignore him," said Mr. Eager sharply, and they all walked rapidly away from the square.

But an Italian can never be ignored, least of all when he has a grievance. His mysterious persecution of Mr. Eager became relentless; the air rang with his threats and lamentations. He appealed to Lucy; would not she intercede? He was poor—he sheltered a family—the tax on bread. He waited, he gibbered, he was recompensed, he was dissatisfied, he did not leave them until he had swept their minds clean of all thoughts whether pleasant or unpleasant.

Shopping was the topic that now ensued. Under the chaplain's guidance they selected many hideous presents and mementoes—florid little picture-frames that seemed fashioned in gilded pastry; other little frames, more severe, that stood on little easels, and were carven out of oak; a blotting book of vellum; a Dante of the same material; cheap mosaic brooches, which the maids, next Christmas, would never tell from real; pins, pots, heraldic saucers, brown art-photographs; Eros and Psyche in alabaster; St. Peter to match—all of which would have cost less in London.

This successful morning left no pleasant impressions on Lucy. She had been a little frightened, both by Miss Lavish and by Mr. Eager, she knew not why. And as they frightened her, she had, strangely enough, ceased to respect them. She doubted that Miss Lavish was a great artist. She doubted that Mr. Eager was as full of spirituality and culture as she had been led to suppose. They were tried by some new test, and they were found wanting. As for Charlotte—as for Charlotte she was exactly the same. It might be possible to be nice to her; it was impossible to love her.

"The son of a labourer; I happen to know it for a fact. A mechanic of some sort himself when he was young; then he took to writing for the Socialistic Press. I came across him at Brixton."

They were talking about the Emersons.

"How wonderfully people rise in these days!" sighed Miss Bartlett, fingering a model of the leaning Tower of Pisa.

"Generally," replied Mr. Eager, "one has only sympathy for their success. The desire for education and for social advance—in these things there is something not wholly vile. There are some working men whom one would be very willing to see out here in Florence—little as they would make of it."

"Is he a journalist now?" Miss Bartlett asked, "He is not; he made an advantageous marriage."

He uttered this remark with a voice full of meaning, and ended with a sigh.

"Oh, so he has a wife."

"Dead, Miss Bartlett, dead. I wonder—yes I wonder how he has the effrontery to look me in the face, to dare to claim acquaintance with me. He was in my London parish long ago. The other day in Santa Croce, when he was with Miss Honeychurch, I snubbed him. Let him beware that he does not get more than a snub."

"What?" cried Lucy, flushing.

"Exposure!" hissed Mr. Eager.

He tried to change the subject; but in scoring a dramatic point he had interested his audience more than he had intended. Miss Bartlett was full of very natural curiosity. Lucy, though she wished never to see the Emersons again, was not disposed to condemn them on a single word.

"Do you mean," she asked, "that he is an irreligious man? We know that already."

"Lucy, dear—" said Miss Bartlett, gently reproving her cousin's penetration.

"I should be astonished if you knew all. The boy—an innocent child at the time—I will exclude. God knows what his education and his inherited qualities may have made him."

"Perhaps," said Miss Bartlett, "it is something that we had better not hear."

"To speak plainly," said Mr. Eager, "it is. I will say no more." For the first time Lucy's rebellious thoughts swept out in words—for the first time in her life.

"You have said very little."

"It was my intention to say very little," was his frigid reply.

He gazed indignantly at the girl, who met him with equal indignation. She turned towards him from the shop counter; her breast heaved quickly. He observed her brow, and the sudden strength of her lips. It was intolerable that she should disbelieve him.

"Murder, if you want to know," he cried angrily. "That man murdered his wife!"

"How?" she retorted.

"To all intents and purposes he murdered her. That day in Santa Croce—did they say anything against me?"

"Not a word, Mr. Eager—not a single word."

"Oh, I thought they had been libelling me to you. But I suppose it is only their personal charms that makes you defend them."

"I'm not defending them," said Lucy, losing her courage, and relapsing into the old chaotic methods. "They're nothing to me."

"How could you think she was defending them?" said Miss Bartlett, much discomfited by the unpleasant scene. The shopman was possibly listening.

"She will find it difficult. For that man has murdered his wife in the sight of God."

The addition of God was striking. But the chaplain was really trying to qualify a rash remark. A silence followed which might have been impressive, but was merely awkward. Then Miss Bartlett hastily purchased the Leaning Tower, and led the way into the street.

"I must be going," said he, shutting his eyes and taking out his watch.

Miss Bartlett thanked him for his kindness, and spoke with enthusiasm of the approaching drive.

"Drive? Oh, is our drive to come off?"

Lucy was recalled to her manners, and after a little exertion the complacency of Mr. Eager was restored.

"Bother the drive!" exclaimed the girl, as soon as he had departed. "It is just the drive we had arranged with Mr. Beebe without any fuss at all. Why should he invite us in that absurd manner? We might as well invite him. We are each paying for ourselves."

Miss Bartlett, who had intended to lament over the Emersons, was launched by this remark into unexpected thoughts.

"If that is so, dear—if the drive we and Mr. Beebe are going with Mr. Eager is really the same as the one we are going with Mr. Beebe, then I foresee a sad kettle of fish."

"How?"

"Because Mr. Beebe has asked Eleanor Lavish to come, too."

"That will mean another carriage."

"Far worse. Mr. Eager does not like Eleanor. She knows it herself. The truth must be told; she is too unconventional for him."

They were now in the newspaper-room at the English bank. Lucy stood by the central table, heedless of Punch and the Graphic, trying to answer, or at all events to formulate the questions rioting in her brain. The well-known world had broken up, and there emerged Florence, a magic city where people thought and did the most extraordinary things. Murder, accusations of murder, A lady clinging to one man and being rude to another—were these the daily incidents of her streets? Was there more in her frank beauty than met the eye—the power, perhaps, to evoke passions, good and bad, and to bring them speedily to a fulfillment?

Happy Charlotte, who, though greatly troubled over things that did not matter, seemed oblivious to things that did; who could conjecture with admirable delicacy "where things might lead to," but apparently lost sight of the goal as she approached it. Now she was crouching in the corner trying to extract a circular note from a kind of linen nose-bag which hung in chaste concealment round her neck. She had been told that this was the only safe way to carry money in Italy; it must only be broached within the walls of the English bank. As she groped she murmured: "Whether it is Mr. Beebe who forgot to tell Mr. Eager, or Mr. Eager who forgot when he told us, or whether they have decided to leave Eleanor out altogether—which they could scarcely do—but in any case we must be prepared. It is you they really want; I am only asked for appearances. You shall go with the two gentlemen, and I and Eleanor will follow behind. A one-horse carriage would do for us. Yet how difficult it is!"

"It is indeed," replied the girl, with a gravity that sounded sympathetic.

"What do you think about it?" asked Miss Bartlett, flushed from the struggle, and buttoning up her dress.

"I don't know what I think, nor what I want."

"Oh, dear, Lucy! I do hope Florence isn't boring you. Speak the word, and, as you know, I would take you to the ends of the earth to-morrow."

"Thank you, Charlotte," said Lucy, and pondered over the offer.

There were letters for her at the bureau—one from her brother, full of athletics and biology; one from her mother, delightful as only her mother's letters could be. She had read in it of the crocuses which had been bought for yellow and were coming up puce, of the new parlour-maid, who had watered the ferns with essence of lemonade, of the semi-detached cottages which were ruining Summer Street, and breaking the heart of Sir Harry Otway. She recalled the free, pleasant life of her home, where she was allowed to do everything, and where nothing ever happened to her. The road up through the pine-woods, the clean drawing-room, the view over the Sussex Weald—all hung before her bright and distinct, but pathetic as the pictures in a gallery to which, after much experience, a traveller returns.

"And the news?" asked Miss Bartlett.

"Mrs. Vyse and her son have gone to Rome," said Lucy, giving the news that interested her least. "Do you know the Vyses?"

"Oh, not that way back. We can never have too much of the dear Piazza Signoria."

"They're nice people, the Vyses. So clever—my idea of what's really clever. Don't you long to be in Rome?"

"I die for it!"

The Piazza Signoria is too stony to be brilliant. It has no grass, no flowers, no frescoes, no glittering walls of marble or comforting patches of ruddy brick. By an odd chance—unless we believe in a presiding genius of places—the statues that relieve its severity suggest, not the innocence of childhood, nor the glorious bewilderment of youth, but the conscious achievements of maturity. Perseus and Judith, Hercules and Thusnelda, they have done or suffered something, and though they are immortal, immortality has come to them after experience, not before. Here, not only in the solitude of Nature, might a hero meet a goddess, or a heroine a god.

"Charlotte!" cried the girl suddenly. "Here's an idea. What if we popped off to Rome to-morrow—straight to the Vyses' hotel? For I do know what I want. I'm sick of Florence. No, you said you'd go to the ends of the earth! Do! Do!"

Miss Bartlett, with equal vivacity, replied:

"Oh, you droll person! Pray, what would become of your drive in the hills?"

Chapter V: Possibilities of a Pleasant Outing

They passed together through the gaunt beauty of the square, laughing over the unpractical suggestion.

Chapter VI: The Reverend Arthur Beebe, the Reverend Cuthbert Eager, Mr. Emerson, Mr. George Emerson, Miss Eleanor Lavish, Miss Charlotte Bartlett, and Miss Lucy Honeychurch Drive Out in Carriages to See a View; Italians Drive Them.

It was Phaethon who drove them to Fiesole that memorable day, a youth all irresponsibility and fire, recklessly urging his master's horses up the stony hill. Mr. Beebe recognized him at once. Neither the Ages of Faith nor the Age of Doubt had touched him; he was Phaethon in Tuscany driving a cab. And it was Persephone whom he asked leave to pick up on the way, saying that she was his sister—Persephone, tall and slender and pale, returning with the Spring to her mother's cottage, and still shading her eyes from the unaccustomed light. To her Mr. Eager objected, saying that here was the thin edge of the wedge, and one must guard against imposition. But the ladies interceded, and when it had been made clear that it was a very great favour, the goddess was allowed to mount beside the god.

Phaethon at once slipped the left rein over her head, thus enabling himself to drive with his arm round her waist. She did not mind. Mr. Eager, who sat with his back to the horses, saw nothing of the indecorous proceeding, and continued his conversation with Lucy. The other two occupants of the carriage were old Mr. Emerson and Miss Lavish. For a dreadful thing had happened: Mr. Beebe, without consulting Mr. Eager, had doubled the size of the party. And though Miss Bartlett and Miss Lavish had planned all the morning how the people were to sit, at the critical moment when the carriages came round they lost their heads, and Miss Lavish got in with Lucy, while Miss Bartlett, with George Emerson and Mr. Beebe, followed on behind.

It was hard on the poor chaplain to have his partie carree thus transformed. Tea at a Renaissance villa, if he had ever meditated it, was now impossible. Lucy and Miss Bartlett had a certain style about them, and Mr. Beebe, though unreliable, was a man of parts. But a shoddy lady writer and a journalist who had murdered his wife in the sight of God—they should enter no villa at his introduction.

Lucy, elegantly dressed in white, sat erect and nervous amid these explosive ingredients, attentive to Mr. Eager, repressive towards Miss Lavish, watchful of old Mr. Emerson, hitherto fortunately asleep, thanks to a heavy lunch and the drowsy atmosphere of Spring. She looked on the expedition as the work of Fate. But for it she would have avoided George Emerson successfully. In an open manner he had shown that he wished to continue their intimacy. She had refused, not because she disliked him, but because she did not know what had happened, and suspected that he did know. And this frightened her.

For the real event—whatever it was—had taken place, not in the Loggia, but by the river. To behave wildly at the sight of death is pardonable. But to discuss it afterwards, to pass from discussion into silence, and through silence into sympathy, that is an error, not of a startled emotion, but of the whole fabric. There was really something blameworthy (she thought) in their joint contemplation of the shadowy stream, in the common impulse which had turned them to the house without the passing of a look or word. This sense of wickedness had been slight at first. She had nearly joined the party to the Torre del Gallo. But each time that she avoided George it became more imperative that she should avoid him again. And now celestial irony, working through her cousin and two clergymen, did not suffer her to leave Florence till she had made this expedition with him through the hills.

Meanwhile Mr. Eager held her in civil converse; their little tiff was over.

"So, Miss Honeychurch, you are travelling? As a student of art?"

"Oh, dear me, no—oh, no!"

"Perhaps as a student of human nature," interposed Miss Lavish, "like myself?"

"Oh, no. I am here as a tourist."

"Oh, indeed," said Mr. Eager. "Are you indeed? If you will not think me rude, we residents sometimes pity you poor tourists not a little—handed about like a parcel of goods from Venice to Florence, from Florence to Rome, living herded together in pensions or hotels, quite unconscious of anything that is outside Baedeker, their one anxiety to get 'done' or 'through' and go on somewhere else. The result is, they mix up towns, rivers, palaces in one inextricable whirl. You know the American girl in Punch who says: 'Say, poppa, what did we see at Rome?' And the father replies: 'Why, guess Rome was the place where we saw the yaller dog.' There's travelling for you. Ha! ha! ha!"

"I quite agree," said Miss Lavish, who had several times tried to interrupt his mordant wit. "The narrowness and superficiality of the Anglo-Saxon tourist is nothing less than a menace."

"Quite so. Now, the English colony at Florence, Miss Honeychurch—and it is of considerable size, though, of course, not all equally—a few are here for trade, for example. But the greater part are students. Lady Helen Laverstock is at present busy over Fra Angelico. I mention her name because we are passing her villa on the left. No, you can only see it if you stand—no, do not stand; you will fall. She is very proud of that thick hedge. Inside, perfect seclusion. One might have gone back six hundred years. Some critics believe that her garden was the scene of The Decameron, which lends it an additional interest, does it not?"

"It does indeed!" cried Miss Lavish. "Tell me, where do they place the scene of that wonderful seventh day?"

But Mr. Eager proceeded to tell Miss Honeychurch that on the right lived Mr. Someone Something, an American of the best type—so rare!—and that the Somebody Elses were farther down the hill. "Doubtless you know her monographs in the series of 'Mediaeval Byways'? He is working at Gemistus Pletho. Sometimes as I take tea in their beautiful grounds I hear, over the wall, the electric tram squealing up the new road with its loads of hot, dusty, unintelligent tourists who are going to 'do' Fiesole in an hour in order that they may say they have been there, and I think—think—I think how little they think what lies so near them."

During this speech the two figures on the box were sporting with each other disgracefully. Lucy had a spasm of envy. Granted that they wished to misbehave, it was pleasant for them to be able to do so. They were probably the only people enjoying the expedition. The carriage swept with agonizing jolts up through the Piazza of Fiesole and into the Settignano road.

"Piano! piano!" said Mr. Eager, elegantly waving his hand over his head.

"Va bene, signore, va bene, va bene," crooned the driver, and whipped his horses up again.

Now Mr. Eager and Miss Lavish began to talk against each other on the subject of Alessio Baldovinetti. Was he a cause of the Renaissance, or was he one of its manifestations? The other carriage was left behind. As the pace increased to a gallop the large, slumbering form of Mr. Emerson was thrown against the chaplain with the regularity of a machine.

"Piano! piano!" said he, with a martyred look at Lucy.

An extra lurch made him turn angrily in his seat. Phaethon, who for some time had been endeavouring to kiss Persephone, had just succeeded.

A little scene ensued, which, as Miss Bartlett said afterwards, was most unpleasant. The horses were stopped, the lovers were ordered to disentangle themselves, the boy was to lose his pourboire, the girl was immediately to get down.

"She is my sister," said he, turning round on them with piteous eyes.

Mr. Eager took the trouble to tell him that he was a liar.

Phaethon hung down his head, not at the matter of the accusation, but at its manner. At this point Mr. Emerson, whom the shock of stopping had awoke, declared that the lovers must on no account be separated, and patted them on the back to signify his approval. And Miss Lavish, though unwilling to ally him, felt bound to support the cause of Bohemianism.

"Most certainly I would let them be," she cried. "But I dare say I shall receive scant support. I have always flown in the face of the conventions all my life. This is what I call an adventure."

"We must not submit," said Mr. Eager. "I knew he was trying it on. He is treating us as if we were a party of Cook's tourists."

"Surely no!" said Miss Lavish, her ardour visibly decreasing.

The other carriage had drawn up behind, and sensible Mr. Beebe called out that after this warning the couple would be sure to behave themselves properly.

"Leave them alone," Mr. Emerson begged the chaplain, of whom he stood in no awe. "Do we find happiness so often that we should turn it off the box when it happens to sit there? To be driven by lovers—A king might envy us, and if we part them it's more like sacrilege than anything I know."

Here the voice of Miss Bartlett was heard saying that a crowd had begun to collect.

Mr. Eager, who suffered from an over-fluent tongue rather than a resolute will, was determined to make himself heard. He addressed the driver again. Italian in the mouth of Italians is a deep-voiced stream, with unexpected cataracts and boulders to preserve it from monotony. In Mr. Eager's mouth it resembled nothing so much as an acid whistling fountain which played ever higher and higher, and quicker and quicker, and more and more shrilly, till abruptly it was turned off with a click.

"Signorina!" said the man to Lucy, when the display had ceased. Why should he appeal to Lucy?

"Signorina!" echoed Persephone in her glorious contralto. She pointed at the other carriage. Why?

For a moment the two girls looked at each other. Then Persephone got down from the box.

"Victory at last!" said Mr. Eager, smiting his hands together as the carriages started again.

"It is not victory," said Mr. Emerson. "It is defeat. You have parted two people who were happy."

Mr. Eager shut his eyes. He was obliged to sit next to Mr. Emerson, but he would not speak to him. The old man was refreshed by sleep, and took up the matter warmly. He commanded Lucy to agree with him; he shouted for support to his son.

"We have tried to buy what cannot be bought with money. He has bargained to drive us, and he is doing it. We have no rights over his soul."

Miss Lavish frowned. It is hard when a person you have classed as typically British speaks out of his character.

"He was not driving us well," she said. "He jolted us."

"That I deny. It was as restful as sleeping. Aha! he is jolting us now. Can you wonder? He would like to throw us out, and most certainly he is justified. And if I were superstitious I'd be frightened of the girl, too. It doesn't do to injure young people. Have you ever heard of Lorenzo de Medici?"

Miss Lavish bristled.

"Most certainly I have. Do you refer to Lorenzo il Magnifico, or to Lorenzo, Duke of Urbino, or to Lorenzo surnamed Lorenzino on account of his diminutive stature?"

"The Lord knows. Possibly he does know, for I refer to Lorenzo the poet. He wrote a line—so I heard yesterday—which runs like this: 'Don't go fighting against the Spring.'"

Mr. Eager could not resist the opportunity for erudition.

"Non fate guerra al Maggio," he murmured. "'War not with the May' would render a correct meaning."

"The point is, we have warred with it. Look." He pointed to the Val d'Arno, which was visible far below them, through the budding trees. "Fifty miles of Spring, and we've come up to admire them. Do you suppose there's any difference between Spring in nature and Spring in man? But there we go, praising the one and condemning the other as improper, ashamed that the same work eternally through both."

No one encouraged him to talk. Presently Mr. Eager gave a signal for the carriages to stop and marshalled the party for their ramble on the hill. A hollow like a great amphitheatre, full of terraced steps and misty olives, now lay between them and the heights of Fiesole, and the road, still following its curve, was about to sweep on to a promontory which stood out in the plain. It was this promontory, uncultivated, wet, covered with bushes and occasional trees, which had caught the fancy of Alessio Baldovinetti nearly five hundred years before. He had ascended it, that diligent and rather obscure master, possibly with an eye to business, possibly for the joy of ascending. Standing there, he had seen that view of the Val d'Arno and distant Florence, which he afterwards had introduced not very effectively into his work. But where exactly had he stood? That was the question which Mr. Eager hoped to solve now. And Miss Lavish, whose nature was attracted by anything problematical, had become equally enthusiastic.

But it is not easy to carry the pictures of Alessio Baldovinetti in your head, even if you have remembered to look at them before starting. And the haze in the valley increased the difficulty of the quest.

The party sprang about from tuft to tuft of grass, their anxiety to keep together being only equalled by their desire to go different directions. Finally they split into groups. Lucy clung to Miss Bartlett and Miss Lavish; the Emersons returned to hold laborious converse with the drivers; while the two clergymen, who were expected to have topics in common, were left to each other.

The two elder ladies soon threw off the mask. In the audible whisper that was now so familiar to Lucy they began to discuss, not Alessio Baldovinetti, but the drive. Miss Bartlett had asked Mr. George Emerson what his profession was, and he had answered "the railway." She was very sorry that she had asked him. She had no idea that it would be such a dreadful answer, or she would not have asked him. Mr. Beebe had turned the conversation so cleverly, and she hoped that the young man was not very much hurt at her asking him.

"The railway!" gasped Miss Lavish. "Oh, but I shall die! Of course it was the railway!" She could not control her mirth. "He is the image of a porter—on, on the South-Eastern."

"Eleanor, be quiet," plucking at her vivacious companion. "Hush! They'll hear—the Emersons—"

"I can't stop. Let me go my wicked way. A porter—"

"Eleanor!"

"I'm sure it's all right," put in Lucy. "The Emersons won't hear, and they wouldn't mind if they did."

Miss Lavish did not seem pleased at this.

"Miss Honeychurch listening!" she said rather crossly. "Pouf! Wouf! You naughty girl! Go away!"

"Oh, Lucy, you ought to be with Mr. Eager, I'm sure."

"I can't find them now, and I don't want to either."

"Mr. Eager will be offended. It is your party."

"Please, I'd rather stop here with you."

"No, I agree," said Miss Lavish. "It's like a school feast; the boys have got separated from the girls. Miss Lucy, you are to go. We wish to converse on high topics unsuited for your ear."

The girl was stubborn. As her time at Florence drew to its close she was only at ease amongst those to whom she felt indifferent. Such a one was Miss Lavish, and such for the moment was Charlotte. She wished she had not called attention to herself; they were both annoyed at her remark and seemed determined to get rid of her.

"How tired one gets," said Miss Bartlett. "Oh, I do wish Freddy and your mother could be here."

Unselfishness with Miss Bartlett had entirely usurped the functions of enthusiasm. Lucy did not look at the view either. She would not enjoy anything till she was safe at Rome.

"Then sit you down," said Miss Lavish. "Observe my foresight."

With many a smile she produced two of those mackintosh squares that protect the frame of the tourist from damp grass or cold marble steps. She sat on one; who was to sit on the other?

"Lucy; without a moment's doubt, Lucy. The ground will do for me. Really I have not had rheumatism for years. If I do feel it coming on I shall stand. Imagine your mother's feelings if I let you sit in the wet in your white linen." She sat down heavily where the ground looked particularly moist. "Here we are, all settled delightfully. Even if my dress is thinner it will not show so much, being brown. Sit down, dear; you are too unselfish; you don't assert yourself enough." She cleared her throat. "Now don't be alarmed; this isn't a cold. It's the tiniest cough, and I have had it three days. It's nothing to do with sitting here at all."

There was only one way of treating the situation. At the end of five minutes Lucy departed in search of Mr. Beebe and Mr. Eager, vanquished by the mackintosh square.

She addressed herself to the drivers, who were sprawling in the carriages, perfuming the cushions with cigars. The miscreant, a bony young man scorched black by the sun, rose to greet her with the courtesy of a host and the assurance of a relative.

"Dove?" said Lucy, after much anxious thought.

His face lit up. Of course he knew where, Not so far either. His arm swept three-fourths of the horizon. He should just think he did know where. He pressed his finger-tips to his forehead and then pushed them towards her, as if oozing with visible extract of knowledge.

More seemed necessary. What was the Italian for "clergyman"?

"Dove buoni uomini?" said she at last.

Good? Scarcely the adjective for those noble beings! He showed her his cigar.

"Uno—piu—piccolo," was her next remark, implying "Has the cigar been given to you by Mr. Beebe, the smaller of the two good men?"

She was correct as usual. He tied the horse to a tree, kicked it to make it stay quiet, dusted the carriage, arranged his hair, remoulded his hat, encouraged his moustache, and in rather less than a quarter of a minute was ready to conduct her. Italians are born knowing the way. It would seem that the whole earth lay before them, not as a map, but as a chess-board, whereon they continually behold the changing pieces as well as the squares. Any one can find places, but the finding of people is a gift from God.

He only stopped once, to pick her some great blue violets. She thanked him with real pleasure. In the company of this common man the world was beautiful and direct. For the first time she felt the influence of Spring. His arm swept the horizon gracefully; violets, like other things, existed in great profusion there; "would she like to see them?"

"Ma buoni uomini."

He bowed. Certainly. Good men first, violets afterwards. They proceeded briskly through the undergrowth, which became thicker and thicker. They were nearing the edge of the promontory, and the view was stealing round them, but the brown network of the bushes shattered it into countless pieces. He was occupied in his cigar, and in holding back the pliant boughs. She was rejoicing in her escape from dullness. Not a step, not a twig, was unimportant to her.

"What is that?"

There was a voice in the wood, in the distance behind them. The voice of Mr. Eager? He shrugged his shoulders. An Italian's ignorance is sometimes more remarkable than his knowledge. She could not make him understand that perhaps they had missed the clergymen. The view was forming at last; she could discern the river, the golden plain, other hills.

"Eccolo!" he exclaimed.

At the same moment the ground gave way, and with a cry she fell out of the wood. Light and beauty enveloped her. She had fallen on to a little open terrace, which was covered with violets from end to end.

"Courage!" cried her companion, now standing some six feet above. "Courage and love."

She did not answer. From her feet the ground sloped sharply into view, and violets ran down in rivulets and streams and cataracts, irrigating the hillside with blue, eddying round the tree stems collecting into pools in the hollows, covering the grass with spots of azure foam. But never again were they in such profusion; this terrace was the well-head, the primal source whence beauty gushed out to water the earth.

Standing at its brink, like a swimmer who prepares, was the good man. But he was not the good man that she had expected, and he was alone.

George had turned at the sound of her arrival. For a moment he contemplated her, as one who had fallen out of heaven. He saw radiant joy in her face, he saw the flowers beat against her dress in blue waves. The bushes above them closed. He stepped quickly forward and kissed her.

Before she could speak, almost before she could feel, a voice called, "Lucy! Lucy! Lucy!" The silence of life had been broken by Miss Bartlett who stood brown against the view.

Chapter VII: They Return

Some complicated game had been playing up and down the hillside all the afternoon. What it was and exactly how the players had sided, Lucy was slow to discover. Mr. Eager had met them with a questioning eye. Charlotte had repulsed him with much small talk. Mr. Emerson, seeking his son, was told whereabouts to find him. Mr. Beebe, who wore the heated aspect of a neutral, was bidden to collect the factions for the return home. There was a general sense of groping and bewilderment. Pan had been amongst them—not the great god Pan, who has been buried these two thousand years, but the little god Pan, who presides over social contretemps and unsuccessful picnics. Mr. Beebe had lost every one, and had consumed in solitude the tea-basket which he had brought up as a pleasant surprise. Miss Lavish had lost Miss Bartlett. Lucy had lost Mr. Eager. Mr. Emerson had lost George. Miss Bartlett had lost a mackintosh square. Phaethon had lost the game.

That last fact was undeniable. He climbed on to the box shivering, with his collar up, prophesying the swift approach of bad weather. "Let us go immediately," he told them. "The signorino will walk."

"All the way? He will be hours," said Mr. Beebe.

"Apparently. I told him it was unwise." He would look no one in the face; perhaps defeat was particularly mortifying for him. He alone had played skilfully, using the whole of his instinct, while the others had used scraps of their intelligence. He alone had divined what things were, and what he wished them to be. He alone had interpreted the message that Lucy had received five days before from the lips of a dying man. Persephone, who spends half her life in the grave—she could interpret it also. Not so these English. They gain knowledge slowly, and perhaps too late.

The thoughts of a cab-driver, however just, seldom affect the lives of his employers. He was the most competent of Miss Bartlett's opponents, but infinitely the least dangerous. Once back in the town, he and his insight and his knowledge would trouble English ladies no more. Of course, it was most unpleasant; she had seen his black head in the bushes; he might make a tavern story out of it. But after all, what have we to do with taverns? Real menace belongs to the drawing-room. It was of drawing-room people that Miss Bartlett thought as she journeyed downwards towards the fading sun. Lucy sat beside her; Mr. Eager sat opposite, trying to catch her eye; he was vaguely suspicious. They spoke of Alessio Baldovinetti.

Rain and darkness came on together. The two ladies huddled together under an inadequate parasol. There was a lightning flash, and Miss Lavish who was nervous, screamed from the carriage in front. At the next flash, Lucy screamed also. Mr. Eager addressed her professionally:

"Courage, Miss Honeychurch, courage and faith. If I might say so, there is something almost blasphemous in this horror of the elements. Are we seriously to suppose that all these clouds, all this immense electrical display, is simply called into existence to extinguish you or me?"

"No—of course—"

"Even from the scientific standpoint the chances against our being struck are enormous. The steel knives, the only articles which might attract the current, are in the other carriage. And, in any case, we are infinitely safer than if we were walking. Courage—courage and faith."

Under the rug, Lucy felt the kindly pressure of her cousin's hand. At times our need for a sympathetic gesture is so great that we care not what exactly it signifies or how much we may have to pay for it afterwards. Miss Bartlett, by this timely exercise of her muscles, gained more than she would have got in hours of preaching or cross examination.

She renewed it when the two carriages stopped, half into Florence.

"Mr. Eager!" called Mr. Beebe. "We want your assistance. Will you interpret for us?"

"George!" cried Mr. Emerson. "Ask your driver which way George went. The boy may lose his way. He may be killed."

"Go, Mr. Eager," said Miss Bartlett, "don't ask our driver; our driver is no help. Go and support poor Mr. Beebe—, he is nearly demented."

"He may be killed!" cried the old man. "He may be killed!"

"Typical behaviour," said the chaplain, as he quitted the carriage. "In the presence of reality that kind of person invariably breaks down."

"What does he know?" whispered Lucy as soon as they were alone. "Charlotte, how much does Mr. Eager know?"

"Nothing, dearest; he knows nothing. But—" she pointed at the driver-"HE knows everything. Dearest, had we better? Shall I?" She took out her purse. "It is dreadful to be entangled with low-class people. He saw it all." Tapping Phaethon's back with her guide-book, she said, "Silenzio!" and offered him a franc.

"Va bene," he replied, and accepted it. As well this ending to his day as any. But Lucy, a mortal maid, was disappointed in him.

There was an explosion up the road. The storm had struck the overhead wire of the tramline, and one of the great supports had fallen. If they had not stopped perhaps they might have been hurt. They chose to regard it as a miraculous preservation, and the floods of love and sincerity, which fructify every hour of life, burst forth in tumult. They descended from the carriages; they embraced each other. It was as joyful to be forgiven past unworthinesses as to forgive them. For a moment they realized vast possibilities of good.

The older people recovered quickly. In the very height of their emotion they knew it to be unmanly or unladylike. Miss Lavish calculated that, even if they had continued, they would not have been caught in the accident. Mr. Eager mumbled a temperate prayer. But the drivers, through miles of dark squalid road, poured out their souls to the dryads and the saints, and Lucy poured out hers to her cousin.

"Charlotte, dear Charlotte, kiss me. Kiss me again. Only you can understand me. You warned me to be careful. And I—I thought I was developing."

"Do not cry, dearest. Take your time."

"I have been obstinate and silly—worse than you know, far worse. Once by the river—Oh, but he isn't killed—he wouldn't be killed, would he?"

The thought disturbed her repentance. As a matter of fact, the storm was worst along the road; but she had been near danger, and so she thought it must be near to every one.

"I trust not. One would always pray against that."

"He is really—I think he was taken by surprise, just as I was before. But this time I'm not to blame; I want you to believe that. I simply slipped into those violets. No, I want to be really truthful. I am a little to blame. I had silly thoughts. The sky, you know, was gold, and the ground all blue, and for a moment he looked like some one in a book."

"In a book?"

"Heroes—gods—the nonsense of schoolgirls."

"And then?"

"But, Charlotte, you know what happened then."

Miss Bartlett was silent. Indeed, she had little more to learn. With a certain amount of insight she drew her young cousin affectionately to her. All the way back Lucy's body was shaken by deep sighs, which nothing could repress.

"I want to be truthful," she whispered. "It is so hard to be absolutely truthful."

"Don't be troubled, dearest. Wait till you are calmer. We will talk it over before bed-time in my room."

So they re-entered the city with hands clasped. It was a shock to the girl to find how far emotion had ebbed in others. The storm had ceased, and Mr. Emerson was easier about his son. Mr. Beebe had regained good humour, and Mr. Eager was already snubbing Miss Lavish. Charlotte alone she was sure of—Charlotte, whose exterior concealed so much insight and love.

The luxury of self-exposure kept her almost happy through the long evening. She thought not so much of what had happened as of how she should describe it. All her sensations, her spasms of courage, her moments of unreasonable joy, her mysterious discontent, should be carefully laid before her cousin. And together in divine confidence they would disentangle and interpret them all.

"At last," thought she, "I shall understand myself. I shan't again be troubled by things that come out of nothing, and mean I don't know what."

Miss Alan asked her to play. She refused vehemently. Music seemed to her the employment of a child. She sat close to her cousin, who, with commendable patience, was listening to a long story about lost luggage. When it was over she capped it by a story of her own. Lucy became rather hysterical with the delay. In vain she tried to check, or at all events to accelerate, the tale. It was not till a late hour that Miss Bartlett had recovered her luggage and could say in her usual tone of gentle reproach:

"Well, dear, I at all events am ready for Bedfordshire. Come into my room, and I will give a good brush to your hair."

With some solemnity the door was shut, and a cane chair placed for the girl. Then Miss Bartlett said "So what is to be done?"

She was unprepared for the question. It had not occurred to her that she would have to do anything. A detailed exhibition of her emotions was all that she had counted upon.

"What is to be done? A point, dearest, which you alone can settle."

The rain was streaming down the black windows, and the great room felt damp and chilly, One candle burnt trembling on the chest of drawers close to Miss Bartlett's toque, which cast monstrous and fantastic shadows on the bolted door. A tram roared by in the dark, and Lucy felt unaccountably sad, though she had long since dried her eyes. She lifted them to the ceiling, where the griffins and bassoons were colourless and vague, the very ghosts of joy.

"It has been raining for nearly four hours," she said at last.

Miss Bartlett ignored the remark.

"How do you propose to silence him?"

"The driver?"

"My dear girl, no; Mr. George Emerson."

Lucy began to pace up and down the room.

"I don't understand," she said at last.

She understood very well, but she no longer wished to be absolutely truthful.

"How are you going to stop him talking about it?"

"I have a feeling that talk is a thing he will never do."

"I, too, intend to judge him charitably. But unfortunately I have met the type before. They seldom keep their exploits to themselves."

"Exploits?" cried Lucy, wincing under the horrible plural.

"My poor dear, did you suppose that this was his first? Come here and listen to me. I am only gathering it from his own remarks. Do you remember that day at lunch when he argued with Miss Alan that liking one person is an extra reason for liking another?"

"Yes," said Lucy, whom at the time the argument had pleased.

"Well, I am no prude. There is no need to call him a wicked young man, but obviously he is thoroughly unrefined. Let us put it down to his deplorable antecedents and education, if you wish. But we are no farther on with our question. What do you propose to do?"

An idea rushed across Lucy's brain, which, had she thought of it sooner and made it part of her, might have proved victorious.

"I propose to speak to him," said she.

Miss Bartlett uttered a cry of genuine alarm.

"You see, Charlotte, your kindness—I shall never forget it. But—as you said—it is my affair. Mine and his."

"And you are going to IMPLORE him, to BEG him to keep silence?"

"Certainly not. There would be no difficulty. Whatever you ask him he answers, yes or no; then it is over. I have been frightened of him. But now I am not one little bit."

"But we fear him for you, dear. You are so young and inexperienced, you have lived among such nice people, that you cannot realize what men can be—how they can take a brutal pleasure in insulting a woman whom her sex does not protect and rally round. This afternoon, for example, if I had not arrived, what would have happened?"

"I can't think," said Lucy gravely.

Something in her voice made Miss Bartlett repeat her question, intoning it more vigorously.

"What would have happened if I hadn't arrived?"

"I can't think," said Lucy again.

"When he insulted you, how would you have replied?"

"I hadn't time to think. You came."

"Yes, but won't you tell me now what you would have done?"

"I should have—" She checked herself, and broke the sentence off. She went up to the dripping window and strained her eyes into the darkness. She could not think what she would have done.

"Come away from the window, dear," said Miss Bartlett. "You will be seen from the road."

Lucy obeyed. She was in her cousin's power. She could not modulate out the key of self-abasement in which she had started. Neither of them referred again to her suggestion that she should speak to George and settle the matter, whatever it was, with him.

Miss Bartlett became plaintive.

"Oh, for a real man! We are only two women, you and I. Mr. Beebe is hopeless. There is Mr. Eager, but you do not trust him. Oh, for your brother! He is young, but I know that his sister's insult would rouse in him a very lion. Thank God, chivalry is not yet dead. There are still left some men who can reverence woman."

As she spoke, she pulled off her rings, of which she wore several, and ranged them upon the pin cushion. Then she blew into her gloves and said:

"It will be a push to catch the morning train, but we must try."

"What train?"

"The train to Rome." She looked at her gloves critically.

The girl received the announcement as easily as it had been given.

"When does the train to Rome go?"

"At eight."

"Signora Bertolini would be upset."

"We must face that," said Miss Bartlett, not liking to say that she had given notice already.

"She will make us pay for a whole week's pension."

"I expect she will. However, we shall be much more comfortable at the Vyses' hotel. Isn't afternoon tea given there for nothing?"

"Yes, but they pay extra for wine." After this remark she remained motionless and silent. To her tired eyes Charlotte throbbed and swelled like a ghostly figure in a dream.

They began to sort their clothes for packing, for there was no time to lose, if they were to catch the train to Rome. Lucy, when admonished, began to move to and fro between the rooms, more conscious of the discomforts of packing by candlelight than of a subtler ill. Charlotte, who was practical without ability, knelt by the side of an empty trunk, vainly endeavouring to pave it with books of varying thickness and size. She gave two or three sighs, for the stooping posture hurt her back, and, for all her diplomacy, she felt that she was growing old. The girl heard her as she entered the room, and was seized with one of those emotional impulses to which she could never attribute a cause. She only felt that the candle would burn better, the packing go easier, the world be happier, if she could give and receive some human love. The impulse had come before to-day, but never so strongly. She knelt down by her cousin's side and took her in her arms.

Miss Bartlett returned the embrace with tenderness and warmth. But she was not a stupid woman, and she knew perfectly well that Lucy did not love her, but needed her to love. For it was in ominous tones that she said, after a long pause:

"Dearest Lucy, how will you ever forgive me?"

Lucy was on her guard at once, knowing by bitter experience what forgiving Miss Bartlett meant. Her emotion relaxed, she modified her embrace a little, and she said:

"Charlotte dear, what do you mean? As if I have anything to forgive!"

"You have a great deal, and I have a very great deal to forgive myself, too. I know well how much I vex you at every turn."

"But no—"

Miss Bartlett assumed her favourite role, that of the prematurely aged martyr.

"Ah, but yes! I feel that our tour together is hardly the success I had hoped. I might have known it would not do. You want some one younger and stronger and more in sympathy with you. I am too uninteresting and old-fashioned—only fit to pack and unpack your things."

"Please—"

"My only consolation was that you found people more to your taste, and were often able to leave me at home. I had my own poor ideas of what a lady ought to do, but I hope I did not inflict them on you more than was necessary. You had your own way about these rooms, at all events."

"You mustn't say these things," said Lucy softly.

She still clung to the hope that she and Charlotte loved each other, heart and soul. They continued to pack in silence.

"I have been a failure," said Miss Bartlett, as she struggled with the straps of Lucy's trunk instead of strapping her own. "Failed to make you happy; failed in my duty to your mother. She has been so generous to me; I shall never face her again after this disaster."

"But mother will understand. It is not your fault, this trouble, and it isn't a disaster either."

"It is my fault, it is a disaster. She will never forgive me, and rightly. Fur instance, what right had I to make friends with Miss Lavish?"

"Every right."

"When I was here for your sake? If I have vexed you it is equally true that I have neglected you. Your mother will see this as clearly as I do, when you tell her."

Lucy, from a cowardly wish to improve the situation, said:

"Why need mother hear of it?"

"But you tell her everything?"

"I suppose I do generally."

"I dare not break your confidence. There is something sacred in it. Unless you feel that it is a thing you could not tell her."

The girl would not be degraded to this.

"Naturally I should have told her. But in case she should blame you in any way, I promise I will not, I am very willing not to. I will never speak of it either to her or to any one."

Her promise brought the long-drawn interview to a sudden close. Miss Bartlett pecked her smartly on both cheeks, wished her good-night, and sent her to her own room.

For a moment the original trouble was in the background. George would seem to have behaved like a cad throughout; perhaps that was the view which one would take eventually. At present she neither acquitted nor condemned him; she did not pass judgment. At the moment when she was about to judge him her cousin's voice had intervened, and, ever since, it was Miss Bartlett who had dominated; Miss Bartlett who, even now, could be heard sighing into a crack in the partition wall; Miss Bartlett, who had really been neither pliable nor humble nor inconsistent. She had worked like a great artist; for a time—indeed, for years—she had been meaningless, but at the end there was presented to the girl the complete picture of a cheerless, loveless world in which the young rush to destruction until they learn better—a shamefaced world of precautions and barriers which may avert evil, but which do not seem to bring good, if we may judge from those who have used them most.

Lucy was suffering from the most grievous wrong which this world has yet discovered: diplomatic advantage had been taken of her sincerity, of her craving for sympathy and love. Such a wrong is not easily forgotten. Never again did she expose herself without due consideration and precaution against rebuff. And such a wrong may react disastrously upon the soul.

The door-bell rang, and she started to the shutters. Before she reached them she hesitated, turned, and blew out the candle. Thus it was that, though she saw some one standing in the wet below, he, though he looked up, did not see her.

To reach his room he had to go by hers. She was still dressed. It struck her that she might slip into the passage and just say that she would be gone before he was up, and that their extraordinary intercourse was over.

Whether she would have dared to do this was never proved. At the critical moment Miss Bartlett opened her own door, and her voice said:

"I wish one word with you in the drawing-room, Mr. Emerson, please."

Soon their footsteps returned, and Miss Bartlett said: "Good-night, Mr. Emerson."

His heavy, tired breathing was the only reply; the chaperon had done her work.

Lucy cried aloud: "It isn't true. It can't all be true. I want not to be muddled. I want to grow older quickly."

Miss Bartlett tapped on the wall.

"Go to bed at once, dear. You need all the rest you can get."

In the morning they left for Rome.

PART TWO

Chapter VIII: Medieval

The drawing-room curtains at Windy Corner had been pulled to meet, for the carpet was new and deserved protection from the August sun. They were heavy curtains, reaching almost to the ground, and the light that filtered through them was subdued and varied. A poet—none was present—might have quoted, "Life like a dome of many coloured glass," or might have compared the curtains to sluice-gates, lowered against the intolerable tides of heaven. Without was poured a sea of radiance; within, the glory, though visible, was tempered to the capacities of man.

Two pleasant people sat in the room. One—a boy of nineteen—was studying a small manual of anatomy, and peering occasionally at a bone which lay upon the piano. From time to time he bounced in his chair and puffed and groaned, for the day was hot and the print small, and the human frame fearfully made; and his mother, who was writing a letter, did continually read out to him what she had written. And continually did she rise from her seat and part the curtains so that a rivulet of light fell across the carpet, and make the remark that they were still there.

"Where aren't they?" said the boy, who was Freddy, Lucy's brother. "I tell you I'm getting fairly sick."

"For goodness' sake go out of my drawing-room, then?" cried Mrs. Honeychurch, who hoped to cure her children of slang by taking it literally.

Freddy did not move or reply.

"I think things are coming to a head," she observed, rather wanting her son's opinion on the situation if she could obtain it without undue supplication.

"Time they did."

"I am glad that Cecil is asking her this once more."

"It's his third go, isn't it?"

"Freddy I do call the way you talk unkind."

"I didn't mean to be unkind." Then he added: "But I do think Lucy might have got this off her chest in Italy. I don't know how girls manage things, but she can't have said 'No' properly before, or she wouldn't have to say it again now. Over the whole thing—I can't explain—I do feel so uncomfortable."

"Do you indeed, dear? How interesting!"

"I feel—never mind."

He returned to his work.

"Just listen to what I have written to Mrs. Vyse. I said: 'Dear Mrs. Vyse.'"

"Yes, mother, you told me. A jolly good letter."

"I said: 'Dear Mrs. Vyse, Cecil has just asked my permission about it, and I should be delighted, if Lucy wishes it. But—'" She stopped reading, "I was rather amused at Cecil asking my permission at all. He has always gone in for unconventionality, and parents nowhere, and so forth. When it comes to the point, he can't get on without me."

"Nor me."

"You?"

Freddy nodded.

"What do you mean?"

"He asked me for my permission also."

She exclaimed: "How very odd of him!"

"Why so?" asked the son and heir. "Why shouldn't my permission be asked?"

"What do you know about Lucy or girls or anything? What ever did you say?"

"I said to Cecil, 'Take her or leave her; it's no business of mine!'"

"What a helpful answer!" But her own answer, though more normal in its wording, had been to the same effect.

"The bother is this," began Freddy.

Then he took up his work again, too shy to say what the bother was. Mrs. Honeychurch went back to the window.

"Freddy, you must come. There they still are!"

"I don't see you ought to go peeping like that."

"Peeping like that! Can't I look out of my own window?"

But she returned to the writing-table, observing, as she passed her son, "Still page 322?" Freddy snorted, and turned over two leaves. For a brief space they were silent. Close by, beyond the curtains, the gentle murmur of a long conversation had never ceased.

"The bother is this: I have put my foot in it with Cecil most awfully." He gave a nervous gulp. "Not content with 'permission', which I did give—that is to say, I said, 'I don't mind'—well, not content with that, he wanted to know whether I wasn't off my head with joy. He practically put it like this: Wasn't it a splendid thing for Lucy and for Windy Corner generally if he married her? And he would have an answer—he said it would strengthen his hand."

"I hope you gave a careful answer, dear."

"I answered 'No'" said the boy, grinding his teeth. "There! Fly into a stew! I can't help it—had to say it. I had to say no. He ought never to have asked me."

"Ridiculous child!" cried his mother. "You think you're so holy and truthful, but really it's only abominable conceit. Do you suppose that a man like Cecil would take the slightest notice of anything you say? I hope he boxed your ears. How dare you say no?"

"Oh, do keep quiet, mother! I had to say no when I couldn't say yes. I tried to laugh as if I didn't mean what I said, and, as Cecil laughed too, and went away, it may be all right. But I feel my foot's in it. Oh, do keep quiet, though, and let a man do some work."

"No," said Mrs. Honeychurch, with the air of one who has considered the subject, "I shall not keep quiet. You know all that has passed between them in Rome; you know why he is down here, and yet you deliberately insult him, and try to turn him out of my house."

"Not a bit!" he pleaded. "I only let out I didn't like him. I don't hate him, but I don't like him. What I mind is that he'll tell Lucy."

He glanced at the curtains dismally.

"Well, I like him," said Mrs. Honeychurch. "I know his mother; he's good, he's clever, he's rich, he's well connected—Oh, you needn't kick the piano! He's well connected—I'll say it again if you like: he's well connected." She paused, as if rehearsing her eulogy, but her face remained dissatisfied. She added: "And he has beautiful manners."

"I liked him till just now. I suppose it's having him spoiling Lucy's first week at home; and it's also something that Mr. Beebe said, not knowing."

"Mr. Beebe?" said his mother, trying to conceal her interest. "I don't see how Mr. Beebe comes in."

"You know Mr. Beebe's funny way, when you never quite know what he means. He said: 'Mr. Vyse is an ideal bachelor.' I was very cute, I asked him what he meant. He said 'Oh, he's like me—better detached.' I couldn't make him say any more, but it set me thinking. Since Cecil has come after Lucy he hasn't been so pleasant, at least—I can't explain."

"You never can, dear. But I can. You are jealous of Cecil because he may stop Lucy knitting you silk ties."

The explanation seemed plausible, and Freddy tried to accept it. But at the back of his brain there lurked a dim mistrust. Cecil praised one too much for being athletic. Was that it? Cecil made one talk in one's own way. This tired one. Was that it? And Cecil was the kind of fellow who would never wear another fellow's cap. Unaware of his own profundity, Freddy checked himself. He must be jealous, or he would not dislike a man for such foolish reasons.

"Will this do?" called his mother. "'Dear Mrs. Vyse,—Cecil has just asked my permission about it, and I should be delighted if Lucy wishes it.' Then I put in at the top, 'and I have told Lucy so.' I must write the letter out again—'and I have told Lucy so. But Lucy seems very uncertain, and in these days young people must decide for themselves.' I said that because I didn't want Mrs. Vyse to think us old-fashioned. She goes in for lectures and improving her mind, and all the time a thick layer of flue under the beds, and the maid's dirty thumb-marks where you turn on the electric light. She keeps that flat abominably—"

"Suppose Lucy marries Cecil, would she live in a flat, or in the country?"

"Don't interrupt so foolishly. Where was I? Oh yes—'Young people must decide for themselves. I know that Lucy likes your son, because she tells me everything, and she wrote to me from Rome when he asked her first.' No, I'll cross that last bit out—it looks patronizing. I'll stop at 'because she tells me everything.' Or shall I cross that out, too?"

"Cross it out, too," said Freddy.

Mrs. Honeychurch left it in.

"Then the whole thing runs: 'Dear Mrs. Vyse.—Cecil has just asked my permission about it, and I should be delighted if Lucy wishes it, and I have told Lucy so. But Lucy seems very uncertain, and in these days young people must decide for themselves. I know that Lucy likes your son, because she tells me everything. But I do not know—'"

"Look out!" cried Freddy.

The curtains parted.

Cecil's first movement was one of irritation. He couldn't bear the Honeychurch habit of sitting in the dark to save the furniture. Instinctively he give the curtains a twitch, and sent them swinging down their poles. Light entered. There was revealed a terrace, such as is owned by many villas with trees each side of it, and on it a little rustic seat, and two flower-beds. But it was transfigured by the view beyond, for Windy Corner was built on the range that overlooks the Sussex Weald. Lucy, who was in the little seat, seemed on the edge of a green magic carpet which hovered in the air above the tremulous world.

Cecil entered.

Appearing thus late in the story, Cecil must be at once described. He was medieval. Like a Gothic statue. Tall and refined, with shoulders that seemed braced square by an effort of the will, and a head that was tilted a little higher than the usual level of vision, he resembled those fastidious saints who guard the portals of a French cathedral. Well educated, well endowed, and not deficient physically, he remained in the grip of a certain devil whom the modern world knows as self-consciousness, and whom the medieval, with dimmer vision, worshipped as asceticism. A Gothic statue implies celibacy, just as a Greek statue implies fruition, and perhaps this was what Mr. Beebe meant. And Freddy, who ignored history and art, perhaps meant the same when he failed to imagine Cecil wearing another fellow's cap.

Mrs. Honeychurch left her letter on the writing table and moved towards her young acquaintance.

"Oh, Cecil!" she exclaimed—"oh, Cecil, do tell me!"

"I promessi sposi," said he.

They stared at him anxiously.

"She has accepted me," he said, and the sound of the thing in English made him flush and smile with pleasure, and look more human.

"I am so glad," said Mrs. Honeychurch, while Freddy proffered a hand that was yellow with chemicals. They wished that they also knew Italian, for our phrases of approval and of amazement are so connected with little occasions that we fear to use them on great ones. We are obliged to become vaguely poetic, or to take refuge in Scriptural reminiscences.

"Welcome as one of the family!" said Mrs. Honeychurch, waving her hand at the furniture. "This is indeed a joyous day! I feel sure that you will make our dear Lucy happy."

"I hope so," replied the young man, shifting his eyes to the ceiling.

"We mothers—" simpered Mrs. Honeychurch, and then realized that she was affected, sentimental, bombastic—all the things she hated most. Why could she not be Freddy, who stood stiff in the middle of the room; looking very cross and almost handsome?

"I say, Lucy!" called Cecil, for conversation seemed to flag.

Lucy rose from the seat. She moved across the lawn and smiled in at them, just as if she was going to ask them to play tennis. Then she saw her brother's face. Her lips parted, and she took him in her arms. He said, "Steady on!"

"Not a kiss for me?" asked her mother.

Lucy kissed her also.

"Would you take them into the garden and tell Mrs. Honeychurch all about it?" Cecil suggested. "And I'd stop here and tell my mother."

"We go with Lucy?" said Freddy, as if taking orders.

"Yes, you go with Lucy."

They passed into the sunlight. Cecil watched them cross the terrace, and descend out of sight by the steps. They would descend—he knew their ways—past the shrubbery, and past the tennis-lawn and the dahlia-bed, until they reached the kitchen garden, and there, in the presence of the potatoes and the peas, the great event would be discussed.

Smiling indulgently, he lit a cigarette, and rehearsed the events that had led to such a happy conclusion.

He had known Lucy for several years, but only as a commonplace girl who happened to be musical. He could still remember his depression that afternoon at Rome, when she and her terrible cousin fell on him out of the blue, and demanded to be taken to St. Peter's. That day she had seemed a typical tourist—shrill, crude, and gaunt with travel. But Italy worked some marvel in her. It gave her light, and—which he held more precious—it gave her shadow. Soon he detected in her a wonderful reticence. She was like a woman of Leonardo da Vinci's, whom we love not so much for herself as for the things that she will not tell us, The things are assuredly not of this life; no woman of Leonardo's could have anything so vulgar as a "story." She did develop most wonderfully day by day.

So it happened that from patronizing civility he had slowly passed if not to passion, at least to a profound uneasiness. Already at Rome he had hinted to her that they might be suitable for each other. It had touched him greatly that she had not broken away at the suggestion. Her refusal had been clear and gentle; after it—as the horrid phrase went—she had been exactly the same to him as before. Three months later, on the margin of Italy, among the flower-clad Alps, he had asked her again in bald, traditional language. She reminded him of a Leonardo more than ever; her sunburnt features were shadowed by fantastic rock; at his words she had turned and stood between him and the light with immeasurable plains behind her. He walked home with her unashamed, feeling not at all like a rejected suitor. The things that really mattered were unshaken.

So now he had asked her once more, and, clear and gentle as ever, she had accepted him, giving no coy reasons for her delay, but simply saying that she loved him and would do her best to make him happy. His mother, too, would be pleased; she had counselled the step; he must write her a long account.

Glancing at his hand, in case any of Freddy's chemicals had come off on it, he moved to the writing table. There he saw "Dear Mrs. Vyse," followed by many erasures. He recoiled without reading any more, and after a little hesitation sat down elsewhere, and pencilled a note on his knee.

Then he lit another cigarette, which did not seem quite as divine as the first, and considered what might be done to make Windy Corner drawing-room more distinctive. With that outlook it should have been a successful room, but the trail of Tottenham Court Road was upon it; he could almost visualize the motor-vans of Messrs. Shoolbred and Messrs. Maple arriving at the door and depositing this chair, those varnished book-cases, that writing-table. The table recalled Mrs. Honeychurch's letter. He did not want to read that letter—his temptations never lay in that direction; but he worried about it none the less. It was his own fault that she was discussing him with his mother; he had wanted her support in his third attempt to win Lucy; he wanted to feel that others, no matter who they were, agreed with him, and so he had asked their permission. Mrs. Honeychurch had been civil, but obtuse in essentials, while as for Freddy—"He is only a boy," he reflected. "I represent all that he despises. Why should he want me for a brother-in-law?"

The Honeychurches were a worthy family, but he began to realize that Lucy was of another clay; and perhaps—he did not put it very definitely—he ought to introduce her into more congenial circles as soon as possible.

"Mr. Beebe!" said the maid, and the new rector of Summer Street was shown in; he had at once started on friendly relations, owing to Lucy's praise of him in her letters from Florence.

Cecil greeted him rather critically.

"I've come for tea, Mr. Vyse. Do you suppose that I shall get it?"

"I should say so. Food is the thing one does get here—Don't sit in that chair; young Honeychurch has left a bone in it."

"Pfui!"

"I know," said Cecil. "I know. I can't think why Mrs. Honeychurch allows it."

For Cecil considered the bone and the Maples' furniture separately; he did not realize that, taken together, they kindled the room into the life that he desired.

"I've come for tea and for gossip. Isn't this news?"

"News? I don't understand you," said Cecil. "News?"

Mr. Beebe, whose news was of a very different nature, prattled forward.

"I met Sir Harry Otway as I came up; I have every reason to hope that I am first in the field. He has bought Cissie and Albert from Mr. Flack!"

"Has he indeed?" said Cecil, trying to recover himself. Into what a grotesque mistake had he fallen! Was it likely that a clergyman and a gentleman would refer to his engagement in a manner so flippant? But his stiffness remained, and, though he asked who Cissie and Albert might be, he still thought Mr. Beebe rather a bounder.

"Unpardonable question! To have stopped a week at Windy Corner and not to have met Cissie and Albert, the semi-detached villas that have been run up opposite the church! I'll set Mrs. Honeychurch after you."

"I'm shockingly stupid over local affairs," said the young man languidly. "I can't even remember the difference between a Parish Council and a Local Government Board. Perhaps there is no difference, or perhaps those aren't the right names. I only go into the country to see my friends and to enjoy the scenery. It is very remiss of me. Italy and London are the only places where I don't feel to exist on sufferance."

Mr. Beebe, distressed at this heavy reception of Cissie and Albert, determined to shift the subject.

"Let me see, Mr. Vyse—I forget—what is your profession?"

"I have no profession," said Cecil. "It is another example of my decadence. My attitude quite an indefensible one—is that so long as I am no trouble to any one I have a right to do as I like. I know I ought to be getting money out of people, or devoting myself to things I don't care a straw about, but somehow, I've not been able to begin."

"You are very fortunate," said Mr. Beebe. "It is a wonderful opportunity, the possession of leisure."

His voice was rather parochial, but he did not quite see his way to answering naturally. He felt, as all who have regular occupation must feel, that others should have it also.

"I am glad that you approve. I daren't face the healthy person—for example, Freddy Honeychurch."

"Oh, Freddy's a good sort, isn't he?"

"Admirable. The sort who has made England what she is."

Cecil wondered at himself. Why, on this day of all others, was he so hopelessly contrary? He tried to get right by inquiring effusively after Mr. Beebe's mother, an old lady for whom he had no particular regard. Then he flattered the clergyman, praised his liberal-mindedness, his enlightened attitude towards philosophy and science.

"Where are the others?" said Mr. Beebe at last, "I insist on extracting tea before evening service."

"I suppose Anne never told them you were here. In this house one is so coached in the servants the day one arrives. The fault of Anne is that she begs your pardon when she hears you perfectly, and kicks the chair-legs with her feet. The faults of Mary—I forget the faults of Mary, but they are very grave. Shall we look in the garden?"

"I know the faults of Mary. She leaves the dust-pans standing on the stairs."

"The fault of Euphemia is that she will not, simply will not, chop the suet sufficiently small."

They both laughed, and things began to go better.

"The faults of Freddy—" Cecil continued.

"Ah, he has too many. No one but his mother can remember the faults of Freddy. Try the faults of Miss Honeychurch; they are not innumerable."

"She has none," said the young man, with grave sincerity.

"I quite agree. At present she has none."

"At present?"

"I'm not cynical. I'm only thinking of my pet theory about Miss Honeychurch. Does it seem reasonable that she should play so wonderfully, and live so quietly? I suspect that one day she will be wonderful in both. The water-tight compartments in her will break down, and music and life will mingle. Then we shall have her heroically good, heroically bad—too heroic, perhaps, to be good or bad."

Cecil found his companion interesting.

"And at present you think her not wonderful as far as life goes?"

"Well, I must say I've only seen her at Tunbridge Wells, where she was not wonderful, and at Florence. Since I came to Summer Street she has been away. You saw her, didn't you, at Rome and in the Alps. Oh, I forgot; of course, you knew her before. No, she wasn't wonderful in Florence either, but I kept on expecting that she would be."

"In what way?"

Conversation had become agreeable to them, and they were pacing up and down the terrace.

"I could as easily tell you what tune she'll play next. There was simply the sense that she had found wings, and meant to use them. I can show you a beautiful picture in my Italian diary: Miss Honeychurch as a kite, Miss Bartlett holding the string. Picture number two: the string breaks."

The sketch was in his diary, but it had been made afterwards, when he viewed things artistically. At the time he had given surreptitious tugs to the string himself.

"But the string never broke?"

"No. I mightn't have seen Miss Honeychurch rise, but I should certainly have heard Miss Bartlett fall."

"It has broken now," said the young man in low, vibrating tones.

Immediately he realized that of all the conceited, ludicrous, contemptible ways of announcing an engagement this was the worst. He cursed his love of metaphor; had he suggested that he was a star and that Lucy was soaring up to reach him?

"Broken? What do you mean?"

"I meant," said Cecil stiffly, "that she is going to marry me."

The clergyman was conscious of some bitter disappointment which he could not keep out of his voice.

"I am sorry; I must apologize. I had no idea you were intimate with her, or I should never have talked in this flippant, superficial way. Mr. Vyse, you ought to have stopped me." And down the garden he saw Lucy herself; yes, he was disappointed.

Cecil, who naturally preferred congratulations to apologies, drew down his mouth at the corners. Was this the reception his action would get from the world? Of course, he despised the world as a whole; every thoughtful man should; it is almost a test of refinement. But he was sensitive to the successive particles of it which he encountered.

Occasionally he could be quite crude.

"I am sorry I have given you a shock," he said dryly. "I fear that Lucy's choice does not meet with your approval."

"Not that. But you ought to have stopped me. I know Miss Honeychurch only a little as time goes. Perhaps I oughtn't to have discussed her so freely with any one; certainly not with you."

"You are conscious of having said something indiscreet?"

Mr. Beebe pulled himself together. Really, Mr. Vyse had the art of placing one in the most tiresome positions. He was driven to use the prerogatives of his profession.

"No, I have said nothing indiscreet. I foresaw at Florence that her quiet, uneventful childhood must end, and it has ended. I realized dimly enough that she might take some momentous step. She has taken it. She has learnt—you will let me talk freely, as I have begun freely—she has learnt what it is to love: the greatest lesson, some people will tell you, that our earthly life provides." It was now time for him to wave his hat at the approaching trio. He did not omit to do so. "She has learnt through you," and if his voice was still clerical, it was now also sincere; "let it be your care that her knowledge is profitable to her."

"Grazie tante!" said Cecil, who did not like parsons.

"Have you heard?" shouted Mrs. Honeychurch as she toiled up the sloping garden. "Oh, Mr. Beebe, have you heard the news?"

Freddy, now full of geniality, whistled the wedding march. Youth seldom criticizes the accomplished fact.

"Indeed I have!" he cried. He looked at Lucy. In her presence he could not act the parson any longer—at all events not without apology. "Mrs. Honeychurch, I'm going to do what I am always supposed to do, but generally I'm too shy. I want to invoke every kind of blessing on them, grave and gay, great and small. I want them all their lives to be supremely good and supremely happy as husband and wife, as father and mother. And now I want my tea."

"You only asked for it just in time," the lady retorted. "How dare you be serious at Windy Corner?"

He took his tone from her. There was no more heavy beneficence, no more attempts to dignify the situation with poetry or the Scriptures. None of them dared or was able to be serious any more.

An engagement is so potent a thing that sooner or later it reduces all who speak of it to this state of cheerful awe. Away from it, in the solitude of their rooms, Mr. Beebe, and even Freddy, might again be critical. But in its presence and in the presence of each other they were sincerely hilarious. It has a strange power, for it compels not only the lips, but the very heart. The chief parallel to compare one great thing with another—is the power over us of a temple of some alien creed. Standing outside, we deride or oppose it, or at the most feel sentimental. Inside, though the saints and gods are not ours, we become true believers, in case any true believer should be present.

So it was that after the gropings and the misgivings of the afternoon they pulled themselves together and settled down to a very pleasant tea-party. If they were hypocrites they did not know it, and their hypocrisy had every chance of setting and of becoming true. Anne, putting down each plate as if it were a wedding present, stimulated them greatly. They could not lag behind that smile of hers which she gave them ere she kicked the drawing-room door. Mr. Beebe chirruped. Freddy was at his wittiest, referring to Cecil as the "Fiasco"—family honoured pun on fiance. Mrs. Honeychurch, amusing and portly, promised well as a mother-in-law. As for Lucy and Cecil, for whom the temple had been built, they also joined in the merry ritual, but waited, as earnest worshippers should, for the disclosure of some holier shrine of joy.

Chapter IX: Lucy As a Work of Art

A few days after the engagement was announced Mrs. Honeychurch made Lucy and her Fiasco come to a little garden-party in the neighbourhood, for naturally she wanted to show people that her daughter was marrying a presentable man.

Cecil was more than presentable; he looked distinguished, and it was very pleasant to see his slim figure keeping step with Lucy, and his long, fair face responding when Lucy spoke to him. People congratulated Mrs. Honeychurch, which is, I believe, a social blunder, but it pleased her, and she introduced Cecil rather indiscriminately to some stuffy dowagers.

At tea a misfortune took place: a cup of coffee was upset over Lucy's figured silk, and though Lucy feigned indifference, her mother feigned nothing of the sort but dragged her indoors to have the frock treated by a sympathetic maid. They were gone some time, and Cecil was left with the dowagers. When they returned he was not as pleasant as he had been.

"Do you go to much of this sort of thing?" he asked when they were driving home.

"Oh, now and then," said Lucy, who had rather enjoyed herself.

"Is it typical of country society?"

"I suppose so. Mother, would it be?"

"Plenty of society," said Mrs. Honeychurch, who was trying to remember the hang of one of the dresses.

Seeing that her thoughts were elsewhere, Cecil bent towards Lucy and said:

"To me it seemed perfectly appalling, disastrous, portentous."

"I am so sorry that you were stranded."

"Not that, but the congratulations. It is so disgusting, the way an engagement is regarded as public property—a kind of waste place where every outsider may shoot his vulgar sentiment. All those old women smirking!"

"One has to go through it, I suppose. They won't notice us so much next time."

"But my point is that their whole attitude is wrong. An engagement—horrid word in the first place—is a private matter, and should be treated as such."

Yet the smirking old women, however wrong individually, were racially correct. The spirit of the generations had smiled through them, rejoicing in the engagement of Cecil and Lucy because it promised the continuance of life on earth. To Cecil and Lucy it promised something quite different—personal love. Hence Cecil's irritation and Lucy's belief that his irritation was just.

"How tiresome!" she said. "Couldn't you have escaped to tennis?"

"I don't play tennis—at least, not in public. The neighbourhood is deprived of the romance of me being athletic. Such romance as I have is that of the Inglese Italianato."

"Inglese Italianato?"

"E un diavolo incarnato! You know the proverb?"

She did not. Nor did it seem applicable to a young man who had spent a quiet winter in Rome with his mother. But Cecil, since his engagement, had taken to affect a cosmopolitan naughtiness which he was far from possessing.

"Well," said he, "I cannot help it if they do disapprove of me. There are certain irremovable barriers between myself and them, and I must accept them."

"We all have our limitations, I suppose," said wise Lucy.

"Sometimes they are forced on us, though," said Cecil, who saw from her remark that she did not quite understand his position.

"How?"

"It makes a difference doesn't it, whether we fully fence ourselves in, or whether we are fenced out by the barriers of others?"

She thought a moment, and agreed that it did make a difference.

"Difference?" cried Mrs. Honeychurch, suddenly alert. "I don't see any difference. Fences are fences, especially when they are in the same place."

"We were speaking of motives," said Cecil, on whom the interruption jarred.

"My dear Cecil, look here." She spread out her knees and perched her card-case on her lap. "This is me. That's Windy Corner. The rest of the pattern is the other people. Motives are all very well, but the fence comes here."

"We weren't talking of real fences," said Lucy, laughing.

"Oh, I see, dear—poetry."

She leant placidly back. Cecil wondered why Lucy had been amused.

"I tell you who has no 'fences,' as you call them," she said, "and that's Mr. Beebe."

"A parson fenceless would mean a parson defenceless."

Lucy was slow to follow what people said, but quick enough to detect what they meant. She missed Cecil's epigram, but grasped the feeling that prompted it.

"Don't you like Mr. Beebe?" she asked thoughtfully.

"I never said so!" he cried. "I consider him far above the average. I only denied—" And he swept off on the subject of fences again, and was brilliant.

"Now, a clergyman that I do hate," said she wanting to say something sympathetic, "a clergyman that does have fences, and the most dreadful ones, is Mr. Eager, the English chaplain at Florence. He was truly insincere—not merely the manner unfortunate. He was a snob, and so conceited, and he did say such unkind things."

"What sort of things?"

"There was an old man at the Bertolini whom he said had murdered his wife."

"Perhaps he had."

"No!"

"Why 'no'?"

"He was such a nice old man, I'm sure."

Cecil laughed at her feminine inconsequence.

"Well, I did try to sift the thing. Mr. Eager would never come to the point. He prefers it vague—said the old man had 'practically' murdered his wife—had murdered her in the sight of God."

"Hush, dear!" said Mrs. Honeychurch absently. "But isn't it intolerable that a person whom we're told to imitate should go round spreading slander? It was, I believe, chiefly owing to him that the old man was dropped. People pretended he was vulgar, but he certainly wasn't that."

"Poor old man! What was his name?"

"Harris," said Lucy glibly.

"Let's hope that Mrs. Harris there warn't no sich person," said her mother.

Cecil nodded intelligently.

"Isn't Mr. Eager a parson of the cultured type?" he asked.

"I don't know. I hate him. I've heard him lecture on Giotto. I hate him. Nothing can hide a petty nature. I HATE him."

"My goodness gracious me, child!" said Mrs. Honeychurch. "You'll blow my head off! Whatever is there to shout over? I forbid you and Cecil to hate any more clergymen."

He smiled. There was indeed something rather incongruous in Lucy's moral outburst over Mr. Eager. It was as if one should see the Leonardo on the ceiling of the Sistine. He longed to hint to her that not here lay her vocation; that a woman's power and charm reside in mystery, not in muscular rant. But possibly rant is a sign of vitality: it mars the beautiful creature, but shows that she is alive. After a moment, he contemplated her flushed face and excited gestures with a certain approval. He forebore to repress the sources of youth.

Nature—simplest of topics, he thought—lay around them. He praised the pine-woods, the deep lasts of bracken, the crimson leaves that spotted the hurt-bushes, the serviceable beauty of the turnpike road. The outdoor world was not very familiar to him, and occasionally he went wrong in a question of fact. Mrs. Honeychurch's mouth twitched when he spoke of the perpetual green of the larch.

"I count myself a lucky person," he concluded, "When I'm in London I feel I could never live out of it. When I'm in the country I feel the same about the country. After all, I do believe that birds and trees and the sky are the most wonderful things in life, and that the people who live amongst them must be the best. It's true that in nine cases out of ten they don't seem to notice anything. The country gentleman and the country labourer are each in their way the most depressing of companions. Yet they may have a tacit sympathy with the workings of Nature which is denied to us of the town. Do you feel that, Mrs. Honeychurch?"

Mrs. Honeychurch started and smiled. She had not been attending. Cecil, who was rather crushed on the front seat of the victoria, felt irritable, and determined not to say anything interesting again.

Lucy had not attended either. Her brow was wrinkled, and she still looked furiously cross—the result, he concluded, of too much moral gymnastics. It was sad to see her thus blind to the beauties of an August wood.

"'Come down, O maid, from yonder mountain height,'" he quoted, and touched her knee with his own.

She flushed again and said: "What height?"

"'Come down, O maid, from yonder mountain height, What pleasure lives in height (the shepherd sang). In height and in the splendour of the hills?' Let us take Mrs. Honeychurch's advice and hate clergymen no more. What's this place?"

"Summer Street, of course," said Lucy, and roused herself.

The woods had opened to leave space for a sloping triangular meadow. Pretty cottages lined it on two sides, and the upper and third side was occupied by a new stone church, expensively simple, a charming shingled spire. Mr. Beebe's house was near the church. In height it scarcely exceeded the cottages. Some great mansions were at hand, but they were hidden in the trees. The scene suggested a Swiss Alp rather than the shrine and centre of a leisured world, and was marred only by two ugly little villas—the villas that had competed with Cecil's engagement, having been acquired by Sir Harry Otway the very afternoon that Lucy had been acquired by Cecil.

"Cissie" was the name of one of these villas, "Albert" of the other. These titles were not only picked out in shaded Gothic on the garden gates, but appeared a second time on the porches, where they followed the semicircular curve of the entrance arch in block capitals. "Albert" was inhabited. His tortured garden was bright with geraniums and lobelias and polished shells. His little windows were chastely swathed in Nottingham lace. "Cissie" was to let. Three notice-boards, belonging to Dorking agents, lolled on her fence and announced the not surprising fact. Her paths were already weedy; her pocket-handkerchief of a lawn was yellow with dandelions.

"The place is ruined!" said the ladies mechanically. "Summer Street will never be the same again."

As the carriage passed, "Cissie's" door opened, and a gentleman came out of her.

"Stop!" cried Mrs. Honeychurch, touching the coachman with her parasol. "Here's Sir Harry. Now we shall know. Sir Harry, pull those things down at once!"

Sir Harry Otway—who need not be described—came to the carriage and said "Mrs. Honeychurch, I meant to. I can't, I really can't turn out Miss Flack."

"Am I not always right? She ought to have gone before the contract was signed. Does she still live rent free, as she did in her nephew's time?"

"But what can I do?" He lowered his voice. "An old lady, so very vulgar, and almost bedridden."

"Turn her out," said Cecil bravely.

Sir Harry sighed, and looked at the villas mournfully. He had had full warning of Mr. Flack's intentions, and might have bought the plot before building commenced: but he was apathetic and dilatory. He had known Summer Street for so many years that he could not imagine it being spoilt. Not till Mrs. Flack had laid the foundation stone, and the apparition of red and cream brick began to rise did he take alarm. He called on Mr. Flack, the local builder,—a most reasonable and respectful man—who agreed that tiles would have made more artistic roof, but pointed out that slates were cheaper. He ventured to differ, however, about the Corinthian columns which were to cling like leeches to the frames of the bow windows, saying that, for his part, he liked to relieve the facade by a bit of decoration. Sir Harry hinted that a column, if possible, should be structural as well as decorative.

Mr. Flack replied that all the columns had been ordered, adding, "and all the capitals different—one with dragons in the foliage, another approaching to the Ionian style, another introducing Mrs. Flack's initials—every one different." For he had read his Ruskin. He built his villas according to his desire; and not until he had inserted an immovable aunt into one of them did Sir Harry buy.

This futile and unprofitable transaction filled the knight with sadness as he leant on Mrs. Honeychurch's carriage. He had failed in his duties to the country-side, and the country-side was laughing at him as well. He had spent money, and yet Summer Street was spoilt as much as ever. All he could do now was to find a desirable tenant for "Cissie"—some one really desirable.

"The rent is absurdly low," he told them, "and perhaps I am an easy landlord. But it is such an awkward size. It is too large for the peasant class and too small for any one the least like ourselves."

Cecil had been hesitating whether he should despise the villas or despise Sir Harry for despising them. The latter impulse seemed the more fruitful.

"You ought to find a tenant at once," he said maliciously. "It would be a perfect paradise for a bank clerk."

"Exactly!" said Sir Harry excitedly. "That is exactly what I fear, Mr. Vyse. It will attract the wrong type of people. The train service has improved—a fatal improvement, to my mind. And what are five miles from a station in these days of bicycles?"

"Rather a strenuous clerk it would be," said Lucy.

Cecil, who had his full share of mediaeval mischievousness, replied that the physique of the lower middle classes was improving at a most appalling rate. She saw that he was laughing at their harmless neighbour, and roused herself to stop him.

"Sir Harry!" she exclaimed, "I have an idea. How would you like spinsters?"

"My dear Lucy, it would be splendid. Do you know any such?"

"Yes; I met them abroad."

"Gentlewomen?" he asked tentatively.

"Yes, indeed, and at the present moment homeless. I heard from them last week—Miss Teresa and Miss Catharine Alan. I'm really not joking. They are quite the right people. Mr. Beebe knows them, too. May I tell them to write to you?"

"Indeed you may!" he cried. "Here we are with the difficulty solved already. How delightful it is! Extra facilities—please tell them they shall have extra facilities, for I shall have no agents' fees. Oh, the agents! The appalling people they have sent me! One woman, when I wrote—a tactful letter, you know—asking her to explain her social position to me, replied that she would pay the rent in advance. As if one cares about that! And several references I took up were most unsatisfactory—people swindlers, or not respectable. And oh, the deceit! I have seen a good deal of the seamy side this last week. The deceit of the most promising people. My dear Lucy, the deceit!"

She nodded.

"My advice," put in Mrs. Honeychurch, "is to have nothing to do with Lucy and her decayed gentlewomen at all. I know the type. Preserve me from people who have seen better days, and bring heirlooms with them that make the house smell stuffy. It's a sad thing, but I'd far rather let to some one who is going up in the world than to some one who has come down."

"I think I follow you," said Sir Harry; "but it is, as you say, a very sad thing."

"The Misses Alan aren't that!" cried Lucy.

"Yes, they are," said Cecil. "I haven't met them but I should say they were a highly unsuitable addition to the neighbourhood."

"Don't listen to him, Sir Harry—he's tiresome."

"It's I who am tiresome," he replied. "I oughtn't to come with my troubles to young people. But really I am so worried, and Lady Otway will only say that I cannot be too careful, which is quite true, but no real help."

"Then may I write to my Misses Alan?"

"Please!"

But his eye wavered when Mrs. Honeychurch exclaimed:

"Beware! They are certain to have canaries. Sir Harry, beware of canaries: they spit the seed out through the bars of the cages and then the mice come. Beware of women altogether. Only let to a man."

"Really—" he murmured gallantly, though he saw the wisdom of her remark.

"Men don't gossip over tea-cups. If they get drunk, there's an end of them—they lie down comfortably and sleep it off. If they're vulgar, they somehow keep it to themselves. It doesn't spread so. Give me a man—of course, provided he's clean."

Sir Harry blushed. Neither he nor Cecil enjoyed these open compliments to their sex. Even the exclusion of the dirty did not leave them much distinction. He suggested that Mrs. Honeychurch, if she had time, should descend from the carriage and inspect "Cissie" for herself. She was delighted. Nature had intended her to be poor and to live in such a house. Domestic arrangements always attracted her, especially when they were on a small scale.

Cecil pulled Lucy back as she followed her mother.

"Mrs. Honeychurch," he said, "what if we two walk home and leave you?"

"Certainly!" was her cordial reply.

Sir Harry likewise seemed almost too glad to get rid of them. He beamed at them knowingly, said, "Aha! young people, young people!" and then hastened to unlock the house.

"Hopeless vulgarian!" exclaimed Cecil, almost before they were out of earshot.

"Oh, Cecil!"

"I can't help it. It would be wrong not to loathe that man."

"He isn't clever, but really he is nice."

"No, Lucy, he stands for all that is bad in country life. In London he would keep his place. He would belong to a brainless club, and his wife would give brainless dinner parties. But down here he acts the little god with his gentility, and his patronage, and his sham aesthetics, and every one—even your mother—is taken in."

"All that you say is quite true," said Lucy, though she felt discouraged. "I wonder whether—whether it matters so very much."

"It matters supremely. Sir Harry is the essence of that garden-party. Oh, goodness, how cross I feel! How I do hope he'll get some vulgar tenant in that villa—some woman so really vulgar that he'll notice it. GENTLEFOLKS! Ugh! with his bald head and retreating chin! But let's forget him."

This Lucy was glad enough to do. If Cecil disliked Sir Harry Otway and Mr. Beebe, what guarantee was there that the people who really mattered to her would escape? For instance, Freddy. Freddy was neither clever, nor subtle, nor beautiful, and what prevented Cecil from saying, any minute, "It would be wrong not to loathe Freddy"? And what would she reply? Further than Freddy she did not go, but he gave her anxiety enough. She could only assure herself that Cecil had known Freddy some time, and that they had always got on pleasantly, except, perhaps, during the last few days, which was an accident, perhaps.

"Which way shall we go?" she asked him.

Nature—simplest of topics, she thought—was around them. Summer Street lay deep in the woods, and she had stopped where a footpath diverged from the highroad.

"Are there two ways?"

"Perhaps the road is more sensible, as we're got up smart."

"I'd rather go through the wood," said Cecil, With that subdued irritation that she had noticed in him all the afternoon. "Why is it, Lucy, that you always say the road? Do you know that you have never once been with me in the fields or the wood since we were engaged?"

"Haven't I? The wood, then," said Lucy, startled at his queerness, but pretty sure that he would explain later; it was not his habit to leave her in doubt as to his meaning.

She led the way into the whispering pines, and sure enough he did explain before they had gone a dozen yards.

"I had got an idea—I dare say wrongly—that you feel more at home with me in a room."

"A room?" she echoed, hopelessly bewildered.

"Yes. Or, at the most, in a garden, or on a road. Never in the real country like this."

"Oh, Cecil, whatever do you mean? I have never felt anything of the sort. You talk as if I was a kind of poetess sort of person."

"I don't know that you aren't. I connect you with a view—a certain type of view. Why shouldn't you connect me with a room?"

She reflected a moment, and then said, laughing:

"Do you know that you're right? I do. I must be a poetess after all. When I think of you it's always as in a room. How funny!"

To her surprise, he seemed annoyed.

"A drawing-room, pray? With no view?"

"Yes, with no view, I fancy. Why not?"

"I'd rather," he said reproachfully, "that connected me with the open air."

She said again, "Oh, Cecil, whatever do you mean?"

As no explanation was forthcoming, she shook off the subject as too difficult for a girl, and led him further into the wood, pausing every now and then at some particularly beautiful or familiar combination of the trees. She had known the wood between Summer Street and Windy Corner ever since she could walk alone; she had played at losing Freddy in it, when Freddy was a purple-faced baby; and though she had been to Italy, it had lost none of its charm.

Presently they came to a little clearing among the pines—another tiny green alp, solitary this time, and holding in its bosom a shallow pool.

She exclaimed, "The Sacred Lake!"

"Why do you call it that?"

"I can't remember why. I suppose it comes out of some book. It's only a puddle now, but you see that stream going through it? Well, a good deal of water comes down after heavy rains, and can't get away at once, and the pool becomes quite large and beautiful. Then Freddy used to bathe there. He is very fond of it."

"And you?"

He meant, "Are you fond of it?" But she answered dreamily, "I bathed here, too, till I was found out. Then there was a row."

At another time he might have been shocked, for he had depths of prudishness within him. But now? with his momentary cult of the fresh air, he was delighted at her admirable simplicity. He looked at her as she stood by the pool's edge. She was got up smart, as she phrased it, and she reminded him of some brilliant flower that has no leaves of its own, but blooms abruptly out of a world of green.

"Who found you out?"

"Charlotte," she murmured. "She was stopping with us. Charlotte—Charlotte."

"Poor girl!"

She smiled gravely. A certain scheme, from which hitherto he had shrank, now appeared practical.

"Lucy!"

"Yes, I suppose we ought to be going," was her reply.

"Lucy, I want to ask something of you that I have never asked before."

At the serious note in his voice she stepped frankly and kindly towards him.

"What, Cecil?"

"Hitherto never—not even that day on the lawn when you agreed to marry me—"

He became self-conscious and kept glancing round to see if they were observed. His courage had gone.

"Yes?"

"Up to now I have never kissed you."

She was as scarlet as if he had put the thing most indelicately.

"No—more you have," she stammered.

"Then I ask you—may I now?"

"Of course, you may, Cecil. You might before. I can't run at you, you know."

At that supreme moment he was conscious of nothing but absurdities. Her reply was inadequate. She gave such a business-like lift to her veil. As he approached her he found time to wish that he could recoil. As he touched her, his gold pince-nez became dislodged and was flattened between them.

Such was the embrace. He considered, with truth, that it had been a failure. Passion should believe itself irresistible. It should forget civility and consideration and all the other curses of a refined nature. Above all, it should never ask for leave where there is a right of way. Why could he not do as any labourer or navvy—nay, as any young man behind the counter would have done? He recast the scene. Lucy was standing flowerlike by the water, he rushed up and took her in his arms; she rebuked him, permitted him and revered him ever after for his manliness. For he believed that women revere men for their manliness.

They left the pool in silence, after this one salutation. He waited for her to make some remark which should show him her inmost thoughts. At last she spoke, and with fitting gravity.

"Emerson was the name, not Harris."

"What name?"

"The old man's."

"What old man?"

"That old man I told you about. The one Mr. Eager was so unkind to."

He could not know that this was the most intimate conversation they had ever had.

Chapter X: Cecil as a Humourist

The society out of which Cecil proposed to rescue Lucy was perhaps no very splendid affair, yet it was more splendid than her antecedents entitled her to. Her father, a prosperous local solicitor, had built Windy Corner, as a speculation at the time the district was opening up, and, falling in love with his own creation, had ended by living there himself. Soon after his marriage the social atmosphere began to alter. Other houses were built on the brow of that steep southern slope and others, again, among the pine-trees behind, and northward on the chalk barrier of the downs. Most of these houses were larger than Windy Corner, and were filled by people who came, not from the district, but from London, and who mistook the Honeychurches for the remnants of an indigenous aristocracy. He was inclined to be frightened, but his wife accepted the situation without either pride or humility. "I cannot think what people are doing," she would say, "but it is extremely fortunate for the children." She called everywhere; her calls were returned with enthusiasm, and by the time people found out that she was not exactly of their milieu, they liked her, and it did not seem to matter. When Mr. Honeychurch died, he had the satisfaction—which few honest solicitors despise—of leaving his family rooted in the best society obtainable.

The best obtainable. Certainly many of the immigrants were rather dull, and Lucy realized this more vividly since her return from Italy. Hitherto she had accepted their ideals without questioning—their kindly affluence, their inexplosive religion, their dislike of paper-bags, orange-peel, and broken bottles. A Radical out and out, she learnt to speak with horror of Suburbia. Life, so far as she troubled to conceive it, was a circle of rich, pleasant people, with identical interests and identical foes. In this circle, one thought, married, and died. Outside it were poverty and vulgarity for ever trying to enter, just as the London fog tries to enter the pine-woods pouring through the gaps in the northern hills. But, in Italy, where any one who chooses may warm himself in equality, as in the sun, this conception of life vanished. Her senses expanded; she felt that there was no one whom she might not get to like, that social barriers were irremovable, doubtless, but not particularly high. You jump over them just as you jump into a peasant's olive-yard in the Apennines, and he is glad to see you. She returned with new eyes.

So did Cecil; but Italy had quickened Cecil, not to tolerance, but to irritation. He saw that the local society was narrow, but, instead of saying, "Does that very much matter?" he rebelled, and tried to substitute for it the society he called broad. He did not realize that Lucy had consecrated her environment by the thousand little civilities that create a tenderness in time, and that though her eyes saw its defects, her heart refused to despise it entirely. Nor did he realize a more important point—that if she was too great for this society, she was too great for all society, and had reached the stage where personal intercourse would alone satisfy her. A rebel she was, but not of the kind he understood—a rebel who desired, not a wider dwelling-room, but equality beside the man she loved. For Italy was offering her the most priceless of all possessions—her own soul.

Playing bumble-puppy with Minnie Beebe, niece to the rector, and aged thirteen—an ancient and most honourable game, which consists in striking tennis-balls high into the air, so that they fall over the net and immoderately bounce; some hit Mrs. Honeychurch; others are lost. The sentence is confused, but the better illustrates Lucy's state of mind, for she was trying to talk to Mr. Beebe at the same time.

"Oh, it has been such a nuisance—first he, then they—no one knowing what they wanted, and every one so tiresome."

"But they really are coming now," said Mr. Beebe. "I wrote to Miss Teresa a few days ago—she was wondering how often the butcher called, and my reply of once a month must have impressed her favourably. They are coming. I heard from them this morning.

"I shall hate those Miss Alans!" Mrs. Honeychurch cried. "Just because they're old and silly one's expected to say 'How sweet!' I hate their 'if'-ing and 'but'-ing and 'and'-ing. And poor Lucy—serve her right—worn to a shadow."

Mr. Beebe watched the shadow springing and shouting over the tennis-court. Cecil was absent—one did not play bumble-puppy when he was there.

"Well, if they are coming—No, Minnie, not Saturn." Saturn was a tennis-ball whose skin was partially unsewn. When in motion his orb was encircled by a ring. "If they are coming, Sir Harry will let them move in before the twenty-ninth, and he will cross out the clause about whitewashing the ceilings, because it made them nervous, and put in the fair wear and tear one.—That doesn't count. I told you not Saturn."

"Saturn's all right for bumble-puppy," cried Freddy, joining them. "Minnie, don't you listen to her."

"Saturn doesn't bounce."

"Saturn bounces enough."

"No, he doesn't."

"Well; he bounces better than the Beautiful White Devil."

"Hush, dear," said Mrs. Honeychurch.

"But look at Lucy—complaining of Saturn, and all the time's got the Beautiful White Devil in her hand, ready to plug it in. That's right, Minnie, go for her—get her over the shins with the racquet—get her over the shins!"

Lucy fell, the Beautiful White Devil rolled from her hand.

Mr. Beebe picked it up, and said: "The name of this ball is Vittoria Corombona, please." But his correction passed unheeded.

Freddy possessed to a high degree the power of lashing little girls to fury, and in half a minute he had transformed Minnie from a well-mannered child into a howling wilderness. Up in the house Cecil heard them, and, though he was full of entertaining news, he did not come down to impart it, in case he got hurt. He was not a coward and bore necessary pain as well as any man. But he hated the physical violence of the young. How right it was! Sure enough it ended in a cry.

"I wish the Miss Alans could see this," observed Mr. Beebe, just as Lucy, who was nursing the injured Minnie, was in turn lifted off her feet by her brother.

"Who are the Miss Alans?" Freddy panted.

"They have taken Cissie Villa."

"That wasn't the name—"

Here his foot slipped, and they all fell most agreeably on to the grass. An interval elapses.

"Wasn't what name?" asked Lucy, with her brother's head in her lap.

"Alan wasn't the name of the people Sir Harry's let to."

"Nonsense, Freddy! You know nothing about it."

"Nonsense yourself! I've this minute seen him. He said to me: 'Ahem! Honeychurch,'"—Freddy was an indifferent mimic—"'ahem! ahem! I have at last procured really dee-sire-rebel tenants.' I said, 'ooray, old boy!' and slapped him on the back."

"Exactly. The Miss Alans?"

"Rather not. More like Anderson."

"Oh, good gracious, there isn't going to be another muddle!" Mrs. Honeychurch exclaimed. "Do you notice, Lucy, I'm always right? I said don't interfere with Cissie Villa. I'm always right. I'm quite uneasy at being always right so often."

"It's only another muddle of Freddy's. Freddy doesn't even know the name of the people he pretends have taken it instead."

"Yes, I do. I've got it. Emerson."

"What name?"

"Emerson. I'll bet you anything you like."

"What a weathercock Sir Harry is," said Lucy quietly. "I wish I had never bothered over it at all."

Then she lay on her back and gazed at the cloudless sky. Mr. Beebe, whose opinion of her rose daily, whispered to his niece that THAT was the proper way to behave if any little thing went wrong.

Meanwhile the name of the new tenants had diverted Mrs. Honeychurch from the contemplation of her own abilities.

"Emerson, Freddy? Do you know what Emersons they are?"

"I don't know whether they're any Emersons," retorted Freddy, who was democratic. Like his sister and like most young people, he was naturally attracted by the idea of equality, and the undeniable fact that there are different kinds of Emersons annoyed him beyond measure.

"I trust they are the right sort of person. All right, Lucy"—she was sitting up again—"I see you looking down your nose and thinking your mother's a snob. But there is a right sort and a wrong sort, and it's affectation to pretend there isn't."

"Emerson's a common enough name," Lucy remarked.

She was gazing sideways. Seated on a promontory herself, she could see the pine-clad promontories descending one beyond another into the Weald. The further one descended the garden, the more glorious was this lateral view.

"I was merely going to remark, Freddy, that I trusted they were no relations of Emerson the philosopher, a most trying man. Pray, does that satisfy you?"

"Oh, yes," he grumbled. "And you will be satisfied, too, for they're friends of Cecil; so"—elaborate irony—"you and the other country families will be able to call in perfect safety."

"CECIL?" exclaimed Lucy.

"Don't be rude, dear," said his mother placidly. "Lucy, don't screech. It's a new bad habit you're getting into."

"But has Cecil—"

"Friends of Cecil's," he repeated, "'and so really dee-sire-rebel. Ahem! Honeychurch, I have just telegraphed to them.'"

She got up from the grass.

It was hard on Lucy. Mr. Beebe sympathized with her very much. While she believed that her snub about the Miss Alans came from Sir Harry Otway, she had borne it like a good girl. She might well "screech" when she heard that it came partly from her lover. Mr. Vyse was a tease—something worse than a tease: he took a malicious pleasure in thwarting people. The clergyman, knowing this, looked at Miss Honeychurch with more than his usual kindness.

When she exclaimed, "But Cecil's Emersons—they can't possibly be the same ones—there is that—" he did not consider that the exclamation was strange, but saw in it an opportunity of diverting the conversation while she recovered her composure. He diverted it as follows:

"The Emersons who were at Florence, do you mean? No, I don't suppose it will prove to be them. It is probably a long cry from them to friends of Mr. Vyse's. Oh, Mrs. Honeychurch, the oddest people! The queerest people! For our part we liked them, didn't we?" He appealed to Lucy. "There was a great scene over some violets. They picked violets and filled all the vases in the room of these very Miss Alans who have failed to come to Cissie Villa. Poor little ladies! So shocked and so pleased. It used to be one of Miss Catharine's great stories. 'My dear sister loves flowers,' it began. They found the whole room a mass of blue—vases and jugs—and the story ends with 'So ungentlemanly and yet so beautiful.' It is all very difficult. Yes, I always connect those Florentine Emersons with violets."

"Fiasco's done you this time," remarked Freddy, not seeing that his sister's face was very red. She could not recover herself. Mr. Beebe saw it, and continued to divert the conversation.

"These particular Emersons consisted of a father and a son—the son a goodly, if not a good young man; not a fool, I fancy, but very immature—pessimism, et cetera. Our special joy was the father—such a sentimental darling, and people declared he had murdered his wife."

In his normal state Mr. Beebe would never have repeated such gossip, but he was trying to shelter Lucy in her little trouble. He repeated any rubbish that came into his head.

"Murdered his wife?" said Mrs. Honeychurch. "Lucy, don't desert us—go on playing bumble-puppy. Really, the Pension Bertolini must have been the oddest place. That's the second murderer I've heard of as being there. Whatever was Charlotte doing to stop? By-the-by, we really must ask Charlotte here some time."

Mr. Beebe could recall no second murderer. He suggested that his hostess was mistaken. At the hint of opposition she warmed. She was perfectly sure that there had been a second tourist of whom the same story had been told. The name escaped her. What was the name? Oh, what was the name? She clasped her knees for the name. Something in Thackeray. She struck her matronly forehead.

Lucy asked her brother whether Cecil was in.

"Oh, don't go!" he cried, and tried to catch her by the ankles.

"I must go," she said gravely. "Don't be silly. You always overdo it when you play."

As she left them her mother's shout of "Harris!" shivered the tranquil air, and reminded her that she had told a lie and had never put it right. Such a senseless lie, too, yet it shattered her nerves and made her connect these Emersons, friends of Cecil's, with a pair of nondescript tourists. Hitherto truth had come to her naturally. She saw that for the future she must be more vigilant, and be—absolutely truthful? Well, at all events, she must not tell lies. She hurried up the garden, still flushed with shame. A word from Cecil would soothe her, she was sure.

"Cecil!"

"Hullo!" he called, and leant out of the smoking-room window. He seemed in high spirits. "I was hoping you'd come. I heard you all bear-gardening, but there's better fun up here. I, even I, have won a great victory for the Comic Muse. George Meredith's right—the cause of Comedy and the cause of Truth are really the same; and I, even I, have found tenants for the distressful Cissie Villa. Don't be angry! Don't be angry! You'll forgive me when you hear it all."

He looked very attractive when his face was bright, and he dispelled her ridiculous forebodings at once.

"I have heard," she said. "Freddy has told us. Naughty Cecil! I suppose I must forgive you. Just think of all the trouble I took for nothing! Certainly the Miss Alans are a little tiresome, and I'd rather have nice friends of yours. But you oughtn't to tease one so."

"Friends of mine?" he laughed. "But, Lucy, the whole joke is to come! Come here." But she remained standing where she was. "Do you know where I met these desirable tenants? In the National Gallery, when I was up to see my mother last week."

"What an odd place to meet people!" she said nervously. "I don't quite understand."

"In the Umbrian Room. Absolute strangers. They were admiring Luca Signorelli—of course, quite stupidly. However, we got talking, and they refreshed me not—a little. They had been to Italy."

"But, Cecil—" proceeded hilariously.

"In the course of conversation they said that they wanted a country cottage—the father to live there, the son to run down for week-ends. I thought, 'What a chance of scoring off Sir Harry!' and I took their address and a London reference, found they weren't actual blackguards—it was great sport—and wrote to him, making out—"

"Cecil! No, it's not fair. I've probably met them before—"

He bore her down.

"Perfectly fair. Anything is fair that punishes a snob. That old man will do the neighbourhood a world of good. Sir Harry is too disgusting with his 'decayed gentlewomen.' I meant to read him a lesson some time. No, Lucy, the classes ought to mix, and before long you'll agree with me. There ought to be intermarriage—all sorts of things. I believe in democracy—"

"No, you don't," she snapped. "You don't know what the word means."

He stared at her, and felt again that she had failed to be Leonardesque. "No, you don't!"

Her face was inartistic—that of a peevish virago.

"It isn't fair, Cecil. I blame you—I blame you very much indeed. You had no business to undo my work about the Miss Alans, and make me look ridiculous. You call it scoring off Sir Harry, but do you realize that it is all at my expense? I consider it most disloyal of you."

She left him.

"Temper!" he thought, raising his eyebrows.

No, it was worse than temper—snobbishness. As long as Lucy thought that his own smart friends were supplanting the Miss Alans, she had not minded. He perceived that these new tenants might be of value educationally. He would tolerate the father and draw out the son, who was silent. In the interests of the Comic Muse and of Truth, he would bring them to Windy Corner.

Chapter XI: In Mrs. Vyse's Well-Appointed Flat

The Comic Muse, though able to look after her own interests, did not disdain the assistance of Mr. Vyse. His idea of bringing the Emersons to Windy Corner struck her as decidedly good, and she carried through the negotiations without a hitch. Sir Harry Otway signed the agreement, met Mr. Emerson, who was duly disillusioned. The Miss Alans were duly offended, and wrote a dignified letter to Lucy, whom they held responsible for the failure. Mr. Beebe planned pleasant moments for the new-comers, and told Mrs. Honeychurch that Freddy must call on them as soon as they arrived. Indeed, so ample was the Muse's equipment that she permitted Mr. Harris, never a very robust criminal, to droop his head, to be forgotten, and to die.

Lucy—to descend from bright heaven to earth, whereon there are shadows because there are hills—Lucy was at first plunged into despair, but settled after a little thought that it did not matter the very least. Now that she was engaged, the Emersons would scarcely insult her and were welcome into the neighbourhood. And Cecil was welcome to bring whom he would into the neighbourhood. Therefore Cecil was welcome to bring the Emersons into the neighbourhood. But, as I say, this took a little thinking, and—so illogical are girls—the event remained rather greater and rather more dreadful than it should have done. She was glad that a visit to Mrs. Vyse now fell due; the tenants moved into Cissie Villa while she was safe in the London flat.

"Cecil—Cecil darling," she whispered the evening she arrived, and crept into his arms.

Cecil, too, became demonstrative. He saw that the needful fire had been kindled in Lucy. At last she longed for attention, as a woman should, and looked up to him because he was a man.

"So you do love me, little thing?" he murmured.

"Oh, Cecil, I do, I do! I don't know what I should do without you."

Several days passed. Then she had a letter from Miss Bartlett. A coolness had sprung up between the two cousins, and they had not corresponded since they parted in August. The coolness dated from what Charlotte would call "the flight to Rome," and in Rome it had increased amazingly. For the companion who is merely uncongenial in the mediaeval world becomes exasperating in the classical. Charlotte, unselfish in the Forum, would have tried a sweeter temper than Lucy's, and once, in the Baths of Caracalla, they had doubted whether they could continue their tour. Lucy had said she would join the Vyses—Mrs. Vyse was an acquaintance of her mother, so there was no impropriety in the plan and Miss Bartlett had replied that she was quite used to being abandoned suddenly. Finally nothing happened; but the coolness remained, and, for Lucy, was even increased when she opened the letter and read as follows. It had been forwarded from Windy Corner.

"Tunbridge Wells,

"September.

"Dearest Lucia,

"I have news of you at last! Miss Lavish has been bicycling in your parts, but was not sure whether a call would be welcome. Puncturing her tire near Summer Street, and it being mended while she sat very woebegone in that pretty churchyard, she saw to her astonishment, a door open opposite and the younger Emerson man come out. He said his father had just taken the house. He SAID he did not know that you lived in the neighbourhood (?). He never suggested giving Eleanor a cup of tea. Dear Lucy, I am much worried, and I advise you to make a clean breast of his past behaviour to your mother, Freddy, and Mr. Vyse, who will forbid him to enter the house, etc. That was a great misfortune, and I dare say you have told them already. Mr. Vyse is so sensitive. I remember how I used to get on his nerves at Rome. I am very sorry about it all, and should not feel easy unless I warned you.

"Believe me,

"Your anxious and loving cousin,

"Charlotte."

Lucy was much annoyed, and replied as follows:

"Beauchamp Mansions, S.W.

"Dear Charlotte,

"Many thanks for your warning. When Mr. Emerson forgot himself on the mountain, you made me promise not to tell mother, because you said she would blame you for not being always with me. I have kept that promise, and cannot possibly tell her now. I have said both to her and Cecil that I met the Emersons at Florence, and that they are respectable people—which I do think—and the reason that he offered Miss Lavish no tea was probably that he had none himself. She should have tried at the Rectory. I cannot begin making a fuss at this stage. You must see that it would be too absurd. If the Emersons heard I had complained of them, they would think themselves of importance, which is exactly what they are not. I like the old father, and look forward to seeing him again. As for the son, I am sorry for him when we meet, rather than for myself. They are known to Cecil, who is very well and spoke of you the other day. We expect to be married in January.

"Miss Lavish cannot have told you much about me, for I am not at Windy Corner at all, but here. Please do not put 'Private' outside your envelope again. No one opens my letters.

"Yours affectionately,

"L. M. Honeychurch."

Secrecy has this disadvantage: we lose the sense of proportion; we cannot tell whether our secret is important or not. Were Lucy and her cousin closeted with a great thing which would destroy Cecil's life if he discovered it, or with a little thing which he would laugh at? Miss Bartlett suggested the former. Perhaps she was right. It had become a great thing now. Left to herself, Lucy would have told her mother and her lover ingenuously, and it would have remained a little thing. "Emerson, not Harris"; it was only that a few weeks ago. She tried to tell Cecil even now when they were laughing about some beautiful lady who had smitten his heart at school. But her body behaved so ridiculously that she stopped.

She and her secret stayed ten days longer in the deserted Metropolis visiting the scenes they were to know so well later on. It did her no harm, Cecil thought, to learn the framework of society, while society itself was absent on the golf-links or the moors. The weather was cool, and it did her no harm. In spite of the season, Mrs. Vyse managed to scrape together a dinner-party consisting entirely of the grandchildren of famous people. The food was poor, but the talk had a witty weariness that impressed the girl. One was tired of everything, it seemed. One launched into enthusiasms only to collapse gracefully, and pick oneself up amid sympathetic laughter. In this atmosphere the Pension Bertolini and Windy Corner appeared equally crude, and Lucy saw that her London career would estrange her a little from all that she had loved in the past.

The grandchildren asked her to play the piano.

She played Schumann. "Now some Beethoven" called Cecil, when the querulous beauty of the music had died. She shook her head and played Schumann again. The melody rose, unprofitably magical. It broke; it was resumed broken, not marching once from the cradle to the grave. The sadness of the incomplete—the sadness that is often Life, but should never be Art—throbbed in its disjected phrases, and made the nerves of the audience throb. Not thus had she played on the little draped piano at the Bertolini, and "Too much Schumann" was not the remark that Mr. Beebe had passed to himself when she returned.

When the guests were gone, and Lucy had gone to bed, Mrs. Vyse paced up and down the drawing-room, discussing her little party with her son. Mrs. Vyse was a nice woman, but her personality, like many another's, had been swamped by London, for it needs a strong head to live among many people. The too vast orb of her fate had crushed her; and she had seen too many seasons, too many cities, too many men, for her abilities, and even with Cecil she was mechanical, and behaved as if he was not one son, but, so to speak, a filial crowd.

"Make Lucy one of us," she said, looking round intelligently at the end of each sentence, and straining her lips apart until she spoke again. "Lucy is becoming wonderful—wonderful."

"Her music always was wonderful."

"Yes, but she is purging off the Honeychurch taint, most excellent Honeychurches, but you know what I mean. She is not always quoting servants, or asking one how the pudding is made."

"Italy has done it."

"Perhaps," she murmured, thinking of the museum that represented Italy to her. "It is just possible. Cecil, mind you marry her next January. She is one of us already."

"But her music!" he exclaimed. "The style of her! How she kept to Schumann when, like an idiot, I wanted Beethoven. Schumann was right for this evening. Schumann was the thing. Do you know, mother, I shall have our children educated just like Lucy. Bring them up among honest country folks for freshness, send them to Italy for subtlety, and then—not till then—let them come to London. I don't believe in these London educations—" He broke off, remembering that he had had one himself, and concluded, "At all events, not for women."

"Make her one of us," repeated Mrs. Vyse, and processed to bed.

As she was dozing off, a cry—the cry of nightmare—rang from Lucy's room. Lucy could ring for the maid if she liked but Mrs. Vyse thought it kind to go herself. She found the girl sitting upright with her hand on her cheek.

"I am so sorry, Mrs. Vyse—it is these dreams."

"Bad dreams?"

"Just dreams."

The elder lady smiled and kissed her, saying very distinctly: "You should have heard us talking about you, dear. He admires you more than ever. Dream of that."

Lucy returned the kiss, still covering one cheek with her hand. Mrs. Vyse recessed to bed. Cecil, whom the cry had not awoke, snored. Darkness enveloped the flat.

Chapter XII: Twelfth Chapter

It was a Saturday afternoon, gay and brilliant after abundant rains, and the spirit of youth dwelt in it, though the season was now autumn. All that was gracious triumphed. As the motorcars passed through Summer Street they raised only a little dust, and their stench was soon dispersed by the wind and replaced by the scent of the wet birches or of the pines. Mr. Beebe, at leisure for life's amenities, leant over his Rectory gate. Freddy leant by him, smoking a pendant pipe.

"Suppose we go and hinder those new people opposite for a little."

"M'm."

"They might amuse you."

Freddy, whom his fellow-creatures never amused, suggested that the new people might be feeling a bit busy, and so on, since they had only just moved in.

"I suggested we should hinder them," said Mr. Beebe. "They are worth it." Unlatching the gate, he sauntered over the triangular green to Cissie Villa. "Hullo!" he cried, shouting in at the open door, through which much squalor was visible.

A grave voice replied, "Hullo!"

"I've brought some one to see you."

"I'll be down in a minute."

The passage was blocked by a wardrobe, which the removal men had failed to carry up the stairs. Mr. Beebe edged round it with difficulty. The sitting-room itself was blocked with books.

"Are these people great readers?" Freddy whispered. "Are they that sort?"

"I fancy they know how to read—a rare accomplishment. What have they got? Byron. Exactly. A Shropshire Lad. Never heard of it. The Way of All Flesh. Never heard of it. Gibbon. Hullo! dear George reads German. Um—um—Schopenhauer, Nietzsche, and so we go on. Well, I suppose your generation knows its own business, Honeychurch."

"Mr. Beebe, look at that," said Freddy in awestruck tones.

On the cornice of the wardrobe, the hand of an amateur had painted this inscription: "Mistrust all enterprises that require new clothes."

"I know. Isn't it jolly? I like that. I'm certain that's the old man's doing."

"How very odd of him!"

"Surely you agree?"

But Freddy was his mother's son and felt that one ought not to go on spoiling the furniture.

"Pictures!" the clergyman continued, scrambling about the room. "Giotto—they got that at Florence, I'll be bound."

"The same as Lucy's got."

"Oh, by-the-by, did Miss Honeychurch enjoy London?"

"She came back yesterday."

"I suppose she had a good time?"

"Yes, very," said Freddy, taking up a book. "She and Cecil are thicker than ever."

"That's good hearing."

"I wish I wasn't such a fool, Mr. Beebe."

Mr. Beebe ignored the remark.

"Lucy used to be nearly as stupid as I am, but it'll be very different now, mother thinks. She will read all kinds of books."

"So will you."

"Only medical books. Not books that you can talk about afterwards. Cecil is teaching Lucy Italian, and he says her playing is wonderful. There are all kinds of things in it that we have never noticed. Cecil says—"

"What on earth are those people doing upstairs? Emerson—we think we'll come another time."

George ran down-stairs and pushed them into the room without speaking.

"Let me introduce Mr. Honeychurch, a neighbour."

Then Freddy hurled one of the thunderbolts of youth. Perhaps he was shy, perhaps he was friendly, or perhaps he thought that George's face wanted washing. At all events he greeted him with, "How d'ye do? Come and have a bathe."

"Oh, all right," said George, impassive.

Mr. Beebe was highly entertained.

"'How d'ye do? how d'ye do? Come and have a bathe,'" he chuckled. "That's the best conversational opening I've ever heard. But I'm afraid it will only act between men. Can you picture a lady who has been introduced to another lady by a third lady opening civilities with 'How do you do? Come and have a bathe'? And yet you will tell me that the sexes are equal."

"I tell you that they shall be," said Mr. Emerson, who had been slowly descending the stairs. "Good afternoon, Mr. Beebe. I tell you they shall be comrades, and George thinks the same."

"We are to raise ladies to our level?" the clergyman inquired.

"The Garden of Eden," pursued Mr. Emerson, still descending, "which you place in the past, is really yet to come. We shall enter it when we no longer despise our bodies."

Mr. Beebe disclaimed placing the Garden of Eden anywhere.

"In this—not in other things—we men are ahead. We despise the body less than women do. But not until we are comrades shall we enter the garden."

"I say, what about this bathe?" murmured Freddy, appalled at the mass of philosophy that was approaching him.

"I believed in a return to Nature once. But how can we return to Nature when we have never been with her? To-day, I believe that we must discover Nature. After many conquests we shall attain simplicity. It is our heritage."

"Let me introduce Mr. Honeychurch, whose sister you will remember at Florence."

"How do you do? Very glad to see you, and that you are taking George for a bathe. Very glad to hear that your sister is going to marry. Marriage is a duty. I am sure that she will be happy, for we know Mr. Vyse, too. He has been most kind. He met us by chance in the National Gallery, and arranged everything about this delightful house. Though I hope I have not vexed Sir Harry Otway. I have met so few Liberal landowners, and I was anxious to compare his attitude towards the game laws with the Conservative attitude. Ah, this wind! You do well to bathe. Yours is a glorious country, Honeychurch!"

"Not a bit!" mumbled Freddy. "I must—that is to say, I have to—have the pleasure of calling on you later on, my mother says, I hope."

"CALL, my lad? Who taught us that drawing-room twaddle? Call on your grandmother! Listen to the wind among the pines! Yours is a glorious country."

Mr. Beebe came to the rescue.

"Mr. Emerson, he will call, I shall call; you or your son will return our calls before ten days have elapsed. I trust that you have realized about the ten days' interval. It does not count that I helped you with the stair-eyes yesterday. It does not count that they are going to bathe this afternoon."

"Yes, go and bathe, George. Why do you dawdle talking? Bring them back to tea. Bring back some milk, cakes, honey. The change will do you good. George has been working very hard at his office. I can't believe he's well."

George bowed his head, dusty and sombre, exhaling the peculiar smell of one who has handled furniture.

"Do you really want this bathe?" Freddy asked him. "It is only a pond, don't you know. I dare say you are used to something better."

"Yes—I have said 'Yes' already."

Mr. Beebe felt bound to assist his young friend, and led the way out of the house and into the pine-woods. How glorious it was! For a little time the voice of old Mr. Emerson pursued them dispensing good wishes and philosophy. It ceased, and they only heard the fair wind blowing the bracken and the trees. Mr. Beebe, who could be silent, but who could not bear silence, was compelled to chatter, since the expedition looked like a failure, and neither of his companions would utter a word. He spoke of Florence. George attended gravely, assenting or dissenting with slight but determined gestures that were as inexplicable as the motions of the tree-tops above their heads.

"And what a coincidence that you should meet Mr. Vyse! Did you realize that you would find all the Pension Bertolini down here?"

"I did not. Miss Lavish told me."

"When I was a young man, I always meant to write a 'History of Coincidence.'"

No enthusiasm.

"Though, as a matter of fact, coincidences are much rarer than we suppose. For example, it isn't purely coincidentally that you are here now, when one comes to reflect."

To his relief, George began to talk.

"It is. I have reflected. It is Fate. Everything is Fate. We are flung together by Fate, drawn apart by Fate—flung together, drawn apart. The twelve winds blow us—we settle nothing—"

"You have not reflected at all," rapped the clergyman. "Let me give you a useful tip, Emerson: attribute nothing to Fate. Don't say, 'I didn't do this,' for you did it, ten to one. Now I'll cross-question you. Where did you first meet Miss Honeychurch and myself?"

"Italy."

"And where did you meet Mr. Vyse, who is going to marry Miss Honeychurch?"

"National Gallery."

"Looking at Italian art. There you are, and yet you talk of coincidence and Fate. You naturally seek out things Italian, and so do we and our friends. This narrows the field immeasurably we meet again in it."

"It is Fate that I am here," persisted George. "But you can call it Italy if it makes you less unhappy."

Mr. Beebe slid away from such heavy treatment of the subject. But he was infinitely tolerant of the young, and had no desire to snub George.

"And so for this and for other reasons my 'History of Coincidence' is still to write."

Silence.

Wishing to round off the episode, he added; "We are all so glad that you have come."

Silence.

"Here we are!" called Freddy.

"Oh, good!" exclaimed Mr. Beebe, mopping his brow.

"In there's the pond. I wish it was bigger," he added apologetically.

They climbed down a slippery bank of pine-needles. There lay the pond, set in its little alp of green—only a pond, but large enough to contain the human body, and pure enough to reflect the sky. On account of the rains, the waters had flooded the surrounding grass, which showed like a beautiful emerald path, tempting these feet towards the central pool.

"It's distinctly successful, as ponds go," said Mr. Beebe. "No apologies are necessary for the pond."

George sat down where the ground was dry, and drearily unlaced his boots.

"Aren't those masses of willow-herb splendid? I love willow-herb in seed. What's the name of this aromatic plant?"

No one knew, or seemed to care.

"These abrupt changes of vegetation—this little spongeous tract of water plants, and on either side of it all the growths are tough or brittle—heather, bracken, hurts, pines. Very charming, very charming.

"Mr. Beebe, aren't you bathing?" called Freddy, as he stripped himself.

Mr. Beebe thought he was not.

"Water's wonderful!" cried Freddy, prancing in.

"Water's water," murmured George. Wetting his hair first—a sure sign of apathy—he followed Freddy into the divine, as indifferent as if he were a statue and the pond a pail of soapsuds. It was necessary to use his muscles. It was necessary to keep clean. Mr. Beebe watched them, and watched the seeds of the willow-herb dance chorically above their heads.

"Apooshoo, apooshoo, apooshoo," went Freddy, swimming for two strokes in either direction, and then becoming involved in reeds or mud.

"Is it worth it?" asked the other, Michelangelesque on the flooded margin.

The bank broke away, and he fell into the pool before he had weighed the question properly.

"Hee-poof—I've swallowed a pollywog, Mr. Beebe, water's wonderful, water's simply ripping."

"Water's not so bad," said George, reappearing from his plunge, and sputtering at the sun.

"Water's wonderful. Mr. Beebe, do."

"Apooshoo, kouf."

Mr. Beebe, who was hot, and who always acquiesced where possible, looked around him. He could detect no parishioners except the pine-trees, rising up steeply on all sides, and gesturing to each other against the blue. How glorious it was! The world of motor-cars and rural Deans receded inimitably. Water, sky, evergreens, a wind—these things not even the seasons can touch, and surely they lie beyond the intrusion of man?

"I may as well wash too"; and soon his garments made a third little pile on the sward, and he too asserted the wonder of the water.

It was ordinary water, nor was there very much of it, and, as Freddy said, it reminded one of swimming in a salad. The three gentlemen rotated in the pool breast high, after the fashion of the nymphs in Gotterdammerung. But either because the rains had given a freshness or because the sun was shedding a most glorious heat, or because two of the gentlemen were young in years and the third young in spirit—for some reason or other a change came over them, and they forgot Italy and Botany and Fate. They began to play. Mr. Beebe and Freddy splashed each other. A little deferentially, they splashed George. He was quiet: they feared they had offended him. Then all the forces of youth burst out. He smiled, flung himself at them, splashed them, ducked them, kicked them, muddied them, and drove them out of the pool.

"Race you round it, then," cried Freddy, and they raced in the sunshine, and George took a short cut and dirtied his shins, and had to bathe a second time. Then Mr. Beebe consented to run—a memorable sight.

They ran to get dry, they bathed to get cool, they played at being Indians in the willow-herbs and in the bracken, they bathed to get clean. And all the time three little bundles lay discreetly on the sward, proclaiming:

"No. We are what matters. Without us shall no enterprise begin. To us shall all flesh turn in the end."

"A try! A try!" yelled Freddy, snatching up George's bundle and placing it beside an imaginary goal-post.

"Socker rules," George retorted, scattering Freddy's bundle with a kick.

"Goal!"

"Goal!"

"Pass!"

"Take care my watch!" cried Mr. Beebe.

Clothes flew in all directions.

"Take care my hat! No, that's enough, Freddy. Dress now. No, I say!"

But the two young men were delirious. Away they twinkled into the trees, Freddy with a clerical waistcoat under his arm, George with a wide-awake hat on his dripping hair.

"That'll do!" shouted Mr. Beebe, remembering that after all he was in his own parish. Then his voice changed as if every pine-tree was a Rural Dean. "Hi! Steady on! I see people coming you fellows!"

Yells, and widening circles over the dappled earth.

"Hi! hi! LADIES!"

Neither George nor Freddy was truly refined. Still, they did not hear Mr. Beebe's last warning or they would have avoided Mrs. Honeychurch, Cecil, and Lucy, who were walking down to call on old Mrs. Butterworth. Freddy dropped the waistcoat at their feet, and dashed into some bracken. George whooped in their faces, turned and scudded away down the path to the pond, still clad in Mr. Beebe's hat.

"Gracious alive!" cried Mrs. Honeychurch. "Whoever were those unfortunate people? Oh, dears, look away! And poor Mr. Beebe, too! Whatever has happened?"

"Come this way immediately," commanded Cecil, who always felt that he must lead women, though knew not whither, and protect them, though he knew not against what. He led them now towards the bracken where Freddy sat concealed.

"Oh, poor Mr. Beebe! Was that his waistcoat we left in the path? Cecil, Mr. Beebe's waistcoat—"

No business of ours, said Cecil, glancing at Lucy, who was all parasol and evidently "minded."

"I fancy Mr. Beebe jumped back into the pond."

"This way, please, Mrs. Honeychurch, this way."

They followed him up the bank attempting the tense yet nonchalant expression that is suitable for ladies on such occasions.

"Well, I can't help it," said a voice close ahead, and Freddy reared a freckled face and a pair of snowy shoulders out of the fronds. "I can't be trodden on, can I?"

"Good gracious me, dear; so it's you! What miserable management! Why not have a comfortable bath at home, with hot and cold laid on?"

"Look here, mother, a fellow must wash, and a fellow's got to dry, and if another fellow—"

"Dear, no doubt you're right as usual, but you are in no position to argue. Come, Lucy." They turned. "Oh, look—don't look! Oh, poor Mr. Beebe! How unfortunate again—"

For Mr. Beebe was just crawling out of the pond, On whose surface garments of an intimate nature did float; while George, the world-weary George, shouted to Freddy that he had hooked a fish.

"And me, I've swallowed one," answered he of the bracken. "I've swallowed a pollywog. It wriggleth in my tummy. I shall die—Emerson you beast, you've got on my bags."

"Hush, dears," said Mrs. Honeychurch, who found it impossible to remain shocked. "And do be sure you dry yourselves thoroughly first. All these colds come of not drying thoroughly."

"Mother, do come away," said Lucy. "Oh for goodness' sake, do come."

"Hullo!" cried George, so that again the ladies stopped.

He regarded himself as dressed. Barefoot, bare-chested, radiant and personable against the shadowy woods, he called:

"Hullo, Miss Honeychurch! Hullo!"

"Bow, Lucy; better bow. Whoever is it? I shall bow."

Miss Honeychurch bowed.

That evening and all that night the water ran away. On the morrow the pool had shrunk to its old size and lost its glory. It had been a call to the blood and to the relaxed will, a passing benediction whose influence did not pass, a holiness, a spell, a momentary chalice for youth.

Chapter XIII: How Miss Bartlett's Boiler Was So Tiresome

How often had Lucy rehearsed this bow, this interview! But she had always rehearsed them indoors, and with certain accessories, which surely we have a right to assume. Who could foretell that she and George would meet in the rout of a civilization, amidst an army of coats and collars and boots that lay wounded over the sunlit earth? She had imagined a young Mr. Emerson, who might be shy or morbid or indifferent or furtively impudent. She was prepared for all of these. But she had never imagined one who would be happy and greet her with the shout of the morning star.

Indoors herself, partaking of tea with old Mrs. Butterworth, she reflected that it is impossible to foretell the future with any degree of accuracy, that it is impossible to rehearse life. A fault in the scenery, a face in the audience, an irruption of the audience on to the stage, and all our carefully planned gestures mean nothing, or mean too much. "I will bow," she had thought. "I will not shake hands with him. That will be just the proper thing." She had bowed—but to whom? To gods, to heroes, to the nonsense of school-girls! She had bowed across the rubbish that cumbers the world.

So ran her thoughts, while her faculties were busy with Cecil. It was another of those dreadful engagement calls. Mrs. Butterworth had wanted to see him, and he did not want to be seen. He did not want to hear about hydrangeas, why they change their colour at the seaside. He did not want to join the C. O. S. When cross he was always elaborate, and made long, clever answers where "Yes" or "No" would have done. Lucy soothed him and tinkered at the conversation in a way that promised well for their married peace. No one is perfect, and surely it is wiser to discover the imperfections before wedlock. Miss Bartlett, indeed, though not in word, had taught the girl that this our life contains nothing satisfactory. Lucy, though she disliked the teacher, regarded the teaching as profound, and applied it to her lover.

"Lucy," said her mother, when they got home, "is anything the matter with Cecil?"

The question was ominous; up till now Mrs. Honeychurch had behaved with charity and restraint.

"No, I don't think so, mother; Cecil's all right."

"Perhaps he's tired."

Lucy compromised: perhaps Cecil was a little tired.

"Because otherwise"—she pulled out her bonnet-pins with gathering displeasure—"because otherwise I cannot account for him."

"I do think Mrs. Butterworth is rather tiresome, if you mean that."

"Cecil has told you to think so. You were devoted to her as a little girl, and nothing will describe her goodness to you through the typhoid fever. No—it is just the same thing everywhere."

"Let me just put your bonnet away, may I?"

"Surely he could answer her civilly for one half-hour?"

"Cecil has a very high standard for people," faltered Lucy, seeing trouble ahead. "It's part of his ideals—it is really that that makes him sometimes seem—"

"Oh, rubbish! If high ideals make a young man rude, the sooner he gets rid of them the better," said Mrs. Honeychurch, handing her the bonnet.

"Now, mother! I've seen you cross with Mrs. Butterworth yourself!"

"Not in that way. At times I could wring her neck. But not in that way. No. It is the same with Cecil all over."

"By-the-by—I never told you. I had a letter from Charlotte while I was away in London."

This attempt to divert the conversation was too puerile, and Mrs. Honeychurch resented it.

"Since Cecil came back from London, nothing appears to please him. Whenever I speak he winces;—I see him, Lucy; it is useless to contradict me. No doubt I am neither artistic nor literary nor intellectual nor musical, but I cannot help the drawing-room furniture; your father bought it and we must put up with it, will Cecil kindly remember."

"I—I see what you mean, and certainly Cecil oughtn't to. But he does not mean to be uncivil—he once explained—it is the things that upset him—he is easily upset by ugly things—he is not uncivil to PEOPLE."

"Is it a thing or a person when Freddy sings?"

"You can't expect a really musical person to enjoy comic songs as we do."

"Then why didn't he leave the room? Why sit wriggling and sneering and spoiling everyone's pleasure?"

"We mustn't be unjust to people," faltered Lucy. Something had enfeebled her, and the case for Cecil, which she had mastered so perfectly in London, would not come forth in an effective form. The two civilizations had clashed—Cecil hinted that they might—and she was dazzled and bewildered, as though the radiance that lies behind all civilization had blinded her eyes. Good taste and bad taste were only catchwords, garments of diverse cut; and music itself dissolved to a whisper through pine-trees, where the song is not distinguishable from the comic song.

She remained in much embarrassment, while Mrs. Honeychurch changed her frock for dinner; and every now and then she said a word, and made things no better. There was no concealing the fact, Cecil had meant to be supercilious, and he had succeeded. And Lucy—she knew not why—wished that the trouble could have come at any other time.

"Go and dress, dear; you'll be late."

"All right, mother—"

"Don't say 'All right' and stop. Go."

She obeyed, but loitered disconsolately at the landing window. It faced north, so there was little view, and no view of the sky. Now, as in the winter, the pine-trees hung close to her eyes. One connected the landing window with depression. No definite problem menaced her, but she sighed to herself, "Oh, dear, what shall I do, what shall I do?" It seemed to her that every one else was behaving very badly. And she ought not to have mentioned Miss Bartlett's letter. She must be more careful; her mother was rather inquisitive, and might have asked what it was about. Oh, dear, should she do?—and then Freddy came bounding up-stairs, and joined the ranks of the ill-behaved.

"I say, those are topping people."

"My dear baby, how tiresome you've been! You have no business to take them bathing in the Sacred it's much too public. It was all right for you but most awkward for every one else. Do be more careful. You forget the place is growing half suburban."

"I say, is anything on to-morrow week?"

"Not that I know of."

"Then I want to ask the Emersons up to Sunday tennis."

"Oh, I wouldn't do that, Freddy, I wouldn't do that with all this muddle."

"What's wrong with the court? They won't mind a bump or two, and I've ordered new balls."

"I meant it's better not. I really mean it."

He seized her by the elbows and humorously danced her up and down the passage. She pretended not to mind, but she could have screamed with temper. Cecil glanced at them as he proceeded to his toilet and they impeded Mary with her brood of hot-water cans. Then Mrs. Honeychurch opened her door and said: "Lucy, what a noise you're making! I have something to say to you. Did you say you had had a letter from Charlotte?" and Freddy ran away.

"Yes. I really can't stop. I must dress too."

"How's Charlotte?"

"All right."

"Lucy!"

The unfortunate girl returned.

"You've a bad habit of hurrying away in the middle of one's sentences. Did Charlotte mention her boiler?"

"Her WHAT?"

"Don't you remember that her boiler was to be had out in October, and her bath cistern cleaned out, and all kinds of terrible to-doings?"

"I can't remember all Charlotte's worries," said Lucy bitterly. "I shall have enough of my own, now that you are not pleased with Cecil."

Mrs. Honeychurch might have flamed out. She did not. She said: "Come here, old lady—thank you for putting away my bonnet—kiss me." And, though nothing is perfect, Lucy felt for the moment that her mother and Windy Corner and the Weald in the declining sun were perfect.

So the grittiness went out of life. It generally did at Windy Corner. At the last minute, when the social machine was clogged hopelessly, one member or other of the family poured in a drop of oil. Cecil despised their methods—perhaps rightly. At all events, they were not his own.

Dinner was at half-past seven. Freddy gabbled the grace, and they drew up their heavy chairs and fell to. Fortunately, the men were hungry. Nothing untoward occurred until the pudding. Then Freddy said:

"Lucy, what's Emerson like?"

"I saw him in Florence," said Lucy, hoping that this would pass for a reply.

"Is he the clever sort, or is he a decent chap?"

"Ask Cecil; it is Cecil who brought him here."

"He is the clever sort, like myself," said Cecil.

Freddy looked at him doubtfully.

"How well did you know them at the Bertolini?" asked Mrs. Honeychurch.

"Oh, very slightly. I mean, Charlotte knew them even less than I did."

"Oh, that reminds me—you never told me what Charlotte said in her letter."

"One thing and another," said Lucy, wondering whether she would get through the meal without a lie. "Among other things, that an awful friend of hers had been bicycling through Summer Street, wondered if she'd come up and see us, and mercifully didn't."

"Lucy, I do call the way you talk unkind."

"She was a novelist," said Lucy craftily. The remark was a happy one, for nothing roused Mrs. Honeychurch so much as literature in the hands of females. She would abandon every topic to inveigh against those women who (instead of minding their houses and their children) seek notoriety by print. Her attitude was: "If books must be written, let them be written by men"; and she developed it at great length, while Cecil yawned and Freddy played at "This year, next year, now, never," with his plum-stones, and Lucy artfully fed the flames of her mother's wrath. But soon the conflagration died down, and the ghosts began to gather in the darkness. There were too many ghosts about. The original ghost—that touch of lips on her cheek—had surely been laid long ago; it could be nothing to her that a man had kissed her on a mountain once. But it had begotten a spectral family—Mr. Harris, Miss Bartlett's letter, Mr. Beebe's memories of violets—and one or other of these was bound to haunt her before Cecil's very eyes. It was Miss Bartlett who returned now, and with appalling vividness.

"I have been thinking, Lucy, of that letter of Charlotte's. How is she?"

"I tore the thing up."

"Didn't she say how she was? How does she sound? Cheerful?"

"Oh, yes I suppose so—no—not very cheerful, I suppose."

"Then, depend upon it, it IS the boiler. I know myself how water preys upon one's mind. I would rather anything else—even a misfortune with the meat."

Cecil laid his hand over his eyes.

"So would I," asserted Freddy, backing his mother up—backing up the spirit of her remark rather than the substance.

"And I have been thinking," she added rather nervously, "surely we could squeeze Charlotte in here next week, and give her a nice holiday while plumbers at Tunbridge Wells finish. I have not seen poor Charlotte for so long."

It was more than her nerves could stand. And she could not protest violently after her mother's goodness to her upstairs.

"Mother, no!" she pleaded. "It's impossible. We can't have Charlotte on the top of the other things; we're squeezed to death as it is. Freddy's got a friend coming Tuesday, there's Cecil, and you've promised to take in Minnie Beebe because of the diphtheria scare. It simply can't be done."

"Nonsense! It can."

"If Minnie sleeps in the bath. Not otherwise."

"Minnie can sleep with you."

"I won't have her."

"Then, if you're so selfish, Mr. Floyd must share a room with Freddy."

"Miss Bartlett, Miss Bartlett, Miss Bartlett," moaned Cecil, again laying his hand over his eyes.

"It's impossible," repeated Lucy. "I don't want to make difficulties, but it really isn't fair on the maids to fill up the house so."

Alas!

"The truth is, dear, you don't like Charlotte."

"No, I don't. And no more does Cecil. She gets on our nerves. You haven't seen her lately, and don't realize how tiresome she can be, though so good. So please, mother, don't worry us this last summer; but spoil us by not asking her to come."

"Hear, hear!" said Cecil.

Mrs. Honeychurch, with more gravity than usual, and with more feeling than she usually permitted herself, replied: "This isn't very kind of you two. You have each other and all these woods to walk in, so full of beautiful things; and poor Charlotte has only the water turned off and plumbers. You are young, dears, and however clever young people are, and however many books they read, they will never guess what it feels like to grow old."

Cecil crumbled his bread.

"I must say Cousin Charlotte was very kind to me that year I called on my bike," put in Freddy. "She thanked me for coming till I felt like such a fool, and fussed round no end to get an egg boiled for my tea just right."

"I know, dear. She is kind to every one, and yet Lucy makes this difficulty when we try to give her some little return."

But Lucy hardened her heart. It was no good being kind to Miss Bartlett. She had tried herself too often and too recently. One might lay up treasure in heaven by the attempt, but one enriched neither Miss Bartlett nor any one else upon earth. She was reduced to saying: "I can't help it, mother. I don't like Charlotte. I admit it's horrid of me."

"From your own account, you told her as much."

"Well, she would leave Florence so stupidly. She flurried—"

The ghosts were returning; they filled Italy, they were even usurping the places she had known as a child. The Sacred Lake would never be the same again, and, on Sunday week, something would even happen to Windy Corner. How would she fight against ghosts? For a moment the visible world faded away, and memories and emotions alone seemed real.

"I suppose Miss Bartlett must come, since she boils eggs so well," said Cecil, who was in rather a happier frame of mind, thanks to the admirable cooking.

"I didn't mean the egg was WELL boiled," corrected Freddy, "because in point of fact she forgot to take it off, and as a matter of fact I don't care for eggs. I only meant how jolly kind she seemed."

Cecil frowned again. Oh, these Honeychurches! Eggs, boilers, hydrangeas, maids—of such were their lives compact. "May me and Lucy get down from our chairs?" he asked, with scarcely veiled insolence. "We don't want no dessert."

Chapter XIV: How Lucy Faced the External Situation Bravely

Of course Miss Bartlett accepted. And, equally of course, she felt sure that she would prove a nuisance, and begged to be given an inferior spare room—something with no view, anything. Her love to Lucy. And, equally of course, George Emerson could come to tennis on the Sunday week.

Lucy faced the situation bravely, though, like most of us, she only faced the situation that encompassed her. She never gazed inwards. If at times strange images rose from the depths, she put them down to nerves. When Cecil brought the Emersons to Summer Street, it had upset her nerves. Charlotte would burnish up past foolishness, and this might upset her nerves. She was nervous at night. When she talked to George—they met again almost immediately at the Rectory—his voice moved her deeply, and she wished to remain near him. How dreadful if she really wished to remain near him! Of course, the wish was due to nerves, which love to play such perverse tricks upon us. Once she had suffered from "things that came out of nothing and meant she didn't know what." Now Cecil had explained psychology to her one wet afternoon, and all the troubles of youth in an unknown world could be dismissed.

It is obvious enough for the reader to conclude, "She loves young Emerson." A reader in Lucy's place would not find it obvious. Life is easy to chronicle, but bewildering to practice, and we welcome "nerves" or any other shibboleth that will cloak our personal desire. She loved Cecil; George made her nervous; will the reader explain to her that the phrases should have been reversed?

But the external situation—she will face that bravely.

The meeting at the Rectory had passed off well enough. Standing between Mr. Beebe and Cecil, she had made a few temperate allusions to Italy, and George had replied. She was anxious to show that she was not shy, and was glad that he did not seem shy either.

"A nice fellow," said Mr. Beebe afterwards "He will work off his crudities in time. I rather mistrust young men who slip into life gracefully."

Lucy said, "He seems in better spirits. He laughs more."

"Yes," replied the clergyman. "He is waking up."

That was all. But, as the week wore on, more of her defences fell, and she entertained an image that had physical beauty. In spite of the clearest directions, Miss Bartlett contrived to bungle her arrival. She was due at the South-Eastern station at Dorking, whither Mrs. Honeychurch drove to meet her. She arrived at the London and Brighton station, and had to hire a cab up. No one was at home except Freddy and his friend, who had to stop their tennis and to entertain her for a solid hour. Cecil and Lucy turned up at four o'clock, and these, with little Minnie Beebe, made a somewhat lugubrious sextette upon the upper lawn for tea.

"I shall never forgive myself," said Miss Bartlett, who kept on rising from her seat, and had to be begged by the united company to remain. "I have upset everything. Bursting in on young people! But I insist on paying for my cab up. Grant that, at any rate."

"Our visitors never do such dreadful things," said Lucy, while her brother, in whose memory the boiled egg had already grown unsubstantial, exclaimed in irritable tones: "Just what I've been trying to convince Cousin Charlotte of, Lucy, for the last half hour."

"I do not feel myself an ordinary visitor," said Miss Bartlett, and looked at her frayed glove.

"All right, if you'd really rather. Five shillings, and I gave a bob to the driver."

Miss Bartlett looked in her purse. Only sovereigns and pennies. Could any one give her change? Freddy had half a quid and his friend had four half-crowns. Miss Bartlett accepted their moneys and then said: "But who am I to give the sovereign to?"

"Let's leave it all till mother comes back," suggested Lucy.

"No, dear; your mother may take quite a long drive now that she is not hampered with me. We all have our little foibles, and mine is the prompt settling of accounts."

Here Freddy's friend, Mr. Floyd, made the one remark of his that need be quoted: he offered to toss Freddy for Miss Bartlett's quid. A solution seemed in sight, and even Cecil, who had been ostentatiously drinking his tea at the view, felt the eternal attraction of Chance, and turned round.

But this did not do, either.

"Please—please—I know I am a sad spoilsport, but it would make me wretched. I should practically be robbing the one who lost."

"Freddy owes me fifteen shillings," interposed Cecil. "So it will work out right if you give the pound to me."

"Fifteen shillings," said Miss Bartlett dubiously. "How is that, Mr. Vyse?"

"Because, don't you see, Freddy paid your cab. Give me the pound, and we shall avoid this deplorable gambling."

Miss Bartlett, who was poor at figures, became bewildered and rendered up the sovereign, amidst the suppressed gurgles of the other youths. For a moment Cecil was happy. He was playing at nonsense among his peers. Then he glanced at Lucy, in whose face petty anxieties had marred the smiles. In January he would rescue his Leonardo from this stupefying twaddle.

"But I don't see that!" exclaimed Minnie Beebe who had narrowly watched the iniquitous transaction. "I don't see why Mr. Vyse is to have the quid."

"Because of the fifteen shillings and the five," they said solemnly. "Fifteen shillings and five shillings make one pound, you see."

"But I don't see—"

They tried to stifle her with cake.

"No, thank you. I'm done. I don't see why—Freddy, don't poke me. Miss Honeychurch, your brother's hurting me. Ow! What about Mr. Floyd's ten shillings? Ow! No, I don't see and I never shall see why Miss What's-her-name shouldn't pay that bob for the driver."'

"I had forgotten the driver," said Miss Bartlett, reddening. "Thank you, dear, for reminding me. A shilling was it? Can any one give me change for half a crown?"

"I'll get it," said the young hostess, rising with decision.

"Cecil, give me that sovereign. No, give me up that sovereign. I'll get Euphemia to change it, and we'll start the whole thing again from the beginning."

"Lucy—Lucy—what a nuisance I am!" protested Miss Bartlett, and followed her across the lawn. Lucy tripped ahead, simulating hilarity. When they were out of earshot Miss Bartlett stopped her wails and said quite briskly: "Have you told him about him yet?"

"No, I haven't," replied Lucy, and then could have bitten her tongue for understanding so quickly what her cousin meant. "Let me see—a sovereign's worth of silver."

She escaped into the kitchen. Miss Bartlett's sudden transitions were too uncanny. It sometimes seemed as if she planned every word she spoke or caused to be spoken; as if all this worry about cabs and change had been a ruse to surprise the soul.

"No, I haven't told Cecil or any one," she remarked, when she returned. "I promised you I shouldn't. Here is your money—all shillings, except two half-crowns. Would you count it? You can settle your debt nicely now."

Miss Bartlett was in the drawing-room, gazing at the photograph of St. John ascending, which had been framed.

"How dreadful!" she murmured, "how more than dreadful, if Mr. Vyse should come to hear of it from some other source."

"Oh, no, Charlotte," said the girl, entering the battle. "George Emerson is all right, and what other source is there?"

Miss Bartlett considered. "For instance, the driver. I saw him looking through the bushes at you, remember he had a violet between his teeth."

Lucy shuddered a little. "We shall get the silly affair on our nerves if we aren't careful. How could a Florentine cab-driver ever get hold of Cecil?"

"We must think of every possibility."

"Oh, it's all right."

"Or perhaps old Mr. Emerson knows. In fact, he is certain to know."

"I don't care if he does. I was grateful to you for your letter, but even if the news does get round, I think I can trust Cecil to laugh at it."

"To contradict it?"

"No, to laugh at it." But she knew in her heart that she could not trust him, for he desired her untouched.

"Very well, dear, you know best. Perhaps gentlemen are different to what they were when I was young. Ladies are certainly different."

"Now, Charlotte!" She struck at her playfully. "You kind, anxious thing. What WOULD you have me do? First you say 'Don't tell'; and then you say, 'Tell'. Which is it to be? Quick!"

Miss Bartlett sighed "I am no match for you in conversation, dearest. I blush when I think how I interfered at Florence, and you so well able to look after yourself, and so much cleverer in all ways than I am. You will never forgive me."

"Shall we go out, then. They will smash all the china if we don't."

For the air rang with the shrieks of Minnie, who was being scalped with a teaspoon.

"Dear, one moment—we may not have this chance for a chat again. Have you seen the young one yet?"

"Yes, I have."

"What happened?"

"We met at the Rectory."

"What line is he taking up?"

"No line. He talked about Italy, like any other person. It is really all right. What advantage would he get from being a cad, to put it bluntly? I do wish I could make you see it my way. He really won't be any nuisance, Charlotte."

"Once a cad, always a cad. That is my poor opinion."

Lucy paused. "Cecil said one day—and I thought it so profound—that there are two kinds of cads—the conscious and the subconscious." She paused again, to be sure of doing justice to Cecil's profundity. Through the window she saw Cecil himself, turning over the pages of a novel. It was a new one from Smith's library. Her mother must have returned from the station.

"Once a cad, always a cad," droned Miss Bartlett.

"What I mean by subconscious is that Emerson lost his head. I fell into all those violets, and he was silly and surprised. I don't think we ought to blame him very much. It makes such a difference when you see a person with beautiful things behind him unexpectedly. It really does; it makes an enormous difference, and he lost his head: he doesn't admire me, or any of that nonsense, one straw. Freddy rather likes him, and has asked him up here on Sunday, so you can judge for yourself. He has improved; he doesn't always look as if he's going to burst into tears. He is a clerk in the General Manager's office at one of the big railways—not a porter! and runs down to his father for week-ends. Papa was to do with journalism, but is rheumatic and has retired. There! Now for the garden." She took hold of her guest by the arm. "Suppose we don't talk about this silly Italian business any more. We want you to have a nice restful visit at Windy Corner, with no worriting."

Lucy thought this rather a good speech. The reader may have detected an unfortunate slip in it. Whether Miss Bartlett detected the slip one cannot say, for it is impossible to penetrate into the minds of elderly people. She might have spoken further, but they were interrupted by the entrance of her hostess. Explanations took place, and in the midst of them Lucy escaped, the images throbbing a little more vividly in her brain.

Chapter XV: The Disaster Within

The Sunday after Miss Bartlett's arrival was a glorious day, like most of the days of that year. In the Weald, autumn approached, breaking up the green monotony of summer, touching the parks with the grey bloom of mist, the beech-trees with russet, the oak-trees with gold. Up on the heights, battalions of black pines witnessed the change, themselves unchangeable. Either country was spanned by a cloudless sky, and in either arose the tinkle of church bells.

The garden of Windy Corners was deserted except for a red book, which lay sunning itself upon the gravel path. From the house came incoherent sounds, as of females preparing for worship. "The men say they won't go"—"Well, I don't blame them"—Minnie says, "need she go?"—"Tell her, no nonsense"—"Anne! Mary! Hook me behind!"—"Dearest Lucia, may I trespass upon you for a pin?" For Miss Bartlett had announced that she at all events was one for church.

The sun rose higher on its journey, guided, not by Phaethon, but by Apollo, competent, unswerving, divine. Its rays fell on the ladies whenever they advanced towards the bedroom windows; on Mr. Beebe down at Summer Street as he smiled over a letter from Miss Catharine Alan; on George Emerson cleaning his father's boots; and lastly, to complete the catalogue of memorable things, on the red book mentioned previously. The ladies move, Mr. Beebe moves, George moves, and movement may engender shadow. But this book lies motionless, to be caressed all the morning by the sun and to raise its covers slightly, as though acknowledging the caress.

Presently Lucy steps out of the drawing-room window. Her new cerise dress has been a failure, and makes her look tawdry and wan. At her throat is a garnet brooch, on her finger a ring set with rubies—an engagement ring. Her eyes are bent to the Weald. She frowns a little—not in anger, but as a brave child frowns when he is trying not to cry. In all that expanse no human eye is looking at her, and she may frown unrebuked and measure the spaces that yet survive between Apollo and the western hills.

"Lucy! Lucy! What's that book? Who's been taking a book out of the shelf and leaving it about to spoil?"

"It's only the library book that Cecil's been reading."

"But pick it up, and don't stand idling there like a flamingo."

Lucy picked up the book and glanced at the title listlessly, Under a Loggia. She no longer read novels herself, devoting all her spare time to solid literature in the hope of catching Cecil up. It was dreadful how little she knew, and even when she thought she knew a thing, like the Italian painters, she found she had forgotten it. Only this morning she had confused Francesco Francia with Piero della Francesca, and Cecil had said, "What! you aren't forgetting your Italy already?" And this too had lent anxiety to her eyes when she saluted the dear view and the dear garden in the foreground, and above them, scarcely conceivable elsewhere, the dear sun.

"Lucy—have you a sixpence for Minnie and a shilling for yourself?"

She hastened in to her mother, who was rapidly working herself into a Sunday fluster.

"It's a special collection—I forget what for. I do beg, no vulgar clinking in the plate with halfpennies; see that Minnie has a nice bright sixpence. Where is the child? Minnie! That book's all warped. (Gracious, how plain you look!) Put it under the Atlas to press. Minnie!"

"Oh, Mrs. Honeychurch—" from the upper regions.

"Minnie, don't be late. Here comes the horse"—it was always the horse, never the carriage. "Where's Charlotte? Run up and hurry her. Why is she so long? She had nothing to do. She never brings anything but blouses. Poor Charlotte—How I do detest blouses! Minnie!"

Paganism is infectious—more infectious than diphtheria or piety—and the Rector's niece was taken to church protesting. As usual, she didn't see why. Why shouldn't she sit in the sun with the young men? The young men, who had now appeared, mocked her with ungenerous words. Mrs. Honeychurch defended orthodoxy, and in the midst of the confusion Miss Bartlett, dressed in the very height of the fashion, came strolling down the stairs.

"Dear Marian, I am very sorry, but I have no small change—nothing but sovereigns and half crowns. Could any one give me—"

"Yes, easily. Jump in. Gracious me, how smart you look! What a lovely frock! You put us all to shame."

"If I did not wear my best rags and tatters now, when should I wear them?" said Miss Bartlett reproachfully. She got into the victoria and placed herself with her back to the horse. The necessary roar ensued, and then they drove off.

"Good-bye! Be good!" called out Cecil.

Lucy bit her lip, for the tone was sneering. On the subject of "church and so on" they had had rather an unsatisfactory conversation. He had said that people ought to overhaul themselves, and she did not want to overhaul herself; she did not know it was done. Honest orthodoxy Cecil respected, but he always assumed that honesty is the result of a spiritual crisis; he could not imagine it as a natural birthright, that might grow heavenward like flowers. All that he said on this subject pained her, though he exuded tolerance from every pore; somehow the Emersons were different.

She saw the Emersons after church. There was a line of carriages down the road, and the Honeychurch vehicle happened to be opposite Cissie Villa. To save time, they walked over the green to it, and found father and son smoking in the garden.

"Introduce me," said her mother. "Unless the young man considers that he knows me already."

He probably did; but Lucy ignored the Sacred Lake and introduced them formally. Old Mr. Emerson claimed her with much warmth, and said how glad he was that she was going to be married. She said yes, she was glad too; and then, as Miss Bartlett and Minnie were lingering behind with Mr. Beebe, she turned the conversation to a less disturbing topic, and asked him how he liked his new house.

"Very much," he replied, but there was a note of offence in his voice; she had never known him offended before. He added: "We find, though, that the Miss Alans were coming, and that we have turned them out. Women mind such a thing. I am very much upset about it."

"I believe that there was some misunderstanding," said Mrs. Honeychurch uneasily.

"Our landlord was told that we should be a different type of person," said George, who seemed disposed to carry the matter further. "He thought we should be artistic. He is disappointed."

"And I wonder whether we ought to write to the Miss Alans and offer to give it up. What do you think?" He appealed to Lucy.

"Oh, stop now you have come," said Lucy lightly. She must avoid censuring Cecil. For it was on Cecil that the little episode turned, though his name was never mentioned.

"So George says. He says that the Miss Alans must go to the wall. Yet it does seem so unkind."

"There is only a certain amount of kindness in the world," said George, watching the sunlight flash on the panels of the passing carriages.

"Yes!" exclaimed Mrs. Honeychurch. "That's exactly what I say. Why all this twiddling and twaddling over two Miss Alans?"

"There is a certain amount of kindness, just as there is a certain amount of light," he continued in measured tones. "We cast a shadow on something wherever we stand, and it is no good moving from place to place to save things; because the shadow always follows. Choose a place where you won't do harm—yes, choose a place where you won't do very much harm, and stand in it for all you are worth, facing the sunshine."

"Oh, Mr. Emerson, I see you're clever!"

"Eh—?"

"I see you're going to be clever. I hope you didn't go behaving like that to poor Freddy."

George's eyes laughed, and Lucy suspected that he and her mother would get on rather well.

"No, I didn't," he said. "He behaved that way to me. It is his philosophy. Only he starts life with it; and I have tried the Note of Interrogation first."

"What DO you mean? No, never mind what you mean. Don't explain. He looks forward to seeing you this afternoon. Do you play tennis? Do you mind tennis on Sunday—?"

"George mind tennis on Sunday! George, after his education, distinguish between Sunday—"

"Very well, George doesn't mind tennis on Sunday. No more do I. That's settled. Mr. Emerson, if you could come with your son we should be so pleased."

He thanked her, but the walk sounded rather far; he could only potter about in these days.

She turned to George: "And then he wants to give up his house to the Miss Alans."

"I know," said George, and put his arm round his father's neck. The kindness that Mr. Beebe and Lucy had always known to exist in him came out suddenly, like sunlight touching a vast landscape—a touch of the morning sun? She remembered that in all his perversities he had never spoken against affection.

Miss Bartlett approached.

"You know our cousin, Miss Bartlett," said Mrs. Honeychurch pleasantly. "You met her with my daughter in Florence."

"Yes, indeed!" said the old man, and made as if he would come out of the garden to meet the lady. Miss Bartlett promptly got into the victoria. Thus entrenched, she emitted a formal bow. It was the pension Bertolini again, the dining-table with the decanters of water and wine. It was the old, old battle of the room with the view.

George did not respond to the bow. Like any boy, he blushed and was ashamed; he knew that the chaperon remembered. He said: "I—I'll come up to tennis if I can manage it," and went into the house. Perhaps anything that he did would have pleased Lucy, but his awkwardness went straight to her heart; men were not gods after all, but as human and as clumsy as girls; even men might suffer from unexplained desires, and need help. To one of her upbringing, and of her destination, the weakness of men was a truth unfamiliar, but she had surmised it at Florence, when George threw her photographs into the River Arno.

"George, don't go," cried his father, who thought it a great treat for people if his son would talk to them. "George has been in such good spirits today, and I am sure he will end by coming up this afternoon."

Lucy caught her cousin's eye. Something in its mute appeal made her reckless. "Yes," she said, raising her voice, "I do hope he will." Then she went to the carriage and murmured, "The old man hasn't been told; I knew it was all right." Mrs. Honeychurch followed her, and they drove away.

Satisfactory that Mr. Emerson had not been told of the Florence escapade; yet Lucy's spirits should not have leapt up as if she had sighted the ramparts of heaven. Satisfactory; yet surely she greeted it with disproportionate joy. All the way home the horses' hoofs sang a tune to her: "He has not told, he has not told." Her brain expanded the melody: "He has not told his father—to whom he tells all things. It was not an exploit. He did not laugh at me when I had gone." She raised her hand to her cheek. "He does not love me. No. How terrible if he did! But he has not told. He will not tell."

She longed to shout the words: "It is all right. It's a secret between us two for ever. Cecil will never hear." She was even glad that Miss Bartlett had made her promise secrecy, that last dark evening at Florence, when they had knelt packing in his room. The secret, big or little, was guarded.

Only three English people knew of it in the world. Thus she interpreted her joy. She greeted Cecil with unusual radiance, because she felt so safe. As he helped her out of the carriage, she said:

"The Emersons have been so nice. George Emerson has improved enormously."

"How are my proteges?" asked Cecil, who took no real interest in them, and had long since forgotten his resolution to bring them to Windy Corner for educational purposes.

"Proteges!" she exclaimed with some warmth. For the only relationship which Cecil conceived was feudal: that of protector and protected. He had no glimpse of the comradeship after which the girl's soul yearned.

"You shall see for yourself how your proteges are. George Emerson is coming up this afternoon. He is a most interesting man to talk to. Only don't—" She nearly said, "Don't protect him." But the bell was ringing for lunch, and, as often happened, Cecil had paid no great attention to her remarks. Charm, not argument, was to be her forte.

Lunch was a cheerful meal. Generally Lucy was depressed at meals. Some one had to be soothed—either Cecil or Miss Bartlett or a Being not visible to the mortal eye—a Being who whispered to her soul: "It will not last, this cheerfulness. In January you must go to London to entertain the grandchildren of celebrated men." But to-day she felt she had received a guarantee. Her mother would always sit there, her brother here. The sun, though it had moved a little since the morning, would never be hidden behind the western hills. After luncheon they asked her to play. She had seen Gluck's Armide that year, and played from memory the music of the enchanted garden—the music to which Renaud approaches, beneath the light of an eternal dawn, the music that never gains, never wanes, but ripples for ever like the tideless seas of fairyland. Such music is not for the piano, and her audience began to get restive, and Cecil, sharing the discontent, called out: "Now play us the other garden—the one in Parsifal."

She closed the instrument.

"Not very dutiful," said her mother's voice.

Fearing that she had offended Cecil, she turned quickly round. There George was. He had crept in without interrupting her.

"Oh, I had no idea!" she exclaimed, getting very red; and then, without a word of greeting, she reopened the piano. Cecil should have the Parsifal, and anything else that he liked.

"Our performer has changed her mind," said Miss Bartlett, perhaps implying, she will play the music to Mr. Emerson. Lucy did not know what to do nor even what she wanted to do. She played a few bars of the Flower Maidens' song very badly and then she stopped.

"I vote tennis," said Freddy, disgusted at the scrappy entertainment.

"Yes, so do I." Once more she closed the unfortunate piano. "I vote you have a men's four."

"All right."

"Not for me, thank you," said Cecil. "I will not spoil the set." He never realized that it may be an act of kindness in a bad player to make up a fourth.

"Oh, come along Cecil. I'm bad, Floyd's rotten, and so I dare say's Emerson."

George corrected him: "I am not bad."

One looked down one's nose at this. "Then certainly I won't play," said Cecil, while Miss Bartlett, under the impression that she was snubbing George, added: "I agree with you, Mr. Vyse. You had much better not play. Much better not."

Minnie, rushing in where Cecil feared to tread, announced that she would play. "I shall miss every ball anyway, so what does it matter?" But Sunday intervened and stamped heavily upon the kindly suggestion.

"Then it will have to be Lucy," said Mrs. Honeychurch; "you must fall back on Lucy. There is no other way out of it. Lucy, go and change your frock."

Lucy's Sabbath was generally of this amphibious nature. She kept it without hypocrisy in the morning, and broke it without reluctance in the afternoon. As she changed her frock, she wondered whether Cecil was sneering at her; really she must overhaul herself and settle everything up before she married him.

Mr. Floyd was her partner. She liked music, but how much better tennis seemed. How much better to run about in comfortable clothes than to sit at the piano and feel girt under the arms. Once more music appeared to her the employment of a child. George served, and surprised her by his anxiety to win. She remembered how he had sighed among the tombs at Santa Croce because things wouldn't fit; how after the death of that obscure Italian he had leant over the parapet by the Arno and said to her: "I shall want to live, I tell you," He wanted to live now, to win at tennis, to stand for all he was worth in the sun—the sun which had begun to decline and was shining in her eyes; and he did win.

Ah, how beautiful the Weald looked! The hills stood out above its radiance, as Fiesole stands above the Tuscan Plain, and the South Downs, if one chose, were the mountains of Carrara. She might be forgetting her Italy, but she was noticing more things in her England. One could play a new game with the view, and try to find in its innumerable folds some town or village that would do for Florence. Ah, how beautiful the Weald looked!

But now Cecil claimed her. He chanced to be in a lucid critical mood, and would not sympathize with exaltation. He had been rather a nuisance all through the tennis, for the novel that he was reading was so bad that he was obliged to read it aloud to others. He would stroll round the precincts of the court and call out: "I say, listen to this, Lucy. Three split infinitives."

"Dreadful!" said Lucy, and missed her stroke. When they had finished their set, he still went on reading; there was some murder scene, and really every one must listen to it. Freddy and Mr. Floyd were obliged to hunt for a lost ball in the laurels, but the other two acquiesced.

"The scene is laid in Florence."

"What fun, Cecil! Read away. Come, Mr. Emerson, sit down after all your energy." She had "forgiven" George, as she put it, and she made a point of being pleasant to him.

He jumped over the net and sat down at her feet asking: "You—and are you tired?"

"Of course I'm not!"

"Do you mind being beaten?"

She was going to answer, "No," when it struck her that she did mind, so she answered, "Yes." She added merrily, "I don't see you're such a splendid player, though. The light was behind you, and it was in my eyes."

"I never said I was."

"Why, you did!"

"You didn't attend."

"You said—oh, don't go in for accuracy at this house. We all exaggerate, and we get very angry with people who don't."

"'The scene is laid in Florence,'" repeated Cecil, with an upward note.

Lucy recollected herself.

"'Sunset. Leonora was speeding—'"

Lucy interrupted. "Leonora? Is Leonora the heroine? Who's the book by?"

"Joseph Emery Prank. 'Sunset. Leonora speeding across the square. Pray the saints she might not arrive too late. Sunset—the sunset of Italy. Under Orcagna's Loggia—the Loggia de' Lanzi, as we sometimes call it now—'"

Lucy burst into laughter. "'Joseph Emery Prank' indeed! Why it's Miss Lavish! It's Miss Lavish's novel, and she's publishing it under somebody else's name."

"Who may Miss Lavish be?"

"Oh, a dreadful person—Mr. Emerson, you remember Miss Lavish?"

Excited by her pleasant afternoon, she clapped her hands.

George looked up. "Of course I do. I saw her the day I arrived at Summer Street. It was she who told me that you lived here."

"Weren't you pleased?" She meant "to see Miss Lavish," but when he bent down to the grass without replying, it struck her that she could mean something else. She watched his head, which was almost resting against her knee, and she thought that the ears were reddening. "No wonder the novel's bad," she added. "I never liked Miss Lavish. But I suppose one ought to read it as one's met her."

"All modern books are bad," said Cecil, who was annoyed at her inattention, and vented his annoyance on literature. "Every one writes for money in these days."

"Oh, Cecil—!"

"It is so. I will inflict Joseph Emery Prank on you no longer."

Cecil, this afternoon seemed such a twittering sparrow. The ups and downs in his voice were noticeable, but they did not affect her. She had dwelt amongst melody and movement, and her nerves refused to answer to the clang of his. Leaving him to be annoyed, she gazed at the black head again. She did not want to stroke it, but she saw herself wanting to stroke it; the sensation was curious.

"How do you like this view of ours, Mr. Emerson?"

"I never notice much difference in views."

"What do you mean?"

"Because they're all alike. Because all that matters in them is distance and air."

"H'm!" said Cecil, uncertain whether the remark was striking or not.

"My father"—he looked up at her (and he was a little flushed)—"says that there is only one perfect view—the view of the sky straight over our heads, and that all these views on earth are but bungled copies of it."

"I expect your father has been reading Dante," said Cecil, fingering the novel, which alone permitted him to lead the conversation.

"He told us another day that views are really crowds—crowds of trees and houses and hills—and are bound to resemble each other, like human crowds—and that the power they have over us is sometimes supernatural, for the same reason."

Lucy's lips parted.

"For a crowd is more than the people who make it up. Something gets added to it—no one knows how—just as something has got added to those hills."

He pointed with his racquet to the South Downs.

"What a splendid idea!" she murmured. "I shall enjoy hearing your father talk again. I'm so sorry he's not so well."

"No, he isn't well."

"There's an absurd account of a view in this book," said Cecil. "Also that men fall into two classes—those who forget views and those who remember them, even in small rooms."

"Mr. Emerson, have you any brothers or sisters?"

"None. Why?"

"You spoke of 'us.'"

"My mother, I was meaning."

Cecil closed the novel with a bang.

"Oh, Cecil—how you made me jump!"

"I will inflict Joseph Emery Prank on you no longer."

"I can just remember us all three going into the country for the day and seeing as far as Hindhead. It is the first thing that I remember."

Cecil got up; the man was ill-bred—he hadn't put on his coat after tennis—he didn't do. He would have strolled away if Lucy had not stopped him.

"Cecil, do read the thing about the view."

"Not while Mr. Emerson is here to entertain us."

"No—read away. I think nothing's funnier than to hear silly things read out loud. If Mr. Emerson thinks us frivolous, he can go."

This struck Cecil as subtle, and pleased him. It put their visitor in the position of a prig. Somewhat mollified, he sat down again.

"Mr. Emerson, go and find tennis balls." She opened the book. Cecil must have his reading and anything else that he liked. But her attention wandered to George's mother, who—according to Mr. Eager—had been murdered in the sight of God according to her son—had seen as far as Hindhead.

"Am I really to go?" asked George.

"No, of course not really," she answered.

"Chapter two," said Cecil, yawning. "Find me chapter two, if it isn't bothering you."

Chapter two was found, and she glanced at its opening sentences.

She thought she had gone mad.

"Here—hand me the book."

She heard her voice saying: "It isn't worth reading—it's too silly to read—I never saw such rubbish—it oughtn't to be allowed to be printed."

He took the book from her.

"'Leonora,'" he read, "'sat pensive and alone. Before her lay the rich champaign of Tuscany, dotted over with many a smiling village. The season was spring.'"

Miss Lavish knew, somehow, and had printed the past in draggled prose, for Cecil to read and for George to hear.

"'A golden haze,'" he read. He read: "'Afar off the towers of Florence, while the bank on which she sat was carpeted with violets. All unobserved Antonio stole up behind her—'"

Lest Cecil should see her face she turned to George and saw his face.

He read: "'There came from his lips no wordy protestation such as formal lovers use. No eloquence was his, nor did he suffer from the lack of it. He simply enfolded her in his manly arms.'"

"This isn't the passage I wanted," he informed them, "there is another much funnier, further on." He turned over the leaves.

"Should we go in to tea?" said Lucy, whose voice remained steady.

She led the way up the garden, Cecil following her, George last. She thought a disaster was averted. But when they entered the shrubbery it came. The book, as if it had not worked mischief enough, had been forgotten, and Cecil must go back for it; and George, who loved passionately, must blunder against her in the narrow path.

"No—" she gasped, and, for the second time, was kissed by him.

As if no more was possible, he slipped back; Cecil rejoined her; they reached the upper lawn alone.

Chapter XVI: Lying to George

But Lucy had developed since the spring. That is to say, she was now better able to stifle the emotions of which the conventions and the world disapprove. Though the danger was greater, she was not shaken by deep sobs. She said to Cecil, "I am not coming in to tea—tell mother—I must write some letters," and went up to her room. Then she prepared for action. Love felt and returned, love which our bodies exact and our hearts have transfigured, love which is the most real thing that we shall ever meet, reappeared now as the world's enemy, and she must stifle it.

She sent for Miss Bartlett.

The contest lay not between love and duty. Perhaps there never is such a contest. It lay between the real and the pretended, and Lucy's first aim was to defeat herself. As her brain clouded over, as the memory of the views grew dim and the words of the book died away, she returned to her old shibboleth of nerves. She "conquered her breakdown." Tampering with the truth, she forgot that the truth had ever been. Remembering that she was engaged to Cecil, she compelled herself to confused remembrances of George; he was nothing to her; he never had been anything; he had behaved abominably; she had never encouraged him. The armour of falsehood is subtly wrought out of darkness, and hides a man not only from others, but from his own soul. In a few moments Lucy was equipped for battle.

"Something too awful has happened," she began, as soon as her cousin arrived. "Do you know anything about Miss Lavish's novel?"

Miss Bartlett looked surprised, and said that she had not read the book, nor known that it was published; Eleanor was a reticent woman at heart.

"There is a scene in it. The hero and heroine make love. Do you know about that?"

"Dear—?"

"Do you know about it, please?" she repeated. "They are on a hillside, and Florence is in the distance."

"My good Lucia, I am all at sea. I know nothing about it whatever."

"There are violets. I cannot believe it is a coincidence. Charlotte, Charlotte, how could you have told her? I have thought before speaking; it must be you."

"Told her what?" she asked, with growing agitation.

"About that dreadful afternoon in February."

Miss Bartlett was genuinely moved. "Oh, Lucy, dearest girl—she hasn't put that in her book?"

Lucy nodded.

"Not so that one could recognize it. Yes."

"Then never—never—never more shall Eleanor Lavish be a friend of mine."

"So you did tell?"

"I did just happen—when I had tea with her at Rome—in the course of conversation—"

"But Charlotte—what about the promise you gave me when we were packing? Why did you tell Miss Lavish, when you wouldn't even let me tell mother?"

"I will never forgive Eleanor. She has betrayed my confidence."

"Why did you tell her, though? This is a most serious thing."

Why does any one tell anything? The question is eternal, and it was not surprising that Miss Bartlett should only sigh faintly in response. She had done wrong—she admitted it, she only hoped that she had not done harm; she had told Eleanor in the strictest confidence.

Lucy stamped with irritation.

"Cecil happened to read out the passage aloud to me and to Mr. Emerson; it upset Mr. Emerson and he insulted me again. Behind Cecil's back. Ugh! Is it possible that men are such brutes? Behind Cecil's back as we were walking up the garden."

Miss Bartlett burst into self-accusations and regrets.

"What is to be done now? Can you tell me?"

"Oh, Lucy—I shall never forgive myself, never to my dying day. Fancy if your prospects—"

"I know," said Lucy, wincing at the word. "I see now why you wanted me to tell Cecil, and what you meant by 'some other source.' You knew that you had told Miss Lavish, and that she was not reliable."

It was Miss Bartlett's turn to wince. "However," said the girl, despising her cousin's shiftiness, "What's done's done. You have put me in a most awkward position. How am I to get out of it?"

Miss Bartlett could not think. The days of her energy were over. She was a visitor, not a chaperon, and a discredited visitor at that. She stood with clasped hands while the girl worked herself into the necessary rage.

"He must—that man must have such a setting down that he won't forget. And who's to give it him? I can't tell mother now—owing to you. Nor Cecil, Charlotte, owing to you. I am caught up every way. I think I shall go mad. I have no one to help me. That's why I've sent for you. What's wanted is a man with a whip."

Miss Bartlett agreed: one wanted a man with a whip.

"Yes—but it's no good agreeing. What's to be DONE. We women go maundering on. What DOES a girl do when she comes across a cad?"

"I always said he was a cad, dear. Give me credit for that, at all events. From the very first moment—when he said his father was having a bath."

"Oh, bother the credit and who's been right or wrong! We've both made a muddle of it. George Emerson is still down the garden there, and is he to be left unpunished, or isn't he? I want to know."

Miss Bartlett was absolutely helpless. Her own exposure had unnerved her, and thoughts were colliding painfully in her brain. She moved feebly to the window, and tried to detect the cad's white flannels among the laurels.

"You were ready enough at the Bertolini when you rushed me off to Rome. Can't you speak again to him now?"

"Willingly would I move heaven and earth—"

"I want something more definite," said Lucy contemptuously. "Will you speak to him? It is the least you can do, surely, considering it all happened because you broke your word."

"Never again shall Eleanor Lavish be a friend of mine."

Really, Charlotte was outdoing herself.

"Yes or no, please; yes or no."

"It is the kind of thing that only a gentleman can settle." George Emerson was coming up the garden with a tennis ball in his hand.

"Very well," said Lucy, with an angry gesture. "No one will help me. I will speak to him myself." And immediately she realized that this was what her cousin had intended all along.

"Hullo, Emerson!" called Freddy from below. "Found the lost ball? Good man! Want any tea?" And there was an irruption from the house on to the terrace.

"Oh, Lucy, but that is brave of you! I admire you—"

They had gathered round George, who beckoned, she felt, over the rubbish, the sloppy thoughts, the furtive yearnings that were beginning to cumber her soul. Her anger faded at the sight of him. Ah! The Emersons were fine people in their way. She had to subdue a rush in her blood before saying:

"Freddy has taken him into the dining-room. The others are going down the garden. Come. Let us get this over quickly. Come. I want you in the room, of course."

"Lucy, do you mind doing it?"

"How can you ask such a ridiculous question?"

"Poor Lucy—" She stretched out her hand. "I seem to bring nothing but misfortune wherever I go." Lucy nodded. She remembered their last evening at Florence—the packing, the candle, the shadow of Miss Bartlett's toque on the door. She was not to be trapped by pathos a second time. Eluding her cousin's caress, she led the way downstairs.

"Try the jam," Freddy was saying. "The jam's jolly good."

George, looking big and dishevelled, was pacing up and down the dining-room. As she entered he stopped, and said:

"No—nothing to eat."

"You go down to the others," said Lucy; "Charlotte and I will give Mr. Emerson all he wants. Where's mother?"

"She's started on her Sunday writing. She's in the drawing-room."

"That's all right. You go away."

He went off singing.

Lucy sat down at the table. Miss Bartlett, who was thoroughly frightened, took up a book and pretended to read.

She would not be drawn into an elaborate speech. She just said: "I can't have it, Mr. Emerson. I cannot even talk to you. Go out of this house, and never come into it again as long as I live here—" flushing as she spoke and pointing to the door. "I hate a row. Go please."

"What—"

"No discussion."

"But I can't—"

She shook her head. "Go, please. I do not want to call in Mr. Vyse."

"You don't mean," he said, absolutely ignoring Miss Bartlett—"you don't mean that you are going to marry that man?"

The line was unexpected.

She shrugged her shoulders, as if his vulgarity wearied her. "You are merely ridiculous," she said quietly.

Then his words rose gravely over hers: "You cannot live with Vyse. He's only for an acquaintance. He is for society and cultivated talk. He should know no one intimately, least of all a woman."

It was a new light on Cecil's character.

"Have you ever talked to Vyse without feeling tired?"

"I can scarcely discuss—"

"No, but have you ever? He is the sort who are all right so long as they keep to things—books, pictures—but kill when they come to people. That's why I'll speak out through all this muddle even now. It's shocking enough to lose you in any case, but generally a man must deny himself joy, and I would have held back if your Cecil had been a different person. I would never have let myself go. But I saw him first in the National Gallery, when he winced because my father mispronounced the names of great painters. Then he brings us here, and we find it is to play some silly trick on a kind neighbour. That is the man all over—playing tricks on people, on the most sacred form of life that he can find. Next, I meet you together, and find him protecting and teaching you and your mother to be shocked, when it was for YOU to settle whether you were shocked or no. Cecil all over again. He daren't let a woman decide. He's the type who's kept Europe back for a thousand years. Every moment of his life he's forming you, telling you what's charming or amusing or ladylike, telling you what a man thinks womanly; and you, you of all women, listen to his voice instead of to your own. So it was at the Rectory, when I met you both again; so it has been the whole of this afternoon. Therefore—not 'therefore I kissed you,' because the book made me do that, and I wish to goodness I had more self-control. I'm not ashamed. I don't apologize. But it has frightened you, and you may not have noticed that I love you. Or would you have told me to go, and dealt with a tremendous thing so lightly? But therefore—therefore I settled to fight him."

Lucy thought of a very good remark.

"You say Mr. Vyse wants me to listen to him, Mr. Emerson. Pardon me for suggesting that you have caught the habit."

And he took the shoddy reproof and touched it into immortality. He said:

"Yes, I have," and sank down as if suddenly weary. "I'm the same kind of brute at bottom. This desire to govern a woman—it lies very deep, and men and women must fight it together before they shall enter the garden. But I do love you surely in a better way than he does." He thought. "Yes—really in a better way. I want you to have your own thoughts even when I hold you in my arms," He stretched them towards her. "Lucy, be quick—there's no time for us to talk now—come to me as you came in the spring, and afterwards I will be gentle and explain. I have cared for you since that man died. I cannot live without you, 'No good,' I thought; 'she is marrying some one else'; but I meet you again when all the world is glorious water and sun. As you came through the wood I saw that nothing else mattered. I called. I wanted to live and have my chance of joy."

"And Mr. Vyse?" said Lucy, who kept commendably calm. "Does he not matter? That I love Cecil and shall be his wife shortly? A detail of no importance, I suppose?"

But he stretched his arms over the table towards her.

"May I ask what you intend to gain by this exhibition?"

He said: "It is our last chance. I shall do all that I can." And as if he had done all else, he turned to Miss Bartlett, who sat like some portent against the skies of the evening. "You wouldn't stop us this second time if you understood," he said. "I have been into the dark, and I am going back into it, unless you will try to understand."

Her long, narrow head drove backwards and forwards, as though demolishing some invisible obstacle. She did not answer.

"It is being young," he said quietly, picking up his racquet from the floor and preparing to go. "It is being certain that Lucy cares for me really. It is that love and youth matter intellectually."

In silence the two women watched him. His last remark, they knew, was nonsense, but was he going after it or not? Would not he, the cad, the charlatan, attempt a more dramatic finish? No. He was apparently content. He left them, carefully closing the front door; and when they looked through the hall window, they saw him go up the drive and begin to climb the slopes of withered fern behind the house. Their tongues were loosed, and they burst into stealthy rejoicings.

"Oh, Lucia—come back here—oh, what an awful man!"

Lucy had no reaction—at least, not yet. "Well, he amuses me," she said. "Either I'm mad, or else he is, and I'm inclined to think it's the latter. One more fuss through with you, Charlotte. Many thanks. I think, though, that this is the last. My admirer will hardly trouble me again."

And Miss Bartlett, too, essayed the roguish:

"Well, it isn't every one who could boast such a conquest, dearest, is it? Oh, one oughtn't to laugh, really. It might have been very serious. But you were so sensible and brave—so unlike the girls of my day."

"Let's go down to them."

But, once in the open air, she paused. Some emotion—pity, terror, love, but the emotion was strong—seized her, and she was aware of autumn. Summer was ending, and the evening brought her odours of decay, the more pathetic because they were reminiscent of spring. That something or other mattered intellectually? A leaf, violently agitated, danced past her, while other leaves lay motionless. That the earth was hastening to re-enter darkness, and the shadows of those trees over Windy Corner?

"Hullo, Lucy! There's still light enough for another set, if you two'll hurry."

"Mr. Emerson has had to go."

"What a nuisance! That spoils the four. I say, Cecil, do play, do, there's a good chap. It's Floyd's last day. Do play tennis with us, just this once."

Cecil's voice came: "My dear Freddy, I am no athlete. As you well remarked this very morning, 'There are some chaps who are no good for anything but books'; I plead guilty to being such a chap, and will not inflict myself on you."

The scales fell from Lucy's eyes. How had she stood Cecil for a moment? He was absolutely intolerable, and the same evening she broke off her engagement.

Chapter XVII: Lying to Cecil

He was bewildered. He had nothing to say. He was not even angry, but stood, with a glass of whiskey between his hands, trying to think what had led her to such a conclusion.

She had chosen the moment before bed, when, in accordance with their bourgeois habit, she always dispensed drinks to the men. Freddy and Mr. Floyd were sure to retire with their glasses, while Cecil invariably lingered, sipping at his while she locked up the sideboard.

"I am very sorry about it," she said; "I have carefully thought things over. We are too different. I must ask you to release me, and try to forget that there ever was such a foolish girl."

It was a suitable speech, but she was more angry than sorry, and her voice showed it.

"Different—how—how—"

"I haven't had a really good education, for one thing," she continued, still on her knees by the sideboard. "My Italian trip came too late, and I am forgetting all that I learnt there. I shall never be able to talk to your friends, or behave as a wife of yours should."

"I don't understand you. You aren't like yourself. You're tired, Lucy."

"Tired!" she retorted, kindling at once. "That is exactly like you. You always think women don't mean what they say."

"Well, you sound tired, as if something has worried you."

"What if I do? It doesn't prevent me from realizing the truth. I can't marry you, and you will thank me for saying so some day."

"You had that bad headache yesterday—All right"—for she had exclaimed indignantly: "I see it's much more than headaches. But give me a moment's time." He closed his eyes. "You must excuse me if I say stupid things, but my brain has gone to pieces. Part of it lives three minutes back, when I was sure that you loved me, and the other part—I find it difficult—I am likely to say the wrong thing."

It struck her that he was not behaving so badly, and her irritation increased. She again desired a struggle, not a discussion. To bring on the crisis, she said:

"There are days when one sees clearly, and this is one of them. Things must come to a breaking-point some time, and it happens to be to-day. If you want to know, quite a little thing decided me to speak to you—when you wouldn't play tennis with Freddy."

"I never do play tennis," said Cecil, painfully bewildered; "I never could play. I don't understand a word you say."

"You can play well enough to make up a four. I thought it abominably selfish of you."

"No, I can't—well, never mind the tennis. Why couldn't you—couldn't you have warned me if you felt anything wrong? You talked of our wedding at lunch—at least, you let me talk."

"I knew you wouldn't understand," said Lucy quite crossly. "I might have known there would have been these dreadful explanations. Of course, it isn't the tennis—that was only the last straw to all I have been feeling for weeks. Surely it was better not to speak until I felt certain." She developed this position. "Often before I have wondered if I was fitted for your wife—for instance, in London; and are you fitted to be my husband? I don't think so. You don't like Freddy, nor my mother. There was always a lot against our engagement, Cecil, but all our relations seemed pleased, and we met so often, and it was no good mentioning it until—well, until all things came to a point. They have to-day. I see clearly. I must speak. That's all."

"I cannot think you were right," said Cecil gently. "I cannot tell why, but though all that you say sounds true, I feel that you are not treating me fairly. It's all too horrible."

"What's the good of a scene?"

"No good. But surely I have a right to hear a little more."

He put down his glass and opened the window. From where she knelt, jangling her keys, she could see a slit of darkness, and, peering into it, as if it would tell him that "little more," his long, thoughtful face.

"Don't open the window; and you'd better draw the curtain, too; Freddy or any one might be outside." He obeyed. "I really think we had better go to bed, if you don't mind. I shall only say things that will make me unhappy afterwards. As you say it is all too horrible, and it is no good talking."

But to Cecil, now that he was about to lose her, she seemed each moment more desirable. He looked at her, instead of through her, for the first time since they were engaged. From a Leonardo she had become a living woman, with mysteries and forces of her own, with qualities that even eluded art. His brain recovered from the shock, and, in a burst of genuine devotion, he cried: "But I love you, and I did think you loved me!"

"I did not," she said. "I thought I did at first. I am sorry, and ought to have refused you this last time, too."

He began to walk up and down the room, and she grew more and more vexed at his dignified behaviour. She had counted on his being petty. It would have made things easier for her. By a cruel irony she was drawing out all that was finest in his disposition.

"You don't love me, evidently. I dare say you are right not to. But it would hurt a little less if I knew why."

"Because"—a phrase came to her, and she accepted it—"you're the sort who can't know any one intimately."

A horrified look came into his eyes.

"I don't mean exactly that. But you will question me, though I beg you not to, and I must say something. It is that, more or less. When we were only acquaintances, you let me be myself, but now you're always protecting me." Her voice swelled. "I won't be protected. I will choose for myself what is ladylike and right. To shield me is an insult. Can't I be trusted to face the truth but I must get it second-hand through you? A woman's place! You despise my mother—I know you do—because she's conventional and bothers over puddings; but, oh goodness!"—she rose to her feet—"conventional, Cecil, you're that, for you may understand beautiful things, but you don't know how to use them; and you wrap yourself up in art and books and music, and would try to wrap up me. I won't be stifled, not by the most glorious music, for people are more glorious, and you hide them from me. That's why I break off my engagement. You were all right as long as you kept to things, but when you came to people—" She stopped.

There was a pause. Then Cecil said with great emotion:

"It is true."

"True on the whole," she corrected, full of some vague shame.

"True, every word. It is a revelation. It is—I."

"Anyhow, those are my reasons for not being your wife."

He repeated: "'The sort that can know no one intimately.' It is true. I fell to pieces the very first day we were engaged. I behaved like a cad to Beebe and to your brother. You are even greater than I thought." She withdrew a step. "I'm not going to worry you. You are far too good to me. I shall never forget your insight; and, dear, I only blame you for this: you might have warned me in the early stages, before you felt you wouldn't marry me, and so have given me a chance to improve. I have never known you till this evening. I have just used you as a peg for my silly notions of what a woman should be. But this evening you are a different person: new thoughts—even a new voice—"

"What do you mean by a new voice?" she asked, seized with incontrollable anger.

"I mean that a new person seems speaking through you," said he.

Then she lost her balance. She cried: "If you think I am in love with some one else, you are very much mistaken."

"Of course I don't think that. You are not that kind, Lucy."

"Oh, yes, you do think it. It's your old idea, the idea that has kept Europe back—I mean the idea that women are always thinking of men. If a girl breaks off her engagement, every one says: 'Oh, she had some one else in her mind; she hopes to get some one else.' It's disgusting, brutal! As if a girl can't break it off for the sake of freedom."

He answered reverently: "I may have said that in the past. I shall never say it again. You have taught me better."

She began to redden, and pretended to examine the windows again. "Of course, there is no question of 'some one else' in this, no 'jilting' or any such nauseous stupidity. I beg your pardon most humbly if my words suggested that there was. I only meant that there was a force in you that I hadn't known of up till now."

"All right, Cecil, that will do. Don't apologize to me. It was my mistake."

"It is a question between ideals, yours and mine—pure abstract ideals, and yours are the nobler. I was bound up in the old vicious notions, and all the time you were splendid and new." His voice broke. "I must actually thank you for what you have done—for showing me what I really am. Solemnly, I thank you for showing me a true woman. Will you shake hands?"

"Of course I will," said Lucy, twisting up her other hand in the curtains. "Good-night, Cecil. Good-bye. That's all right. I'm sorry about it. Thank you very much for your gentleness."

"Let me light your candle, shall I?"

They went into the hall.

"Thank you. Good-night again. God bless you, Lucy!"

"Good-bye, Cecil."

She watched him steal up-stairs, while the shadows from three banisters passed over her face like the beat of wings. On the landing he paused strong in his renunciation, and gave her a look of memorable beauty. For all his culture, Cecil was an ascetic at heart, and nothing in his love became him like the leaving of it.

She could never marry. In the tumult of her soul, that stood firm. Cecil believed in her; she must some day believe in herself. She must be one of the women whom she had praised so eloquently, who care for liberty and not for men; she must forget that George loved her, that George had been thinking through her and gained her this honourable release, that George had gone away into—what was it?—the darkness.

She put out the lamp.

It did not do to think, nor, for the matter of that to feel. She gave up trying to understand herself, and the vast armies of the benighted, who follow neither the heart nor the brain, and march to their destiny by catch-words. The armies are full of pleasant and pious folk. But they have yielded to the only enemy that matters—the enemy within. They have sinned against passion and truth, and vain will be their strife after virtue. As the years pass, they are censured. Their pleasantry and their piety show cracks, their wit becomes cynicism, their unselfishness hypocrisy; they feel and produce discomfort wherever they go. They have sinned against Eros and against Pallas Athene, and not by any heavenly intervention, but by the ordinary course of nature, those allied deities will be avenged.

Lucy entered this army when she pretended to George that she did not love him, and pretended to Cecil that she loved no one. The night received her, as it had received Miss Bartlett thirty years before.

Chapter XVIII: Lying to Mr. Beebe, Mrs. Honey-church, Freddy, and The Servants

Windy Corner lay, not on the summit of the ridge, but a few hundred feet down the southern slope, at the springing of one of the great buttresses that supported the hill. On either side of it was a shallow ravine, filled with ferns and pine-trees, and down the ravine on the left ran the highway into the Weald.

Whenever Mr. Beebe crossed the ridge and caught sight of these noble dispositions of the earth, and, poised in the middle of them, Windy Corner,—he laughed. The situation was so glorious, the house so commonplace, not to say impertinent. The late Mr. Honeychurch had affected the cube, because it gave him the most accommodation for his money, and the only addition made by his widow had been a small turret, shaped like a rhinoceros' horn, where she could sit in wet weather and watch the carts going up and down the road. So impertinent—and yet the house "did," for it was the home of people who loved their surroundings honestly. Other houses in the neighborhood had been built by expensive architects, over others their inmates had fidgeted sedulously, yet all these suggested the accidental, the temporary; while Windy Corner seemed as inevitable as an ugliness of Nature's own creation. One might laugh at the house, but one never shuddered. Mr. Beebe was bicycling over this Monday afternoon with a piece of gossip. He had heard from the Miss Alans. These admirable ladies, since they could not go to Cissie Villa, had changed their plans. They were going to Greece instead.

"Since Florence did my poor sister so much good," wrote Miss Catharine, "we do not see why we should not try Athens this winter. Of course, Athens is a plunge, and the doctor has ordered her special digestive bread; but, after all, we can take that with us, and it is only getting first into a steamer and then into a train. But is there an English Church?" And the letter went on to say: "I do not expect we shall go any further than Athens, but if you knew of a really comfortable pension at Constantinople, we should be so grateful."

Lucy would enjoy this letter, and the smile with which Mr. Beebe greeted Windy Corner was partly for her. She would see the fun of it, and some of its beauty, for she must see some beauty. Though she was hopeless about pictures, and though she dressed so unevenly—oh, that cerise frock yesterday at church!—she must see some beauty in life, or she could not play the piano as she did. He had a theory that musicians are incredibly complex, and know far less than other artists what they want and what they are; that they puzzle themselves as well as their friends; that their psychology is a modern development, and has not yet been understood. This theory, had he known it, had possibly just been illustrated by facts. Ignorant of the events of yesterday he was only riding over to get some tea, to see his niece, and to observe whether Miss Honeychurch saw anything beautiful in the desire of two old ladies to visit Athens.

A carriage was drawn up outside Windy Corner, and just as he caught sight of the house it started, bowled up the drive, and stopped abruptly when it reached the main road. Therefore it must be the horse, who always expected people to walk up the hill in case they tired him. The door opened obediently, and two men emerged, whom Mr. Beebe recognized as Cecil and Freddy. They were an odd couple to go driving; but he saw a trunk beside the coachman's legs. Cecil, who wore a bowler, must be going away, while Freddy (a cap)—was seeing him to the station. They walked rapidly, taking the short cuts, and reached the summit while the carriage was still pursuing the windings of the road.

They shook hands with the clergyman, but did not speak.

"So you're off for a minute, Mr. Vyse?" he asked.

Cecil said, "Yes," while Freddy edged away.

"I was coming to show you this delightful letter from those friends of Miss Honeychurch." He quoted from it. "Isn't it wonderful? Isn't it romance? most certainly they will go to Constantinople. They are taken in a snare that cannot fail. They will end by going round the world."

Cecil listened civilly, and said he was sure that Lucy would be amused and interested.

"Isn't Romance capricious! I never notice it in you young people; you do nothing but play lawn tennis, and say that romance is dead, while the Miss Alans are struggling with all the weapons of propriety against the terrible thing. 'A really comfortable pension at Constantinople!' So they call it out of decency, but in their hearts they want a pension with magic windows opening on the foam of perilous seas in fairyland forlorn! No ordinary view will content the Miss Alans. They want the Pension Keats."

"I'm awfully sorry to interrupt, Mr. Beebe," said Freddy, "but have you any matches?"

"I have," said Cecil, and it did not escape Mr. Beebe's notice that he spoke to the boy more kindly.

"You have never met these Miss Alans, have you, Mr. Vyse?"

"Never."

"Then you don't see the wonder of this Greek visit. I haven't been to Greece myself, and don't mean to go, and I can't imagine any of my friends going. It is altogether too big for our little lot. Don't you think so? Italy is just about as much as we can manage. Italy is heroic, but Greece is godlike or devilish—I am not sure which, and in either case absolutely out of our suburban focus. All right, Freddy—I am not being clever, upon my word I am not—I took the idea from another fellow; and give me those matches when you've done with them." He lit a cigarette, and went on talking to the two young men. "I was saying, if our poor little Cockney lives must have a background, let it be Italian. Big enough in all conscience. The ceiling of the Sistine Chapel for me. There the contrast is just as much as I can realize. But not the Parthenon, not the frieze of Phidias at any price; and here comes the victoria."

"You're quite right," said Cecil. "Greece is not for our little lot"; and he got in. Freddy followed, nodding to the clergyman, whom he trusted not to be pulling one's leg, really. And before they had gone a dozen yards he jumped out, and came running back for Vyse's match-box, which had not been returned. As he took it, he said: "I'm so glad you only talked about books. Cecil's hard hit. Lucy won't marry him. If you'd gone on about her, as you did about them, he might have broken down."

"But when—"

"Late last night. I must go."

"Perhaps they won't want me down there."

"No—go on. Good-bye."

"Thank goodness!" exclaimed Mr. Beebe to himself, and struck the saddle of his bicycle approvingly, "It was the one foolish thing she ever did. Oh, what a glorious riddance!" And, after a little thought, he negotiated the slope into Windy Corner, light of heart. The house was again as it ought to be—cut off forever from Cecil's pretentious world.

He would find Miss Minnie down in the garden.

In the drawing-room Lucy was tinkling at a Mozart Sonata. He hesitated a moment, but went down the garden as requested. There he found a mournful company. It was a blustering day, and the wind had taken and broken the dahlias. Mrs. Honeychurch, who looked cross, was tying them up, while Miss Bartlett, unsuitably dressed, impeded her with offers of assistance. At a little distance stood Minnie and the "garden-child," a minute importation, each holding either end of a long piece of bass.

"Oh, how do you do, Mr. Beebe? Gracious what a mess everything is! Look at my scarlet pompons, and the wind blowing your skirts about, and the ground so hard that not a prop will stick in, and then the carriage having to go out, when I had counted on having Powell, who—give every one their due—does tie up dahlias properly."

Evidently Mrs. Honeychurch was shattered.

"How do you do?" said Miss Bartlett, with a meaning glance, as though conveying that more than dahlias had been broken off by the autumn gales.

"Here, Lennie, the bass," cried Mrs. Honeychurch. The garden-child, who did not know what bass was, stood rooted to the path with horror. Minnie slipped to her uncle and whispered that every one was very disagreeable to-day, and that it was not her fault if dahlia-strings would tear longways instead of across.

"Come for a walk with me," he told her. "You have worried them as much as they can stand. Mrs. Honeychurch, I only called in aimlessly. I shall take her up to tea at the Beehive Tavern, if I may."

"Oh, must you? Yes do.—Not the scissors, thank you, Charlotte, when both my hands are full already—I'm perfectly certain that the orange cactus will go before I can get to it."

Mr. Beebe, who was an adept at relieving situations, invited Miss Bartlett to accompany them to this mild festivity.

"Yes, Charlotte, I don't want you—do go; there's nothing to stop about for, either in the house or out of it."

Miss Bartlett said that her duty lay in the dahlia bed, but when she had exasperated every one, except Minnie, by a refusal, she turned round and exasperated Minnie by an acceptance. As they walked up the garden, the orange cactus fell, and Mr. Beebe's last vision was of the garden-child clasping it like a lover, his dark head buried in a wealth of blossom.

"It is terrible, this havoc among the flowers," he remarked.

"It is always terrible when the promise of months is destroyed in a moment," enunciated Miss Bartlett.

"Perhaps we ought to send Miss Honeychurch down to her mother. Or will she come with us?"

"I think we had better leave Lucy to herself, and to her own pursuits."

"They're angry with Miss Honeychurch because she was late for breakfast," whispered Minnie, "and Floyd has gone, and Mr. Vyse has gone, and Freddy won't play with me. In fact, Uncle Arthur, the house is not AT ALL what it was yesterday."

"Don't be a prig," said her Uncle Arthur. "Go and put on your boots."

He stepped into the drawing-room, where Lucy was still attentively pursuing the Sonatas of Mozart. She stopped when he entered.

"How do you do? Miss Bartlett and Minnie are coming with me to tea at the Beehive. Would you come too?"

"I don't think I will, thank you."

"No, I didn't suppose you would care to much."

Lucy turned to the piano and struck a few chords.

"How delicate those Sonatas are!" said Mr. Beebe, though at the bottom of his heart, he thought them silly little things.

Lucy passed into Schumann.

"Miss Honeychurch!"

"Yes."

"I met them on the hill. Your brother told me."

"Oh he did?" She sounded annoyed. Mr. Beebe felt hurt, for he had thought that she would like him to be told.

"I needn't say that it will go no further."

"Mother, Charlotte, Cecil, Freddy, you," said Lucy, playing a note for each person who knew, and then playing a sixth note.

"If you'll let me say so, I am very glad, and I am certain that you have done the right thing."

"So I hoped other people would think, but they don't seem to."

"I could see that Miss Bartlett thought it unwise."

"So does mother. Mother minds dreadfully."

"I am very sorry for that," said Mr. Beebe with feeling.

Mrs. Honeychurch, who hated all changes, did mind, but not nearly as much as her daughter pretended, and only for the minute. It was really a ruse of Lucy's to justify her despondency—a ruse of which she was not herself conscious, for she was marching in the armies of darkness.

"And Freddy minds."

"Still, Freddy never hit it off with Vyse much, did he? I gathered that he disliked the engagement, and felt it might separate him from you."

"Boys are so odd."

Minnie could be heard arguing with Miss Bartlett through the floor. Tea at the Beehive apparently involved a complete change of apparel. Mr. Beebe saw that Lucy—very properly—did not wish to discuss her action, so after a sincere expression of sympathy, he said, "I have had an absurd letter from Miss Alan. That was really what brought me over. I thought it might amuse you all."

"How delightful!" said Lucy, in a dull voice.

For the sake of something to do, he began to read her the letter. After a few words her eyes grew alert, and soon she interrupted him with "Going abroad? When do they start?"

"Next week, I gather."

"Did Freddy say whether he was driving straight back?"

"No, he didn't."

"Because I do hope he won't go gossiping."

So she did want to talk about her broken engagement. Always complaisant, he put the letter away. But she, at once exclaimed in a high voice, "Oh, do tell me more about the Miss Alans! How perfectly splendid of them to go abroad!"

"I want them to start from Venice, and go in a cargo steamer down the Illyrian coast!"

She laughed heartily. "Oh, delightful! I wish they'd take me."

"Has Italy filled you with the fever of travel? Perhaps George Emerson is right. He says that 'Italy is only an euphuism for Fate.'"

"Oh, not Italy, but Constantinople. I have always longed to go to Constantinople. Constantinople is practically Asia, isn't it?"

Mr. Beebe reminded her that Constantinople was still unlikely, and that the Miss Alans only aimed at Athens, "with Delphi, perhaps, if the roads are safe." But this made no difference to her enthusiasm. She had always longed to go to Greece even more, it seemed. He saw, to his surprise, that she was apparently serious.

"I didn't realize that you and the Miss Alans were still such friends, after Cissie Villa."

"Oh, that's nothing; I assure you Cissie Villa's nothing to me; I would give anything to go with them."

"Would your mother spare you again so soon? You have scarcely been home three months."

"She MUST spare me!" cried Lucy, in growing excitement. "I simply MUST go away. I have to." She ran her fingers hysterically through her hair. "Don't you see that I HAVE to go away? I didn't realize at the time—and of course I want to see Constantinople so particularly."

"You mean that since you have broken off your engagement you feel—"

"Yes, yes. I knew you'd understand."

Mr. Beebe did not quite understand. Why could not Miss Honeychurch repose in the bosom of her family? Cecil had evidently taken up the dignified line, and was not going to annoy her. Then it struck him that her family itself might be annoying. He hinted this to her, and she accepted the hint eagerly.

"Yes, of course; to go to Constantinople until they are used to the idea and everything has calmed down."

"I am afraid it has been a bothersome business," he said gently.

"No, not at all. Cecil was very kind indeed; only—I had better tell you the whole truth, since you have heard a little—it was that he is so masterful. I found that he wouldn't let me go my own way. He would improve me in places where I can't be improved. Cecil won't let a woman decide for herself—in fact, he daren't. What nonsense I do talk! but that is the kind of thing."

"It is what I gathered from my own observation of Mr. Vyse; it is what I gather from all that I have known of you. I do sympathize and agree most profoundly. I agree so much that you must let me make one little criticism: Is it worth while rushing off to Greece?"

"But I must go somewhere!" she cried. "I have been worrying all the morning, and here comes the very thing." She struck her knees with clenched fists, and repeated: "I must! And the time I shall have with mother, and all the money she spent on me last spring. You all think much too highly of me. I wish you weren't so kind." At this moment Miss Bartlett entered, and her nervousness increased. "I must get away, ever so far. I must know my own mind and where I want to go."

"Come along; tea, tea, tea," said Mr. Beebe, and bustled his guests out of the front-door. He hustled them so quickly that he forgot his hat. When he returned for it he heard, to his relief and surprise, the tinkling of a Mozart Sonata.

"She is playing again," he said to Miss Bartlett.

"Lucy can always play," was the acid reply.

"One is very thankful that she has such a resource. She is evidently much worried, as, of course, she ought to be. I know all about it. The marriage was so near that it must have been a hard struggle before she could wind herself up to speak."

Miss Bartlett gave a kind of wriggle, and he prepared for a discussion. He had never fathomed Miss Bartlett. As he had put it to himself at Florence, "she might yet reveal depths of strangeness, if not of meaning." But she was so unsympathetic that she must be reliable. He assumed that much, and he had no hesitation in discussing Lucy with her. Minnie was fortunately collecting ferns.

She opened the discussion with: "We had much better let the matter drop."

"I wonder."

"It is of the highest importance that there should be no gossip in Summer Street. It would be DEATH to gossip about Mr. Vyse's dismissal at the present moment."

Mr. Beebe raised his eyebrows. Death is a strong word—surely too strong. There was no question of tragedy. He said: "Of course, Miss Honeychurch will make the fact public in her own way, and when she chooses. Freddy only told me because he knew she would not mind."

"I know," said Miss Bartlett civilly. "Yet Freddy ought not to have told even you. One cannot be too careful."

"Quite so."

"I do implore absolute secrecy. A chance word to a chattering friend, and—"

"Exactly." He was used to these nervous old maids and to the exaggerated importance that they attach to words. A rector lives in a web of petty secrets, and confidences and warnings, and the wiser he is the less he will regard them. He will change the subject, as did Mr. Beebe, saying cheerfully: "Have you heard from any Bertolini people lately? I believe you keep up with Miss Lavish. It is odd how we of that pension, who seemed such a fortuitous collection, have been working into one another's lives. Two, three, four, six of us—no, eight; I had forgotten the Emersons—have kept more or less in touch. We must really give the Signora a testimonial."

And, Miss Bartlett not favouring the scheme, they walked up the hill in a silence which was only broken by the rector naming some fern. On the summit they paused. The sky had grown wilder since he stood there last hour, giving to the land a tragic greatness that is rare in Surrey. Grey clouds were charging across tissues of white, which stretched and shredded and tore slowly, until through their final layers there gleamed a hint of the disappearing blue. Summer was retreating. The wind roared, the trees groaned, yet the noise seemed insufficient for those vast operations in heaven. The weather was breaking up, breaking, broken, and it is a sense of the fit rather than of the supernatural that equips such crises with the salvos of angelic artillery. Mr. Beebe's eyes rested on Windy Corner, where Lucy sat, practising Mozart. No smile came to his lips, and, changing the subject again, he said: "We shan't have rain, but we shall have darkness, so let us hurry on. The darkness last night was appalling."

They reached the Beehive Tavern at about five o'clock. That amiable hostelry possesses a verandah, in which the young and the unwise do dearly love to sit, while guests of more mature years seek a pleasant sanded room, and have tea at a table comfortably. Mr. Beebe saw that Miss Bartlett would be cold if she sat out, and that Minnie would be dull if she sat in, so he proposed a division of forces. They would hand the child her food through the window. Thus he was incidentally enabled to discuss the fortunes of Lucy.

"I have been thinking, Miss Bartlett," he said, "and, unless you very much object, I would like to reopen that discussion." She bowed. "Nothing about the past. I know little and care less about that; I am absolutely certain that it is to your cousin's credit. She has acted loftily and rightly, and it is like her gentle modesty to say that we think too highly of her. But the future. Seriously, what do you think of this Greek plan?" He pulled out the letter again. "I don't know whether you overheard, but she wants to join the Miss Alans in their mad career. It's all—I can't explain—it's wrong."

Miss Bartlett read the letter in silence, laid it down, seemed to hesitate, and then read it again.

"I can't see the point of it myself."

To his astonishment, she replied: "There I cannot agree with you. In it I spy Lucy's salvation."

"Really. Now, why?"

"She wanted to leave Windy Corner."

"I know—but it seems so odd, so unlike her, so—I was going to say—selfish."

"It is natural, surely—after such painful scenes—that she should desire a change."

Here, apparently, was one of those points that the male intellect misses. Mr. Beebe exclaimed: "So she says herself, and since another lady agrees with her, I must own that I am partially convinced. Perhaps she must have a change. I have no sisters or—and I don't understand these things. But why need she go as far as Greece?"

"You may well ask that," replied Miss Bartlett, who was evidently interested, and had almost dropped her evasive manner. "Why Greece? (What is it, Minnie dear—jam?) Why not Tunbridge Wells? Oh, Mr. Beebe! I had a long and most unsatisfactory interview with dear Lucy this morning. I cannot help her. I will say no more. Perhaps I have already said too much. I am not to talk. I wanted her to spend six months with me at Tunbridge Wells, and she refused."

Mr. Beebe poked at a crumb with his knife.

"But my feelings are of no importance. I know too well that I get on Lucy's nerves. Our tour was a failure. She wanted to leave Florence, and when we got to Rome she did not want to be in Rome, and all the time I felt that I was spending her mother's money—."

"Let us keep to the future, though," interrupted Mr. Beebe. "I want your advice."

"Very well," said Charlotte, with a choky abruptness that was new to him, though familiar to Lucy. "I for one will help her to go to Greece. Will you?"

Mr. Beebe considered.

"It is absolutely necessary," she continued, lowering her veil and whispering through it with a passion, an intensity, that surprised him. "I know—I know." The darkness was coming on, and he felt that this odd woman really did know. "She must not stop here a moment, and we must keep quiet till she goes. I trust that the servants know nothing. Afterwards—but I may have said too much already. Only,

Lucy and I are helpless against Mrs. Honeychurch alone. If you help we may succeed. Otherwise—"

"Otherwise—?"

"Otherwise," she repeated as if the word held finality.

"Yes, I will help her," said the clergyman, setting his jaw firm. "Come, let us go back now, and settle the whole thing up."

Miss Bartlett burst into florid gratitude. The tavern sign—a beehive trimmed evenly with bees—creaked in the wind outside as she thanked him. Mr. Beebe did not quite understand the situation; but then, he did not desire to understand it, nor to jump to the conclusion of "another man" that would have attracted a grosser mind. He only felt that Miss Bartlett knew of some vague influence from which the girl desired to be delivered, and which might well be clothed in the fleshly form. Its very vagueness spurred him into knight-errantry. His belief in celibacy, so reticent, so carefully concealed beneath his tolerance and culture, now came to the surface and expanded like some delicate flower. "They that marry do well, but they that refrain do better." So ran his belief, and he never heard that an engagement was broken off but with a slight feeling of pleasure. In the case of Lucy, the feeling was intensified through dislike of Cecil; and he was willing to go further—to place her out of danger until she could confirm her resolution of virginity. The feeling was very subtle and quite undogmatic, and he never imparted it to any other of the characters in this entanglement. Yet it existed, and it alone explains his action subsequently, and his influence on the action of others. The compact that he made with Miss Bartlett in the tavern, was to help not only Lucy, but religion also.

They hurried home through a world of black and grey. He conversed on indifferent topics: the Emersons' need of a housekeeper; servants; Italian servants; novels about Italy; novels with a purpose; could literature influence life? Windy Corner glimmered. In the garden, Mrs. Honeychurch, now helped by Freddy, still wrestled with the lives of her flowers.

"It gets too dark," she said hopelessly. "This comes of putting off. We might have known the weather would break up soon; and now Lucy wants to go to Greece. I don't know what the world's coming to."

"Mrs. Honeychurch," he said, "go to Greece she must. Come up to the house and let's talk it over. Do you, in the first place, mind her breaking with Vyse?"

"Mr. Beebe, I'm thankful—simply thankful."

"So am I," said Freddy.

"Good. Now come up to the house."

They conferred in the dining-room for half an hour.

Lucy would never have carried the Greek scheme alone. It was expensive and dramatic—both qualities that her mother loathed. Nor would Charlotte have succeeded. The honours of the day rested with Mr. Beebe. By his tact and common sense, and by his influence as a clergyman—for a clergyman who was not a fool influenced Mrs. Honeychurch greatly—he bent her to their purpose, "I don't see why Greece is necessary," she said; "but as you do, I suppose it is all right. It must be something I can't understand. Lucy! Let's tell her. Lucy!"

"She is playing the piano," Mr. Beebe said. He opened the door, and heard the words of a song:

> *"Look not thou on beauty's charming."*

"I didn't know that Miss Honeychurch sang, too."

> *"Sit thou still when kings are arming,*
> *Taste not when the wine-cup glistens—"*

"It's a song that Cecil gave her. How odd girls are!"

"What's that?" called Lucy, stopping short.

"All right, dear," said Mrs. Honeychurch kindly. She went into the drawing-room, and Mr. Beebe heard her kiss Lucy and say: "I am sorry I was so cross about Greece, but it came on the top of the dahlias."

Rather a hard voice said: "Thank you, mother; that doesn't matter a bit."

"And you are right, too—Greece will be all right; you can go if the Miss Alans will have you."

"Oh, splendid! Oh, thank you!"

Mr. Beebe followed. Lucy still sat at the piano with her hands over the keys. She was glad, but he had expected greater gladness. Her mother bent over her. Freddy, to whom she had been singing, reclined on the floor with his head against her, and an unlit pipe between his lips. Oddly enough, the group was beautiful. Mr. Beebe, who loved the art of the past, was reminded of a favourite theme, the Santa Conversazione, in which people who care for one another are painted chatting together about noble things—a theme neither sensual nor sensational, and therefore ignored by the art of to-day. Why should Lucy want either to marry or to travel when she had such friends at home?

> *"Taste not when the wine-cup glistens, Speak not when the people listens,"*

she continued.

"Here's Mr. Beebe."

"Mr. Beebe knows my rude ways."

"It's a beautiful song and a wise one," said he. "Go on."

"It isn't very good," she said listlessly. "I forget why—harmony or something."

"I suspected it was unscholarly. It's so beautiful."

"The tune's right enough," said Freddy, "but the words are rotten. Why throw up the sponge?"

"How stupidly you talk!" said his sister. The Santa Conversazione was broken up. After all, there was no reason that Lucy should talk about Greece or thank him for persuading her mother, so he said good-bye.

Freddy lit his bicycle lamp for him in the porch, and with his usual felicity of phrase, said: "This has been a day and a half."

"Stop thine ear against the singer—"

"Wait a minute; she is finishing."

"From the red gold keep thy finger;
Vacant heart and hand and eye
Easy live and quiet die."

"I love weather like this," said Freddy.

Mr. Beebe passed into it.

The two main facts were clear. She had behaved splendidly, and he had helped her. He could not expect to master the details of so big a change in a girl's life. If here and there he was dissatisfied or puzzled, he must acquiesce; she was choosing the better part.

"Vacant heart and hand and eye—"

Perhaps the song stated "the better part" rather too strongly. He half fancied that the soaring accompaniment—which he did not lose in the shout of the gale—really agreed with Freddy, and was gently criticizing the words that it adorned:

"Vacant heart and hand and eye
Easy live and quiet die."

However, for the fourth time Windy Corner lay poised below him—now as a beacon in the roaring tides of darkness.

Chapter XIX: Lying to Mr. Emerson

The Miss Alans were found in their beloved temperance hotel near Bloomsbury—a clean, airless establishment much patronized by provincial England. They always perched there before crossing the great seas, and for a week or two would fidget gently over clothes, guide-books, mackintosh squares, digestive bread, and other Continental necessaries. That there are shops abroad, even in Athens, never occurred to them, for they regarded travel as a species of warfare, only to be undertaken by those who have been fully armed at the Haymarket Stores. Miss Honeychurch, they trusted, would take care to equip herself duly. Quinine could now be obtained in tabloids; paper soap was a great help towards freshening up one's face in the train. Lucy promised, a little depressed.

"But, of course, you know all about these things, and you have Mr. Vyse to help you. A gentleman is such a stand-by."

Mrs. Honeychurch, who had come up to town with her daughter, began to drum nervously upon her card-case.

"We think it so good of Mr. Vyse to spare you," Miss Catharine continued. "It is not every young man who would be so unselfish. But perhaps he will come out and join you later on."

"Or does his work keep him in London?" said Miss Teresa, the more acute and less kindly of the two sisters.

"However, we shall see him when he sees you off. I do so long to see him."

"No one will see Lucy off," interposed Mrs. Honeychurch. "She doesn't like it."

"No, I hate seeings-off," said Lucy.

"Really? How funny! I should have thought that in this case—"

"Oh, Mrs. Honeychurch, you aren't going? It is such a pleasure to have met you!"

They escaped, and Lucy said with relief: "That's all right. We just got through that time."

But her mother was annoyed. "I should be told, dear, that I am unsympathetic. But I cannot see why you didn't tell your friends about Cecil and be done with it. There all the time we had to sit fencing, and almost telling lies, and be seen through, too, I dare say, which is most unpleasant."

Lucy had plenty to say in reply. She described the Miss Alans' character: they were such gossips, and if one told them, the news would be everywhere in no time.

"But why shouldn't it be everywhere in no time?"

"Because I settled with Cecil not to announce it until I left England. I shall tell them then. It's much pleasanter. How wet it is! Let's turn in here."

"Here" was the British Museum. Mrs. Honeychurch refused. If they must take shelter, let it be in a shop. Lucy felt contemptuous, for she was on the tack of caring for Greek sculpture, and had already borrowed a mythical dictionary from Mr. Beebe to get up the names of the goddesses and gods.

"Oh, well, let it be shop, then. Let's go to Mudie's. I'll buy a guide-book."

"You know, Lucy, you and Charlotte and Mr. Beebe all tell me I'm so stupid, so I suppose I am, but I shall never understand this hole-and-corner work. You've got rid of Cecil—well and good, and I'm thankful he's gone, though I did feel angry for the minute. But why not announce it? Why this hushing up and tiptoeing?"

"It's only for a few days."

"But why at all?"

Lucy was silent. She was drifting away from her mother. It was quite easy to say, "Because George Emerson has been bothering me, and if he hears I've given up Cecil may begin again"—quite easy, and it had the incidental advantage of being true. But she could not say it. She disliked confidences, for they might lead to self-knowledge and to that king of terrors—Light. Ever since that last evening at Florence she had deemed it unwise to reveal her soul.

Mrs. Honeychurch, too, was silent. She was thinking, "My daughter won't answer me; she would rather be with those inquisitive old maids than with Freddy and me. Any rag, tag, and bobtail apparently does if she can leave her home." And as in her case thoughts never remained unspoken long, she burst out with: "You're tired of Windy Corner."

This was perfectly true. Lucy had hoped to return to Windy Corner when she escaped from Cecil, but she discovered that her home existed no longer. It might exist for Freddy, who still lived and thought straight, but not for one who had deliberately warped the brain. She did not acknowledge that her brain was warped, for the brain itself must assist in that acknowledgment, and she was disordering the very instruments of life. She only felt, "I do not love George; I broke off my engagement because I did not love George; I must go to Greece because I do not love George; it is more important that I should look up gods in the dictionary than that I should help my mother; every one else is behaving very badly." She only felt irritable and petulant, and anxious to do what she was not expected to do, and in this spirit she proceeded with the conversation.

"Oh, mother, what rubbish you talk! Of course I'm not tired of Windy Corner."

"Then why not say so at once, instead of considering half an hour?"

She laughed faintly, "Half a minute would be nearer."

"Perhaps you would like to stay away from your home altogether?"

"Hush, mother! People will hear you"; for they had entered Mudie's. She bought Baedeker, and then continued: "Of course I want to live at home; but as we are talking about it, I may as well say that I shall want to be away in the future more than I have been. You see, I come into my money next year."

Tears came into her mother's eyes.

Driven by nameless bewilderment, by what is in older people termed "eccentricity," Lucy determined to make this point clear. "I've seen the world so little—I felt so out of things in Italy. I have seen so little of life; one ought to come up to London more—not a cheap ticket like to-day, but to stop. I might even share a flat for a little with some other girl."

"And mess with typewriters and latch-keys," exploded Mrs. Honeychurch. "And agitate and scream, and be carried off kicking by the police. And call it a Mission—when no one wants you! And call it Duty—when it means that you can't stand your own home! And call it Work—when thousands of men are starving with the competition as it is! And then to prepare yourself, find two doddering old ladies, and go abroad with them."

"I want more independence," said Lucy lamely; she knew that she wanted something, and independence is a useful cry; we can always say that we have not got it. She tried to remember her emotions in Florence: those had been sincere and passionate, and had suggested beauty rather than short skirts and latch-keys. But independence was certainly her cue.

"Very well. Take your independence and be gone. Rush up and down and round the world, and come back as thin as a lath with the bad food. Despise the house that your father built and the garden that he planted, and our dear view—and then share a flat with another girl."

Lucy screwed up her mouth and said: "Perhaps I spoke hastily."

"Oh, goodness!" her mother flashed. "How you do remind me of Charlotte Bartlett!"

"Charlotte!" flashed Lucy in her turn, pierced at last by a vivid pain.

"More every moment."

"I don't know what you mean, mother; Charlotte and I are not the very least alike."

"Well, I see the likeness. The same eternal worrying, the same taking back of words. You and Charlotte trying to divide two apples among three people last night might be sisters."

"What rubbish! And if you dislike Charlotte so, it's rather a pity you asked her to stop. I warned you about her; I begged you, implored you not to, but of course it was not listened to."

"There you go."

"I beg your pardon?"

"Charlotte again, my dear; that's all; her very words."

Lucy clenched her teeth. "My point is that you oughtn't to have asked Charlotte to stop. I wish you would keep to the point." And the conversation died off into a wrangle.

She and her mother shopped in silence, spoke little in the train, little again in the carriage, which met them at Dorking Station. It had poured all day and as they ascended through the deep Surrey lanes showers of water fell from the overhanging beech-trees and rattled on the hood. Lucy complained that the hood was stuffy. Leaning forward, she looked out into the steaming dusk, and watched the carriage-lamp pass like a search-light over mud and leaves, and reveal nothing beautiful. "The crush when Charlotte gets in will be abominable," she remarked. For they were to pick up Miss Bartlett at Summer Street, where she had been dropped as the carriage went down, to pay a call on Mr. Beebe's old mother. "We shall have to sit three a side, because the trees drop, and yet it isn't raining. Oh, for a little air!" Then she listened to the horse's hoofs—"He has not told—he has not told." That melody was blurred by the soft road. "CAN'T we have the hood down?" she demanded, and her mother, with sudden tenderness, said: "Very well, old lady, stop the horse." And the horse was stopped, and Lucy and Powell wrestled with the hood, and squirted water down Mrs. Honeychurch's neck. But now that the hood was down, she did see something that she would have missed—there were no lights in the windows of Cissie Villa, and round the garden gate she fancied she saw a padlock.

"Is that house to let again, Powell?" she called.

"Yes, miss," he replied.

"Have they gone?"

"It is too far out of town for the young gentleman, and his father's rheumatism has come on, so he can't stop on alone, so they are trying to let furnished," was the answer.

"They have gone, then?"

"Yes, miss, they have gone."

Lucy sank back. The carriage stopped at the Rectory. She got out to call for Miss Bartlett. So the Emersons had gone, and all this bother about Greece had been unnecessary. Waste! That word seemed to sum up the whole of life. Wasted plans, wasted money, wasted love, and she had wounded her mother. Was it possible that she had muddled things away? Quite possible. Other people had. When the maid opened the door, she was unable to speak, and stared stupidly into the hall.

Miss Bartlett at once came forward, and after a long preamble asked a great favour: might she go to church? Mr. Beebe and his mother had already gone, but she had refused to start until she obtained her hostess's full sanction, for it would mean keeping the horse waiting a good ten minutes more.

"Certainly," said the hostess wearily. "I forgot it was Friday. Let's all go. Powell can go round to the stables."

"Lucy dearest—"

"No church for me, thank you."

A sigh, and they departed. The church was invisible, but up in the darkness to the left there was a hint of colour. This was a stained window, through which some feeble light was shining, and when the door opened Lucy heard Mr. Beebe's voice running through the litany to a minute congregation. Even their church, built upon the slope of the hill so artfully, with its beautiful raised transept and its spire of silvery shingle—even their church had lost its charm; and the thing one never talked about—religion—was fading like all the other things.

She followed the maid into the Rectory.

Would she object to sitting in Mr. Beebe's study? There was only that one fire.

She would not object.

Some one was there already, for Lucy heard the words: "A lady to wait, sir."

Old Mr. Emerson was sitting by the fire, with his foot upon a gout-stool.

"Oh, Miss Honeychurch, that you should come!" he quavered; and Lucy saw an alteration in him since last Sunday.

Not a word would come to her lips. George she had faced, and could have faced again, but she had forgotten how to treat his father.

"Miss Honeychurch, dear, we are so sorry! George is so sorry! He thought he had a right to try. I cannot blame my boy, and yet I wish he had told me first. He ought not to have tried. I knew nothing about it at all."

If only she could remember how to behave!

He held up his hand. "But you must not scold him."

Lucy turned her back, and began to look at Mr. Beebe's books.

"I taught him," he quavered, "to trust in love. I said: 'When love comes, that is reality.' I said: 'Passion does not blind. No. Passion is sanity, and the woman you love, she is the only person you will ever really understand.'" He sighed: "True, everlastingly true, though my day is over, and though there is the result. Poor boy! He is so sorry! He said he knew it was madness when you brought your cousin in; that whatever you felt you did not mean. Yet"—his voice gathered strength: he spoke out to make certain—"Miss Honeychurch, do you remember Italy?"

Lucy selected a book—a volume of Old Testament commentaries. Holding it up to her eyes, she said: "I have no wish to discuss Italy or any subject connected with your son."

"But you do remember it?"

"He has misbehaved himself from the first."

"I only was told that he loved you last Sunday. I never could judge behaviour. I—I—suppose he has."

Feeling a little steadier, she put the book back and turned round to him. His face was drooping and swollen, but his eyes, though they were sunken deep, gleamed with a child's courage.

"Why, he has behaved abominably," she said. "I am glad he is sorry. Do you know what he did?"

"Not 'abominably,'" was the gentle correction. "He only tried when he should not have tried. You have all you want, Miss Honeychurch: you are going to marry the man you love. Do not go out of George's life saying he is abominable."

"No, of course," said Lucy, ashamed at the reference to Cecil. "'Abominable' is much too strong. I am sorry I used it about your son. I think I will go to church, after all. My mother and my cousin have gone. I shall not be so very late—"

"Especially as he has gone under," he said quietly.

"What was that?"

"Gone under naturally." He beat his palms together in silence; his head fell on his chest.

"I don't understand."

"As his mother did."

"But, Mr. Emerson—MR. EMERSON—what are you talking about?"

"When I wouldn't have George baptized," said he.

Lucy was frightened.

"And she agreed that baptism was nothing, but he caught that fever when he was twelve and she turned round. She thought it a judgment." He shuddered. "Oh, horrible, when we had given up that sort of thing and broken away from her parents. Oh, horrible—worst of all—worse than death, when you have made a little clearing in the wilderness, planted your little garden, let in your sunlight, and then the weeds creep in again! A judgment! And our boy had typhoid because no clergyman had dropped water on him in church! Is it possible, Miss Honeychurch? Shall we slip back into the darkness for ever?"

"I don't know," gasped Lucy. "I don't understand this sort of thing. I was not meant to understand it."

"But Mr. Eager—he came when I was out, and acted according to his principles. I don't blame him or any one... but by the time George was well she was ill. He made her think about sin, and she went under thinking about it."

It was thus that Mr. Emerson had murdered his wife in the sight of God.

"Oh, how terrible!" said Lucy, forgetting her own affairs at last.

"He was not baptized," said the old man. "I did hold firm." And he looked with unwavering eyes at the rows of books, as if—at what cost!—he had won a victory over them. "My boy shall go back to the earth untouched."

She asked whether young Mr. Emerson was ill.

"Oh—last Sunday." He started into the present. "George last Sunday—no, not ill: just gone under. He is never ill. But he is his mother's son. Her eyes were his, and she had that forehead that I think so beautiful, and he will not think it worth while to live. It was always touch and go. He will live; but he will not think it worth while to live. He will never think anything worth while. You remember that church at Florence?"

Lucy did remember, and how she had suggested that George should collect postage stamps.

"After you left Florence—horrible. Then we took the house here, and he goes bathing with your brother, and became better. You saw him bathing?"

"I am so sorry, but it is no good discussing this affair. I am deeply sorry about it."

"Then there came something about a novel. I didn't follow it at all; I had to hear so much, and he minded telling me; he finds me too old. Ah, well, one must have failures. George comes down to-morrow, and takes me up to his London rooms. He can't bear to be about here, and I must be where he is."

"Mr. Emerson," cried the girl, "don't leave at least, not on my account. I am going to Greece. Don't leave your comfortable house."

It was the first time her voice had been kind and he smiled. "How good every one is! And look at Mr. Beebe housing me—came over this morning and heard I was going! Here I am so comfortable with a fire."

"Yes, but you won't go back to London. It's absurd."

"I must be with George; I must make him care to live, and down here he can't. He says the thought of seeing you and of hearing about you—I am not justifying him: I am only saying what has happened."

"Oh, Mr. Emerson"—she took hold of his hand—"you mustn't. I've been bother enough to the world by now. I can't have you moving out of your house when you like it, and perhaps losing money through it—all on my account. You must stop! I am just going to Greece."

"All the way to Greece?"

Her manner altered.

"To Greece?"

"So you must stop. You won't talk about this business, I know. I can trust you both."

"Certainly you can. We either have you in our lives, or leave you to the life that you have chosen."

"I shouldn't want—"

"I suppose Mr. Vyse is very angry with George? No, it was wrong of George to try. We have pushed our beliefs too far. I fancy that we deserve sorrow."

She looked at the books again—black, brown, and that acrid theological blue. They surrounded the visitors on every side; they were piled on the tables, they pressed against the very ceiling. To Lucy who could not see that Mr. Emerson was profoundly religious, and differed from Mr. Beebe chiefly by his acknowledgment of passion—it seemed dreadful that the old man should crawl into such a sanctum, when he was unhappy, and be dependent on the bounty of a clergyman.

More certain than ever that she was tired, he offered her his chair.

"No, please sit still. I think I will sit in the carriage."

"Miss Honeychurch, you do sound tired."

"Not a bit," said Lucy, with trembling lips.

"But you are, and there's a look of George about you. And what were you saying about going abroad?"

She was silent.

"Greece"—and she saw that he was thinking the word over—"Greece; but you were to be married this year, I thought."

"Not till January, it wasn't," said Lucy, clasping her hands. Would she tell an actual lie when it came to the point?

"I suppose that Mr. Vyse is going with you. I hope—it isn't because George spoke that you are both going?"

"No."

"I hope that you will enjoy Greece with Mr. Vyse."

"Thank you."

At that moment Mr. Beebe came back from church. His cassock was covered with rain. "That's all right," he said kindly. "I counted on you two keeping each other company. It's pouring again. The entire congregation, which consists of your cousin, your mother, and my mother, stands waiting in the church, till the carriage fetches it. Did Powell go round?"

"I think so; I'll see."

"No—of course, I'll see. How are the Miss Alans?"

"Very well, thank you."

"Did you tell Mr. Emerson about Greece?"

"I—I did."

"Don't you think it very plucky of her, Mr. Emerson, to undertake the two Miss Alans? Now, Miss Honeychurch, go back—keep warm. I think three is such a courageous number to go travelling." And he hurried off to the stables.

"He is not going," she said hoarsely. "I made a slip. Mr. Vyse does stop behind in England."

Somehow it was impossible to cheat this old man. To George, to Cecil, she would have lied again; but he seemed so near the end of things, so dignified in his approach to the gulf, of which he gave one account, and the books that surrounded him another, so mild to the rough paths that he had traversed, that the true chivalry—not the worn-out chivalry of sex, but the true chivalry that all the young may show to all the old—awoke in her, and, at whatever risk, she told him that Cecil was not her companion to Greece. And she spoke so seriously that the risk became a certainty, and he, lifting his eyes, said: "You are leaving him? You are leaving the man you love?"

"I—I had to."

"Why, Miss Honeychurch, why?"

Terror came over her, and she lied again. She made the long, convincing speech that she had made to Mr. Beebe, and intended to make to the world when she announced that her engagement was no more. He heard her in silence, and then said: "My dear, I am worried about you. It seems to me"—dreamily; she was not alarmed—"that you are in a muddle."

She shook her head.

"Take an old man's word; there's nothing worse than a muddle in all the world. It is easy to face Death and Fate, and the things that sound so dreadful. It is on my muddles that I look back with horror—on the things that I might have avoided. We can help one another but little. I used to think I could teach young people the whole of life, but I know better now, and all my teaching of George has come down to this: beware of muddle. Do you remember in that church, when you pretended to be annoyed with me and weren't? Do you remember before, when you refused the room with the view? Those were muddles—little, but ominous—and I am fearing that you are in one now." She was silent. "Don't trust me, Miss Honeychurch. Though life is very glorious, it is difficult." She was still silent. "'Life' wrote a friend of mine, 'is a public performance on the violin, in which you must learn the instrument as you go along.' I think he puts it well. Man has to pick up the use of his functions as he goes along—especially the function of Love." Then he burst out excitedly; "That's it; that's what I mean. You love George!" And after his long preamble, the three words burst against Lucy like waves from the open sea.

"But you do," he went on, not waiting for contradiction. "You love the boy body and soul, plainly, directly, as he loves you, and no other word expresses it. You won't marry the other man for his sake."

"How dare you!" gasped Lucy, with the roaring of waters in her ears. "Oh, how like a man!—I mean, to suppose that a woman is always thinking about a man."

"But you are."

She summoned physical disgust.

"You're shocked, but I mean to shock you. It's the only hope at times. I can reach you no other way. You must marry, or your life will be wasted. You have gone too far to retreat. I have no time for the tenderness, and the comradeship, and the poetry, and the things that really matter, and for which you marry. I know that, with George, you will find them, and that you love him. Then be his wife. He is already part of you. Though you fly to Greece, and never see him again, or forget his very name, George will work in your thoughts till you die. It isn't possible to love and to part. You will wish that it was. You can transmute love, ignore it, muddle it, but you can never pull it out of you. I know by experience that the poets are right: love is eternal."

Lucy began to cry with anger, and though her anger passed away soon, her tears remained.

"I only wish poets would say this, too: love is of the body; not the body, but of the body. Ah! the misery that would be saved if we confessed that! Ah! for a little directness to liberate the soul! Your soul, dear Lucy! I hate the word now, because of all the cant with which superstition has wrapped it round. But we have souls. I cannot say how they came nor whither they go, but we have them, and I see you ruining yours. I cannot bear it. It is again the darkness creeping in; it is hell." Then he checked himself. "What nonsense I have talked—how abstract and remote! And I have made you cry! Dear girl, forgive my prosiness; marry my boy. When I think what life is, and how seldom love is answered by love—Marry him; it is one of the moments for which the world was made."

She could not understand him; the words were indeed remote. Yet as he spoke the darkness was withdrawn, veil after veil, and she saw to the bottom of her soul.

"Then, Lucy—"

"You've frightened me," she moaned. "Cecil—Mr. Beebe—the ticket's bought—everything." She fell sobbing into the chair. "I'm caught in the tangle. I must suffer and grow old away from him. I cannot break the whole of life for his sake. They trusted me."

A carriage drew up at the front-door.

"Give George my love—once only. Tell him 'muddle.'" Then she arranged her veil, while the tears poured over her cheeks inside.

"Lucy—"

"No—they are in the hall—oh, please not, Mr. Emerson—they trust me—"

"But why should they, when you have deceived them?"

Mr. Beebe opened the door, saying: "Here's my mother."

"You're not worthy of their trust."

"What's that?" said Mr. Beebe sharply.

"I was saying, why should you trust her when she deceived you?"

"One minute, mother." He came in and shut the door.

"I don't follow you, Mr. Emerson. To whom do you refer? Trust whom?"

"I mean she has pretended to you that she did not love George. They have loved one another all along."

Mr. Beebe looked at the sobbing girl. He was very quiet, and his white face, with its ruddy whiskers, seemed suddenly inhuman. A long black column, he stood and awaited her reply.

"I shall never marry him," quavered Lucy.

A look of contempt came over him, and he said, "Why not?"

"Mr. Beebe—I have misled you—I have misled myself—"

"Oh, rubbish, Miss Honeychurch!"

"It is not rubbish!" said the old man hotly. "It's the part of people that you don't understand."

Mr. Beebe laid his hand on the old man's shoulder pleasantly.

"Lucy! Lucy!" called voices from the carriage.

"Mr. Beebe, could you help me?"

He looked amazed at the request, and said in a low, stern voice: "I am more grieved than I can possibly express. It is lamentable, lamentable—incredible."

"What's wrong with the boy?" fired up the other again.

"Nothing, Mr. Emerson, except that he no longer interests me. Marry George, Miss Honeychurch. He will do admirably."

He walked out and left them. They heard him guiding his mother up-stairs.

"Lucy!" the voices called.

She turned to Mr. Emerson in despair. But his face revived her. It was the face of a saint who understood.

"Now it is all dark. Now Beauty and Passion seem never to have existed. I know. But remember the mountains over Florence and the view. Ah, dear, if I were George, and gave you one kiss, it would make you brave. You have to go cold into a battle that needs warmth, out into the muddle that you have made yourself; and your mother and all your friends will despise you, oh, my darling, and rightly, if it is ever right to despise. George still dark, all the tussle and the misery without a word from him. Am I justified?" Into his own eyes tears came. "Yes, for we fight for more than Love or Pleasure; there is Truth. Truth counts, Truth does count."

"You kiss me," said the girl. "You kiss me. I will try."

He gave her a sense of deities reconciled, a feeling that, in gaining the man she loved, she would gain something for the whole world. Throughout the squalor of her homeward drive—she spoke at once—his salutation remained. He had robbed the body of its taint, the world's taunts of their sting; he had shown her the holiness of direct desire. She "never exactly understood," she would say in after years, "how he managed to strengthen her. It was as if he had made her see the whole of everything at once."

Chapter XX: The End of the Middle Ages

The Miss Alans did go to Greece, but they went by themselves. They alone of this little company will double Malea and plough the waters of the Saronic gulf. They alone will visit Athens and Delphi, and either shrine of intellectual song—that upon the Acropolis, encircled by blue seas; that under Parnassus, where the eagles build and the bronze charioteer drives undismayed towards infinity. Trembling, anxious, cumbered with much digestive bread, they did proceed to Constantinople, they did go round the world. The rest of us must be contented with a fair, but a less arduous, goal. Italiam petimus: we return to the Pension Bertolini.

George said it was his old room.

"No, it isn't," said Lucy; "because it is the room I had, and I had your father's room. I forget why; Charlotte made me, for some reason."

He knelt on the tiled floor, and laid his face in her lap.

"George, you baby, get up."

"Why shouldn't I be a baby?" murmured George.

Unable to answer this question, she put down his sock, which she was trying to mend, and gazed out through the window. It was evening and again the spring.

"Oh, bother Charlotte," she said thoughtfully. "What can such people be made of?"

"Same stuff as parsons are made of."

"Nonsense!"

"Quite right. It is nonsense."

"Now you get up off the cold floor, or you'll be starting rheumatism next, and you stop laughing and being so silly."

"Why shouldn't I laugh?" he asked, pinning her with his elbows, and advancing his face to hers. "What's there to cry at? Kiss me here." He indicated the spot where a kiss would be welcome.

He was a boy after all. When it came to the point, it was she who remembered the past, she into whose soul the iron had entered, she who knew whose room this had been last year. It endeared him to her strangely that he should be sometimes wrong.

"Any letters?" he asked.

"Just a line from Freddy."

"Now kiss me here; then here."

Then, threatened again with rheumatism, he strolled to the window, opened it (as the English will), and leant out. There was the parapet, there the river, there to the left the beginnings of the hills. The cab-driver, who at once saluted him with the hiss of a serpent, might be that very Phaethon who had set this happiness in motion twelve months ago. A passion of gratitude—all feelings grow to passions in the South—came over the husband, and he blessed the people and the things who had taken so much trouble about a young fool. He had helped himself, it is true, but how stupidly!

All the fighting that mattered had been done by others—by Italy, by his father, by his wife.

"Lucy, you come and look at the cypresses; and the church, whatever its name is, still shows."

"San Miniato. I'll just finish your sock."

"Signorino, domani faremo uno giro," called the cabman, with engaging certainty.

George told him that he was mistaken; they had no money to throw away on driving.

And the people who had not meant to help—the Miss Lavishes, the Cecils, the Miss Bartletts! Ever prone to magnify Fate, George counted up the forces that had swept him into this contentment.

"Anything good in Freddy's letter?"

"Not yet."

His own content was absolute, but hers held bitterness: the Honeychurches had not forgiven them; they were disgusted at her past hypocrisy; she had alienated Windy Corner, perhaps for ever.

"What does he say?"

"Silly boy! He thinks he's being dignified. He knew we should go off in the spring—he has known it for six months—that if mother wouldn't give her consent we should take the thing into our own hands. They had fair warning, and now he calls it an elopement. Ridiculous boy—"

"Signorino, domani faremo uno giro—"

"But it will all come right in the end. He has to build us both up from the beginning again. I wish, though, that Cecil had not turned so cynical about women. He has, for the second time, quite altered. Why will men have theories about women? I haven't any about men. I wish, too, that Mr. Beebe—"

"You may well wish that."

"He will never forgive us—I mean, he will never be interested in us again. I wish that he did not influence them so much at Windy Corner. I wish he hadn't—But if we act the truth, the people who really love us are sure to come back to us in the long run."

"Perhaps." Then he said more gently: "Well, I acted the truth—the only thing I did do—and you came back to me. So possibly you know." He turned back into the room. "Nonsense with that sock." He carried her to the window, so that she, too, saw all the view. They sank upon their knees, invisible from the road, they hoped, and began to whisper one another's names. Ah! it was worth while; it was the great joy that they had expected, and countless little joys of which they had never dreamt. They were silent.

"Signorino, domani faremo—"

"Oh, bother that man!"

But Lucy remembered the vendor of photographs and said, "No, don't be rude to him." Then with a catching of her breath, she murmured: "Mr. Eager and Charlotte, dreadful frozen Charlotte. How cruel she would be to a man like that!"

"Look at the lights going over the bridge."

"But this room reminds me of Charlotte. How horrible to grow old in Charlotte's way! To think that evening at the rectory that she shouldn't have heard your father was in the house. For she would have stopped me going in, and he was the only person alive who could have made me see sense. You couldn't have made me. When I am very happy"—she kissed him—"I remember on how little it all hangs. If Charlotte had only known, she would have stopped me going in, and I should have gone to silly Greece, and become different for ever."

"But she did know," said George; "she did see my father, surely. He said so."

"Oh, no, she didn't see him. She was upstairs with old Mrs. Beebe, don't you remember, and then went straight to the church. She said so."

George was obstinate again. "My father," said he, "saw her, and I prefer his word. He was dozing by the study fire, and he opened his eyes, and there was Miss Bartlett. A few minutes before you came in. She was turning to go as he woke up. He didn't speak to her."

Then they spoke of other things—the desultory talk of those who have been fighting to reach one another, and whose reward is to rest quietly in each other's arms. It was long ere they returned to Miss Bartlett, but when they did her behaviour seemed more interesting. George, who disliked any darkness, said: "It's clear that she knew. Then, why did she risk the meeting? She knew he was there, and yet she went to church."

They tried to piece the thing together.

As they talked, an incredible solution came into Lucy's mind. She rejected it, and said: "How like Charlotte to undo her work by a feeble muddle at the last moment." But something in the dying evening, in the roar of the river, in their very embrace warned them that her words fell short of life, and George whispered: "Or did she mean it?"

"Mean what?"

"Signorino, domani faremo uno giro—"

Lucy bent forward and said with gentleness: "Lascia, prego, lascia. Siamo sposati."

"Scusi tanto, signora," he replied in tones as gentle and whipped up his horse.

"Buona sera—e grazie."

"Niente."

The cabman drove away singing.

"Mean what, George?"

He whispered: "Is it this? Is this possible? I'll put a marvel to you. That your cousin has always hoped. That from the very first moment we met, she hoped, far down in her mind, that we should be like this—of course, very far down. That she fought us on the surface, and yet she hoped. I can't explain her any other way. Can you? Look how she kept me alive in you all the summer; how she gave you no peace; how month after month she became more eccentric and unreliable. The sight of us haunted her—or she couldn't have described us as she did to her friend. There are details—it burnt. I read the book afterwards. She is not frozen, Lucy, she is not withered up all through. She tore us apart twice, but in the rectory that evening she was given one more chance to make us happy. We can never make friends with her or thank her. But I do believe that, far down in her heart, far below all speech and behaviour, she is glad."

"It is impossible," murmured Lucy, and then, remembering the experiences of her own heart, she said: "No—it is just possible."

Youth enwrapped them; the song of Phaethon announced passion requited, love attained. But they were conscious of a love more mysterious than this. The song died away; they heard the river, bearing down the snows of winter into the Mediterranean.

HOWARDS END

Chapter 1

One may as well begin with Helen's letters to her sister.

Howards End,
Tuesday.

Dearest Meg,

It isn't going to be what we expected. It is old and little, and altogether delightful--red brick. We can scarcely pack in as it is, and the dear knows what will happen when Paul (younger son) arrives to-morrow. From hall you go right or left into dining-room or drawing-room. Hall itself is practically a room. You open another door in it, and there are the stairs going up in a sort of tunnel to the first-floor. Three bedrooms in a row there, and three attics in a row above. That isn't all the house really, but it's all that one notices--nine windows as you look up from the front garden.

Then there's a very big wych-elm--to the left as you look up--leaning a little over the house, and standing on the boundary between the garden and meadow. I quite love that tree already. Also ordinary elms, oaks--no nastier than ordinary oaks--pear-trees, apple-trees, and a vine. No silver birches, though. However, I must get on to my host and hostess. I only wanted to show that it isn't the least what we expected. Why did we settle that their house would be all gables and wiggles, and their garden all gamboge-coloured paths? I believe simply because we associate them with expensive hotels--Mrs. Wilcox trailing in beautiful dresses down long corridors, Mr. Wilcox bullying porters, etc. We females are that unjust.

I shall be back Saturday; will let you know train later. They are as angry as I am that you did not come too; really Tibby is too tiresome, he starts a new mortal disease every month. How could he have got hay fever in London? and even if he could, it seems hard that you should give up a visit to hear a schoolboy sneeze. Tell him that Charles Wilcox (the son who is here) has hay fever too, but he's brave, and gets quite cross when we inquire after it. Men like the

Wilcoxes would do Tibby a power of good. But you won't agree, and I'd better change the subject.

This long letter is because I'm writing before breakfast. Oh, the beautiful vine leaves! The house is covered with a vine. I looked out earlier, and Mrs. Wilcox was already in the garden. She evidently loves it. No wonder she sometimes looks tired. She was watching the large red poppies come out. Then she walked off the lawn to the meadow, whose corner to the right I can just see. Trail, trail, went her long dress over the sopping grass, and she came back with her hands full of the hay that was cut yesterday--I suppose for rabbits or something, as she kept on smelling it. The air here is delicious. Later on I heard the noise of croquet balls, and looked out again, and it was Charles Wilcox practising; they are keen on all games. Presently he started sneezing and had to stop. Then I hear more clicketing, and it is Mr. Wilcox practising, and then, 'a-tissue, a-tissue': he has to stop too. Then Evie comes out, and does some calisthenic exercises on a machine that is tacked on to a greengage-tree--they put everything to use--and then she says 'a-tissue,' and in she goes. And finally Mrs. Wilcox reappears, trail, trail, still smelling hay and looking at the flowers. I inflict all this on you because once you said that life is sometimes life and sometimes only a drama, and one must learn to distinguish t'other from which, and up to now I have always put that down as 'Meg's clever nonsense.' But this morning, it really does seem not life but a play, and it did amuse me enormously to watch the W's. Now Mrs. Wilcox has come in.

I am going to wear [omission]. Last night Mrs. Wilcox wore an [omission], and Evie [omission]. So it isn't exactly a go-as-you-please place, and if you shut your eyes it still seems the wiggly hotel that we expected. Not if you open them. The dog-roses are too sweet. There is a great hedge of them over the lawn--magnificently tall, so that they fall down in garlands, and nice and thin at the bottom, so that you can see ducks through it and a cow. These belong to the farm, which is the only house near us. There goes the breakfast gong. Much love. Modified love to Tibby. Love to Aunt Juley; how good of her to come and keep you company, but what a bore. Burn this. Will write again Thursday.

Helen

Howards End,
Friday.

Dearest Meg,

I am having a glorious time. I like them all. Mrs. Wilcox, if quieter than in Germany, is sweeter than ever, and I never saw anything like her steady unselfishness, and the best of it is that the others do not take advantage of her. They are the very happiest, jolliest family that you can imagine. I do really feel that we are making friends. The fun of it is that they think me a noodle, and say so--at least Mr. Wilcox does--and when that happens, and one doesn't mind, it's a pretty sure test, isn't it? He says the most horrid things about women's suffrage so nicely, and when I said I believed in equality he just folded his arms and gave me such a setting down as I've never had. Meg, shall we ever learn to talk less? I never felt so ashamed of myself in my life. I couldn't point to a time when men had been equal, nor even to a time when the wish to be equal had made them happier in other ways. I couldn't say a word. I had just picked up the notion that equality is good from some book--probably from poetry, or you. Anyhow, it's been knocked into pieces, and, like all people who are really strong, Mr. Wilcox did it without hurting me. On the other hand, I laugh at them for catching hay fever. We live like fighting-cocks, and Charles takes us out every day in the motor--a tomb with trees in it, a hermit's house, a wonderful road that was made by the Kings of Mercia--tennis--a cricket match--bridge--and at night we squeeze up in this lovely house. The whole clan's here now--it's like a rabbit warren. Evie is a dear. They want me to stop over Sunday--I suppose it won't matter if I do. Marvellous weather and the view's marvellous--views westward to the high ground. Thank you for your letter. Burn this.

Your affectionate
Helen

Howards End,
Sunday.

Dearest, dearest Meg,--I do not know what you will say: Paul and I are in love--the younger son who only came here Wednesday.

Chapter 2

Margaret glanced at her sister's note and pushed it over the breakfast-table to her aunt. There was a moment's hush, and then the flood-gates opened.

"I can tell you nothing, Aunt Juley. I know no more than you do. We met--we only met the father and mother abroad last spring. I know so little that I didn't even know their son's name. It's all so--" She waved her hand and laughed a little.

"In that case it is far too sudden."

"Who knows, Aunt Juley, who knows?"

"But, Margaret dear, I mean we mustn't be unpractical now that we've come to facts. It is too sudden, surely."

"Who knows!"

"But Margaret dear--"

"I'll go for her other letters," said Margaret. "No, I won't, I'll finish my breakfast. In fact, I haven't them. We met the Wilcoxes on an awful expedition that we made from Heidelberg to Speyer. Helen and I had got it into our heads that there was a grand old cathedral at Speyer--the Archbishop of Speyer was one of the seven electors--you know--'Speyer, Maintz, and Köln.' Those three sees once commanded the Rhine Valley and got it the name of Priest Street."

"I still feel quite uneasy about this business, Margaret."

"The train crossed by a bridge of boats, and at first sight it looked quite fine. But oh, in five minutes we had seen the whole thing. The cathedral had been ruined, absolutely ruined, by restoration; not an inch left of the original structure. We wasted a whole day, and came across the Wilcoxes as we were eating our sandwiches in the public gardens. They too, poor things, had been taken in--they were actually stopping at Speyer--and they rather liked Helen insisting that they must fly with us to Heidelberg. As a matter of fact, they did come on next day. We all took some drives together. They knew us well enough to ask Helen to come and see them--at least, I was asked too, but Tibby's illness prevented me, so last Monday she went alone. That's all. You know as much as I do now. It's a young man out the unknown. She was to have come back Saturday, but put off till Monday, perhaps on account of--I don't know.

She broke off, and listened to the sounds of a London morning. Their house was in Wickham Place, and fairly quiet, for a lofty promontory of buildings separated it from the main thoroughfare. One had the sense of a backwater, or rather of an estuary, whose waters flowed in from the invisible sea, and ebbed into a profound silence while the waves without were still beating. Though the promontory consisted of flats--expensive, with cavernous entrance halls, full of concierges and palms--it fulfilled its purpose, and gained for the older houses opposite a certain measure of peace. These, too, would be swept away in time, and another promontory would rise upon their site, as humanity piled itself higher and higher on the precious soil of London.

Mrs. Munt had her own method of interpreting her nieces. She decided that Margaret was a little hysterical, and was trying to gain time by a torrent of talk. Feeling very diplomatic, she lamented the fate of Speyer, and declared that never, never should she be so misguided as to visit it, and added of her own accord that the principles of restoration were ill understood in Germany. "The Germans," she said, "are too thorough, and this is all very well sometimes, but at other times it does not do."

"Exactly," said Margaret; "Germans are too thorough." And her eyes began to shine.

"Of course I regard you Schlegels as English," said Mrs. Munt hastily--"English to the backbone."

Margaret leaned forward and stroked her hand.

"And that reminds me--Helen's letter--"

"Oh, yes, Aunt Juley, I am thinking all right about Helen's letter. I know--I must go down and see her. I am thinking about her all right. I am meaning to go down"

"But go with some plan," said Mrs. Munt, admitting into her kindly voice a note of exasperation. "Margaret, if I may interfere, don't be taken by surprise. What do you think of the Wilcoxes? Are they our sort? Are they likely people? Could they appreciate Helen, who is to my mind a very special sort of person? Do they care about Literature and Art? That is most important when you come to think of it. Literature and Art. Most important. How old would the son be? She says 'younger son.' Would he be in a position to marry? Is he likely to make Helen happy? Did you gather--"

"I gathered nothing."

They began to talk at once.

"Then in that case--"

"In that case I can make no plans, don't you see."

"On the contrary--"

"I hate plans. I hate lines of action. Helen isn't a baby."

"Then in that case, my dear, why go down?"

Margaret was silent. If her aunt could not see why she must go down, she was not going to tell her. She was not going to say "I love my dear sister; I must be near her at this crisis of her life." The affections are more reticent than the passions, and their expression more subtle. If she herself should ever fall in love with a man, she, like Helen, would proclaim it from the house-tops, but as she only loved a sister she used the voiceless language of sympathy.

"I consider you odd girls," continued Mrs. Munt, "and very wonderful girls, and in many ways far older than your years. But--you won't be offended? --frankly I feel you are not up to this business. It requires an older person. Dear, I have nothing to call me back to Swanage." She spread out her plump arms. "I am all at your disposal. Let me go down to this house whose name I forget instead of you."

"Aunt Juley"--she jumped up and kissed her--"I must, must go to Howards End myself. You don't exactly understand, though I can never thank you properly for offering."

"I do understand," retorted Mrs. Munt, with immense confidence. "I go down in no spirit of interference, but to make inquiries. Inquiries are necessary. Now, I am going to be rude. You would say the wrong thing; to a certainty you would. In your anxiety for Helen's happiness you would offend the whole of these Wilcoxes by asking one of your impetuous questions--not that one minds offending them."

"I shall ask no questions. I have it in Helen's writing that she and a man are in love. There is no question to ask as long as she keeps to that. All the rest isn't worth a straw. A long engagement if you like, but inquiries, questions, plans, lines of action--no, Aunt Juley, no."

Away she hurried, not beautiful, not supremely brilliant, but filled with something that took the place of both qualities--something best described as a profound vivacity, a continual and sincere response to all that she encountered in her path through life.

"If Helen had written the same to me about a shop-assistant or a penniless clerk--"

"Dear Margaret, do come into the library and shut the door. Your good maids are dusting the banisters."

"--or if she had wanted to marry the man who calls for Carter Paterson, I should have said the same." Then, with one of those turns that convinced her aunt that she was not mad really and convinced observers of another type that she was not a barren theorist, she added: "Though in the case of Carter Paterson I should want it to be a very long engagement indeed, I must say."

"I should think so," said Mrs. Munt; "and, indeed, I can scarcely follow you. Now, just imagine if you said anything of that sort to the Wilcoxes. I understand it, but most good people would think you mad. Imagine how disconcerting for Helen! What is wanted is a person who will go slowly, slowly in this business, and see how things are and where they are likely to lead to."

Margaret was down on this.

"But you implied just now that the engagement must be broken off."

"I think probably it must; but slowly."

"Can you break an engagement off slowly?" Her eyes lit up. "What's an engagement made of, do you suppose? I think it's made of some hard stuff, that may snap, but can't break. It is different to the other ties of life. They stretch or bend. They admit of degree. They're different."

"Exactly so. But won't you let me just run down to Howards House, and save you all the discomfort? I will really not interfere, but I do so thoroughly understand the kind of thing you Schlegels want that one quiet look round will be enough for me."

Margaret again thanked her, again kissed her, and then ran upstairs to see her brother.

He was not so well.

The hay fever had worried him a good deal all night. His head ached, his eyes were wet, his mucous membrane, he informed her, was in a most unsatisfactory condition. The only thing that made life worth living was the thought of Walter Savage Landor, from whose *Imaginary Conversations* she had promised to read at frequent intervals during the day.

It was rather difficult. Something must be done about Helen. She must be assured that it is not a criminal offence to love at first sight. A telegram to this effect would be cold and cryptic, a personal visit seemed each moment more impossible. Now the doctor arrived, and said that Tibby was quite bad. Might it really be best to accept Aunt Juley's kind offer, and to send her down to Howards End with a note?

Certainly Margaret was impulsive. She did swing rapidly from one decision to another. Running downstairs into the library, she cried--"Yes, I have changed my mind; I do wish that you would go."

There was a train from King's Cross at eleven. At half-past ten Tibby, with rare self-effacement, fell asleep, and Margaret was able to drive her aunt to the station.

"You will remember, Aunt Juley, not to be drawn into discussing the engagement. Give my letter to Helen, and say whatever you feel yourself, but do keep clear of the relatives. We have scarcely got their names straight yet, and besides, that sort of thing is so uncivilized and wrong.

"So uncivilized?" queried Mrs. Munt, fearing that she was losing the point of some brilliant remark.

"Oh, I used an affected word. I only meant would you please only talk the thing over with Helen."

"Only with Helen."

"Because--" But it was no moment to expound the personal nature of love. Even Margaret shrank from it, and contented herself with stroking her good aunt's hand, and with meditating, half sensibly and half poetically, on the journey that was about to begin from King's Cross.

Like many others who have lived long in a great capital, she had strong feelings about the various railway termini. They are our gates to the glorious and the unknown. Through them we pass out into adventure and sunshine, to them alas! we return. In Paddington all Cornwall is latent and the remoter west; down the inclines of Liverpool Street lie fenlands and the illimitable Broads; Scotland is through the pylons of Euston; Wessex behind the poised chaos of Waterloo. Italians realize this, as is natural; those of them who are so unfortunate as to serve as waiters in Berlin call the Anhalt Bahnhof the Stazione d'Italia, because by it they must return to their homes. And he is a chilly Londoner who does not endow his stations with some personality, and extend to them, however shyly, the emotions of fear and love.

To Margaret--I hope that it will not set the reader against her--the station of King's Cross had always suggested Infinity. Its very situation--withdrawn a little behind the facile splendours of St. Pancras--implied a comment on the materialism of life. Those two great arches, colourless, indifferent, shouldering between them an unlovely clock, were fit portals for some eternal adventure, whose issue might be prosperous, but would certainly not be expressed in the ordinary language of prosperity. If you think this ridiculous, remember that it is not Margaret who is telling you about it; and let me hasten to add that they were in plenty of time for the train; that Mrs. Munt, though she took a second-class ticket, was put by the guard into a first (only two seconds on the train, one smoking and the other babies--one cannot be expected to travel with babies); and that Margaret, on her return to Wickham Place, was confronted with the following telegram:

> All over. Wish I had never written. Tell no one.
>
> --Helen

But Aunt Juley was gone--gone irrevocably, and no power on earth could stop her.

Chapter 3

Most complacently did Mrs. Munt rehearse her mission. Her nieces were independent young women, and it was not often that she was able to help them. Emily's daughters had never been quite like other girls. They had been left motherless when Tibby was born, when Helen was five and Margaret herself but thirteen. It was before the passing of the Deceased Wife's Sister Bill, so Mrs. Munt could without impropriety offer to go and keep house at Wickham Place. But her brother-in-law, who was peculiar and a German, had referred the question to Margaret, who with the crudity of youth had answered, "No, they could manage much better alone." Five years later Mr. Schlegel had died too, and Mrs. Munt had repeated her offer. Margaret, crude no longer, had been grateful and extremely nice, but the substance of her answer had been the same. "I must not interfere a third time," thought Mrs. Munt. However, of course she did. She learnt, to her horror, that Margaret, now of age, was taking her money out of the old safe investments and putting it into Foreign Things, which always smash. Silence would have been criminal. Her own fortune was invested in Home Rails, and most ardently did she beg her niece to imitate her. "Then we should be together, dear." Margaret, out of politeness, invested a few hundreds in the Nottingham and Derby Railway, and though the Foreign Things did admirably and the Nottingham and Derby declined with the steady dignity of which only Home Rails are capable, Mrs. Munt never ceased to rejoice, and to say, "I did manage that, at all events. When the smash comes poor Margaret will have a nest-egg to fall back upon." This year Helen came of age, and exactly the same thing happened in Helen's case; she also would shift her money out of Consols, but she, too, almost without being pressed, consecrated a fraction of it to the Nottingham and Derby Railway. So far so good, but in social matters their aunt had accomplished nothing. Sooner or later the girls would enter on the process known as throwing themselves away, and if they had delayed hitherto, it was only that they might throw themselves more vehemently in the future. They saw too many people at Wickham Place--unshaven musicians, an actress even, German cousins (one knows what foreigners are), acquaintances picked up at Continental hotels (one knows what they are too). It was interesting, and down at Swanage no one appreciated culture more than Mrs. Munt; but it was dangerous, and disaster was bound to come. How right she was, and how lucky to be on the spot when the disaster came!

The train sped northward, under innumerable tunnels. It was only an hour's journey, but Mrs. Munt had to raise and lower the window again and again. She passed through the South Welwyn Tunnel, saw light for a moment, and entered the North Welwyn Tunnel, of tragic fame. She traversed the immense viaduct, whose arches span untroubled meadows and the dreamy flow of Tewin Water. She skirted the parks of politicians. At times the Great North Road accompanied her, more suggestive of infinity than any railway, awakening, after a nap of a hundred years, to such life as is conferred by the stench of motor-cars, and to such culture as is implied by the advertisements of antibilious pills. To history, to tragedy, to the past, to the future, Mrs. Munt remained equally indifferent; hers but to concentrate on the end of her journey, and to rescue poor Helen from this dreadful mess.

The station for Howards End was at Hilton, one of the large villages that are strung so frequently along the North Road, and that owe their size to the traffic of coaching and pre-coaching days. Being near London, it had not shared in the rural decay, and its long High Street had budded out right and left into residential estates. For about a mile a series of tiled and slated houses passed before Mrs. Munt's inattentive eyes, a series broken at one point by six Danish tumuli that stood shoulder to shoulder along the highroad, tombs of soldiers. Beyond these tumuli habitations thickened, and the train came to a standstill in a tangle that was almost a town.

The station, like the scenery, like Helen's letters, struck an indeterminate note. Into which country will it lead, England or Suburbia? It was new, it had island platforms and a subway, and the superficial comfort exacted by business men. But it held hints of local life, personal intercourse, as even Mrs. Munt was to discover.

"I want a house," she confided to the ticket boy. "Its name is Howards Lodge. Do you know where it is?"

"Mr. Wilcox!" the boy called.

A young man in front of them turned round.

"She's wanting Howards End."

There was nothing for it but to go forward, though Mrs. Munt was too much agitated even to stare at the stranger. But remembering that there were two brothers, she had the sense to say to him, "Excuse me asking, but are you the younger Mr. Wilcox or the elder?"

"The younger. Can I do anything for you?"

"Oh, well"--she controlled herself with difficulty. "Really. Are you? I--" She moved away from the ticket boy and lowered her voice. "I am Miss Schlegels aunt. I ought to introduce myself, oughtn't I? My name is Mrs. Munt."

She was conscious that he raised his cap and said quite coolly, "Oh, rather; Miss Schlegel is stopping with us. Did you want to see her?"

"Possibly--"

"I'll call you a cab. No; wait a mo--" He thought. "Our motor's here. I'll run you up in it."

"That is very kind--"

"Not at all, if you'll just wait till they bring out a parcel from the office. This way."

"My niece is not with you by any chance?"

"No; I came over with my father. He has gone on north in your train. You'll see Miss Schlegel at lunch. You're coming up to lunch, I hope?"

"I should like to come *up*," said Mrs. Munt, not committing herself to nourishment until she had studied Helen's lover a little more. He seemed a gentleman, but had so rattled her round that her powers of observation were numbed. She glanced at him stealthily. To a feminine eye there was nothing amiss in the sharp depressions at the corners of his mouth, nor in the rather box-like construction of his forehead. He was dark, clean-shaven and seemed accustomed to command.

"In front or behind? Which do you prefer? It may be windy in front."

"In front if I may; then we can talk."

"But excuse me one moment--I can't think what they're doing with that parcel." He strode into the booking-office and called with a new voice: "Hi! hi, you there! Are you going to keep me waiting all day? Parcel for Wilcox, Howards End. Just look sharp!" Emerging, he said in quieter tones: "This station's abominably organized; if I had my way, the whole lot of 'em should get the sack. May I help you in?"

"This is very good of you," said Mrs. Munt, as she settled herself into a luxurious cavern of red leather, and suffered her person to be padded with rugs and shawls. She was more civil than she had intended, but really this young man was very kind. Moreover, she was a little afraid of him: his self-possession was extraordinary. "Very good indeed," she repeated, adding: "It is just what I should have wished."

"Very good of you to say so," he replied, with a slight look of surprise, which, like most slight looks, escaped Mrs. Munt's attention. "I was just tooling my father over to catch the down train."

"You see, we heard from Helen this morning."

Young Wilcox was pouring in petrol, starting his engine, and performing other actions with which this story has no concern. The great car began to rock, and the form of Mrs. Munt, trying to explain things, sprang agreeably up and down among the red cushions. "The mater will be very glad to see you," he mumbled. "Hi! I say. Parcel for Howards End. Bring it out. Hi!"

A bearded porter emerged with the parcel in one hand and an entry book in the other. With the gathering whir of the motor these ejaculations mingled: "Sign, must I? Why the--should I sign after all this bother? Not even got a pencil on you? Remember next time I report you to the station-master. My time's of value, though yours mayn't be. Here"--here being a tip.

"Extremely sorry, Mrs. Munt."

"Not at all, Mr. Wilcox."

"And do you object to going through the village? It is rather a longer spin, but I have one or two commissions."

"I should love going through the village. Naturally I am very anxious to talk things over with you."

As she said this she felt ashamed, for she was disobeying Margaret's instructions. Only disobeying them in the letter, surely. Margaret had only warned her against discussing the incident with outsiders. Surely it was not "uncivilized or wrong" to discuss it with the young man himself, since chance had thrown them together.

A reticent fellow, he made no reply. Mounting by her side, he put on gloves and spectacles, and off they drove, the bearded porter--life is a mysterious business--looking after them with admiration.

The wind was in their faces down the station road, blowing the dust into Mrs. Munt's eyes. But as soon as they turned into the Great North Road she opened fire. "You can well imagine," she said, "that the news was a great shock to us."

"What news?"

"Mr. Wilcox," she said frankly. "Margaret has told me everything--everything. I have seen Helen's letter."

He could not look her in the face, as his eyes were fixed on his work; he was travelling as quickly as he dared down the High Street. But he inclined his head in her direction, and said, "I beg your pardon; I didn't catch."

"About Helen. Helen, of course. Helen is a very exceptional person--I am sure you will let me say this, feeling towards her as you do--indeed, all the Schlegels are exceptional. I come in no spirit of interference, but it was a great shock."

They drew up opposite a draper's. Without replying, he turned round in his seat, and contemplated the cloud of dust that they had raised in their passage through the village. It was settling again, but not all into the road from which he had taken it. Some of it had percolated through the open windows, some had whitened the roses and gooseberries of the wayside gardens, while a certain proportion had entered the lungs of the villagers. "I wonder when they'll learn wisdom and tar the roads," was his comment. Then a man ran out of the draper's with a roll of oilcloth, and off they went again.

"Margaret could not come herself, on account of poor Tibby, so I am here to represent her and to have a good talk."

"I'm sorry to be so dense," said the young man, again drawing up outside a shop. "But I still haven't quite understood."

"Helen, Mr. Wilcox--my niece and you."

He pushed up his goggles and gazed at her, absolutely bewildered. Horror smote her to the heart, for even she began to suspect that they were at cross-purposes, and that she had commenced her mission by some hideous blunder.

"Miss Schlegel and myself." he asked, compressing his lips.

"I trust there has been no misunderstanding," quavered Mrs. Munt. "Her letter certainly read that way."

"What way?"

"That you and she--" She paused, then drooped her eyelids.

"I think I catch your meaning," he said stickily. "What an extraordinary mistake!"

"Then you didn't the least--" she stammered, getting blood-red in the face, and wishing she had never been born.

"Scarcely, as I am already engaged to another lady." There was a moment's silence, and then he caught his breath and exploded with, "Oh, good God! Don't tell me it's some silliness of Paul's."

"But you are Paul."

"I'm not."

"Then why did you say so at the station?"

"I said nothing of the sort."

"I beg your pardon, you did."

"I beg your pardon, I did not. My name is Charles."

"Younger" may mean son as opposed to father, or second brother as opposed to first. There is much to be said for either view, and later on they said it. But they had other questions before them now.

"Do you mean to tell me that Paul--"

But she did not like his voice. He sounded as if he was talking to a porter, and, certain that he had deceived her at the station, she too grew angry.

"Do you mean to tell me that Paul and your niece--"

Mrs. Munt--such is human nature--determined that she would champion the lovers. She was not going to be bullied by a severe young man. "Yes, they care for one another very much indeed," she said. "I dare say they will tell you about it by-and-by. We heard this morning."

And Charles clenched his fist and cried, "The idiot, the idiot, the little fool!"

Mrs. Munt tried to divest herself of her rugs. "If that is your attitude, Mr. Wilcox, I prefer to walk."

"I beg you will do no such thing. I'll take you up this moment to the house. Let me tell you the thing's impossible, and must be stopped."

Mrs. Munt did not often lose her temper, and when she did it was only to protect those whom she loved. On this occasion she blazed out. "I quite agree, sir. The thing is impossible, and I will come up and stop it. My niece is a very exceptional person, and I am not inclined to sit still while she throws herself away on those who will not appreciate her."

Charles worked his jaws.

"Considering she has only known your brother since Wednesday, and only met your father and mother at a stray hotel--"

"Could you possibly lower your voice? The shopman will overhear."

"Esprit de classe"--if one may coin the phrase--was strong in Mrs. Munt. She sat quivering while a member of the lower orders deposited a metal funnel, a saucepan, and a garden squirt beside the roll of oilcloth.

"Right behind?"

"Yes, sir." And the lower orders vanished in a cloud of dust.

"I warn you: Paul hasn't a penny; it's useless."

"No need to warn us, Mr. Wilcox, I assure you. The warning is all the other way. My niece has been very foolish, and I shall give her a good scolding and take her back to London with me."

"He has to make his way out in Nigeria. He couldn't think of marrying for years and when he does it must be a woman who can stand the climate, and is in other ways--Why hasn't he told us? Of course he's ashamed. He knows he's been a fool. And so he has--a damned fool."

She grew furious.

"Whereas Miss Schlegel has lost no time in publishing the news."

"If I were a man, Mr. Wilcox, for that last remark I'd box your ears. You're not fit to clean my niece's boots, to sit in the same room with her, and you dare--you actually dare--I decline to argue with such a person."

"All I know is, she's spread the thing and he hasn't, and my father's away and I--"

"And all that I know is--"

"Might I finish my sentence, please?"

"No."

Charles clenched his teeth and sent the motor swerving all over the lane.

She screamed.

So they played the game of Capping Families, a round of which is always played when love would unite two members of our race. But they played it with unusual vigour, stating in so many words that Schlegels were better than Wilcoxes, Wilcoxes better than Schlegels. They flung decency aside. The man was young, the woman deeply stirred; in both a vein of coarseness was latent. Their quarrel was no more surprising than are most quarrels--inevitable at the time, incredible afterwards. But it was more than usually futile. A few minutes, and they were enlightened. The motor drew up at Howards End, and Helen, looking very pale, ran out to meet her aunt.

"Aunt Juley, I have just had a telegram from Margaret; I--I meant to stop your coming. It isn't--it's over."

The climax was too much for Mrs. Munt. She burst into tears.

"Aunt Juley dear, don't. Don't let them know I've been so silly. It wasn't anything. Do bear up for my sake."

"Paul," cried Charles Wilcox, pulling his gloves off.

"Don't let them know. They are never to know."

"Oh, my darling Helen--"

"Paul! Paul!"

A very young man came out of the house.

"Paul, is there any truth in this?"

"I didn't--I don't--"

"Yes or no, man; plain question, plain answer. Did or didn't Miss Schlegel--"

"Charles dear," said a voice from the garden. "Charles, dear Charles, one doesn't ask plain questions. There aren't such things."

They were all silent. It was Mrs. Wilcox.

Chapter 3

She approached just as Helen's letter had described her, trailing noiselessly over the lawn, and there was actually a wisp of hay in her hands. She seemed to belong not to the young people and their motor, but to the house, and to the tree that overshadowed it. One knew that she worshipped the past, and that the instinctive wisdom the past can alone bestow had descended upon her--that wisdom to which we give the clumsy name of aristocracy. High born she might not be. But assuredly she cared about her ancestors, and let them help her. When she saw Charles angry, Paul frightened, and Mrs. Munt in tears, she heard her ancestors say, "Separate those human beings who will hurt each other most. The rest can wait." So she did not ask questions. Still less did she pretend that nothing had happened, as a competent society hostess would have done. She said, "Miss Schlegel, would you take your aunt up to your room or to my room, whichever you think best. Paul, do find Evie, and tell her lunch for six, but I'm not sure whether we shall all be downstairs for it." And when they had obeyed her, she turned to her elder son, who still stood in the throbbing stinking car, and smiled at him with tenderness, and without a word, turned away from him towards her flowers.

"Mother," he called, "are you aware that Paul has been playing the fool again?"

"It's all right, dear. They have broken off the engagement."

"Engagement--!"

"They do not love any longer, if you prefer it put that way," said Mrs. Wilcox, stooping down to smell a rose.

Chapter 4

Helen and her aunt returned to Wickham Place in a state of collapse, and for a little time Margaret had three invalids on her hands. Mrs. Munt soon recovered. She possessed to a remarkable degree the power of distorting the past, and before many days were over she had forgotten the part played by her own imprudence in the catastrophe. Even at the crisis she had cried, "Thank goodness, poor Margaret is saved this!" which during the journey to London evolved into, "It had to be gone through by someone," which in its turn ripened into the permanent form of "The one time I really did help Emily's girls was over the Wilcox business." But Helen was a more serious patient. New ideas had burst upon her like a thunder clap, and by them and by her reverberations she had been stunned.

The truth was that she had fallen in love, not with an individual, but with a family.

Before Paul arrived she had, as it were, been tuned up into his key. The energy of the Wilcoxes had fascinated her, had created new images of beauty in her responsive mind. To be all day with them in the open air, to sleep at night under their roof, had seemed the supreme joy of life, and had led to that abandonment of personality that is a possible prelude to love. She had liked giving in to Mr. Wilcox, or Evie, or Charles; she had liked being told that her notions of life were sheltered or academic; that Equality was nonsense, Votes for Women nonsense, Socialism nonsense, Art and Literature, except when conducive to strengthening the character, nonsense. One by one the Schlegel fetiches had been overthrown, and, though professing to defend them, she had rejoiced. When Mr. Wilcox said that one sound man of business did more good to the world than a dozen of your social reformers, she had swallowed the curious assertion without a gasp, and had leant back luxuriously among the cushions of his motor-car. When Charles said, "Why be so polite to servants? they don't understand it," she had not given the Schlegel retort of, "If they don't understand it, I do." No; she had vowed to be less polite to servants in the future. "I am swathed in cant," she thought, "and it is good for me to be stripped of it." And all that she thought or did or breathed was a quiet preparation for Paul. Paul was inevitable. Charles was taken up with another girl, Mr. Wilcox was so old, Evie so young, Mrs. Wilcox so different. Round the absent brother she began to throw the halo of Romance, to irradiate him with all the splendour of those happy days, to feel that in him she should draw nearest to the robust ideal. He and she were about the same age, Evie said. Most people thought Paul handsomer than his brother. He was certainly a better shot, though not so good at golf. And when Paul appeared, flushed with the triumph of getting through an examination, and ready to flirt with any pretty girl, Helen met him halfway, or more than halfway, and turned towards him on the Sunday evening.

He had been talking of his approaching exile in Nigeria, and he should have continued to talk of it, and allowed their guest to recover. But the heave of her bosom flattered him. Passion was possible, and he became passionate. Deep down in him something whispered, "This girl would let you kiss her; you might not have such a chance again."

That was "how it happened," or, rather, how Helen described it to her sister, using words even more unsympathetic than my own. But the poetry of that kiss, the wonder of it, the magic that there was in life for hours after it--who can describe that? It is so easy for an Englishman to sneer at these chance collisions of human beings. To the insular cynic and the insular moralist they offer an equal opportunity. It is so easy to talk of "passing emotion," and how to forget how vivid the emotion was ere it passed. Our impulse to sneer, to forget, is at root a good one. We recognize that emotion is not enough, and that men and women are personalities capable of sustained relations, not mere opportunities for an electrical discharge. Yet we rate the impulse too highly. We do not admit that by collisions of this trivial sort the doors of heaven may be shaken open. To Helen, at all events, her life was to bring nothing more intense than the embrace of this boy who played no part in it. He had drawn her out of the house, where there was danger of surprise and light; he had led her by a path he knew, until they stood under the column of the vast wych-elm. A man in the darkness, he had whispered "I love you" when she was desiring love. In time his slender personality faded, the scene that he had evoked endured. In all the variable years that followed she never saw the like of it again.

"I understand," said Margaret--"at least, I understand as much as ever is understood of these things. Tell me now what happened on the Monday morning."

"It was over at once."

"How, Helen?"

"I was still happy while I dressed, but as I came downstairs I got nervous, and when I went into the dining-room I knew it was no good. There was Evie--I can't explain--managing the tea-urn, and Mr. Wilcox reading the *Times*."

"Was Paul there?"

"Yes; and Charles was talking to him about Stocks and Shares, and he looked frightened."

By slight indications the sisters could convey much to each other. Margaret saw horror latent in the scene, and Helen's next remark did not surprise her.

"Somehow, when that kind of man looks frightened it is too awful. It is all right for us to be frightened, or for men of another sort--father, for instance; but for men like that! When I saw all the others so placid, and Paul mad with terror in case I said the wrong thing, I felt for a moment that the whole Wilcox family was a fraud, just a wall of newspapers and motor-cars and golf-clubs, and that if it fell I should find nothing behind it but panic and emptiness. "

"I don't think that. The Wilcoxes struck me as being genuine people, particularly the wife."

"No, I don't really think that. But Paul was so broad-shouldered; all kinds of extraordinary things made it worse, and I knew that it would never do--never. I said to him after breakfast, when the others were practising strokes, 'We rather lost our heads,' and he looked better at once, though frightfully ashamed. He began a speech about having no money to marry on, but it hurt him to make it, and I--stopped him. Then he said, 'I must beg your pardon over this, Miss Schlegel; I can't think what came over me last night.' And I said, 'Nor what over me; never mind.' And then we parted--at least, until I remembered that I had written straight off to tell you the night before, and that frightened him again. I asked him to send a telegram for me, for he knew you would be coming or something; and he tried to get hold of the motor, but Charles and Mr. Wilcox wanted it to go to the station; and Charles offered to send the telegram for me, and then I had to say that the telegram was of no consequence, for Paul said Charles might read it, and though I wrote it out several times, he always said people would suspect something. He took it himself at last, pretending that he must walk down to get cartridges, and, what with one thing and the other, it was not handed in at the Post Office until too late. It was the most terrible morning. Paul disliked me more and more, and Evie talked cricket averages till I nearly screamed. I cannot think how I stood her all the other days. At last Charles and his father started for the station, and then came your telegram warning me that Aunt Juley was coming by that train, and Paul--oh, rather horrible--said that I had muddled it. But Mrs. Wilcox knew."

"Knew what?"

"Everything; though we neither of us told her a word, and had known all along, I think."

"Oh, she must have overheard you."

"I suppose so, but it seemed wonderful. When Charles and Aunt Juley drove up, calling each other names, Mrs. Wilcox stepped in from the garden and made everything less terrible. Ugh! but it has been a disgusting business. To think that--" She sighed.

"To think that because you and a young man meet for a moment, there must be all these telegrams and anger," supplied Margaret.

Helen nodded.

"I've often thought about it, Helen. It's one of the most interesting things in the world. The truth is that there is a great outer life that you and I have never touched--a life in which telegrams and anger count. Personal relations, that we think supreme, are not supreme there. There love means marriage settlements, death, death duties. So far I'm clear. But here my difficulty. This outer life, though obviously horrid, often seems the real one--there's grit in it. It does breed character. Do personal relations lead to sloppiness in the end?"

"Oh, Meg, that's what I felt, only not so clearly, when the Wilcoxes were so competent, and seemed to have their hands on all the ropes. "

"Don't you feel it now?"

"I remember Paul at breakfast," said Helen quietly. "I shall never forget him. He had nothing to fall back upon. I know that personal relations are the real life, for ever and ever.

"Amen!"

So the Wilcox episode fell into the background, leaving behind it memories of sweetness and horror that mingled, and the sisters pursued the life that Helen had commended. They talked to each other and to other people, they filled the tall thin house at Wickham Place with those whom they liked or could befriend. They even attended public meetings. In their own fashion they cared deeply about politics, though not as politicians would have us care; they desired that public life should mirror whatever is good in the life within. Temperance, tolerance, and sexual equality were intelligible cries to them; whereas they did not follow our Forward Policy in Thibet with the keen attention that it merits, and would at times dismiss the whole British Empire with a puzzled, if reverent, sigh. Not out of them are the shows of history erected: the world would be a grey, bloodless place were it entirely composed of Miss Schlegels. But the world being what it is, perhaps they shine out in it like stars.

A word on their origin. They were not "English to the backbone," as their aunt had piously asserted. But, on the other band, they were not "Germans of the dreadful sort." Their father had belonged to a type that was more prominent in Germany fifty years ago than now. He was not the aggressive German, so dear to the English journalist, nor the domestic German, so dear to the English wit. If one classed him at all it would be as the countryman of Hegel and Kant, as the idealist, inclined to be dreamy, whose Imperialism was the Imperialism of the air. Not that his life had been inactive. He had fought like blazes against Denmark, Austria, France. But he had fought without visualizing the results of victory. A hint of the truth broke on him after Sedan, when he saw the dyed moustaches of Napoleon going grey; another when he entered Paris, and saw the smashed windows of the Tuileries. Peace came--it was all very immense, one had turned into an Empire--but he knew that some quality had vanished for which not all Alsace-Lorraine could compensate him. Germany a commercial Power, Germany a naval Power, Germany with colonies here and a Forward Policy there, and legitimate aspirations in the other place, might appeal to others, and be fitly served by them; for his own part, he abstained from the fruits of victory, and naturalized himself in England. The more earnest members of his family never forgave him, and knew that his children, though scarcely English of the dreadful sort, would never be German to the backbone. He had obtained work in one of our provincial Universities, and there married Poor Emily (or Die Engländerin as the case may be), and as she had money, they proceeded to London, and came to know a good many people. But his gaze was always fixed beyond the sea. It was his hope that the clouds of materialism obscuring the Fatherland would part in time, and the mild intellectual light re-emerge. "Do you imply that we Germans are stupid, Uncle Ernst?" exclaimed a haughty and magnificent nephew. Uncle Ernst replied, "To my mind. You use the intellect, but you no longer care about it. That I call stupidity." As the haughty nephew did not follow, he continued, "You only care about the' things that you can use, and therefore arrange them in the following order: Money, supremely useful; intellect, rather useful; imagination, of no use at all. No"--for the other had protested--"your Pan-Germanism is no more imaginative than is our Imperialism over here. It is the vice of a vulgar mind to be thrilled by bigness, to think that a thousand square miles are a thousand times more wonderful than one square mile, and that a million square miles are almost the same as heaven. That is not imagination. No, it kills it. When their poets over here try to celebrate bigness they are dead at once, and naturally. Your poets too are dying, your philosophers, your musicians, to whom Europe has listened for two hundred years. Gone. Gone with the little courts that nurtured them--gone with Esterhaz and Weimar. What? What's that? Your Universities? Oh, yes, you have learned men, who collect more facts than do the learned men of England. They collect facts, and facts, and empires of facts. But which of them will rekindle the light within?"

To all this Margaret listened, sitting on the haughty nephew's knee.

It was a unique education for the little girls. The haughty nephew would be at Wickham Place one day, bringing with him an even haughtier wife, both convinced that Germany was appointed by God to govern the world. Aunt Juley would come the next day, convinced that Great Britain had been appointed to the same post by the same authority. Were both these loud-voiced parties right? On one occasion they had met, and Margaret with clasped hands had implored them to argue the subject out in her presence. Whereat they blushed, and began to talk about the weather. "Papa" she cried--she was a most offensive child--"why will they not discuss this most clear question?" Her father, surveying the parties grimly, replied that he did not know. Putting her head on one side, Margaret then remarked, "To me one of two things is very clear; either God does not know his own mind about England and Germany, or else these do not know the mind of God." A hateful little girl, but at thirteen she had grasped a dilemma that most people travel through life without perceiving. Her brain darted up and down; it grew pliant and strong. Her conclusion was, that any human being lies nearer to the unseen than any organization, and from this she never varied.

Helen advanced along the same lines, though with a more irresponsible tread. In character she resembled her sister, but she was pretty, and so apt to have a more amusing time. People gathered round her more readily, especially when they were new acquaintances, and she did enjoy a little homage very much. When their father died and they ruled alone at Wickham Place, she often absorbed the whole of the company, while Margaret--both were tremendous talkers--fell flat. Neither sister bothered about this. Helen never apologized afterwards, Margaret did not feel the slightest rancour. But looks have their influence upon character. The sisters were alike as little girls, but at the time of the Wilcox episode their methods were beginning to diverge; the younger was rather apt to entice people, and, in enticing them, to be herself enticed; the elder went straight ahead, and accepted an occasional failure as part of the game.

Little need be premised about Tibby. He was now an intelligent man of sixteen, but dyspeptic and difficile.

Chapter 5

It will be generally admitted that Beethoven's Fifth Symphony is the most sublime noise that has ever penetrated into the ear of man. All sorts and conditions are satisfied by it. Whether you are like Mrs. Munt, and tap surreptitiously when the tunes come--of course, not so as to disturb the others--; or like Helen, who can see heroes and shipwrecks in the music's flood; or like Margaret, who can only see the music; or like Tibby, who is profoundly versed in counterpoint, and holds the full score open on his knee; or like their cousin, Fräulein Mosebach, who remembers all the time that Beethoven is "echt Deutsch"; or like Fräulein Mosebach's young man, who can remember nothing but Fräulein Mosebach: in any case, the passion of your life becomes more vivid, and you are bound to admit that such a noise is cheap at two shillings. It is cheap, even if you hear it in the Queen's Hall, dreariest music-room in London, though not as dreary as the Free Trade Hall, Manchester; and even if you sit on the extreme left of that hall, so that the brass bumps at you before the rest of the orchestra arrives, it is still cheap.

"Who is Margaret talking to?" said Mrs. Munt, at the conclusion of the first movement. She was again in London on a visit to Wickham Place.

Helen looked down the long line of their party, and said that she did not know.

"Would it be some young man or other whom she takes an interest in?"

"I expect so," Helen replied. Music enwrapped her, and she could not enter into the distinction that divides young men whom one takes an interest in from young men whom one knows.

"You girls are so wonderful in always having--Oh dear! one mustn't talk."

For the Andante had begun--very beautiful, but bearing a family likeness to all the other beautiful Andantes that Beethoven had written, and, to Helen's mind, rather disconnecting the heroes and shipwrecks of the first movement from the heroes and goblins of the third. She heard the tune through once, and then her attention wandered, and she gazed at the audience, or the organ, or the architecture. Much did she censure the attenuated Cupids who encircle the ceiling of the Queen's Hall, inclining each to each with vapid gesture, and clad in sallow pantaloons, on which the October sunlight struck. "How awful to marry a man like those Cupids!" thought Helen. Here Beethoven started decorating his tune, so she heard him through once more, and then she smiled at her cousin Frieda. But Frieda, listening to Classical Music, could not respond. Herr Liesecke, too, looked as if wild horses could not make him inattentive; there were lines across his forehead, his lips were parted, his pince-nez at right angles to his nose, and he had laid a thick, white hand on either knee. And next to her was Aunt Juley, so British, and wanting to tap. How interesting that row of people was! What diverse influences had gone to the making! Here Beethoven, after humming and hawing with great sweetness, said "Heigho," and the Andante came to an end. Applause, and a round of "wunderschöning" and "prachtvolleying" from the German contingent. Margaret started talking to her new young man; Helen said to her aunt: "Now comes the wonderful movement: first of all the goblins, and then a trio of elephants dancing;" and Tibby implored the company generally to look out for the transitional passage on the drum.

"On the what, dear?"

"On the *drum*, Aunt Juley."

"No; look out for the part where you think you have done with the goblins and they come back," breathed Helen, as the music started with a goblin walking quietly over the universe, from end to end. Others followed him. They were not aggressive creatures; it was that that made them so terrible to Helen. They merely observed in passing that there was no such thing as splendour or heroism in the world. After the interlude of elephants dancing, they returned and made the observation for the second time. Helen could not contradict them, for, once at all events, she had felt the same, and had seen the reliable walls of youth collapse. Panic and emptiness! Panic and emptiness! The goblins were right.

Her brother raised his finger: it was the transitional passage on the drum.

For, as if things were going too far, Beethoven took hold of the goblins and made them do what he wanted. He appeared in person. He gave them a little push, and they began to walk in major key instead of in a minor, and then--he blew with his mouth and they were scattered! Gusts of splendour, gods and demigods contending with vast swords, colour and fragrance broadcast on the field of battle, magnificent victory, magnificent death! Oh, it all burst before the girl, and she even stretched out her gloved hands as if it was tangible. Any fate was titanic; any contest desirable; conqueror and conquered would alike be applauded by the angels of the utmost stars.

And the goblins--they had not really been there at all? They were only the phantoms of cowardice and unbelief? One healthy human impulse would dispel them? Men like the Wilcoxes, or President Roosevelt, would say yes. Beethoven knew better. The goblins really had been there. They might return--and they did. It was as if the splendour of life might boil over--and waste to steam and froth. In its dissolution one heard the terrible, ominous note, and a goblin, with increased malignity, walked quietly over the universe from end to end. Panic and emptiness! Panic and emptiness! Even the flaming ramparts of the world might fall.

Beethoven chose to make all right in the end. He built the ramparts up. He blew with his mouth for the second time, and again the goblins were scattered. He brought back the gusts of splendour, the heroism, the youth, the magnificence of life and of death, and, amid vast roarings of a superhuman joy, he led his Fifth

Symphony to its conclusion. But the goblins were there. They could return. He had said so bravely, and that is why one can trust Beethoven when he says other things.

Helen pushed her way out during the applause. She desired to be alone. The music summed up to her all that had happened or could happen in her career. She read it as a tangible statement, which could never be superseded. The notes meant this and that to her, and they could have no other meaning, and life could have no other meaning. She pushed right out of the building, and walked slowly down the outside staircase, breathing the autumnal air, and then she strolled home.

"Margaret," called Mrs. Munt, "is Helen all right?"

"Oh yes."

"She is always going away in the middle of a programme," said Tibby.

"The music has evidently moved her deeply," said Fräulein Mosebach.

"Excuse me," said Margaret's young man, who had for some time been preparing a sentence, "but that lady has, quite inadvertently, taken my umbrella."

"Oh, good gracious me! --I am so sorry. Tibby, run after Helen."

"I shall miss the Four Serious Songs if I do."

"Tibby love, you must go."

"It isn't of any consequence," said the young man, in truth a little uneasy about his umbrella.

"But of course it is. Tibby! Tibby!"

Tibby rose to his feet, and wilfully caught his person on the backs of the chairs. By the time he had tipped up the seat and had found his hat, and had deposited his full score in safety, it was "too late" to go after Helen. The Four Serious Songs had begun, and one could not move during their performance.

"My sister is so careless," whispered Margaret.

"Not at all," replied the young man; but his voice was dead and cold.

"If you would give me your address--"

"Oh, not at all, not at all;" and he wrapped his greatcoat over his knees.

Then the Four Serious Songs rang shallow in Margaret's ears. Brahms, for all his grumbling and grizzling, had never guessed what it felt like to be suspected of stealing an umbrella. For this fool of a young man thought that she and Helen and Tibby had been playing the confidence trick on him, and that if he gave his address they would break into his rooms some midnight or other and steal his walkingstick too. Most ladies would have laughed, but Margaret really minded, for it gave her a glimpse into squalor. To trust people is a luxury in which only the wealthy can indulge; the poor cannot afford it. As soon as Brahms had grunted himself out, she gave him her card and said, "That is where we live; if you preferred, you could call for the umbrella after the concert, but I didn't like to trouble you when it has all been our fault."

His face brightened a little when he saw that Wickham Place was W. It was sad to see him corroded with suspicion, and yet not daring to be impolite, in case these well-dressed people were honest after all. She took it as a good sign that he said to her, "It's a fine programme this afternoon, is it not?" for this was the remark with which he had originally opened, before the umbrella intervened.

"The Beethoven's fine," said Margaret, who was not a female of the encouraging type. "I don't like the Brahms, though, nor the Mendelssohn that came first--and ugh! I don't like this Elgar that's coming."

"What, what?" called Herr Liesecke, overhearing. "The *Pomp and Circumstance* will not be fine?"

"Oh, Margaret, you tiresome girl!" cried her aunt. "Here have I been persuading Herr Liesecke to stop for *Pomp and Circumstance*, and you are undoing all my work. I am so anxious for him to hear what we are doing in music. Oh, you mustn't run down our English composers, Margaret."

"For my part, I have heard the composition at Stettin," said Fräulein Mosebach. "On two occasions. It is dramatic, a little."

"Frieda, you despise English music. You know you do. And English art. And English Literature, except Shakespeare and he's a German. Very well, Frieda, you may go."

The lovers laughed and glanced at each other. Moved by a common impulse, they rose to their feet and fled from *Pomp and Circumstance*.

"We have this call to play in Finsbury Circus, it is true," said Herr Liesecke, as he edged past her and reached the gangway just as the music started.

"Margaret--" loudly whispered by Aunt Juley. "Margaret, Margaret! Fräulein Mosebach has left her beautiful little bag behind her on the seat."

Sure enough, there was Frieda's reticule, containing her address book, her pocket dictionary, her map of London, and her money.

"Oh, what a bother--what a family we are! Fr-Frieda!"

"Hush!" said all those who thought the music fine.

"But it's the number they want in Finsbury Circus--"

"Might I--couldn't I--" said the suspicious young man, and got very red.

"Oh, I would be so grateful."

He took the bag--money clinking inside it--and slipped up the gangway with it. He was just in time to catch them at the swing-door, and he received a pretty smile from the German girl and a fine bow from her cavalier. He returned to his seat up-sides with the world. The trust that they had reposed in him was trivial, but he felt that it cancelled his mistrust for them, and that probably he would not be "had" over his umbrella. This young man had been "had" in the past--badly, perhaps overwhelmingly--and now most of his energies went in defending himself against the unknown. But this afternoon--perhaps on account of music--he perceived that one must slack off occasionally, or what is the good of being alive? Wickham Place, W., though a risk, was as safe as most things, and he would risk it.

So when the concert was over and Margaret said, "We live quite near; I am going there now. Could you walk around with me, and we'll find your umbrella?" he said, "Thank you," peaceably, and followed her out of the Queen's Hall. She wished that he was not so anxious to hand a lady downstairs, or to carry a lady's programme for her--his class was near enough her own for its manners to vex her. But she found him interesting on the whole--every one interested the Schlegels on the whole at that time--and while her lips talked culture, her heart was planning to invite him to tea.

"How tired one gets after music!" she began.

"Do you find the atmosphere of Queen's Hall oppressive?"

"Yes, horribly."

"But surely the atmosphere of Covent Garden is even more oppressive."

"Do you go there much?"

"When my work permits, I attend the gallery for, the Royal Opera."

Helen would have exclaimed, "So do I. I love the gallery," and thus have endeared herself to the young man. Helen could do these things. But Margaret had an almost morbid horror of "drawing people out," of "making things go." She had been to the gallery at Covent Garden, but she did not "attend" it, preferring the more expensive seats; still less did she love it. So she made no reply.

"This year I have been three times--to *Faust*, *Tosca*, and--" Was it "Tannhouser" or "Tannhoyser"? Better not risk the word.

Margaret disliked *Tosca* and *Faust*. And so, for one reason and another, they walked on in silence, chaperoned by the voice of Mrs. Munt, who was getting into difficulties with her nephew.

"I do in a *way* remember the passage, Tibby, but when every instrument is so beautiful, it is difficult to pick out one thing rather than another. I am sure that you and Helen take me to the very nicest concerts. Not a dull note from beginning to end. I only wish that our German friends would have stayed till it finished."

"But surely you haven't forgotten the drum steadily beating on the low C, Aunt Juley?" came Tibby's voice. "No one could. It's unmistakable."

"A specially loud part?" hazarded Mrs. Munt. "Of course I do not go in for being musical," she added, the shot failing. "I only care for music--a very different thing. But still I will say this for myself--I do know when I like a thing and when I don't. Some people are the same about pictures. They can go into a picture gallery--Miss Conder can--and say straight off what they feel, all round the wall. I never could do that. But music is so different to pictures, to my mind. When it comes to music I am as safe as houses, and I assure you, Tibby, I am by no means pleased by everything. There was a thing--something about a faun in French--which Helen went into ecstasies over, but I thought it most tinkling and superficial, and said so, and I held to my opinion too."

"Do you agree?" asked Margaret. "Do you think music is so different to pictures?"

"I--I should have thought so, kind of," he said.

"So should I. Now, my sister declares they're just the same. We have great arguments over it. She says I'm dense; I say she's sloppy." Getting under way, she cried: "Now, doesn't it seem absurd to you? What is the good of the Arts if they are interchangeable? What is the good of the ear if it tells you the same as the eye? Helen's one aim is to translate tunes into the language of painting, and pictures into the language of music. It's very ingenious, and she says several pretty things in the process, but what's gained, I'd like to know? Oh, it's all rubbish, radically false. If Monet's really Debussy, and Debussy's really Monet, neither gentleman is worth his salt--that's my opinion.

Evidently these sisters quarrelled.

"Now, this very symphony that we've just been having--she won't let it alone. She labels it with meanings from start to finish; turns it into literature. I wonder if the day will ever return when music will be treated as music. Yet I don't know. There's my brother--behind us. He treats music as music, and oh, my goodness! He makes me angrier than anyone, simply furious. With him I daren't even argue."

An unhappy family, if talented.

"But, of course, the real villain is Wagner. He has done more than any man in the nineteenth century towards the muddling of arts. I do feel that music is in a very serious state just now, though extraordinarily interesting. Every now and then in history there do come these terrible geniuses, like Wagner, who stir up all the wells of thought at once. For a moment it's splendid. Such a splash as never was. But afterwards--such a lot of mud; and the wells--as it were, they communicate with each other too easily now, and not one of them will run quite clear. That's what Wagner's done."

Her speeches fluttered away from the young man like birds. If only he could talk like this, he would have caught the world. Oh to acquire culture! Oh, to pronounce foreign names correctly! Oh, to be well informed, discoursing at ease on every subject that a lady started! But it would take one years. With an hour at lunch and a few shattered hours in the evening, how was it possible to catch up with leisured women, who had been reading steadily from childhood? His brain might be full of names, he might have even heard of Monet and Debussy; the trouble was that he could not string them together into a sentence, he could not make them "tell," he could not quite forget about his stolen umbrella. Yes, the umbrella was the real trouble. Behind Monet and Debussy the umbrella persisted, with the steady beat of a drum. "I suppose my umbrella will be all right," he was thinking. "I don't really mind about it. I will think about music instead. I suppose my umbrella will be all right." Earlier in the afternoon he had worried about seats. Ought he to have paid as much as two shillings? Earlier still he had wondered, "Shall I try to do without a programme?" There had always been something to worry him ever since he could remember, always something that distracted him in the pursuit of beauty. For he did pursue beauty, and therefore, Margaret's speeches did flutter away from him like birds.

Margaret talked ahead, occasionally saying, "Don't you think so? don't you feel the same?" And once she stopped, and said "Oh, do interrupt me!" which terrified him. She did not attract him, though she filled him with awe. Her figure was meagre, her face seemed all teeth and eyes, her references to her sister and brother were uncharitable. For all her cleverness and culture, she was probably one of those soulless, atheistical women who have been so shown up by Miss Corelli. It was surprising (and alarming) that she should suddenly say, "I do hope that you'll come in and have some tea."

"I do hope that you'll come in and have some tea. We should be so glad. I have dragged you so far out of your way."

They had arrived at Wickham Place. The sun had set, and the backwater, in deep shadow, was filling with a gentle haze. To the right of the fantastic skyline of the flats towered black against the hues of evening; to the left the older houses raised a square-cut, irregular parapet against the grey. Margaret fumbled for her latchkey. Of course she had forgotten it. So, grasping her umbrella by its ferrule, she leant over the area and tapped at the dining-room window.

"Helen! Let us in!"

"All right," said a voice.

"You've been taking this gentleman's umbrella."

"Taken a what?" said Helen, opening the door. "Oh, what's that? Do come in! How do you do?"

"Helen, you must not be so ramshackly. You took this gentleman's umbrella away from Queen's Hall, and he has had the trouble of coming for it."

"Oh, I am so sorry!" cried Helen, all her hair flying. She had pulled off her hat as soon as she returned, and had flung herself into the big dining-room chair. "I do nothing but steal umbrellas. I am so very sorry! Do come in and choose one. Is yours a hooky or a nobbly? Mine's a nobbly--at least, I *think* it is."

The light was turned on, and they began to search the hall, Helen, who had abruptly parted with the Fifth Symphony, commenting with shrill little cries.

"Don't you talk, Meg! You stole an old gentleman's silk top-hat. Yes, she did, Aunt Juley. It is a positive fact. She thought it was a muff. Oh, heavens! I've knocked the In and Out card down. Where's Frieda? Tibby, why don't you ever-- No, I can't remember what I was going to say. That wasn't it, but do tell the maids to hurry tea up. What about this umbrella?" She opened it. "No, it's all gone along the seams. It's an appalling umbrella. It must be mine."

But it was not.

He took it from her, murmured a few words of thanks, and then fled, with the lilting step of the clerk.

"But if you will stop--" cried Margaret. "Now, Helen, how stupid you've been!"

"Whatever have I done?"

"Don't you see that you've frightened him away? I meant him to stop to tea. You oughtn't to talk about stealing or holes in an umbrella. I saw his nice eyes getting so miserable. No, it's not a bit of good now." For Helen had darted out into the street, shouting, "Oh, do stop!"

"I dare say it is all for the best," opined Mrs. Munt. "We know nothing about the young man, Margaret, and your drawing-room is full of very tempting little things."

But Helen cried: "Aunt Juley, how can you! You make me more and more ashamed. I'd rather he *had* been a thief and taken all the apostle spoons than that I--Well, I must shut the front-door, I suppose. One more failure for Helen."

"Yes, I think the apostle spoons could have gone as rent," said Margaret. Seeing that her aunt did not understand, she added: "You remember 'rent.' It was one of father's words--Rent to the ideal, to his own faith in human nature. You remember how he would trust strangers, and if they fooled him he would say, 'It's better to be fooled than to be suspicious'--that the confidence trick is the work of man, but the want-of-confidence-trick is the work of the devil."

"I remember something of the sort now," said Mrs. Munt, rather tartly, for she longed to add, "It was lucky that your father married a wife with money." But this was unkind, and she contented herself with, "Why, he might have stolen the little Ricketts picture as well."

"Better that he had," said Helen stoutly.

"No, I agree with Aunt Juley," said Margaret. "I'd rather mistrust people than lose my little Ricketts. There are limits."

Their brother, finding the incident commonplace, had stolen upstairs to see whether there were scones for tea. He warmed the teapot--almost too deftly--rejected the Orange Pekoe that the parlour-maid had provided, poured in five spoonfuls of a superior blend, filled up with really boiling water, and now called to the ladies to be quick or they would lose the aroma.

"All right, Auntie Tibby," called Helen, while Margaret, thoughtful again, said: "In a way, I wish we had a real boy in the house--the kind of boy who cares for men. It would make entertaining so much easier."

"So do I," said her sister. "Tibby only cares for cultured females singing Brahms." And when they joined him she said rather sharply: "Why didn't you make that young man welcome, Tibby? You must do the host a little, you know. You ought to have taken his hat and coaxed him into stopping, instead of letting him be swamped by screaming women."

Tibby sighed, and drew a long strand of hair over his forehead.

"Oh, it's no good looking superior. I mean what I say."

"Leave Tibby alone!" said Margaret, who could not bear her brother to be scolded.

"Here's the house a regular hen-coop!" grumbled Helen.

"Oh, my dear!" protested Mrs. Munt. "How can you say such dreadful things! The number of men you get here has always astonished me. If there is any danger it's the other way round."

"Yes, but it's the wrong sort of men, Helen means."

"No, I don't," corrected Helen. "We get the right sort of man, but the wrong side of him, and I say that's Tibby's fault. There ought to be a something about the house--an--I don't know what."

"A touch of the W.'s, perhaps?"

Helen put out her tongue.

"Who are the W.'s?" asked Tibby.

"The W.'s are things I and Meg and Aunt Juley know about and you don't, so there!"

"I suppose that ours is a female house," said Margaret, "and one must just accept it. No, Aunt Juley, I don't mean that this house is full of women. I am trying to say something much more clever. I mean that it was irrevocably feminine, even in father's time. Now I'm sure you understand! Well, I'll give you another example. It'll shock you, but I don't care. Suppose Queen Victoria gave a dinner-party, and that the guests had been Leighton, Millais, Swinburne, Rossetti, Meredith, Fitzgerald, etc. Do you suppose that the atmosphere of that dinner would have been artistic? Heavens no! The very chairs on which they sat would have seen to that. So with our house--it must be feminine, and all we can do is to see that it isn't effeminate. Just as another house that I can mention, but I won't, sounded irrevocably masculine, and all its inmates can do is to see that it isn't brutal."

"That house being the W.'s house, I presume," said Tibby.

"You're not going to be told about the W.'s, my child," Helen cried, "so don't you think it. And on the other hand, I don't the least mind if you find out, so don't you think you've done anything clever, in either case. Give me a cigarette."

"You do what you can for the house," said Margaret. "The drawing-room reeks of smoke."

"If you smoked too, the house might suddenly turn masculine. Atmosphere is probably a question of touch and go. Even at Queen Victoria's dinner-party--if something had been just a little different--perhaps if she'd worn a clinging Liberty tea-gown instead of a magenta satin--"

"With an Indian shawl over her shoulders--"

"Fastened at the bosom with a Cairngorm-pin--"

Bursts of disloyal laughter--you must remember that they are half German--greeted these suggestions, and Margaret said pensively, "How inconceivable it would be if the Royal Family cared about Art." And the conversation drifted away and away, and Helen's cigarette turned to a spot in the darkness, and the great flats opposite were sown with lighted windows, which vanished and were relit again, and vanished incessantly. Beyond them the thoroughfare roared gently--a tide that could never be quiet, while in the east, invisible behind the smokes of Wapping, the moon was rising.

"That reminds me, Margaret. We might have taken that young man into the dining-room, at all events. Only the majolica plate--and that is so firmly set in the wall. I am really distressed that he had no tea."

For that little incident had impressed the three women more than might be supposed. It remained as a goblin football, as a hint that all is not for the best in the best of all possible worlds, and that beneath these superstructures of wealth and art there wanders an ill-fed boy, who has recovered his umbrella indeed, but who has left no address behind him, and no name.

Chapter 6

We are not concerned with the very poor. They are unthinkable, and only to be approached by the statistician or the poet. This story deals with gentlefolk, or with those who are obliged to pretend that they are gentlefolk.

The boy, Leonard Bast, stood at the extreme verge of gentility. He was not in the abyss, but he could see it, and at times people whom he knew had dropped in, and counted no more. He knew that he was poor, and would admit it: he would have died sooner than confess any inferiority to the rich. This may be splendid of him. But he was inferior to most rich people, there is not the least doubt of it. He was not as courteous as the average rich man, nor as intelligent, nor as healthy, nor as lovable. His mind and his body had been alike underfed, because he was poor, and because he was modern they were always craving better food. Had he lived some centuries ago, in the brightly coloured civilizations of the past, he would have had a definite status, his rank and his income would have corresponded. But in his day the angel of Democracy had arisen, enshadowing the classes with leathern wings, and proclaiming, "All men are equal--all men, that is to say, who possess umbrellas," and so he was obliged to assert gentility, lest he slipped into the abyss where nothing counts, and the statements of Democracy are inaudible.

As he walked away from Wickham Place, his first care was to prove that he was as good as the Miss Schlegels. Obscurely wounded in his pride, he tried to wound them in return. They were probably not ladies. Would real ladies have asked him to tea? They were certainly ill-natured and cold. At each step his feeling of superiority increased. Would a real lady have talked about stealing an umbrella? Perhaps they were thieves after all, and if he had gone into the house they could have clapped a chloroformed handkerchief over his face. He walked on complacently as far as the Houses of Parliament. There an empty stomach asserted itself, and told him he was a fool.

"Evening, Mr. Bast."

"Evening, Mr. Dealtry."

"Nice evening."

"Evening."

Mr. Dealtry, a fellow clerk, passed on, and Leonard stood wondering whether he would take the tram as far as a penny would take him, or whether he would walk. He decided to walk--it is no good giving in, and he had spent money enough at Queen's Hall--and he walked over Westminster Bridge, in front of St. Thomas's Hospital, and through the immense tunnel that passes under the South-Western main line at Vauxhall. In the tunnel he paused and listened to the roar of the trains. A sharp pain darted through his head, and he was conscious of the exact form of his eye sockets. He pushed on for another mile, and did not slacken speed until he stood at the entrance of a road called Camelia Road, which was at present his home.

Here he stopped again, and glanced suspiciously to right and left, like a rabbit that is going to bolt into its hole. A block of flats, constructed with extreme cheapness, towered on either hand. Farther down the road two more blocks were being built, and beyond these an old house was being demolished to accommodate another pair. It was the kind of scene that may be observed all over London, whatever the locality--bricks and mortar rising and falling with the restlessness of the water in a fountain, as the city receives more and more men upon her soil. Camelia Road would soon stand out like a fortress, and command, for a little, an extensive view. Only for a little. Plans were out for the erection of flats in Magnolia Road also. And again a few years, and all the flats in either road might be pulled down, and new buildings, of a vastness at present unimaginable, might arise where they had fallen.

"Evening, Mr. Bast."

"Evening, Mr. Cunningham."

"Very serious thing this decline of the birth-rate in Manchester."

"I beg your pardon?"

"Very serious thing this decline of the birth-rate in Manchester," repeated Mr. Cunningham, tapping the Sunday paper, in which the calamity in question had just been announced to him.

"Ah, yes," said Leonard, who was not going to let on that he had not bought a Sunday paper.

"If this kind of thing goes on the population of England will be stationary in 1960."

"You don't say so."

"I call it a very serious thing, eh?"

"Good-evening, Mr. Cunningham."

"Good-evening, Mr. Bast."

Then Leonard entered Block B of the flats, and turned, not upstairs, but down, into what is known to house agents as a semi-basement, and to other men as a cellar. He opened the door, and cried "Hullo!" with the pseudo-geniality of the Cockney. There was no reply. "Hullo!" he repeated. The sitting-room was empty, though the electric light had been left burning. A look of relief came over his face, and he flung himself into the armchair.

The sitting-room contained, besides the armchair, two other chairs, a piano, a three-legged table, and a cosy corner. Of the walls, one was occupied by the window, the other by a draped mantelshelf bristling with Cupids. Opposite the window was the door, and beside the door a bookcase, while over the piano there extended one of the masterpieces of Maud Goodman. It was an amorous and not unpleasant little hole when the curtains were drawn, and the lights turned on, and the gas-stove unlit. But it struck that shallow makeshift note that is so often heard in the modem dwelling-place. It had been too easily gained, and could be relinquished too easily.

As Leonard was kicking off his boots he jarred the three-legged table, and a photograph frame, honourably poised upon it, slid sideways, fell off into the fireplace, and smashed. He swore in a colourless sort of way, and picked the photograph up. It represented a young lady called Jacky, and had been taken at the time when young ladies called Jacky were often photographed with their mouths open. Teeth of dazzling whiteness extended along either of Jacky's jaws, and positively weighted her head sideways, so large were they and so numerous. Take my word for it, that smile was simply stunning, and it is only you and I who will be fastidious, and complain that true joy begins in the eyes, and that the eyes of Jacky did not accord with her smile, but were anxious and hungry.

Leonard tried to pull out the fragments of glass, and cut his fingers and swore again. A drop of blood fell on the frame, another followed, spilling over on to the exposed photograph. He swore more vigorously, and dashed to the kitchen, where he bathed his hands. The kitchen was the same size as the sitting room; through it was a bedroom. This completed his home. He was renting the flat furnished: of all the objects that encumbered it none were his own except the photograph frame, the Cupids, and the books.

"Damn, damn, damnation!" he murmured, together with such other words as he had learnt from older men. Then he raised his hand to his forehead and said, "Oh, damn it all--" which meant something different. He pulled himself together. He drank a little tea, black and silent, that still survived upon an upper shelf. He swallowed some dusty crumbs of cake. Then he went back to the sitting-room, settled himself anew, and began to read a volume of Ruskin.

"Seven miles to the north of Venice--"

How perfectly the famous chapter opens! How supreme its command of admonition and of poetry! The rich man is speaking to us from his gondola.

"Seven miles to the north of Venice the banks of sand which nearer the city rise little above low-water mark attain by degrees a higher level, and knit themselves at last into fields of salt morass, raised here and there into shapeless mounds, and intercepted by narrow creeks of sea."

Leonard was trying to form his style on Ruskin: he understood him to be the greatest master of English Prose. He read forward steadily, occasionally making a few notes.

"Let us consider a little each of these characters in succession, and first (for of the shafts enough has been said already), what is very peculiar to this church--its luminousness."

Was there anything to be learnt from this fine sentence? Could he adapt it to the needs of daily life? Could he introduce it, with modifications, when he next wrote a letter to his brother, the lay-reader? For example--

"Let us consider a little each of these characters in succession, and first (for of the absence of ventilation enough has been said already), what is very peculiar to this flat--its obscurity. "

Something told him that the modifications would not do; and that something, had he known it, was the spirit of English Prose. "My flat is dark as well as stuffy." Those were the words for him.

And the voice in the gondola rolled on, piping melodiously of Effort and Self-Sacrifice, full of high purpose, full of beauty, full even of sympathy and the love of men, yet somehow eluding all that was actual and insistent in Leonard's life. For it was the voice of one who had never been dirty or hungry, and had not guessed successfully what dirt and hunger are.

Leonard listened to it with reverence. He felt that he was being done good to, and that if he kept on with Ruskin, and the Queen's Hall Concerts, and some pictures by Watts, he would one day push his head out of the grey waters and see the universe. He believed in sudden conversion, a belief which may be right, but which is peculiarly attractive to a half-baked mind. It is the bias of much popular religion: in the domain of business it dominates the Stock Exchange, and becomes that "bit of luck" by which all successes and failures are explained. "If only I had a bit of luck, the whole thing would come straight. . . . He's got a most magnificent place down at Streatham and a 20 h.-p. Fiat, but then, mind you, he's had luck. . . . I'm sorry the wife's so late, but she never has any luck over catching trains." Leonard was superior to these people; he did believe in effort and in a steady preparation for the change that he desired. But of a heritage that may expand gradually, he had no conception: he hoped to come to Culture suddenly, much as the Revivalist hopes to come to Jesus. Those Miss Schlegels had come to it; they had done the trick; their hands were upon the ropes, once and for all. And meanwhile, his flat was dark, as well as stuffy.

Presently there was a noise on the staircase. He shut up Margaret's card in the pages of Ruskin, and opened the door. A woman entered, of whom it is simplest to say that she was not respectable. Her appearance was awesome. She seemed all strings and bell-pulls--ribbons, chains, bead necklaces that clinked and caught--and a boa of azure feathers hung round her neck, with the ends uneven. Her throat was bare, wound with a double row of pearls, her arms were bare to the elbows, and might again be detected at the shoulder, through cheap lace. Her hat, which was flowery, resembled those punnets, covered with flannel, which we sowed with mustard and cress in our childhood, and which germinated here yes, and there no. She wore it on the back of her head. As for her hair, or rather hairs, they are too complicated to describe, but one system went down her back, lying in a thick pad there, while another, created for a lighter destiny, rippled around her forehead. The face--the face does not signify. It was the face of the photograph, but older, and the teeth were not so numerous as the photographer had suggested, and certainly not so white. Yes, Jacky was past her prime, whatever that prime may have been. She was descending quicker than most women into the colourless years, and the look in her eyes confessed it.

"What ho!" said Leonard, greeting that apparition with much spirit, and helping it off with its boa.

Jacky, in husky tones, replied, "What ho!"

"Been out?" he asked. The question sounds superfluous, but it cannot have been really, for the lady answered, "No," adding, "Oh, I am so tired."

"You tired?"

"Eh?"

"I'm tired," said he, hanging the boa up.

"Oh, Len, I am so tired."

"I've been to that classical concert I told you about," said Leonard.

"What's that?"

"I came back as soon as it was over."

"Any one been round to our place?" asked Jacky.

"Not that I've seen. I met Mr. Cunningham outside, and we passed a few remarks."

"What, not Mr. Cunnginham?"

"Yes."

"Oh, you mean Mr. Cunningham."

"Yes. Mr. Cunningham."

"I've been out to tea at a lady friend's."

Her secret being at last given to the world, and the name of the lady-friend being even adumbrated, Jacky made no further experiments in the difficult and tiring art of conversation. She never had been a great talker. Even in her photographic days she had relied upon her smile and her figure to attract, and now that she was--

"On the shelf,
On the shelf,
Boys, boys, I'm on the shelf,"

she was not likely to find her tongue. Occasional bursts of song (of which the above is an example) still issued from her lips, but the spoken word was rare.

She sat down on Leonard's knee, and began to fondle him. She was now a massive woman of thirty-three, and her weight hurt him, but he could not very well say anything. Then she said, "Is that a book you're reading?" and he said, "That's a book," and drew it from her unreluctant grasp. Margaret's card fell out of it. It fell face downwards, and he murmured, "Bookmarker."

"Len--"

"What is it?" he asked, a little wearily, for she only had one topic of conversation when she sat upon his knee.

"You do love me?"

"Jacky, you know that I do. How can you ask such questions!"

"But you do love me, Len, don't you?"

"Of course I do."

A pause. The other remark was still due.

"Len--"

"Well? What is it?"

"Len, you will make it all right?"

"I can't have you ask me that again," said the boy, flaring up into a sudden passion. "I've promised to marry you when I'm of age, and that's enough. My word's my word. I've promised to marry you as soon as ever I'm twenty-one, and I can't keep on being worried. I've worries enough. It isn't likely I'd throw you over, let alone my word, when I've spent all this money. Besides, I'm an Englishman, and I never go back on my word. Jacky, do be reasonable. Of course I'll marry you. Only do stop badgering me."

"When's your birthday, Len?"

"I've told you again and again, the eleventh of November next. Now get off my knee a bit; someone must get supper, I suppose."

Jacky went through to the bedroom, and began to see to her hat. This meant blowing at it with short sharp puffs. Leonard tidied up the sitting-room, and began to prepare their evening meal. He put a penny into the slot of the gas-meter, and soon the flat was reeking with metallic fumes. Somehow he could not recover his temper, and all the time he was cooking he continued to complain bitterly.

"It really is too bad when a fellow isn't trusted. It makes one feel so wild, when I've pretended to the people here that you're my wife--all right, you shall be my wife--and I've bought you the ring to wear, and I've taken this flat furnished, and it's far more than I can afford, and yet you aren't content, and I've also not told the truth when I've written home." He lowered his voice. "He'd stop it." In a tone of horror, that was a little luxurious, he repeated: "My brother'd stop it. I'm going against the whole world, Jacky.

"That's what I am, Jacky. I don't take any heed of what anyone says. I just go straight forward, I do. That's always been my way. I'm not one of your weak knock-kneed chaps. If a woman's in trouble, I don't leave her in the lurch. That's not my street. No, thank you.

"I'll tell you another thing too. I care a good deal about improving myself by means of Literature and Art, and so getting a wider outlook. For instance, when you came in I was reading Ruskin's *Stones of Venice*. I don't say this to boast, but just to show you the kind of man I am. I can tell you, I enjoyed that classical concert this afternoon."

To all his moods Jacky remained equally indifferent. When supper was ready--and not before--she emerged from the bedroom, saying: "But you do love me, don't you?"

They began with a soup square, which Leonard had just dissolved in some hot water. It was followed by the tongue--a freckled cylinder of meat, with a little jelly at the top, and a great deal of yellow fat at the bottom--ending with another square dissolved in water (jelly: pineapple), which Leonard had prepared earlier in the day. Jacky ate contentedly enough, occasionally looking at her man with those anxious eyes, to which nothing else in her appearance corresponded, and which yet seemed to mirror her soul. And Leonard managed to convince his stomach that it was having a nourishing meal.

After supper they smoked cigarettes and exchanged a few statements. She observed that her "likeness" had been broken. He found occasion to remark, for the second time, that he had come straight back home after the concert at Queen's Hall. Presently she sat upon his knee. The inhabitants of Camelia Road tramped to and fro outside the window, just on a level with their heads, and the family in the flat on the ground-floor began to sing, "Hark, my soul, it is the Lord."

"That tune fairly gives me the hump," said Leonard.

Jacky followed this, and said that, for her part, she thought it a lovely tune.

"No; I'll play you something lovely. Get up, dear, for a minute."

He went to the piano and jingled out a little Grieg. He played badly and vulgarly, but the performance was not without its effect, for Jacky said she thought she'd be going to bed. As she receded, a new set of interests possessed the boy, and he began to think of what had been said about music by that odd Miss Schlegel--the one that twisted her face about so when she spoke. Then the thoughts grew sad and envious. There was the girl named Helen, who had pinched his umbrella, and the German girl who had smiled at him pleasantly, and Herr someone, and Aunt someone, and the brother--all, all with their hands on the ropes. They had all passed up that narrow, rich staircase at Wickham Place, to some ample room, whither he could never follow them, not if he read for ten hours a day. Oh, it was not good, this continual aspiration. Some are born cultured; the rest had better go in for whatever comes easy. To see life steadily and to see it whole was not for the likes of him.

From the darkness beyond the kitchen a voice called, "Len?"

"You in bed?" he asked, his forehead twitching.

"M'm."

"All right."

Presently she called him again.

"I must clean my boots ready for the morning," he answered.

Presently she called him again.

"I rather want to get this chapter done."

"What?"

He closed his ears against her.

"What's that?"

"All right, Jacky, nothing; I'm reading a book."

"What?"

"What?" he answered, catching her degraded deafness.

Presently she called him again.

Ruskin had visited Torcello by this time, and was ordering his gondoliers to take him to Murano. It occurred to him, as he glided over the whispering lagoons, that the power of Nature could not be shortened by the folly, nor her beauty altogether saddened by the misery, of such as Leonard.

Chapter 7

"Oh, Margaret," cried her aunt next morning, "such a most unfortunate thing has happened. I could not get you alone."

The most unfortunate thing was not very serious. One of the flats in the ornate block opposite had been taken furnished by the Wilcox family, "coming up, no doubt, in the hope of getting into London society." That Mrs. Munt should be the first to discover the misfortune was not remarkable, for she was so interested in the flats, that she watched their every mutation with unwearying care. In theory she despised them--they took away that old-world look--they cut off the sun--flats house a flashy type of person. But if the truth had been known, she found her visits to Wickham Place twice as amusing since Wickham Mansions had arisen, and would in a couple of days learn more about them than her nieces in a couple of months, or her nephew in a couple of years. She would stroll across and make friends with the porters, and inquire what the rents were, exclaiming for example: "What! a hundred and twenty for a basement? You'll never get it!" And they would answer: "One can but try, madam." The passenger lifts, the provision lifts, the arrangement for coals (a great temptation for a dishonest porter), were all familiar matters to her, and perhaps a relief from the politico-economical-æsthetic atmosphere that reigned at the Schlegels'.

Margaret received the information calmly, and did not agree that it would throw a cloud over poor Helen's life.

"Oh, but Helen isn't a girl with no interests," she explained. "She has plenty of other things and other people to think about. She made a false start with the Wilcoxes, and she'll be as willing as we are to have nothing more to do with them."

"For a clever girl, dear, how very oddly you do talk. Helen'll *have* to have something more to do with them, now that they're all opposite. She may meet that Paul in the street. She cannot very well not bow."

"Of course she must bow. But look here; let's do the flowers. I was going to say, the will to be interested in him has died, and what else matters? I look on that disastrous episode (over which you were so kind) as the killing of a nerve in Helen. It's dead, and she'll never be troubled with it again. The only things that matter are the things that interest one. Bowing, even calling and leaving cards, even a dinner-party--we can do all those things to the Wilcoxes, if they find it agreeable; but the other thing, the one important thing--never again. Don't you see?"

Mrs. Munt did not see, and indeed Margaret was making a most questionable statement--that any emotion, any interest once vividly aroused, can wholly die.

"I also have the honour to inform you that the Wilcoxes are bored with us. I didn't tell you at the time--it might have made you angry, and you had enough to worry you--but I wrote a letter to Mrs. W., and apologized for the trouble that Helen had given them. She didn't answer it."

"How very rude!"

"I wonder. Or was it sensible?"

"No, Margaret, most rude."

"In either case one can class it as reassuring."

Mrs. Munt sighed. She was going back to Swanage on the morrow, just as her nieces were wanting her most. Other regrets crowded upon her: for instance, how magnificently she would have cut Charles if she had met him face to face. She had already seen him, giving an order to the porter--and very common he looked in a tall hat. But unfortunately his back was turned to her, and though she had cut his back, she could not regard this as a telling snub.

"But you will be careful, won't you?" she exhorted.

"Oh, certainly. Fiendishly careful."

"And Helen must be careful, too,"

"Careful over what?" cried Helen, at that moment coming into the room with her cousin.

"Nothing," said Margaret, seized with a momentary awkwardness.

"Careful over what, Aunt Juley?"

Mrs. Munt assumed a cryptic air. "It is only that a certain family, whom we know by name but do not mention, as you said yourself last night after the concert, have taken the flat opposite from the Mathesons--where the plants are in the balcony."

Helen began some laughing reply, and then disconcerted them all by blushing. Mrs. Munt was so disconcerted that she exclaimed, "What, Helen, you don't mind them coming, do you?" and deepened the blush to crimson.

"Of course I don't mind," said Helen a little crossly. "It is that you and Meg are both so absurdly grave about it, when there's nothing to be grave about at all."

"I'm not grave," protested Margaret, a little cross in her turn.

"Well, you look grave; doesn't she, Frieda?"

"I don't feel grave, that's all I can say; you're going quite on the wrong tack."

"No, she does not feel grave," echoed Mrs. Munt. "I can bear witness to that. She disagrees--"

"Hark!" interrupted Fräulein Mosebach. "I hear Bruno entering the hall."

For Herr Liesecke was due at Wickham Place to call for the two younger girls. He was not entering the hall--in fact, he did not enter it for quite five minutes. But Frieda detected a delicate situation, and said that she and Helen had much better wait for Bruno down below, and leave Margaret and Mrs. Munt to finish arranging the flowers. Helen acquiesced. But, as if to prove that the situation was not delicate really, she stopped in the doorway and said:

"Did you say the Mathesons' flat, Aunt Juley? How wonderful you are! I never knew that the woman who laced too tightly's name was Matheson."

"Come, Helen," said her cousin.

"Go, Helen," said her aunt; and continued to Margaret almost in the same breath: "Helen cannot deceive me, She does mind."

"Oh, hush!" breathed Margaret. "Frieda'll hear you, and she can be so tiresome."

"She minds," persisted Mrs. Munt, moving thoughtfully about the room, and pulling the dead chrysanthemums out of the vases. "I knew she'd mind--and I'm sure a girl ought to! Such an experience! Such awful coarse-grained people! I know more about them than you do, which you forget, and if Charles had taken you that motor drive--well, you'd have reached the house a perfect wreck. Oh, Margaret, you don't know what you are in for. They're all bottled up against the drawing-room window. There's Mrs. Wilcox--I've seen her. There's Paul. There's Evie, who is a minx. There's Charles--I saw him to start with. And who would an elderly man with a moustache and a copper-coloured face be?"

"Mr. Wilcox, possibly."

"I knew it. And there's Mr. Wilcox."

"It's a shame to call his face copper colour," complained Margaret. "He has a remarkably good complexion for a man of his age."

Mrs. Munt, triumphant elsewhere, could afford to concede Mr. Wilcox his complexion. She passed on from it to the plan of campaign that her nieces should pursue in the future. Margaret tried to stop her.

"Helen did not take the news quite as I expected, but the Wilcox nerve is dead in her really, so there's no need for plans."

"It's as well to be prepared."

"No--it's as well not to be prepared."

"Because--'

Her thought drew being from the obscure borderland. She could not explain in so many words, but she felt that those who prepare for all the emergencies of life beforehand may equip themselves at the expense of joy. It is necessary to prepare for an examination, or a dinner-party, or a possible fall in the price of stock: those who attempt human relations must adopt another method, or fail. "Because I'd sooner risk it," was her lame conclusion.

"But imagine the evenings," exclaimed her aunt, pointing to the Mansions with the spout of the watering-can. "Turn the electric light on her or there, and it's almost the same room. One evening they may forget to draw their blinds down, and you'll see them; and the next, you yours, and they'll see you. Impossible to sit out on the balconies. Impossible to water the plants, or even speak. Imagine going out of the front-door, and they come out opposite at the same moment. And yet you tell me that plans are unnecessary, and you'd rather risk it."

"I hope to risk things all my life."

"Oh, Margaret, most dangerous."

"But after all," she continued with a smile, "there's never any great risk as long as you have money."

"Oh, shame! What a shocking speech!"

"Money pads the edges of things," said Miss Schlegel. "God help those who have none."

"But this is something quite new!" said Mrs. Munt, who collected new ideas as a squirrel collects nuts, and was especially attracted by those that are portable.

"New for me; sensible people have acknowledged it for years. You and I and the Wilcoxes stand upon money as upon islands. It is so firm beneath our feet that we forget its very existence. It's only when we see someone near us tottering that we realize all that an independent income means. Last night, when we were talking up here round the fire, I began to think that the very soul of the world is economic, and that the lowest abyss is not the absence of love, but the absence of coin."

"I call that rather cynical."

"So do I. But Helen and I, we ought to remember, when we are tempted to criticize others, that we are standing on these islands, and that most of the others, are down below the surface of the sea. The poor cannot always reach those whom they want to love, and they can hardly ever escape from those whom they love no longer. We rich can. Imagine the tragedy last June, if Helen and Paul Wilcox had been poor people, and couldn't invoke railways and motor-cars to part them."

"That's more like Socialism," said Mrs. Munt suspiciously.

"Call it what you like. I call it going through life with one's hand spread open on the table. I'm tired of these rich people who pretend to be poor, and think it shows a nice mind to ignore the piles of money that keep their feet above the waves. I stand each year upon six hundred pounds, and Helen upon the same, and Tibby will stand upon eight, and as fast as our pounds crumble away into the sea they are renewed--from the sea, yes, from the sea. And all our thoughts are the thoughts of six-hundred-pounders, and all our speeches; and because we don't want to steal umbrellas ourselves, we forget that below the sea people do want to steal them, and do steal them sometimes, and that what's a joke up here is down there reality--"

"There they go--there goes Fräulein Mosebach. Really, for a German she does dress charmingly. Oh--!"

"What is it?"

"Helen was looking up at the Wilcoxes' flat."

"Why shouldn't she?"

"I beg your pardon, I interrupted you. What was it you were saying about reality?"

"I had worked round to myself, as usual," answered Margaret in tones that were suddenly preoccupied.

"Do tell me this, at all events. Are you for the rich or for the poor?"

"Too difficult. Ask me another. Am I for poverty or for riches? For riches. Hurrah for riches!"

"For riches!" echoed Mrs. Munt, having, as it were, at last secured her nut.

"Yes. For riches. Money for ever!"

"So am I, and so, I am afraid, are most of my acquaintances at Swanage, but I am surprised that you agree with us."

"Thank you so much, Aunt Juley. While I have talked theories, you have done the flowers."

"Not at all, dear. I wish you would let me help you in more important things."

"Well, would you be very kind? Would you come round with me to the registry office? There's a housemaid who won't say yes but doesn't say no."

On their way thither they too looked up at the Wilcoxes' flat. Evie was in the balcony, "staring most rudely," according to Mrs. Munt. Oh yes, it was a nuisance, there was no doubt of it. Helen was proof against a passing encounter but--Margaret began to lose confidence. Might it reawake the dying nerve if the family were living close against her eyes? And Frieda Mosebach was stopping with them for another fortnight, and Frieda was sharp, abominably sharp, and quite capable of remarking, "You love one of the young gentlemen opposite, yes?" The remark would be untrue, but of the kind which, if stated often enough, may become true; just as the remark, "England and Germany are bound to fight," renders war a little more likely each time that it is made, and is therefore made the more readily by the gutter press of either nation. Have the private emotions also their gutter press? Margaret thought so, and feared that good Aunt Juley and Frieda were typical specimens of it. They might, by continual chatter, lead Helen into a repetition of the desires of June. Into a repetition--they could not do more; they could not lead her into lasting love. They were--she saw it clearly--Journalism; her father, with all his defects and wrong-headedness, had been Literature, and had he lived, he would have persuaded his daughter rightly.

The registry office was holding its morning reception. A string of carriages filled the street. Miss Schlegel waited her turn, and finally had to be content with an insidious "temporary," being rejected by genuine housemaids on the ground of her numerous stairs. Her failure depressed her, and though she forgot the failure, the depression remained. On her way home she again glanced up at the Wilcoxes' flat, and took the rather matronly step of speaking about the matter to Helen.

"Helen, you must tell me whether this thing worries you."

"If what?" said Helen, who was washing her hands for lunch.

"The W.'s coming."

"No, of course not."

"Really?"

"Really." Then she admitted that she was a little worried on Mrs. Wilcox's account; she implied that Mrs. Wilcox might reach backward into deep feelings, and be pained by things that never touched the other members of that clan. "I shan't mind if Paul points at our house and says, 'There lives the girl who tried to catch me.' But she might."

"If even that worries you, we could arrange something. There's no reason we should be near people who displease us or whom we displease, thanks to our money. We might even go away for a little."

"Well, I am going away. Frieda's just asked me to Stettin, and I shan't be back till after the New Year. Will that do? Or must I fly the country altogether? Really, Meg, what has come over you to make such a fuss?"

"Oh, I'm getting an old maid, I suppose. I thought I minded nothing, but really I--I should be bored if you fell in love with the same man twice and"--she cleared her throat--"you did go red, you know, when Aunt Juley attacked you this morning. I shouldn't have referred to it otherwise."

But Helen's laugh rang true, as she raised a soapy hand to heaven and swore that never, nowhere and nohow, would she again fall in love with any of the Wilcox family, down to its remotest collaterals.

Chapter 8

The friendship between Margaret and Mrs. Wilcox, which was to develop so--quickly and with such strange results, may perhaps have had its beginnings at Speyer, in the spring. Perhaps the elder lady, as she gazed at the vulgar, ruddy cathedral, and listened to the talk of Helen and her husband, may have detected in the other and less charming of the sisters a deeper sympathy, a sounder judgment. She was capable of detecting such things. Perhaps it was she who had desired the Miss Schlegels to be invited to Howards End, and Margaret whose presence she had particularly desired. All this is speculation: Mrs. Wilcox has left few clear indications behind her. It is certain that she came to call at Wickham Place a fortnight later, the very day that Helen was going with her cousin to Stettin.

"Helen!" cried Fräulein Mosebach in awestruck tones (she was now in her cousin's confidence)--"his mother has forgiven you!" And then, remembering that in England the new-comer ought not to call before she is called upon, she changed her tone from awe to disapproval, and opined that Mrs. Wilcox was "keine Dame."

"Bother the whole family!" snapped Margaret. "Helen, stop giggling and pirouetting, and go and finish your packing. Why can't the woman leave us alone?"

"I don't know what I shall do with Meg," Helen retorted, collapsing upon the stairs. "She's got Wilcox and Box upon the brain. Meg, Meg, I don't love the young gentleman; I don't love the young gentleman, Meg, Meg. Can a body speak plainer?"

"Most certainly her love has died," asserted Fräulein Mosebach.

"Most certainly it has, Frieda, but that will not prevent me from being bored with the Wilcoxes if I return the call."

Then Helen simulated tears, and Fräulein Mosebach, who thought her extremely amusing, did the same. "Oh, boo hoo! boo hoo hoo! Meg's going to return the call, and I can't. 'Cos why? 'Cos I'm going to German-eye."

"If you are going to Germany, go and pack; if you aren't, go and call on the Wilcoxes instead of me."

"But, Meg, Meg, I don't love the young gentleman; I don't love the young--O lud, who's that coming down the stairs? I vow 'tis my brother. O crimini!"

A male--even such a male as Tibby--was enough to stop the foolery. The barrier of sex, though decreasing among the civilized, is still high, and higher on the side of women. Helen could tell her sister all, and her cousin much about Paul; she told her brother nothing. It was not prudishness, for she now spoke of "the Wilcox ideal" with laughter, and even with a growing brutality. Nor was it precaution, for Tibby seldom repeated any news that did not concern himself. It was rather the feeling that she betrayed a secret into the camp of men, and that, however trivial it was on this side of the barrier, it would become important on that. So she stopped, or rather began to fool on other subjects, until her long-suffering relatives drove her upstairs. Fräulein Mosebach followed her, but lingered to say heavily over the banisters to Margaret, "It is all right--she does not love the young man--he has not been worthy of her."

"Yes, I know; thanks very much."

"I thought I did right to tell you."

"Ever so many thanks."

"What's that?" asked Tibby. No one told him, and he proceeded into the dining-room, to eat Elvas plums.

That evening Margaret took decisive action. The house was very quiet, and the fog--we are in November now--pressed against the windows like an excluded ghost. Frieda and Helen and all their luggage had gone. Tibby, who was not feeling well, lay stretched on a sofa by the fire. Margaret sat by him, thinking. Her mind darted from impulse to impulse, and finally marshalled them all in review. The practical person, who knows what he wants at once, and generally knows nothing else, will excuse her of indecision. But this was the way her mind worked. And when she did act, no one could accuse her of indecision then. She hit out as lustily as if she had not considered the matter at all. The letter that she wrote Mrs. Wilcox glowed with the native hue of resolution. The pale cast of thought was with her a breath rather than a tarnish, a breath that leaves the colours all the more vivid when it has been wiped away.

> Dear Mrs. Wilcox,
>
> I have to write something discourteous. It would be better if we did not meet. Both my sister and my aunt have given displeasure to your family, and, in my sister's case, the grounds for displeasure might recur. As far as I know, she no longer occupies her thoughts with your son. But it would not be fair, either to her or to you, if they met, and it is therefore right that our acquaintance which began so pleasantly, should end.
>
> I fear that you will not agree with this; indeed, I know that you will not, since you have been good enough to call on us. It is only an instinct on my part, and no doubt the instinct is wrong. My sister would, undoubtedly, say that it is wrong. I write without her knowledge, and I hope that you will not associate her with my discourtesy.
>
> Believe me,
> Yours truly,
> M. J. Schlegel

Margaret sent this letter round by post. Next morning she received the following reply by hand:

> Dear Miss Schlegel,
>
> You should not have written me such a letter. I called to tell you that Paul has gone abroad.
>
> Ruth Wilcox

Margaret's cheeks burnt. She could not finish her breakfast. She was on fire with shame. Helen had told her that the youth was leaving England, but other things had seemed more important, and she had forgotten. All her absurd anxieties fell to the ground, and in their place arose the certainty that she had been rude to Mrs. Wilcox. Rudeness affected Margaret like a bitter taste in the mouth. It poisoned life. At times it is necessary, but woe to those who employ it without due need. She flung on a hat and shawl, just like a poor woman, and plunged into the fog, which still continued. Her lips were compressed, the letter remained in her hand, and in this state she crossed the street, entered the marble vestibule of the flats, eluded the concierges, and ran up the stairs till she reached the second-floor.

She sent in her name, and to her surprise was shown straight into Mrs. Wilcox's bedroom.

"Oh, Mrs. Wilcox, I have made the baddest blunder. I am more, more ashamed and sorry than I can say."

Mrs. Wilcox bowed gravely. She was offended, and did not pretend to the contrary. She was sitting up in bed, writing letters on an invalid table that spanned her knees. A breakfast tray was on another table beside her. The light of the fire, the light from the window, and the light of a candle-lamp, which threw a quivering halo round her hands, combined to create a strange atmosphere of dissolution.

"I knew he was going to India in November, but I forgot."

"He sailed on the 17th for Nigeria, in Africa."

"I knew--I know. I have been too absurd all through. I am very much ashamed."

Mrs. Wilcox did not answer.

"I am more sorry than I can say, and I hope that you will forgive me."

"It doesn't matter, Miss Schlegel. It is good of you to have come round so promptly."

"It does matter," cried Margaret. "I have been rude to you; and my sister is not even at home, so there was not even that excuse.

"Indeed?"

"She has just gone to Germany."

"She gone as well," murmured the other. "Yes, certainly, it is quite safe--safe, absolutely, now."

"You've been worrying too!" exclaimed Margaret, getting more and more excited, and taking a chair without invitation. "How perfectly extraordinary! I can see that you have. You felt as I do; Helen mustn't meet him again."

"I did think it best."

"Now why?"

"That's a most difficult question," said Mrs. Wilcox, smiling, and a little losing her expression of annoyance. "I think you put it best in your letter--it was an instinct, which may be wrong."

"It wasn't that your son still--"

"Oh no; he often--my Paul is very young, you see."

"Then what was it?"

She repeated: "An instinct which may be wrong."

"In other words, they belong to types that can fall in love, but couldn't live together. That's dreadfully probable. I'm afraid that in nine cases out of ten Nature pulls one way and human nature another."

"These are indeed 'other words,'" said Mrs. Wilcox." I had nothing so coherent in my head. I was merely alarmed when I knew that my boy cared for your sister."

"Ah, I have always been wanting to ask you. How did you know? Helen was so surprised when our aunt drove up, and you stepped forward and arranged things. Did Paul tell you?"

"There is nothing to be gained by discussing that," said Mrs. Wilcox after a moment's pause.

"Mrs. Wilcox, were you very angry with us last June? I wrote you a letter and you didn't answer it."

"I was certainly against taking Mrs. Matheson's flat. I knew it was opposite your house."

"But it's all right now?"

"I think so."

"You only think? You aren't sure? I do love these little muddles tidied up?"

"Oh yes, I'm sure," said Mrs. Wilcox, moving with uneasiness beneath the clothes. "I always sound uncertain over things. It is my way of speaking."

"That's all right, and I'm sure too."

Here the maid came in to remove the breakfast-tray. They were interrupted, and when they resumed conversation it was on more normal lines.

"I must say good-bye now--you will be getting up."

"No--please stop a little longer--I am taking a day in bed. Now and then I do."

"I thought of you as one of the early risers."

"At Howards End--yes; there is nothing to get up for in London."

"Nothing to get up for?" cried the scandalized Margaret. "When there are all the autumn exhibitions, and Ysaye playing in the afternoon! Not to mention people."

"The truth is, I am a little tired. First came the wedding, and then Paul went off, and, instead of resting yesterday, I paid a round of calls."

"A wedding?"

"Yes; Charles, my elder son, is married."

"Indeed!"

"We took the flat chiefly on that account, and also that Paul could get his African outfit. The flat belongs to a cousin of my husband's, and she most kindly offered it to us. So before the day came we were able to make the acquaintance of Dolly's people, which we had not yet done."

Margaret asked who Dolly's people were.

"Fussell. The father is in the Indian army--retired; the brother is in the army. The mother is dead."

So perhaps these were the "chinless sunburnt men" whom Helen had espied one afternoon through the window. Margaret felt mildly interested in the fortunes of the Wilcox family. She had acquired the habit on Helen's account, and it still clung to her. She asked for more information about Miss Dolly Fussell that was, and was given it in even, unemotional tones. Mrs. Wilcox's voice, though sweet and compelling, had little range of expression. It suggested that pictures, concerts, and people are all of small and equal value. Only once had it quickened--when speaking of Howards End.

"Charles and Albert Fussell have known one another some time. They belong to the same club, and are both devoted to golf. Dolly plays golf too, though I believe not so well, and they first met in a mixed foursome. We all like her, and are very much pleased. They were married on the 11th, a few days before Paul sailed. Charles was very anxious to have his brother as best man, so he made a great point of having it on the 11th. The Fussells would have preferred it after Christmas, but they were very nice about it. There is Dolly's photograph--in that double frame."

"Are you quite certain that I'm not interrupting, Mrs. Wilcox?"

"Yes, quite."

"Then I will stay. I'm enjoying this."

Dolly's photograph was now examined. It was signed "For dear Mims," which Mrs. Wilcox interpreted as "the name she and Charles had settled that she should call me." Dolly looked silly, and had one of those triangular faces that so often prove attractive to a robust man. She was very pretty. From her Margaret passed to Charles, whose features prevailed opposite. She speculated on the forces that had drawn the two together till God parted them. She found time to hope that they would be happy.

"They have gone to Naples for their honeymoon."

"Lucky people!"

"I can hardly imagine Charles in Italy."

"Doesn't he care for travelling?"

"He likes travel, but he does see through foreigners so. What he enjoys most is a motor tour in England, and I think that would have carried the day if the weather had not been so abominable. His father gave him a car of his own for a wedding present, which for the present is being stored at Howards End."

"I suppose you have a garage there?"

"Yes. My husband built a little one only last month, to the west of the house, not far from the wych-elm, in what used to be the paddock for the pony."

The last words had an indescribable ring about them.

"Where's the pony gone?" asked Margaret after a pause.

"The pony? Oh, dead, ever so long ago." "The wych-elm I remember. Helen spoke of it as a very splendid tree."

"It is the finest wych-elm in Hertfordshire. Did your sister tell you about the teeth?"

"No."

"Oh, it might interest you. There are pigs' teeth stuck into the trunk, about four feet from the ground. The country people put them in long ago, and they think that if they chew a piece of the bark, it will cure the toothache. The teeth are almost grown over now, and no one comes to the tree."

"I should. I love folklore and all festering superstitions."

"Do you think that the tree really did cure toothache, if one believed in it?"

"Of course it did. It would cure anything--once."

"Certainly I remember cases--you see I lived at Howards End long, long before Mr. Wilcox knew it. I was born there."

The conversation again shifted. At the time it seemed little more than aimless chatter. She was interested when her hostess explained that Howards End was her own property. She was bored when too minute an account was given of the Fussell family, of the anxieties of Charles concerning Naples, of the movements of Mr. Wilcox and Evie, who were motoring in Yorkshire. Margaret could not bear being bored. She grew inattentive, played with the photograph frame, dropped it, smashed Dolly's glass, apologized, was pardoned, cut her finger thereon, was pitied, and finally said she must be going--there was all the housekeeping to do, and she had to interview Tibby's riding-master.

Then the curious note was struck again.

"Good-bye, Miss Schlegel, good-bye. Thank you for coming. You have cheered me up."

"I'm so glad!"

"I--I wonder whether you ever think about yourself.?"

"I think of nothing else," said Margaret, blushing, but letting her hand remain in that of the invalid.

"I wonder. I wondered at Heidelberg."

"*I'm* sure!"

"I almost think--"

"Yes?" asked Margaret, for there was a long pause--a pause that was somehow akin to the flicker of the fire, the quiver of the reading-lamp upon their hands, the white blur from the window; a pause of shifting and eternal shadows.

"I almost think you forget you're a girl."

Margaret was startled and a little annoyed. "I'm twenty-nine," she remarked. "That not so wildly girlish."

Mrs. Wilcox smiled.

"What makes you say that? Do you mean that I have been gauche and rude?"

A shake of the head. "I only meant that I am fifty-one, and that to me both of you--Read it all in some book or other; I cannot put things clearly."

"Oh, I've got it--inexperience. I'm no better than Helen, you mean, and yet I presume to advise her."

"Yes. You have got it. Inexperience is the word."

"Inexperience," repeated Margaret, in serious yet buoyant tones. "Of course, I have everything to learn--absolutely everything--just as much as Helen. Life's very difficult and full of surprises. At all events, I've got as far as that. To be humble and kind, to go straight ahead, to love people rather than pity them, to remember the submerged--well, one can't do all these things at once, worse luck, because they're so contradictory. It's then that proportion comes in--to live by proportion. Don't *begin* with proportion. Only prigs do that. Let proportion come in as a last resource, when the better things have failed, and a deadlock--Gracious me, I've started preaching!"

"Indeed, you put the difficulties of life splendidly," said Mrs. Wilcox, withdrawing her hand into the deeper shadows. "It is just what I should have liked to say about them myself."

Chapter 9

Mrs. Wilcox cannot be accused of giving Margaret much information about life. And Margaret, on the other hand, has made a fair show of modesty, and has pretended to an inexperience that she certainly did not feel. She had kept house for over ten years; she had entertained, almost with distinction; she had brought up a charming sister, and was bringing up a brother. Surely, if experience is attainable, she had attained it.

Yet the little luncheon-party that she gave in Mrs. Wilcox's honour was not a success. The new friend did not blend with the "one or two delightful people" who had been asked to meet her, and the atmosphere was one of polite bewilderment. Her tastes were simple, her knowledge of culture slight, and she was not interested in the New English Art Club, nor in the dividing-line between Journalism and Literature, which was started as a conversational hare. The delightful people darted after it with cries of joy, Margaret leading them, and not till the meal was half over did they realize that the principal guest had taken no part in the chase. There was no common topic. Mrs. Wilcox, whose life had been spent in the service of husband and sons, had little to say to strangers who had never shared it, and whose age was half her own. Clever talk alarmed her, and withered her delicate imaginings; it was the social; counterpart of a motorcar, all jerks, and she was a wisp of hay, a flower. Twice she deplored the weather, twice criticized the train service on the Great Northern Railway. They vigorously assented, and rushed on, and when she inquired whether there was any news of Helen, her hostess was too much occupied in placing Rothenstein to answer. The question was repeated: "I hope that your sister is safe in Germany by now." Margaret checked herself and said, "Yes, thank you; I heard on Tuesday." But the demon of vociferation was in her, and the next moment she was off again.

"Only on Tuesday, for they live right away at Stettin. Did you ever know any one living at Stettin?"

"Never," said Mrs. Wilcox gravely, while her neighbour, a young man low down in the Education Office, began to discuss what people who lived at Stettin ought to look like. Was there such a thing as Stettininity? Margaret swept on.

"People at Stettin drop things into boats out of overhanging warehouses. At least, our cousins do, but aren't particularly rich. The town isn't interesting, except for a clock that rolls its eyes, and the view of the Oder, which truly is something special. Oh, Mrs. Wilcox, you would love the Oder! The river, or rather rivers--there seem to be dozens of them--are intense blue, and the plain they run through an intensest green."

"Indeed! That sounds like a most beautiful view, Miss Schlegel."

"So I say, but Helen, who will muddle things, says no, it's like music. The course of the Oder is to be like music. It's obliged to remind her of a symphonic poem. The part by the landing-stage is in B minor, if I remember rightly, but lower down things get extremely mixed. There is a slodgy theme in several keys at once, meaning mud-banks, and another for the navigable canal, and the exit into the Baltic is in C sharp major, pianissimo."

"What do the overhanging warehouses make of that?" asked the man, laughing.

"They make a great deal of it," replied Margaret, unexpectedly rushing off on a new track. "I think it's affectation to compare the Oder to music, and so do you, but the overhanging warehouses of Stettin take beauty seriously, which we don't, and the average Englishman doesn't, and despises all who do. Now don't say 'Germans have no taste,' or I shall scream. They haven't. But--but--such a tremendous but! --they take poetry seriously. They do take poetry seriously.

"Is anything gained by that?"

"Yes, yes. The German is always on the lookout for beauty. He may miss it through stupidity, or misinterpret it, but he is always asking beauty to enter his life, and I believe that in the end it will come. At Heidelberg I met a fat veterinary surgeon whose voice broke with sobs as he repeated some mawkish poetry. So easy for me to laugh--I, who never repeat poetry, good or bad, and cannot remember one fragment of verse to thrill myself with. My blood boils--well, I'm half German, so put it down to patriotism--when I listen to the tasteful contempt of the average islander for things Teutonic, whether they're Böcklin or my veterinary surgeon. 'Oh, Böcklin,' they say; 'he strains after beauty, he peoples Nature with gods too consciously.' Of course Böcklin strains, because he wants something--beauty and all the other intangible gifts that are floating about the world. So his landscapes don't come off, and Leader's do."

"I am not sure that I agree. Do you?" said he, turning to Mrs. Wilcox.

She replied: "I think Miss Schlegel puts everything splendidly"; and a chill fell on the conversation.

"Oh, Mrs. Wilcox, say something nicer than that. It's such a snub to be told you put things splendidly. "

"I do not mean it as a snub. Your last speech interested me so much. Generally people do not seem quite to like Germany. I have long wanted to hear what is said on the other side."

"The other side? Then you do disagree. Oh, good! Give us your side."

"I have no side. But my husband"--her voice softened, the chill increased--"has very little faith in the Continent, and our children have all taken after him."

"On what grounds? Do they feel that the Continent is in bad form?"

Mrs. Wilcox had no idea; she paid little attention to grounds. She was not intellectual, nor even alert, and it was odd that, all the same, she should give the idea of greatness. Margaret, zigzagging with her friends over Thought and Art, was conscious of a personality that transcended their own and dwarfed their activities. There was no bitterness in Mrs. Wilcox; there was not even criticism; she was lovable, and no ungracious or uncharitable word had passed her lips. Yet she and daily life were out of focus: one or the other must show blurred. And at lunch she seemed more out of focus than usual, and nearer the line that divides life from a life that may be of greater importance.

"You will admit, though, that the Continent--it seems silly to speak of 'the Continent,' but really it is all more like itself than any part of it is like England. England is unique. Do have another jelly first. I was going to say that the Continent, for good or for evil, is interested in ideas. Its Literature and Art have what one might call the kink of the unseen about them, and this persists even through decadence and affectation. There is more liberty of action in England, but for liberty of thought go to bureaucratic Prussia. People will there discuss with humility vital questions that we here think ourselves too good to touch with tongs."

"I do not want to go to Prussian" said Mrs. Wilcox--"not even to see that interesting view that you were describing. And for discussing with humility I am too old. We never discuss anything at Howards End."

"Then you ought to!" said Margaret. "Discussion keeps a house alive. It cannot stand by bricks and mortar alone."

"It cannot stand without them," said Mrs. Wilcox, unexpectedly catching on to the thought, and rousing, for the first and last time, a faint hope in the breasts of the delightful people. "It cannot stand without them, and I sometimes think--But I cannot expect your generation to agree, for even my daughter disagrees with me here."

"Never mind us or her. Do say!"

"I sometimes think that it is wiser to leave action and discussion to men."

There was a little silence.

"One admits that the arguments against the suffrage are extraordinarily strong," said a girl opposite, leaning forward and crumbling her bread.

"Are they? I never follow any arguments. I am only too thankful not to have a vote myself."

"We didn't mean the vote, though, did we?" supplied Margaret. "Aren't we differing on something much wider, Mrs. Wilcox? Whether women are to remain what they have been since the dawn of history; or whether, since men have moved forward so far, they too may move forward a little now. I say they may. I would even admit a biological change."

"I don't know, I don't know."

"I must be getting back to my overhanging warehouse," said the man. "They've turned disgracefully strict.

Mrs. Wilcox also rose.

"Oh, but come upstairs for a little. Miss Quested plays. Do you like MacDowell? Do you mind him only having two noises? If you must really go, I'll see you out. Won't you even have coffee?"

They left the dining-room, closing the door behind them, and as Mrs. Wilcox buttoned up her jacket, she said: "What an interesting life you all lead in London!"

"No, we don't," said Margaret, with a sudden revulsion. "We lead the lives of gibbering monkeys. Mrs. Wilcox--really--We have something quiet and stable at the bottom. We really have. All my friends have. Don't pretend you enjoyed lunch, for you loathed it, but forgive me by coming again, alone, or by asking me to you."

"I am used to young people," said Mrs. Wilcox, and with each word she spoke the outlines of known things grew dim. "I hear a great deal of chatter at home, for we, like you, entertain a great deal. With us it is more sport and politics, but--I enjoyed my lunch very much, Miss Schlegel, dear, and am not pretending, and only wish I could have joined in more. For one thing, I'm not particularly well just today. For another, you younger people move so quickly that it dazes me. Charles is the same, Dolly the same. But we are all in the same boat, old and young. I never forget that."

They were silent for a moment. Then, with a newborn emotion, they shook hands. The conversation ceased suddenly when Margaret re-entered the dining-room: her friends had been talking over her new friend, and had dismissed her as uninteresting.

Chapter 10

Several days passed.

Was Mrs. Wilcox one of the unsatisfactory people--there are many of them--who dangle intimacy and then withdraw it? They evoke our interests and affections, and keep the life of the spirit dawdling round them. Then they withdraw. When physical passion is involved, there is a definite name for such behaviour--flirting--and if carried far enough it is punishable by law. But no law--not public opinion even--punishes those who coquette with friendship, though the dull ache that they inflict, the sense of misdirected effort and exhaustion, may be as intolerable. Was she one of these?

Margaret feared so at first, for, with a Londoner's impatience, she wanted everything to be settled up immediately. She mistrusted the periods of quiet that are essential to true growth. Desiring to book Mrs. Wilcox as a friend, she pressed on the ceremony, pencil, as it were, in hand, pressing the more because the rest of the family were away, and the opportunity seemed favourable. But the elder woman would not be hurried. She refused to fit in with the Wickham Place set, or to reopen discussion of Helen and Paul, whom Margaret would have utilized as a short-cut. She took her time, or perhaps let time take her, and when the crisis did come all was ready.

The crisis opened with a message: would Miss Schlegel come shopping? Christmas was nearing, and Mrs. Wilcox felt behind-hand with the presents. She had taken some more days in bed, and must make up for lost time. Margaret accepted, and at eleven o'clock one cheerless morning they started out in a brougham.

"First of all," began Margaret, "we must make a list and tick off the people's names. My aunt always does, and this fog may thicken up any moment. Have you any ideas?"

"I thought we would go to Harrod's or the Haymarket Stores," said Mrs. Wilcox rather hopelessly. "Everything is sure to be there. I am not a good shopper. The din is so confusing, and your aunt is quite right--one ought to make a list. Take my notebook, then, and write your own name at the top of the page."

"Oh, hooray!" said Margaret, writing it. "How very kind of you to start with me!" But she did not want to receive anything expensive. Their acquaintance was singular rather than intimate, and she divined that the Wilcox clan would resent any expenditure on outsiders; the more compact families do. She did not want to be thought a second Helen, who would snatch presents since she could not snatch young men, nor to be exposed, like a second Aunt Juley, to the insults of Charles. A certain austerity of demeanour was best, and she added: "I don't really want a Yuletide gift, though. In fact, I'd rather not."

"Why?"

"Because I've odd ideas about Christmas. Because I have all that money can buy. I want more people, but no more things."

"I should like to give you something worth your acquaintance, Miss Schlegel, in memory of your kindness to me during my lonely fortnight. It has so happened that I have been left alone, and you have stopped me from brooding. I am too apt to brood."

"If that is so," said Margaret, "if I have happened to be of use to you, which I didn't know, you cannot pay me back with anything tangible."

" I suppose not, but one would like to. Perhaps I shall think of something as we go about."

Her name remained at the head of the list, but nothing was written opposite it. They drove from shop to shop. The air was white, and when they alighted it tasted like cold pennies. At times they passed through a clot of grey. Mrs. Wilcox's vitality was low that morning, and it was Margaret who decided on a horse for this little girl, a golliwog for that, for the rector's wife a copper warming-tray. "We always give the servants money." "Yes, do you, yes, much easier," replied Margaret, but felt the grotesque impact of the unseen upon the seen, and saw issuing from a forgotten manger at Bethlehem this torrent of coins and toys. Vulgarity reigned. Public-houses, besides their usual exhortation against temperance reform, invited men to "Join our Christmas goose club"--one bottle of gin, etc., or two, according to subscription. A poster of a woman in tights heralded the Christmas pantomime, and little red devils, who had come in again that year, were prevalent upon the Christmas-cards. Margaret was no morbid idealist. She did not wish this spate of business and self-advertisement checked. It was only the occasion of it that struck her with amazement annually. How many of these vacillating shoppers and tired shop-assistants realized that it was a divine event that drew them together? She realized it, though standing outside in the matter. She was not a Christian in the accepted sense; she did not believe that God had ever worked among us as a young artisan. These people, or most of them, believed it, and if pressed, would affirm it in words. But the visible signs of their belief were Regent Street or Drury Lane, a little mud displaced, a little money spent, a little food cooked, eaten, and forgotten. Inadequate. But in public who shall express the unseen adequately? It is private life that holds out the mirror to infinity; personal intercourse, and that alone, that ever hints at a personality beyond our daily vision.

"No, I do like Christmas on the whole," she announced. "In its clumsy way, it does approach Peace and Goodwill. But oh, it is clumsier every year."

"Is it? I am only used to country Christmases."

"We are usually in London, and play the game with vigour--carols at the Abbey, clumsy midday meal, clumsy dinner for the maids, followed by Christmas-tree and dancing of poor children, with songs from Helen. The drawing-room does very well for that. We put the tree in the powder-closet, and draw a curtain when the candles are lighted, and with the looking-glass behind it looks quite pretty. I wish we might have a powder-closet in our next house. Of course, the tree has to be very small, and the presents don't hang on it. No; the presents reside in a sort of rocky landscape made of crumpled brown paper."

"You spoke of your 'next house,' Miss Schlegel. Then are you leaving Wickham Place?"

"Yes, in two or three years, when the lease expires. We must."

"Have you been there long?"

"All our lives."

"You will be very sorry to leave it."

"I suppose so. We scarcely realize it yet. My father--" She broke off, for they had reached the stationery department of the Haymarket Stores, and Mrs. Wilcox wanted to order some private greeting cards.

"If possible, something distinctive," she sighed. At the counter she found a friend, bent on the same errand, and conversed with her insipidly, wasting much time. "My husband and our daughter are motoring."

"Bertha too? Oh, fancy, what a coincidence!" Margaret, though not practical, could shine in such company as this. While they talked, she went through a volume of specimen cards, and submitted one for Mrs. Wilcox's inspection. Mrs. Wilcox was delighted--so original, words so sweet; she would order a hundred like that, and could never be sufficiently grateful. Then, just as the assistant was booking the order, she said: "Do you know, I'll wait. On second thoughts, I'll wait. There's plenty of time still, isn't there, and I shall be able to get Evie's opinion."

They returned to the carriage by devious paths; when they were in, she said, "But couldn't you get it renewed?"

"I beg your pardon?" asked Margaret.

"The lease, I mean."

"Oh, the lease! Have you been thinking of that all the time? How very kind of you!"

"Surely something could be done."

"No; values have risen too enormously. They mean to pull down Wickham Place, and build flats like yours."

"But how horrible!"

"Landlords are horrible."

Then she said vehemently: "It is monstrous, Miss Schlegel; it isn't right. I had no idea that this was hanging over you. I do pity you from the bottom of my heart. To be parted from your house, your father's house--it oughtn't to be allowed. It is worse than dying. I would rather die than--Oh, poor girls! Can what they call civilization be right, if people mayn't die in the room where they were born? My dear, I am so sorry--"

Margaret did not know what to say. Mrs. Wilcox had been overtired by the shopping, and was inclined to hysteria.

"Howards End was nearly pulled down once. It would have killed me."

"Howards End must be a very different house to ours. We are fond of ours, but there is nothing distinctive about it. As you saw, it is an ordinary London house. We shall easily find another."

"So you think."

"Again my lack of experience, I suppose!" said Margaret, easing away from the subject. "I can't say anything when you take up that line, Mrs. Wilcox. I wish I could see myself as you see me--foreshortened into a backfisch. Quite the ingénue. Very charming--wonderfully well read for my age, but incapable--"

Mrs. Wilcox would not be deterred. "Come down with me to Howards End now," she said, more vehemently than ever. "I want you to see it. You have never seen it. I want to hear what you say about it, for you do put things so wonderfully."

Margaret glanced at the pitiless air and then at the tired face of her companion. "Later on I should love it," she continued, "but it's hardly the weather for such an expedition, and we ought to start when we're fresh. Isn't the house shut up, too?"

She received no answer. Mrs. Wilcox appeared to be annoyed.

"Might I come some other day?"

Mrs. Wilcox bent forward and tapped the glass. "Back to Wickham Place, please!" was her order to the coachman. Margaret had been snubbed.

"A thousand thanks, Miss Schlegel, for all your help."

"Not at all."

"It is such a comfort to get the presents off my mind--the Christmas-cards especially. I do admire your choice."

It was her turn to receive no answer. In her turn Margaret became annoyed.

"My husband and Evie will be back the day after tomorrow. That is why I dragged you out shopping today. I stayed in town chiefly to shop, but got through nothing, and now he writes that they must cut their tour short, the weather is so bad, and the police-traps have been so bad--nearly as bad as in Surrey. Ours is such a careful chauffeur, and my husband feels it particularly hard that they should be treated like roadhogs."

"Why?"

"Well, naturally he--he isn't a road-hog."

"He was exceeding the speed-limit, I conclude. He must expect to suffer with the lower animals."

Mrs. Wilcox was silenced. In growing discomfort they drove homewards. The city seemed Satanic, the narrower streets oppressing like the galleries of a mine. No harm was done by the fog to trade, for it lay high, and the lighted windows of the shops were thronged with customers. It was rather a darkening of the spirit which fell back upon itself, to find a more grievous darkness within. Margaret nearly spoke a dozen times, but something throttled her. She felt petty and awkward, and her meditations on Christmas grew more cynical. Peace? It may bring other gifts, but is there a single Londoner to whom Christmas is peaceful? The craving for excitement and for elaboration has ruined that blessing. Goodwill? Had she seen any example of it in the hordes of purchasers? Or in herself. She had failed to respond to this invitation merely because it was a little queer and imaginative--she, whose birthright it was to nourish imagination! Better to have accepted, to have tired themselves a little by the journey, than coldly to reply, "Might I come some other day?" Her cynicism left her. There would be no other day. This shadowy woman would never ask her again.

They parted at the Mansions. Mrs. Wilcox went in after due civilities, and Margaret watched the tall, lonely figure sweep up the hall to the lift. As the glass doors closed on it she had the sense of an imprisonment. The beautiful head disappeared first, still buried in the muff, the long trailing skirt followed. A woman of undefinable rarity was going up heaven-ward, like a specimen in a bottle. And into what a heaven--a vault as of hell, sooty black, from which soots descended!

At lunch her brother, seeing her inclined for silence, insisted on talking. Tibby was not ill-natured, but from babyhood something drove him to do the unwelcome and the unexpected. Now he gave her a long account of the day-school that he sometimes patronized. The account was interesting, and she had often pressed him for it before, but she could not attend now, for her mind was focussed on the invisible. She discerned that Mrs. Wilcox, though a loving wife and mother, had only one passion in life--her house--and that the moment was solemn when she invited a friend to share this passion with her. To answer "another day" was to answer as a fool. "Another day" will do for brick and mortar, but not for the Holy of Holies into which Howards End had been transfigured. Her own curiosity was slight. She had heard more than enough about it in the summer. The nine windows, the vine, and the wych-elm had no pleasant connections for her, and she would have preferred to spend the afternoon at a concert. But imagination triumphed. While her brother held forth she determined to go, at whatever cost, and to compel Mrs. Wilcox to go, too. When lunch was over she stepped over to the flats.

Mrs. Wilcox had just gone away for the night.

Margaret said that it was of no consequence, hurried downstairs, and took a hansom to King's Cross. She was convinced that the escapade was important, though it would have puzzled her to say why. There was a question of imprisonment and escape, and though she did not know the time of the train, she strained her eyes for the St. Pancras' clock.

Then the clock of King's Cross swung into sight, a second moon in that infernal sky, and her cab drew up at the station. There was a train for Hilton in five minutes. She took a ticket, asking in her agitation for a single. As she did so, a grave and happy voice saluted her and thanked her.

"I will come if I still may," said Margaret, laughing nervously.

"You are coming to sleep, dear, too. It is in the morning that my house is most beautiful. You are coming to stop. I cannot show you my meadow properly except at sunrise. These fogs"--she pointed at the station roof--"never spread far. I dare say they are sitting in the sun in Hertfordshire, and you will never repent joining them.

"I shall never repent joining you."

"It is the same."

They began the walk up the long platform. Far at its end stood the train, breasting the darkness without. They never reached it. Before imagination could triumph, there were cries of "Mother! Mother!" and a heavy-browed girl darted out of the cloak-room and seized Mrs. Wilcox by the arm.

"Evie!" she gasped. "Evie, my pet--"

The girl called, "Father! I say! look who's here."

"Evie, dearest girl, why aren't you in Yorkshire?"

"No--motor smash--changed plans--Father's coming."

"Why, Ruth!" cried Mr. Wilcox, joining them. "What in the name of all that's wonderful are you doing here, Ruth?"

Mrs. Wilcox had recovered herself.

"Oh, Henry dear! --here's a lovely surprise--but let me introduce--but I think you know Miss Schlegel."

"Oh, yes," he replied, not greatly interested. "But how's yourself, Ruth?"

"Fit as a fiddle," she answered gaily.

"So are we and so was our car, which ran A-1 as far as Ripon, but there a wretched horse and cart which a fool of a driver--"

"Miss Schlegel, our little outing must be for another day."

"I was saying that this fool of a driver, as the policeman himself admits--"

"Another day, Mrs. Wilcox. Of course."

"--But as we've insured against third party risks, it won't so much matter--"

"--Cart and car being practically at right angles--"

The voices of the happy family rose high. Margaret was left alone. No one wanted her. Mrs. Wilcox walked out of King's Cross between her husband and her daughter, listening to both of them.

Chapter 11

The funeral was over. The carriages rolled away through the soft mud, and only the poor remained. They approached to the newly-dug shaft and looked their last at the coffin, now almost hidden beneath the spadefuls of clay. It was their moment. Most of them were women from the dead woman's district, to whom black garments had been served out by Mr. Wilcox's orders. Pure curiosity had brought others. They thrilled with the excitement of a death, and of a rapid death, and stood in groups or moved between the graves, like drops of ink. The son of one of them, a wood-cutter, was perched high above their heads, pollarding one of the churchyard elms. From where he sat he could see the village of Hilton, strung upon the North Road, with its accreting suburbs; the sunset beyond, scarlet and orange, winking at him beneath brows of grey; the church; the plantations; and behind him an unspoilt country of fields and farms. But he, too, was rolling the event luxuriously in his mouth. He tried to tell his mother down below all that he had felt when he saw the coffin approaching: how he could not leave his work, and yet did not like to go on with it; how he had almost slipped out of the tree, he was so upset; the rooks had cawed, and no wonder--it was as if rooks knew too. His mother claimed the prophetic power herself--she had seen a strange look about Mrs. Wilcox for some time. London had done the mischief, said others. She had been a kind lady; her grandmother had been kind, too--a plainer person, but very kind. Ah, the old sort was dying out! Mr. Wilcox, he was a kind gentleman. They advanced to the topic again and again, dully, but with exaltation. The funeral of a rich person was to them what the funeral of Alcestis or Ophelia is to the educated. It was Art; though remote from life, it enhanced life's values, and they witnessed it avidly.

The grave-diggers, who had kept up an undercurrent of disapproval--they disliked Charles; it was not a moment to speak of such things, but they did not like Charles Wilcox--the grave-diggers finished their work and piled up the wreaths and crosses above it. The sun set over Hilton: the grey brows of the evening flushed a little, and were cleft with one scarlet frown. Chattering sadly to each other, the mourners passed through the lych-gate and traversed the chestnut avenues that led down to the village. The young wood-cutter stayed a little longer, poised above the silence and swaying rhythmically. At last the bough fell beneath his saw. With a grunt, he descended, his thoughts dwelling no longer on death, but on love, for he was mating. He stopped as he passed the new grave; a sheaf of tawny chrysanthemums had caught his eye. "They didn't ought to have coloured flowers at buryings," he reflected. Trudging on a few steps, he stopped again, looked furtively at the dusk, turned back, wrenched a chrysanthemum from the sheaf, and hid it in his pocket.

After him came silence absolute. The cottage that abutted on the churchyard was empty, and no other house stood near. Hour after hour the scene of the interment remained without an eye to witness it. Clouds drifted over it from the west; or the church may have been a ship, high-prowed, steering with all its company towards infinity. Towards morning the air grew colder, the sky clearer, the surface of the earth hard and sparkling above the prostrate dead. The woodcutter, returning after a night of joy, reflected: "They lilies, they chrysants; it's a pity I didn't take them all."

Up at Howards End they were attempting breakfast. Charles and Evie sat in the dining-room, with Mrs. Charles. Their father, who could not bear to see a face, breakfasted upstairs. He suffered acutely. Pain came over him in spasms, as if it was physical, and even while he was about to eat, his eyes would fill with tears, and he would lay down the morsel untasted.

He remembered his wife's even goodness during thirty years. Not anything in detail--not courtship or early raptures--but just the unvarying virtue, that seemed to him a woman's noblest quality. So many women are capricious, breaking into odd flaws of passion or frivolity. Not so his wife. Year after year, summer and winter, as bride and mother, she had been the same, he had always trusted her. Her tenderness! Her innocence! The wonderful innocence that was hers by the gift of God. Ruth knew no more of worldly wickedness and wisdom than did the flowers in her garden, or the grass in her field. Her idea of business--"Henry, why do people who have enough money try to get more money?" Her idea of politics--"I am sure that if the mothers of various nations could meet, there would be no more wars." Her idea of religion--ah, this had been a cloud, but a cloud that passed. She came of Quaker stock, and he and his family, formerly Dissenters, were now members of the Church of England. The rector's sermons had at first repelled her, and she had expressed a desire for "a more inward light," adding, "not so much for myself as for baby" (Charles). Inward light must have been granted, for he heard no complaints in later years. They brought up their three children without dispute. They had never disputed.

She lay under the earth now. She had gone, and as if to make her going the more bitter, had gone with a touch of mystery that was all unlike her. "Why didn't you tell me you knew of it?" he had moaned, and her faint voice had answered: "I didn't want to, Henry--I might have been wrong--and every one hates illnesses." He had been told of the horror by a strange doctor, whom she had consulted during his absence from town. Was this altogether just? Without fully explaining, she had died. It was a fault on her part, and--tears rushed into his eyes--what a little fault! It was the only time she had deceived him in those thirty years.

He rose to his feet and looked out of the window, for Evie had come in with the letters, and he could meet no one's eye. Ah yes--she had been a good woman--she had been steady. He chose the word deliberately. To him steadiness included all praise.

He himself, gazing at the wintry garden, is in appearance a steady man. His face was not as square as his son's, and, indeed, the chin, though firm enough in outline, retreated a little, and the lips, ambiguous, were curtained by a moustache. But there was no external hint of weakness. The eyes, if capable of kindness and goodfellowship, if ruddy for the moment with tears, were the eyes of one who could not be driven. The forehead, too, was like Charles's. High and straight, brown and polished, merging abruptly into temples and skull, it has the effect of a bastion that protected his head from the world. At times it had the effect of a blank wall. He had dwelt behind it, intact and happy, for fifty years.

"The post's come, Father," said Evie awkwardly.

"Thanks. Put it down."

"Has the breakfast been all right?"

"Yes, thanks."

The girl glanced at him and at it with constraint. She did not know what to do.

"Charles says do you want the *Times*?"

"No, I'll read it later."

"Ring if you want anything, Father, won't you?"

"I've all I want."

Having sorted the letters from the circulars, she went back to the dining-room.

"Father's eaten nothing," she announced, sitting down with wrinkled brows behind the tea-urn--

Charles did not answer, but after a moment he ran quickly upstairs, opened the door, and said: "Look here, Father, you must eat, you know"; and having paused for a reply that did not come, stole down again. "He's going to read his letters first, I think," he said evasively; "I dare say he will go on with his breakfast afterwards." Then he took up the *Times*, and for some time there was no sound except the clink of cup against saucer and of knife on plate.

Poor Mrs. Charles sat between her silent companions, terrified at the course of events, and a little bored. She was a rubbishy little creature, and she knew it. A telegram had dragged her from Naples to the death-bed of a woman whom she had scarcely known. A word from her husband had plunged her into mourning. She desired to mourn inwardly as well, but she wished that Mrs. Wilcox, since fated to die, could have died before the marriage, for then less would have been expected of her. Crumbling her toast, and too nervous to ask for the butter, she remained almost motionless, thankful only for this, that her father-in-law was having his breakfast upstairs.

At last Charles spoke. "They had no business to be pollarding those elms yesterday," he said to his sister.

"No indeed."

"I must make a note of that," he continued. "I am surprised that the rector allowed it."

"Perhaps it may not be the rector's affair."

"Whose else could it be?"

"The lord of the manor."

"Impossible."

"Butter, Dolly?"

"Thank you, Evie dear. Charles--"

"Yes, dear?"

"I didn't know one could pollard elms. I thought one only pollarded willows."

"Oh no, one can pollard elms."

"Then why oughtn't the elms in the churchyard to be pollarded?"

Charles frowned a little, and turned again to his sister. "Another point. I must speak to Chalkeley."

"Yes, rather; you must complain to Chalkeley.

"It's no good him saying he is not responsible for those men. He is responsible."

"Yes, rather."

Brother and sister were not callous. They spoke thus, partly because they desired to keep Chalkeley up to the mark--a healthy desire in its way--partly because they avoided the personal note in life. All Wilcoxes did. It did not seem to them of supreme importance. Or it may be as Helen supposed: they realized its importance, but were afraid of it. Panic and emptiness, could one glance behind. They were not callous, and they left the breakfast-table with aching hearts. Their mother never had come in to breakfast. It was in the other rooms, and especially in the garden, that they felt her loss most. As Charles went out to the garage, he was reminded at every step of the woman who had loved him and whom he could never replace. What battles he had fought against her gentle conservatism! How she had disliked improvements, yet how loyally she had accepted them when made! He and his father--what trouble they had had to get this very garage! With what difficulty had they persuaded her to yield them to the paddock for it--the paddock that she loved more dearly than the garden itself! The vine--she had got her way about the vine. It still encumbered the south wall with its unproductive branches. And so with Evie, as she stood talking to the cook. Though she could take up her mother's work inside the house, just as the man could take it up without, she felt that something unique had fallen out of her life. Their grief, though less poignant than their father's, grew from deeper roots, for a wife may be replaced; a mother never.

Charles would go back to the office. There was little to do at Howards End. The contents of his mother's will had been long known to them. There were no legacies, no annuities, none of the posthumous bustle with which some of the dead prolong their activities. Trusting her husband, she had left him everything without reserve. She was quite a poor woman--the house had been all her dowry, and the house would come to Charles in time. Her water-colours Mr. Wilcox intended to reserve for Paul, while Evie would take the jewellery and lace. How easily she slipped out of life! Charles thought the habit laudable, though he did not intend to adopt it himself, whereas Margaret would have seen in it an almost culpable indifference to earthly fame. Cynicism--not the superficial cynicism that snarls and sneers, but the cynicism that can go with courtesy and tenderness--that was the note of Mrs. Wilcox's will. She wanted not to vex people. That accomplished, the earth might freeze over her for ever.

No, there was nothing for Charles to wait for. He could not go on with his honeymoon, so he would go up to London and work--he felt too miserable hanging about. He and Dolly would have the furnished flat while his father rested quietly in the country with Evie. He could also keep an eye on his own little house, which was being painted and decorated for him in one of the Surrey suburbs, and in which he hoped to install himself soon after Christmas. Yes, he would go up after lunch in his new motor, and the town servants, who had come down for the funeral, would go up by train.

He found his father's chauffeur in the garage, said, "Morning" without looking at the man's face, and, bending over the car, continued: "Hullo! my new car's been driven!"

"Has it, sir?"

"Yes," said Charles, getting rather red; "and whoever's driven it hasn't cleaned it properly, for there's mud on the axle. Take it off."

The man went for the cloths without a word. He was a chauffeur as ugly as sin--not that this did him disservice with Charles, who thought charm in a man rather rot, and had soon got rid of the little Italian beast with whom they had started.

"Charles--" His bride was tripping after him over the hoar-frost, a dainty black column, her little face and elaborate mourning hat forming the capital thereof.

"One minute, I'm busy. Well, Crane, who's been driving it, do you suppose?"

"Don't know, I'm sure, sir. No one's driven it since I've been back, but, of course, there's the fortnight I've been away with the other car in Yorkshire."

The mud came off easily.

"Charles, your father's down. Something's happened. He wants you in the house at once. Oh, Charles!"

"Wait, dear, wait a minute. Who had the key to the garage while you were away, Crane?"

"The gardener, sir."

"Do you mean to tell me that old Penny can drive a motor?"

"No, sir; no one's had the motor out, sir."

"Then how do you account for the mud on the axle?"

"I can't, of course, say for the time I've been in Yorkshire. No more mud now, sir."

Charles was vexed. The man was treating him as a fool, and if his heart had not been so heavy he would have reported him to his father. But it was not a morning for complaints. Ordering the motor to be round after lunch, he joined his wife, who had all the while been pouring out some incoherent story about a letter and a Miss Schlegel.

"Now, Dolly, I can attend to you. Miss Schlegel? What does she want?"

When people wrote a letter Charles always asked what they wanted. Want was to him the only cause of action. And the question in this case was correct, for his wife replied, "She wants Howards End."

"Howards End? Now, Crane, just don't forget to put on the Stepney wheel."

"No, sir."

"Now, mind you don't forget, for I--Come, little woman." When they were out of the chauffeur's sight he put his arm around her waist and pressed her against him. All his affection and half his attention--it was what he granted her throughout their happy married life.

"But you haven't listened, Charles--"

"What's wrong?"

"I keep on telling you--Howards End. Miss Schlegels got it."

"Got what?" asked Charles, unclasping her. "What the dickens are you talking about?"

"Now, Charles, you promised not to say those naughty--"

"Look here, I'm in no mood for foolery. It's no morning for it either."

"I tell you--I keep on telling you--Miss Schlegel--she's got it--your mother's left it to her--and you've all got to move out!"

"*Howards End?*"

"*Howards End!*" she screamed, mimicking him, and as she did so Evie came dashing out of the shrubbery.

"Dolly, go back at once! My father's much annoyed with you. Charles"--she hit herself wildly--"come in at once to Father. He's had a letter that's too awful."

Charles began to run, but checked himself, and stepped heavily across the gravel path. There the house was--the nine windows, the unprolific vine. He exclaimed, "Schlegels again!" and as if to complete chaos, Dolly said, "Oh no, the matron of the nursing home has written instead of her."

"Come in, all three of you!" cried his father, no longer inert. "Dolly, why have you disobeyed me?"

"Oh, Mr. Wilcox--"

"I told you not to go out to the garage. I've heard you all shouting in the garden. I won't have it. Come in."

He stood in the porch, transformed, letters in his hand.

"Into the dining-room, every one of you. We can't discuss private matters in the middle of all the servants. Here, Charles, here; read these. See what you make."

Charles took two letters, and read them as he followed the procession. The first was a covering note from the matron. Mrs. Wilcox had desired her, when the funeral should be over, to forward the enclosed. The enclosed--it was from his mother herself. She had written: "To my husband: I should like Miss Schlegel (Margaret) to have Howards End."

"I suppose we're going to have a talk about this?" he remarked, ominously calm.

"Certainly. I was coming out to you when Dolly--"

"Well, let's sit down."

"Come, Evie, don't waste time, sit down."

In silence they drew up to the breakfast-table. The events of yesterday--indeed, of this morning--suddenly receded into a past so remote that they seemed scarcely to have lived in it. Heavy breathings were heard. They were calming themselves. Charles, to steady them further, read the enclosure out loud: "A note in my mother's handwriting, in an envelope addressed to my father, sealed. Inside: 'I should like Miss Schlegel (Margaret) to have Howards End.' No date, no signature. Forwarded through the matron of that nursing home. Now, the question is--"

Dolly interrupted him. "But I say that note isn't legal. Houses ought to be done by a lawyer, Charles, surely."

Her husband worked his jaw severely. Little lumps appeared in front of either ear--a symptom that she had not yet learnt to respect, and she asked whether she might see the note. Charles looked at his father for permission, who said abstractedly, "Give it her." She seized it, and at once exclaimed: "Why, it's only in pencil! I said so. Pencil never counts."

"We know that it is not legally binding, Dolly," said Mr. Wilcox, speaking from out of his fortress. "We are aware of that. Legally, I should be justified in tearing it up and throwing it into the fire. Of course, my dear, we consider you as one of the family, but it will be better if you do not interfere with what you do not understand."

Charles, vexed both with his father and his wife, then repeated: "The question is--" He had cleared a space of the breakfast-table from plates and knives, so that he could draw patterns on the tablecloth. "The question is whether Miss Schlegel, during the fortnight we were all away, whether she unduly--" He stopped.

"I don't think that," said his father, whose nature was nobler than his son's

"Don't think what?"

"That she would have--that it is a case of undue influence. No, to my mind the question is the--the invalid's condition at the time she wrote."

"My dear father, consult an expert if you like, but I don't admit it is my mother's writing."

"Why, you just said it was!" cried Dolly.

"Never mind if I did," he blazed out; "and hold your tongue."

The poor little wife coloured at this, and, drawing her handkerchief from her pocket, shed a few tears. No one noticed her. Evie was scowling like an angry boy. The two men were gradually assuming the manner of the committee-room. They were both at their best when serving on committees. They did not make the mistake of handling human affairs in the bulk, but disposed of them item by item, sharply. Calligraphy was the item before them now, and on it they turned their well-trained brains. Charles, after a little demur, accepted the writing as genuine, and they passed on to the next point. It is the best--perhaps the only--way of dodging emotion. They were the average human article, and had they considered the note as a whole it would have driven them miserable or mad. Considered item by item, the emotional content was minimized, and all went forward smoothly. The clock ticked, the coals blazed higher, and contended with the white radiance that poured in through the windows. Unnoticed, the sun occupied his sky, and the shadows of the tree stems, extraordinarily solid, fell like trenches of purple across the frosted lawn. It was a glorious winter morning. Evie's fox terrier, who had passed for white, was only a dirty grey dog now, so intense was the purity that surrounded him. He was discredited, but the blackbirds that he was chasing glowed with Arabian darkness, for all the conventional colouring of life had been altered. Inside, the clock struck ten with a rich and confident note. Other clocks confirmed it, and the discussion moved towards its close.

To follow it is unnecessary. It is rather a moment when the commentator should step forward. Ought the Wilcoxes to have offered their home to Margaret? I think not. The appeal was too flimsy. It was not legal; it had been written in illness, and under the spell of a sudden friendship; it was contrary to the dead woman's intentions in the past, contrary to her very nature, so far as that nature was understood by them. To them Howards End was a house: they could not know that to her it had been a spirit, for which she sought a spiritual heir. And--pushing one step farther in these mists--may they not have decided even better than they supposed? Is it credible that the possessions of the spirit can be bequeathed at all? Has the soul offspring? A wych-elm tree, a vine, a wisp of hay with dew on it--can passion for such things be transmitted where there is no bond of blood? No; the Wilcoxes are not to be blamed. The problem is too terrific, and they could not even perceive a problem. No; it is natural and fitting that after due debate they should tear the note up and throw it on to their dining-room fire. The practical moralist may acquit them absolutely. He who strives to look deeper may acquit them--almost. For one hard fact remains. They did neglect a personal appeal. The woman who had died did say to them, "Do this," and they answered, "We will not."

The incident made a most painful impression on them. Grief mounted into the brain and worked there disquietingly. Yesterday they had lamented: "She was a dear mother, a true wife: in our absence she neglected her health and died." Today they thought: "She was not as true, as dear, as we supposed." The desire for a more inward light had found expression at last, the unseen had impacted on the seen, and all that they could say was "Treachery." Mrs. Wilcox had been treacherous to the family, to the laws of property, to her own written word. How did she expect Howards End to be conveyed to Miss Schlegel? Was her husband, to whom it legally belonged, to make it over to her as a free gift? Was the said Miss Schlegel to have a life interest in it, or to own it absolutely? Was there to be no compensation for the garage and other improvements that they had made under the assumption that all would be theirs some day? Treacherous! treacherous and absurd! When we think the dead both treacherous and absurd, we have gone far towards reconciling ourselves to their departure. That note, scribbled in pencil, sent through the matron, was unbusinesslike as well as cruel, and decreased at once the value of the woman who had written it.

"Ah, well!" said Mr. Wilcox, rising from the table. "I shouldn't have thought it possible."

"Mother couldn't have meant it," said Evie, still frowning.

"No, my girl, of course not."

"Mother believed so in ancestors too--it isn't like her to leave anything to an outsider, who'd never appreciate. "

"The whole thing is unlike her," he announced. "If Miss Schlegel had been poor, if she had wanted a house, I could understand it a little. But she has a house of her own. Why should she want another? She wouldn't have any use of Howards End."

"That time may prove," murmured Charles.

"How?" asked his sister.

"Presumably she knows--mother will have told her. She got twice or three times into the nursing home. Presumably she is awaiting developments."

"What a horrid woman!" And Dolly, who had recovered, cried, "Why, she may be coming down to turn us out now!"

Charles put her right. "I wish she would," he said ominously. "I could then deal with her."

"So could I," echoed his father, who was feeling rather in the cold. Charles had been kind in undertaking the funeral arrangements and in telling him to eat his breakfast, but the boy as he grew up was a little dictatorial, and assumed the post of chairman too readily. "I could deal with her, if she comes, but she won't come. You're all a bit hard on Miss Schlegel."

"That Paul business was pretty scandalous, though."

"I want no more of the Paul business, Charles, as I said at the time, and besides, it is quite apart from this business. Margaret Schlegel has been officious and tiresome during this terrible week, and we have all suffered under her, but upon my soul she's honest. She's not in collusion with the matron. I'm absolutely certain of it. Nor was she with the doctor. I'm equally certain of that. She did not hide anything from us, for up to that very afternoon she was as ignorant as we are. She, like ourselves, was a dupe--" He stopped for a moment. "You see, Charles, in her terrible pain your poor mother put us all in false positions. Paul would not have left England, you would not have gone to Italy, nor Evie and I into Yorkshire, if only we had known. Well, Miss Schlegel's position has been equally false. Take all in all, she has not come out of it badly."

Evie said: "But those chrysanthemums--"

"Or coming down to the funeral at all--" echoed Dolly.

"Why shouldn't she come down? She had the right to, and she stood far back among the Hilton women. The flowers--certainly we should not have sent such flowers, but they may have seemed the right thing to her, Evie, and for all you know they may be the custom in Germany. "

"Oh, I forget she isn't really English," cried Evie. "That would explain a lot."

"She's a cosmopolitan," said Charles, looking at his watch. "I admit I'm rather down on cosmopolitans. My fault, doubtless. I cannot stand them, and a German cosmopolitan is the limit. I think that's about all, isn't it? I want to run down and see Chalkeley. A bicycle will do. And, by the way, I wish you'd speak to Crane some time. I'm certain he's had my new car out."

"Has he done it any harm?"

"No."

"In that case I shall let it pass. It's not worth while having a row."

Charles and his father sometimes disagreed. But they always parted with an increased regard for one another, and each desired no doughtier comrade when it was necessary to voyage for a little past the emotions. So the sailors of Ulysses voyaged past the Sirens, having first stopped one another's ears with wool.

Chapter 12

Charles need not have been anxious. Miss Schlegel had never heard of his mother's strange request. She was to hear of it in after years, when she had built up her life differently, and it was to fit into position as the headstone of the corner. Her mind was bent on other questions now, and by her also it would have been rejected as the fantasy of an invalid.

She was parting from these Wilcoxes for the second time. Paul and his mother, ripple and great wave, had flowed into her life and ebbed out of it for ever. The ripple had left no traces behind: the wave had strewn at her feet fragments torn from the unknown. A curious seeker, she stood for a while at the verge of the sea that tells so little, but tells a little, and watched the outgoing of this last tremendous tide. Her friend had vanished in agony, but not, she believed, in degradation. Her withdrawal had hinted at other things besides disease and pain. Some leave our life with tears, others with an insane frigidity; Mrs. Wilcox had taken the middle course, which only rarer natures can pursue. She had kept proportion. She had told a little of her grim secret to her friends, but not too much; she had shut up her heart--almost, but not entirely. It is thus, if there is any rule, that we ought to die--neither as victim nor as fanatic, but as the seafarer who can greet with an equal eye the deep that he is entering, and the shore that he must leave.

The last word--whatever it would be--had certainly not been said in Hilton churchyard. She had not died there. A funeral is not death, any more than baptism is birth or marriage union. All three are the clumsy devices, coming now too late, now too early, by which Society would register the quick motions of man. In Margaret's eyes Mrs. Wilcox had escaped registration. She had gone out of life vividly, her own way, and no dust was so truly dust as the contents of that heavy coffin, lowered with ceremonial until it rested on the dust of the earth, no flowers so utterly wasted as the chrysanthemums that the frost must have withered before morning. Margaret had once said she "loved superstition." It was not true. Few women had tried more earnestly to pierce the accretions in which body and soul are enwrapped. The death of Mrs. Wilcox had helped her in her work. She saw a little more clearly than hitherto what a human being is, and to what he may aspire. Truer relationships gleamed. Perhaps the last word would be hope--hope even on this side of the grave.

Meanwhile, she could take an interest in the survivors. In spite of her Christmas duties, in spite of her brother, the Wilcoxes continued to play a considerable part in her thoughts. She had seen so much of them in the final week. They were not "her sort," they were often suspicious and stupid, and deficient where she excelled; but collision with them stimulated her, and she felt an interest that verged into liking, even for Charles. She desired to protect them, and often felt that they could protect her, excelling where she was deficient. Once past the rocks of emotion, they knew so well what to do, whom to send for; their hands were on all the ropes, they had grit as well as grittiness, and she valued grit enormously. They led a life that she could not attain to--the outer life of "telegrams and anger," which had detonated when Helen and Paul had touched in June, and had detonated again the other week. To Margaret this life was to remain a real force. She could not despise it, as Helen and Tibby affected to do. It fostered such virtues as neatness, decision, and obedience, virtues of the second rank, no doubt, but they have formed our civilization. They form character, too; Margaret could not doubt it: they keep the soul from becoming sloppy. How dare Schlegels despise Wilcoxes, when it takes all sorts to make a world?

"Don't brood too much," she wrote to Helen, "on the superiority of the unseen to the seen. It's true, but to brood on it is mediaeval. Our business is not to contrast the two, but to reconcile them."

Helen replied that she had no intention of brooding on such a dull subject. What did her sister take her for? The weather was magnificent. She and the Mosebachs had gone tobogganing on the only hill that Pomerania boasted. It was fun, but overcrowded, for the rest of Pomerania had gone there too. Helen loved the country, and her letter glowed with physical exercise and poetry. She spoke of the scenery, quiet, yet august; of the snow-clad fields, with their scampering herds of deer; of the river and its quaint entrance into the Baltic Sea; of the Oderberge, only three hundred feet high, from which one slid all too quickly back into the Pomeranian plains, and yet these Oderberge were real mountains, with pine-forests, streams, and views complete. "It isn't size that counts so much as the way things are arranged." In another paragraph she referred to Mrs. Wilcox sympathetically, but the news had not bitten into her. She had not realized the accessories of death, which are in a sense more memorable than death itself. The atmosphere of precautions and recriminations, and in the midst a human body growing more vivid because it was in pain; the end of that body in Hilton churchyard; the survival of something that suggested hope, vivid in its turn against life's workaday cheerfulness;--all these were lost to Helen, who only felt that a pleasant lady could now be pleasant no longer. She returned to Wickham Place full of her own affairs--she had had another proposal--and Margaret, after a moment's hesitation, was content that this should be so.

The proposal had not been a serious matter. It was the work of Fräulein Mosebach, who had conceived the large and patriotic notion of winning back her cousins to the Fatherland by matrimony. England had played Paul Wilcox, and lost; Germany played Herr Förstmeister someone--Helen could not remember his name.

Herr Förstmeister lived in a wood, and standing on the summit of the Oderberge, he had pointed out his house to Helen, or rather, had pointed out the wedge of pines in which it lay. She had exclaimed, "Oh, how lovely! That's the place for me!" and in the evening Frieda appeared in her bedroom. "I have a message, dear Helen," etc., and so she had, but had been very nice when Helen laughed; quite understood--a forest too solitary and damp--quite agreed, but Herr Förstmeister believed he had assurance to the contrary. Germany had lost, but with good-humour; holding the manhood of the world, she felt bound to win. "And there will even be someone for Tibby," concluded Helen. "There now, Tibby, think of that; Frieda is saving up a little girl for you, in pig-tails and white worsted stockings, but the feet of the stockings are pink, as if the little girl had trodden in strawberries. I've talked too much. My head aches. Now you talk."

Tibby consented to talk. He too was full of his own affairs, for he had just been up to try for a scholarship at Oxford. The men were down, and the candidates had been housed in various colleges, and had dined in hall. Tibby was sensitive to beauty, the experience was new, and he gave a description of his visit that was almost glowing. The august and mellow University, soaked with the richness of the western counties that it has served for a thousand years, appealed at once to the boy's taste: it was the kind of thing he could understand, and he understood it all the better because it was empty. Oxford is--Oxford: not a mere receptacle for youth, like Cambridge. Perhaps it wants its inmates to love it rather than to love one another: such at all events was to be its effect on Tibby. His sisters sent him there that he might make friends, for they knew that his education had been cranky, and had severed him from other boys and men. He made no friends. His Oxford remained Oxford empty, and he took into life with him, not the memory of a radiance, but the memory of a colour scheme.

It pleased Margaret to hear her brother and sister talking. They did not get on overwell as a rule. For a few moments she listened to them, feeling elderly and benign. Then something occurred to her, and she interrupted:

"Helen, I told you about poor Mrs. Wilcox; that sad business?"

"Yes."

"I have had a correspondence with her son. He was winding up the estate, and wrote to ask me whether his mother had wanted me to have anything. I thought it good of him, considering I knew her so little. I said that she had once spoken of giving me a Christmas present, but we both forgot about it afterwards."

"I hope Charles took the hint."

"Yes--that is to say, her husband wrote later on, and thanked me for being a little kind to her, and actually gave me her silver vinaigrette. Don't you think that is extraordinarily generous? It has made me like him very much. He hopes that this will not be the end of our acquaintance, but that you and I will go and stop with Evie some time in the future. I like Mr. Wilcox. He is taking up his work--rubber--it is a big business. I gather he is launching out rather. Charles is in it, too. Charles is married--a pretty little creature, but she doesn't seem wise. They took on the flat, but now they have gone off to a house of their own."

Helen, after a decent pause, continued her account of Stettin. How quickly a situation changes! In June she had been in a crisis; even in November she could blush and be unnatural; now it was January, and the whole affair lay forgotten. Looking back on the past six months, Margaret realized the chaotic nature of our daily life, and its difference from the orderly sequence that has been fabricated by historians. Actual life is full of false clues and sign-posts that lead nowhere. With infinite effort we nerve ourselves for a crisis that never comes. The most successful career must show a waste of strength that might have removed mountains, and the most unsuccessful is not that of the man who is taken unprepared, but of him who has prepared and is never taken. On a tragedy of that kind our national morality is duly silent. It assumes that preparation against danger is in itself a good, and that men, like nations, are the better for staggering through life fully armed. The tragedy of preparedness has scarcely been handled, save by the Greeks. Life is indeed dangerous, but not in the way morality would have us believe. It is indeed unmanageable, but the essence of it is not a battle. It is unmanageable because it is a romance, and its essence is romantic beauty.

Margaret hoped that for the future she would be less cautious, not more cautious, than she had been in the past.

Chapter 13

Over two years passed, and the Schlegel household continued to lead its life of cultured but not ignoble ease, still swimming gracefully on the grey tides of London. Concerts and plays swept past them, money had been spent and renewed, reputations won and lost, and the city herself, emblematic of their lives, rose and fell in a continual flux, while her shallows washed more widely against the hills of Surrey and over the fields of Hertfordshire. This famous building had arisen, that was doomed. Today Whitehall had been transformed: it would be the turn of Regent Street tomorrow. And month by month the roads smelt more strongly of petrol, and were more difficult to cross, and human beings heard each other speak with greater difficulty, breathed less of the air, and saw less of the sky. Nature withdrew: the leaves were falling by midsummer; the sun shone through dirt with an admired obscurity.

To speak against London is no longer fashionable. The Earth as an artistic cult has had its day, and the literature of the near future will probably ignore the country and seek inspiration from the town. One can understand the reaction. Of Pan and the elemental forces, the public has heard a little too much--they seem Victorian, while London is Georgian--and those who care for the earth with sincerity may wait long ere the pendulum swings back to her again. Certainly London fascinates. One visualizes it as a tract of quivering grey, intelligent without purpose, and excitable without love; as a spirit that has altered before it can be chronicled; as a heart that certainly beats, but with no pulsation of humanity. It lies beyond everything: Nature, with all her cruelty, comes nearer to us than do these crowds of men. A friend explains himself: the earth is explicable--from her we came, and we must return to her. But who can explain Westminster Bridge Road or Liverpool Street in the morning--the city inhaling--or the same thoroughfares in the evening--the city exhaling her exhausted air? We reach in desperation beyond the fog, beyond the very stars, the voids of the universe are ransacked to justify the monster, and stamped with a human face. London is religion's opportunity--not the decorous religion of theologians, but anthropomorphic, crude. Yes, the continuous flow would be tolerable if a man of our own sort--not anyone pompous or tearful--were caring for us up in the sky.

The Londoner seldom understands his city until it sweeps him, too, away from his moorings, and Margaret's eyes were not opened until the lease of Wickham

Place expired. She had always known that it must expire, but the knowledge only became vivid about nine months before the event. Then the house was suddenly ringed with pathos. It had seen so much happiness. Why had it to be swept away? In the streets of the city she noted for the first time the architecture of hurry, and heard the language of hurry on the mouths of its inhabitants--clipped words, formless sentences, potted expressions of approval or disgust. Month by month things were stepping livelier, but to what goal? The population still rose, but what was the quality of the men born? The particular millionaire who owned the freehold of Wickham Place, and desired to erect Babylonian flats upon it--what right had he to stir so large a portion of the quivering jelly? He was not a fool--she had heard him expose Socialism--but true insight began just where his intelligence ended, and one gathered that this was the case with most millionaires. What right had such men--But Margaret checked herself. That way lies madness. Thank goodness she, too, had some money, and could purchase a new home.

Tibby, now in his second year at Oxford, was down for the Easter vacation, and Margaret took the opportunity of having a serious talk with him. Did he at all know where he wanted to live? Tibby didn't know that he did know. Did he at all know what he wanted to do? He was equally uncertain, but when pressed remarked that he should prefer to be quite free of any profession. Margaret was not shocked, but went on sewing for a few minutes before she replied:

"I was thinking of Mr. Vyse. He never strikes me as particularly happy."

"Ye-es," said Tibby, and then held his mouth open in a curious quiver, as if he, too, had thoughts of Mr. Vyse, had seen round, through, over, and beyond Mr. Vyse, had weighed Mr. Vyse, grouped him, and finally dismissed him as having no possible bearing on the subject under discussion. That bleat of Tibby's infuriated Helen. But Helen was now down in the dining-room preparing a speech about political economy. At times her voice could be heard declaiming through the floor.

"But Mr. Vyse is rather a wretched, weedy man, don't you think? Then there's Guy. That was a pitiful business. Besides"--shifting to the general--" every one is the better for some regular work."

Groans.

"I shall stick to it," she continued, smiling. "I am not saying it to educate you; it is what I really think. I believe that in the last century men have developed the desire for work, and they must not starve it. It's a new desire. It goes with a great deal that's bad, but in itself it's good, and I hope that for women, too, 'not to work' will soon become as shocking as 'not to be married' was a hundred years ago."

"I have no experience of this profound desire to which you allude," enunciated Tibby.

"Then we'll leave the subject till you do. I'm not going to rattle you round. Take your time. Only do think over the lives of the men you like most, and see how they've arranged them."

"I like Guy and Mr. Vyse most," said Tibby faintly, and leant so far back in his chair that he extended in a horizontal line from knees to throat.

"And don't think I'm not serious because I don't use the traditional arguments--making money, a sphere awaiting you, and so on--all of which are, for various reasons, cant." She sewed on. "I'm only your sister. I haven't any authority over you, and I don't want to have any. Just to put before you what I think the truth. You see"--she shook off the pince-nez to which she had recently taken--"in a few years we shall be the same age practically, and I shall want you to help me. Men are so much nicer than women."

"Labouring under such a delusion, why do you not marry?"

"I sometimes jolly well think I would if I got the chance."

"Has nobody arst you?"

"Only ninnies."

"Do people ask Helen?"

"Plentifully."

"Tell me about them."

"No."

"Tell me about your ninnies, then."

"They were men who had nothing better to do," said his sister, feeling that she was entitled to score this point. "So take warning: you must work, or else you must pretend to work, which is what I do. Work, work, work if you'd save your soul and your body. It is honestly a necessity, dear boy. Look at the Wilcoxes, look at Mr. Pembroke. With all their defects of temper and understanding, such men give me more pleasure than many who are better equipped and I think it is because they have worked regularly and honestly.

"Spare me the Wilcoxes," he moaned.

"I shall not. They are the right sort."

"Oh, goodness me, Meg!" he protested, suddenly sitting up, alert and angry. Tibby, for all his defects, had a genuine personality.

"Well, they're as near the right sort as you can imagine."

"No, no--oh, no!"

"I was thinking of the younger son, whom I once classed as a ninny, but who came back so ill from Nigeria. He's gone out there again, Evie Wilcox tells me--out to his duty."

"Duty" always elicited a groan.

"He doesn't want the money, it is work he wants, though it is beastly work--dull country, dishonest natives, an eternal fidget over fresh water and food. A nation who can produce men of that sort may well be proud. No wonder England has become an Empire."

"*Empire!*"

"I can't bother over results," said Margaret, a little sadly. "They are too difficult for me. I can only look at the men. An Empire bores me, so far, but I can appreciate the heroism that builds it up. London bores me, but what thousands of splendid people are labouring to make London--"

"What it is," he sneered.

"What it is, worse luck. I want activity without civilization. How paradoxical! Yet I expect that is what we shall find in heaven."

"And I," said Tibby, "want civilization without activity, which, I expect, is what we shall find in the other place."

"You needn't go as far as the other place, Tibbi-kins, if you want that. You can find it at Oxford."

"Stupid--"

"If I'm stupid, get me back to the house-hunting. I'll even live in Oxford if you like--North Oxford. I'll live anywhere except Bournemouth, Torquay, and Cheltenham. Oh yes, or Ilfracombe and Swanage and Tunbridge Wells and Surbiton and Bedford. There on no account."

"London, then."

"I agree, but Helen rather wants to get away from London. However, there's no reason we shouldn't have a house in the country and also a flat in town, provided we all stick together and contribute. Though of course--Oh, how one does maunder on, and to think, to think of the people who are really poor. How do they live? Not to move about the world would kill me."

As she spoke, the door was flung open, and Helen burst in in a state of extreme excitement.

"Oh, my dears, what do you think? You'll never guess. A woman's been here asking me for her husband. Her *what?*" (Helen was fond of supplying her own surprise.) "Yes, for her husband, and it really is so."

"Not anything to do with Bracknell?" cried Margaret, who had lately taken on an unemployed of that name to clean the knives and boots.

"I offered Bracknell, and he was rejected. So was Tibby. (Cheer up, Tibby!) It's no one we know. I said, 'Hunt, my good woman; have a good look round, hunt under the tables, poke up the chimney, shake out the antimacassars. Husband? husband?' Oh, and she so magnificently dressed and tinkling like a chandelier."

"Now, Helen, what did happen really?"

"What I say. I was, as it were, orating my speech. Annie opens the door like a fool, and shows a female straight in on me, with my mouth open. Then we began--very civilly. 'I want my husband, what I have reason to believe is here.' No--how unjust one is. She said 'whom,' not 'what.' She got it perfectly. So I said, 'Name, please?' and she said, 'Lan, Miss,' and there we were.

"Lan?"

"Lan or Len. We were not nice about our vowels. Lanoline."

"But what an extraordinary--"

"I said, 'My good Mrs. Lanoline, we have some grave misunderstanding here. Beautiful as I am, my modesty is even more remarkable than my beauty, and never, never has Mr. Lanoline rested his eyes on mine.'"

"I hope you were pleased," said Tibby.

"Of course," Helen squeaked. "A perfectly delightful experience. Oh, Mrs. Lanoline's a dear--she asked for a husband as if he was an umbrella. She mislaid him Saturday afternoon--and for a long time suffered no inconvenience. But all night, and all this morning her apprehensions grew. Breakfast didn't seem the same--no, no more did lunch, and so she strolled up to 2, Wickham Place as being the most likely place for the missing article."

"But how on earth--"

"Don't begin how on earthing. 'I know what I know,' she kept repeating, not uncivilly, but with extreme gloom. In vain I asked her what she did know. Some knew what others knew, and others didn't, and if they didn't, then others again had better be careful. Oh dear, she was incompetent! She had a face like a silkworm, and the dining-room reeks of orris-root. We chatted pleasantly a little about husbands, and I wondered where hers was too, and advised her to go to the police. She thanked me. We agreed that Mr. Lanoline's a notty, notty man, and hasn't no business to go on the lardy-da. But I think she suspected me up to the last. Bags I writing to Aunt Juley about this. Now, Meg, remember--bags I."

"Bag it by all means," murmured Margaret, putting down her work. "I'm not sure that this is so funny, Helen. It means some horrible volcano smoking somewhere, doesn't it?"

"I don't think so--she doesn't really mind. The admirable creature isn't capable of tragedy."

"Her husband may be, though," said Margaret, moving to the window.

"Oh, no, not likely. No one capable of tragedy could have married Mrs. Lanoline."

"Was she pretty?"

"Her figure may have been good once."

The flats, their only outlook, hung like an ornate curtain between Margaret and the welter of London. Her thoughts turned sadly to house-hunting. Wickham Place had been so safe. She feared, fantastically, that her own little flock might be moving into turmoil and squalor, into nearer contact with such episodes as these.

"Tibby and I have again been wondering where we'll live next September," she said at last.

"Tibby had better first wonder what he'll do," retorted Helen; and that topic was resumed, but with acrimony. Then tea came, and after tea Helen went on preparing her speech, and Margaret prepared one, too, for they were going out to a discussion society on the morrow. But her thoughts were poisoned. Mrs. Lanoline had risen out of the abyss, like a faint smell, a goblin football, telling of a life where love and hatred had both decayed.

Chapter 14

The mystery, like so many mysteries, was explained. Next day, just as they were dressed to go out to dinner, a Mr. Bast called. He was a clerk in the employment of the Porphyrion Fire Insurance Company. Thus much from his card. He had come "about the lady yesterday." Thus much from Annie, who had shown him into the dining-room.

"Cheers, children!" cried Helen. "It's Mrs. Lanoline."

Tibby was interested. The three hurried downstairs, to find, not the gay dog they expected, but a young man, colourless, toneless, who had already the mournful eyes above a drooping moustache that are so common in London, and that haunt some streets of the city like accusing presences. One guessed him as the third generation, grandson to the shepherd or ploughboy whom civilization had sucked into the town; as one of the thousands who have lost the life of the body and failed to reach the life of the spirit. Hints of robustness survived in him, more than a hint of primitive good looks, and Margaret, noting the spine that might have been straight, and the chest that might have broadened, wondered whether it paid to give up the glory of the animal for a tail coat and a couple of ideas. Culture had worked in her own case, but during the last few weeks she had doubted whether it humanized the majority, so wide and so widening is the gulf that stretches between the natural and the philosophic man, so many the good chaps who are wrecked in trying to cross it. She knew this type very well--the vague aspirations, the mental dishonesty, the familiarity with the outsides of books. She knew the very tones in which he would address her. She was only unprepared for an example of her own visiting-card.

"You wouldn't remember giving me this, Miss Schlegel?" said he, uneasily familiar.

"No; I can't say I do."

"Well, that was how it happened, you see."

"Where did we meet, Mr. Bast? For the minute I don't remember."

"It was a concert at the Queen's Hall. I think you will recollect," he added pretentiously, "when I tell you that it included a performance of the Fifth Symphony of Beethoven."

"We hear the Fifth practically every time it's done, so I'm not sure--do you remember, Helen?"

"Was it the time the sandy cat walked round the balustrade?"

He thought not.

"Then I don't remember. That's the only Beethoven I ever remember specially."

"And you, if I may say so, took away my umbrella, inadvertently of course."

"Likely enough," Helen laughed, "for I steal umbrellas even oftener than I hear Beethoven. Did you get it back?"

"Yes, thank you, Miss Schlegel."

"The mistake arose out of my card, did it?" interposed Margaret.

"Yes, the mistake arose--it was a mistake."

"The lady who called here yesterday thought that you were calling too, and that she could find you?" she continued, pushing him forward, for, though he had promised an explanation, he seemed unable to give one.

"That's so, calling too--a mistake."

"Then why--?" began Helen, but Margaret laid a hand on her arm.

"I said to my wife," he continued more rapidly--"I said to Mrs. Bast, 'I have to pay a call on some friends,' and Mrs. Bast said to me, 'Do go.' While I was gone, however, she wanted me on important business, and thought I had come here, owing to the card, and so came after me, and I beg to tender my apologies, and hers as well, for any inconvenience we may have inadvertently caused you."

"No inconvenience," said Helen; "but I still don't understand."

An air of evasion characterized Mr. Bast. He explained again, but was obviously lying, and Helen didn't see why he should get off. She had the cruelty of youth. Neglecting her sister's pressure, she said, "I still don't understand. When did you say you paid this call?"

"Call? What call?" said he, staring as if her question had been a foolish one, a favourite device of those in mid-stream.

"This afternoon call."

"In the afternoon, of course!" he replied, and looked at Tibby to see how the repartee went. But Tibby, himself a repartee, was unsympathetic, and said, "Saturday afternoon or Sunday afternoon?"

"S-Saturday."

"Really!" said Helen; "and you were still calling on Sunday, when your wife came here. A long visit."

"I don't call that fair," said Mr. Bast, going scarlet and handsome. There was fight in his eyes." I know what you mean, and it isn't so."

"Oh, don't let us mind," said Margaret, distressed again by odours from the abyss.

"It was something else," he asserted, his elaborate manner breaking down. "I was somewhere else to what you think, so there!"

"It was good of you to come and explain," she said. "The rest is naturally no concern of ours."

"Yes, but I want--I wanted--have you ever read *The Ordeal of Richard Feverel?*"

Margaret nodded.

"It's a beautiful book. I wanted to get back to the Earth, don't you see, like Richard does in the end. Or have you ever read Stevenson's *Prince Otto?*"

Helen and Tibby groaned gently.

"That's another beautiful book. You get back to the Earth in that. I wanted--" He mouthed affectedly. Then through the mists of his culture came a hard fact, hard as a pebble. "I walked all the Saturday night," said Leonard. "I walked." A thrill of approval ran through the sisters. But culture closed in again. He asked whether they had ever read E. V. Lucas's *Open Road.*

Said Helen, "No doubt it's another beautiful book, but I'd rather hear about your road."

"Oh, I walked."

"How far?"

"I don't know, nor for how long. It got too dark to see my watch."

"Were you walking alone, may I ask?"

"Yes," he said, straightening himself; "but we'd been talking it over at the office. There's been a lot of talk at the office lately about these things. The fellows there said one steers by the Pole Star, and I looked it up in the celestial atlas, but once out of doors everything gets so mixed--"

"Don't talk to me about the Pole Star," interrupted Helen, who was becoming interested. "I know its little ways. It goes round and round, and you go round after it."

"Well, I lost it entirely. First of all the street lamps, then the trees, and towards morning it got cloudy."

Tibby, who preferred his comedy undiluted, slipped from the room. He knew that this fellow would never attain to poetry, and did not want to hear him trying. Margaret and Helen remained. Their brother influenced them more than they knew: in his absence they were stirred to enthusiasm more easily.

"Where did you start from?" cried Margaret. "Do tell us more."

"I took the Underground to Wimbledon. As I came out of the office I said to myself, 'I must have a walk once in a way. If I don't take this walk now, I shall never take it.' I had a bit of dinner at Wimbledon, and then--"

"But not good country there, is it?"

"It was gas-lamps for hours. Still, I had all the night, and being out was the great thing. I did get into woods, too, presently."

"Yes, go on," said Helen.

"You've no idea how difficult uneven ground is when it's dark."

"Did you actually go off the roads?"

"Oh yes. I always meant to go off the roads, but the worst of it is that it's more difficult to find one's way."

"Mr. Bast, you're a born adventurer," laughed Margaret. "No professional athlete would have attempted what you've done. It's a wonder your walk didn't end in a broken neck. Whatever did your wife say?"

"Professional athletes never move without lanterns and compasses," said Helen. "Besides, they can't walk. It tires them. Go on."

"I felt like R. L. S. You probably remember how in *Virginibus*--"

"Yes, but the wood. This 'ere wood. How did you get out of it?"

"I managed one wood, and found a road the other side which went a good bit uphill. I rather fancy it was those North Downs, for the road went off into grass, and I got into another wood. That was awful, with gorse bushes. I did wish I'd never come, but suddenly it got light--just while I seemed going under one tree. Then I found a road down to a station, and took the first train I could back to London."

"But was the dawn wonderful?" asked Helen.

With unforgettable sincerity he replied, "No." The word flew again like a pebble from the sling. Down toppled all that had seemed ignoble or literary in his talk, down toppled tiresome R. L. S. and the "love of the earth" and his silk top-hat. In the presence of these women Leonard had arrived, and he spoke with a flow, an exultation, that he had seldom known.

"The dawn was only grey, it was nothing to mention--"

"Just a grey evening turned upside down. I know."

"--and I was too tired to lift up my head to look at it, and so cold too. I'm glad I did it, and yet at the time it bored me more than I can say. And besides--you can believe me or not as you choose--I was very hungry. That dinner at Wimbledon--I meant it to last me all night like other dinners. I never thought that walking would make such a difference. Why, when you're walking you want, as it were, a breakfast and luncheon and tea during the night as well, and I'd nothing but a packet of Woodbines. Lord, I did feel bad! Looking back, it wasn't what you may call enjoyment. It was more a case of sticking to it. I did stick. I--I was determined. Oh, hang it all! what's the good--I mean, the good of living in a room for ever? There one goes on day after day, same old game, same up and down to town, until you forget there is any other game. You ought to see once in a way what's going on outside, if it's only nothing particular after all."

"I should just think you ought," said Helen, sitting on the edge of the table.

The sound of a lady's voice recalled him from sincerity, and he said: "Curious it should all come about from reading something of Richard Jefferies."

"Excuse me, Mr. Bast, but you're wrong there. It didn't. It came from something far greater."

But she could not stop him. Borrow was imminent after Jefferies--Borrow, Thoreau, and sorrow. R. L. S. brought up the rear, and the outburst ended in a swamp of books. No disrespect to these great names. The fault is ours, not theirs. They mean us to use them for sign-posts, and are not to blame if, in our weakness, we mistake the sign-post for the destination. And Leonard had reached the destination. He had visited the county of Surrey when darkness covered its amenities, and its cosy villas had re-entered ancient night. Every twelve hours this miracle happens, but he had troubled to go and see for himself. Within his cramped little mind dwelt something that was greater than Jefferies' books--the spirit that led Jefferies to write them; and his dawn, though revealing nothing but monotones, was part of the eternal sunrise that shows George Borrow Stonehenge.

"Then you don't think I was foolish?" he asked, becoming again the naïve and sweet-tempered boy for whom Nature had intended him.

"Heavens, no!" replied Margaret.

"Heaven help us if we do!" replied Helen.

"I'm very glad you say that. Now, my wife would never understand--not if I explained for days."

"No, it wasn't foolish!" cried Helen, her eyes aflame. "You've pushed back the boundaries; I think it splendid of you."

"You've not been content to dream as we have--"

"Though we have walked, too--"

"I must show you a picture upstairs--"

Here the door-bell rang. The hansom had come to take them to their evening party.

"Oh, bother, not to say dash--I had forgotten we were dining out; but do, do, come round again and have a talk."

"Yes, you must--do," echoed Margaret.

Leonard, with extreme sentiment, replied: "No, I shall not. It's better like this."

"Why better?" asked Margaret.

"No, it is better not to risk a second interview. I shall always look back on this talk with you as one of the finest things in my life. Really. I mean this. We can never repeat. It has done me real good, and there we had better leave it."

"That's rather a sad view of life, surely."

"Things so often get spoiled."

"I know," flashed Helen, "but people don't."

He could not understand this. He continued in a vein which mingled true imagination and false. What he said wasn't wrong, but it wasn't right, and a false note jarred. One little twist, they felt, and the instrument might be in tune. One little strain, and it might be silent for ever. He thanked the ladies very much, but he would not call again. There was a moment's awkwardness, and then Helen said: "Go, then; perhaps you know best; but never forget you're better than Jefferies." And he went. Their hansom caught him up at the corner, passed with a waving of hands, and vanished with its accomplished load into the evening.

London was beginning to illuminate herself against the night. Electric lights sizzled and jagged in the main thoroughfares, gas-lamps in the side streets glimmered a canary gold or green. The sky was a crimson battlefield of spring, but London was not afraid. Her smoke mitigated the splendour, and the clouds down Oxford Street were a delicately painted ceiling, which adorned while it did not distract. She has never known the clear-cut armies of the purer air. Leonard hurried through her tinted wonders, very much part of the picture. His was a grey life, and to brighten it he had ruled off a few corners for romance. The Miss

Schlegels--or, to speak more accurately, his interview with them--were to fill such a corner, nor was it by any means the first time that he had talked intimately to strangers. The habit was analogous to a debauch, an outlet, though the worst of outlets, for instincts that would not be denied. Terrifying him, it would beat down his suspicions and prudence until he was confiding secrets to people whom he had scarcely seen. It brought him many fears and some pleasant memories. Perhaps the keenest happiness he had ever known was during a railway journey to Cambridge, where a decent-mannered undergraduate had spoken to him. They had got into conversation, and gradually Leonard flung reticence aside, told some of his domestic troubles, and hinted at the rest. The undergraduate, supposing they could start a friendship, asked him to "coffee after hall," which he accepted, but afterwards grew shy, and took care not to stir from the commercial hotel where he lodged. He did not want Romance to collide with the Porphyrion, still less with Jacky, and people with fuller, happier lives are slow to understand this. To the Schlegels, as to the undergraduate, he was an interesting creature, of whom they wanted to see more. But they to him were denizens of Romance, who must keep to the corner he had assigned them, pictures that must not walk out of their frames.

His behaviour over Margaret's visiting-card had been typical. His had scarcely been a tragic marriage. Where there is no money and no inclination to violence tragedy cannot be generated. He could not leave his wife, and he did not want to hit her. Petulance and squalor were enough. Here "that card" had come in. Leonard, though furtive, was untidy, and left it lying about. Jacky found it, and then began, "What's that card, eh?" "Yes, don't you wish you knew what that card was?" "Len, who's Miss Schlegel?" etc. Months passed, and the card, now as a joke, now as a grievance, was handed about, getting dirtier and dirtier. It followed them when they moved from Cornelia Road to Tulse Hill. It was submitted to third parties. A few inches of pasteboard, it became the battlefield on which the souls of Leonard and his wife contended. Why did he not say, "A lady took my umbrella, another gave me this that I might call for my umbrella"? Because Jacky would have disbelieved him? Partly, but chiefly because he was sentimental. No affection gathered round the card, but it symbolized the life of culture, that Jacky should never spoil. At night he would say to himself, "Well, at all events, she doesn't know about that card. Yah! done her there!"

Poor Jacky! she was not a bad sort, and had a great deal to bear. She drew her own conclusion--she was only capable of drawing one conclusion--and in the fulness of time she acted upon it. All the Friday Leonard had refused to speak to her, and had spent the evening observing the stars. On the Saturday he went up, as usual, to town, but he came not back Saturday night nor Sunday morning, nor Sunday afternoon. The inconvenience grew intolerable, and though she was now of a retiring habit, and shy of women, she went up to Wickham Place. Leonard returned in her absence. The card, the fatal card, was gone from the pages of Ruskin, and he guessed what had happened.

"Well?" he had exclaimed, greeting her with peals of laughter. "I know where you've been, but you don't know where I've been. "

Jacky sighed, said, "Len, I do think you might explain," and resumed domesticity.

Explanations were difficult at this stage, and Leonard was too silly--or it is tempting to write, too sound a chap to attempt them. His reticence was not entirely the shoddy article that a business life promotes, the reticence that pretends that nothing is something, and hides behind the *Daily Telegraph*. The adventurer, also, is reticent, and it is an adventure for a clerk to walk for a few hours in darkness. You may laugh at him, you who have slept nights on the veldt, with your rifle beside you and all the atmosphere of adventure past. And you also may laugh who think adventures silly. But do not be surprised if Leonard is shy whenever he meets you, and if the Schlegels rather than Jacky hear about the dawn.

That the Schlegels had not thought him foolish became a permanent joy. He was at his best when he thought of them. It buoyed him as he journeyed home beneath fading heavens. Somehow the barriers of wealth had fallen, and there had been--he could not phrase it--a general assertion of the wonder of the world. "My conviction," says the mystic, "gains infinitely the moment another soul will believe in it," and they had agreed that there was something beyond life's daily grey. He took off his top-hat and smoothed it thoughtfully. He had hitherto supposed the unknown to be books, literature, clever conversation, culture. One raised oneself by study, and got upsides with the world. But in that quick interchange a new light dawned. Was that something" walking in the dark among the surburban hills?

He discovered that he was going bareheaded down Regent Street. London came back with a rush. Few were about at this hour, but all whom he passed looked at him with a hostility that was the more impressive because it was unconscious. He put his hat on. It was too big; his head disappeared like a pudding into a basin, the ears bending outwards at the touch of the curly brim. He wore it a little backwards, and its effect was greatly to elongate the face and to bring out the distance between the eyes and the moustache. Thus equipped, he escaped criticism. No one felt uneasy as he titupped along the pavements, the heart of a man ticking fast in his chest.

Chapter 15

The sisters went out to dinner full of their adventure, and when they were both full of the same subject, there were few dinner-parties that could stand up against them. This particular one, which was all ladies, had more kick in it than most, but succumbed after a struggle. Helen at one part of the table, Margaret at the other, would talk of Mr. Bast and of no one else, and somewhere about the entree their monologues collided, fell ruining, and became common property. Nor was this all. The dinner-party was really an informal discussion club; there was a paper after it, read amid coffee-cups and laughter in the drawing-room, but dealing more or less thoughtfully with some topic of general interest. After the paper came a debate, and in this debate Mr. Bast also figured, appearing now as a bright spot in civilization, now as a dark spot, according to the temperament of the speaker. The subject of the paper had been, "How ought I to dispose of my money?" the reader professing to be a millionaire on the point of death, inclined to bequeath her fortune for the foundation of local art galleries, but open to conviction from other sources. The various parts had been assigned beforehand, and some of the speeches were amusing. The hostess assumed the ungrateful role of "the millionaire's eldest son," and implored her expiring parent not to dislocate Society by allowing such vast sums to pass out of the family. Money was the fruit of self-denial, and the second generation had a right to profit by the self-denial of the first. What right had "Mr. Bast" to profit? The National Gallery was good enough for the likes of him. After property had had its say--a saying that is necessarily ungracious--the various philanthropists stepped forward. Something must be done for "Mr. Bast": his conditions must be improved without impairing his independence; he must have a free library, or free tennis-courts; his rent must be paid in such a way that he did not know it was being paid; it must be made worth his while to join the Territorials; he must be forcibly parted from his uninspiring wife, the money going to her as compensation; he must be assigned a Twin Star, some member of the leisured classes who would watch over him ceaselessly (groans from Helen); he must be given food but no clothes, clothes but no food, a third-return ticket to Venice, without either food or clothes when he arrived there. In short, he might be given anything and everything so long as it was not the money itself.

And here Margaret interrupted.

"Order, order, Miss Schlegel!" said the reader of the paper. "You are here, I understand, to advise me in the interests of the Society for the Preservation of Places of Historic Interest or Natural Beauty. I cannot have you speaking out of your role. It makes my poor head go round, and I think you forget that I am very ill."

"Your head won't go round if only you'll listen to my argument," said Margaret. "Why not give him the money itself. You're supposed to have about thirty thousand a year."

"Have I? I thought I had a million."

"Wasn't a million your capital? Dear me! we ought to have settled that. Still, it doesn't matter. Whatever you've got, I order you to give as many poor men as you can three hundred a year each. "

"But that would be pauperizing them," said an earnest girl, who liked the Schlegels, but thought them a little unspiritual at times.

"Not if you gave them so much. A big windfall would not pauperize a man. It is these little driblets, distributed among too many, that do the harm. Money's educational. It's far more educational than the things it buys." There was a protest. "In a sense," added Margaret, but the protest continued. "Well, isn't the most civilized thing going, the man who has learnt to wear his income properly?"

"Exactly what your Mr. Basts won't do."

"Give them a chance. Give them money. Don't dole them out poetry-books and railway-tickets like babies. Give them the wherewithal to buy these things. When your Socialism comes it may be different, and we may think in terms of commodities instead of cash. Till it comes give people cash, for it is the warp of civilization, whatever the woof may be. The imagination ought to play upon money and realize it vividly, for it's the--the second most important thing in the world. It is so sluffed over and hushed up, there is so little clear thinking--oh, political economy, of course, but so few of us think clearly about our own private incomes, and admit that independent thoughts are in nine cases out of ten the result of independent means. Money: give Mr. Bast money, and don't bother about his ideals. He'll pick up those for himself."

She leant back while the more earnest members of the club began to misconstrue her. The female mind, though cruelly practical in daily life, cannot bear to hear ideals belittled in conversation, and Miss Schlegel was asked however she could say such dreadful things, and what it would profit Mr. Bast if he gained the whole world and lost his own soul. She answered, "Nothing, but he would not gain his soul until he had gained a little of the world." Then they said, "No they did not believe it," and she admitted that an overworked clerk may save his soul in the superterrestrial sense, where the effort will be taken for the deed, but she denied that he will ever explore the spiritual resources of this world, will ever know the rarer joys of the body, or attain to clear and passionate intercourse with his fellows. Others had attacked the fabric of Society-Property, Interest, etc.; she only fixed her eyes on a few human beings, to see how, under present conditions, they could be made happier. Doing good to humanity was useless: the many-coloured efforts thereto spreading over the vast area like films and resulting in an universal grey. To do good to one, or, as in this case, to a few, was the utmost she dare hope for.

Between the idealists, and the political economists, Margaret had a bad time. Disagreeing elsewhere, they agreed in disowning her, and in keeping the administration of the millionaire's money in their own hands. The earnest girl brought forward a scheme of "personal supervision and mutual help," the effect of which was to alter poor people until they became exactly like people who were not so poor. The hostess pertinently remarked that she, as eldest son, might surely rank among the millionaire's legatees. Margaret weakly admitted the claim, and another claim was at once set up by Helen, who declared that she had been the millionaire's housemaid for over forty years, overfed and underpaid; was nothing to be done for her, so corpulent and poor? The millionaire then read out her last will and testament, in which she left the whole of her fortune to the Chancellor of the Exchequer. Then she died. The serious parts of the discussion had been of higher merit than the playful--in a men's debate is the reverse more general? --but the meeting broke up hilariously enough, and a dozen happy ladies dispersed to their homes.

Helen and Margaret walked the earnest girl as far as Battersea Bridge Station, arguing copiously all the way. When she had gone they were conscious of an alleviation, and of the great beauty of the evening. They turned back towards Oakley Street. The lamps and the plane-trees, following the line of the embankment, struck a note of dignity that is rare in English cities. The seats, almost deserted, were here and there occupied by gentlefolk in evening dress, who had strolled out from the houses behind to enjoy fresh air and the whisper of the rising tide. There is something continental about Chelsea Embankment. It is an open space used rightly, a blessing more frequent in Germany than here. As Margaret and Helen sat down, the city behind them seemed to be a vast theatre, an opera-house in which some endless trilogy was performing, and they themselves a pair of satisfied subscribers, who did not mind losing a little of the second act.

"Cold?"

"No."

"Tired?"

"Doesn't matter."

The earnest girl's train rumbled away over the bridge.

"I say, Helen--"

"Well?"

"Are we really going to follow up Mr. Bast?"

"I don't know."

"I think we won't."

"As you like."

"It's no good, I think, unless you really mean to know people. The discussion brought that home to me. We got on well enough with him in a spirit of excitement, but think of rational intercourse. We mustn't play at friendship. No, it's no good."

"There's Mrs. Lanoline, too," Helen yawned. "So dull."

"Just so, and possibly worse than dull."

"I should like to know how he got hold of your card."

"But he said--something about a concert and an umbrella--"

"Then did the card see the wife--"

"Helen, come to bed."

"No, just a little longer, it is so beautiful. Tell me; oh yes; did you say money is the warp of the world?"

"Yes."

"Then what's the woof?"

"Very much what one chooses," said Margaret. "It's something that isn't money--one can't say more."

"Walking at night?"

"Probably."

"For Tibby, Oxford?"

"It seems so."

"For you?"

"Now that we have to leave Wickham Place, I begin to think it's that. For Mrs. Wilcox it was certainly Howards End."

One's own name will carry immense distances. Mr. Wilcox, who was sitting with friends many seats away, heard his, rose to his feet, and strolled along towards the speakers.

"It is sad to suppose that places may ever be more important than people," continued Margaret.

"Why, Meg? They're so much nicer generally. I'd rather think of that forester's house in Pomerania than of the fat Herr Förstmeister who lived in it."

"I believe we shall come to care about people less and less, Helen. The more people one knows the easier it becomes to replace them. It's one of the curses of London. I quite expect to end my life caring most for a place."

Here Mr. Wilcox reached them. It was several weeks since they had met.

"How do you do?" he cried. "I thought I recognized your voices. Whatever are you both doing down here?"

His tones were protective. He implied that one ought not to sit out on Chelsea Embankment without a male escort. Helen resented this, but Margaret accepted it as part of the good man's equipment.

"What an age it is since I've seen you, Mr. Wilcox. I met Evie in the Tube, though, lately. I hope you have good news of your son."

"Paul?" said Mr. Wilcox, extinguishing his cigarette, and sitting down between them. "Oh, Paul's all right. We had a line from Madeira. He'll be at work again by now."

"Ugh--" said Helen, shuddering from complex causes.

"I beg your pardon?"

"Isn't the climate of Nigeria too horrible?"

"Someone's got to go," he said simply. "England will never keep her trade overseas unless she is prepared to make sacrifices. Unless we get firm in West Africa, Ger--untold complications may follow. Now tell me all your news."

"Oh, we've had a splendid evening," cried Helen, who always woke up at the advent of a visitor. "We belong to a kind of club that reads papers, Margaret and I--all women, but there is a discussion after. This evening it was on how one ought to leave one's money--whether to one's family, or to the poor, and if so how--oh, most interesting."

The man of business smiled. Since his wife's death he had almost doubled his income. He was an important figure at last, a reassuring name on company prospectuses, and life had treated him very well. The world seemed in his grasp as he listened to the River Thames, which still flowed inland from the sea. So wonderful to the girls, it held no mysteries for him. He had helped to shorten its long tidal trough by taking shares in the lock at Teddington, and if he and other capitalists thought good, some day it could be shortened again. With a good dinner inside him and an amiable but academic woman on either flank, he felt that his hands were on all the ropes of life, and that what he did not know could not be worth knowing.

"Sounds a most original entertainment!" he exclaimed, and laughed in his pleasant way. "I wish Evie would go to that sort of thing. But she hasn't the time. She's taken to breed Aberdeen terriers--jolly little dogs.

"I expect we'd better be doing the same, really."

"We pretend we're improving ourselves, you see," said Helen a little sharply, for the Wilcox glamour is not of the kind that returns, and she had bitter memories of the days when a speech such as he had just made would have impressed her favourably. "We suppose it is a good thing to waste an evening once a fortnight over a debate, but, as my sister says, it may be better to breed dogs."

"Not at all. I don't agree with your sister. There's nothing like a debate to teach one quickness. I often wish I had gone in for them when I was a youngster. It would have helped me no end."

"Quickness--?"

"Yes. Quickness in argument. Time after time I've missed scoring a point because the other man has had the gift of the gab and I haven't. Oh, I believe in these discussions."

The patronizing tone thought Margaret, came well enough from a man who was old enough to be their father. She had always maintained that Mr. Wilcox had a charm. In times of sorrow or emotion his inadequacy had pained her, but it was pleasant to listen to him now, and to watch his thick brown moustache and high forehead confronting the stars. But Helen was nettled. The aim of *their* debates she implied was Truth.

"Oh yes, it doesn't much matter what subject you take," said he.

Margaret laughed and said, "But this is going to be far better than the debate itself." Helen recovered herself and laughed too. "No, I won't go on," she declared. "I'll just put our special case to Mr. Wilcox."

"About Mr. Bast? Yes, do. He'll be more lenient to a special case.

"But, Mr. Wilcox, do first light another cigarette. It's this. We've just come across a young fellow, who's evidently very poor, and who seems interest--"

"What's his profession?"

"Clerk."

"What in?"

"Do you remember, Margaret?"

"Porphyrion Fire Insurance Company."

"Oh yes; the nice people who gave Aunt Juley a new hearth-rug. He seems interesting, in some ways very, and one wishes one could help him. He is married to a wife whom he doesn't seem to care for much. He likes books, and what one may roughly call adventure, and if he had a chance--But he is so poor. He lives a life where all the money is apt to go on nonsense and clothes. One is so afraid that circumstances will be too strong for him and that he will sink. Well, he got mixed up in our debate. He wasn't the subject of it, but it seemed to bear on his point. Suppose a millionaire died, and desired to leave money to help such a man. How should he be helped? Should he be given three hundred pounds a year direct, which was Margaret's plan? Most of them thought this would pauperize him. Should he and those like him be given free libraries? I said 'No!' He doesn't want more books to read, but to read books rightly. My suggestion was he should be given something every year towards a summer holiday, but then there is his wife, and they said she would have to go too. Nothing seemed quite right! Now what do you think? Imagine that you were a millionaire, and wanted to help the poor. What would you do?"

Mr. Wilcox, whose fortune was not so very far below the standard indicated, laughed exuberantly. "My dear Miss Schlegel, I will not rush in where your sex has been unable to tread. I will not add another plan to the numerous excellent ones that have been already suggested. My only contribution is this: let your young friend clear out of the Porphyrion Fire Insurance Company with all possible speed."

"Why?" said Margaret.

He lowered his voice. "This is between friends. It'll be in the Receiver's hands before Christmas. It'll smash," he added, thinking that she had not understood.

"Dear me, Helen, listen to that. And he'll have to get another place!"

"*Will* have? Let him leave the ship before it sinks. Let him get one now."

"Rather than wait, to make sure?"

"Decidedly."

"Why's that?"

Again the Olympian laugh, and the lowered voice. "Naturally the man who's in a situation when he applies stands a better chance, is in a stronger position, than the man who isn't. It looks as if he's worth something. I know by myself--(this is letting you into the State secrets)--it affects an employer greatly. Human nature, I'm afraid."

"I hadn't thought of that," murmured Margaret, while Helen said, "Our human nature appears to be the other way round. We employ people because they're unemployed. The boot man, for instance."

"And how does he clean the boots?"

"Not well," confessed Margaret.

"There you are!"

"Then do you really advise us to tell this youth--"

"I advise nothing," he interrupted, glancing up and down the Embankment, in case his indiscretion had been overheard. "I oughtn't to have spoken--but I happen to know, being more or less behind the scenes. The Porphyrion's a bad, bad concern--Now, don't say I said so. It's outside the Tariff Ring."

"Certainly I won't say. In fact, I don't know what that means."

"I thought an insurance company never smashed," was Helen's contribution. "Don't the others always run in and save them?"

"You're thinking of reinsurance," said Mr. Wilcox mildly. "It is exactly there that the Porphyrion is weak. It has tried to undercut, has been badly hit by a long series of small fires, and it hasn't been able to reinsure. I'm afraid that public companies don't save one another for love."

"'Human nature,' I suppose," quoted Helen, and he laughed and agreed that it was. When Margaret said that she supposed that clerks, like every one else, found it extremely difficult to get situations in these days, he replied, "Yes, extremely," and rose to rejoin his friends. He knew by his own office--seldom a vacant post, and hundreds of applicants for it; at present no vacant post.

"And how's Howards End looking?" said Margaret, wishing to change the subject before they parted. Mr. Wilcox was a little apt to think one wanted to get something out of him.

"It's let."

"Really. And you wandering homeless in long-haired Chelsea? How strange are the ways of Fate!"

"No; it's let unfurnished. We've moved."

"Why, I thought of you both as anchored there for ever. Evie never told me."

"I dare say when you met Evie the thing wasn't settled. We only moved a week ago. Paul has rather a feeling for the old place, and we held on for him to have his holiday there; but, really, it is impossibly small. Endless drawbacks. I forget whether you've been up to it?"

"As far as the house, never."

"Well, Howards End is one of those converted farms. They don't really do, spend what you will on them. We messed away with a garage all among the wych-elm roots, and last year we enclosed a bit of the meadow and attempted a mockery. Evie got rather keen on Alpine plants. But it didn't do--no, it didn't do. You remember, or your sister will remember, the farm with those abominable guinea-fowls, and the hedge that the old woman never would cut properly, so that it all went thin at the bottom. And, inside the house, the beams--and the staircase through a door--picturesque enough, but not a place to live in." He glanced over the parapet cheerfully. "Full tide. And the position wasn't right either. The neighbourhood's getting suburban. Either be in London or out of it, I say; so we've taken a house in Ducie Street, close to Sloane Street, and a place right down in Shropshire--Oniton Grange. Ever heard of Oniton? Do come and see us--right away from everywhere, up towards Wales. "

"What a change!" said Margaret. But the change was in her own voice, which had become most sad. "I can't imagine Howards End or Hilton without you."

"Hilton isn't without us," he replied. "Charles is there still."

"Still?" said Margaret, who had not kept up with the Charles'. "But I thought he was still at Epsom. They were furnishing that Christmas--one Christmas. How everything alters! I used to admire Mrs. Charles from our windows very often. Wasn't it Epsom?"

"Yes, but they moved eighteen months ago. Charles, the good chap"--his voice dropped--"thought I should be lonely. I didn't want him to move, but he would, and took a house at the other end of Hilton, down by the Six Hills. He had a motor, too. There they all are, a very jolly party--he and she and the two grand-children."

"I manage other people's affairs so much better than they manage them themselves," said Margaret as they shook hands. "When you moved out of Howards End, I should have moved Mr. Charles Wilcox into it. I should have kept so remarkable a place in the family."

"So it is," he replied. "I haven't sold it, and don't mean to."

"No; but none of you are there."

"Oh, we've got a splendid tenant--Hamar Bryce, an invalid. If Charles ever wanted it--but he won't. Dolly is so dependent on modern conveniences. No, we have all decided against Howards End. We like it in a way, but now we feel that it is neither one thing nor the other. One must have one thing or the other."

"And some people are lucky enough to have both. You're doing yourself proud, Mr. Wilcox. My congratulations."

"And mine," said Helen.

"Do remind Evie to come and see us--two, Wickham Place. We shan't be there very long, either."

"You, too, on the move?"

"Next September," Margaret sighed.

"Every one moving! Good-bye."

The tide had begun to ebb. Margaret leant over the parapet and watched it sadly. Mr. Wilcox had forgotten his wife, Helen her lover; she herself was probably forgetting. Every one moving. Is it worth while attempting the past when there is this continual flux even in the hearts of men?

Helen roused her by saying: "What a prosperous vulgarian Mr. Wilcox has grown! I have very little use for him in these days. However, he did tell us about the Porphyrion. Let us write to Mr. Bast as soon as ever we get home, and tell him to clear out of it at once."

"Do; yes, that's worth doing. Let us."

"Let's ask him to tea."

Chapter 16

Leonard accepted the invitation to tea next Saturday. But he was right; the visit proved a conspicuous failure.

"Sugar?" said Margaret.

"Cake?" said Helen. "The big cake or the little deadlies? I'm afraid you thought my letter rather odd, but we'll explain--we aren't odd, really--not affected, really. We're over-expressive: that's all. "

As a lady's lap-dog Leonard did not excel. He was not an Italian, still less a Frenchman, in whose blood there runs the very spirit of persiflage and of gracious repartee. His wit was the Cockney's; it opened no doors into imagination, and Helen was drawn up short by "The more a lady has to say, the better," administered waggishly.

"Oh, yes," she said.

"Ladies brighten--"

"Yes, I know. The darlings are regular sunbeams. Let me give you a plate."

"How do you like your work?" interposed Margaret.

He, too, was drawn up short. He would not have these women prying into his work. They were Romance, and so was the room to which he had at last penetrated, with the queer sketches of people bathing upon its walls, and so were the very tea-cups, with their delicate borders of wild strawberries. But he would not let Romance interfere with his life. There is the devil to pay then.

"Oh, well enough," he answered.

"Your company is the Porphyrion, isn't it?"

"Yes, that's so"--becoming rather offended. "It's funny how things get round."

"Why funny?" asked Helen, who did not follow the workings of his mind. "It was written as large as life on your card, and considering we wrote to you there, and that you replied on the stamped paper--"

"Would you call the Porphyrion one of the big Insurance Companies?" pursued Margaret.

"It depends what you call big."

"I mean by big, a solid, well-established concern, that offers a reasonably good career to its employés."

"I couldn't say--some would tell you one thing and others another," said the employe uneasily. "For my own part"--he shook his head--"I only believe half I hear. Not that even; it's safer. Those clever ones come to the worse grief, I've often noticed. Ah, you can't be too careful."

He drank, and wiped his moustache, which was going to be one of those moustaches that always droop into tea-cups--more bother than they're worth, surely, and not fashionable either.

"I quite agree, and that's why I was curious to know: is it a solid, well-established concern?"

Leonard had no idea. He understood his own corner of the machine, but nothing beyond it. He desired to confess neither knowledge nor ignorance, and under these circumstances, another motion of the head seemed safest. To him, as to the British public, the Porphyrion was the Porphyrion of the advertisement--a giant, in the classical style, but draped sufficiently, who held in one hand a burning torch, and pointed with the other to St. Paul's and Windsor Castle. A large sum of money was inscribed below, and you drew your own conclusions. This giant caused Leonard to do arithmetic and write letters, to explain the regulations to new clients, and re-explain them to old ones. A giant was of an impulsive morality--one knew that much. He would pay for Mrs. Munt's hearth-rug with ostentatious haste, a large claim he would repudiate quietly, and fight court by court. But his true fighting weight, his antecedents, his amours with other members of the commercial Pantheon--all these were as uncertain to ordinary mortals as were the escapades of Zeus. While the gods are powerful, we learn little about them. It is only in the days of their decadence that a strong light beats into heaven.

"We were told the Porphyrion's no go," blurted Helen. "We wanted to tell you; that's why we wrote."

"A friend of ours did think that it is unsufficiently reinsured," said Margaret.

Now Leonard had his clue. He must praise the Porphyrion. "You can tell your friend," he said, "that he's quite wrong."

"Oh, good!"

The young man coloured a little. In his circle to be wrong was fatal. The Miss Schlegels did not mind being wrong. They were genuinely glad that they had been misinformed. To them nothing was fatal but evil.

"Wrong, so to speak," he added.

"How 'so to speak'?"

"I mean I wouldn't say he's right altogether."

But this was a blunder. "Then he is right partly," said the elder woman, quick as lightning.

Leonard replied that every one was right partly, if it came to that.

"Mr. Bast, I don't understand business, and I dare say my questions are stupid, but can you tell me what makes a concern 'right' or 'wrong'?"

Leonard sat back with a sigh.

"Our friend, who is also a business man, was so positive. He said before Christmas--"

"And advised you to clear out of it," concluded Helen. "But I don't see why he should know better than you do."

Leonard rubbed his hands. He was tempted to say that he knew nothing about the thing at all. But a commercial training was too strong for him. Nor could he say it was a bad thing, for this would be giving it away; nor yet that it was good, for this would be giving it away equally. He attempted to suggest that it was something between the two, with vast possibilities in either direction, but broke down under the gaze of four sincere eyes. As yet he scarcely distinguished between the two sisters. One was more beautiful and more lively, but "the Miss Schlegels" still remained a composite Indian god, whose waving arms and contradictory speeches were the product of a single mind.

"One can but see," he remarked, adding, "as Ibsen says, 'things happen.'" He was itching to talk about books and make the most of his romantic hour. Minute after minute slipped away, while the ladies, with imperfect skill, discussed the subject of reinsurance or praised their anonymous friend. Leonard grew annoyed--perhaps rightly. He made vague remarks about not being one of those who minded their affairs being talked over by others, but they did not take the hint. Men might have shown more tact. Women, however tactful elsewhere, are heavy-handed here. They cannot see why we should shroud our incomes and our prospects in a veil. "How much exactly have you, and how much do you expect to have next June?" And these were women with a theory, who held that reticence about money matters is absurd, and that life would be truer if each would state the exact size of the golden island upon which he stands, the exact stretch of warp over which he throws the woof that is not money. How can we do justice to the pattern otherwise?

And the precious minutes slipped away, and Jacky and squalor came nearer. At last he could bear it no longer, and broke in, reciting the names of books feverishly. There was a moment of piercing joy when Margaret said, "So *you* like Carlyle," and then the door opened, and "Mr. Wilcox, Miss Wilcox" entered, preceded by two prancing puppies.

"Oh, the dears! Oh, Evie, how too impossibly sweet!" screamed Helen, falling on her hands and knees.

"We brought the little fellows round," said Mr. Wilcox.

"I bred 'em myself."

"Oh, really! Mr. Bast, come and play with puppies."

"I've got to be going now," said Leonard sourly.

"But play with puppies a little first."

"This is Ahab, that's Jezebel," said Evie, who was one of those who name animals after the less successful characters of Old Testament history.

"I've got to be going."

Helen was too much occupied with puppies to notice him.

"Mr. Wilcox, Mr. Ba--Must you be really? Good-bye!"

"Come again," said Helen from the floor.

Then Leonard's gorge arose. Why should he come again? What was the good of it? He said roundly: "No, I shan't; I knew it would be a failure."

Most people would have let him go. "A little mistake. We tried knowing another class--impossible." But the Schlegels had never played with life. They had attempted friendship, and they would take the consequences. Helen retorted, "I call that a very rude remark. What do you want to turn on me like that for?" and suddenly the drawing-room re-echoed to a vulgar row.

"You ask me why I turn on you?"

"Yes."

"What do you want to have me here for?"

"To help you, you silly boy!" cried Helen. "And don't shout."

"I don't want your patronage. I don't want your tea. I was quite happy. What do you want to unsettle me for?" He turned to Mr. Wilcox. "I put it to this gentleman. I ask you, sir, am to have my brain picked?"

Mr. Wilcox turned to Margaret with the air of humorous strength that he could so well command. "Are we intruding, Miss Schlegel? Can we be of any use or shall we go?"

But Margaret ignored him.

"I'm connected with a leading insurance company, sir. I receive what I take to be an invitation from these--ladies" (he drawled the word). "I come, and it's to have my brain picked. I ask you, is it fair?"

"Highly unfair," said Mr. Wilcox, drawing a gasp from Evie, who knew that her father was becoming dangerous.

"There, you hear that? Most unfair, the gentleman says. There! Not content with"--pointing at Margaret--"you can't deny it." His voice rose: he was falling into the rhythm of a scene with Jacky. "But as soon as I'm useful it's a very different thing. 'Oh yes, send for him. Cross-question him. Pick his brains.' Oh yes. Now, take me on the whole, I'm a quiet fellow: I'm law-abiding, I don't wish any unpleasantness; but I--I--"

"You," said Margaret--"you--you--"

Laughter from Evie, as at a repartee.

"You are the man who tried to walk by the Pole Star."

More laughter.

"You saw the sunrise."

Laughter.

"You tried to get away from the fogs that are stifling us all--away past books and houses to the truth. You were looking for a real home. "

"I fail to see the connection," said Leonard, hot with stupid anger.

"So do I." There was a pause. "You were that last Sunday--you are this today. Mr. Bast! I and my sister have talked you over. We wanted to help you; we also supposed you might help us. We did not have you here out of charity--which bores us--but because we hoped there would be a connection between last Sunday and other days. What is the good of your stars and trees, your sunrise and the wind, if they do not enter into our daily lives? They have never entered into mine, but into yours, we thought--Haven't we all to struggle against life's daily greyness, against pettiness, against mechanical cheerfulness, against suspicion? I struggle by remembering my friends; others I have known by remembering some place--some beloved place or tree--we thought you one of these."

"Of course, if there's been any misunderstanding," mumbled Leonard, "all I can do is to go. But I beg to state--" He paused. Ahab and Jezebel danced at his boots and made him look ridiculous. "You were picking my brain for official information--I can prove it--I--He blew his nose and left them.

"Can I help you now?" said Mr. Wilcox, turning to Margaret. "May I have one quiet word with him in the hall?"

"Helen, go after him--do anything--*anything*--to make the noodle understand."

Helen hesitated.

"But really--" said their visitor. "Ought she to?"

At once she went.

He resumed. "I would have chimed in, but I felt that you could polish him off for yourselves--I didn't interfere. You were splendid, Miss Schlegel--absolutely splendid. You can take my word for it, but there are very few women who could have managed him."

"Oh yes," said Margaret distractedly.

"Bowling him over with those long sentences was what fetched me," cried Evie.

"Yes, indeed," chuckled her father; "all that part about 'mechanical cheerfulness'--oh, fine!"

"I'm very sorry," said Margaret, collecting herself. "He's a nice creature really. I cannot think what set him off. It has been most unpleasant for you."

"Oh, *I* didn't mind." Then he changed his mood. He asked if he might speak as an old friend, and, permission given, said: "Oughtn't you really to be more careful?"

Margaret laughed, though her thoughts still strayed after Helen. "Do you realize that it's all your fault?" she said. "You're responsible."

"I?"

"This is the young man whom we were to warn against the Porphyrion. We warn him, and--look!"

Mr. Wilcox was annoyed. "I hardly consider that a fair deduction," he said.

"Obviously unfair," said Margaret. "I was only thinking how tangled things are. It's our fault mostly--neither yours nor his."

"Not his?"

"No."

"Miss Schlegel, you are too kind."

"Yes, indeed," nodded Evie, a little contemptuously.

"You behave much too well to people, and then they impose on you. I know the world and that type of man, and as soon as I entered the room I saw you had not been treating him properly. You must keep that type at a distance. Otherwise they forget themselves. Sad, but true. They aren't our sort, and one must face the fact."

"Ye-es."

"Do admit that we should never have had the outburst if he was a gentleman."

"I admit it willingly," said Margaret, who was pacing up and down the room. "A gentleman would have kept his suspicions to himself."

Mr. Wilcox watched her with a vague uneasiness.

"What did he suspect you of?"

"Of wanting to make money out of him."

"Intolerable brute! But how were you to benefit?"

"Exactly. How indeed! Just horrible, corroding suspicion. One touch of thought or of goodwill would have brushed it away. Just the senseless fear that does make men intolerable brutes."

"I come back to my original point. You ought to be more careful, Miss Schlegel. Your servants ought to have orders not to let such people in."

She turned to him frankly. "Let me explain exactly why we like this man, and want to see him again."

"That's your clever way of thinking. I shall never believe you like him."

"I do. Firstly, because he cares for physical adventure, just as you do. Yes, you go motoring and shooting; he would like to go camping out. Secondly, he cares for something special *in* adventure. It is quickest to call that special something poetry--"

"Oh, he's one of that writer sort."

"No--oh no! I mean he may be, but it would be loathsome stiff. His brain is filled with the husks of books, culture--horrible; we want him to wash out his brain and go to the real thing. We want to show him how he may get upsides with life. As I said, either friends or the country, some"--she hesitated--"either some very dear person or some very dear place seems necessary to relieve life's daily grey, and to show that it is grey. If possible, one should have both."

Some of her words ran past Mr. Wilcox. He let them run past. Others he caught and criticized with admirable lucidity.

"Your mistake is this, and it is a very common mistake. This young bounder has a life of his own. What right have you to conclude it is an unsuccessful life, or, as you call it, 'grey'?"

"Because--"

"One minute. You know nothing about him. He probably has his own joys and interests--wife, children, snug little home. That's where we practical fellows"--he smiled--"are more tolerant than you intellectuals. We live and let live, and assume that things are jogging on fairly well elsewhere, and that the ordinary plain man may be trusted to look after his own affairs. I quite grant--I look at the faces of the clerks in my own office, and observe them to be dull, but I don't know what's going on beneath. So, by the way, with London. I have heard you rail against London, Miss Schlegel, and it seems a funny thing to say but I was very angry with you. What do you know about London? You only see civilization from the outside. I don't say in your case, but in too many cases that attitude leads to morbidity, discontent, and Socialism."

She admitted the strength of his position, though it undermined imagination. As he spoke, some outposts of poetry and perhaps of sympathy fell ruining, and she retreated to what she called her "second line"--to the special facts of the case.

"His wife is an old bore," she said simply. "He never came home last Saturday night because he wanted to be alone, and she thought he was with us."

"With *you?*"

"Yes." Evie tittered. "He hasn't got the cosy home that you assumed. He needs outside interests."

"Naughty young man!" cried the girl.

"Naughty?" said Margaret, who hated naughtiness more than sin. "When you're married, Miss Wilcox, won't you want outside interests?"

"He has apparently got them," put in Mr. Wilcox slyly.

"Yes, indeed, Father."

"He was tramping in Surrey, if you mean that," said Margaret, pacing away rather crossly.

"Oh, I dare say!"

"Miss Wilcox, he was!"

"M-m-m-m!" from Mr. Wilcox, who thought the episode amusing, if risqué. With most ladies he would not have discussed it, but he was trading on Margaret's reputation as an emanicipated woman.

"He said so, and about such a thing he wouldn't lie."

They both began to laugh.

"That's where I differ from you. Men lie about their positions and prospects, but not about a thing of that sort."

He shook his head. "Miss Schlegel, excuse me, but I know the type."

"I said before--he isn't a type. He cares about adventures rightly. He's certain that our smug existence isn't all. He's vulgar and hysterical and bookish, but I don't think that sums him up. There's manhood in him as well. Yes, that's what I'm trying to say. He's a real man."

As she spoke their eyes met, and it was as if Mr. Wilcox's defences fell. She saw back to the real man in him. Unwittingly she had touched his emotions. A woman and two men--they had formed the magic triangle of sex, and the male was thrilled to jealousy, in case the female was attracted by another male. Love, say the ascetics, reveals our shameful kinship with the beasts. Be it so: one can bear that; jealousy is the real shame. It is jealousy, not love, that connects us with the farmyard intolerably, and calls up visions of two angry cocks and a complacent hen. Margaret crushed complacency down because she was civilized. Mr. Wilcox, uncivilized, continued to feel anger long after he had rebuilt his defences, and was again presenting a bastion to the world.

"Miss Schlegel, you're a pair of dear creatures, but you really *must* be careful in this uncharitable world. What does your brother say?"

"I forget."

"Surely he has some opinion?"

"He laughs, if I remember correctly."

"He's very clever, isn't he?" said Evie, who had met and detested Tibby at Oxford.

"Yes, pretty well--but I wonder what Helen's doing."

"She is very young to undertake this sort of thing," said Mr. Wilcox.

Margaret went out into the landing. She heard no sound, and Mr. Bast's topper was missing from the hall.

"Helen!" she called.

"Yes!" replied a voice from the library.

"You in there?"

"Yes--he's gone some time."

Margaret went to her. "Why, you're all alone," she said.

"Yes--it's all right, Meg--Poor, poor creature--"

"Come back to the Wilcoxes and tell me later--Mr. W. much concerned, and slightly titillated."

"Oh, I've no patience with him. I hate him. Poor dear Mr. Bast! he wanted to talk literature, and we would talk business. Such a muddle of a man, and yet so worth pulling through. I like him extraordinarily. "

"Well done," said Margaret, kissing her, "but come into the drawing-room now, and don't talk about him to the Wilcoxes. Make light of the whole thing."

Helen came and behaved with a cheerfulness that reassured their visitor--this hen at all events was fancy-free.

"He's gone with my blessing," she cried, "and now for puppies."

As they drove away, Mr. Wilcox said to his daughter:

"I am really concerned at the way those girls go on. They are as clever as you make 'em, but unpractical--God bless me! One of these days they'll go too far. Girls like that oughtn't to live alone in London. Until they marry, they ought to have someone to look after them. We must look in more often--we're better than no one. You like them, don't you, Evie?"

Evie replied: "Helen's right enough, but I can't stand the toothy one. And I shouldn't have called either of them girls."

Evie had grown up handsome. Dark-eyed, with the glow of youth under sunburn, built firmly and firm-lipped, she was the best the Wilcoxes could do in the way of feminine beauty. For the present, puppies and her father were the only things she loved, but the net of matrimony was being prepared for her, and a few days later she was attracted to a Mr. Percy Cahill, an uncle of Mrs. Charles, and he was attracted to her.

Chapter 17

The Age of Property holds bitter moments even for a proprietor. When a move is imminent, furniture becomes ridiculous, and Margaret now lay awake at nights wondering where, where on earth they and all their belongings would be deposited in September next. Chairs, tables, pictures, books, that had rumbled down to them through the generations, must rumble forward again like a slide of rubbish to which she longed to give the final push, and send toppling into the sea. But there were all their father's books--they never read them, but they were their father's, and must be kept. There was the marble-topped chiffonier--their mother had set store by it, they could not remember why. Round every knob and cushion in the house sentiment gathered, a sentiment that was at times personal, but more often a faint piety to the dead, a prolongation of rites that might have ended at the grave.

It was absurd, if you came to think of it; Helen and Tibby came to think of it: Margaret was too busy with the house-agents. The feudal ownership of land did bring dignity, whereas the modern ownership of movables is reducing us again to a nomadic horde. We are reverting to the civilization of luggage, and historians of the future will note how the middle classes accreted possessions without taking root in the earth, and may find in this the secret of their imaginative poverty. The Schlegels were certainly the poorer for the loss of Wickham Place. It had helped to balance their lives, and almost to counsel them. Nor is their ground-landlord spiritually the richer. He has built flats on its site, his motor-cars grow swifter, his exposures of Socialism more trenchant. But he has spilt the precious distillation of the years, and no chemistry of his can give it back to society again.

Margaret grew depressed; she was anxious to settle on a house before they left town to pay their annual visit to Mrs. Munt. She enjoyed this visit, and wanted to have her mind at ease for it. Swanage, though dull, was stable, and this year she longed more than usual for its fresh air and for the magnificent downs that guard it on the north. But London thwarted her; in its atmosphere she could not concentrate. London only stimulates, it cannot sustain; and Margaret, hurrying over its surface for a house without knowing what sort of a house she wanted, was paying for many a thrilling sensation in the past. She could not even break loose from culture, and her time was wasted by concerts which it would be a sin to miss, and invitations which it would never do to refuse. At last she grew desperate; she resolved that she would go nowhere and be at home to no one until she found a house, and broke the resolution in half an hour.

Once she had humorously lamented that she had never been to Simpson's restaurant in the Strand. Now a note arrived from Miss Wilcox, asking her to lunch there. Mr. Cahill was coming, and the three would have such a jolly chat, and perhaps end up at the Hippodrome. Margaret had no strong regard for Evie, and no desire to meet her fiancé, and she was surprised that Helen, who had been far funnier about Simpson's, had not been asked instead. But the invitation touched her by its intimate tone. She must know Evie Wilcox better than she supposed, and declaring that she "simply must," she accepted.

But when she saw Evie at the entrance of the restaurant, staring fiercely at nothing after the fashion of athletic women, her heart failed her anew. Miss Wilcox had changed perceptibly since her engagement. Her voice was gruffer, her manner more downright, and she was inclined to patronize the more foolish virgin. Margaret was silly enough to be pained at this. Depressed at her isolation, she saw not only houses and furniture, but the vessel of life itself slipping past her, with people like Evie and Mr. Cahill on board.

There are moments when virtue and wisdom fail us, and one of them came to her at Simpson's in the Strand. As she trod the staircase, narrow, but carpeted thickly, as she entered the eating-room, where saddles of mutton were being trundled up to expectant clergymen, she had a strong, if erroneous, conviction of her own futility, and wished she had never come out of her backwater, where nothing happened except art and literature, and where no one ever got married or succeeded in remaining engaged. Then came a little surprise. "Father might be of the party--yes, Father was." With a smile of pleasure she moved forward to greet him, and her feeling of loneliness vanished.

"I thought I'd get round if I could," said he. "Evie told me of her little plan, so I just slipped in and secured a table. Always secure a table first. Evie, don't pretend you want to sit by your old father, because you don't. Miss Schlegel, come in my side, out of pity. My goodness, but you look tired! Been worrying round after your young clerks?"

"No, after houses," said Margaret, edging past him into the box. "I'm hungry, not tired; I want to eat heaps."

"That's good. What'll you have?"

"Fish pie," said she, with a glance at the menu.

"Fish pie! Fancy coming for fish pie to Simpson's. It's not a bit the thing to go for here. "

"Go for something for me, then," said Margaret, pulling off her gloves. Her spirits were rising, and his reference to Leonard Bast had warmed her curiously.

"Saddle of mutton," said he after profound reflection: "and cider to drink. That's the type of thing. I like this place, for a joke, once in a way. It is so thoroughly Old English. Don't you agree?"

"Yes," said Margaret, who didn't. The order was given, the joint rolled up, and the carver, under Mr. Wilcox's direction, cut the meat where it was succulent, and piled their plates high. Mr. Cahill insisted on sirloin, but admitted that he had made a mistake later on. He and Evie soon fell into a conversation of the "No, I didn't; yes, you did" type--conversation which, though fascinating to those who are engaged in it, neither desires nor deserves the attention of others.

"It's a golden rule to tip the carver. Tip everywhere's my motto."

"Perhaps it does make life more human."

"Then the fellows know one again. Especially in the East, if you tip, they remember you from year's end to year's end.

"Have you been in the East?"

"Oh, Greece and the Levant. I used to go out for sport and business to Cyprus; some military society of a sort there. A few piastres, properly distributed, help to keep one's memory green. But you, of course, think this shockingly cynical. How's your discussion society getting on? Any new Utopias lately?"

"No, I'm house-hunting, Mr. Wilcox, as I've already told you once. Do you know of any houses?"

"Afraid I don't."

"Well, what's the point of being practical if you can't find two distressed females a house? We merely want a small house with large rooms, and plenty of them."

"Evie, I like that! Miss Schlegel expects me to turn house agent for her!"

"What's that, Father?

"I want a new home in September, and someone must find it. I can't."

"Percy, do you know of anything?"

"I can't say I do," said Mr. Cahill.

"How like you! You're never any good."

"Never any good. Just listen to her! Never any good. Oh, come!"

"Well, you aren't. Miss Schlegel, is he?"

The torrent of their love, having splashed these drops at Margaret, swept away on its habitual course. She sympathized with it now, for a little comfort had restored her geniality. Speech and silence pleased her equally, and while Mr. Wilcox made some preliminary inquiries about cheese, her eyes surveyed the restaurant, and admired its well-calculated tributes to the solidity of our past. Though no more Old English than the works of Kipling, it had selected its reminiscences so adroitly that her criticism was lulled, and the guests whom it was nourishing for imperial purposes bore the outer semblance of Parson Adams or Tom Jones. Scraps of their talk jarred oddly on the ear. "Right you are! I'll cable out to Uganda this evening," came from the table behind. "Their Emperor wants war; well, let him have it," was the opinion of a clergyman. She smiled at such incongruities. "Next time," she said to Mr. Wilcox, "you shall come to lunch with me at Mr. Eustace Miles's."

"With pleasure."

"No, you'd hate it," she said, pushing her glass towards him for some more cider. "It's all proteids and body-buildings, and people come up to you and beg your pardon, but you have such a beautiful aura."

"A what?"

"Never heard of an aura? Oh, happy, happy man! I scrub at mine for hours. Nor of an astral plane?"

He had heard of astral planes, and censured them.

"Just so. Luckily it was Helen's aura, not mine, and she had to chaperone it and do the politenesses. I just sat with my handkerchief in my mouth till the man went."

"Funny experiences seem to come to you two girls. No one's ever asked me about my--what d'ye call it? Perhaps I've not got one."

"You're bound to have one, but it may be such a terrible colour that no one dares mention it."

"Tell me, though, Miss Schlegel, do you really believe in the supernatural and all that?"

"Too difficult a question."

"Why's that? Gruyère or Stilton?"

"Gruyère, please."

"Better have Stilton."

"Stilton. Because, though I don't believe in auras, and think Theosophy's only a halfway-house--"

"--Yet there may be something in it all the same," he concluded, with a frown.

"Not even that. It may be halfway in the wrong direction. I can't explain. I don't believe in all these fads, and yet I don't like saying that I don't believe in them."

He seemed unsatisfied, and said: "So you wouldn't give me your word that you *don't* hold with astral bodies and all the rest of it?"

"I could," said Margaret, surprised that the point was of any importance to him. "Indeed, I will. When I talked about scrubbing my aura, I was only trying to be funny. But why do you want this settled?"

"I don't know."

"Now, Mr. Wilcox, you do know."

"Yes, I am," "No, you're not," burst from the lovers opposite. Margaret was silent for a moment, and then changed the subject.

"How's your house?"

"Much the same as when you honoured it last week."

"I don't mean Ducie Street. Howards End, of course."

"Why 'of course'?"

"Can't you turn out your tenant and let it to us? We're nearly demented."

"Let me think. I wish I could help you. But I thought you wanted to be in town. One bit of advice: fix your district, then fix your price, and then don't budge. That's how I got both Ducie Street and Oniton. I said to myself, 'I mean to be exactly here,' and I was, and Oniton's a place in a thousand."

"But I do budge. Gentlemen seem to mesmerize houses--cow them with an eye, and up they come, trembling. Ladies can't. It's the houses that are mesmerizing me. I've no control over the saucy things. Houses are alive. No?"

"I'm out of my depth," he said, and added: "Didn't you talk rather like that to your office boy?"

"Did I? --I mean I did, more or less. I talk the same way to every one--or try to."

"Yes, I know. And how much do you suppose that he understood of it?"

"That's his lookout. I don't believe in suiting my conversation to my company. One can doubtless hit upon some medium of exchange that seems to do well enough, but it's no more like the real thing than money is like food. There's no nourishment in it. You pass it to the lower classes, and they pass it back to you, and this you call 'social intercourse' or 'mutual endeavour,' when it's mutual priggishness if it's anything. Our friends at Chelsea don't see this. They say one ought to be at all costs intelligible, and sacrifice--"

"Lower classes," interrupted Mr. Wilcox, as it were thrusting his hand into her speech. "Well, you do admit that there are rich and poor. That's something."

Margaret could not reply. Was he incredibly stupid, or did he understand her better than she understood herself?

"You do admit that, if wealth was divided up equally, in a few years there would be rich and poor again just the same. The hard-working man would come to the top, the wastrel sink to the bottom."

"Every one admits that."

"Your Socialists don't."

"My Socialists do. Yours mayn't; but I strongly suspect yours of being not Socialists, but ninepins, which you have constructed for your own amusement. I can't imagine any living creature who would bowl over quite so easily."

He would have resented this had she not been a woman. But women may say anything--it was one of his holiest beliefs--and he only retorted, with a gay smile: "I don't care. You've made two damaging admissions, and I'm heartily with you in both."

In time they finished lunch, and Margaret, who had excused herself from the Hippodrome, took her leave. Evie had scarcely addressed her, and she suspected that the entertainment had been planned by the father. He and she were advancing out of their respective families towards a more intimate acquaintance. It had begun long ago. She had been his wife's friend, and, as such, he had given her that silver vinaigrette as a memento. It was pretty of him to have given that vinaigrette, and he had always preferred her to Helen--unlike most men. But the advance had been astonishing lately. They had done more in a week than in two years, and were really beginning to know each other.

She did not forget his promise to sample Eustace Miles, and asked him as soon as she could secure Tibby as his chaperon. He came, and partook of body-building dishes with humility.

Next morning the Schlegels left for Swanage. They had not succeeded in finding a new home.

Chapter 18

As they were seated at Aunt Juley's breakfast-table at The Bays, parrying her excessive hospitality and enjoying the view of the bay, a letter came for Margaret and threw her into perturbation. It was from Mr. Wilcox. It announced an "important change" in his plans. Owing to Evie's marriage, he had decided to give up his house in Ducie Street, and was willing to let it on a yearly tenancy. It was a businesslike letter, and stated frankly what he would do for them and what he would not do. Also the rent. If they approved, Margaret was to come up *at once*--the words were underlined, as is necessary when dealing with women--and to go over the house with him. If they disapproved, a wire would oblige, as he should put it into the hands of an agent.

The letter perturbed, because she was not sure what it meant. If he liked her, if he had manoeuvred to get her to Simpson's, might this be a manoeuvre to get her to London, and result in an offer of marriage? She put it to herself as indelicately as possible, in the hope that her brain would cry, "Rubbish, you're a self-conscious fool!" But her brain only tingled a little and was silent, and for a time she sat gazing at the mincing waves, and wondering whether the news would seem strange to the others.

As soon as she began speaking, the sound of her own voice reassured her. There could be nothing in it. The replies also were typical, and in the buff of conversation her fears vanished.

"You needn't go though--" began her hostess.

"I needn't, but hadn't I better? It's really getting rather serious. We let chance after chance slip, and the end of it is we shall be bundled out bag and baggage into the street. We don't know what we *want*, that's the mischief with us--"

"No, we have no real ties," said Helen, helping herself to toast.

"Shan't I go up to town today, take the house if it's the least possible, and then come down by the afternoon train tomorrow, and start enjoying myself. I shall be no fun to myself or to others until this business is off my mind."

"But you won't do anything rash, Margaret?"

"There's nothing rash to do."

"Who *are* the Wilcoxes?" said Tibby, a question that sounds silly, but was really extremely subtle, as his aunt found to her cost when she tried to answer it. "I don't *manage* the Wilcoxes; I don't see where they come *in*."

"No more do I," agreed Helen. "It's funny that we just don't lose sight of them. Out of all our hotel acquaintances, Mr. Wilcox is the only one who has stuck. It is now over three years, and we have drifted away from far more interesting people in that time.

"Interesting people don't get one houses."

"Meg, if you start in your honest-English vein, I shall throw the treacle at you."

"It's a better vein than the cosmopolitan," said Margaret, getting up. "Now, children, which is it to be? You know the Ducie Street house. Shall I say yes or shall I say no? Tibby love--which? I'm specially anxious to pin you both."

"It all depends what meaning you attach to the word 'possi--'"

"It depends on nothing of the sort. Say 'yes.'"

"Say 'no.'"

Then Margaret spoke rather seriously. "I think," she said, "that our race is degenerating. We cannot settle even this little thing; what will it be like when we have to settle a big one?"

"It will be as easy as eating," returned Helen.

"I was thinking of Father. How could he settle to leave Germany as he did, when he had fought for it as a young man, and all his feelings and friends were Prussian? How could he break loose with Patriotism and begin aiming at something else? It would have killed me. When he was nearly forty he could change countries and ideals--and we, at our age, can't change houses. It's humiliating."

"Your father may have been able to change countries," said Mrs. Munt with asperity, "and that may or may not be a good thing. But he could change houses no better than you can, in fact, much worse. Never shall I forget what poor Emily suffered in the move from Manchester."

"I knew it," cried Helen. "I told you so. It is the little things one bungles at. The big, real ones are nothing when they come."

"Bungle, my dear! You are too little to recollect--in fact, you weren't there. But the furniture was actually in the vans and on the move before the lease for Wickham Place was signed, and Emily took train with baby--who was Margaret then--and the smaller luggage for London, without so much as knowing where her new home would be. Getting away from that house may be hard, but it is nothing to the misery that we all went through getting you into it."

Helen, with her mouth full, cried: "And that's the man who beat the Austrians, and the Danes, and the French, and who beat the Germans that were inside himself. And we're like him."

"Speak for yourself," said Tibby. "Remember that I am cosmopolitan, please."

"Helen may be right."

"Of course she's right," said Helen.

Helen might be right, but she did not go up to London. Margaret did that. An interrupted holiday is the worst of the minor worries, and one may be pardoned for feeling morbid when a business letter snatches one away from the sea and friends. She could not believe that her father had ever felt the same. Her eyes had been troubling her lately, so that she could not read in the train, and it bored her to look at the landscape, which she had seen but yesterday. At Southampton she "waved" to Frieda: Frieda was on her way down to join them at Swanage, and Mrs. Munt had calculated that their trains would cross. But Frieda was looking the other way, and Margaret travelled on to town feeling solitary and old-maidish. How like an old maid to fancy that Mr. Wilcox was courting her! She had once visited a spinster--poor, silly, and unattractive--whose mania it was that every man who approached her fell in love. How Margaret's heart had bled for the deluded thing! How she had lectured, reasoned, and in despair acquiesced! "I may have been deceived by the curate, my dear, but the young fellow who brings the midday post really is fond of me, and has, as a matter fact--" It had always seemed to her the most hideous corner of old age, yet she might be driven into it herself by the mere pressure of virginity.

Mr. Wilcox met her at Waterloo himself. She felt certain that he was not the same as usual; for one thing, he took offence at everything she said.

"This is awfully kind of you," she began, "but I'm afraid it's not going to do. The house has not been built that suits the Schlegel family."

"What! Have you come up determined not to deal?"

"Not exactly."

"Not exactly? In that case let's be starting."

She lingered to admire the motor, which was new and a fairer creature than the vermilion giant that had borne Aunt Juley to her doom three years before.

"Presumably it's very beautiful," she said. "How do you like it, Crane?"

"Come, let's be starting," repeated her host. "How on earth did you know that my chauffeur was called Crane?"

"Why, I know Crane: I've been for a drive with Evie once. I know that you've got a parlourmaid called Milton. I know all sorts of things."

"Evie!" he echoed in injured tones. "You won't see her. She's gone out with Cahill. It's no fun, I can tell you, being left so much alone. I've got my work all day--indeed, a great deal too much of it--but when I come home in the evening, I tell you, I can't stand the house."

"In my absurd way, I'm lonely too," Margaret replied. "It's heart-breaking to leave one's old home. I scarcely remember anything before Wickham Place, and Helen and Tibby were born there. Helen says--"

"You, too, feel lonely?"

"Horribly. Hullo, Parliament's back!"

Mr. Wilcox glanced at Parliament contemptuously. The more important ropes of life lay elsewhere. "Yes, they are talking again." said he. "But you were going to say--"

"Only some rubbish about furniture. Helen says it alone endures while men and houses perish, and that in the end the world will be a desert of chairs and sofas--just imagine it! --rolling through infinity with no one to sit upon them."

"Your sister always likes her little joke.

"She says 'Yes,' my brother says 'No,' to Ducie Street. It's no fun helping us, Mr. Wilcox, I assure you."

"You are not as unpractical as you pretend. I shall never believe it."

Margaret laughed. But she was--quite as unpractical. She could not concentrate on details. Parliament, the Thames, the irresponsive chauffeur, would flash into the field of house-hunting, and all demand some comment or response. It is impossible to see modern life steadily and see it whole, and she had chosen to see it whole. Mr. Wilcox saw steadily. He never bothered over the mysterious or the private. The Thames might run inland from the sea, the chauffeur might conceal all passion and philosophy beneath his unhealthy skin. They knew their own business, and he knew his.

Yet she liked being with him. He was not a rebuke, but a stimulus, and banished morbidity. Some twenty years her senior, he preserved a gift that she supposed herself to have already lost--not youth's creative power, but its self-confidence and optimism. He was so sure that it was a very pleasant world. His complexion was robust, his hair had receded but not thinned, the thick moustache and the eyes that Helen had compared to brandy-balls had an agreeable menace in them, whether they were turned towards the slums or towards the stars. Some day--in the millennium--there may be no need for his type. At present, homage is due to it from those who think themselves superior, and who possibly are."

"At all events you responded to my telegram promptly," he remarked.

"Oh, even I know a good thing when I see it."

"I'm glad you don't despise the goods of this world."

"Heavens, no! Only idiots and prigs do that."

"I am glad, very glad," he repeated, suddenly softening and turning to her, as if the remark had pleased him. "There is so much cant talked in would-be intellectual circles. I am glad you don't share it. Self-denial is all very well as a means of strengthening the character. But I can't stand those people who run down comforts. They have usually some axe to grind. Can you?"

"Comforts are of two kinds," said Margaret, who was keeping herself in hand--"those we can share with others, like fire, weather, or music; and those we can't--food, for instance. It depends."

"I mean reasonable comforts, of course. I shouldn't like to think that you--" He bent nearer; the sentence died unfinished. Margaret's head turned very stupid, and the inside of it seemed to revolve like the beacon in a lighthouse. He did not kiss her, for the hour was half-past twelve, and the car was passing by the stables of Buckingham Palace. But the atmosphere was so charged with emotion that people only seemed to exist on her account, and she was surprised that Crane did not realize this, and turn round. Idiot though she might be, surely Mr. Wilcox was more--how should one put it? --more psychological than usual. Always a good judge of character for business purposes, he seemed this afternoon to enlarge his field, and to note qualities outside neatness, obedience, and decision.

"I want to go over the whole house," she announced when they arrived. "As soon as I get back to Swanage, which will be tomorrow afternoon, I'll talk it over once more with Helen and Tibby, and wire you 'yes' or 'no.'"

"Right. The dining-room." And they began their survey.

The dining-room was big, but over-furnished. Chelsea would have moaned aloud. Mr. Wilcox had eschewed those decorative schemes that wince, and relent, and refrain, and achieve beauty by sacrificing comfort and pluck. After so much self-colour and self-denial, Margaret viewed with relief the sumptuous dado, the frieze, the gilded wall-paper, amid whose foliage parrots sang. It would never do with her own furniture, but those heavy chairs, that immense side-board loaded with presentation plate, stood up against its pressure like men. The room suggested men, and Margaret, keen to derive the modern capitalist from the warriors and hunters of the past, saw it as an ancient guest-hall, where the lord sat at meat among his thanes. Even the Bible--the Dutch Bible that Charles had brought back from the Boer War--fell into position. Such a room admitted loot.

"Now the entrance-hall."

The entrance-hall was paved.

"Here we fellows smoke."

We fellows smoked in chairs of maroon leather. It was as if a motor-car had spawned. "Oh, jolly!" said Margaret, sinking into one of them.

"You do like it?" he said, fixing his eyes on her upturned face, and surely betraying an almost intimate note. "It's all rubbish not making oneself comfortable. Isn't it?"

"Ye-es. Semi-rubbish. Are those Cruikshanks?"

"Gillrays. Shall we go on upstairs?"

"Does all this furniture come from Howards End?"

"The Howards End furniture has all gone to Oniton."

"Does--However, I'm concerned with the house, not the furniture. How big is this smoking-room?"

"Thirty by fifteen. No, wait a minute. Fifteen and a half?."

"Ah, well. Mr. Wilcox, aren't you ever amused at the solemnity with which we middle classes approach the subject of houses?"

They proceeded to the drawing-room. Chelsea managed better here. It was sallow and ineffective. One could visualize the ladies withdrawing to it, while their lords discussed life's realities below, to the accompaniment of cigars. Had Mrs. Wilcox's drawing-room looked thus at Howards End? Just as this thought entered Margaret's brain, Mr. Wilcox did ask her to be his wife, and the knowledge that she had been right so overcame her that she nearly fainted.

But the proposal was not to rank among the world's great love scenes.

"Miss Schlegel"--his voice was firm--"I have had you up on false pretences. I want to speak about a much more serious matter than a house."

Margaret almost answered: "I know--"

"Could you be induced to share my--is it probable--"

"Oh, Mr. Wilcox!" she interrupted, holding the piano and averting her eyes. "I see, I see. I will write to you afterwards if I may."

He began to stammer. "Miss Schlegel--Margaret--you don't understand."

"Oh yes! Indeed, yes!" said Margaret.

"I am asking you to be my wife."

So deep already was her sympathy, that when he said, "I am asking you to be my wife," she made herself give a little start. She must show surprise if he expected it. An immense joy came over her. It was indescribable. It had nothing to do with humanity, and most resembled the all-pervading happiness of fine weather. Fine weather is due to the sun, but Margaret could think of no central radiance here. She stood in his drawing-room happy, and longing to give happiness. On leaving him she realized that the central radiance had been love.

"You aren't offended, Miss Schlegel?"

"How could I be offended?"

There was a moment's pause. He was anxious to get rid of her, and she knew it. She had too much intuition to look at him as he struggled for possessions that money cannot buy. He desired comradeship and affection, but he feared them, and she, who had taught herself only to desire, and could have clothed the struggle with beauty, held back, and hesitated with him.

"Good-bye," she continued. "You will have a letter from me--I am going back to Swanage tomorrow.

"Thank you."

"Good-bye, and it's you I thank."

"I may order the motor round, mayn't I?"

"That would be most kind."

"I wish I had written instead. Ought I to have written?"

"Not at all."

"There's just one question--"

She shook her head. He looked a little bewildered, and they parted.

They parted without shaking hands: she had kept the interview, for his sake, in tints of the quietest grey. Yet she thrilled with happiness ere she reached her own house. Others had loved her in the past, if one may apply to their brief desires so grave a word, but those others had been "ninnies"--young men who had nothing to do, old men who could find nobody better. And she had often "loved," too, but only so far as the facts of sex demanded: mere yearnings for the masculine, to be dismissed for what they were worth, with a smile. Never before had her personality been touched. She was not young or very rich, and it amazed her that a man of any standing should take her seriously. As she sat trying to do accounts in her empty house, amidst beautiful pictures and noble books, waves of emotion broke, as if a tide of passion was flowing through the night air. She shook her head, tried to concentrate her attention, and failed. In vain did she repeat: "But I've been through this sort of thing before." She had never been through it; the big machinery, as opposed to the little, had been set in motion, and the idea that Mr. Wilcox loved, obsessed her before she came to love him in return.

Chapter 18

She would come to no decision yet. "Oh, sir, this is so sudden"--that prudish phrase exactly expressed her when her time came. Premonitions are not preparation. She must examine more closely her own nature and his; she must talk it over judicially with Helen. It had been a strange love-scene--the central radiance unacknowledged from first to last. She, in his place, would have said "Ich liebe dich," but perhaps it was not his habit to open the heart. He might have done it if she had pressed him--as a matter of duty, perhaps; England expects every man to open his heart once; but the effort would have jarred him, and never, if she could avoid it, should he lose those defences that he had chosen to raise against the world. He must never be bothered with emotional talk, or with a display of sympathy. He was an elderly man now, and it would be futile and impudent to correct him.

Mrs. Wilcox strayed in and out, ever a welcome ghost; surveying the scene, thought Margaret, without one hint of bitterness.

Chapter 19

If one wanted to show a foreigner England, perhaps the wisest course would be to take him to the final section of the Purbeck Hills, and stand him on their summit, a few miles to the east of Corfe. Then system after system of our island would roll together under his feet. Beneath him is the valley of the Frome, and all the wild lands that come tossing down from Dorchester, black and gold, to mirror their gorse in the expanses of Poole. The valley of the Stour is beyond, unaccountable stream, dirty at Blandford, pure at Wimborne--the Stour, sliding out of fat fields, to marry the Avon beneath the tower of Christchurch. The valley of the Avon--invisible, but far to the north the trained eye may see Clearbury Ring that guards it, and the imagination may leap beyond that on to Salisbury Plain itself, and beyond the Plain to all the glorious downs of Central England. Nor is Suburbia absent. Bournemouth's ignoble coast cowers to the right, heralding the pine-trees that mean, for all their beauty, red houses, and the Stock Exchange, and extend to the gates of London itself. So tremendous is the City's trail! But the cliffs of Freshwater it shall never touch, and the island will guard the Island's purity till the end of time. Seen from the west, the Wight is beautiful beyond all laws of beauty. It is as if a fragment of England floated forward to greet the foreigner--chalk of our chalk, turf of our turf, epitome of what will follow. And behind the fragment lies Southampton, hostess to the nations, and Portsmouth, a latent fire, and all around it, with double and treble collision of tides, swirls the sea. How many villages appear in this view! How many castles! How many churches, vanished or triumphant! How many ships, railways, and roads! What incredible variety of men working beneath that lucent sky to what final end! The reason fails, like a wave on the Swanage beach; the imagination swells, spreads, and deepens, until it becomes geographic and encircles England.

So Frieda Mosebach, now Frau Architect Liesecke, and mother to her husband's baby, was brought up to these heights to be impressed, and, after a prolonged gaze, she said that the hills were more swelling here than in Pomerania, which was true, but did not seem to Mrs. Munt apposite. Poole Harbour was dry, which led her to praise the absence of muddy foreshore at Friedrich Wilhelms Bad, Rügen, where beech-trees hang over the tideless Baltic, and cows may contemplate the brine. Rather unhealthy Mrs. Munt thought this would be, water being safer when it moved about.

"And your English lakes--Vindermere, Grasmere--are they, then, unhealthy?"

"No, Frau Liesecke; but that is because they are fresh water, and different. Salt water ought to have tides, and go up and down a great deal, or else it smells. Look, for instance, at an aquarium."

"An aquarium! Oh, *Meesis* Munt, you mean to tell me that fresh aquariums stink less than salt? Why, when Victor, my brother-in-law, collected many tadpoles--"

"You are not to say 'stink,'" interrupted Helen; "at least, you may say it, but you must pretend you are being funny while you say it."

"Then 'smell.' And the mud of your Pool down there--does it not smell, or may I say 'stink, ha, ha'?"

"There always has been mud in Poole Harbour," said Mrs. Munt, with a slight frown. "The rivers bring it down, and a most valuable oyster-fishery depends upon it."

"Yes, that is so," conceded Frieda; and another international incident was closed.

"'Bournemouth is,'" resumed their hostess, quoting a local rhyme to which she was much attached--" 'Bournemouth is, Poole was, and Swanage is to be the most important town of all and biggest of the three.' Now, Frau Liesecke, I have shown you Bournemouth, and I have shown you Poole, so let us walk backward a little, and look down again at Swanage."

"Aunt Juley, wouldn't that be Meg's train?"

A tiny puff of smoke had been circling the harbour, and now was bearing southwards towards them over the black and the gold.

"Oh, dearest Margaret, I do hope she won't be overtired."

"Oh, I do wonder--I do wonder whether she's taken the house."

"I hope she hasn't been hasty."

"So do I--oh, so do I."

"Will it be as beautiful as Wickham Place?" Frieda asked.

"I should think it would. Trust Mr. Wilcox for doing himself proud. All those Ducie Street houses are beautiful in their modern way, and I can't think why he doesn't keep on with it. But it's really for Evie that he went there, and now that Evie's going to be married--"

"Ah!"

"You've never seen Miss Wilcox, Frieda. How absurdly matrimonial you are!"

"But sister to that Paul?"

"Yes."

"And to that Charles," said Mrs. Munt with feeling. "Oh, Helen, Helen, what a time that was!"

Helen laughed. "Meg and I haven't got such tender hearts. If there's a chance of a cheap house, we go for it."

"Now look, Frau Liesecke, at my niece's train. You see, it is coming towards us--coming, coming; and, when it gets to Corfe, it will actually go *through* the downs, on which we are standing, so that, if we walk over, as I suggested, and look down on Swanage, we shall see it coming on the other side. Shall we?"

Frieda assented, and in a few minutes they had crossed the ridge and exchanged the greater view for the lesser. Rather a dull valley lay below, backed by the slope of the coastward downs. They were looking across the Isle of Purbeck and on to Swanage, soon to be the most important town of all, and ugliest of the three. Margaret's train reappeared as promised, and was greeted with approval by her aunt. It came to a standstill in the middle distance, and there it had been planned that Tibby should meet her, and drive her, and a tea-basket, up to join them.

"You see," continued Helen to her cousin, "the Wilcoxes collect houses as your Victor collects tadpoles. They have, one, Ducie Street; two, Howards End, where my great rumpus was; three, a country seat in Shropshire; four, Charles has a house in Hilton; and five, another near Epsom; and six, Evie will have a house when she marries, and probably a pied-à-terre in the country--which makes seven. Oh yes, and Paul a hut in Africa makes eight. I wish we could get Howards End. That was something like a dear little house! Didn't you think so, Aunt Juley?"

" I had too much to do, dear, to look at it," said Mrs. Munt, with a gracious dignity. "I had everything to settle and explain, and Charles Wilcox to keep in his place besides. It isn't likely I should remember much. I just remember having lunch in your bedroom."

"Yes so do I. But, oh dear, dear, how dead it all seems! And in the autumn there began this anti-Pauline movement--you, and Frieda, and Meg, and Mrs. Wilcox, all obsessed with the idea that I might yet marry Paul."

"You yet may," said Frieda despondently.

Helen shook her head. "The Great Wilcox Peril will never return. If I'm certain of anything it's of that."

"One is certain of nothing but the truth of one's own emotions."

The remark fell damply on the conversation. But Helen slipped her arm round her cousin, somehow liking her the better for making it. It was not an original remark, nor had Frieda appropriated it passionately, for she had a patriotic rather than a philosophic mind. Yet it betrayed that interest in the universal which the average Teuton possesses and the average Englishman does not. It was, however illogically, the good, the beautiful, the true, as opposed to the respectable, the pretty, the adequate. It was a landscape of Böcklin's beside a landscape of Leader's, strident and ill-considered, but quivering into supernatural life. It sharpened idealism, stirred the soul. It may have been a bad preparation for what followed.

"Look!" cried Aunt Juley, hurrying away from generalities over the narrow summit of the down. "Stand where I stand, and you will see the pony-cart coming. I see the pony-cart coming."

They stood and saw the pony-cart coming. Margaret and Tibby were presently seen coming in it. Leaving the outskirts of Swanage, it drove for a little through the budding lanes, and then began the ascent.

Chapter 19

"Have you got the house?" they shouted, long before she could possibly hear.

Helen ran down to meet her. The highroad passed over a saddle, and a track went thence at right angles along the ridge of the down.

"Have you got the house?"

Margaret shook her head.

"Oh, what a nuisance! So we're as we were?"

"Not exactly."

She got out, looking tired.

"Some mystery," said Tibby. "We are to be enlightened presently."

Margaret came close up to her and whispered that she had had a proposal of marriage from Mr. Wilcox.

Helen was amused. She opened the gate on to the downs so that her brother might lead the pony through. "It's just like a widower," she remarked. "They've cheek enough for anything, and invariably select one of their first wife's friends."

Margaret's face flashed despair.

"That type--" She broke off with a cry. "Meg, not anything wrong with you?"

"Wait one minute," said Margaret, whispering always.

"But you've never conceivably--you've never--" She pulled herself together. "Tibby, hurry up through; I can't hold this gate indefinitely. Aunt Juley! I say, Aunt Juley, make the tea, will you, and Frieda; we've got to talk houses, and I'll come on afterwards." And then, turning her face to her sister's, she burst into tears.

Margaret was stupefied. She heard herself saying, "Oh, really--" She felt herself touched with a hand that trembled.

"Don't," sobbed Helen, "don't, don't, Meg, don't!" She seemed incapable of saying any other word. Margaret, trembling herself, led her forward up the road, till they strayed through another gate on to the down.

"Don't, don't do such a thing! I tell you not to--don't! I know--don't!"

"What do you know?"

"Panic and emptiness," sobbed Helen. "Don't!"

Then Margaret thought, "Helen is a little selfish. I have never behaved like this when there has seemed a chance of her marrying. She said: "But we would still see each other very often, and--"

"It's not a thing like that," sobbed Helen. And she broke right away and wandered distractedly upwards, stretching her hands towards the view and crying.

"What's happened to you?" called Margaret, following through the wind that gathers at sundown on the northern slopes of hills. "But it's stupid!" And suddenly stupidity seized her, and the immense landscape was blurred. But Helen turned back.

" Meg--"

"I don't know what's happened to either of us," said Margaret, wiping her eyes. "We must both have gone mad." Then Helen wiped hers, and they even laughed a little.

"Look here, sit down."

"All right; I'll sit down if you'll sit down."

"There. (One kiss.) Now, whatever, whatever is the matter?"

"I do mean what I said. Don't; it wouldn't do."

"Oh, Helen, stop saying 'don't'! It's ignorant. It's as if your head wasn't out of the slime. 'Don't' is probably what Mrs. Bast says all the day to Mr. Bast."

Helen was silent.

"Well?"

"Tell me about it first, and meanwhile perhaps I'll have got my head out of the slime."

"That's better. Well, where shall I begin? When I arrived at Waterloo--no, I'll go back before that, because I'm anxious you should know everything from the first. The 'first' was about ten days ago. It was the day Mr. Bast came to tea and lost his temper. I was defending him, and Mr. Wilcox became jealous about me, however slightly. I thought it was the involuntary thing, which men can't help any more than we can. You know--at least, I know in my own case--when a man has said to me, 'So-and-so's a pretty girl,' I am seized with a momentary sourness against So-and-so, and long to tweak her ear. It's a tiresome feeling, but not an important one, and one easily manages it. But it wasn't only this in Mr. Wilcox's case, I gather now."

"Then you love him?"

Margaret considered. "It is wonderful knowing that a real man cares for you," she said. "The mere fact of that grows more tremendous. Remember, I've known and liked him steadily for nearly three years.

"But loved him?"

Margaret peered into her past. It is pleasant to analyze feelings while they are still only feelings, and unembodied in the social fabric. With her arm round Helen, and her eyes shifting over the view, as if this county or that could reveal the secret of her own heart, she meditated honestly, and said, "No."

"But you will?"

"Yes," said Margaret, "of that I'm pretty sure. Indeed, I began the moment he spoke to me."

"And have settled to marry him?"

"I had, but am wanting a long talk about it now. What is it against him, Helen? You must try and say."

Helen, in her turn, looked outwards. "It is ever since Paul," she said finally.

"But what has Mr. Wilcox to do with Paul?"

"But he was there, they were all there that morning when I came down to breakfast, and saw that Paul was frightened--the man who loved me frightened and all his paraphernalia fallen, so that I knew it was impossible, because personal relations are the important thing for ever and ever, and not this outer life of telegrams and anger."

She poured the sentence forth in one breath, but her sister understood it, because it touched on thoughts that were familiar between them.

"That's foolish. In the first place, I disagree about the outer life. Well, we've often argued that. The real point is that there is the widest gulf between my love-making and yours. Yours--was romance; mine will be prose. I'm not running it down--a very good kind of prose, but well considered, well thought out. For instance, I know all Mr. Wilcox's faults. He's afraid of emotion. He cares too much about success, too little about the past. His sympathy lacks poetry, and so isn't sympathy really. I'd even say"--she looked at the shining lagoons--"that, spiritually, he's not as honest as I am. Doesn't that satisfy you?"

"No, it doesn't," said Helen. "It makes me feel worse and worse. You must be mad."

Margaret made a movement of irritation.

"I don't intend him, or any man or any woman, to be all my life--good heavens, no! There are heaps of things in me that he doesn't, and shall never, understand."

Thus she spoke before the wedding ceremony and the physical union, before the astonishing glass shade had fallen that interposes between married couples and the world. She was to keep her independence more than do most women as yet. Marriage was to alter her fortunes rather than her character, and she was not far wrong in boasting that she understood her future husband. Yet he did alter her character--a little. There was an unforeseen surprise, a cessation of the winds and odours of life, a social pressure that would have her think conjugally.

"So with him," she continued. "There are heaps of things in him--more especially things that he does--that will always be hidden from me. He has all those public qualities which you so despise and enable all this--" She waved her hand at the landscape, which confirmed anything. "If Wilcoxes hadn't worked and died in England for thousands of years, you and I couldn't sit here without having our throats cut. There would be no trains, no ships to carry us literary people about in, no fields even. Just savagery. No--perhaps not even that. Without their spirit life might never have moved out of protoplasm. More and more do I refuse to draw my income and sneer at those who guarantee it. There are times when it seems to me--"

"And to me, and to all women. So one kissed Paul."

"That's brutal," said Margaret. "Mine is an absolutely different case. I've thought things out."

"It makes no difference thinking things out. They come to the same."

" Rubbish!"

There was a long silence, during which the tide returned into Poole Harbour. "One would lose something," murmured Helen, apparently to herself. The water crept over the mud-flats towards the gorse and the blackened heather. Branksea Island lost its immense foreshores, and became a sombre episode of trees. Frome was forced inward towards Dorchester, Stour against Wimborne, Avon towards Salisbury, and over the immense displacement the sun presided, leading it to triumph ere he sank to rest. England was alive, throbbing through all her estuaries, crying for joy through the mouths of all her gulls, and the north wind, with contrary motion, blew stronger against her rising seas. What did it mean? For what end are her fair complexities, her changes of soil, her sinuous coast? Does she belong to those who have moulded her and made her feared by other lands, or to those who have added nothing to her power, but have somehow seen her, seen the whole island at once, lying as a jewel in a silver sea, sailing as a ship of souls, with all the brave world's fleet accompanying her towards eternity?

Chapter 20

Margaret had often wondered at the disturbance that takes place in the world's waters, when Love, who seems so tiny a pebble, slips in. Whom does Love concern beyond the beloved and the lover? Yet his impact deluges a hundred shores. No doubt the disturbance is really the spirit of the generations, welcoming the new generation, and chafing against the ultimate Fate, who holds all the seas in the palm of her hand. But Love cannot understand this. He cannot comprehend another's infinity; he is conscious only of his own--flying sunbeam, falling rose, pebble that asks for one quiet plunge below the fretting interplay of space and time. He knows that he will survive at the end of things, and be gathered by Fate as a jewel from the slime, and be handed with admiration round the assembly of the gods. "Men did produce this," they will say, and, saying, they will give men immortality. But meanwhile--what agitations meanwhile! The foundations of Property and Propriety are laid bare, twin rocks; Family Pride flounders to the surface, puffing and blowing, and refusing to be comforted; Theology, vaguely ascetic, gets up a nasty ground swell. Then the lawyers are aroused--cold brood--and creep out of their holes. They do what they can; they tidy up Property and Propriety, reassure Theology and Family Pride. Half-guineas are poured on the troubled waters, the lawyers creep back, and, if all has gone well, Love joins one man and woman together in Matrimony.

Margaret had expected the disturbance, and was not irritated by it. For a sensitive woman she had steady nerves, and could bear with the incongruous and the grotesque; and, besides, there was nothing excessive about her love-affair. Good-humour was the dominant note of her relations with Mr. Wilcox, or, as I must now call him, Henry. Henry did not encourage romance, and she was no girl to fidget for it. An acquaintance had become a lover, might become a husband, but would retain all that she had noted in the acquaintance; and love must confirm an old relation rather than reveal a new one.

In this spirit she promised to marry him.

He was in Swanage on the morrow, bearing the engagement-ring. They greeted one another with a hearty cordiality that impressed Aunt Juley. Henry dined at The Bays, but he had engaged a bedroom in the principal hotel: he was one of those men who knew the principal hotel by instinct. After dinner he asked Margaret if she wouldn't care for a turn on the Parade. She accepted, and could not repress a little tremor; it would be her first real love scene. But as she put on her hat she burst out laughing. Love was so unlike the article served up in books: the joy, though genuine, was different; the mystery an unexpected mystery. For one thing, Mr. Wilcox still seemed a stranger.

For a time they talked about the ring; then she said:

"Do you remember the Embankment at Chelsea? It can't be ten days ago."

"Yes," he said, laughing. "And you and your sister were head and ears deep in some Quixotic scheme. Ah well!"

"I little thought then, certainly. Did you?"

"I don't know about that; I shouldn't like to say."

"Why, was it earlier?" she cried. "Did you think of me this way earlier! How extraordinarily interesting, Henry! Tell me."

But Henry had no intention of telling. Perhaps he could not have told, for his mental states became obscure as soon as he had passed through them. He misliked the very word "interesting," connoting it with wasted energy and even with morbidity. Hard facts were enough for him.

"I didn't think of it," she pursued. "No; when you spoke to me in the drawing-room, that was practically the first. It was all so different from what it's supposed to be. On the stage, or in books, a proposal is--how shall I put it? --a full-blown affair, a kind of bouquet; it loses its literal meaning. But in life a proposal really is a proposal--"

"By the way--"

"--a suggestion, a seed," she concluded; and the thought flew away into darkness.

"I was thinking, if you didn't mind, that we ought to spend this evening in a business talk; there will be so much to settle."

"I think so too. Tell me, in the first place, how did you get on with Tibby?"

"With your brother?"

"Yes, during cigarettes."

"Oh, very well."

"I am so glad," she answered, a little surprised. "What did you talk about? Me, presumably."

"About Greece too."

"Greece was a very good card, Henry. Tibby's only a boy still, and one has to pick and choose subjects a little. Well done."

"I was telling him I have shares in a currant-farm near Calamata.

"What a delightful thing to have shares in! Can't we go there for our honeymoon?"

"What to do?"

"To eat the currants. And isn't there marvellous scenery?"

"Moderately, but it's not the kind of place one could possibly go to with a lady."

"Why not?"

"No hotels."

"Some ladies do without hotels. Are you aware that Helen and I have walked alone over the Apennines, with our luggage on our backs?"

"I wasn't aware, and, if I can manage it, you will never do such a thing again."

She said more gravely: "You haven't found time for a talk with Helen yet, I suppose?"

"No."

"Do, before you go. I am so anxious you two should be friends."

"Your sister and I have always hit it off," he said negligently. "But we're drifting away from our business. Let me begin at the beginning. You know that Evie is going to marry Percy Cahill."

"Dolly's uncle."

"Exactly. The girl's madly in love with him. A very good sort of fellow, but he demands--and rightly--a suitable provision with her. And in the second place, you will naturally understand, there is Charles. Before leaving town, I wrote Charles a very careful letter. You see, he has an increasing family and increasing expenses, and the I. and W. A. is nothing particular just now, though capable of development.

"Poor fellow!" murmured Margaret, looking out to sea, and not understanding.

"Charles being the elder son, some day Charles will have Howards End; but I am anxious, in my own happiness, not to be unjust to others."

"Of course not," she began, and then gave a little cry. "You mean money. How stupid I am! Of course not!"

Oddly enough, he winced a little at the word. "Yes. Money, since you put it so frankly. I am determined to be just to all--just to you, just to them. I am determined that my children shall have no case against me."

"Be generous to them," she said sharply. "Bother justice!"

"I am determined--and have already written to Charles to that effect--"

"But how much have you got?"

"What?"

"How much have you a year? I've six hundred."

"My income?"

"Yes. We must begin with how much you have, before we can settle how much you can give Charles. Justice, and even generosity, depend on that."

"I must say you're a downright young woman," he observed, patting her arm and laughing a little. "What a question to spring on a fellow!"

"Don't you know your income? Or don't you want to tell it me?"

"I--"

"That's all right"--now she patted him--"don't tell me. I don't want to know. I can do the sum just as well by proportion. Divide your income into ten parts. How many parts would you give to Evie, how many to Charles, how many to Paul?"

"The fact is, my dear, I hadn't any intention of bothering you with details. I only wanted to let you know that--well, that something must be done for the others, and you've understood me perfectly, so let's pass on to the next point."

"Yes, we've settled that," said Margaret, undisturbed by his strategic blunderings. "Go ahead; give away all you can, bearing in mind I've a clear six hundred. What a mercy it is to have all this money about one!"

"We've none too much, I assure you; you're marrying a poor man.

"Helen wouldn't agree with me here," she continued. "Helen daren't slang the rich, being rich herself, but she would like to. There's an odd notion, that I haven't yet got hold of, running about at the back of her brain, that poverty is somehow 'real.' She dislikes all organization, and probably confuses wealth with the technique of wealth. Sovereigns in a stocking wouldn't bother her; cheques do. Helen is too relentless. One can't deal in her high-handed manner with the world."

"There's this other point, and then I must go back to my hotel and write some letters. What's to be done now about the house in Ducie Street?"

"Keep it on--at least, it depends. When do you want to marry me?"

She raised her voice, as too often, and some youths, who were also taking the evening air, overheard her. "Getting a bit hot, eh?" said one. Mr. Wilcox turned on them, and said sharply, "I say!" There was silence. "Take care I don't report you to the police." They moved away quietly enough, but were only biding their time, and the rest of the conversation was punctuated by peals of ungovernable laughter.

Lowering his voice and infusing a hint of reproof into it, he said: "Evie will probably be married in September. We could scarcely think of anything before then."

"The earlier the nicer, Henry. Females are not supposed to say such things, but the earlier the nicer."

"How about September for us too?" he asked, rather dryly.

"Right. Shall we go into Ducie Street ourselves in September? Or shall we try to bounce Helen and Tibby into it? That's rather an idea. They are so unbusiness-like, we could make them do anything by judicious management. Look here--yes. We'll do that. And we ourselves could live at Howards End or Shropshire."

He blew out his cheeks. "Heavens! how you women do fly round! My head's in a whirl. Point by point, Margaret. Howards End's impossible. I let it to Hamar Bryce on a three years' agreement last March. Don't you remember? Oniton. Well, that is much, much too far away to rely on entirely. You will be able to be down there entertaining a certain amount, but we must have a house within easy reach of Town. Only Ducie Street has huge drawbacks. There's a mews behind."

Margaret could not help laughing. It was the first she had heard of the mews behind Ducie Street. When she was a possible tenant it had suppressed itself, not consciously, but automatically. The breezy Wilcox manner, though genuine, lacked the clearness of vision that is imperative for truth. When Henry lived in Ducie Street he remembered the mews; when he tried to let he forgot it; and if anyone had remarked that the mews must be either there or not, he would have felt annoyed, and afterwards have found some opportunity of stigmatizing the speaker as academic. So does my grocer stigmatize me when I complain of the quality of his sultanas, and he answers in one breath that they are the best sultanas, and how can I expect the best sultanas at that price? It is a flaw inherent in the business mind, and Margaret may do well to be tender to it, considering all that the business mind has done for England.

"Yes, in summer especially, the mews is a serious nuisance. The smoking room, too, is an abominable little den. The house opposite has been taken by operatic people. Ducie Street's going down, it's my private opinion."

"How sad! It's only a few years since they built those pretty houses."

"Shows things are moving. Good for trade."

"I hate this continual flux of London. It is an epitome of us at our worst--eternal formlessness; all the qualities, good, bad, and indifferent, streaming away--streaming, streaming for ever. That's why I dread it so. I mistrust rivers, even in scenery. Now, the sea--"

"High tide, yes."

"Hoy toid"--from the promenading youths.

"And these are the men to whom we give the vote," observed Mr. Wilcox, omitting to add that they were also the men to whom he gave work as clerks--work that scarcely encouraged them to grow into other men. "However, they have their own lives and interests. Let's get on."

He turned as he spoke, and prepared to see her back to The Bays. The business was over. His hotel was in the opposite direction, and if he accompanied her his letters would be late for the post. She implored him not to come, but he was obdurate.

"A nice beginning, if your aunt saw you slip in alone!"

"But I always do go about alone. Considering I've walked over the Apennines, it's common sense. You will make me so angry. I don't the least take it as a compliment."

He laughed, and lit a cigar. "It isn't meant as a compliment, my dear. I just won't have you going about in the dark. Such people about too! It's dangerous. "

"Can't I look after myself? I do wish--"

"Come along, Margaret; no wheedling."

A younger woman might have resented his masterly ways, but Margaret had too firm a grip of life to make a fuss. She was, in her own way, as masterly. If he was a fortress she was a mountain peak, whom all might tread, but whom the snows made nightly virginal. Disdaining the heroic outfit, excitable in her methods, garrulous, episodical, shrill, she misled her lover much as she had misled her aunt. He mistook her fertility for weakness. He supposed her "as clever as they make 'em," but no more, not realizing that she was penetrating to the depths of his soul, and approving of what she found there.

And if insight were sufficient, if the inner life were the whole of life, their happiness has been assured.

They walked ahead briskly. The parade and the road after it were well lighted, but it was darker in Aunt Juley's garden. As they were going up by the side-paths, through some rhododendrons, Mr. Wilcox, who was in front, said "Margaret" rather huskily, turned, dropped his cigar, and took her in his arms.

She was startled, and nearly screamed, but recovered herself at once, and kissed with genuine love the lips that were pressed against her own. It was their first kiss, and when it was over he saw her safely to the door and rang the bell for her, but disappeared into the night before the maid answered it. On looking back, the incident displeased her. It was so isolated. Nothing in their previous conversation had heralded it, and, worse still, no tenderness had ensued. If a man cannot lead up to passion he can at all events lead down from it, and she had hoped, after her complaisance, for some interchange of gentle words. But he had hurried away as if ashamed, and for an instant she was reminded of Helen and Paul.

Chapter 21

Charles had just been scolding his Dolly. She deserved the scolding, and had bent before it, but her head, though bloody, was unsubdued, and her chirrupings began to mingle with his retreating thunder.

"You've woken the baby. I knew you would. (Rum-ti-foo, Rackety-tackety Tompkin!) I'm not responsible for what Uncle Percy does, nor for anybody else or anything, so there!"

"Who asked him while I was away? Who asked my sister down to meet him? Who sent them out in the motor day after day?"

"Charles, that reminds me of some poem."

"Does it indeed? We shall all be dancing to a very different music presently. Miss Schlegel has fairly got us on toast."

"I could simply scratch that woman's eyes out, and to say it's my fault is most unfair."

"It's your fault, and five months ago you admitted it."

"I didn't."

"You did."

"Tootle, tootle, playing on the pootle!" exclaimed Dolly, suddenly devoting herself to the child.

"It's all very well to turn the conversation, but Father would never have dreamt of marrying as long as Evie was there to make him comfortable. But you must needs start match-making. Besides, Cahill's too old."

"Of course, if you're going to be rude to Uncle Percy--"

"Miss Schlegel always meant to get hold of Howards End, and, thanks to you, she's got it."

"I call the way you twist things round and make them hang together most unfair. You couldn't have been nastier if you'd caught me flirting. Could he, diddums?"

"We're in a bad hole, and must make the best of it. I shall answer the pater's letter civilly. He's evidently anxious to do the decent thing. But I do not intend to forget these Schlegels in a hurry. As long as they're on their best behaviour--Dolly, are you listening? --we'll behave, too. But if I find them giving themselves airs, or monopolizing my father, or at all ill-treating him, or worrying him with their artistic beastliness, I intend to put my foot down, yes, firmly. Taking my mother's place! Heaven knows what poor old Paul will say when the news reaches him."

The interlude closes. It has taken place in Charles's garden at Hilton. He and Dolly are sitting in deck-chairs, and their motor is regarding them placidly from its garage across the lawn. A short-frocked edition of Charles also regards them placidly; a perambulator edition is squeaking; a third edition is expected shortly. Nature is turning out Wilcoxes in this peaceful abode, so that they may inherit the earth.

Chapter 22

Margaret greeted her lord with peculiar tenderness on the morrow. Mature as he was, she might yet be able to help him to the building of the rainbow bridge that should connect the prose in us with the passion. Without it we are meaningless fragments, half monks, half beasts, unconnected arches that have never joined into a man. With it love is born, and alights on the highest curve, glowing against the grey, sober against the fire. Happy the man who sees from either aspect the glory of these outspread wings. The roads of his soul lie clear, and he and his friends shall find easy-going.

It was hard-going in the roads of Mr. Wilcox's soul. From boyhood he had neglected them. "I am not a fellow who bothers about my own inside." Outwardly he was cheerful, reliable, and brave; but within, all had reverted to chaos, ruled, so far as it was ruled at all, by an incomplete asceticism. Whether as boy, husband, or widower, he had always the sneaking belief that bodily passion is bad, a belief that is desirable only when held passionately. Religion had confirmed him. The words that were read aloud on Sunday to him and to other respectable men were the words that had once kindled the souls of St. Catharine and St. Francis into a white-hot hatred of the carnal. He could-not be as the saints and love the Infinite with a seraphic ardour, but he could be a little ashamed of loving a wife. "Amabat, amare timebat." And it was here that Margaret hoped to help him.

It did not seem so difficult. She need trouble him with no gift of her own. She would only point out the salvation that was latent in his own soul, and in the soul of every man. Only connect! That was the whole of her sermon. Only connect the prose and the passion, and both will be exalted, and human love will be seen at its height. Live in fragments no longer. Only connect, and the beast and the monk, robbed of the isolation that is life to either, will die.

Nor was the message difficult to give. It need not take the form of a good "talking." By quiet indications the bridge would be built and span their lives with beauty.

But she failed. For there was one quality in Henry for which she was never prepared, however much she reminded herself of it: his obtuseness. He simply did not notice things, and there was no more to be said. He never noticed that Helen and Frieda were hostile, or that Tibby was not interested in currant plantations; he never noticed the lights and shades that exist in the grayest conversation, the finger-posts, the milestones, the collisions, the illimitable views. Once--on another occasion--she scolded him about it. He was puzzled, but replied with a laugh: "My motto is Concentrate. I've no intention of frittering away my strength on that sort of thing." "It isn't frittering away the strength," she protested. "It's enlarging the space in which you may be strong." He answered: "You're a clever little woman, but my motto's Concentrate." And this morning he concentrated with a vengeance.

They met in the rhododendrons of yesterday. In the daylight the bushes were inconsiderable and the path was bright in the morning sun. She was with Helen, who had been ominously quiet since the affair was settled. "Here we all are!" she cried, and took him by one hand, retaining her sister's in the other.

"Here we are. Good-morning, Helen."

Helen replied, "Good-morning, Mr. Wilcox."

"Henry, she has had such a nice letter from the queer, cross boy--Do you remember him? He had a sad moustache, but the back of his head was young."

"I have had a letter too. Not a nice one--I want to talk it over with you:" for Leonard Bast was nothing to him now that she had given him her word; the triangle of sex was broken for ever.

"Thanks to your hint, he's clearing out of the Porphyrion."

"Not a bad business that Porphyrion," he said absently, as he took his own letter out of his pocket.

"Not a *bad*--" she exclaimed, dropping his hand. "Surely, on Chelsea Embankment--"

"Here's our hostess. Good-morning, Mrs. Munt. Fine rhododendrons. Good morning, Frau Liesecke; we manage to grow flowers in England, don't we?"

"Not a *bad* business?"

"No. My letter's about Howards End. Bryce has been ordered abroad, and wants to sublet it. I am far from sure that I shall give him permission. There was no clause in the agreement. In my opinion, subletting is a mistake. If he can find me another tenant, whom I consider suitable, I may cancel the agreement. Morning, Schlegel. Don't you think that's better than subletting?"

Helen had dropped her hand now, and he had steered her past the whole party to the seaward side of the house. Beneath them was the bourgeois little bay, which must have yearned all through the centuries for just such a watering-place as Swanage to be built on its margin. The waves were colourless, and the Bournemouth steamer gave a further touch of insipidity, drawn up against the pier and hooting wildly for excursionists.

"When there is a sublet I find that damage--"

"Do excuse me, but about the Porphyrion. I don't feel easy--might I just bother you, Henry?"

Her manner was so serious that he stopped, and asked her a little sharply what she wanted.

"You said on Chelsea Embankment, surely, that it was a bad concern, so we advised this clerk to clear out. He writes this morning that he's taken our advice, and now you say it's not a bad concern. "

"A clerk who clears out of any concern, good or bad, without securing a berth somewhere else first, is a fool, and I've no pity for him."

"He has not done that. He's going into a bank in Camden Town, he says. The salary's much lower, but he hopes to manage--a branch of Dempster's Bank. Is that all right?"

"Dempster! My goodness me, yes."

"More right than the Porphyrion?"

"Yes, yes, yes; safe as houses--safer."

"Very many thanks. I'm sorry--if you sublet--?"

"If he sublets, I shan't have the same control. In theory there should be no more damage done at Howards End; in practice there will be. Things may be done for which no money can compensate. For instance, I shouldn't want that fine wych-elm spoilt. It hangs--Margaret, we must go and see the old place some time. It's pretty in its way. We'll motor down and have lunch with Charles."

"I should enjoy that," said Margaret bravely.

"What about next Wednesday?"

"Wednesday? No, I couldn't well do that. Aunt Juley expects us to stop here another week at least."

"But you can give that up now."

"Er--no," said Margaret, after a moment's thought.

"Oh, that'll be all right. I'll speak to her."

"This visit is a high solemnity. My aunt counts on it year after year. She turns the house upside down for us; she invites our special friends--she scarcely knows Frieda, and we can't leave her on her hands. I missed one day, and she would be so hurt if I didn't stay the full ten."

"But I'll say a word to her. Don't you bother."

"Henry, I won't go. Don't bully me."

"You want to see the house, though?"

"Very much--I've heard so much about it, one way or the other. Aren't there pigs' teeth in the wych-elm?"

"*Pigs' teeth?*"

"And you chew the bark for toothache."

"What a rum notion! Of course not!"

"Perhaps I have confused it with some other tree. There are still a great number of sacred trees in England, it seems."

But he left her to intercept Mrs. Munt, whose voice could be heard in the distance: to be intercepted himself by Helen.

"Oh, Mr. Wilcox, about the Porphyrion--" she began, and went scarlet all over her face.

"It's all right," called Margaret, catching them up. "Dempster's Bank's better."

"But I think you told us the Porphyrion was bad, and would smash before Christmas."

"Did I? It was still outside the Tariff Ring, and had to take rotten policies. Lately it came in--safe as houses now."

"In other words, Mr. Bast need never have left it."

"No, the fellow needn't."

"--and needn't have started life elsewhere at a greatly reduced salary."

"He only says 'reduced,'" corrected Margaret, seeing trouble ahead.

"With a man so poor, every reduction must be great. I consider it a deplorable misfortune."

Mr. Wilcox, intent on his business with Mrs. Munt, was going steadily on, but the last remark made him say: "What? What's that? Do you mean that I'm responsible?"

"You're ridiculous, Helen."

"You seem to think--" He looked at his watch. "Let me explain the point to you. It is like this. You seem to assume, when a business concern is conducting a delicate negotiation, it ought to keep the public informed stage by stage. The Porphyrion, according to you, was bound to say, 'I am trying all I can to get into the Tariff Ring. I am not sure that I shall succeed, but it is the only thing that will save me from insolvency, and I am trying.' My dear Helen--"

"Is that your point? A man who had little money has less--that's mine."

"I am grieved for your clerk. But it is all in the day's work. It's part of the battle of life."

"A man who had little money," she repeated, "has less, owing to us. Under these circumstances I do not consider 'the battle of life' a happy expression."

"Oh come, come!" he protested pleasantly. "You're not to blame. No one's to blame."

"Is no one to blame for anything?"

"I wouldn't say that, but you're taking it far too seriously. Who is this fellow?"

"We have told you about the fellow twice already," said Helen. "You have even met the fellow. He is very poor and his wife is an extravagant imbecile. He is capable of better things. We--we, the upper classes--thought we would help him from the height of our superior knowledge--and here's the result!"

He raised his finger. "Now, a word of advice."

"I require no more advice."

"A word of advice. Don't take up that sentimental attitude over the poor. See that she doesn't, Margaret. The poor are poor, and one's sorry for them, but there it is. As civilization moves forward, the shoe is bound to pinch in places, and it's absurd to pretend that anyone is responsible personally. Neither you, nor I, nor my informant, nor the man who informed him, nor the directors of the Porphyrion, are to blame for this clerk's loss of salary. It's just the shoe pinching--no one can help it; and it might easily have been worse."

Helen quivered with indignation.

Chapter 22

"By all means subscribe to charities--subscribe to them largely--but don't get carried away by absurd schemes of Social Reform. I see a good deal behind the scenes, and you can take it from me that there is no Social Question--except for a few journalists who try to get a living out of the phrase. There are just rich and poor, as there always have been and always will be. Point me out a time when men have been equal--"

"I didn't say--"

"Point me out a time when desire for equality has made them happier. No, no. You can't. There always have been rich and poor. I'm no fatalist. Heaven forbid! But our civilization is moulded by great impersonal forces" (his voice grew complacent; it always did when he eliminated the personal), "and there always will be rich and poor. You can't deny it" (and now it was a respectful voice)--"and you can't deny that, in spite of all, the tendency of civilization has on the whole been upward."

"Owing to God, I suppose," flashed Helen.

He stared at her.

"You grab the dollars. God does the rest."

It was no good instructing the girl if she was going to talk about God in that neurotic modern way. Fraternal to the last, he left her for the quieter company of Mrs. Munt. He thought, "She rather reminds me of Dolly."

Helen looked out at the sea.

"Don't even discuss political economy with Henry," advised her sister. "It'll only end in a cry."

"But he must be one of those men who have reconciled science with religion," said Helen slowly. "I don't like those men. They are scientific themselves, and talk of the survival of the fittest, and cut down the salaries of their clerks, and stunt the independence of all who may menace their comfort, but yet they believe that somehow good--and it is always that sloppy 'somehow'--will be the outcome, and that in some mystical way the Mr. Basts of the future will benefit because the Mr. Basts of today are in pain."

"He is such a man in theory. But oh, Helen, in theory!"

"But oh, Meg, what a theory!"

"Why should you put things so bitterly, dearie?"

"Because I'm an old maid," said Helen, biting her lip. "I can't think why I go on like this myself." She shook off her sister's hand and went into the house. Margaret, distressed at the day's beginning, followed the Bournemouth steamer with her eyes. She saw that Helen's nerves were exasperated by the unlucky Bast business beyond the bounds of politeness. There might at any minute be a real explosion, which even Henry would notice. Henry must be removed.

"Margaret!" her aunt called. "Magsy! It isn't true, surely, what Mr. Wilcox says, that you want to go away early next week?"

"Not 'want,'" was Margaret's prompt reply; "but there is so much to be settled, and I do want to see the Charles'."

"But going away without taking the Weymouth trip, or even the Lulworth?" said Mrs. Munt, coming nearer. "Without going once more up Nine Barrows Down?"

"I'm afraid so."

Mr. Wilcox rejoined her with, "Good! I did the breaking of the ice."

A wave of tenderness came over her. She put a hand on either shoulder, and looked deeply into the black, bright eyes. What was behind their competent stare? She knew, but was not disquieted.

Chapter 23

Margaret had no intention of letting things slide, and the evening before she left Swanage she gave her sister a thorough scolding. She censured her, not for disapproving of the engagement, but for throwing over her disapproval a veil of mystery. Helen was equally frank. "Yes," she said, with the air of one looking inwards, "there is a mystery. I can't help it. It's not my fault. It's the way life has been made." Helen in those days was over-interested in the subconscious self. She exaggerated the Punch and Judy aspect of life, and spoke of mankind as puppets, whom an invisible showman twitches into love and war. Margaret pointed out that if she dwelt on this she, too, would eliminate the personal. Helen was silent for a minute, and then burst into a queer speech, which cleared the air. "Go on and marry him. I think you're splendid; and if anyone can pull it off, you will." Margaret denied that there was anything to "pull off," but she continued: "Yes, there is, and I wasn't up to it with Paul. I can only do what's easy. I can only entice and be enticed. I can't, and won't attempt difficult relations. If I marry, it will either be a man who's strong enough to boss me or whom I'm strong enough to boss. So I shan't ever marry, for there aren't such men. And Heaven help any one whom I do marry, for I shall certainly run away from him before you can say 'Jack Robinson.' There! Because I'm uneducated. But you, you're different; you're a heroine."

"Oh, Helen! Am I? Will it be as dreadful for poor Henry as all that?"

"You mean to keep proportion, and that's heroic, it's Greek, and I don't see why it shouldn't succeed with you. Go on and fight with him and help him. Don't ask *me* for help, or even for sympathy. Henceforward I'm going my own way. I mean to be thorough, because thoroughness is easy. I mean to dislike your husband, and to tell him so. I mean to make no concessions to Tibby. If Tibby wants to live with me, he must lump me. I mean to love *you* more than ever. Yes, I do. You and I have built up something real, because it is purely spiritual. There's no veil of mystery over us. Unreality and mystery begin as soon as one touches the body. The popular view is, as usual, exactly the wrong one. Our bothers are over tangible things--money, husbands, house-hunting. But Heaven will work of itself."

Margaret was grateful for this expression of affection, and answered, "Perhaps." All vistas close in the unseen--no one doubts it--but Helen closed them rather too quickly for her taste. At every turn of speech one was confronted with reality and the absolute. Perhaps Margaret grew too old for metaphysics, perhaps Henry was weaning her from them, but she felt that there was something a little unbalanced in the mind that so readily shreds the visible. The business man who assumes that this life is everything, and the mystic who asserts that it is nothing, fail, on this side and on that, to hit the truth. "Yes, I see, dear; it's about halfway between," Aunt Juley had hazarded in earlier years. No; truth, being alive, was not halfway between anything. It was only to be found by continuous excursions into either realm, and though proportion is the final secret, to espouse it at the outset is to insure sterility.

Helen, agreeing here, disagreeing there, would have talked till midnight, but Margaret, with her packing to do, focussed the conversation on Henry. She might abuse Henry behind his back, but please would she always, be civil to him in company? "I definitely dislike him, but I'll do what I can," promised Helen. "Do what you can with my friends in return."

This conversation made Margaret easier. Their inner life was so safe that they could bargain over externals in a way that would have been incredible to Aunt Juley, and impossible for Tibby or Charles. There are moments when the inner life actually "pays," when years of self-scrutiny, conducted for no ulterior motive, are suddenly of practical use. Such moments are still rare in the West; that they come at all promises a fairer future. Margaret, though unable to understand her sister, was assured against estrangement, and returned to London with a more peaceful mind.

The following morning, at eleven o'clock, she presented herself at the offices of the Imperial and West African Rubber Company. She was glad to go there, for Henry had implied his business rather than described it, and the formlessness and vagueness that one associates with Africa had hitherto brooded over the main sources of his wealth. Not that a visit to the office cleared things up. There was just the ordinary surface scum of ledgers and polished counters and brass bars that began and stopped for no possible reason, of electric-light globes blossoming in triplets, of little rabbit hutches faced with glass or wire, of little rabbits. And even when she penetrated to the inner depths, she found only the ordinary table and Turkey carpet, and though the map over the fireplace did depict a helping of West Africa, it was a very ordinary map. Another map hung opposite, on which the whole continent appeared, looking like a whale marked out for blubber, and by its side was a door, shut, but Henry's voice came through it, dictating a "strong" letter. She might have been at the Porphyrion, or Dempster's Bank, or her own wine-merchant's. Everything seems just alike in these days. But perhaps she was seeing the Imperial side of the company rather than its West African, and Imperialism always had been one of her difficulties.

"One minute!" called Mr. Wilcox on receiving her name. He touched a bell, the effect of which was to produce Charles.

Chapter 23

Charles had written his father an adequate letter--more adequate than Evie's, through which a girlish indignation throbbed. And he greeted his future step-mother with propriety.

"I hope that my wife--how do you do? --will give you a decent lunch," was his opening. "I left instructions, but we live in a rough-and-ready way. She expects you back to tea, too, after you have had a look at Howards End. I wonder what you'll think of the place. I wouldn't touch it with tongs myself. Do sit down! It's a measly little place."

"I shall enjoy seeing it," said Margaret, feeling, for the first time, shy.

"You'll see it at its worst, for Bryce decamped abroad last Monday without even arranging for a charwoman to clear up after him. I never saw such a disgraceful mess. It's unbelievable. He wasn't in the house a month."

"I've more than a little bone to pick with Bryce," called Henry from the inner chamber.

"Why did he go so suddenly?"

"Invalid type; couldn't sleep."

"Poor fellow!"

"Poor fiddlesticks!" said Mr. Wilcox, joining them. "He had the impudence to put up notice-boards without as much as saying with your leave or by your leave. Charles flung them down."

"Yes, I flung them down," said Charles modestly.

"I've sent a telegram after him, and a pretty sharp one, too. He, and he in person is responsible for the upkeep of that house for the next three years."

"The keys are at the farm; we wouldn't have the keys."

"Quite right."

"Dolly would have taken them, but I was in, fortunately."

"What's Mr. Bryce like?" asked Margaret.

But nobody cared. Mr. Bryce was the tenant, who had no right to sublet; to have defined him further was a waste of time. On his misdeeds they descanted profusely, until the girl who had been typing the strong letter came out with it. Mr. Wilcox added his signature. "Now we'll be off," said he.

A motor-drive, a form of felicity detested by Margaret, awaited her. Charles saw them in, civil to the last, and in a moment the offices of the Imperial and West African Rubber Company faded away. But it was not an impressive drive. Perhaps the weather was to blame, being grey and banked high with weary clouds. Perhaps Hertfordshire is scarcely intended for motorists. Did not a gentleman once motor so quickly through Westmoreland that he missed it? and if Westmoreland can be missed, it will fare ill with a county whose delicate structure particularly needs the attentive eye. Hertfordshire is England at its quietest, with little emphasis of river and hill; it is England meditative. If Drayton were with us again to write a new edition of his incomparable poem, he would sing the nymphs of Hertfordshire as indeterminate of feature, with hair obfuscated by the London smoke. Their eyes would be sad, and averted from their fate towards the Northern flats, their leader not Isis or Sabrina, but the slowly flowing Lea. No glory of raiment would be theirs, no urgency of dance; but they would be real nymphs.

The chauffeur could not travel as quickly as he had hoped, for the Great North Road was full of Easter traffic. But he went quite quick enough for Margaret, a poor-spirited creature, who had chickens and children on the brain.

"They're all right," said Mr. Wilcox. "They'll learn--like the swallows and the telegraph-wires."

"Yes, but, while they're learning--"

"The motor's come to stay," he answered. "One must get about. There's a pretty church--oh, you aren't sharp enough. Well, look out, if the road worries you--right outward at the scenery. "

She looked at the scenery. It heaved and merged like porridge. Presently it congealed. They had arrived.

Charles's house on the left; on the right the swelling forms of the Six Hills. Their appearance in such a neighbourhood surprised her. They interrupted the stream of residences that was thickening up towards Hilton. Beyond them she saw meadows and a wood, and beneath them she settled that soldiers of the best kind lay buried. She hated war and liked soldiers--it was one of her amiable inconsistencies.

But here was Dolly, dressed up to the nines, standing at the door to greet them, and here were the first drops of the rain. They ran in gaily, and after a long wait in the drawing-room sat down to the rough-and-ready lunch, every dish in which concealed or exuded cream. Mr. Bryce was the chief topic of conversation. Dolly described his visit with the key, while her father-in-law gave satisfaction by chaffing her and contradicting all she said. It was evidently the custom to laugh at Dolly. He chaffed Margaret, too, and Margaret, roused from a grave meditation, was pleased, and chaffed him back. Dolly seemed surprised, and eyed her curiously. After lunch the two children came down. Margaret disliked babies, but hit it off better with the two-year-old, and sent Dolly into fits of laughter by talking sense to him. "Kiss them now, and come away," said Mr. Wilcox. She came, but refused to kiss them: it was such hard luck on the little things, she said, and though Dolly proffered Chorly-worly and Porgly-woggles in turn, she was obdurate.

By this time it was raining steadily. The car came round with the hood up, and again she lost all sense of space. In a few minutes they stopped, and Crane opened the door of the car.

"What's happened?" asked Margaret.

"What do you suppose?" said Henry.

A little porch was close up against her face.

"Are we there already?"

"We are."

"Well, I never! In years ago it seemed so far away."

Smiling, but somehow disillusioned, she jumped out, and her impetus carried her to the front-door. She was about to open it, when Henry said: "That's no good; it's locked. Who's got the key?"

As he had himself forgotten to call for the key at the farm, no one replied. He also wanted to know who had left the front gate open, since a cow had strayed in from the road, and was spoiling the croquet lawn. Then he said rather crossly: "Margaret, you wait in the dry. I'll go down for the key. It isn't a hundred yards.

"Mayn't I come too?"

"No; I shall be back before I'm gone."

Then the car turned away, and it was as if a curtain had risen. For the second time that day she saw the appearance of the earth.

There were the greengage-trees that Helen had once described, there the tennis lawn, there the hedge that would be glorious with dog-roses in June, but the vision now was of black and palest green. Down by the dell-hole more vivid colours were awakening, and Lent Lilies stood sentinel on its margin, or advanced in battalions over the grass. Tulips were a tray of jewels. She could not see the wych-elm tree, but a branch of the celebrated vine, studded with velvet knobs, had covered the porch. She was struck by the fertility of the soil; she had seldom been in a garden where the flowers looked so well, and even the weeds she was idly plucking out of the porch were intensely green. Why had poor Mr. Bryce fled from all this beauty? For she had already decided that the place was beautiful.

"Naughty cow! Go away!" cried Margaret to the cow, but without indignation.

Harder came the rain, pouring out of a windless sky, and spattering up from the notice-boards of the house-agents, which lay in a row on the lawn where Charles had hurled them. She must have interviewed Charles in another world--where one did have interviews. How Helen would revel in such a notion! Charles dead, all people dead, nothing alive but houses and gardens. The obvious dead, the intangible alive, and--no connection at all between them! Margaret smiled. Would that her own fancies were as clear-cut! Would that she could deal as high-handedly with the world! Smiling and sighing, she laid her hand upon the door. It opened. The house was not locked up at all.

She hesitated. Ought she to wait for Henry? He felt strongly about property, and might prefer to show her over himself. On the other hand, he had told her to keep in the dry, and the porch was beginning to drip. So she went in, and the drought from inside slammed the door behind.

Desolation greeted her. Dirty finger-prints were on the hall-windows, flue and rubbish on its unwashed boards. The civilization of luggage had been here for a month, and then decamped. Dining-room and drawing room--right and left--were guessed only by their wall-papers. They were just rooms where one could shelter from the rain. Across the ceiling of each ran a great beam. The dining-room and hall revealed theirs openly, but the drawing-room's was match-boarded--because the facts of life must be concealed from ladies? Drawing-room, dining-room, and hall--how petty the names sounded! Here were simply three rooms where children could play and friends shelter from the rain. Yes, and they were beautiful.

Then she opened one of the doors opposite--there were two--and exchanged wall-papers for whitewash. It was the servants' part, though she scarcely realized that: just rooms again, where friends might shelter. The garden at the back was full of flowering cherries and plums. Farther on were hints of the meadow and a black cliff of pines. Yes, the meadow was beautiful.

Penned in by the desolate weather, she recaptured the sense of space which the motor had tried to rob from her. She remembered again that ten square miles are not ten times as wonderful as one square mile, that a thousand square miles are not practically the same as heaven. The phantom of bigness, which London encourages, was laid for ever when she paced from the hall at Howards End to its kitchen and heard the rains run this way and that where the watershed of the roof divided them.

Now Helen came to her mind, scrutinizing half Wessex from the ridge of the Purbeck Downs, and saying: "You will have to lose something." She was not so sure. For instance, she would double her kingdom by opening the door that concealed the stairs.

Now she thought of the map of Africa; of empires; of her father; of the two supreme nations, streams of whose life warmed her blood, but, mingling, had cooled her brain. She paced back into the hall, and as she did so the house reverberated.

"Is that you, Henry?" she called.

There was no answer, but the house reverberated again.

"Henry, have you got in?"

But it was the heart of the house beating, faintly at first, then loudly, martially. It dominated the rain.

It is the starved imagination, not the well-nourished, that is afraid. Margaret flung open the door to the stairs. A noise as of drums seemed to deafen her. A woman, an old woman, was descending, with figure erect, with face impassive, with lips that parted and said dryly:

"Oh! Well, I took you for Ruth Wilcox."

Margaret stammered: "I--Mrs. Wilcox--I?"

"In fancy, of course--in fancy. You had her way of walking. Good-day." And the old woman passed out into the rain.

Chapter 24

"It gave her quite a turn," said Mr. Wilcox, when retailing the incident to Dolly at tea-time. "None of you girls have any nerves, really. Of course, a word from me put it all right, but silly old Miss Avery--she frightened you, didn't she, Margaret? There you stood clutching a bunch of weeds. She might have said something, instead of coming down the stairs with that alarming bonnet on. I passed her as I came in. Enough to make the car shy. I believe Miss Avery goes in for being a character; some old maids do." He lit a cigarette. "It is their last resource. Heaven knows what she was doing in the place; but that's Bryce's business, not mine."

"I wasn't as foolish as you suggest," said Margaret. "She only startled me, for the house had been silent so long."

"Did you take her for a spook?" asked Dolly, for whom "spooks" and "going to church" summarized the unseen.

"Not exactly."

"She really did frighten you," said Henry, who was far from discouraging timidity in females. "Poor Margaret! And very naturally. Uneducated classes are so stupid."

"Is Miss Avery uneducated classes?" Margaret asked, and found herself looking at the decoration scheme of Dolly's drawing-room.

"She's just one of the crew at the farm. People like that always assume things. She assumed you'd know who she was. She left all the Howards End keys in the front lobby, and assumed that you'd seen them as you came in, that you'd lock up the house when you'd done, and would bring them on down to her. And there was her niece hunting for them down at the farm. Lack of education makes people very casual. Hilton was full of women like Miss Avery once."

"I shouldn't have disliked it, perhaps."

"Or Miss Avery giving me a wedding present," said Dolly.

Which was illogical but interesting. Through Dolly, Margaret was destined to learn a good deal.

"But Charles said I must try not to mind, because she had known his grandmother."

"As usual, you've got the story wrong, my good Dorothea."

"I mean great-grandmother--the one who left Mrs. Wilcox the house. Weren't both of them and Miss Avery friends when Howards End, too, was a farm?"

Her father-in-law blew out a shaft of smoke. His attitude to his dead wife was curious. He would allude to her, and hear her discussed, but never mentioned her by name. Nor was he interested in the dim, bucolic past. Dolly was--for the following reason.

"Then hadn't Mrs. Wilcox a brother--or was it an uncle? Anyhow, he popped the question, and Miss Avery, she said 'No.' Just imagine, if she'd said 'Yes,' she would have been Charles's aunt. (Oh, I say,--that's rather good! 'Charlie's Aunt'! I must chaff him about that this evening.) And the man went out and was killed. Yes, I'm certain I've got it right now. Tom Howard--he was the last of them."

"I believe so," said Mr. Wilcox negligently.

"I say! Howards End--Howard's Ended!" cried Dolly. "I'm rather on the spot this evening, eh?"

"I wish you'd ask whether Crane's ended."

"Oh, Mr. Wilcox, how *can* you?"

"Because, if he has had enough tea, we ought to go.--Dolly's a good little woman," he continued, "but a little of her goes a long way. I couldn't live near her if you paid me."

Margaret smiled. Though presenting a firm front to outsiders, no Wilcox could live near, or near the possessions of, any other Wilcox. They had the colonial spirit, and were always making for some spot where the white man might carry his burden unobserved. Of course, Howards End was impossible, so long as the younger couple were established in Hilton. His objections to the house were plain as daylight now.

Crane had had enough tea, and was sent to the garage, where their car had been trickling muddy water over Charles's. The downpour had surely penetrated the Six Hills by now, bringing news of our restless civilization. "Curious mounds," said, Henry, "but in with you now; another time." He had to be up in London by seven--if possible, by six-thirty. Once more she lost the sense of space; once more trees, houses, people, animals, hills, merged and heaved into one dirtiness, and she was at Wickham Place.

Her evening was pleasant. The sense of flux which had haunted her all the year disappeared for a time. She forgot the luggage and the motor-cars, and the hurrying men who know so much and connect so little. She recaptured the sense of space, which is the basis of all earthly beauty, and, starting from Howards End, she attempted to realize England. She failed--visions do not come when we try, though they may come through trying. But an unexpected love of the island awoke in her, connecting on this side with the joys of the flesh, on that with the inconceivable. Helen and her father had known this love, poor Leonard Bast was groping after it, but it had been hidden from Margaret till this afternoon. It had certainly come through the house and old Miss Avery. Through them: the notion of "through" persisted; her mind trembled towards a conclusion which only the unwise have put into words. Then, veering back into warmth, it dwelt on ruddy bricks, flowering plum-trees, and all the tangible joys of, spring.

Henry, after allaying her agitation, had taken her over his property, and had explained to her the use and dimensions of the various rooms. He had sketched the history of the little estate. "It is so unlucky," ran the monologue, "that money wasn't put into it about fifty years ago. Then it had four--five-times the land--thirty acres at least. One could have made something out of it then--a small park, or at all events shrubberies, and rebuilt the house farther away from the road. What's the good of taking it in hand now? Nothing but the meadow left, and even that was heavily mortgaged when I first had to do with things--yes, and the house too. Oh, it was no joke." She saw two women as he spoke, one old, the other young, watching their inheritance melt away. She saw them greet him as a deliverer. "Mismanagement did it--besides, the days for small farms are over. It doesn't pay--except with intensive cultivation. Small holdings, back to the land--ah! philanthropic bunkum. Take it as a rule that nothing pays on a small scale. Most of the land you see (they were standing at an upper window, the only one which faced west) belongs to the people at the Park--they made their pile over copper--good chaps. Avery's Farm, Sishe's--what they call the Common, where you see that ruined oak--one after the other fell in, and so did this, as near as is no matter. "But Henry had saved it; without fine feelings or deep insight, but he had saved it, and she loved him for the deed. "When I had more control I did what I could: sold off the two and a half animals, and the mangy pony, and the superannuated tools; pulled down the outhouses; drained; thinned out I don't know how many guelder-roses and elder-trees; and inside the house I turned the old kitchen into a hall, and made a kitchen behind where the dairy was. Garage and so on came later. But one could still tell it's been an old farm. And yet it isn't the place that would fetch one of your artistic crew." No, it wasn't; and if he did not quite understand it, the artistic crew would still less: it was English, and the wych-elm that she saw from the window was an English tree. No report had prepared her for its peculiar glory. It was neither warrior, nor lover, nor god; in none of these roles do the English excel. It was a comrade, bending over the house, strength and adventure in its roots, but in its utmost fingers tenderness, and the girth, that a dozen men could not have spanned, became in the end evanescent, till pale bud clusters seemed to float in the air. It was a comrade. House and tree transcended any similes of sex. Margaret thought of them now, and was to think of them through many a windy night and London day, but to compare either to man, to woman, always dwarfed the vision. Yet they kept within limits of the human. Their message was not of eternity, but of hope on this side of the grave. As she stood in the one, gazing at the other, truer relationship had gleamed.

Another touch, and the account of her day is finished. They entered the garden for a minute, and to Mr. Wilcox's surprise she was right. Teeth, pigs' teeth, could be seen in the bark of the wych-elm tree--just the white tips of them showing. "Extraordinary!" he cried. "Who told you?"

"I heard of it one winter in London," was her answer, for she, too, avoided mentioning Mrs. Wilcox by name.

Chapter 25

Evie heard of her father's engagement when she was in for a tennis tournament, and her play went simply to pot. That she should marry and leave him had seemed natural enough; that he, left alone, should do the same was deceitful; and now Charles and Dolly said that it was all her fault. "But I never dreamt of such a thing," she grumbled. "Dad took me to call now and then, and made me ask her to Simpson's. Well, I'm altogether off Dad." It was also an insult to their mother's memory; there they were agreed, and Evie had the idea of returning Mrs. Wilcox's lace and jewellery "as a protest." Against what it would protest she was not clear; but being only eighteen, the idea of renunciation appealed to her, the more as she did not care for jewellery or lace. Dolly then suggested that she and Uncle Percy should pretend to break off their engagement, and then perhaps Mr. Wilcox would quarrel with Miss Schlegel, and break off his; or Paul might be cabled for. But at this point Charles told them not to talk nonsense. So Evie settled to marry as soon as possible; it was no good hanging about with these Schlegels eyeing her. The date of her wedding was consequently put forward from September to August, and in the intoxication of presents she recovered much of her good-humour.

Margaret found that she was expected to figure at this function, and to figure largely; it would be such an opportunity, said Henry, for her to get to know his set. Sir James Bidder would be there, and all the Cahills and the Fussells, and his sister-in-law, Mrs. Warrington Wilcox, had fortunately got back from her tour round the world. Henry she loved, but his set promised to be another matter. He had not the knack of surrounding himself with nice people--indeed, for a man of ability and virtue his choice had been singularly unfortunate; he had no guiding principle beyond a certain preference for mediocrity; he was content to settle one of the greatest things in life haphazard, and so, while his investments went right, his friends generally went wrong. She would be told, "Oh, So-and-so's a good sort--a thundering good sort," and find, on meeting him, that he was a brute or a bore. If Henry had shown real affection, she would have understood, for affection explains everything. But he seemed without sentiment. The "thundering good sort" might at any moment become "a fellow for whom I never did have much use, and have less now," and be shaken off cheerily into oblivion. Margaret had done the same as a schoolgirl. Now she never forgot anyone for whom she had once cared; she connected, though the connection might be bitter, and she hoped that some day Henry would do the same.

Evie was not to be married from Ducie Street. She had a fancy for something rural, and, besides, no one would be in London then, so she left her boxes for a few weeks at Oniton Grange, and her banns were duly published in the parish church, and for a couple of days the little town, dreaming between the ruddy hills, was roused by the clang of our civilization, and drew up by the roadside to let the motors pass. Oniton had been a discovery of Mr. Wilcox's--a discovery of which he was not altogether proud. It was up towards the Welsh border, and so difficult of access that he had concluded it must be something special. A ruined castle stood in the grounds. But having got there, what was one to do? The shooting was bad, the fishing indifferent, and women-folk reported the scenery as nothing much. The place turned out to be in the wrong part of Shropshire, damn it, and though he never damned his own property aloud, he was only waiting to get it off his hands, and then to let fly. Evie's marriage was its last appearance in public. As soon as a tenant was found, it became a house for which he never had had much use, and had less now, and, like Howards End, faded into Limbo.

But on Margaret Oniton was destined to make a lasting impression. She regarded it as her future home, and was anxious to start straight with the clergy, etc., and, if possible, to see something of the local life. It was a market-town--as tiny a one as England possesses--and had for ages served that lonely valley, and guarded our marches against the Kelt. In spite of the occasion, in spite of the numbing hilarity that greeted her as soon as she got into the reserved saloon at Paddington, her senses were awake and watching, and though Oniton was to prove one of her innumerable false starts, she never forgot it, nor the things that happened there.

The London party only numbered eight--the Fussells, father and son, two Anglo-Indian ladies named Mrs. Plynlimmon and Lady Edser, Mrs. Warrington Wilcox and her daughter, and lastly, the little girl, very smart and quiet, who figures at so many weddings, and who kept a watchful eye on Margaret, the bride-elect, Dolly was absent--a domestic event detained her at Hilton; Paul had cabled a humorous message; Charles was to meet them with a trio of motors at Shrewsbury. Helen had refused her invitation; Tibby had never answered his. The management was excellent, as was to be expected with anything that Henry undertook; one was conscious of his sensible and generous brain in the background. They were his guests as soon as they reached the train; a special label for their luggage; a courier; a special lunch; they had only to look pleasant and, where possible, pretty. Margaret thought with dismay of her own nuptials--presumably under the management of Tibby. "Mr. Theobald Schlegel and Miss Helen Schlegel request the pleasure of Mrs. Plynlimmon's company on the occasion of the marriage of their sister Margaret." The formula was incredible, but it must soon be printed and sent, and though Wickham Place need not compete with Oniton, it must feed its guests properly, and provide them with sufficient chairs. Her wedding would either be ramshackly or bourgeois--she hoped the latter. Such an affair as the present, staged with a deftness that was almost beautiful, lay beyond her powers and those of her friends.

The low rich purr of a Great Western express is not the worst background for conversation, and the journey passed pleasantly enough. Nothing could have exceeded the kindness of the two men. They raised windows for some ladies, and lowered them for others, they rang the bell for the servant, they identified the colleges as the train slipped past Oxford, they caught books or bag-purses in the act of tumbling on to the floor. Yet there was nothing finicky about their politeness: it had the Public School touch, and, though sedulous, was virile. More battles than Waterloo have been won on our playing-fields, and Margaret bowed to a charm of which she did not wholly approve, and said nothing when the Oxford colleges were identified wrongly. "Male and female created He them"; the journey to Shrewsbury confirmed this questionable statement, and the long glass saloon, that moved so easily and felt so comfortable, became a forcing-house for the idea of sex.

At Shrewsbury came fresh air. Margaret was all for sight-seeing, and while the others were finishing their tea at the Raven, she annexed a motor and hurried over the astonishing city. Her chauffeur was not the faithful Crane, but an Italian, who dearly loved making her late. Charles, watch in hand, though with a level brow, was standing in front of the hotel when they returned. It was perfectly all right, he told her; she was by no means the last. And then he dived into the coffee-room, and she heard him say, "For God's sake, hurry the women up; we shall never be off," and Albert Fussell reply, "Not I; I've done my share," and Colonel Fussell opine that the ladies were getting themselves up to kill. Presently Myra (Mrs. Warrington's daughter) appeared, and as she was his cousin, Charles blew her up a little: she had been changing her smart traveling hat for a smart motor hat. Then Mrs. Warrington herself, leading the quiet child; the two Anglo-Indian ladies were always last. Maids, courier, heavy luggage, had already gone on by a branch-line to a station nearer Oniton, but there were five hat-boxes and four dressing-bags to be packed, and five dust-cloaks to be put on, and to be put off at the last moment, because Charles declared them not necessary. The men presided over everything with unfailing good-humour. By half-past five the party was ready, and went out of Shrewsbury by the Welsh Bridge.

Shropshire had not the reticence of Hertfordshire. Though robbed of half its magic by swift movement, it still conveyed the sense of hills. They were nearing the buttresses that force the Severn eastern and make it an English stream, and the sun, sinking over the Sentinels of Wales, was straight in their eyes. Having picked up another guest, they turned southward, avoiding the greater mountains, but conscious of an occasional summit, rounded and mild, whose colouring differed in quality from that of the lower earth, and whose contours altered more slowly. Quiet mysteries were in progress behind those tossing horizons: the West, as ever, was retreating with some secret which may not be worth the discovery, but which no practical man will ever discover.

They spoke of Tariff Reform.

Mrs. Warrington was just back from the Colonies. Like many other critics of Empire, her mouth had been stopped with food, and she could only exclaim at the hospitality with which she had been received, and warn the Mother Country against trifling with young Titans. "They threaten to cut the painter," she cried, "and where shall we be then? Miss Schlegel, you'll undertake to keep Henry sound about Tariff Reform? It is our last hope."

Margaret playfully confessed herself on the other side, and they began to quote from their respective hand-books while the motor carried them deep into the hills. Curious these were, rather than impressive, for their outlines lacked beauty, and the pink fields--on their summits suggested the handkerchiefs of a giant spread out to dry. An occasional outcrop of rock, an occasional wood, an occasional "forest," treeless and brown, all hinted at wildness to follow, but the main colour was an agricultural green. The air grew cooler; they had surmounted the last gradient, and Oniton lay below them with its church, its radiating houses, its castle, its river-girt peninsula. Close to the castle was a grey mansion, unintellectual but kindly, stretching with its grounds across the peninsula's neck--the sort of mansion that was built all over England in the beginning of the last century, while architecture was still an expression of the national character. That was the Grange, remarked Albert, over his shoulder, and then he jammed the brake on, and the motor slowed down and stopped. "I'm sorry," said he, turning round. "Do you mind getting out--by the door on the right? Steady on!"

"What's happened?" asked Mrs. Warrington.

Then the car behind them drew up, and the voice of Charles was heard saying: "Get out the women at once." There was a concourse of males, and Margaret and her companions were hustled out and received into the second car. What had happened? As it started off again, the door of a cottage opened, and a girl screamed wildly at them.

"What is it?" the ladies cried.

Charles drove them a hundred yards without speaking. Then he said: "It's all right. Your car just touched a dog."

"But stop!" cried Margaret, horrified.

"It didn't hurt him."

"Didn't really hurt him?" asked Myra.

"No."

"Do *please* stop!" said Margaret, leaning forward. She was standing up in the car, the other occupants holding her knees to steady her. "I want to go back, please."

Charles took no notice.

"We've left Mr. Fussell behind," said another; "and Angelo, and Crane."

"Yes, but no woman."

"I expect a little of"--Mrs. Warrington scratched her palm--" will be more to the point than one of us!"

"The insurance company sees to that," remarked Charles, "and Albert will do the talking."

"I want to go back, though, I say!" repeated Margaret, getting angry.

Charles took no notice. The motor, loaded with refugees, continued to travel very slowly down the hill. "The men are there," chorused the others. "Men will see to it."

"The men *can't* see to it. Oh, this is ridiculous! Charles, I ask you to stop."

"Stopping's no good," drawled Charles.

"Isn't it?" said Margaret, and jumped straight out of the car.

She fell on her knees, cut her gloves, shook her hat over her ear. Cries of alarm followed her. "You've hurt yourself," exclaimed Charles, jumping after her.

"Of course I've hurt myself!" she retorted.

"May I ask what--"

"There's nothing to ask," said Margaret.

"Your hand's bleeding."

"I know."

"I'm in for a frightful row from the pater."

"You should have thought of that sooner, Charles."

Charles had never been in such a position before. It was a woman in revolt who was hobbling away from him, and the sight was too strange to leave any room for anger. He recovered himself when the others caught them up: their sort he understood. He commanded them to go back.

Albert Fussell was seen walking towards them.

"It's all right!" he called. "It wasn't a dog, it was a cat."

"There!" exclaimed Charles triumphantly. "It's only a rotten cat.

"Got room in your car for a little un? I cut as soon as I saw it wasn't a dog; the chauffeurs are tackling the girl." But Margaret walked forward steadily. Why should the chauffeurs tackle the girl? Ladies sheltering behind men, men sheltering behind servants--the whole system's wrong, and she must challenge it.

"Miss Schlegel! 'Pon my word, you've hurt your hand."

"I'm just going to see," said Margaret. "Don't you wait, Mr. Fussell."

The second motor came round the corner. "It is all right, madam," said Crane in his turn. He had taken to calling her madam.

"What's all right? The cat?"

"Yes, madam. The girl will receive compensation for it."

"She was a very ruda girla," said Angelo from the third motor thoughtfully.

"Wouldn't you have been rude?"

The Italian spread out his hands, implying that he had not thought of rudeness, but would produce it if it pleased her. The situation became absurd. The gentlemen were again buzzing round Miss Schlegel with offers of assistance, and Lady Edser began to bind up her hand. She yielded, apologizing slightly, and was led back to the car, and soon the landscape resumed its motion, the lonely cottage disappeared, the castle swelled on its cushion of turf, and they had arrived. No doubt she had disgraced herself. But she felt their whole journey from London had been unreal. They had no part with the earth and its emotions. They were dust, and a stink, and cosmopolitan chatter, and the girl whose cat had been killed had lived more deeply than they.

"Oh, Henry," she exclaimed, "I have been so naughty," for she had decided to take up this line. "We ran over a cat. Charles told me not to jump out, but I would, and look!" She held out her bandaged hand. "Your poor Meg went such a flop."

Mr. Wilcox looked bewildered. In evening dress, he was standing to welcome his guests in the hall.

"Thinking it was a dog," added Mrs. Warrington.

"Ah, a dog's a companion!" said Colonel Fussell. "A dog'll remember you."

"Have you hurt yourself, Margaret?"

"Not to speak about; and it's my left hand."

"Well, hurry up and change."

She obeyed, as did the others. Mr. Wilcox then turned to his son.

"Now, Charles, what's happened?"

Charles was absolutely honest. He described what he believed to have happened. Albert had flattened out a cat, and Miss Schlegel had lost her nerve, as any woman might. She had been got safely into the other car, but when it was in motion had leapt out--again, in spite of all that they could say. After walking a little on the road, she had calmed down and had said that she was sorry. His father accepted this explanation, and neither knew that Margaret had artfully prepared the way for it. It fitted in too well with their view of feminine nature. In the smoking-room, after dinner, the Colonel put forward the view that Miss Schlegel had jumped it out of devilry. Well he remembered as a young man, in the harbour of Gibraltar once, how a girl--a handsome girl, too--had jumped overboard for a bet. He could see her now, and all the lads overboard after her. But Charles and Mr. Wilcox agreed it was much more probably nerves in Miss Schlegel's case. Charles was depressed. That woman had a tongue. She would bring worse disgrace on his father before she had done with them. He strolled out on to the castle mound to think the matter over. The evening was exquisite. On three sides of him a little river whispered, full of messages from the west; above his head the ruins made patterns against the sky. He carefully reviewed their dealings with this family, until he fitted Helen, and Margaret, and Aunt Juley into an orderly conspiracy. Paternity had made him suspicious. He had two children to look after, and more coming, and day by day they seemed less likely to grow up rich men. "It is all very well," he reflected, "the pater saying that he will be just to all, but one can't be just indefinitely. Money isn't elastic. What's to happen if Evie has a family? And, come to that, so may the pater. There'll not be enough to go round, for there's none coming in, either through Dolly or Percy. It's damnable!" He looked enviously at the Grange, whose windows poured light and laughter. First and last, this wedding would cost a pretty penny. Two ladies were strolling up and down the garden terrace, and as the syllables "Imperialism" were wafted to his ears, he guessed that one of them was his aunt. She might have helped him, if she too had not had a family to provide for. "Every one for himself," he repeated--a maxim which had cheered him in the past, but which rang grimly enough among the ruins of Oniton. He lacked his father's ability in business, and so had an ever higher regard for money; unless he could inherit plenty, he feared to leave his children poor.

As he sat thinking, one of the ladies left the terrace and walked into the meadow; he recognized her as Margaret by the white bandage that gleamed on her arm, and put out his cigar, lest the gleam should betray him. She climbed up the mound in zigzags, and at times stooped down, as if she was stroking the turf. It sounds absolutely incredible, but for a moment Charles thought that she was in love with him, and had come out to tempt him. Charles believed in temptresses, who are indeed the strong man's necessary complement, and having no sense of humour, he could not purge himself of the thought by a smile. Margaret, who was engaged to his father, and his sister's wedding-guest, kept on her way without noticing him, and he admitted that he had wronged her on this point. But what was she doing? Why was she stumbling about amongst the rubble and catching her dress in brambles and burrs? As she edged round the keep, she must have got to leeward and smelt his cigar-smoke, for she exclaimed, "Hullo! Who's that?"

Charles made no answer.

"Saxon or Kelt?" she continued, laughing in the darkness. "But it doesn't matter. Whichever you are, you will have to listen to me. I love this place. I love Shropshire. I hate London. I am glad that this will be my home. Ah, dear"--she was now moving back towards the house--"what a comfort to have arrived!"

"That woman means mischief," thought Charles, and compressed his lips. In a few minutes he followed her indoors, as the ground was getting damp. Mists were rising from the river, and presently it became invisible, though it whispered more loudly. There had been a heavy downpour in the Welsh hills.

Chapter 26

Next morning a fine mist covered the peninsula. The weather promised well, and the outline of the castle mound grew clearer each moment that Margaret watched it. Presently she saw the keep, and the sun painted the rubble gold, and charged the white sky with blue. The shadow of the house gathered itself together and fell over the garden. A cat looked up at her window and mewed. Lastly the river appeared, still holding the mists between its banks and its overhanging alders, and only visible as far as a hill, which cut off its upper reaches.

Margaret was fascinated by Oniton. She had said that she loved it, but it was rather its romantic tension that held her. The rounded Druids of whom she had caught glimpses in her drive, the rivers hurrying down from them to England, the carelessly modelled masses of the lower hills, thrilled her with poetry. The house was insignificant, but the prospect from it would be an eternal joy, and she thought of all the friends she would have to stop in it, and of the conversion of Henry himself to a rural life. Society, too, promised favourably. The rector of the parish had dined with them last night, and she found that he was a friend of her father's, and so knew what to find in her. She liked him. He would introduce her to the town. While, on her other side, Sir James Bidder sat, repeating that she only had to give the word, and he would whip up the county families for twenty miles round. Whether Sir James, who was Garden Seeds, had promised what he could perform, she doubted, but so long as Henry mistook them for the county families when they did call, she was content.

Charles and Albert Fussell now crossed the lawn. They were going for a morning dip, and a servant followed them with their bathing-dresses. She had meant to take a stroll herself before breakfast, but saw that the day was still sacred to men, and amused herself by watching their contretemps. In the first place the key of the bathing-shed could not be found. Charles stood by the riverside with folded hands, tragical, while the servant shouted, and was misunderstood by another servant in the garden. Then came a difficulty about a spring-board, and soon three people were running backwards and forwards over the meadow, with orders and counter orders and recriminations and apologies. If Margaret wanted to jump from a motor-car, she jumped; if Tibby thought paddling would benefit his ankles, he paddled; if a clerk desired adventure, he took a walk in the dark. But these athletes seemed paralysed. They could not bathe without their appliances, though the morning sun was calling and the last mists were rising from the dimpling stream. Had they found the life of the body after all? Could not the men whom they despised as milksops beat them, even on their own ground?

She thought of the bathing arrangements as they should be in her day--no worrying of servants, no appliances, beyond good sense. Her reflections were disturbed by the quiet child, who had come out to speak to the cat, but was now watching her watch the men. She called, "Good-morning, dear," a little sharply. Her voice spread consternation. Charles looked round, and though completely attired in indigo blue, vanished into the shed, and was seen no more.

"Miss Wilcox is up--" the child whispered, and then became unintelligible.

"What's that?"

It sounded like, "--cut-yoke--sack back--"

"I can't hear."

"--On the bed--tissue-paper--"

Gathering that the wedding-dress was on view, and that a visit would be seemly, she went to Evie's room. All was hilarity here. Evie, in a petticoat, was dancing with one of the Anglo-Indian ladies, while the other was adoring yards of white satin. They screamed, they laughed, they sang, and the dog barked.

Margaret screamed a little too, but without conviction. She could not feel that a wedding was so funny. Perhaps something was missing in her equipment.

Evie gasped: "Dolly is a rotter not to be here! Oh, we would rag just then!" Then Margaret went down to breakfast.

Henry was already installed; he ate slowly and spoke little, and was, in Margaret's eyes, the only member of their party who dodged emotion successfully. She could not suppose him indifferent either to the loss of his daughter or to the presence of his future wife. Yet he dwelt intact, only issuing orders occasionally--orders that promoted the comfort of his guests. He inquired after her hand; he set her to pour out the coffee and Mrs. Warrington to pour out the tea. When Evie came down there was a moment's awkwardness, and both ladies rose to vacate their places. "Burton," called Henry, "serve tea and coffee from the side-board!" It wasn't genuine tact, but it was tact, of a sort--the sort that is as useful as the genuine, and saves even more situations at Board meetings. Henry treated a marriage like a funeral, item by item, never raising his eyes to the whole, and "Death, where is thy sting? Love, where is thy victory?" one would exclaim at the close.

After breakfast she claimed a few words with him. It was always best to approach him formally. She asked for the interview, because he was going on to shoot grouse tomorrow, and she was returning to Helen in town.

"Certainly, dear," said he. "Of course, I have the time. What do you want?"

"Nothing."

"I was afraid something had gone wrong."

"No; I have nothing to say, but you may talk."

Glancing at his watch, he talked of the nasty curve at the lych-gate. She heard him with interest. Her surface could always respond to his without contempt, though all her deeper being might be yearning to help him. She had abandoned any plan of action. Love is the best, and the more she let herself love him, the more chance was there that he would set his soul in order. Such a moment as this, when they sat under fair weather by the walks of their future home, was so sweet to her that its sweetness would surely pierce to him. Each lift of his eyes, each parting of the thatched lip from the clean-shaven, must prelude the tenderness that kills the Monk and the Beast at a single blow. Disappointed a hundred times, she still hoped. She loved him with too clear a vision to fear his cloudiness. Whether he droned trivialities, as today, or sprang kisses on her in the twilight, she could pardon him, she could respond.

"If there is this nasty curve," she suggested, "couldn't we walk to the church? Not, of course, you and Evie; but the rest of us might very well go on first, and that would mean fewer carriages."

"One can't have ladies walking through the Market Square. The Fussells wouldn't like it; they were awfully particular at Charles's wedding. My--she--one of our party was anxious to walk, and certainly the church was just round the corner, and I shouldn't have minded; but the Colonel made a great point of it."

"You men shouldn't be so chivalrous," said Margaret thoughtfully.

"Why not?"

She knew why not, but said that she did not know.

He then announced that, unless she had anything special to say, he must visit the wine-cellar, and they went off together in search of Burton. Though clumsy and a little inconvenient, Oniton was a genuine country house. They clattered down flagged passages, looking into room after room, and scaring unknown maids from the performance of obscure duties. The wedding-breakfast must be in readiness when they came back from church, and tea would be served in the garden. The sight of so many agitated and serious people made Margaret smile, but she reflected that they were paid to be serious, and enjoyed being agitated. Here were the lower wheels of the machine that was tossing Evie up into nuptial glory. A little boy blocked their way with pig-tails. His mind could not grasp their greatness, and he said: "By your leave; let me pass, please." Henry asked him where Burton was. But the servants were so new that they did not know one another's names. In the still-room sat the band, who had stipulated for champagne as part of their fee, and who were already drinking beer. Scents of Araby came from the kitchen, mingled with cries. Margaret knew what had happened there, for it happened at Wickham Place. One of the wedding dishes had boiled over, and the cook was throwing cedar-shavings to hide the smell. At last they came upon the butler. Henry gave him the keys, and handed Margaret down the cellar-stairs. Two doors were unlocked. She, who kept all her wine at the bottom of the linen-cupboard, was astonished at the sight. "We shall never get through it!" she cried, and the two men were suddenly drawn into brotherhood, and exchanged smiles. She felt as if she had again jumped out of the car while it was moving.

Certainly Oniton would take some digesting. It would be no small business to remain herself, and yet to assimilate such an establishment. She must remain herself, for his sake as well as her own, since a shadowy wife degrades the husband whom she accompanies; and she must assimilate for reasons of common honesty, since she had no right to marry a man and make him uncomfortable. Her only ally was the power of Home. The loss of Wickham Place had taught her more than its possession. Howards End had repeated the lesson. She was determined to create new sanctities among these hills.

After visiting the wine-cellar, she dressed, and then came the wedding, which seemed a small affair when compared with the preparations for it. Everything went like one o'clock. Mr. Cahill materialized out of space, and was waiting for his bride at the church door. No one dropped the ring or mispronounced the responses, or trod on Evie's train, or cried. In a few minutes--the clergymen performed their duty, the register was signed, and they were back in their carriages, negotiating the dangerous curve by the lych-gate. Margaret was convinced that they had not been married at all, and that the Norman church had been intent all the time on other business.

There were more documents to sign at the house, and the breakfast to eat, and then a few more people dropped in for the garden party. There had been a great many refusals, and after all it was not a very big affair--not as big as Margaret's would be. She noted the dishes and the strips of red carpet, that outwardly she might give Henry what was proper. But inwardly she hoped for something better than this blend of Sunday church and fox-hunting. If only someone had been upset! But this wedding had gone off so particularly well--"quite like a Durbar" in the opinion of Lady Edser, and she thoroughly agreed with her.

So the wasted day lumbered forward, the bride and bridegroom drove off, yelling with laughter, and for the second time the sun retreated towards the hills of Wales. Henry, who was more tired than he owned, came up to her in the castle meadow, and, in tones of unusual softness, said that he was pleased. Everything had gone off so well. She felt that he was praising her, too, and blushed; certainly she had done all she could with his intractable friends, and had made a special point of kowtowing to the men. They were breaking camp this evening: only the Warringtons and quiet child would stay the night, and the others were already moving towards the house to finish their packing. "I think it did go off well," she agreed. "Since I had to jump out of the motor, I'm thankful I lighted on my left hand. I am so very glad about it, Henry dear; I only hope that the guests at ours may be half as comfortable. You must all remember that we have no practical person among us, except my aunt, and she is not used to entertainments on a large scale."

"I know," he said gravely. "Under the circumstances, it would be better to put everything into the hands of Harrod's or Whiteley's, or even to go to some hotel."

"You desire a hotel?"

"Yes, because--well, I mustn't interfere with you. No doubt you want to be married from your old home."

"My old home's falling into pieces, Henry. I only want my new. Isn't it a perfect evening--"

"The Alexandrina isn't bad--"

"The Alexandrina," she echoed, more occupied with the threads of smoke that were issuing from their chimneys, and ruling the sunlit slopes with parallels of grey.

"It's off Curzon Street."

"Is it? Let's be married from off Curzon Street."

Then she turned westward, to gaze at the swirling gold. Just where the river rounded the hill the sun caught it. Fairyland must lie above the bend, and its precious liquid was pouring towards them past Charles's bathing-shed. She gazed so long that her eyes were dazzled, and when they moved back to the house, she could not recognize the faces of people who were coming out of it. A parlourmaid was preceding them.

"Who are those people?" she asked.

"They're callers!" exclaimed Henry. "It's too late for callers."

"Perhaps they're town people who want to see the wedding presents."

"I'm not at home yet to townees."

"Well, hide among the ruins, and if I can stop them, I will."

He thanked her.

Margaret went forward, smiling socially. She supposed that these were unpunctual guests, who would have to be content with vicarious civility, since Evie and Charles were gone, Henry tired, and the others in their rooms. She assumed the airs of a hostess; not for long. For one of the group was Helen--Helen in her oldest clothes, and dominated by that tense, wounding excitement that had made her a terror in their nursery days.

"What is it?" she called. "Oh, what's wrong? Is Tibby ill?"

Helen spoke to her two companions, who fell back. Then she bore forward furiously.

"They're starving!" she shouted. "I found them starving!"

"Who? Why have you come?"

"The Basts."

"Oh, Helen!" moaned Margaret. "Whatever have you done now?"

"He has lost his place. He has been turned out of his bank. Yes, he's done for. We upper classes have ruined him, and I suppose you'll tell me it's the battle of life. Starving. His wife is ill. Starving. She fainted in the train."

"Helen, are you mad?"

"Perhaps. Yes. If you like, I'm mad. But I've brought them. I'll stand injustice no longer. I'll show up the wretchedness that lies under this luxury, this talk of impersonal forces, this cant about God doing what we're too slack to do ourselves."

"Have you actually brought two starving people from London to Shropshire, Helen?"

Helen was checked. She had not thought of this, and her hysteria abated. "There was a restaurant car on the train," she said.

"Don't be absurd. They aren't starving, and you know it. Now, begin from the beginning. I won't have such theatrical nonsense. How dare you! Yes, how dare you!" she repeated, as anger filled her, "bursting in to Evie's wedding in this heartless way. My goodness! but you've a perverted notion of philanthropy. Look"--she indicated the house--"servants, people out of the windows. They think it's some vulgar scandal, and I must explain, 'Oh no, it's only my sister screaming, and only two hangers-on of ours, whom she has brought here for no conceivable reason.'"

"Kindly take back that word 'hangers-on,'" said Helen, ominously calm.

"Very well," conceded Margaret, who for all her wrath was determined to avoid a real quarrel. "I, too, am sorry about them, but it beats me why you've brought them here, or why you're here yourself.

"It's our last chance of seeing Mr. Wilcox."

Margaret moved towards the house at this. She was determined not to worry Henry.

"He's going to Scotland. I know he is. I insist on seeing him."

"Yes, tomorrow."

"I knew it was our last chance."

"How do you do, Mr. Bast?" said Margaret, trying to control her voice. "This is an odd business. What view do you take of it?"

"There is Mrs. Bast, too," prompted Helen.

Jacky also shook hands. She, like her husband, was shy, and, furthermore, ill, and furthermore, so bestially stupid that she could not grasp what was happening. She only knew that the lady had swept down like a whirlwind last night, had paid the rent, redeemed the furniture, provided them with a dinner and breakfast, and ordered them to meet her at Paddington next morning. Leonard had feebly protested, and when the morning came, had suggested that they shouldn't go. But she, half mesmerized, had obeyed. The lady had told them to, and they must, and their bed-sitting-room had accordingly changed into Paddington, and Paddington into a railway carriage, that shook, and grew hot, and grew cold, and vanished entirely, and reappeared amid torrents of expensive scent. "You have fainted," said the lady in an awe-struck voice. "Perhaps the air will do you good." And perhaps it had, for here she was, feeling rather better among a lot of flowers.

"I'm sure I don't want to intrude," began Leonard, in answer to Margaret's question. "But you have been so kind to me in the past in warning me about the Porphyrion that I wondered--why, I wondered whether--"

"Whether we could get him back into the Porphyrion again," supplied Helen. "Meg, this has been a cheerful business. A bright evening's work that was on Chelsea Embankment."

Margaret shook her head and returned to Mr. Bast.

"I don't understand. You left the Porphyrion because we suggested it was a bad concern, didn't you?"

"That's right."

"And went into a bank instead?"

"I told you all that," said Helen; "and they reduced their staff after he had been in a month, and now he's penniless, and I consider that we and our informant are directly to blame."

"I hate all this," Leonard muttered.

"I hope you do, Mr. Bast. But it's no good mincing matters. You have done yourself no good by coming here. If you intend to confront Mr. Wilcox, and to call him to account for a chance remark, you will make a very great mistake."

"I brought them. I did it all," cried Helen.

"I can only advise you to go at once. My sister has put you in a false position, and it is kindest to tell you so. It's too late to get to town, but you'll find a comfortable hotel in Oniton, where Mrs. Bast can rest, and I hope you'll be my guests there."

"That isn't what I want, Miss Schlegel," said Leonard. "You're very kind, and no doubt it's a false position, but you make me miserable. I seem no good at all."

"It's work he wants," interpreted Helen. "Can't you see?"

Then he said: "Jacky, let's go. We're more bother than we're worth. We're costing these ladies pounds and pounds already to get work for us, and they never will. There's nothing we're good enough to do."

"We would like to find you work," said Margaret rather conventionally. "We want to--I, like my sister. You're only down in your luck. Go to the hotel, have a good night's rest, and some day you shall pay me back the bill, if you prefer it."

But Leonard was near the abyss, and at such moments men see clearly. "You don't know what you're talking about," he said. "I shall never get work now. If rich people fail at one profession, they can try another. Not I. I had my groove, and I've got out of it. I could do one particular branch of insurance in one particular office well enough to command a salary, but that's all. Poetry's nothing, Miss Schlegel. One's thoughts about this and that are nothing. Your money, too, is nothing, if you'll understand me. I mean if a man over twenty once loses his own particular job, it's all over with him. I have seen it happen to others. Their friends gave them money for a little, but in the end they fall over the edge. It's no good. It's the whole world pulling. There always will be rich and poor."

He ceased.

"Won't you have something to eat?" said Margaret. "I don't know what to do. It isn't my house, and though Mr. Wilcox would have been glad to see you at any other time--as I say, I don't know what to do, but I undertake to do what I can for you. Helen, offer them something. Do try a sandwich, Mrs. Bast."

They moved to a long table behind which a servant was still standing. Iced cakes, sandwiches innumerable, coffee, claret-cup, champagne, remained almost intact: their overfed guests could do no more. Leonard refused. Jacky thought she could manage a little. Margaret left them whispering together and had a few more words with Helen.

She said: "Helen, I like Mr. Bast. I agree that he's worth helping. I agree that we are directly responsible."

"No, indirectly. Via Mr. Wilcox."

"Let me tell you once for all that if you take up that attitude, I'll do nothing. No doubt you're right logically, and are entitled to say a great many scathing things about Henry. Only, I won't have it. So choose.

Helen looked at the sunset.

"If you promise to take them quietly to the George, I will speak to Henry about them--in my own way, mind; there is to be none of this absurd screaming about justice. I have no use for justice. If it was only a question of money, we could do it ourselves. But he wants work, and that we can't give him, but possibly Henry can."

"It's his duty to," grumbled Helen.

"Nor am I concerned with duty. I'm concerned with the characters of various people whom we know, and how, things being as they are, things may be made a little better. Mr. Wilcox hates being asked favours: all business men do. But I am going to ask him, at the risk of a rebuff, because I want to make things a little better."

"Very well. I promise. You take it very calmly. "

"Take them off to the George, then, and I'll try. Poor creatures! but they look tried." As they parted, she added: "I haven't nearly done with you, though, Helen. You have been most self-indulgent. I can't get over it. You have less restraint rather than more as you grow older. Think it over and alter yourself, or we shan't have happy lives."

She rejoined Henry. Fortunately he had been sitting down: these physical matters were important. "Was it townees?" he asked, greeting her with a pleasant smile.

"You'll never believe me," said Margaret, sitting down beside him. "It's all right now, but it was my sister."

"Helen here?" he cried, preparing to rise. "But she refused the invitation. I thought she despised weddings."

"Don't get up. She has not come to the wedding. I've bundled her off to the George."

Inherently hospitable, he protested.

"No; she has two of her protégés with her, and must keep with them."

"Let 'em all come."

"My dear Henry, did you see them?"

"I did catch sight of a brown bunch of a woman, certainly.

"The brown bunch was Helen, but did you catch sight of a sea-green and salmon bunch?"

"What! are they out beanfeasting?"

"No; business. They wanted to see me, and later on I want to talk to you about them."

She was ashamed of her own diplomacy. In dealing with a Wilcox, how tempting it was to lapse from comradeship, and to give him the kind of woman that he desired! Henry took the hint at once, and said: "Why later on? Tell me now. No time like the present."

"Shall I?"

"If it isn't a long story."

"Oh, not five minutes; but there's a sting at the end of it, for I want you to find the man some work in your office."

"What are his qualifications?"

"I don't know. He's a clerk."

"How old?"

"Twenty-five, perhaps."

"What's his name?"

"Bast," said Margaret, and was about to remind him that they had met at Wickham Place, but stopped herself. It had not been a successful meeting.

"Where was he before?"

"Dempster's Bank."

"Why did he leave?" he asked, still remembering nothing.

"They reduced their staff."

"All right; I'll see him."

It was the reward of her tact and devotion through the day. Now she understood why some women prefer influence to rights. Mrs. Plynlimmon, when condemning suffragettes, had said: "The woman who can't influence her husband to vote the way she wants ought to be ashamed of herself." Margaret had winced, but she was influencing Henry now, and though pleased at her little victory, she knew that she had won it by the methods of the harem.

"I should be glad if you took him," she said, "but I don't know whether he's qualified."

"I'll do what I can. But, Margaret, this mustn't be taken as a precedent."

"No, of course--of course--"

"I can't fit in your protégés every day. Business would suffer."

"I can promise you he's the last. He--he's rather a special case."

"Protégés always are."

She let it stand at that. He rose with a little extra touch of complacency, and held out his hand to help her up. How wide the gulf between Henry as he was and Henry as Helen thought he ought to be! And she herself--hovering as usual between the two, now accepting men as they are, now yearning with her sister for Truth. Love and Truth--their warfare seems eternal. Perhaps the whole visible world rests on it, and if they were one, life itself, like the spirits when Prospero was reconciled to his brother, might vanish into air, into thin air.

"Your protégé has made us late," said he. "The Fussells will just be starting."

On the whole she sided with men as they are. Henry would save the Basts as he had saved Howards End, while Helen and her friends were discussing the ethics of salvation. His was a slap-dash method, but the world has been built slap-dash, and the beauty of mountain and river and sunset may be but the varnish with which the unskilled artificer hides his joins. Oniton, like herself, was imperfect. Its apple-trees were stunted, its castle ruinous. It, too, had suffered in the border warfare between the Anglo Saxon and the Kelt, between things as they are and as they ought to be. Once more the west was retreating, once again the orderly stars were dotting the eastern sky. There is certainly no rest for us on the earth. But there is happiness, and as Margaret descended the mound on her lover's arm, she felt that she was having her share.

To her annoyance, Mrs. Bast was still in the garden; the husband and Helen had left her there to finish her meal while they went to engage rooms. Margaret found this woman repellent. She had felt, when shaking her hand, an overpowering shame. She remembered the motive of her call at Wickham Place, and smelt again odours from the abyss--odours the more disturbing because they were involuntary. For there was no malice in Jacky. There she sat, a piece of cake in one hand, an empty champagne glass in the other, doing no harm to anybody.

"She's overtired," Margaret whispered.

"She's something else," said Henry. "This won't do. I can't have her in my garden in this state."

"Is she--" Margaret hesitated to add "drunk." Now that she was going to marry him, he had grown particular. He discountenanced risqué conversations now.

Henry went up to the woman. She raised her face, which gleamed in the twilight like a puff-ball.

"Madam, you will be more comfortable at the hotel," he said sharply.

Jacky replied: "If it isn't Hen!"

"Ne crois pas que le mari lui ressemble," apologized Margaret. "Il est tout à fait différent."

"Henry!" she repeated, quite distinctly.

Mr. Wilcox was much annoyed. "I can't congratulate you on your protégés," he remarked.

"Hen, don't go. You do love me, dear, don't you?"

"Bless us, what a person!" sighed Margaret, gathering up her skirts.

Jacky pointed with her cake. "You're a nice boy, you are." She yawned. "There now, I love you."

"Henry, I am awfully sorry."

"And pray why?" he asked, and looked at her so sternly that she feared he was ill. He seemed more scandalized than the facts demanded.

"To have brought this down on you."

"Pray don't apologize."

The voice continued.

"Why does she call you 'Hen'?" said Margaret innocently. "Has she ever seen you before?"

"Seen Hen before!" said Jacky. "Who hasn't seen Hen? He's serving you like me, my dear. These boys! You wait--Still we love 'em."

"Are you now satisfied?" Henry asked.

Margaret began to grow frightened. "I don't know what it is all about," she said. "Let's come in."

But he thought she was acting. He thought he was trapped. He saw his whole life crumbling. "Don't you indeed?" he said bitingly. "I do. Allow me to congratulate you on the success of your plan."

"This is Helen's plan, not mine."

"I now understand your interest in the Basts. Very well thought out. I am amused at your caution, Margaret. You are quite right--it was necessary. I am a man, and have lived a man's past. I have the honour to release you from your engagement."

Still she could not understand. She knew of life's seamy side as a theory; she could not grasp it as a fact. More words from Jacky were necessary--words unequivocal, undenied.

"So that--" burst from her, and she went indoors. She stopped herself from saying more.

"So what?" asked Colonel Fussell, who was getting ready to start in the hall.

"We were saying--Henry and I were just having the fiercest argument, my point being--" Seizing his fur coat from a footman, she offered to help him on. He protested, and there was a playful little scene.

"No, let me do that," said Henry, following.

"Thanks so much! You see--he has forgiven me!"

The Colonel said gallantly: "I don't expect there's much to forgive.

He got into the car. The ladies followed him after an interval. Maids, courier, and heavier luggage had been sent on earlier by the branch--line. Still chattering, still thanking their host and patronizing their future hostess, the guests were home away.

Then Margaret continued: "So that woman has been your mistress?"

"You put it with your usual delicacy," he replied.

"When, please?"

"Why?"

"When, please?"

"Ten years ago."

She left him without a word. For it was not her tragedy: it was Mrs. Wilcox's.

Chapter 27

Helen began to wonder why she had spent a matter of eight pounds in making some people ill and others angry. Now that the wave of excitement was ebbing, and had left her, Mr. Bast, and Mrs. Bast stranded for the night in a Shropshire hotel, she asked herself what forces had made the wave flow. At all events, no harm was done. Margaret would play the game properly now, and though Helen disapproved of her sister's methods, she knew that the Basts would benefit by them in the long run.

"Mr. Wilcox is so illogical," she explained to Leonard, who had put his wife to bed, and was sitting with her in the empty coffee-room. "If we told him it was his duty to take you on, he might refuse to do it. The fact is, he isn't properly educated. I don't want to set you against him, but you'll find him a trial."

"I can never thank you sufficiently, Miss Schlegel," was all that Leonard felt equal to.

"I believe in personal responsibility. Don't you? And in personal everything. I hate--I suppose I oughtn't to say that--but the Wilcoxes are on the wrong tack surely. Or perhaps it isn't their fault. Perhaps the little thing that says 'I' is missing out of the middle of their heads, and then it's a waste of time to blame them. There's a nightmare of a theory that says a special race is being born which will rule the rest of us in the future just because it lacks the little thing that says 'I.' Had you heard that?"

"I get no time for reading."

"Had you thought it, then? That there are two kinds of people--our kind, who live straight from the middle of their heads, and the other kind who can't, because their heads have no middle? They can't say 'I.' They *aren't* in fact, and so they're supermen. Pierpont Morgan has never said 'I' in his life."

Leonard roused himself. If his benefactress wanted intellectual conversation, she must have it. She was more important than his ruined past. "I never got on to Nietzsche," he said. "But I always understood that those supermen were rather what you may call egoists."

"Oh, no, that's wrong," replied Helen. "No superman ever said 'I want,' because 'I want' must lead to the question, 'Who am I?' and so to Pity and to Justice. He only says 'want.' 'Want Europe,' if he's Napoleon; 'want wives,' if he's Bluebeard; 'want Botticelli,' if he's Pierpont Morgan. Never the 'I'; and if you could pierce through him, you'd find panic and emptiness in the middle."

Leonard was silent for a moment. Then he said: "May I take it, Miss Schlegel, that you and I are both the sort that say 'I'?"

"Of course."

"And your sister too?"

"Of course," repeated Helen, a little sharply. She was annoyed with Margaret, but did not want her discussed. "All presentable people say 'I.'"

"But Mr. Wilcox--he is not perhaps--"

"I don't know that it's any good discussing Mr. Wilcox either."

"Quite so, quite so," he agreed. Helen asked herself why she had snubbed him. Once or twice during the day she had encouraged him to criticize, and then had pulled him up short. Was she afraid of him presuming? If so, it was disgusting of her.

But he was thinking the snub quite natural. Everything she did was natural, and incapable of causing offence. While the Miss Schlegels were together he had felt them scarcely human--a sort of admonitory whirligig. But a Miss Schlegel alone was different. She was in Helen's case unmarried, in Margaret's about to be married, in neither case an echo of her sister. A light had fallen at last into this rich upper world, and he saw that it was full of men and women, some of whom were more friendly to him than others. Helen had become "his" Miss Schlegel, who scolded him and corresponded with him, and had swept down yesterday with grateful vehemence. Margaret, though not unkind, was severe and remote. He would not presume to help her, for instance. He had never liked her, and began to think that his original impression was true, and that her sister did not like her either. Helen was certainly lonely. She, who gave away so much, was receiving too little. Leonard was pleased to think that he could spare her vexation by holding his tongue and concealing what he knew about Mr. Wilcox. Jacky had announced her discovery when he fetched her from the lawn. After the first shock, he did not mind for himself. By now he had no illusions about his wife, and this was only one new stain on the face of a love that had never been pure. To keep perfection perfect, that should be his ideal, if the future gave him time to have ideals. Helen, and Margaret for Helen's sake, must not know.

Helen disconcerted him by fuming the conversation to his wife. "Mrs. Bast--does she ever say 'I'?" she asked, half mischievously, and then, "Is she very tired?"

"It's better she stops in her room," said Leonard.

"Shall I sit up with her?"

"No, thank you; she does not need company."

"Mr. Bast, what kind of woman is your wife?"

Leonard blushed up to his eyes.

"You ought to know my ways by now. Does that question offend you?"

"No, oh no, Miss Schlegel, no."

"Because I love honesty. Don't pretend your marriage has been a happy one. You and she can have nothing in common."

He did not deny it, but said shyly: "I suppose that's pretty obvious; but Jacky never meant to do anybody any harm. When things went wrong, or I heard things, I used to think it was her fault, but, looking back, it's more mine. I needn't have married her, but as I have I must stick to her and keep her."

"How long have you been married?"

"Nearly three years."

"What did your people say?"

"They will not have anything to do with us. They had a sort of family council when they heard I was married, and cut us off altogether."

Helen began to pace up and down the room. "My good boy, what a mess!" she said gently. "Who are your people?"

He could answer this. His parents, who were dead, had been in trade; his sisters had married commercial travellers; his brother was a lay-reader.

"And your grandparents?"

Leonard told her a secret that he had held shameful up to now. "They were just nothing at all," he said, "--agricultural labourers and that sort."

"So! From which part?"

"Lincolnshire mostly, but my mother's father--he, oddly enough, came from these parts round here."

"From this very Shropshire. Yes, that is odd. My mother's people were Lancashire. But why do your brother and your sisters object to Mrs. Bast?"

"Oh, I don't know."

"Excuse me, you do know. I am not a baby. I can bear anything you tell me, and the more you tell the more I shall be able to help. Have they heard anything against her?"

He was silent.

"I think I have guessed now," said Helen very gravely.

"I don't think so, Miss Schlegel; I hope not."

"We must be honest, even over these things. I have guessed. I am frightfully, dreadfully sorry, but it does not make the least difference to me. I shall feel just the same to both of you. I blame, not your wife for these things, but men."

Leonard left it at that--so long as she did not guess the man. She stood at the window and slowly pulled up the blinds. The hotel looked over a dark square. The mists had begun. When she turned back to him her eyes were shining.

"Don't you worry," he pleaded. "I can't bear that. We shall be all right if I get work. If I could only get work--something regular to do. Then it wouldn't be so bad again. I don't trouble after books as I used. I can imagine that with regular work we should settle down again. It stops one thinking. "

"Settle down to what?"

"Oh, just settle down."

"And that's to be life!" said Helen, with a catch in her throat. "How can you, with all the beautiful things to see and do--with music--with walking at night--"

"Walking is well enough when a man's in work," he answered. "Oh, I did talk a lot of nonsense once, but there's nothing like a bailiff in the house to drive it out of you. When I saw him fingering my Ruskins and Stevensons, I seemed to see life straight real, and it isn't a pretty sight. My books are back again, thanks to you, but they'll never be the same to me again, and I shan't ever again think night in the woods is wonderful."

"Why not?" asked Helen, throwing up the window.

"Because I see one must have money."

"Well, you're wrong."

"I wish I was wrong, but--the clergyman--he has money of his own, or else he's paid; the poet or the musician--just the same; the tramp--he's no different. The tramp goes to the workhouse in the end, and is paid for with other people's money. Miss Schlegel, the real thing's money and all the rest is a dream."

"You're still wrong. You've forgotten Death."

Leonard could not understand.

"If we lived for ever what you say would be true. But we have to die, we have to leave life presently. Injustice and greed would be the real thing if we lived for ever. As it is, we must hold to other things, because Death is coming. I love Death--not morbidly, but because He explains. He shows me the emptiness of Money. Death and Money are the eternal foes. Not Death and Life. Never mind what lies behind Death, Mr. Bast, but be sure that the poet and the musician and the tramp will be happier in it than the man who has never learnt to say, 'I am I.'"

"I wonder."

"We are all in a mist--I know but I can help you this far--men like the Wilcoxes are deeper in the mist than any. Sane, sound Englishmen! building up empires, levelling all the world into what they call common sense. But mention Death to them and they're offended, because Death's really Imperial, and He cries out against them for ever."

"I am as afraid of Death as any one."

"But not of the idea of Death."

"But what is the difference?"

"Infinite difference," said Helen, more gravely than before.

Leonard looked at her wondering, and had the sense of great things sweeping out of the shrouded night. But he could not receive them, because his heart was still full of little things. As the lost umbrella had spoilt the concert at Queen's Hall, so the lost situation was obscuring the diviner harmonies now. Death, Life and Materialism were fine words, but would Mr. Wilcox take him on as a clerk? Talk as one would, Mr. Wilcox was king of this world, the superman, with his own morality, whose head remained in the clouds.

"I must be stupid," he said apologetically.

While to Helen the paradox became clearer and clearer. "Death destroys a man: the idea of Death saves him." Behind the coffins and the skeletons that stay the vulgar mind lies something so immense that all that is great in us responds to it. Men of the world may recoil from the charnel-house that they will one day enter, but Love knows better. Death is his foe, but his peer, and in their age-long struggle the thews of Love have been strengthened, and his vision cleared, until there is no one who can stand against him.

"So never give in," continued the girl, and restated again and again the vague yet convincing plea that the Invisible lodges against the Visible. Her excitement grew as she tried to cut the rope that fastened Leonard to the earth. Woven of bitter experience, it resisted her. Presently the waitress entered and gave her a letter from Margaret. Another note, addressed to Leonard, was inside. They read them, listening to the murmurings of the river.

Chapter 28

For many hours Margaret did nothing; then she controlled herself, and wrote some letters. She was too bruised to speak to Henry; she could pity him, and even determine to marry him, but as yet all lay too deep in her heart for speech. On the surface the sense of his degradation was too strong. She could not command voice or look, and the gentle words that she forced out through her pen seemed to proceed from some other person.

"My dearest boy," she began, "this is not to part us. It is everything or nothing, and I mean it to be nothing. It happened long before we ever met, and even if it had happened since, I should be writing the same, I hope. I do understand."

But she crossed out "I do understand"; it struck a false note. Henry could not bear to be understood. She also crossed out, "It is everything or nothing. "Henry would resent so strong a grasp of the situation. She must not comment; comment is unfeminine.

"I think that'll about do," she thought.

Then the sense of his degradation choked her. Was he worth all this bother? To have yielded to a woman of that sort was everything, yes, it was, and she could not be his wife. She tried to translate his temptation into her own language, and her brain reeled. Men must be different, even to want to yield to such a temptation. Her belief in comradeship was stifled, and she saw life as from that glass saloon on the Great Western, which sheltered male and female alike from the fresh air. Are the sexes really races, each with its own code of morality, and their mutual love a mere device of Nature to keep things going? Strip human intercourse of the proprieties, and is it reduced to this? Her judgment told her no. She knew that out of Nature's device we have built a magic that will win us immortality. Far more mysterious than the call of sex to sex is the tenderness that we throw into that call; far wider is the gulf between us and the farmyard than between the farm-yard and the garbage that nourishes it. We are evolving, in ways that Science cannot measure, to ends that Theology dares not contemplate. "Men did produce one jewel," the gods will say, and, saying, will give us immortality. Margaret knew all this, but for the moment she could not feel it, and transformed the marriage of Evie and Mr. Cahill into a carnival of fools, and her own marriage--too miserable to think of that, she tore up the letter, and then wrote another:

Chapter 28

Dear Mr. Bast,

I have spoken to Mr. Wilcox about you, as I promised, and am sorry to say that he has no vacancy for you.

Yours truly,
M. J. Schlegel

She enclosed this in a note to Helen, over which she took less trouble than she might have done; but her head was aching, and she could not stop to pick her words:

Dear Helen,

Give him this. The Basts are no good. Henry found the woman drunk on the lawn. I am having a room got ready for you here, and will you please come round at once on getting this? The Basts are not at all the type we should trouble about. I may go round to them myself in the morning, and do anything that is fair.

M

In writing this, Margaret felt that she was being practical. Something might be arranged for the Basts later on, but they must be silenced for the moment. She hoped to avoid a conversation between the woman and Helen. She rang the bell for a servant, but no one answered it; Mr. Wilcox and the Warringtons were gone to bed, and the kitchen was abandoned to Saturnalia. Consequently she went over to the George herself. She did not enter the hotel, for discussion would have been perilous, and, saying that the letter was important, she gave it to the waitress. As she recrossed the square she saw Helen and Mr. Bast looking out of the window of the coffee-room, and feared she was already too late. Her task was not yet over; she ought to tell Henry what she had done.

This came easily, for she saw him in the hall. The night wind had been rattling the pictures against the wall, and the noise had disturbed him.

"Who's there?" he called, quite the householder.

Margaret walked in and past him.

"I have asked Helen to sleep," she said. "She is best here; so don't lock the front-door."

"I thought someone had got in," said Henry.

"At the same time I told the man that we could do nothing for him. I don't know about later, but now the Basts must clearly go."

"Did you say that your sister is sleeping here, after all?"

"Probably."

"Is she to be shown up to your room?"

"I have naturally nothing to say to her; I am going to bed. Will you tell the servants about Helen? Could someone go to carry her bag?"

He tapped a little gong, which had been bought to summon the servants.

"You must make more noise than that if you want them to hear."

Henry opened a door, and down the corridor came shouts of laughter. "Far too much screaming there," he said, and strode towards it. Margaret went upstairs, uncertain whether to be glad that they had met, or sorry. They had behaved as if nothing had happened, and her deepest instincts told her that this was wrong. For his own sake, some explanation was due.

And yet--what could an explanation tell her? A date, a place, a few details, which she could imagine all too clearly. Now that the first shock was over, she saw that there was every reason to premise a Mrs. Bast. Henry's inner life had long laid open to her--his intellectual confusion, his obtuseness to personal influence, his strong but furtive passions. Should she refuse him because his outer life corresponded? Perhaps. Perhaps, if the dishonour had been done to her, but it was done long before her day. She struggled against the feeling. She told herself that Mrs. Wilcox's wrong was her own. But she was not a bargain theorist. As she undressed, her anger, her regard for the dead, her desire for a scene, all grew weak. Henry must have it as he liked, for she loved him, and some day she would use her love to make him a better man.

Pity was at the bottom of her actions all through this crisis. Pity, if one may generalize, is at the bottom of woman. When men like us, it is for our better qualities, and however tender their liking, we dare not be unworthy of it, or they will quietly let us go. But unworthiness stimulates woman. It brings out her deeper nature, for good or for evil.

Here was the core of the question. Henry must be forgiven, and made better by love; nothing else mattered. Mrs. Wilcox, that unquiet yet kindly ghost, must be left to her own wrong. To her everything was in proportion now, and she, too, would pity the man who was blundering up and down their lives. Had Mrs. Wilcox known of his trespass? An interesting question, but Margaret fell asleep, tethered by affection, and lulled by the murmurs of the river that descended all the night from Wales. She felt herself at one with her future home, colouring it and coloured by it, and awoke to see, for the second time, Oniton Castle conquering the morning mists.

Chapter 29

"Henry dear--" was her greeting.

He had finished his breakfast, and was beginning the *Times*. His sister-in-law was packing. She knelt by him and took the paper from him, feeling that it was unusually heavy and thick. Then, putting her face where it had been, she looked up in his eyes.

"Henry dear, look at me. No, I won't have you shirking. Look at me. There. That's all."

"You're referring to last evening," he said huskily. "I have released you from your engagement. I could find excuses, but I won't. No, I won't. A thousand times no. I'm a bad lot, and must be left at that."

Expelled from his old fortress, Mr. Wilcox was building a new one. He could no longer appear respectable to her, so he defended himself instead in a lurid past. It was not true repentance.

"Leave it where you will, boy. It's not going to trouble us: I know what I'm talking about, and it will make no difference."

"No difference?" he inquired. "No difference, when you find that I am not the fellow you thought?" He was annoyed with Miss Schlegel here. He would have preferred her to be prostrated by the blow, or even to rage. Against the tide of his sin flowed the feeling that she was not altogether womanly. Her eyes gazed too straight; they had read books that are suitable for men only. And though he had dreaded a scene, and though she had determined against one, there was a scene, all the same. It was somehow imperative.

"I am unworthy of you," he began. "Had I been worthy, I should not have released you from your engagement. I know what I am talking about. I can't bear to talk of such things. We had better leave it. "

She kissed his hand. He jerked it from her, and, rising to his feet, went on: "You, with your sheltered life, and refined pursuits, and friends, and books, you and your sister, and women like you--I say, how can you guess the temptations that lie round a man?"

"It is difficult for us," said Margaret; "but if we are worth marrying, we do guess."

"Cut off from decent society and family ties, what do you suppose happens to thousands of young fellows overseas? Isolated. No one near. I know by bitter experience, and yet you say it makes 'no difference.'"

"Not to me."

He laughed bitterly. Margaret went to the side-board and helped herself to one of the breakfast dishes. Being the last down, she turned out the spirit-lamp that kept them warm. She was tender, but grave. She knew that Henry was not so much confessing his soul as pointing out the gulf between the male soul and the female, and she did not desire to hear him on this point.

"Did Helen come?" she asked.

He shook his head.

"But that won't do at all, at all! We don't want her gossiping with Mrs. Bast."

"Good God! no!" he exclaimed, suddenly natural. Then he caught himself up. "Let them gossip. My game's up, though I thank you for your unselfishness--little as my thanks are worth."

"Didn't she send me a message or anything?"

"I heard of none."

"Would you ring the bell, please?"

"What to do?"

"Why, to inquire."

He swaggered up to it tragically, and sounded a peal. Margaret poured herself out some coffee. The butler came, and said that Miss Schlegel had slept at the George, so far as he had heard. Should he go round to the George?

"I'll go, thank you," said Margaret, and dismissed him.

"It is no good," said Henry. "Those things leak out; you cannot stop a story once it has started. I have known cases of other men--I despised them once, I thought that *I'm* different, I shall never be tempted. Oh, Margaret--" He came and sat down near her, improvising emotion. She could not bear to listen to him. "We fellows all come to grief once in our time. Will you believe that? There are moments when the strongest man--'Let him who standeth, take heed lest he fall.' That's true, isn't it? If you knew all, you would excuse me. I was far from good influences--far even from England. I was very, very lonely, and longed for a woman's voice. That's enough. I have told you too much already for you to forgive me now."

"Yes, that's enough, dear."

"I have"--he lowered his voice--"I have been through hell."

Gravely she considered this claim. Had he? Had he suffered tortures of remorse, or had it been, "There! that's over. Now for respectable life again"? The latter, if she read him rightly. A man who has been through hell does not boast of his virility. He is humble and hides it, if, indeed, it still exists. Only in legend does the sinner come forth penitent, but terrible, to conquer pure woman by his resistless power. Henry was anxious to be terrible, but had not got it in him. He was a good average Englishman, who had slipped. The really culpable point--his faithlessness to Mrs. Wilcox--never seemed to strike him. She longed to mention Mrs. Wilcox.

And bit by bit the story was told her. It was a very simple story. Ten years ago was the time, a garrison town in Cyprus the place. Now and then he asked her whether she could possibly forgive him, and she answered, "I have already forgiven you, Henry." She chose her words carefully, and so saved him from panic. She played the girl, until he could rebuild his fortress and hide his soul from the world. When the butler came to clear away, Henry was in a very different mood--asked the fellow what he was in such a hurry for, complained of the noise last night in the servants' hall. Margaret looked intently at the butler. He, as a handsome young man, was faintly attractive to her as a woman--an attraction so faint as scarcely to be perceptible, yet the skies would have fallen if she had mentioned it to Henry.

On her return from the George the building operations were complete, and the old Henry fronted her, competent, cynical, and kind. He had made a clean breast, had been forgiven, and the great thing now was to forget his failure, and to send it the way of other unsuccessful investments. Jacky rejoined Howards End and Ducie Street, and the vermilion motor-car, and the Argentine Hard Dollars, and all the things and people for whom he had never had much use and had less now. Their memory hampered him. He could scarcely attend to Margaret who brought back disquieting news from the George. Helen and her clients had gone.

"Well, let them go--the man and his wife, I mean, for the more we see of your sister the better."

"But they have gone separately--Helen very early, the Basts just before I arrived. They have left no message. They have answered neither of my notes. I don't like to think what it all means."

"What did you say in the notes?"

"I told you last night."

"Oh--ah--yes! Dear, would you like one turn in the garden?"

Margaret took his arm. The beautiful weather soothed her. But the wheels of Evie's wedding were still at work, tossing the guests outwards as deftly as they had drawn them in, and she could not be with him long. It had been arranged that they should motor to Shrewsbury, whence he would go north, and she back to London with the Warringtons. For a fraction of time she was happy. Then her brain recommenced.

"I am afraid there has been gossiping of some kind at the George. Helen would not have left unless she had heard something. I mismanaged that. It is wretched. I ought to--have parted her from that woman at once.

"Margaret!" he exclaimed, loosing her arm impressively.

"Yes--yes, Henry?"

"I am far from a saint--in fact, the reverse--but you have taken me, for better or worse. Bygones must be bygones. You have promised to forgive me. Margaret, a promise is a promise. Never mention that woman again."

"Except for some practical reason--never."

"Practical! You practical!"

"Yes, I'm practical," she murmured, stooping over the mowing-machine and playing with the grass which trickled through her fingers like sand.

He had silenced her, but her fears made him uneasy. Not for the first time, he was threatened with blackmail. He was rich and supposed to be moral; the Basts knew that he was not, and might find it profitable to hint as much.

"At all events, you mustn't worry," he said. "This is a man's business." He thought intently. "On no account mention it to anybody."

Margaret flushed at advice so elementary, but he was really paving the way for a lie. If necessary he would deny that he had ever known Mrs. Bast, and prosecute her for libel. Perhaps he never had known her. Here was Margaret, who behaved as if he had not. There the house. Round them were half a dozen gardeners, clearing up after his daughter's wedding. All was so solid and spruce, that the past flew up out of sight like a spring-blind, leaving only the last five minutes unrolled.

Glancing at these, he saw that the car would be round during the next five, and plunged into action. Gongs were tapped, orders issued, Margaret was sent to dress, and the housemaid to sweep up the long trickle of grass that she had left across the hall. As is Man to the Universe, so was the mind of Mr. Wilcox to the minds of some men--a concentrated light upon a tiny spot, a little Ten Minutes moving self-contained through its appointed years. No Pagan he, who lives for the Now, and may be wiser than all philosophers. He lived for the five minutes that have past, and the five to come; he had the business mind.

How did he stand now, as his motor slipped out of Oniton and breasted the great round hills? Margaret had heard a certain rumour, but was all right. She had forgiven him, God bless her, and he felt the manlier for it. Charles and Evie had not heard it, and never must hear. No more must Paul. Over his children he felt great tenderness, which he did not try to track to a cause: Mrs. Wilcox was too far back in his life. He did not connect her with the sudden aching love that he felt for Evie. Poor little Evie! he trusted that Cahill would make her a decent husband.

And Margaret? How did she stand?

She had several minor worries. Clearly her sister had heard something. She dreaded meeting her in town. And she was anxious about Leonard, for whom they certainly were responsible. Nor ought Mrs. Bast to starve. But the main situation had not altered. She still loved Henry. His actions, not his disposition, had disappointed her, and she could bear that. And she loved her future home. Standing up in the car, just where she had leapt from it two days before, she gazed back with deep emotion upon Oniton. Besides the Grange and the Castle keep, she could now pick out the church and the black-and-white gables of the George. There was the bridge, and the river nibbling its green peninsula. She could even see the bathing-shed, but while she was looking for Charles's new springboard, the forehead of the hill rose up and hid the whole scene.

Chapter 29

She never saw it again. Day and night the river flows down into England, day after day the sun retreats into the Welsh mountains, and the tower chimes, "See the Conquering Hero." But the Wilcoxes have no part in the place, nor in any place. It is not their names that recur in the parish register. It is not their ghosts that sigh among the alders at evening. They have swept into the valley and swept out of it, leaving a little dust and a little money behind.

Chapter 30

Tibby was now approaching his last year at Oxford. He had moved out of college, and was contemplating the Universe, or such portions of it as concerned him, from his comfortable lodgings in Long Wall. He was not concerned with much. When a young man is untroubled by passions and sincerely indifferent to public opinion, his outlook is necessarily limited. Tibby neither wished to strengthen the position of the rich nor to improve that of the poor, and so was well content to watch the elms nodding behind the mildly embattled parapets of Magdalen. There are worse lives. Though selfish, he was never cruel; though affected in manner, he never posed. Like Margaret, he disdained the heroic equipment, and it was only after many visits that men discovered Schlegel to possess a character and a brain. He had done well in Mods, much to the surprise of those who attended lectures and took proper exercise, and was now glancing disdainfully at Chinese in case he should some day consent to qualify as a Student Interpreter. To him thus employed Helen entered. A telegram had preceded her.

He noticed, in a distant way, that his sister had altered. As a rule he found her too pronounced, and had never come across this look of appeal, pathetic yet dignified--the look of a sailor who has lost everything at sea.

"I have come from Oniton," she began. "There has been a great deal of trouble there."

"Who's for lunch?" said Tibby, picking up the claret, which was warming in the hearth. Helen sat down submissively at the table. "Why such an early start?" he asked.

"Sunrise or something--when I could get away."

"So I surmise. Why?"

"I don't know what's to be done, Tibby. I am very much upset at a piece of news that concerns Meg, and do not want to face her, and I am not going back to Wickham Place. I stopped here to tell you this."

The landlady came in with the cutlets. Tibby put a marker in the leaves of his Chinese Grammar and helped them. Oxford--the Oxford of the vacation--dreamed and rustled outside, and indoors the little fire was coated with grey where the sunshine touched it. Helen continued her odd story.

"Give Meg my love and say that I want to be alone. I mean to go to Munich or else Bonn."

"Such a message is easily given," said her brother.

"As regards Wickham Place and my share of the furniture, you and she are to do exactly as you like. My own feeling is that everything may just as well be sold. What does one want with dusty economic, books, which have made the world no better, or with mother's hideous chiffoniers? I have also another commission for you. I want you to deliver a letter." She got up. "I haven't written it yet. Why shouldn't I post it, though?" She sat down again. "My head is rather wretched. I hope that none of your friends are likely to come in."

Tibby locked the door. His friends often found it in this condition. Then he asked whether anything had gone wrong at Evie's wedding.

"Not there," said Helen, and burst into tears.

He had known her hysterical--it was one of her aspects with which he had no concern--and yet these tears touched him as something unusual. They were nearer the things that did concern him, such as music. He laid down his knife and looked at her curiously. Then, as she continued to sob, he went on with his lunch.

The time came for the second course, and she was still crying. Apple Charlotte was to follow, which spoils by waiting. "Do you mind Mrs. Martlett coming in?" he asked, "or shall I take it from her at the door?"

"Could I bathe my eyes, Tibby?"

He took her to his bedroom, and introduced the pudding in her absence. Having helped himself, he put it down to warm in the hearth. His hand stretched towards the Grammar, and soon he was turning over the pages, raising his eyebrows scornfully, perhaps at human nature, perhaps at Chinese. To him thus employed Helen returned. She had pulled herself together, but the grave appeal had not vanished from her eyes.

"Now for the explanation," she said. "Why didn't I begin with it? I have found out something about Mr. Wilcox. He has behaved very wrongly indeed, and ruined two people's lives. It all came on me very suddenly last night; I am very much upset, and I do not know what to do. Mrs. Bast--"

"Oh, those people!"

Helen seemed silenced.

"Shall I lock the door again?"

"No, thanks, Tibbikins. You're being very good to me. I want to tell you the story before I go abroad. You must do exactly what you like--treat it as part of the furniture. Meg cannot have heard it yet, I think. But I cannot face her and tell her that the man she is going to marry has misconducted himself. I don't even know whether she ought to be told. Knowing as she does that I dislike him, she will suspect me, and think that I want to ruin her match. I simply don't know what to make of such a thing. I trust your judgment. What would you do?"

"I gather he has had a mistress," said Tibby.

Helen flushed with shame and anger. "And ruined two people's lives. And goes about saying that personal actions count for nothing, and there always will be rich and poor. He met her when he was trying to get rich out in Cyprus--I don't wish to make him worse than he is, and no doubt she was ready enough to meet him. But there it is. They met. He goes his way and she goes hers. What do you suppose is the end of such women?"

He conceded that it was a bad business.

"They end in two ways: Either they sink till the lunatic asylums and the work-houses are full of them, and cause Mr. Wilcox to write letters to the papers complaining of our national degeneracy, or else they entrap a boy into marriage before it is too late. She--I can't blame her.

"But this isn't all," she continued after a long pause, during which the landlady served them with coffee. "I come now to the business that took us to Oniton. We went all three. Acting on Mr. Wilcox's advice, the man throws up a secure situation and takes an insecure one, from which he is dismissed. There are certain excuses, but in the main Mr. Wilcox is to blame, as Meg herself admitted. It is only common justice that he should employ the man himself. But he meets the woman, and, like the cur that he is, he refuses, and tries to get rid of them. He makes Meg write. Two notes came from her late that evening--one for me, one for Leonard, dismissing him with barely a reason. I couldn't understand. Then it comes out that Mrs. Bast had spoken to Mr. Wilcox on the lawn while we left her to get rooms, and was still speaking about him when Leonard came back to her. This Leonard knew all along. He thought it natural he should be ruined twice. Natural! Could you have contained yourself?.

"It is certainly a very bad business," said Tibby.

His reply seemed to calm his sister. "I was afraid that I saw it out of proportion. But you are right outside it, and you must know. In a day or two--or perhaps a week--take whatever steps you think fit. I leave it in your hands."

She concluded her charge.

"The facts as they touch Meg are all before you," she added; and Tibby sighed and felt it rather hard that, because of his open mind, he should be empanelled to serve as a juror. He had never been interested in human beings, for which one must blame him, but he had had rather too much of them at Wickham Place. Just as some people cease to attend when books are mentioned, so Tibby's attention wandered when "personal relations" came under discussion. Ought Margaret to know what Helen knew the Basts to know? Similar questions had vexed him from infancy, and at Oxford he had learned to say that the importance of human beings has been vastly overrated by specialists. The epigram, with its faint whiff of the eighties, meant nothing. But he might have let it off now if his sister had not been ceaselessly beautiful.

"You see, Helen--have a cigarette--I don't see what I'm to do."

"Then there's nothing to be done. I dare say you are right. Let them marry. There remains the question of compensation. "

"Do you want me to adjudicate that too? Had you not better consult an expert?"

"This part is in confidence," said Helen. "It has nothing to do with Meg, and do not mention it to her. The compensation--I do not see who is to pay it if I don't, and I have already decided on the minimum sum. As soon as possible I am placing it to your account, and when I am in Germany you will pay it over for me. I shall never forget your kindness, Tibbikins, if you do this."

"What is the sum?"

"Five thousand."

"Good God alive!" said Tibby, and went crimson.

"Now, what is the good of driblets? To go through life having done one thing--to have raised one person from the abyss: not these puny gifts of shillings and blankets--making the grey more grey. No doubt people will think me extraordinary."

"I don't care a damn what people think!" cried he, heated to unusual manliness of diction. "But it's half what you have."

"Not nearly half." She spread out her hands over her soiled skirt. "I have far too much, and we settled at Chelsea last spring that three hundred a year is necessary to set a man on his feet. What I give will bring in a hundred and fifty between two. It isn't enough."

He could not recover. He was not angry or even shocked, and he saw that Helen would still have plenty to live on. But it amazed him to think what haycocks people can make of their lives. His delicate intonations would not work, and he could only blurt out that the five thousand pounds would mean a great deal of bother for him personally.

"I didn't expect you to understand me."

"I? I understand nobody."

"But you'll do it?"

"Apparently."

"I leave you two commissions, then. The first concerns Mr. Wilcox, and you are to use your discretion. The second concerns the money, and is to be mentioned to no one, and carried out literally. You will send a hundred pounds on account tomorrow."

He walked with her to the station, passing through those streets whose serried beauty never bewildered him and never fatigued. The lovely creature raised domes and spires into the cloudless blue, and only the ganglion of vulgarity round Carfax showed how evanescent was the phantom, how faint its claim to represent England. Helen, rehearsing her commission, noticed nothing: the Basts were in her brain, and she retold the crisis in a meditative way, which might have made other men curious. She was seeing whether it would hold. He asked her once why she had taken the Basts right into the heart of Evie's wedding. She stopped like a frightened animal and said, "Does that seem to you so odd?" Her eyes, the hand laid on the mouth, quite haunted him, until they were absorbed into the figure of St. Mary the Virgin, before whom he paused for a moment on the walk home.

It is convenient to follow him in the discharge of his duties. Margaret summoned him the next day. She was terrified at Helen's flight, and he had to say that she had called in at Oxford. Then she said: "Did she seem worried at any rumour about Henry?" He answered, "Yes." "I knew it was that!" she exclaimed. "I'll write to her." Tibby was relieved.

He then sent the cheque to the address that Helen gave him, and stated that later on he was instructed to forward five thousand pounds. An answer came back, very civil and quiet in tone--such an answer as Tibby himself would have given. The cheque was returned, the legacy refused, the writer being in no need of money. Tibby forwarded this to Helen, adding in the fulness of his heart that Leonard Bast seemed somewhat a monumental person after all. Helen's reply was frantic. He was to take no notice. He was to go down at once and say that she commanded acceptance. He went. A scurf of books and china ornaments awaited them. The Basts had just been evicted for not paying their rent, and had wandered no one knew whither. Helen had begun bungling with her money by this time, and had even sold out her shares in the Nottingham and Derby Railway. For some weeks she did nothing. Then she reinvested, and, owing to the good advice of her stockbrokers, became rather richer than she had been before.

Chapter 31

Houses have their own ways of dying, falling as variously as the generations of men, some with a tragic roar, some quietly, but to an after-life in the city of ghosts, while from others--and thus was the death of Wickham Place--the spirit slips before the body perishes. It had decayed in the spring, disintegrating the girls more than they knew, and causing either to accost unfamiliar regions. By September it was a corpse, void of emotion, and scarcely hallowed by the memories of thirty years of happiness. Through its round-topped doorway passed furniture, and pictures, and books, until the last room was gutted and the last van had rumbled away. It stood for a week or two longer, open-eyed, as if astonished at its own emptiness. Then it fell. Navvies came, and spilt it back into the grey. With their muscles and their beery good temper, they were not the worst of undertakers for a house which had always been human, and had not mistaken culture for an end.

The furniture, with a few exceptions, went down into Hertfordshire, Mr. Wilcox having most kindly offered Howards End as a warehouse. Mr. Bryce had died abroad--an unsatisfactory affair--and as there seemed little guarantee that the rent would be paid regularly, he cancelled the agreement, and resumed possession himself. Until he relet the house, the Schlegels were welcome to stack their furniture in the garage and lower rooms. Margaret demurred, but Tibby accepted the offer gladly; it saved him from coming to any decision about the future. The plate and the more valuable pictures found a safer home in London, but the bulk of the things went country-ways, and were entrusted to the guardianship of Miss Avery.

Shortly before the move, our hero and heroine were married. They have weathered the storm, and may reasonably expect peace. To have no illusions and yet to love--what stronger surety can a woman find? She had seen her husband's past as well as his heart. She knew her own heart with a thoroughness that commonplace people believe impossible. The heart of Mrs. Wilcox was alone hidden, and perhaps it is superstitious to speculate on the feelings of the dead. They were married quietly--really quietly, for as the day approached she refused to go through another Oniton. Her brother gave her away, her aunt, who was out of health, presided over a few colourless refreshments. The Wilcoxes were represented by Charles, who witnessed the marriage settlement, and by Mr. Cahill. Paul did send a cablegram. In a few minutes, and without the aid of music, the clergyman made them man and wife, and soon the glass shade had fallen that cuts off married couples from the world. She, a monogamist, regretted the cessation of some of life's innocent odours; he, whose instincts were polygamous, felt morally braced by the change, and less liable to the temptations that had assailed him in the past.

They spent their honeymoon near Innsbruck. Henry knew of a reliable hotel there, and Margaret hoped for a meeting with her sister. In this she was disappointed. As they came south, Helen retreated over the Brenner, and wrote an unsatisfactory postcard from the shores of the Lake of Garda, saying that her plans were uncertain and had better be ignored. Evidently she disliked meeting Henry. Two months are surely enough to accustom an outsider to a situation which a wife has accepted in two days, and Margaret had again to regret her sister's lack of self-control. In a long letter she pointed out the need of charity in sexual matters: so little is known about them; it is hard enough for those who are personally touched to judge; then how futile must be the verdict of Society. "I don't say there is no standard, for that would destroy morality; only that there can be no standard until our impulses are classified and better understood." Helen thanked her for her kind letter--rather a curious reply. She moved south again, and spoke of wintering in Naples.

Mr. Wilcox was not sorry that the meeting failed. Helen left him time to grow skin over his wound. There were still moments when it pained him. Had he only known that Margaret was awaiting him--Margaret, so lively and intelligent, and yet so submissive--he would have kept himself worthier of her. Incapable of grouping the past, he confused the episode of Jacky with another episode that had taken place in the days of his bachelorhood. The two made one crop of wild oats, for which he was heartily sorry, and he could not see that those oats are of a darker stock which are rooted in another's dishonour. Unchastity and infidelity were as confused to him as to the Middle Ages, his only moral teacher. Ruth (poor old Ruth!) did not enter into his calculations at all, for poor old Ruth had never found him out.

His affection for his present wife grew steadily. Her cleverness gave him no trouble, and, indeed, he liked to see her reading poetry or something about social questions; it distinguished her from the wives of other men. He had only to call, and she clapped the book up and was ready to do what he wished. Then they would argue so jollily, and once or twice she had him in quite a tight corner, but as soon as he grew really serious, she gave in. Man is for war, woman for the recreation of the warrior, but he does not dislike it if she makes a show of fight. She cannot win in a real battle, having no muscles, only nerves. Nerves make her jump out of a moving motor-car, or refuse to be married fashionably. The warrior may well allow her to triumph on such occasions; they move not the imperishable plinth of things that touch his peace.

Margaret had a bad attack of these nerves during the honeymoon. He told her--casually, as was his habit--that Oniton Grange was let. She showed her annoyance, and asked rather crossly why she had not been consulted.

"I didn't want to bother you," he replied. "Besides, I have only heard for certain this morning."

"Where are we to live?" said Margaret, trying to laugh. "I loved the place extraordinarily. Don't you believe in having a permanent home, Henry?"

He assured her that she misunderstood him. It is home life that distinguishes us from the foreigner. But he did not believe in a damp home.

"This is news. I never heard till this minute that Oniton was damp."

"My dear girl!"--he flung out his hand--"have you eyes? have you a skin? How could it be anything but damp in such a situation? In the first place, the Grange is on clay, and built where the castle moat must have been; then there's that destestable little river, steaming all night like a kettle. Feel the cellar walls; look up under the eaves. Ask Sir James or anyone. Those Shropshire valleys are notorious. The only possible place for a house in Shropshire is on a hill; but, for my part, I think the country is too far from London, and the scenery nothing special. "

Margaret could not resist saying, "Why did you go there, then?"

"I--because--" He drew his head back and grew rather angry. "Why have we come to the Tyrol, if it comes to that? One might go on asking such questions indefinitely."

One might; but he was only gaining time for a plausible answer. Out it came, and he believed it as soon as it was spoken.

"The truth is, I took Oniton on account of Evie. Don't let this go any further."

"Certainly not."

"I shouldn't like her to know that she nearly let me in for a very bad bargain. No sooner did I sign the agreement than she got engaged. Poor little girl! She was so keen on it all, and wouldn't even wait to make proper inquiries about the shooting. Afraid it would get snapped up--just like all of your sex. Well, no harm's done. She has had her country wedding, and I've got rid of my house to some fellows who are starting a preparatory school."

"Where shall we live, then, Henry? I should enjoy living somewhere."

"I have not yet decided. What about Norfolk?"

Margaret was silent. Marriage had not saved her from the sense of flux. London was but a foretaste of this nomadic civilization which is altering human nature so profoundly, and throws upon personal relations a stress greater than they have ever borne before. Under cosmopolitanism, if it comes, we shall receive no help from the earth. Trees and meadows and mountains will only be a spectacle, and the binding force that they once exercised on character must be entrusted to Love alone. May Love be equal to the task!

"It is now what?" continued Henry. "Nearly October. Let us camp for the winter at Ducie Street, and look out for something in the spring.

"If possible, something permanent. I can't be as young as I was, for these alterations don't suit me. "

"But, my dear, which would you rather have--alterations or rheumatism?"

"I see your point," said Margaret, getting up. "If Oniton is really damp, it is impossible, and must be inhabited by little boys. Only, in the spring, let us look before we leap. I will take warning by Evie, and not hurry you. Remember that you have a free hand this time. These endless moves must be bad for the furniture, and are certainly expensive."

"What a practical little woman it is! What's it been reading? Theo--theo--how much?"

"Theosophy."

So Ducie Street was her first fate--a pleasant enough fate. The house, being only a little larger than Wickham Place, trained her for the immense establishment that was promised in the spring. They were frequently away, but at home life ran fairly regularly. In the morning Henry went to the business, and his sandwich--a relic this of some prehistoric craving--was always cut by her own hand. He did not rely upon the sandwich for lunch, but liked to have it by him in case he grew hungry at eleven. When he had gone, there was the house to look after, and the servants to humanize, and several kettles of Helen's to keep on the boil. Her conscience pricked her a little about the Basts; she was not sorry to have lost sight of them. No doubt Leonard was worth helping, but being Henry's wife, she preferred to help someone else. As for theatres and discussion societies, they attracted her less and less. She began to "miss" new movements, and to spend her spare time re-reading or thinking, rather to the concern of her Chelsea friends. They attributed the change to her marriage, and perhaps some deep instinct did warn her not to travel further from her husband than was inevitable. Yet the main cause lay deeper still; she had outgrown stimulants, and was passing from words to things. It was doubtless a pity not to keep up with Wedekind or John, but some closing of the gates is inevitable after thirty, if the mind itself is to become a creative power.

Chapter 32

She was looking at plans one day in the following spring--they had finally decided to go down into Sussex and build--when Mrs. Charles Wilcox was announced.

"Have you heard the news?" Dolly cried, as soon as she entered the room. "Charles is so ang--I mean he is sure you know about it, or rather, that you don't know."

"Why, Dolly!" said Margaret, placidly kissing her. "Here's a surprise! How are the boys and the baby?"

Boys and the baby were well, and in describing a great row that there had been at Hilton Tennis Club, Dolly forgot her news. The wrong people had tried to get in. The rector, as representing the older inhabitants, had said--Charles had said--the tax-collector had said--Charles had regretted not saying--and she closed the description with, "But lucky you, with four courts of your own at Midhurst."

"It will be very jolly," replied Margaret.

"Are those the plans? Does it matter me seeing them?"

"Of course not."

"Charles has never seen the plans."

"They have only just arrived. Here is the ground floor--no, that's rather difficult. Try the elevation. We are to have a good many gables and a picturesque sky-line."

"What makes it smell so funny?" said Dolly, after a moment's inspection. She was incapable of understanding plans or maps.

"I suppose the paper."

"And *which* way up is it?"

"Just the ordinary way up. That's the sky-line, and the part that smells strongest is the sky."

"Well, ask me another. Margaret--oh--what was I going to say? How's Helen?"

"Quite well."

"Is she never coming back to England? Every one thinks it's awfully odd she doesn't."

"So it is," said Margaret, trying to conceal her vexation. She was getting rather sore on this point. "Helen is odd, awfully. She has now been away eight months.

"But hasn't she any address?"

"A poste restante somewhere in Bavaria is her address. Do write her a line. I will look it up for you."

"No, don't bother. That's eight months she has been away, surely?"

"Exactly. She left just after Evie's wedding. It would be eight months."

"Just when baby was born, then?"

"Just so."

Dolly sighed, and stared enviously round the drawing-room. She was beginning to lose her brightness and good looks. The Charles' were not well off, for Mr. Wilcox, having brought up his children with expensive tastes, believed in letting them shift for themselves. After all, he had not treated them generously. Yet another baby was expected, she told Margaret, and they would have to give up the motor. Margaret sympathized, but in a formal fashion, and Dolly little imagined that the step-mother was urging Mr. Wilcox to make them a more liberal allowance. She sighed again, and at last the particular grievance was remembered. "Oh yes," she cried, "that is it: Miss Avery has been unpacking your packing-cases."

"Why has she done that? How unnecessary!"

"Ask another. I suppose you ordered her to."

"I gave no such orders. Perhaps she was airing the things. She did undertake to light an occasional fire."

"It was far more than an air," said Dolly solemnly. "The floor sounds covered with books. Charles sent me to know what is to be done, for he feels certain you don't know."

"Books!" cried Margaret, moved by the holy word. "Dolly, are you serious? Has she been touching our books?"

"Hasn't she, though! What used to be the hall's full of them. Charles thought for certain you knew of it."

"I am very much obliged to you, Dolly. What can have come over Miss Avery? I must go down about it at once. Some of the books are my brother's, and are quite valuable. She had no right to open any of the cases."

"I say she's dotty. She was the one that never got married, you know. Oh, I say, perhaps she thinks your books are wedding-presents to herself. Old maids are taken that way sometimes. Miss Avery hates us all like poison ever since her frightful dust-up with Evie."

"I hadn't heard of that," said Margaret. A visit from Dolly had its compensations.

"Didn't you know she gave Evie a present last August, and Evie returned it, and then--oh, goloshes! You never read such a letter as Miss Avery wrote."

"But it was wrong of Evie to return it. It wasn't like her to do such a heartless thing."

"But the present was so expensive."

"Why does that make any difference, Dolly?"

"Still, when it costs over five pounds--I didn't see it, but it was a lovely enamel pendant from a Bond Street shop. You can't very well accept that kind of thing from a farm woman. Now, can you?"

"You accepted a present from Miss Avery when you were married.

"Oh, mine was old earthenware stuff--not worth a halfpenny. Evie's was quite different. You'd have to ask anyone to the wedding who gave you a pendant like that. Uncle Percy and Albert and father and Charles all said it was quite impossible, and when four men agree, what is a girl to do? Evie didn't want to upset the old thing, so thought a sort of joking letter best, and returned the pendant straight to the shop to save Miss Avery trouble."

"But Miss Avery said--"

Dolly's eyes grew round. "It was a perfectly awful letter. Charles said it was the letter of a madman. In the end she had the pendant back again from the shop and threw it into the duckpond.

"Did she give any reasons?"

"We think she meant to be invited to Oniton, and so climb into society."

"She's rather old for that," said Margaret pensively. "May not she have given the present to Evie in remembrance of her mother?"

"That's a notion. Give every one their due, eh? Well, I suppose I ought to be toddling. Come along, Mr. Muff--you want a new coat, but I don't know who'll give it you, I'm sure;" and addressing her apparel with mournful humour, Dolly moved from the room.

Margaret followed her to ask whether Henry knew about Miss Avery's rudeness.

"Oh yes."

"I wonder, then, why he let me ask her to look after the house."

"But she's only a farm woman," said Dolly, and her explanation proved correct. Henry only censured the lower classes when it suited him. He bore with Miss Avery as with Crane--because he could get good value out of them. "I have patience with a man who knows his job," he would say, really having patience with the job, and not the man. Paradoxical as it may sound, he had something of the artist about him; he would pass over an insult to his daughter sooner than lose a good charwoman for his wife.

Margaret judged it better to settle the little trouble herself. Parties were evidently ruffled. With Henry's permission, she wrote a pleasant note to Miss Avery, asking her to leave the cases untouched. Then, at the first convenient opportunity, she went down herself, intending to repack her belongings and store them properly in the local warehouse: the plan had been amateurish and a failure. Tibby promised to accompany her, but at the last moment begged to be excused. So, for the second time in her life, she entered the house alone.

Chapter 33

The day of her visit was exquisite, and the last of unclouded happiness that she was to have for many months. Her anxiety about Helen's extraordinary absence was still dormant, and as for a possible brush with Miss Avery--that only gave zest to the expedition. She had also eluded Dolly's invitation to luncheon. Walking straight up from the station, she crossed the village green and entered the long chestnut avenue that connects it with the church. The church itself stood in the village once. But it there attracted so many worshippers that the devil, in a pet, snatched it from its foundations, and poised it on an inconvenient knoll, three-quarters of a mile away. If this story is true, the chestnut avenue must have been planted by the angels. No more tempting approach could be imagined for the luke-warm Christian, and if he still finds the walk too long, the devil is defeated all the same, Science having built Holy Trinity, a Chapel of Ease, near the Charles', and roofed it with tin.

Up the avenue Margaret strolled slowly, stopping to watch the sky that gleamed through the upper branches of the chestnuts, or to finger the little horse-shoes on the lower branches. Why has not England a great mythology? Our folklore has never advanced beyond daintiness, and the greater melodies about our country-side have all issued through the pipes of Greece. Deep and true as the native imagination can be, it seems to have failed here. It has stopped with the witches and the fairies. It cannot vivify one fraction of a summer field, or give names to half a dozen stars. England still waits for the supreme moment of her literature--for the great poet who shall voice her, or, better still, for the thousand little poets whose voices shall pass into our common talk.

At the church the scenery changed. The chestnut avenue opened into a road, smooth but narrow, which led into the untouched country. She followed it for over a mile. Its little hesitations pleased her. Having no urgent destiny, it strolled downhill or up as it wished, taking no trouble about the gradients, nor about the view, which nevertheless expanded. The great estates that throttle the south of Hertfordshire were less obtrusive here, and the appearance of the land was neither aristocratic nor suburban. To define it was difficult, but Margaret knew what it was not: it was not snobbish. Though its contours were slight, there was a touch of freedom in their sweep to which Surrey will never attain, and the distant brow of the Chilterns towered like a mountain. "Left to itself," was Margaret's opinion, "this county would vote Liberal." The comradeship, not passionate, that is our highest gift as a nation, was promised by it, as by the low brick farm where she called for the key.

But the inside of the farm was disappointing. A most finished young person received her. "Yes, Mrs. Wilcox; no, Mrs. Wilcox; oh yes, Mrs. Wilcox, auntie received your letter quite duly. Auntie has gone up to your little place at the present moment. Shall I send the servant to direct you?" Followed by: "Of course, auntie does not generally look after your place; she only does it to oblige a neighbour as something exceptional. It gives her something to do. She spends quite a lot of her time there. My husband says to me sometimes, 'Where's auntie?' I say, 'Need you ask? She's at Howards End.' Yes, Mrs. Wilcox. Mrs. Wilcox, could I prevail upon you to accept a piece of cake? Not if I cut it for you?"

Margaret refused the cake, but unfortunately this acquired her gentility in the eyes of Miss Avery's niece.

"I cannot let you go on alone. Now don't. You really mustn't. I will direct you myself if it comes to that. I must get my hat. Now"--roguishly--"Mrs. Wilcox, don't you move while I'm gone."

Stunned, Margaret did not move from the best parlour, over which the touch of art nouveau had fallen. But the other rooms looked in keeping, though they conveyed the peculiar sadness of a rural interior. Here had lived an elder race, to which we look back with disquietude. The country which we visit at week-ends was really a home to it, and the graver sides of life, the deaths, the partings, the yearnings for love, have their deepest expression in the heart of the fields. All was not sadness. The sun was shining without. The thrush sang his two syllables on the budding guelder-rose. Some children were playing uproariously in heaps of golden straw. It was the presence of sadness at all that surprised Margaret, and ended by giving her a feeling of completeness. In these English farms, if anywhere, one might see life steadily and see it whole, group in one vision its transitoriness and its eternal youth, connect--connect without bitterness until all men are brothers. But her thoughts were interrupted by the return of Miss Avery's niece, and were so tranquillizing that she suffered the interruption gladly.

It was quicker to go out by the back door, and, after due explanations, they went out by it. The niece was now mortified by unnumerable chickens, who rushed up to her feet for food, and by a shameless and maternal sow. She did not know what animals were coming to. But her gentility withered at the touch of the sweet air. The wind was rising, scattering the straw and ruffling the tails of the ducks as they floated in families over Evie's pendant. One of those delicious gales of spring, in which leaves stiff in bud seem to rustle, swept over the land and then fell silent. "Georgia," sang the thrush. "Cuckoo," came furtively from the cliff of pine-trees. "Georgia, pretty Georgia," and the other birds joined in with nonsense. The hedge was a half-painted picture which would be finished in a few days. Celandines grew on its banks, lords and ladies and primroses in the defended hollows; the wild rose-bushes, still bearing their withered hips, showed also the promise of blossom. Spring had come, clad in no classical garb, yet fairer than all springs; fairer even than she who walks through the myrtles of Tuscany with the graces before her and the zephyr behind.

The two women walked up the lane full of outward civility. But Margaret was thinking how difficult it was to be earnest about furniture on such a day, and the niece was thinking about hats. Thus engaged, they reached Howards End. Petulant cries of "Auntie!" severed the air. There was no reply, and the front door was locked.

"Are you sure that Miss Avery is up here?" asked Margaret.

"Oh yes, Mrs. Wilcox, quite sure. She is here daily."

Margaret tried to look in through the dining-room window, but the curtain inside was drawn tightly. So with the drawing-room and the hall. The appearance of these curtains was familiar, yet she did not remember them being there on her other visit: her impression was that Mr. Bryce had taken everything away. They tried the back. Here again they received no answer, and could see nothing; the kitchen-window was fitted with a blind, while the pantry and scullery had pieces of wood propped up against them, which looked ominously like the lids of packing-cases. Margaret thought of her books, and she lifted up her voice also. At the first cry she succeeded.

"Well, well!" replied someone inside the house. "If it isn't Mrs. Wilcox come at last!"

"Have you got the key, auntie?"

"Madge, go away," said Miss Avery, still invisible.

"Auntie, it's Mrs. Wilcox--"

Margaret supported her. "Your niece and I have come together--"

"Madge, go away. This is no moment for your hat."

The poor woman went red. "Auntie gets more eccentric lately," she said nervously.

"Miss Avery!" called Margaret. "I have come about the furniture. Could you kindly let me in?"

"Yes, Mrs. Wilcox," said the voice, "of course." But after that came silence. They called again without response. They walked round the house disconsolately.

"I hope Miss Avery is not ill," hazarded Margaret.

"Well, if you'll excuse me," said Madge, "perhaps I ought to be leaving you now. The servants need seeing to at the farm. Auntie is so odd at times." Gathering up her elegancies, she retired defeated, and, as if her departure had loosed a spring, the front door opened at once.

Miss Avery said, "Well, come right in, Mrs. Wilcox!" quite pleasantly and calmly.

"Thank you so much," began Margaret, but broke off at the sight of an umbrella-stand. It was her own.

"Come right into the hall first," said Miss Avery. She drew the curtain, and Margaret uttered a cry of despair. For an appalling thing had happened. The hall was fitted up with the contents of the library from Wickham Place. The carpet had been laid, the big work-table drawn up near the window; the bookcases filled the wall opposite the fireplace, and her father's sword--this is what bewildered her particularly--had been drawn from its scabbard and hung naked amongst the sober volumes. Miss Avery must have worked for days.

"I'm afraid this isn't what we meant," she began. "Mr. Wilcox and I never intended the cases to be touched. For instance, these books are my brother's. We are storing them for him and for my sister, who is abroad. When you kindly undertook to look after things, we never expected you to do so much."

"The house has been empty long enough," said the old woman.

Margaret refused to argue. "I dare say we didn't explain," she said civilly. "It has been a mistake, and very likely our mistake."

"Mrs. Wilcox, it has been mistake upon mistake for fifty years. The house is Mrs. Wilcox's, and she would not desire it to stand empty any longer."

To help the poor decaying brain, Margaret said:

"Yes, Mrs. Wilcox's house, the mother of Mr. Charles."

"Mistake upon mistake," said Miss Avery. "Mistake upon mistake."

"Well, I don't know," said Margaret, sitting down in one of her own chairs. "I really don't know what's to be done." She could not help laughing.

The other said: "Yes, it should be a merry house enough."

"I don't know--I dare say. Well, thank you very much, Miss Avery. Yes, that's all right. Delightful."

"There is still the parlour." She went through the door opposite and drew a curtain. Light flooded the drawing-room and the drawing-room furniture from Wickham Place. "And the dining-room." More curtains were drawn, more windows were flung open to the spring. "Then through here--" Miss Avery continued passing and repassing through the hall. Her voice was lost, but Margaret heard her pulling up the kitchen blind. "I've not finished here yet," she announced, returning. "There's still a deal to do. The farm lads will carry your great wardrobes upstairs, for there is no need to go into expense at Hilton."

"It is all a mistake," repeated Margaret, feeling that she must put her foot down. "A misunderstanding. Mr. Wilcox and I are not going to live at Howards End."

"Oh, indeed. On account of his hay fever?"

"We have settled to build a new home for ourselves in Sussex, and part of this furniture--my part--will go down there presently." She looked at Miss Avery intently, trying to understand the kink in her brain. Here was no maundering old woman. Her wrinkles were shrewd and humorous. She looked capable of scathing wit and also of high but unostentatious nobility.

"You think that you won't come back to live here, Mrs. Wilcox, but you will."

"That remains to be seen," said Margaret, smiling. "We have no intention of doing so for the present. We happen to need a much larger house. Circumstances oblige us to give big parties. Of course, some day--one never knows, does one?"

Miss Avery retorted: "Some day! Tcha! tcha! Don't talk about some day. You are living here now."

"Am I?"

"You are living here, and have been for the last ten minutes, if you ask me."

It was a senseless remark, but with a queer feeling of disloyalty Margaret rose from her chair. She felt that Henry had been obscurely censured. They went into the dining-room, where the sunlight poured in upon her mother's chiffonier, and upstairs, where many an old god peeped from a new niche. The furniture fitted extraordinarily well. In the central room--over the hall, the room that Helen had slept in four years ago--Miss Avery had placed Tibby's old bassinette.

"The nursery," she said.

Margaret turned away without speaking.

At last everything was seen. The kitchen and lobby were still stacked with furniture and straw, but, as far as she could make out, nothing had been broken or scratched. A pathetic display of ingenuity! Then they took a friendly stroll in the garden. It had gone wild since her last visit. The gravel sweep was weedy, and grass had sprung up at the very jaws of the garage. And Evie's rockery was only bumps. Perhaps Evie was responsible for Miss Avery's oddness. But Margaret suspected that the cause lay deeper, and that the girl's silly letter had but loosed the irritation of years.

"It's a beautiful meadow," she remarked. It was one of those open-air drawing-rooms that have been formed, hundreds of years ago, out of the smaller fields. So the boundary hedge zigzagged down the hill at right angles, and at the bottom there was a little green annex--a sort of powder-closet for the cows.

"Yes, the maidy's well enough," said Miss Avery, "for those that is, who don't suffer from sneezing." And she cackled maliciously. "I've seen Charlie Wilcox go out to my lads in hay time--oh, they ought to do this--they mustn't do that--he'd learn them to be lads. And just then the tickling took him. He has it from his father, with other things. There's not one Wilcox that can stand up against a field in June--I laughed fit to burst while he was courting Ruth."

"My brother gets hay fever too," said Margaret.

"This house lies too much on the land for them. Naturally, they were glad enough to slip in at first. But Wilcoxes are better than nothing, as I see you've found."

Margaret laughed.

"They keep a place going, don't they? Yes, it is just that."

"They keep England going, it is my opinion."

But Miss Avery upset her by replying: "Ay, they breed like rabbits. Well, well, it's a funny world. But He who made it knows what He wants in it, I suppose. If Mrs. Charlie is expecting her fourth, it isn't for us to repine."

"They breed and they also work," said Margaret, conscious of some invitation to disloyalty, which was echoed by the very breeze and by the songs of the birds. "It certainly is a funny world, but so long as men like my husband and his sons govern it, I think it'll never be a bad one--never really bad."

"No, better'n nothing," said Miss Avery, and turned to the wych-elm.

On their way back to the farm she spoke of her old friend much more clearly than before. In the house Margaret had wondered whether she quite distinguished the first wife from the second. Now she said: "I never saw much of Ruth after her grandmother died, but we stayed civil. It was a very civil family. Old Mrs. Howard never spoke against anybody, nor let anyone be turned away without food. Then it was never 'Trespassers will be prosecuted' in their land, but would people please not come in. Mrs. Howard was never created to run a farm."

"Had they no men to help them?" Margaret asked.

Miss Avery replied: "Things went on until there were no men."

"Until Mr. Wilcox came along," corrected Margaret, anxious that her husband should receive his dues.

"I suppose so; but Ruth should have married a--no disrespect to you to say this, for I take it you were intended to get Wilcox any way, whether she got him first or no."

"Whom should she have married?"

"A soldier!" exclaimed the old woman. "Some real soldier."

Margaret was silent. It was a criticism of Henry's character far more trenchant than any of her own. She felt dissatisfied.

"But that's all over," she went on. "A better time is coming now, though you've kept me long enough waiting. In a couple of weeks I'll see your lights shining through the hedge of an evening. Have you ordered in coals?"

"We are not coming," said Margaret firmly. She respected Miss Avery too much to humour her. "No. Not coming. Never coming. It has all been a mistake. The furniture must be repacked at once, and I am very sorry but I am making other arrangements, and must ask you to give me the keys."

"Certainly, Mrs. Wilcox," said Miss Avery, and resigned her duties with a smile.

Relieved at this conclusion, and having sent her compliments to Madge, Margaret walked back to the station. She had intended to go to the furniture warehouse and give directions for removal, but the muddle had turned out more extensive than she expected, so she decided to consult Henry. It was as well that she did this. He was strongly against employing the local man whom he had previously recommended, and advised her to store in London after all.

But before this could be done an unexpected trouble fell upon her.

Chapter 34

It was not unexpected entirely. Aunt Juley's health had been bad all the winter. She had had a long series of colds and coughs, and had been too busy to get rid of them. She had scarcely promised her niece "to really take my tiresome chest in hand," when she caught a chill and developed acute pneumonia. Margaret and Tibby went down to Swanage. Helen was telegraphed for, and that spring party that after all gathered in that hospitable house had all the pathos of fair memories. On a perfect day, when the sky seemed blue porcelain, and the waves of the discreet little bay beat gentlest of tattoos upon the sand, Margaret hurried up through the rhododendrons, confronted again by the senselessness of Death. One death may explain itself, but it throws no light upon another: the groping inquiry must begin anew. Preachers or scientists may generalize, but we know that no generality is possible about those whom we love; not one heaven awaits them, not even one oblivion. Aunt Juley, incapable of tragedy, slipped out of life with odd little laughs and apologies for having stopped in it so long. She was very weak; she could not rise to the occasion, or realize the great mystery which all agree must await her; it only seemed to her that she was quite done up--more done up than ever before; that she saw and heard and felt less every moment; and that, unless something changed, she would soon feel nothing. Her spare strength she devoted to plans: could not Margaret take some steamer expeditions? were mackerel cooked as Tibby liked them? She worried herself about Helen's absence, and also that she could be the cause of Helen's return. The nurses seemed to think such interests quite natural, and perhaps hers was an average approach to the Great Gate. But Margaret saw Death stripped of any false romance; whatever the idea of Death may contain, the process can be trivial and hideous.

"Important--Margaret dear, take the Lulworth when Helen comes."

"Helen won't be able to stop, Aunt Juley. She has telegraphed that she can only get away just to see you. She must go back to Germany as soon as you are well."

"How very odd of Helen! Mr. Wilcox--"

"Yes, dear?"

"Can he spare you?"

Henry wished her to come, and had been very kind. Yet again Margaret said so.

Chapter 34

Mrs. Munt did not die. Quite outside her will, a more dignified power took hold of her and checked her on the downward slope. She returned, without emotion, as fidgety as ever. On the fourth day she was out of danger.

"Margaret--important," it went on: "I should like you to have some companion to take walks with. Do try Miss Conder."

"I have been a little walk with Miss Conder."

"But she is not really interesting. If only you had Helen."

"I have Tibby, Aunt Juley."

"No, but he has to do his Chinese. Some real companion is what you need. Really, Helen is odd."

"Helen is odd, very," agreed Margaret.

"Not content with going abroad, why does she want to go back there at once?"

"No doubt she will change her mind when she sees us. She has not the least balance."

That was the stock criticism about Helen, but Margaret's voice trembled as she made it. By now she was deeply pained at her sister's behaviour. It may be unbalanced to fly out of England, but to stop away eight months argues that the heart is awry as well as the head. A sick-bed could recall Helen, but she was deaf to more human calls; after a glimpse at her aunt, she would retire into her nebulous life behind some poste restante. She scarcely existed; her letters had become dull and infrequent; she had no wants and no curiosity. And it was all put down to poor Henry's account! Henry, long pardoned by his wife, was still too infamous to be greeted by his sister-in-law. It was morbid, and, to her alarm, Margaret fancied that she could trace the growth of morbidity back in Helen's life for nearly four years. The flight from Oniton; the unbalanced patronage of the Basts; the explosion of grief up on the Downs--all connected with Paul, an insignificant boy whose lips had kissed hers for a fraction of time. Margaret and Mrs. Wilcox had feared that they might kiss again. Foolishly: the real danger was reaction. Reaction against the Wilcoxes had eaten into her life until she was scarcely sane. At twenty-five she had an idée fixe. What hope was there for her as an old woman?

The more Margaret thought about it the more alarmed she became. For many months she had put the subject away, but it was too big to be slighted now. There was almost a taint of madness. Were all Helen's actions to be governed by a tiny mishap, such as may happen to any young man or woman? Can human nature be constructed on lines so insignificant? The blundering little encounter at Howards End was vital. It propagated itself where graver intercourse lay barren; it was stronger than sisterly intimacy, stronger than reason or books. In one of her moods Helen had confessed that she still "enjoyed" it in a certain sense. Paul had faded, but the magic of his caress endured. And where there is enjoyment of the past there may also be reaction--propagation at both ends.

Well, it is odd and sad that our minds should be such seed-beds, and we without power to choose the seed. But man is an odd, sad creature as yet, intent on pilfering the earth, and heedless of the growths within himself. He cannot be bored about psychology. He leaves it to the specialist, which is as if he should leave his dinner to be eaten by a steam-engine. He cannot be bothered to digest his own soul. Margaret and Helen have been more patient, and it is suggested that Margaret has succeeded--so far as success is yet possible. She does understand herself, she has some rudimentary control over her own growth. Whether Helen has succeeded one cannot say.

The day that Mrs. Munt rallied Helen's letter arrived. She had posted it at Munich, and would be in London herself on the morrow. It was a disquieting letter, though the opening was affectionate and sane.

> Dearest Meg,
>
> Give Helen's love to Aunt Juley. Tell her that I love, and have loved, her ever since I can remember. I shall be in London Thursday.
>
> My address will be care of the bankers. I have not yet settled on a hotel, so write or wire to me there and give me detailed news. If Aunt Juley is much better, or if, for a terrible reason, it would be no good my coming down to Swanage, you must not think it odd if I do not come. I have all sorts of plans in my head. I am living abroad at present, and want to get back as quickly as possible. Will you please tell me where our furniture is. I should like to take out one or two books; the rest are for you.
>
> Forgive me, dearest Meg. This must read like rather a tiresome letter, but all letters are from your loving
>
> Helen

It was a tiresome letter, for it tempted Margaret to tell a lie. If she wrote that Aunt Juley was still in danger her sister would come. Unhealthiness is contagious. We cannot be in contact with those who are in a morbid state without ourselves deteriorating. To "act for the best" might do Helen good, but would do herself harm, and, at the risk of disaster, she kept her colours flying a little longer. She replied that their aunt was much better, and awaited developments.

Tibby approved of her reply. Mellowing rapidly, he was a pleasanter companion than before. Oxford had done much for him. He had lost his peevishness, and could hide his indifference to people and his interest in food. But he had not grown more human. The years between eighteen and twenty-two, so magical for most, were leading him gently from boyhood to middle age. He had never known young-manliness, that quality which warms the heart till death, and gives Mr. Wilcox an imperishable charm. He was frigid, through no fault of his own, and without cruelty. He thought Helen wrong and Margaret right, but the family trouble was for him what a scene behind footlights is for most people. He had only one suggestion to make, and that was characteristic.

"Why don't you tell Mr. Wilcox?"

"About Helen?"

"Perhaps he has come across that sort of thing."

"He would do all he could, but--"

"Oh, you know best. But he is practical."

It was the student's belief in experts. Margaret demurred for one or two reasons. Presently Helen's answer came. She sent a telegram requesting the address of the furniture, as she would now return at once. Margaret replied, "Certainly not; meet me at the bankers at four." She and Tibby went up to London. Helen was not at the bankers, and they were refused her address. Helen had passed into chaos.

Margaret put her arm round her brother. He was all that she had left, and never had he seemed more unsubstantial.

"Tibby love, what next?"

He replied: "It is extraordinary."

"Dear, your judgment's often clearer than mine. Have you any notion what's at the back?"

"None, unless it's something mental."

"Oh--that!" said Margaret. "Quite impossible." But the suggestion had been uttered, and in a few minutes she took it up herself. Nothing else explained. And London agreed with Tibby. The mask fell off the city, and she saw it for what it really is--a caricature of infinity. The familiar barriers, the streets along which she moved, the houses between which she had made her little journeys for so many years, became negligible suddenly. Helen seemed one with grimy trees and the traffic and the slowly-flowing slabs of mud. She had accomplished a hideous act of renunciation and returned to the One. Margaret's own faith held firm. She knew the human soul will be merged, if it be merged at all, with the stars and the sea. Yet she felt that her sister had been going amiss for many years. It was symbolic the catastrophe should come now, on a London afternoon, while rain fell slowly.

Henry was the only hope. Henry was definite. He might know of some paths in the chaos that were hidden from them, and she determined to take Tibby's advice and lay the whole matter in his hands. They must call at his office. He could not well make it worse. She went for a few moments into St. Paul's, whose dome stands out of the welter so bravely, as if preaching the gospel of form. But within, St. Paul's is as its surroundings--echoes and whispers, inaudible songs, invisible mosaics, wet footmarks crossing and recrossing the floor. Si monumentum requiris, circumspice: it points us back to London. There was no hope of Helen here.

Henry was unsatisfactory at first. That she had expected. He was overjoyed to see her back from Swanage, and slow to admit the growth of a new trouble. When they told him of their search, he only chaffed Tibby and the Schlegels generally, and declared that it was "just like Helen" to lead her relatives a dance.

"That is what we all say," replied Margaret. "But why should it be just like Helen? Why should she be allowed to be so queer, and to grow queerer?"

"Don't ask me. I'm a plain man of business. I live and let live. My advice to you both is, don't worry. Margaret, you've got black marks again under your eyes. You know that's strictly forbidden. First your aunt--then your sister. No, we aren't going to have it. Are we, Theobald?" He rang the bell. "I'll give you some tea, and then you go straight to Ducie Street. I can't have my girl looking as old as her husband."

"All the same, you have not quite seen our point," said Tibby.

Mr. Wilcox, who was in good spirits, retorted, "I don't suppose I ever shall." He leant back, laughing at the gifted but ridiculous family, while the fire flickered over the map of Africa. Margaret motioned to her brother to go on. Rather diffident, he obeyed her.

"Margaret's point is this," he said. "Our sister may be mad."

Charles, who was working in the inner room, looked round.

"Come in, Charles," said Margaret kindly. "Could you help us at all? We are again in trouble."

"I'm afraid I cannot. What are the facts? We are all mad more or less, you know, in these days."

"The facts are as follows," replied Tibby, who had at times a pedantic lucidity. "The facts are that she has been in England for three days and will not see us. She has forbidden the bankers to give us her address. She refuses to answer questions. Margaret finds her letters colourless. There are other facts, but these are the most striking."

"She has never behaved like this before, then?" asked Henry.

"Of course not!" said his wife, with a frown.

"Well, my dear, how am I to know?"

A senseless spasm of annoyance came over her. "You know quite well that Helen never sins against affection," she said. "You must have noticed that much in her, surely."

"Oh yes; she and I have always hit it off together."

"No, Henry--can't you see? --I don't mean that."

She recovered herself, but not before Charles had observed her. Stupid and attentive, he was watching the scene.

"I was meaning that when she was eccentric in the past, one could trace it back to the heart in the long run. She behaved oddly because she cared for someone, or wanted to help them. There's no possible excuse for her now. She is grieving us deeply, and that is why I am sure that she is not well. 'Mad' is too terrible a word, but she is not well. I shall never believe it. I shouldn't discuss my sister with you if I thought she was well--trouble you about her, I mean."

Henry began to grow serious. Ill-health was to him something perfectly definite. Generally well himself, he could not realize that we sink to it by slow gradations. The sick had no rights; they were outside the pale; one could lie to them remorselessly. When his first wife was seized, he had promised to take her down into Hertfordshire, but meanwhile arranged with a nursing-home instead. Helen, too, was ill. And the plan that he sketched out for her capture, clever and well-meaning as it was, drew its ethics from the wolf-pack.

"You want to get hold of her?" he said. "That's the problem, isn't it? She has got to see a doctor."

"For all I know she has seen one already."

"Yes, yes; don't interrupt." He rose to his feet and thought intently. The genial, tentative host disappeared, and they saw instead the man who had carved money out of Greece and Africa, and bought forests from the natives for a few bottles of gin. "I've got it," he said at last. "It's perfectly easy. Leave it to me. We'll send her down to Howards End."

"How will you do that?"

"After her books. Tell her that she must unpack them herself. Then you can meet her there."

"But, Henry, that's just what she won't let me do. It's part of her--whatever it is--never to see me."

"Of course you won't tell her you're going. When she is there, looking at the cases, you'll just stroll in. If nothing is wrong with her, so much the better. But there'll be the motor round the corner, and we can run her up to a specialist in no time."

Margaret shook her head. "It's quite impossible."

"Why?"

"It doesn't seem impossible to me," said Tibby; "it is surely a very tippy plan."

"It is impossible, because--" She looked at her husband sadly. "It's not the particular language that Helen and I talk if you see my meaning. It would do splendidly for other people, whom I don't blame."

"But Helen doesn't talk," said Tibby. "That's our whole difficulty. She won't talk your particular language, and on that account you think she's ill."

"No, Henry; it's sweet of you, but I couldn't."

"I see," he said; "you have scruples."

"I suppose so."

"And sooner than go against them you would have your sister suffer. You could have got her down to Swanage by a word, but you had scruples. And scruples are all very well. I am as scrupulous as any man alive, I hope; but when it is a case like this, when there is a question of madness--"

"I deny it's madness."

"You said just now--"

"It's madness when I say it, but not when you say it."

Henry shrugged his shoulders. "Margaret! Margaret!" he groaned. "No education can teach a woman logic. Now, my dear, my time is valuable. Do you want me to help you or not?"

"Not in that way."

"Answer my question. Plain question, plain answer. Do--"

Charles surprised them by interrupting. "Pater, we may as well keep Howards End out of it," he said.

"Why, Charles?"

Charles could give no reason; but Margaret felt as if, over tremendous distance, a salutation had passed between them.

"The whole house is at sixes and sevens," he said crossly. "We don't want any more mess."

"Who's 'we'?" asked his father. "My boy, pray, who's 'we'?"

"I am sure I beg your pardon," said Charles. "I appear always to be intruding."

By now Margaret wished she had never mentioned her trouble to her husband. Retreat was impossible. He was determined to push the matter to a satisfactory conclusion, and Helen faded as he talked. Her fair, flying hair and eager eyes counted for nothing, for she was ill, without rights, and any of her friends might hunt her. Sick at heart, Margaret joined in the chase. She wrote her sister a lying letter, at her husband's dictation; she said the furniture was all at Howards End, but could be seen on Monday next at 3 p.m., when a charwoman would be in attendance. It was a cold letter, and the more plausible for that. Helen would think she was offended. And on Monday next she and Henry were to lunch with Dolly, and then ambush themselves in the garden.

After they had gone, Mr. Wilcox said to his son: "I can't have this sort of behaviour, my boy. Margaret's too sweet-natured to mind, but I mind for her."

Charles made no answer.

"Is anything wrong with you, Charles, this afternoon?"

"No, pater; but you may be taking on a bigger business than you reckon."

"How?"

"Don't ask me."

Chapter 35

One speaks of the moods of spring, but the days that are her true children have only one mood; they are all full of the rising and dropping of winds, and the whistling of birds. New flowers may come out, the green embroidery of the hedges increase, but the same heaven broods overhead, soft, thick, and blue, the same figures, seen and unseen, are wandering by coppice and meadow. The morning that Margaret had spent with Miss Avery, and the afternoon she set out to entrap Helen, were the scales of a single balance. Time might never have moved, rain never have fallen, and man alone, with his schemes and ailments, was troubling Nature until he saw her through a veil of tears.

She protested no more. Whether Henry was right or wrong, he was most kind, and she knew of no other standard by which to judge him. She must trust him absolutely. As soon as he had taken up a business, his obtuseness vanished. He profited by the slightest indications, and the capture of Helen promised to be staged as deftly as the marriage of Evie.

They went down in the morning as arranged, and he discovered that their victim was actually in Hilton. On his arrival he called at all the livery-stables in the village, and had a few minutes' serious conversation with the proprietors. What he said, Margaret did not know--perhaps not the truth; but news arrived after lunch that a lady had come by the London train, and had taken a fly to Howards End.

"She was bound to drive," said Henry. "There will be her books.

"I cannot make it out," said Margaret for the hundredth time.

"Finish your coffee, dear. We must be off."

"Yes, Margaret, you know you must take plenty," said Dolly.

Margaret tried, but suddenly lifted her hand to her eyes. Dolly stole glances at her father-in-law which he did not answer. In the silence the motor came round to the door.

"You're not fit for it," he said anxiously. "Let me go alone. I know exactly what to do."

"Oh yes, I am fit," said Margaret, uncovering her face. "Only most frightfully worried. I cannot feel that Helen is really alive. Her letters and telegrams seem to have come from someone else. Her voice isn't in them. I don't believe your driver really saw her at the station. I wish I'd never mentioned it. I know that

Charles is vexed. Yes, he is--" She seized Dolly's hand and kissed it. "There, Dolly will forgive me. There. Now we'll be off."

Henry had been looking at her closely. He did not like this breakdown.

"Don't you want to tidy yourself?" he asked.

"Have I time?"

"Yes, plenty."

She went to the lavatory by the front door, and as soon as the bolt slipped, Mr. Wilcox said quietly:

"Dolly, I'm going without her."

Dolly's eyes lit up with vulgar excitement. She followed him on tip-toe out to the car.

"Tell her I thought it best."

"Yes, Mr. Wilcox, I see."

"Say anything you like. All right."

The car started well, and with ordinary luck would have got away. But Porgly-woggles, who was playing in the garden, chose this moment to sit down in the middle of the path. Crane, in trying to pass him, ran one wheel over a bed of wallflowers. Dolly screamed. Margaret, hearing the noise, rushed out hatless, and was in time to jump on the footboard. She said not a single word: he was only treating her as she had treated Helen, and her rage at his dishonesty only helped to indicate what Helen would feel against them. She thought, "I deserve it: I am punished for lowering my colours." And she accepted his apologies with a calmness that astonished him.

"I still consider you are not fit for it," he kept saying.

"Perhaps I was not at lunch. But the whole thing is spread clearly before me now."

"I was meaning to act for the best."

"Just lend me your scarf, will you? This wind takes one's hair so."

"Certainly, dear girl. Are you all right now?"

"Look! My hands have stopped trembling."

"And have quite forgiven me? Then listen. Her cab should already have arrived at Howards End. (We're a little late, but no matter.) Our first move will be to send it down to wait at the farm, as, if possible, one doesn't want a scene before servants. A certain gentleman"--he pointed at Crane's back--"won't drive in, but will wait a little short of the front gate, behind the laurels. Have you still the keys of the house?"

"Yes."

"Well, they aren't wanted. Do you remember how the house stands?"

"Yes."

"If we don't find her in the porch, we can stroll round into the garden. Our object--"

Here they stopped to pick up the doctor.

"I was just saying to my wife, Mansbridge, that our main object is not to frighten Miss Schlegel. The house, as you know, is my property, so it should seem quite natural for us to be there. The trouble is evidently nervous--wouldn't you say so, Margaret?"

The doctor, a very young man, began to ask questions about Helen. Was she normal? Was there anything congenital or hereditary? Had anything occurred that was likely to alienate her from her family?

"Nothing," answered Margaret, wondering what would have happened if she had added: "Though she did resent my husband's immorality."

"She always was highly strung," pursued Henry, leaning back in the car as it shot past the church. "A tendency to spiritualism and those things, though nothing serious. Musical, literary, artistic, but I should say normal--a very charming girl."

Margaret's anger and terror increased every moment. How dare these men label her sister! What horrors lay ahead! What impertinences that shelter under the name of science! The pack was turning on Helen, to deny her human rights, and it seemed to Margaret that all Schlegels were threatened with her. "Were they normal?" What a question to ask! And it is always those who know nothing about human nature, who are bored by psychology and shocked by physiology, who ask it. However piteous her sister's state, she knew that she must be on her side. They would be mad together if the world chose to consider them so.

It was now five minutes past three. The car slowed down by the farm, in the yard of which Miss Avery was standing. Henry asked her whether a cab had gone past. She nodded, and the next moment they caught sight of it, at the end of the lane. The car ran silently like a beast of prey. So unsuspicious was Helen that she was sitting on the porch, with her back to the road. She had come. Only her head and shoulders were visible. She sat framed in the vine, and one of her hands played with the buds. The wind ruffled her hair, the sun glorified it; she was as she had always been.

Margaret was seated next to the door. Before her husband could prevent her, she slipped out. She ran to the garden gate, which was shut, passed through it, and deliberately pushed it in his face. The noise alarmed Helen. Margaret saw her rise with an unfamiliar movement, and, rushing into the porch, learnt the simple explanation of all their fears--her sister was with child.

"Is the truant all right?" called Henry.

She had time to whisper: "Oh, my darling--" The keys of the house were in her hand. She unlocked Howards End and thrust Helen into it. "Yes, all right," she said, and stood with her back to the door.

Chapter 36

"Margaret, you look upset!" said Henry. Mansbridge had followed. Crane was at the gate, and the flyman had stood up on the box. Margaret shook her head at them; she could not speak any more. She remained clutching the keys, as if all their future depended on them. Henry was asking more questions. She shook her head again. His words had no sense. She heard him wonder why she had let Helen in. "You might have given me a knock with the gate," was another of his remarks. Presently she heard herself speaking. She, or someone for her, said "Go away." Henry came nearer. He repeated, "Margaret, you look upset again. My dear, give me the keys. What are you doing with Helen?"

"Oh, dearest, do go away, and I will manage it all."

"Manage what?"

He stretched out his hand for the keys. She might have obeyed if it had not been for the doctor.

"Stop that at least," she said piteously; the doctor had turned back, and was questioning the driver of Helen's cab. A new feeling came over her; she was fighting for women against men. She did not care about rights, but if men came into Howards End, it should be over her body.

"Come, this is an odd beginning," said her husband.

The doctor came forward now, and whispered two words to Mr. Wilcox--the scandal was out. Sincerely horrified, Henry stood gazing at the earth.

"I cannot help it," said Margaret. "Do wait. It's not my fault. Please all four of you to go away now."

Now the flyman was whispering to Crane.

"We are relying on you to help us, Mrs. Wilcox," said the young doctor. "Could you go in and persuade your sister to come out?"

"On what grounds?" said Margaret, suddenly looking him straight in the eyes.

Thinking it professional to prevaricate, he murmured something about a nervous breakdown.

"I beg your pardon, but it is nothing of the sort. You are not qualified to attend my sister, Mr. Mansbridge. If we require your services, we will let you know."

"I can diagnose the case more bluntly if you wish," he retorted.

"You could, but you have not. You are, therefore, not qualified to attend my sister."

"Come, come, Margaret!" said Henry, never raising his eyes. "This is a terrible business, an appalling business. It's doctor's orders. Open the door."

"Forgive me, but I will not."

"I don't agree."

Margaret was silent.

"This business is as broad as it's long," contributed the doctor. "We had better all work together. You need us, Mrs. Wilcox, and we need you."

"Quite so," said Henry.

"I do not need you in the least," said Margaret.

The two men looked at each other anxiously.

"No more does my sister, who is still many weeks from her confinement."

"Margaret, Margaret!"

"Well, Henry, send your doctor away. What possible use is he now?"

Mr. Wilcox ran his eye over the house. He had a vague feeling that he must stand firm and support the doctor. He himself might need support, for there was trouble ahead.

"It all turns on affection now," said Margaret. "Affection. Don't you see?" Resuming her usual methods, she wrote the word on the house with her finger. "Surely you see. I like Helen very much, you not so much. Mr. Mansbridge doesn't know her. That's all. And affection, when reciprocated, gives rights. Put that down in your notebook, Mr. Mansbridge. It's a useful formula."

Henry told her to be calm.

"You don't know what you want yourselves," said Margaret, folding her arms. "For one sensible remark I will let you in. But you cannot make it. You would trouble my sister for no reason. I will not permit it. I'll stand here all the day sooner."

"Mansbridge," said Henry in a low voice, "perhaps not now."

The pack was breaking up. At a sign from his master, Crane also went back into the car.

"Now, Henry, you," she said gently. None of her bitterness had been directed at him. "Go away now, dear. I shall want your advice later, no doubt. Forgive me if I have been cross. But, seriously, you must go."

He was too stupid to leave her. Now it was Mr. Mansbridge who called in a low voice to him.

"I shall soon find you down at Dolly's," she called, as the gate at last clanged between them. The fly moved out of the way, the motor backed, turned a little, backed again, and turned in the narrow road. A string of farm carts came up in the middle; but she waited through all, for there was no hurry. When all was over and the car had started, she opened the door. "Oh, my darling!" she said. "My darling, forgive me." Helen was standing in the hall.

Chapter 37

Margaret bolted the door on the inside. Then she would have kissed her sister, but Helen, in a dignified voice, that came strangely from her, said:

"Convenient! You did not tell me that the books were unpacked. I have found nearly everything that I want.

"I told you nothing that was true."

"It has been a great surprise, certainly. Has Aunt Juley been ill?"

"Helen, you wouldn't think I'd invent that?"

"I suppose not," said Helen, turning away, and crying a very little. "But one loses faith in everything after this."

"We thought it was illness, but even then--I haven't behaved worthily."

Helen selected another book.

"I ought not to have consulted anyone. What would our father have thought of me?"

She did not think of questioning her sister, nor of rebuking her. Both might be necessary in the future, but she had first to purge a greater crime than any that Helen could have committed--that want of confidence that is the work of the devil.

"Yes, I am annoyed," replied Helen. "My wishes should have been respected. I would have gone through this meeting if it was necessary, but after Aunt Juley recovered, it was not necessary. Planning my life, as I now have to do--"

"Come away from those books," called Margaret. "Helen, do talk to me."

"I was just saying that I have stopped living haphazard. One can't go through a great deal of"--she missed out the noun--"without planning one's actions in advance. I am going to have a child in June, and in the first place conversations, discussions, excitement, are not good for me. I will go through them if necessary, but only then. In the second place I have no right to trouble people. I cannot fit in with England as I know it. I have done something that the English never pardon. It would not be right for them to pardon it. So I must live where I am not known."

"But why didn't you tell me, dearest?"

"Yes," replied Helen judicially. "I might have, but decided to wait."

" I believe you would never have told me."

"Oh yes, I should. We have taken a flat in Munich."

Margaret glanced out of window.

"By 'we' I mean myself and Monica. But for her, I am and have been and always wish to be alone."

"I have not heard of Monica."

"You wouldn't have. She's an Italian--by birth at least. She makes her living by journalism. I met her originally on Garda. Monica is much the best person to see me through."

"You are very fond of her, then."

"She has been extraordinarily sensible with me."

Margaret guessed at Monica's type--"Italiano Inglesiato" they had named it: the crude feminist of the South, whom one respects but avoids. And Helen had turned to it in her need!

"You must not think that we shall never meet," said Helen, with a measured kindness. "I shall always have a room for you when you can be spared, and the longer you can be with me the better. But you haven't understood yet, Meg, and of course it is very difficult for you. This is a shock to you. It isn't to me, who have been thinking over our futures for many months, and they won't be changed by a slight contretemps, such as this. I cannot live in England."

"Helen, you've not forgiven me for my treachery. You *couldn't* talk like this to me if you had."

"Oh, Meg dear, why do we talk at all?" She dropped a book and sighed wearily. Then, recovering herself, she said: "Tell me, how is it that all the books are down here?"

"Series of mistakes."

"And a great deal of the furniture has been unpacked."

"All."

"Who lives here, then?"

"No one."

"I suppose you are letting it though--"

"The house is dead," said Margaret with a frown. "Why worry on about it?"

"But I am interested. You talk as if I had lost all my interest in life. I am still Helen, I hope. Now this hasn't the feel of a dead house. The hall seems more alive even than in the old days, when it held the Wilcoxes' own things."

"Interested, are you? Very well, I must tell you, I suppose. My husband lent it on condition we--but by a mistake all our things were unpacked, and Miss Avery, instead of--" She stopped. "Look here, I can't go on like this. I warn you I won't. Helen, why should you be so miserably unkind to me, simply because you hate Henry?"

"I don't hate him now," said Helen. "I have stopped being a schoolgirl, and, Meg, once again, I'm not being unkind. But as for fitting in with your English life--no, put it out of your head at once. Imagine a visit from me at Ducie Street! It's unthinkable."

Margaret could not contradict her. It was appalling to see her quietly moving forward with her plans, not bitter or excitable, neither asserting innocence nor confessing guilt, merely desiring freedom and the company of those who would not blame her. She had been through--how much? Margaret did not know. But it was enough to part her from old habits as well as old friends.

"Tell me about yourself," said Helen, who had chosen her books, and was lingering over the furniture.

"There's nothing to tell."

"But your marriage has been happy, Meg?"

"Yes, but I don't feel inclined to talk."

"You feel as I do."

"Not that, but I can't."

"No more can I. It is a nuisance, but no good trying."

Something had come between them. Perhaps it was Society, which henceforward would exclude Helen. Perhaps it was a third life, already potent as a spirit. They could find no meeting-place. Both suffered acutely, and were not comforted by the knowledge that affection survived.

"Look here, Meg, is the coast clear?"

"You mean that you want to go away from me?"

"I suppose so--dear old lady! it isn't any use. I knew we should have nothing to say. Give my love to Aunt Juley and Tibby, and take more yourself than I can say. Promise to come and see me in Munich later."

"Certainly, dearest."

"For that is all we can do."

It seemed so. Most ghastly of all was Helen's common sense: Monica had been extraordinarily good for her.

"I am glad to have seen you and the things." She looked at the bookcase lovingly, as if she was saying farewell to the past.

Margaret unbolted the door. She remarked: "The car has gone, and here's your cab."

She led the way to it, glancing at the leaves and the sky. The spring had never seemed more beautiful. The driver, who was leaning on the gate, called out, "Please, lady, a message," and handed her Henry's visiting-card through the bars.

"How did this come?" she asked.

Crane had returned with it almost at once.

She read the card with annoyance. It was covered with instructions in domestic French. When she and her sister had talked she was to come back for the night to Dolly's. "Il faut dormir sur ce sujet." While Helen was to be found "une comfortable chambre à l'hôtel." The final sentence displeased her greatly until she remembered that the Charles' had only one spare room, and so could not invite a third guest.

"Henry would have done what he could," she interpreted.

Helen had not followed her into the garden. The door once open, she lost her inclination to fly. She remained in the hall, going from bookcase to table. She grew more like the old Helen, irresponsible and charming.

"This is Mr. Wilcox's house?" she inquired.

"Surely you remember Howards End?"

"Remember? I who remember everything! But it looks to be ours now."

"Miss Avery was extraordinary," said Margaret, her own spirits lightening a little. Again she was invaded by a slight feeling of disloyalty. But it brought her relief, and she yielded to it. "She loved Mrs. Wilcox, and would rather furnish her house with our things than think of it empty. In consequence here are all the library books. "

"Not all the books. She hasn't unpacked the Art Books, in which she may show her sense. And we never used to have the sword here."

"The sword looks well, though."

"Magnificent."

"Yes, doesn't it?"

"Where's the piano, Meg?"

"I warehoused that in London. Why?"

"Nothing."

"Curious, too, that the carpet fits."

"The carpet's a mistake," announced Helen. "I know that we had it in London, but this floor ought to be bare. It is far too beautiful."

"You still have a mania for under-furnishing. Would you care to come into the dining-room before you start? There's no carpet there.

They went in, and each minute their talk became more natural.

"Oh, *what* a place for mother's chiffonier!" cried Helen.

"Look at the chairs, though."

"Oh, look at them! Wickham Place faced north, didn't it?"

"North-west."

"Anyhow, it is thirty years since any of those chairs have felt the sun. Feel. Their little backs are quite warm."

"But why has Miss Avery made them set to partners? I shall just--"

"Over here, Meg. Put it so that any one sitting will see the lawn."

Margaret moved a chair. Helen sat down in it.

"Ye-es. The window's too high."

"Try a drawing-room chair."

"No, I don't like the drawing-room so much. The beam has been match-boarded. It would have been so beautiful otherwise. "

"Helen, what a memory you have for some things! You're perfectly right. It's a room that men have spoilt through trying to make it nice for women. Men don't know what we want--"

"And never will."

"I don't agree. In two thousand years they'll know."

"But the chairs show up wonderfully. Look where Tibby spilt the soup."

"Coffee. It was coffee surely."

Helen shook her head. "Impossible. Tibby was far too young to be given coffee at that time."

"Was Father alive?"

"Yes."

"Then you're right and it must have been soup. I was thinking of much later--that unsuccessful visit of Aunt Juley's, when she didn't realize that Tibby had grown up. It was coffee then, for he threw it down on purpose. There was some rhyme, 'Tea, coffee--coffee, tea,' that she said to him every morning at breakfast. Wait a minute--how did it go?"

"I know--no, I don't. What a detestable boy Tibby was!"

"But the rhyme was simply awful. No decent person could have put up with it."

"Ah, that greengage tree," cried Helen, as if the garden was also part of their childhood. "Why do I connect it with dumbbells? And there come the chickens. The grass wants cutting. I love yellow-hammers--"

Margaret interrupted her. "I have got it," she announced.

'Tea, tea, coffee, tea,
Or chocolaritee.'

"That every morning for three weeks. No wonder Tibby was wild."

"Tibby is moderately a dear now," said Helen.

"There! I knew you'd say that in the end. Of course he's a dear."

A bell rang.

"Listen! what's that?"

Helen said, "Perhaps the Wilcoxes are beginning the siege."

"What nonsense--listen!"

And the triviality faded from their faces, though it left something behind--the knowledge that they never could be parted because their love was rooted in common things. Explanations and appeals had failed; they had tried for a common meeting-ground, and had only made each other unhappy. And all the time their salvation was lying round them--the past sanctifying the present; the present, with wild heart-throb, declaring that there would after all be a future, with laughter and the voices of children. Helen, still smiling, came up to her sister. She said, "It is always Meg." They looked into each other's eyes. The inner life had paid.

Solemnly the clapper tolled. No one was in the front. Margaret went to the kitchen, and struggled between packing-cases to the window. Their visitor was only a little boy with a tin can. And triviality returned.

"Little boy, what do you want?"

"Please, I am the milk."

"Did Miss Avery send you?" said Margaret, rather sharply.

"Yes, please."

"Then take it back and say we require no milk." While she called to Helen, "No, it's not the siege, but possibly an attempt to provision us against one."

"But I like milk," cried Helen. "Why send it away?"

"Do you? Oh, very well. But we've nothing to put it in, and he wants the can."

"Please, I'm to call in the morning for the can," said the boy.

"The house will be locked up then."

"In the morning would I bring eggs, too?"

"Are you the boy whom I saw playing in the stacks last week?"

The child hung his head.

"Well, run away and do it again."

"Nice little boy," whispered Helen. "I say, what's your name? Mine's Helen."

"Tom."

That was Helen all over. The Wilcoxes, too, would ask a child its name, but they never told their names in return.

"Tom, this one here is Margaret. And at home we've another called Tibby."

"Mine are lop-eared," replied Tom, supposing Tibby to be a rabbit.

"You're a very good and rather a clever little boy. Mind you come again.--Isn't he charming?"

"Undoubtedly," said Margaret. "He is probably the son of Madge, and Madge is dreadful. But this place has wonderful powers."

"What do you mean?"

"I don't know."

"Because I probably agree with you."

"It kills what is dreadful and makes what is beautiful live."

"I do agree," said Helen, as she sipped the milk. "But you said that the house was dead not half an hour ago."

"Meaning that I was dead. I felt it."

"Yes, the house has a surer life than we, even if it was empty, and, as it is, I can't get over that for thirty years the sun has never shone full on our furniture. After all, Wickham Place was a grave. Meg, I've a startling idea."

"What is it?"

"Drink some milk to steady you."

Margaret obeyed.

"No, I won't tell you yet," said Helen, "because you may laugh or be angry. Let's go upstairs first and give the rooms an airing."

They opened window after window, till the inside, too, was rustling to the spring. Curtains blew, picture-frames tapped cheerfully. Helen uttered cries of excitement as she found this bed obviously in its right place, that in its wrong one. She was angry with Miss Avery for not having moved the wardrobes up. "Then one would see really." She admired the view. She was the Helen who had written the memorable letters four years ago. As they leant out, looking westward, she said: "About my idea. Couldn't you and I camp out in this house for the night?"

"I don't think we could well do that," said Margaret.

"Here are beds, tables, towels--"

"I know; but the house isn't supposed to be slept in, and Henry's suggestion was--"

"I require no suggestions. I shall not alter anything in my plans. But it would give me so much pleasure to have one night here with you. It will be something to look back on. Oh, Meg lovey, do let's!"

"But, Helen, my pet," said Margaret, "we can't without getting Henry's leave. Of course, he would give it, but you said yourself that you couldn't visit at Ducie Street now, and this is equally intimate."

"Ducie Street is his house. This is ours. Our furniture, our sort of people coming to the door. Do let us camp out, just one night, and Tom shall feed us on eggs and milk. Why not? It's a moon."

Margaret hesitated. "I feel Charles wouldn't like it," she said at last. "Even our furniture annoyed him, and I was going to clear it out when Aunt Juley's illness prevented me. I sympathize with Charles. He feels it's his mother's house. He loves it in rather an untaking way. Henry I could answer for--not Charles."

"I know he won't like it," said Helen. "But I am going to pass out of their lives. What difference will it make in the long run if they say, 'And she even spent the night at Howards End'?"

"How do you know you'll pass out of their lives? We have thought that twice before."

"Because my plans--"

"--which you change in a moment."

"Then because my life is great and theirs are little," said Helen, taking fire. "I know of things they can't know of, and so do you. We know that there's poetry. We know that there's death. They can only take them on hearsay. We know this is our house, because it feels ours. Oh, they may take the title-deeds and the doorkeys, but for this one night we are at home."

"It would be lovely to have you once more alone," said Margaret. "It may be a chance in a thousand."

"Yes, and we could talk." She dropped her voice. "It won't be a very glorious story. But under that wych-elm--honestly, I see little happiness ahead. Cannot I have this one night with you?"

"I needn't say how much it would mean to me."

"Then let us."

"It is no good hesitating. Shall I drive down to Hilton now and get leave?"

"Oh, we don't want leave."

But Margaret was a loyal wife. In spite of imagination and poetry--perhaps on account of them--she could sympathize with the technical attitude that Henry would adopt. If possible, she would be technical, too. A night's lodging--and they demanded no more--need not involve the discussion of general principles.

"Charles may say no," grumbled Helen.

"We shan't consult him."

"Go if you like; I should have stopped without leave."

It was the touch of selfishness, which was not enough to mar Helen's character, and even added to its beauty. She would have stopped without leave, and escaped to Germany the next morning. Margaret kissed her.

"Expect me back before dark. I am looking forward to it so much. It is like you to have thought of such a beautiful thing."

"Not a thing, only an ending," said Helen rather sadly; and the sense of tragedy closed in on Margaret again as soon as she left the house.

She was afraid of Miss Avery. It is disquieting to fulfil a prophecy, however superficially. She was glad to see no watching figure as she drove past the farm, but only little Tom, turning somersaults in the straw.

Chapter 38

The tragedy began quietly enough, and like many another talk, by the man's deft assertion of his superiority. Henry heard her arguing with the driver, stepped out and settled the fellow, who was inclined to be rude, and then led the way to some chairs on the lawn. Dolly, who had not been "told," ran out with offers of tea. He refused them, and ordered her to wheel baby's perambulator away, as they desired to be alone.

"But the diddums can't listen; he isn't nine months old," she pleaded.

"That's not what I was saying," retorted her father-in-law.

Baby was wheeled out of earshot, and did not hear about the crisis till later years. It was now the turn of Margaret.

"Is it what we feared?" he asked.

"It is."

"Dear girl," he began, "there is a troublesome business ahead of us, and nothing but the most absolute honesty and plain speech will see us through." Margaret bent her head. "I am obliged to question you on subjects we'd both prefer to leave untouched. As you know, I am not one of your Bernard Shaws who consider nothing sacred. To speak as I must will pain me, but there are occasions--We are husband and wife, not children. I am a man of the world, and you are a most exceptional woman."

All Margaret's senses forsook her. She blushed, and looked past him at the Six Hills, covered with spring herbage. Noting her colour, he grew still more kind.

"I see that you feel as I felt when--My poor little wife! Oh, be brave! Just one or two questions, and I have done with you. Was your sister wearing a wedding-ring?"

Margaret stammered a "No."

There was an appalling silence.

"Henry, I really came to ask a favour about Howards End."

"One point at a time. I am now obliged to ask for the name of her seducer."

She rose to her feet and held the chair between them. Her colour had ebbed, and she was grey. It did not displease him that she should receive his question thus.

"Take your time," he counselled her. "Remember that this is far worse for me than for you."

She swayed; he feared she was going to faint. Then speech came, and she said slowly: "Seducer? No; I do not know her seducer's name."

"Would she not tell you?"

"I never even asked her who seduced her," said Margaret, dwelling on the hateful word thoughtfully.

"That is singular." Then he changed his mind. "Natural perhaps, dear girl, that you shouldn't ask. But until his name is known, nothing can be done. Sit down. How terrible it is to see you so upset! I knew you weren't fit for it. I wish I hadn't taken you."

Margaret answered, "I like to stand, if you don't mind, for it gives me a pleasant view of the Six Hills."

"As you like."

"Have you anything else to ask me, Henry?"

"Next you must tell me whether you have gathered anything. I have often noticed your insight, dear. I only wish my own was as good. You may have guessed something, even though your sister said nothing. The slightest hint would help us."

"Who is 'we'?"

"I thought it best to ring up Charles."

"That was unnecessary," said Margaret, growing warmer. "This news will give Charles disproportionate pain."

"He has at once gone to call on your brother."

"That too was unnecessary."

"Let me explain, dear, how the matter stands. You don't think that I and my son are other than gentlemen? It is in Helen's interests that we are acting. It is still not too late to save her name."

Then Margaret hit out for the first time. "Are we to make her seducer marry her?" she asked.

"If possible. Yes."

"But, Henry, suppose he turned out to be married already? One has heard of such cases."

"In that case he must pay heavily for his misconduct, and be thrashed within an inch of his life."

So her first blow missed. She was thankful of it. What had tempted her to imperil both of their lives? Henry's obtuseness had saved her as well as himself. Exhausted with anger, she sat down again, blinking at him as he told her as much as he thought fit. At last she said: "May I ask you my question now?"

"Certainly, my dear."

"Tomorrow Helen goes to Munich--"

"Well, possibly she is right."

"Henry, let a lady finish. Tomorrow she goes; tonight, with your permission, she would like to sleep at Howards End."

It was the crisis of his life. Again she would have recalled the words as soon as they were uttered. She had not led up to them with sufficient care. She longed to warn him that they were far more important than he supposed. She saw him weighing them, as if they were a business proposition.

"Why Howards End?" he said at last. "Would she not be more comfortable, as I suggested, at the hotel?"

Margaret hastened to give him reasons. "It is an odd request, but you know what Helen is and what women in her state are." He frowned, and moved irritably. "She has the idea that one night in your house would give her pleasure and do her good. I think she's right. Being one of those imaginative girls, the presence of all our books and furniture soothes her. This is a fact. It is the end of her girlhood. Her last words to me were, 'A beautiful ending.'"

"She values the old furniture for sentimental reasons, in fact."

"Exactly. You have quite understood. It is her last hope of being with it."

"I don't agree there, my dear! Helen will have her share of the goods wherever she goes--possibly more than her share, for you are so fond of her that you'd give her anything of yours that she fancies, wouldn't you? and I'd raise no objection. I could understand it if it was her old home, because a home, or a house"--he changed the word, designedly; he had thought of a telling point--"because a house in which one has once lived becomes in a sort of way sacred, I don't know why. Associations and so on. Now Helen has no associations with Howards End, though I and Charles and Evie have. I do not see why she wants to stay the night there. She will only catch cold."

"Leave it that you don't see," cried Margaret. "Call it fancy. But realize that fancy is a scientific fact. Helen is fanciful, and wants to."

Then he surprised her--a rare occurrence. He shot an unexpected bolt. "If she wants to sleep one night, she may want to sleep two. We shall never get her out of the house, perhaps."

"Well?" said Margaret, with the precipice in sight. "And suppose we don't get her out of the house? Would it matter? She would do no one any harm."

Again the irritated gesture.

"No, Henry," she panted, receding. "I didn't mean that. We will only trouble Howards End for this one night. I take her to London tomorrow--"

"Do you intend to sleep in a damp house, too?"

"She cannot be left alone."

"That's quite impossible! Madness. You must be here to meet Charles."

"I have already told you that your message to Charles was unnecessary, and I have no desire to meet him."

"Margaret--my Margaret--"

"What has this business to do with Charles? If it concerns me little, it concerns you less, and Charles not at all."

"As the future owner of Howards End," said Mr. Wilcox, arching his fingers, "I should say that it did concern Charles."

"In what way? Will Helen's condition depreciate the property?"

"My dear, you are forgetting yourself."

"I think you yourself recommended plain speaking."

They looked at each other in amazement. The precipice was at their feet now.

"Helen commands my sympathy," said Henry. "As your husband, I shall do all for her that I can, and I have no doubt that she will prove more sinned against than sinning. But I cannot treat her as if nothing has happened. I should be false to my position in society if I did."

She controlled herself for the last time. "No, let us go back to Helen's request," she said. "It is unreasonable, but the request of an unhappy girl. Tomorrow she will go to Germany, and trouble society no longer. Tonight she asks to sleep in your empty house--a house which you do not care about, and which you have not occupied for over a year. May she? Will you give my sister leave? Will you forgive her--as you hope to be forgiven, and as you have actually been forgiven? Forgive her for one night only. That will be enough."

"As I have actually been forgiven--?"

"Never mind for the moment what I mean by that," said Margaret. "Answer my question."

Perhaps some hint of her meaning did dawn on him. If so, he blotted it out. Straight from his fortress he answered: "I seem rather unaccommodating, but I have some experience of life, and know how one thing leads to another. I am afraid that your sister had better sleep at the hotel. I have my children and the memory of my dear wife to consider. I am sorry, but see that she leaves my house at once."

"You mentioned Mrs. Wilcox."

"I beg your pardon?"

"A rare occurrence. In reply, may I mention Mrs. Bast?"

"You have not been yourself all day," said Henry, and rose from his seat with face unmoved. Margaret rushed at him and seized both his hands. She was transfigured.

"Not any more of this!" she cried. "You shall see the connection if it kills you, Henry! You have had a mistress--I forgave you. My sister has a lover--you drive her from the house. Do you see the connection? Stupid, hypocritical, cruel--oh, contemptible! --a man who insults his wife when she's alive and cants with her memory when she's dead. A man who ruins a woman for his pleasure, and casts her off to ruin other men. And gives bad financial advice, and then says he is not responsible. These, man, are you. You can't recognize them, because you cannot connect. I've had enough of your unweeded kindness. I've spoilt you long enough. All your life you have been spoiled. Mrs. Wilcox spoiled you. No one has ever told what you are--muddled, criminally muddled. Men like you use repentance as a blind, so don't repent. Only say to yourself, 'What Helen has done, I've done.'"

"The two cases are different," Henry stammered. His real retort was not quite ready. His brain was still in a whirl, and he wanted a little longer.

"In what way different? You have betrayed Mrs. Wilcox, Helen only herself. You remain in society, Helen can't. You have had only pleasure, she may die. You have the insolence to talk to me of differences, Henry?"

Oh, the uselessness of it! Henry's retort came.

"I perceive you are attempting blackmail. It is scarcely a pretty weapon for a wife to use against her husband. My rule through life has been never to pay the least attention to threats, and I can only repeat what I said before: I do not give you and your sister leave to sleep at Howards End."

Margaret loosed his hands. He went into the house, wiping first one and then the other on his handkerchief. For a little she stood looking at the Six Hills, tombs of warriors, breasts of the spring. Then she passed out into what was now the evening.

Chapter 39

Charles and Tibby met at Ducie Street, where the latter was staying. Their interview was short and absurd. They had nothing in common but the English language, and tried by its help to express what neither of them understood. Charles saw in Helen the family foe. He had singled her out as the most dangerous of the Schlegels, and, angry as he was, looked forward to telling his wife how right he had been. His mind was made up at once: the girl must be got out of the way before she disgraced them farther. If occasion offered she might be married to a villain or, possibly, to a fool. But this was a concession to morality, it formed no part of his main scheme. Honest and hearty was Charles's dislike, and the past spread itself out very clearly before him; hatred is a skilful compositor. As if they were heads in a note-book, he ran through all the incidents of the Schlegels' campaign: the attempt to compromise his brother, his mother's legacy, his father's marriage, the introduction of the furniture, the unpacking of the same. He had not yet heard of the request to sleep at Howards End; that was to be their masterstroke and the opportunity for his. But he already felt that Howards End was the objective, and, though he disliked the house, was determined to defend it.

Tibby, on the other hand, had no opinions. He stood above the conventions: his sister had a right to do what she thought right. It is not difficult to stand above the conventions when we leave no hostages among them; men can always be more unconventional than women, and a bachelor of independent means need encounter no difficulties at all. Unlike Charles, Tibby had money enough; his ancestors had earned it for him, and if he shocked the people in one set of lodgings he had only to move into another. His was the leisure without sympathy--an attitude as fatal as the strenuous: a little cold culture may be raised on it, but no art. His sisters had seen the family danger, and had never forgotten to discount the gold islets that raised them from the sea. Tibby gave all the praise to himself, and so despised the struggling and the submerged.

Hence the absurdity of the interview; the gulf between them was economic as well as spiritual. But several facts passed: Charles pressed for them with an impertinence that the undergraduate could not withstand. On what date had Helen gone abroad? To whom? (Charles was anxious to fasten the scandal on Germany.) Then, changing his tactics, he said roughly: "I suppose you realize that you are your sister's protector?"

"In what sense?"

"If a man played about with my sister, I'd send a bullet through him, but perhaps you don't mind."

"I mind very much," protested Tibby.

"Who d'ye suspect, then? Speak out, man. One always suspects someone."

"No one. I don't think so." Involuntarily he blushed. He had remembered the scene in his Oxford rooms.

"You are hiding something," said Charles. As interviews go, he got the best of this one. "When you saw her last, did she mention anyone's name? Yes, or no!" he thundered, so that Tibby started.

"In my rooms she mentioned some friends, called the Basts--"

"Who are the Basts?"

"People--friends of hers at Evie's wedding."

"I don't remember. But, by great Scott! I do. My aunt told me about some tag-rag. Was she full of them when you saw her? Is there a man? Did she speak of the man? Or--look here--have you had any dealings with him?"

Tibby was silent. Without intending it, he had betrayed his sister's confidence; he was not enough interested in human life to see where things will lead to. He had a strong regard for honesty, and his word, once given, had always been kept up to now. He was deeply vexed, not only for the harm he had done Helen, but for the flaw he had discovered in his own equipment.

"I see--you are in his confidence. They met at your rooms. Oh, what a family, what a family! God help the poor pater--"

And Tibby found himself alone.

Chapter 40

Leonard--he would figure at length in a newspaper report, but that evening he did not count for much. The foot of the tree was in shadow, since the moon was still hidden behind the house. But above, to right, to left, down the long meadow the moonlight was streaming. Leonard seemed not a man, but a cause.

Perhaps it was Helen's way of falling in love--a curious way to Margaret, whose agony and whose contempt of Henry were yet imprinted with his image. Helen forgot people. They were husks that had enclosed her emotion. She could pity, or sacrifice herself, or have instincts, but had she ever loved in the noblest way, where man and woman, having lost themselves in sex, desire to lose sex itself in comradeship?

Margaret wondered, but said no word of blame. This was Helen's evening. Troubles enough lay ahead of her--the loss of friends and of social advantages, the agony, the supreme agony, of motherhood, which is even yet not a matter of common knowledge. For the present let the moon shine brightly and the breezes of the spring blow gently, dying away from the gale of the day, and let the earth, who brings increase, bring peace. Not even to herself dare she blame Helen. She could not assess her trespass by any moral code; it was everything or nothing. Morality can tell us that murder is worse than stealing, and group most sins in an order all must approve, but it cannot group Helen. The surer its pronouncements on this point, the surer may we be that morality is not speaking. Christ was evasive when they questioned Him. It is those that cannot connect who hasten to cast the first stone.

This was Helen's evening--won at what cost, and not to be marred by the sorrows of others. Of her own tragedy Margaret never uttered a word.

"One isolates," said Helen slowly. "I isolated Mr. Wilcox from the other forces that were pulling Leonard downhill. Consequently, I was full of pity, and almost of revenge. For weeks I had blamed Mr. Wilcox only, and so, when your letters came--"

"I need never have written them," sighed Margaret. "They never shielded Henry. How hopeless it is to tidy away the past, even for others!"

"I did not know that it was your own idea to dismiss the Basts."

"Looking back, that was wrong of me."

"Looking back, darling, I know that it was right. It is right to save the man whom one loves. I am less enthusiastic about justice now. But we both thought you wrote at his dictation. It seemed the last touch of his callousness. Being very much wrought up by this time--and Mrs. Bast was upstairs. I had not seen her, and had talked for a long time to Leonard--I had snubbed him for no reason, and that should have warned me I was in danger. So when the notes came I wanted us to go to you for an explanation. He said that he guessed the explanation--he knew of it, and you mustn't know. I pressed him to tell me. He said no one must know; it was something to do with his wife. Right up to the end we were Mr. Bast and Miss Schlegel. I was going to tell him that he must be frank with me when I saw his eyes, and guessed that Mr. Wilcox had ruined him in two ways, not one. I drew him to me. I made him tell me. I felt very lonely myself. He is not to blame. He would have gone on worshipping me. I want never to see him again, though it sounds appalling. I wanted to give him money and feel finished. Oh, Meg, the little that is known about these things!"

She laid her face against the tree.

"The little, too, that is known about growth! Both times it was loneliness, and the night, and panic afterwards. Did Leonard grow out of Paul?"

Margaret did not speak for a moment. So tired was she that her attention had actually wandered to the teeth--the teeth that had been thrust into the tree's bark to medicate it. From where she sat she could see them gleam. She had been trying to count them. "Leonard is a better growth than madness," she said. "I was afraid that you would react against Paul until you went over the verge."

"I did react until I found poor Leonard. I am steady now. I shan't ever like your Henry, dearest Meg, or even speak kindly about him, but all that blinding hate is over. I shall never rave against Wilcoxes any more. I understand how you married him, and you will now be very happy."

Margaret did not reply.

"Yes," repeated Helen, her voice growing more tender, "I do at last understand."

"Except Mrs. Wilcox, dearest, no one understands our little movements."

"Because in death--I agree."

"Not quite. I feel that you and I and Henry are only fragments of that woman's mind. She knows everything. She is everything. She is the house, and the tree that leans over it. People have their own deaths as well as their own lives, and even if there is nothing beyond death, we shall differ in our nothingness. I cannot believe that knowledge such as hers will perish with knowledge such as mine. She knew about realities. She knew when people were in love, though she was not in the room. I don't doubt that she knew when Henry deceived her."

"Good-night, Mrs. Wilcox," called a voice.

"Oh, good-night, Miss Avery."

"Why should Miss Avery work for us?" Helen murmured.

"Why, indeed?"

Chapter 40

Miss Avery crossed the lawn and merged into the hedge that divided it from the farm. An old gap, which Mr. Wilcox had filled up, had reappeared, and her track through the dew followed the path that he had turfed over, when he improved the garden and made it possible for games.

"This is not quite our house yet," said Helen. "When Miss Avery called, I felt we are only a couple of tourists."

"We shall be that everywhere, and for ever."

"But affectionate tourists--"

"But tourists who pretend each hotel is their home."

"I can't pretend very long," said Helen. "Sitting under this tree one forgets, but I know that tomorrow I shall see the moon rise out of Germany. Not all your goodness can alter the facts of the case. Unless you will come with me."

Margaret thought for a moment. In the past year she had grown so fond of England that to leave it was a real grief. Yet what detained her? No doubt Henry would pardon her outburst, and go on blustering and muddling into a ripe old age. But what was the good? She had just as soon vanish from his mind.

"Are you serious in asking me, Helen? Should I get on with your Monica?"

"You would not, but I am serious in asking you."

"Still, no more plans now. And no more reminiscences."

They were silent for a little. It was Helen's evening.

The present flowed by them like a stream. The tree rustled. It had made music before they were born, and would continue after their deaths, but its song was of the moment. The moment had passed. The tree rustled again. Their senses were sharpened, and they seemed to apprehend life. Life passed. The tree nestled again.

"Sleep now," said Margaret.

The peace of the country was entering into her. It has no commerce with memory, and little with hope. Least of all is it concerned with the hopes of the next five minutes. It is the peace of the present, which passes understanding. Its murmur came "now," and "now" once more as they trod the gravel, and "now," as the moonlight fell upon their father's sword. They passed upstairs, kissed, and amidst the endless iterations fell asleep. The house had enshadowed the tree at first, but as the moon rose higher the two disentangled, and were clear for a few moments at midnight. Margaret awoke and looked into the garden. How incomprehensible that Leonard Bast should have won her this night of peace! Was he also part of Mrs. Wilcox's mind?

Chapter 41

Far different was Leonard's development. The months after Oniton, whatever minor troubles they might bring him, were all overshadowed by Remorse. When Helen looked back she could philosophize, or she could look into the future and plan for her child. But the father saw nothing beyond his own sin. Weeks afterwards, in the midst of other occupations, he would suddenly cry out, "Brute--you brute, I couldn't have--" and be rent into two people who held dialogues. Or brown rain would descend, blotting out faces and the sky. Even Jacky noticed the change in him. Most terrible were his sufferings when he awoke from sleep. Sometimes he was happy at first, but grew conscious of a burden hanging to him and weighing down his thoughts when they would move. Or little irons scorched his body. Or a sword stabbed him. He would sit at the edge of his bed, holding his heart and moaning, "Oh what *shall* I do, whatever *shall* I do?" Nothing brought ease. He could put distance between him and the trespass, but it grew in his soul.

Remorse is not among the eternal verities. The Greeks were right to dethrone her. Her action is too capricious, as though the Erinyes selected for punishment only certain men and certain sins. And of all means to regeneration Remorse is surely the most wasteful. It cuts away healthy tissues with the poisoned. It is a knife that probes far deeper than the evil. Leonard was driven straight through its torments and emerged pure, but enfeebled--a better man, who would never lose control of himself again, but also a smaller, who had less to control. Nor did purity mean peace. The use of the knife can become a habit as hard to shake off as passion itself, and Leonard continued to start with a cry out of dreams.

He built up a situation that was far enough from the truth. It never occurred to him that Helen was to blame. He forgot the intensity of their talk, the charm that had been lent him by sincerity, the magic of Oniton under darkness and of the whispering river. Helen loved the absolute. Leonard had been ruined absolutely, and had appeared to her as a man apart, isolated from the world. A real man, who cared for adventure and beauty, who desired to live decently and pay his way, who could have travelled more gloriously through life than the Juggernaut car that was crushing him. Memories of Evie's wedding had warped her, the starched servants, the yards of uneaten food, the rustle of overdressed women, motor-cars oozing grease on the gravel, rubbish on a pretentious band. She had tasted the lees of this on her arrival: in the darkness, after failure, they intoxicated her. She and the victim seemed alone in a world of unreality, and she loved him absolutely, perhaps for half an hour.

In the morning she was gone. The note that she left, tender and hysterical in tone, and intended to be most kind, hurt her lover terribly. It was as if some work of art had been broken by him, some picture in the National Gallery slashed out of its frame. When he recalled her talents and her social position, he felt that the first passerby had a right to shoot him down. He was afraid of the waitress and the porters at the railway-station. He was afraid at first of his wife, though later he was to regard her with a strange new tenderness, and to think, "There is nothing to choose between us, after all."

The expedition to Shropshire crippled the Basts permanently. Helen in her flight forgot to settle the hotel bill, and took their return tickets away with her; they had to pawn Jacky's bangles to get home, and the smash came a few days afterwards. It is true that Helen offered him five thousands pounds, but such a sum meant nothing to him. He could not see that the girl was desperately righting herself, and trying to save something out of the disaster, if it was only five thousand pounds. But he had to live somehow. He turned to his family, and degraded himself to a professional beggar. There was nothing else for him to do.

"A letter from Leonard," thought Blanche, his sister; "and after all this time." She hid it, so that her husband should not see, and when he had gone to his work read it with some emotion, and sent the prodigal a little money out of her dress allowance.

"A letter from Leonard!" said the other sister, Laura, a few days later. She showed it to her husband. He wrote a cruel insolent reply, but sent more money than Blanche, so Leonard soon wrote to him again.

And during the winter the system was developed. Leonard realized that they need never starve, because it would be too painful for his relatives. Society is based on the family, and the clever wastrel can exploit this indefinitely. Without a generous thought on either side, pounds and pounds passed. The donors disliked Leonard, and he grew to hate them intensely. When Laura censured his immoral marriage, he thought bitterly, "She minds that! What would she say if she knew the truth?" When Blanche's husband offered him work, he found some pretext for avoiding it. He had wanted work keenly at Oniton, but too much anxiety had shattered him; he was joining the unemployable. When his brother, the lay-reader, did not reply to a letter, he wrote again, saying that he and Jacky would come down to his village on foot. He did not intend this as blackmail. Still, the brother sent a postal order, and it became part of the system. And so passed his winter and his spring.

In the horror there are two bright spots. He never confused the past. He remained alive, and blessed are those who live, if it is only to a sense of sinfulness. The anodyne of muddledom, by which most men blur and blend their mistakes, never passed Leonard's lips--

And if I drink oblivion of a day,

So shorten I the stature of my soul.

It is a hard saying, and a hard man wrote it, but it lies at the foot of all character.

And the other bright spot was his tenderness for Jacky. He pitied her with nobility now--not the contemptuous pity of a man who sticks to a woman through thick and thin. He tried to be less irritable. He wondered what her hungry eyes desired--nothing that she could express, or that he or any man could give her. Would she ever receive the justice that is mercy--the justice for by-products that the world is too busy to bestow? She was fond of flowers, generous with money, and not revengeful. If she had borne him a child he might have cared for her. Unmarried, Leonard would never have begged; he would have flickered out and died. But the whole of life is mixed. He had to provide for Jacky, and went down dirty paths that she might have a few feathers and dishes of food that suited her.

One day he caught sight of Margaret and her brother. He was in St. Paul's. He had entered the cathedral partly to avoid the rain and partly to see a picture that had educated him in former years. But the light was bad, the picture ill placed, and Time and Judgment were inside him now. Death alone still charmed him, with her lap of poppies, on which all men shall sleep. He took one glance, and turned aimlessly away towards a chair. Then down the nave he saw Miss Schlegel and her brother. They stood in the fairway of passengers, and their faces were extremely grave. He was perfectly certain that they were in trouble about their sister.

Once outside--and he fled immediately--he wished that he had spoken to them. What was his life? What were a few angry words, or even imprisonment? He had done wrong--that was the true terror. Whatever they might know, he would tell them everything he knew. He re-entered St. Paul's. But they had moved in his absence, and had gone to lay their difficulties before Mr. Wilcox and Charles.

The sight of Margaret turned remorse into new channels. He desired to confess, and though the desire is proof of a weakened nature, which is about to lose the essence of human intercourse, it did not take an ignoble form. He did not suppose that confession would bring him happiness. It was rather that he yearned to get clear of the tangle. So does the suicide yearn. The impulses are akin, and the crime of suicide lies rather in its disregard for the feelings of those whom we leave behind. Confession need harm no one--it can satisfy that test--and though it was un-English, and ignored by our Anglican cathedral, Leonard had a right to decide upon it.

Moreover, he trusted Margaret. He wanted her hardness now. That cold, intellectual nature of hers would be just, if unkind. He would do whatever she told him, even if he had to see Helen. That was the supreme punishment she would exact. And perhaps she would tell him how Helen was. That was the supreme reward.

He knew nothing about Margaret, not even whether she was married to Mr. Wilcox, and tracking her out took several days. That evening he toiled through the wet to Wickham Place, where the new flats were now appearing. Was he also the cause of their move? Were they expelled from society on his account? Thence to a public library, but could find no satisfactory Schlegel in the directory. On the morrow he searched again. He hung about outside Mr. Wilcox's office at lunch time, and, as the clerks came out said: "Excuse me, sir, but is your boss married?" Most of them stared, some said, "What's that to you?" but one, who had not yet acquired reticence, told him what he wished. Leonard could not learn the private address. That necessitated more trouble with directories and tubes. Ducie Street was not discovered till the Monday, the day that Margaret and her husband went down on their hunting expedition to Howards End.

He called at about four o'clock. The weather had changed, and the sun shone gaily on the ornamental steps--black and white marble in triangles. Leonard lowered his eyes to them after ringing the bell. He felt in curious health: doors seemed to be opening and shutting inside his body, and he had been obliged to steep sitting up in bed, with his back propped against the wall. When the parlourmaid came he could not see her face; the brown rain had descended suddenly.

"Does Mrs. Wilcox live here?" he asked.

"She's out," was the answer.

"When will she be back?"

"I'll ask," said the parlourmaid.

Margaret had given instructions that no one who mentioned her name should ever be rebuffed. Putting the door on the chain--for Leonard's appearance demanded this--she went through to the smoking-room, which was occupied by Tibby. Tibby was asleep. He had had a good lunch. Charles Wilcox had not yet rung him up for the distracting interview. He said drowsily: "I don't know. Hilton. Howards End. Who is it?"

"I'll ask, sir."

"No, don't bother."

"They have taken the car to Howards End," said the parlourmaid to Leonard.

He thanked her, and asked whereabouts that place was.

"You appear to want to know a good deal," she remarked. But Margaret had forbidden her to be mysterious. She told him against her better judgment that Howards End was in Hertfordshire.

"Is it a village, please?"

"Village! It's Mr. Wilcox's private house--at least, it's one of them. Mrs. Wilcox keeps her furniture there. Hilton is the village."

"Yes. And when will they be back?"

"Mr. Schlegel doesn't know. We can't know everything, can we?" She shut him out, and went to attend to the telephone, which was ringing furiously.

He loitered away another night of agony. Confession grew more difficult. As soon as possible he went to bed. He watched a patch of moonlight cross the floor of their lodging, and, as sometimes happens when the mind is overtaxed, he fell asleep for the rest of the room, but kept awake for the patch of moonlight. Horrible! Then began one of those disintegrating dialogues. Part of him said: "Why horrible? It's ordinary light from the room." "But it moves." "So does the moon." "But it is a clenched fist." "Why not?" "But it is going to touch me." "Let it." And, seeming to gather motion, the patch ran up his blanket. Presently a blue snake appeared; then another, parallel to it. "Is there life in the moon?" "Of course." "But I thought it was uninhabited." "Not by Time, Death, Judgment, and the smaller snakes." "Smaller snakes!" said Leonard indignantly and aloud. "What a notion!" By a rending effort of the will he woke the rest of the room up. Jacky, the bed, their food, their clothes on the chair, gradually entered his consciousness, and the horror vanished outwards, like a ring that is spreading through water.

"I say, Jacky, I'm going out for a bit."

She was breathing regularly. The patch of light fell clear of the striped blanket, and began to cover the shawl that lay over her feet. Why had he been afraid? He went to the window, and saw that the moon was descending through a clear sky. He saw her volcanoes, and the bright expanses that a gracious error has named seas. They paled, for the sun, who had lit them up, was coming to light the earth. Sea of Serenity, Sea of Tranquillity, Ocean of the Lunar Storms, merged into one lucent drop, itself to slip into the sempiternal dawn. And he had been afraid of the moon!

He dressed among the contending lights, and went through his money. It was running low again, but enough for a return ticket to Hilton. As it clinked Jacky opened her eyes.

"Hullo, Len! What ho, Len!"

"What ho, Jacky! see you again later."

She turned over and slept.

The house was unlocked, their landlord being a salesman at Convent Garden. Leonard passed out and made his way down to the station. The train, though it did not start for an hour, was already drawn up at the end of the platform, and he lay down in it and slept. With the first jolt he was in daylight; they had left the gateways of King's Cross, and were under blue sky. Tunnels followed, and after each the sky grew bluer, and from the embankment at Finsbury Park he had his first sight of the sun. It rolled along behind the eastern smokes--a wheel, whose fellow was the descending moon--and as yet it seemed the servant of the blue sky, not its lord. He dozed again. Over Tewin Water it was day. To the left fell the shadow of the embankment and its arches; to the right Leonard saw up into the Tewin Woods and towards the church, with its wild legend of immortality. Six forest trees--that is a fact--grow out of one of the graves in Tewin churchyard. The grave's occupant--that is the legend--is an atheist, who declared that if God existed, six forest trees would grow out of her grave. These things in Hertfordshire; and farther afield lay the house of a hermit--Mrs. Wilcox had known him--who barred himself up, and wrote prophecies, and gave all he had to the poor. While, powdered in between, were the villas of business men, who saw life more steadily, though with the steadiness of the half-closed eye. Over all the sun was streaming, to all the birds were singing, to all the primroses were yellow, and the speedwell blue, and the country, however they interpreted her, was uttering her cry of "now." She did not free Leonard yet, and the knife plunged deeper into his heart as the train drew up at Hilton. But remorse had become beautiful.

Hilton was asleep, or at the earliest, breakfasting. Leonard noticed the contrast when he stepped out of it into the country. Here men had been up since dawn. Their hours were ruled, not by a London office, but by the movements of the crops and the sun. That they were men of the finest type only the sentimentalist can declare. But they kept to the life of daylight. They are England's hope. Clumsily they carry forward the torch of the sun, until such time as the nation sees fit to take it up. Half clodhopper, half board-school prig, they can still throw back to a nobler stock, and breed yeomen.

At the chalk pit a motor passed him. In it was another type, whom Nature favours--the Imperial. Healthy, ever in motion, it hopes to inherit the earth. It breeds as quickly as the yeoman, and as soundly; strong is the temptation to acclaim it as a super-yeoman, who carries his country's virtue overseas. But the Imperialist is not what he thinks or seems. He is a destroyer. He prepares the way for cosmopolitanism, and though his ambitions may be fulfilled, the earth that he inherits will be grey.

To Leonard, intent on his private sin, there came the conviction of innate goodness elsewhere. It was not the optimism which he had been taught at school. Again and again must the drums tap, and the goblins stalk over the universe before joy can be purged of the superficial. It was rather paradoxical, and arose from his sorrow. Death destroys a man, but the idea of death saves him--that is the best account of it that has yet been given. Squalor and tragedy can beckon to all that is great in us, and strengthen the wings of love. They can beckon; it is not certain that they will, for they are not love's servants. But they can beckon, and the knowledge of this incredible truth comforted him.

As he approached the house all thought stopped. Contradictory notions stood side by side in his mind. He was terrified but happy, ashamed, but had done no sin. He knew the confession: "Mrs. Wilcox, I have done wrong," but sunrise had robbed its meaning, and he felt rather on a supreme adventure.

He entered a garden, steadied himself against a motor-car that he found in it, found a door open and entered a house. Yes, it would be very easy. From a room to the left he heard voices, Margaret's amongst them. His own name was called aloud, and a man whom he had never seen said, "Oh, is he there? I am not surprised. I now thrash him within an inch of his life."

"Mrs. Wilcox," said Leonard, "I have done wrong."

The man took him by the collar and cried, "Bring me a stick." Women were screaming. A stick, very bright, descended. It hurt him, not where it descended, but in the heart. Books fell over him in a shower. Nothing had sense.

"Get some water," commanded Charles, who had all through kept very calm. "He's shamming. Of course I only used the blade. Here, carry him out into the air."

Thinking that he understood these things, Margaret obeyed him. They laid Leonard, who was dead, on the gravel; Helen poured water over him.

"That's enough," said Charles.

"Yes, murder's enough," said Miss Avery, coming out of the house with the sword.

Chapter 42

When Charles left Ducie Street he had caught the first train home, but had no inkling of the newest development until late at night. Then his father, who had dined alone, sent for him, and in very grave tones inquired for Margaret.

"I don't know where she is, pater," said Charles. "Dolly kept back dinner nearly an hour for her."

"Tell me when she comes in--."

Another hour passed. The servants went to bed, and Charles visited his father again, to receive further instructions. Mrs. Wilcox had still not returned.

"I'll sit up for her as late as you like, but she can hardly be coming. Isn't she stopping with her sister at the hotel?"

"Perhaps," said Mr. Wilcox thoughtfully--"perhaps."

"Can I do anything for you, sir?"

"Not tonight, my boy."

Mr. Wilcox liked being called sir. He raised his eyes and gave his son more open a look of tenderness than he usually ventured. He saw Charles as little boy and strong man in one. Though his wife had proved unstable his children were left to him.

After midnight he tapped on Charles's door. "I can't sleep," he said. "I had better have a talk with you and get it over."

He complained of the heat. Charles took him out into the garden, and they paced up and down in their dressing-gowns. Charles became very quiet as the story unrolled; he had known all along that Margaret was as bad as her sister.

"She will feel differently in the morning," said Mr. Wilcox, who had of course said nothing about Mrs. Bast. "But I cannot let this kind of thing continue without comment. I am morally certain that she is with her sister at Howards End. The house is mine--and, Charles, it will be yours--and when I say that no one is to live there, I mean that no one is to live there. I won't have it." He looked angrily at the moon. "To my mind this question is connected with something far greater, the rights of property itself."

"Undoubtedly," said Charles.

Mr. Wilcox linked his arm in his son's, but somehow liked him less as he told him more. "I don't want you to conclude that my wife and I had anything of the nature of a quarrel. She was only over-wrought, as who would not be? I shall do what I can for Helen, but on the understanding that they clear out of the house at once. Do you see? That is a sine qua non."

"Then at eight tomorrow I may go up in the car?"

"Eight or earlier. Say that you are acting as my representative, and, of course, use no violence, Charles."

On the morrow, as Charles returned, leaving Leonard dead upon the gravel, it did not seem to him that he had used violence. Death was due to heart disease. His stepmother herself had said so, and even Miss Avery had acknowledged that he only used the flat of the sword. On his way through the village he informed the police, who thanked him, and said there must be an inquest. He found his father in the garden shading his eyes from the sun.

"It has been pretty horrible," said Charles gravely. "They were there, and they had the man up there with them too."

"What--what man?"

"I told you last night. His name was Bast."

"My God, is it possible?" said Mr. Wilcox. "In your mother's house! Charles, in your mother's house!"

"I know, pater. That was what I felt. As a matter of fact, there is no need to trouble about the man. He was in the last stages of heart disease, and just before I could show him what I thought of him he went off. The police are seeing about it at this moment."

Mr. Wilcox listened attentively.

"I got up there--oh, it couldn't have been more than half-past seven. The Avery woman was lighting a fire for them. They were still upstairs. I waited in the drawing-room. We were all moderately civil and collected, though I had my suspicions. I gave them your message, and Mrs. Wilcox said, 'Oh yes, I see; yes,' in that way of hers."

"Nothing else?"

"I promised to tell you, 'with her love,' that she was going to Germany with her sister this evening. That was all we had time for."

Mr. Wilcox seemed relieved.

"Because by then I suppose the man got tired of hiding, for suddenly Mrs. Wilcox screamed out his name. I recognized it, and I went for him in the hall. Was I right, pater? I thought things were going a little too far."

"Right, my dear boy? I don't know. But you would have been no son of mine if you hadn't. Then did he just--just--crumple up as you said?" He shrunk from the simple word.

"He caught hold of the bookcase, which came down over him. So I merely put the sword down and carried him into the garden. We all thought he was shamming. However, he's dead right enough. Awful business!"

"Sword?" cried his father, with anxiety in his voice. "What sword? Whose sword?"

"A sword of theirs."

"What were you doing with it?"

"Well, didn't you see, pater, I had to snatch up the first thing handy I hadn't a riding-whip or stick. I caught him once or twice over the shoulders with the flat of their old German sword."

"Then what?"

"He pulled over the bookcase, as I said, and fell," said Charles, with a sigh. It was no fun doing errands for his father, who was never quite satisfied.

"But the real cause was heart disease? Of that you're sure?"

"That or a fit. However, we shall hear more than enough at the inquest on such unsavoury topics."

They went into breakfast. Charles had a racking headache, consequent on motoring before food. He was also anxious about the future, reflecting that the police must detain Helen and Margaret for the inquest and ferret the whole thing out. He saw himself obliged to leave Hilton. One could not afford to live near the scene of a scandal--it was not fair on one's wife. His comfort was that the pater's eyes were opened at last. There would be a horrible smash up, and probably a separation from Margaret; then they would all start again, more as they had been in his mother's time.

"I think I'll go round to the police-station," said his father when breakfast was over.

"What for?" cried Dolly, who had still not been "told."

"Very well, sir. Which car will you have?"

"I think I'll walk."

"It's a good half-mile," said Charles, stepping into the garden. "The sun's very hot for April. Shan't I take you up, and then, perhaps, a little spin round by Tewin?"

"You go on as if I didn't know my own mind," said Mr. Wilcox fretfully. Charles hardened his mouth. "You young fellows' one idea is to get into a motor. I tell you, I want to walk: I'm very fond of walking."

"Oh, all right; I'm about the house if you want me for anything. I thought of not going up to the office today, if that is your wish."

"It is, indeed, my boy," said Mr. Wilcox, and laid a hand on his sleeve.

Charles did not like it; he was uneasy about his father, who did not seem himself this morning. There was a petulant touch about him--more like a woman. Could it be that he was growing old? The Wilcoxes were not lacking in affection; they had it royally, but they did not know how to use it. It was the talent in the napkin, and, for a warm-hearted man, Charles had conveyed very little joy. As he watched his father shuffling up the road, he had a vague regret--a wish that something had been different somewhere--a wish (though he did not express it thus) that he had been taught to say "I" in his youth. He meant to make up for Margaret's defection, but knew that his father had been very happy with her until yesterday. How had she done it? By some dishonest trick, no doubt--but how?

Mr. Wilcox reappeared at eleven, looking very tired. There was to be an inquest on Leonard's' body tomorrow, and the police required his son to attend.

"I expected that," said Charles. "I shall naturally be the most important witness there."

Chapter 43

Out of the turmoil and horror that had begun with Aunt Juley's illness and was not even to end with Leonard's death, it seemed impossible to Margaret that healthy life should re-emerge. Events succeeded in a logical, yet senseless, train. People lost their humanity, and took values as arbitrary as those in a pack of playing-cards. It was natural that Henry should do this and cause Helen to do that, and then think her wrong for doing it; natural that she herself should think him wrong; natural that Leonard should want to know how Helen was, and come, and Charles be angry with him for coming--natural, but unreal. In this jangle of causes and effects what had become of their true selves? Here Leonard lay dead in the garden, from natural causes; yet life was a deep, deep river, death a blue sky, life was a house, death a wisp of hay, a flower, a tower, life and death were anything and everything, except this ordered insanity, where the king takes the queen, and the ace the king. Ah, no; there was beauty and adventure behind, such as the man at her feet had yearned for; there was hope this side of the grave; there were truer relationships beyond the limits that fetter us now. As a prisoner looks up and sees stars beckoning, so she, from the turmoil and horror of those days, caught glimpses of the diviner wheels.

And Helen, dumb with fright, but trying to keep calm for the child's sake, and Miss Avery, calm, but murmuring tenderly, "No one ever told the lad he'll have a child"--they also reminded her that horror is not the end. To what ultimate harmony we tend she did not know, but there seemed great chance that a child would be born into the world, to take the great chances of beauty and adventure that the world offers. She moved through the sunlit garden, gathering narcissi, crimson-eyed and white. There was nothing else to be done; the time for telegrams and anger was over, and it seemed wisest that the hands of Leonard should be folded on his breast and be filled with flowers. Here was the father; leave it at that. Let Squalor be turned into Tragedy, whose eyes are the stars, and whose hands hold the sunset and the dawn.

And even the influx of officials, even the return of the doctor, vulgar and acute, could not shake her belief in the eternity of beauty. Science explained people, but could not understand them. After long centuries among the bones and muscles it might be advancing to knowledge of the nerves, but this would never give understanding. One could open the heart to Mr. Mansbridge and his sort without discovering its secrets to them, for they wanted everything down in black and white, and black and white was exactly what they were left with.

They questioned her closely about Charles. She never suspected why. Death had come, and the doctor agreed that it was due to heart disease. They asked to see her father's sword. She explained that Charles's anger was natural, but mistaken. Miserable questions about Leonard followed, all of which she answered unfalteringly. Then back to Charles again. "No doubt Mr. Wilcox may have induced death," she said; "but if it wasn't one thing it would have been another, as you yourselves know." At last they thanked her, and took the sword and the body down to Hilton. She began to pick up the books from the floor.

Helen had gone to the farm. It was the best place for her, since she had to wait for the inquest. Though, as if things were not hard enough, Madge and her husband had raised trouble; they did not see why they should receive the offscourings of Howards End. And, of course, they were right. The whole world was going to be right, and amply avenge any brave talk against the conventions. "Nothing matters," the Schlegels had said in the past, "except one's self-respect and that of one's friends." When the time came, other things mattered terribly. However, Madge had yielded, and Helen was assured of peace for one day and night, and tomorrow she would return to Germany.

As for herself, she determined to go too. No message came from Henry; perhaps he expected her to apologize. Now that she had time to think over her own tragedy, she was unrepentant. She neither forgave him for his behaviour nor wished to forgive him. Her speech to him seemed perfect. She would not have altered a word. It had to be uttered once in a life, to adjust the lopsidedness of the world. It was spoken not only to her husband, but to thousands of men like him--a protest against the inner darkness in high places that comes with a commercial age. Though he would build up his life without hers, she could not apologize. He had refused to connect, on the clearest issue that can be laid before a man, and their love must take the consequences.

No, there was nothing more to be done. They had tried not to go over the precipice but perhaps the fall was inevitable. And it comforted her to think that the future was certainly inevitable: cause and effect would go jangling forward to some goal doubtless, but to none that she could imagine. At such moments the soul retires within, to float upon the bosom of a deeper stream, and has communion with the dead, and sees the world's glory not diminished, but different in kind to what she has supposed. She alters her focus until trivial things are blurred. Margaret had been tending this way all the winter. Leonard's death brought her to the goal. Alas! that Henry should fade, away as reality emerged, and only her love for him should remain clear, stamped with his image like the cameos we rescue out of dreams.

With unfaltering eye she traced his future. He would soon present a healthy mind to the world again, and what did he or the world care if he was rotten at the core? He would grow into a rich, jolly old man, at times a little sentimental about women, but emptying his glass with anyone. Tenacious of power, he would keep

Charles and the rest dependent, and retire from business reluctantly and at a vanced age. He would settle down--though she could not realize this. In her Henry was always moving and causing others to move, until the ends of the met. But in time he must get too tired to move, and settle down. What next? inevitable word. The release of the soul to its appropriate Heaven.

Would they meet in it? Margaret believed in immortality for herself. An nal future had always seemed natural to her. And Henry believed in i himself. Yet, would they meet again? Are there not rather endless levels be the grave, as the theory that he had censured teaches? And his level, wh higher or lower, could it possibly be the same as hers?

Thus gravely meditating, she was summoned by him. He sent up Crane i motor. Other servants passed like water, but the chauffeur remained, thoug pertinent and disloyal. Margaret disliked Crane, and he knew it.

"Is it the keys that Mr. Wilcox wants?" she asked.

"He didn't say, madam."

"You haven't any note for me?"

"He didn't say, madam."

After a moment's thought she locked up Howards End. It was pitiable to s it the stirrings of warmth that would be quenched for ever. She raked out th that was blazing in the kitchen, and spread the coals in the gravelled yard. closed the windows and drew the curtains. Henry would probably sell the now.

She was determined not to spare him, for nothing new had happened as they were concerned. Her mood might never have altered from yesterday ing. He was standing a little outside Charles's gate, and motioned the car to When his wife got out he said hoarsely: "I prefer to discuss things with you side."

"It will be more appropriate in the road, I am afraid," said Margaret. "Di get my message?"

"What about?"

"I am going to Germany with my sister. I must tell you now that I shall it my permanent home. Our talk last night was more important than you realized. I am unable to forgive you and am leaving you."

"I am extremely tired," said Henry, in injured tones. "I have been wa about all the morning, and wish to sit down."

"Certainly, if you will consent to sit on the grass."

The Great North Road should have been bordered all its length with gl Henry's kind had filched most of it. She moved to the scrap opposite, wh were the Six Hills. They sat down on the farther side, so that they could n seen by Charles or Dolly.

"Here are your keys," said Margaret. She tossed them towards him. They on the sunlit slope of grass, and he did not pick them up.

"I have something to tell you," he said gently.

She knew this superficial gentleness, this confession of hastiness, that was only intended to enhance her admiration of the male.

"I don't want to hear it," she replied. "My sister is going to be ill. My life is going to be with her now. We must manage to build up something, she and I and her child."

"Where are you going?"

"Munich. We start after the inquest, if she is not too ill."

"After the inquest?"

"Yes."

"Have you realized what the verdict at the inquest will be?"

"Yes, heart disease."

"No, my dear; manslaughter."

Margaret drove her fingers through the grass. The hill beneath her moved as if it was alive.

"Manslaughter," repeated Mr. Wilcox. "Charles may go to prison. I dare not tell him. I don't know what to do--what to do. I'm broken--I'm ended. "

No sudden warmth arose in her. She did not see that to break him was her only hope. She did not enfold the sufferer in her arms. But all through that day and the next a new life began to move. The verdict was brought in. Charles was committed for trial. It was against all reason that he should be punished, but the law, being made in his image, sentenced him to three years' imprisonment. Then Henry's fortress gave way. He could bear no one but his wife, he shambled up to Margaret afterwards and asked her to do what she could with him. She did what seemed easiest--she took him down to recruit at Howards End.

Chapter 44

Tom's father was cutting the big meadow. He passed again and again amid whirring blades and sweet odours of grass, encompassing with narrowing circles the sacred centre of the field. Tom was negotiating with Helen.

"I haven't any idea," she replied. "Do you suppose baby may, Meg?"

Margaret put down her work and regarded them absently. "What was that?" she asked.

"Tom wants to know whether baby is old enough to play with hay?"

"I haven't the least notion," answered Margaret, and took up her work again.

"Now, Tom, baby is not to stand; he is not to lie on his face; he is not to lie so that his head wags; he is not to be teased or tickled; and he is not to be cut into two or more pieces by the cutter. Will you be as careful as all that?"

Tom held out his arms.

"That child is a wonderful nursemaid," remarked Margaret.

"He is fond of baby. That's why he does it!" was Helen's answer. They're going to be lifelong friends."

"Starting at the ages of six and one?"

"Of course. It will be a great thing for Tom."

"It may be a greater thing for baby."

Fourteen months had passed, but Margaret still stopped at Howards End. No better plan had occurred to her. The meadow was being recut, the great red poppies were reopening in the garden. July would follow with the little red poppies among the wheat, August with the cutting of the wheat. These little events would become part of her year after year. Every summer she would fear lest the well should give out, every winter lest the pipes should freeze; every westerly gale might blow the wych-elm down and bring the end of all things, and so she could not read or talk during a westerly gale. The air was tranquil now. She and her sister were sitting on the remains of Evie's mockery, where the lawn merged into the field.

"What a time they all are!" said Helen. "What can they be doing inside?" Margaret, who was growing less talkative, made no answer. The noise of the cutter came intermittently, like the breaking of waves. Close by them a man was preparing to scythe out one of the dell-holes.

"I wish Henry was out to enjoy this," said Helen. "This lovely weather and to be shut up in the house! It's very hard."

"It has to be," said Margaret. "The hay-fever is his chief objection against living here, but he thinks it worth while."

"Meg, is or isn't he ill? I can't make out."

"Not ill. Eternally tired. He has worked very hard all his life, and noticed nothing. Those are the people who collapse when they do notice a thing."

"I suppose he worries dreadfully about his part of the tangle."

"Dreadfully. That is why I wish Dolly had not come, too, today. Still, he wanted them all to come. It has to be."

"Why does he want them?"

Margaret did not answer.

"Meg, may I tell you something? I like Henry."

"You'd be odd if you didn't," said Margaret.

"I usen't to."

"Usen't!" She lowered her eyes a moment to the black abyss of the past. They had crossed it, always excepting Leonard and Charles. They were building up a new life, obscure, yet gilded with tranquillity. Leonard was dead; Charles had two years more in prison. One usen't always to see clearly before that time. It was different now.

"I like Henry because he does worry."

"And he likes you because you don't."

Helen sighed. She seemed humiliated, and buried her face in her hands. After a time she said: "Above love," a transition less abrupt than it appeared.

Margaret never stopped working.

"I mean a woman's love for a man. I supposed I should hang my life on to that once, and was driven up and down and about as if something was worrying through me. But everything is peaceful now; I seem cured. That Herr Förstmeister, whom Frieda keeps writing about, must be a noble character, but he doesn't see that I shall never marry him or anyone. It isn't shame or mistrust of myself. I simply couldn't. I'm ended. I used to be so dreamy about a man's love as a girl, and think that for good or evil love must be the great thing. But it hasn't been; it has been itself a dream. Do you agree?"

"I do not agree. I do not."

"I ought to remember Leonard as my lover," said Helen, stepping down into the field. "I tempted him, and killed him and it is surely the least I can do. I would like to throw out all my heart to Leonard on such an afternoon as this. But I cannot. It is no good pretending. I am forgetting him." Her eyes filled with tears. "How nothing seems to match--how, my darling, my precious--" She broke off. "Tommy!"

"Yes, please?"

"Baby's not to try and stand.--There's something wanting in me. I see you loving Henry, and understanding him better daily, and I know that death wouldn't part you in the least. But I--Is it some awful appalling, criminal defect?"

Margaret silenced her. She said: "It is only that people are far more different than is pretended. All over the world men and women are worrying because they cannot develop as they are supposed to develop. Here and there they have the matter out, and it comforts them. Don't fret yourself, Helen. Develop what you have; love your child. I do not love children. I am thankful to have none. I can play with their beauty and charm, but that is all--nothing real, not one scrap of what there ought to be. And others--others go farther still, and move outside humanity altogether. A place, as well as a person, may catch the glow. Don't you see that all this leads to comfort in the end? It is part of the battle against sameness. Differences--eternal differences, planted by God in a single family, so that there may always be colour; sorrow perhaps, but colour in the daily grey. Then I can't have you worrying about Leonard. Don't drag in the personal when it will not come. Forget him."

"Yes, yes, but what has Leonard got out of life?"

"Perhaps an adventure."

"Is that enough?"

"Not for us. But for him."

Helen took up a bunch of grass. She looked at the sorrel, and the red and white and yellow clover, and the quaker grass, and the daisies, and the bents that composed it. She raised it to her face.

"Is it sweetening yet?" asked Margaret.

"No, only withered."

"It will sweeten tomorrow."

Helen smiled. "Oh, Meg, you are a person," she said. "Think of the racket and torture this time last year. But now I couldn't stop unhappy if I tried. What a change--and all through you!"

"Oh, we merely settled down. You and Henry learnt to understand one another and to forgive, all through the autumn and the winter."

"Yes, but who settled us down?"

Margaret did not reply. The scything had begun, and she took off her pince-nez to watch it.

"You!" cried Helen. "You did it all, sweetest, though you're too stupid to see. Living here was your plan--I wanted you; he wanted you; and every one said it was impossible, but you knew. Just think of our lives without you, Meg--I and baby with Monica, revolting by theory, he handed about from Dolly to Evie. But you picked up the pieces, and made us a home. Can't it strike you--even for a moment--that your life has been heroic? Can't you remember the two months after Charles's arrest, when you began to act, and did all?"

"You were both ill at the time," said Margaret. "I did the obvious things. I had two invalids to nurse. Here was a house, ready furnished and empty. It was obvious. I didn't know myself it would turn into a permanent home. No doubt I have done a little towards straightening the tangle, but things that I can't phrase have helped me."

"I hope it will be permanent," said Helen, drifting away to other thoughts.

"I think so. There are moments when I feel Howards End peculiarly our own."

"All the same, London's creeping."

She pointed over the meadow--over eight or nine meadows, but at the end of them was a red rust.

"You see that in Surrey and even Hampshire now," she continued. "I can see it from the Purbeck Downs. And London is only part of something else, I'm afraid. Life's going to be melted down, all over the world."

Margaret knew that her sister spoke truly. Howards End, Oniton, the Purbeck Downs, the Oderberge, were all survivals, and the melting-pot was being prepared for them. Logically, they had no right to be alive. One's hope was in the weakness of logic. Were they possibly the earth beating time?

"Because a thing is going strong now, it need not go strong for ever," she said. "This craze for motion has only set in during the last hundred years. It may be followed by a civilization that won't be a movement, because it will rest on the earth. All the signs are against it now, but I can't help hoping, and very early in the morning in the garden I feel that our house is the future as well as the past."

They turned and looked at it. Their own memories coloured it now, for Helen's child had been born in the central room of the nine. Then Margaret said, "Oh, take care--!" for something moved behind the window of the hall, and the door opened.

"The conclave's breaking at last. I'll go."

It was Paul.

Helen retreated with the children far into the field. Friendly voices greeted her. Margaret rose, to encounter a man with a heavy black moustache.

"My father has asked for you," he said with hostility. She took her work and followed him.

"We have been talking business," he continued, "but I dare say you knew all about it beforehand."

"Yes, I did."

Clumsy of movement--for he had spent all his life in the saddle--Paul drove his foot against the paint of the front door. Mrs. Wilcox gave a little cry of annoyance. She did not like anything scratched; she stopped in the hall to take Dolly's boa and gloves out of a vase.

Her husband was lying in a great leather chair in the dining-room, and by his side, holding his hand rather ostentatiously, was Evie. Dolly, dressed in purple, sat near the window. The room was a little dark and airless; they were obliged to keep it like this until the carting of the hay. Margaret joined the family without speaking; the five of them had met already at tea, and she knew quite well what was going to be said. Averse to wasting her time, she went on sewing. The clock struck six.

"Is this going to suit every one?" said Henry in a weary voice. He used the old phrases, but their effect was unexpected and shadowy. "Because I don't want you all coming here later on and complaining that I have been unfair."

"It's apparently got to suit us," said Paul.

"I beg your pardon, my boy. You have only to speak, and I will leave the house to you instead."

Paul frowned ill-temperedly, and began scratching at his arm. "As I've given up the outdoor life that suited me, and I have come home to look after the business, it's no good my settling down here," he said at last. "It's not really the country, and it's not the town."

"Very well. Does my arrangement suit you, Evie?"

"Of course, Father."

"And you, Dolly?"

Dolly raised her faded little face, which sorrow could wither but not steady. "Perfectly splendidly," she said. "I thought Charles wanted it for the boys, but last time I saw him he said no, because we cannot possibly live in this part of England again. Charles says we ought to change our name, but I cannot think what to, for Wilcox just suits Charles and me, and I can't think of any other name."

There was a general silence. Dolly looked nervously round, fearing that she had been inappropriate. Paul continued to scratch his arm.

"Then I leave Howards End to my wife absolutely," said Henry. "And let every one understand that; and after I am dead let there be no jealousy and no surprise."

Margaret did not answer. There was something uncanny in her triumph. She, who had never expected to conquer anyone, had charged straight through these Wilcoxes and broken up their lives.

"In consequence, I leave my wife no money," said Henry. "That is her own wish. All that she would have had will be divided among you. I am also giving you a great deal in my lifetime, so that you may be independent of me. That is her wish, too. She also is giving away a great deal of money. She intends to diminish her income by half during the next ten years; she intends when she dies to leave the house to her--to her nephew, down in the field. Is all that clear? Does every one understand?"

Paul rose to his feet. He was accustomed to natives, and a very little shook him out of the Englishman. Feeling manly and cynical, he said: "Down in the field? Oh, come! I think we might have had the whole establishment, piccaninnies included."

Mrs. Cahill whispered: "Don't, Paul. You promised you'd take care." Feeling a woman of the world, she rose and prepared to take her leave.

Her father kissed her. "Good-bye, old girl," he said; "don't you worry about me. "

"Good-bye, Dad."

Then it was Dolly's turn. Anxious to contribute, she laughed nervously, and said: "Good-bye, Mr. Wilcox. It does seem curious that Mrs. Wilcox should have left Margaret Howards End, and yet she get it, after all."

From Evie came a sharply-drawn breath. "Good-bye," she said to Margaret, and kissed her.

And again and again fell the word, like the ebb of a dying sea.

"Good-bye."

"Good-bye, Dolly."

"So long, Father."

"Good-bye, my boy; always take care of yourself."

"Good-bye, Mrs. Wilcox."

"Good-bye.

Margaret saw their visitors to the gate. Then she returned to her husband and laid her head in his hands. He was pitiably tired. But Dolly's remark had interested her. At last she said: "Could you tell me, Henry, what was that about Mrs. Wilcox having left me Howards End?"

Tranquilly he replied: "Yes, she did. But that is a very old story. When she was ill and you were so kind to her she wanted to make you some return, and, not being herself at the time, scribbled 'Howards End' on a piece of paper. I went into it thoroughly, and, as it was clearly fanciful, I set it aside, little knowing what my Margaret would be to me in the future."

Margaret was silent. Something shook her life in its inmost recesses, and she shivered.

"I didn't do wrong, did I?" he asked, bending down.

"You didn't, darling. Nothing has been done wrong."

From the garden came laughter. "Here they are at last!" exclaimed Henry, disengaging himself with a smile. Helen rushed into the gloom, holding Tom by one hand and carrying her baby on the other. There were shouts of infectious joy.

"The field's cut!" Helen cried excitedly--"the big meadow! We've seen to the very end, and it'll be such a crop of hay as never!"

Weybridge, 1908-1910.

THE LONGEST JOURNEY

PART 1 — CAMBRIDGE

I

"The cow is there," said Ansell, lighting a match and holding it out over the carpet. No one spoke. He waited till the end of the match fell off. Then he said again, "She is there, the cow. There, now."

"You have not proved it," said a voice.

"I have proved it to myself."

"I have proved to myself that she isn't," said the voice. "The cow is not there." Ansell frowned and lit another match.

"She's there for me," he declared. "I don't care whether she's there for you or not. Whether I'm in Cambridge or Iceland or dead, the cow will be there."

It was philosophy. They were discussing the existence of objects. Do they exist only when there is some one to look at them? Or have they a real existence of their own? It is all very interesting, but at the same time it is difficult. Hence the cow. She seemed to make things easier. She was so familiar, so solid, that surely the truths that she illustrated would in time become familiar and solid also. Is the cow there or not? This was better than deciding between objectivity and subjectivity. So at Oxford, just at the same time, one was asking, "What do our rooms look like in the vac.?"

"Look here, Ansell. I'm there—in the meadow—the cow's there. You're there—the cow's there. Do you agree so far?" "Well?"

"Well, if you go, the cow stops; but if I go, the cow goes. Then what will happen if you stop and I go?"

Several voices cried out that this was quibbling.

"I know it is," said the speaker brightly, and silence descended again, while they tried honestly to think the matter out.

Rickie, on whose carpet the matches were being dropped, did not like to join in the discussion. It was too difficult for him. He could not even quibble. If he spoke, he should simply make himself a fool. He preferred to listen, and to watch the tobacco-smoke stealing out past the window-seat into the tranquil October air. He could see the court too, and the college cat teasing the college tortoise, and the kitchen-men with supper-trays upon their heads. Hot food for one—that must be for the geographical don, who never came in for Hall; cold food for three, apparently at half-a-crown a head, for some one he did not know; hot food, a la carte—obviously for the ladies haunting the next staircase; cold food for two, at two shillings—going to Ansell's rooms for himself and Ansell, and as it passed under the lamp he saw that it was meringues again. Then the bedmakers began to arrive, chatting to each other pleasantly, and he could hear Ansell's bedmaker say, "Oh dang!" when she found she had to lay Ansell's tablecloth; for there was not a breath stirring. The great elms were motionless, and seemed still in the glory of midsummer, for the darkness hid the yellow blotches on their leaves, and their outlines were still rounded against the tender sky. Those elms were Dryads—so Rickie believed or pretended, and the line between the two is subtler than we admit. At all events they were lady trees, and had for generations fooled the college statutes by their residence in the haunts of youth.

But what about the cow? He returned to her with a start, for this would never do. He also would try to think the matter out. Was she there or not? The cow. There or not. He strained his eyes into the night.

Either way it was attractive. If she was there, other cows were there too. The darkness of Europe was dotted with them, and in the far East their flanks were shining in the rising sun. Great herds of them stood browsing in pastures where no man came nor need ever come, or plashed knee-deep by the brink of impassable rivers. And this, moreover, was the view of Ansell. Yet Tilliard's view had a good deal in it. One might do worse than follow Tilliard, and suppose the cow not to be there unless oneself was there to see her. A cowless world, then, stretched round him on every side. Yet he had only to peep into a field, and, click! it would at once become radiant with bovine life.

Suddenly he realized that this, again, would never do. As usual, he had missed the whole point, and was overlaying philosophy with gross and senseless details. For if the cow was not there, the world and the fields were not there either. And what would Ansell care about sunlit flanks or impassable streams? Rickie rebuked his own groveling soul, and turned his eyes away from the night, which had led him to such absurd conclusions.

The fire was dancing, and the shadow of Ansell, who stood close up to it, seemed to dominate the little room. He was still talking, or rather jerking, and he was still lighting matches and dropping their ends upon the carpet. Now and then he would make a motion with his feet as if he were running quickly backward upstairs, and would tread on the edge of the fender, so that the fire-irons went flying and the buttered-bun dishes crashed against each other in the hearth. The other philosophers were crouched in odd shapes on the sofa and table and chairs, and one, who was a little bored, had crawled to the piano and was timidly trying the Prelude to Rhinegold with his knee upon the soft pedal. The air was heavy with good tobacco-smoke and the pleasant warmth of tea, and as Rickie became more sleepy the events of the day seemed to float one by one before his acquiescent eyes. In the morning he had read Theocritus, whom he believed to be the greatest of Greek poets; he had lunched with a merry don and had tasted Zwieback biscuits; then he had walked with people he liked, and had walked just long enough; and now his room was full of other people whom he liked, and when they left he would go and have supper with Ansell, whom he liked as well as any one. A year ago he had known none of these joys. He had crept cold and friendless and ignorant out of a great public school, preparing for a silent and solitary journey, and praying as a highest favour that he might be left alone. Cambridge had not answered his prayer. She had taken and soothed him, and warmed him, and had laughed at him a little, saying that he must not be so tragic yet awhile, for his boyhood had been but a dusty corridor that led to the spacious halls of youth. In one year he had made many friends and learnt much, and he might learn even more if he could but concentrate his attention on that cow.

The fire had died down, and in the gloom the man by the piano ventured to ask what would happen if an objective cow had a subjective calf. Ansell gave an angry sigh, and at that moment there was a tap on the door.

"Come in!" said Rickie.

The door opened. A tall young woman stood framed in the light that fell from the passage.

"Ladies!" whispered every-one in great agitation.

"Yes?" he said nervously, limping towards the door (he was rather lame). "Yes? Please come in. Can I be any good—"

"Wicked boy!" exclaimed the young lady, advancing a gloved finger into the room. "Wicked, wicked boy!"

He clasped his head with his hands.

"Agnes! Oh how perfectly awful!"

"Wicked, intolerable boy!" She turned on the electric light. The philosophers were revealed with unpleasing suddenness. "My goodness, a tea-party! Oh really, Rickie, you are too bad! I say again: wicked, abominable, intolerable boy! I'll have you horsewhipped. If you please"—she turned to the symposium, which had now risen to its feet "If you please, he asks me and my brother for the week-end. We accept. At the station, no Rickie. We drive to where his old lodgings were—Trumpery Road or some such name—and he's left them. I'm furious, and before I can stop my brother, he's paid off the cab and there we are stranded. I've walked—walked for miles. Pray can you tell me what is to be done with Rickie?"

"He must indeed be horsewhipped," said Tilliard pleasantly. Then he made a bolt for the door.

"Tilliard—do stop—let me introduce Miss Pembroke—don't all go!" For his friends were flying from his visitor like mists before the sun. "Oh, Agnes, I am so sorry; I've nothing to say. I simply forgot you were coming, and everything about you."

"Thank you, thank you! And how soon will you remember to ask where Herbert is?"

"Where is he, then?"

"I shall not tell you."

"But didn't he walk with you?"

"I shall not tell, Rickie. It's part of your punishment. You are not really sorry yet. I shall punish you again later."

She was quite right. Rickie was not as much upset as he ought to have been. He was sorry that he had forgotten, and that he had caused his visitors inconvenience. But he did not feel profoundly degraded, as a young man should who has acted discourteously to a young lady. Had he acted discourteously to his bedmaker or his gyp, he would have minded just as much, which was not polite of him.

"First, I'll go and get food. Do sit down and rest. Oh, let me introduce—"

Ansell was now the sole remnant of the discussion party. He still stood on the hearthrug with a burnt match in his hand. Miss Pembroke's arrival had never disturbed him.

"Let me introduce Mr. Ansell—Miss Pembroke."

There came an awful moment—a moment when he almost regretted that he had a clever friend. Ansell remained absolutely motionless, moving neither hand nor head. Such behaviour is so unknown that Miss Pembroke did not realize what had happened, and kept her own hand stretched out longer than is maidenly.

"Coming to supper?" asked Ansell in low, grave tones.

"I don't think so," said Rickie helplessly.

Ansell departed without another word.

"Don't mind us," said Miss Pembroke pleasantly. "Why shouldn't you keep your engagement with your friend? Herbert's finding lodgings,—that's why he's not here,—and they're sure to be able to give us some dinner. What jolly rooms you've got!"

"Oh no—not a bit. I say, I am sorry. I am sorry. I am most awfully sorry."

"What about?"

"Ansell" Then he burst forth. "Ansell isn't a gentleman. His father's a draper. His uncles are farmers. He's here because he's so clever—just on account of his brains. Now, sit down. He isn't a gentleman at all." And he hurried off to order some dinner.

"What a snob the boy is getting!" thought Agnes, a good deal mollified. It never struck her that those could be the words of affection—that Rickie would never have spoken them about a person whom he disliked. Nor did it strike her that Ansell's humble birth scarcely explained the quality of his rudeness. She was willing to find life full of trivialities. Six months ago and she might have minded; but now—she cared not what men might do unto her, for she had her own splendid lover, who could have knocked all these unhealthy undergraduates into a cocked-hat. She dared not tell Gerald a word of what had happened: he might have come up from wherever he was and half killed Ansell. And she determined not to tell her brother either, for her nature was kindly, and it pleased her to pass things over.

She took off her gloves, and then she took off her ear-rings and began to admire them. These ear-rings were a freak of hers—her only freak. She had always wanted some, and the day Gerald asked her to marry him she went to a shop and had her ears pierced. In some wonderful way she knew that it was right. And he had given her the rings—little gold knobs, copied, the jeweller told them, from something prehistoric and he had kissed the spots of blood on her handkerchief. Herbert, as usual, had been shocked.

"I can't help it," she cried, springing up. "I'm not like other girls." She began to pace about Rickie's room, for she hated to keep quiet. There was nothing much to see in it. The pictures were not attractive, nor did they attract her—school groups, Watts' "Sir Percival," a dog running after a rabbit, a man running after a maid, a cheap brown Madonna in a cheap green frame—in short, a collection where one mediocrity was generally cancelled by another. Over the door there hung a long photograph of a city with waterways, which Agnes, who had never been to Venice, took to be Venice, but which people who had been to Stockholm knew to be Stockholm. Rickie's mother, looking rather sweet, was standing on the mantelpiece. Some more pictures had just arrived from the framers and were leaning with their faces to the wall, but she did not bother to turn them round. On the table were dirty teacups, a flat chocolate cake, and Omar Khayyam, with an Oswego biscuit between his pages. Also a vase filled with the crimson leaves of autumn. This made her smile.

Then she saw her host's shoes: he had left them lying on the sofa. Rickie was slightly deformed, and so the shoes were not the same size, and one of them had a thick heel to help him towards an even walk. "Ugh!" she exclaimed, and removed them gingerly to the bedroom. There she saw other shoes and boots and pumps, a whole row of them, all deformed. "Ugh! Poor boy! It is too bad. Why shouldn't he be like other people? This hereditary business is too awful." She shut the door with a sigh. Then she recalled the perfect form of Gerald, his athletic walk, the poise of his shoulders, his arms stretched forward to receive her. Gradually she was comforted.

"I beg your pardon, miss, but might I ask how many to lay?" It was the bedmaker, Mrs. Aberdeen.

"Three, I think," said Agnes, smiling pleasantly. "Mr. Elliot'll be back in a minute. He has gone to order dinner.

"Thank you, miss."

"Plenty of teacups to wash up!"

"But teacups is easy washing, particularly Mr. Elliot's."

"Why are his so easy?"

"Because no nasty corners in them to hold the dirt. Mr. Anderson—he's below-has crinkly noctagons, and one wouldn't believe the difference. It was I bought these for Mr. Elliot. His one thought is to save one trouble. I never seed such a thoughtful gentleman. The world, I say, will be the better for him." She took the teacups into the gyp room, and then returned with the tablecloth, and added, "if he's spared."

"I'm afraid he isn't strong," said Agnes.

"Oh, miss, his nose! I don't know what he'd say if he knew I mentioned his nose, but really I must speak to someone, and he has neither father nor mother. His nose! It poured twice with blood in the Long."

"Yes?"

"It's a thing that ought to be known. I assure you, that little room!... And in any case, Mr. Elliot's a gentleman that can ill afford to lose it. Luckily his friends were up; and I always say they're more like brothers than anything else."

"Nice for him. He has no real brothers."

"Oh, Mr. Hornblower, he is a merry gentleman, and Mr. Tilliard too! And Mr. Elliot himself likes his romp at times. Why, it's the merriest staircase in the buildings! Last night the bedmaker from W said to me, 'What are you doing to my gentlemen? Here's Mr. Ansell come back 'ot with his collar flopping.' I said, 'And a good thing.' Some bedders keep their gentlemen just so; but surely, miss, the world being what it is, the longer one is able to laugh in it the better."

Bedmakers have to be comic and dishonest. It is expected of them. In a picture of university life it is their only function. So when we meet one who has the face of a lady, and feelings of which a lady might be proud, we pass her by.

"Yes?" said Miss Pembroke, and then their talk was stopped by the arrival of her brother.

"It is too bad!" he exclaimed. "It is really too bad."

"Now, Bertie boy, Bertie boy! I'll have no peevishness."

"I am not peevish, Agnes, but I have a full right to be. Pray, why did he not meet us? Why did he not provide rooms? And pray, why did you leave me to do all the settling? All the lodgings I knew are full, and our bedrooms look into a mews. I cannot help it. And then—look here! It really is too bad." He held up his foot like a wounded dog. It was dripping with water.

"Oho! This explains the peevishness. Off with it at once. It'll be another of your colds."

"I really think I had better." He sat down by the fire and daintily unlaced his boot. "I notice a great change in university tone. I can never remember swaggering three abreast along the pavement and charging inoffensive visitors into a gutter when I was an undergraduate. One of the men, too, wore an Eton tie. But the others, I should say, came from very queer schools, if they came from any schools at all."

Mr. Pembroke was nearly twenty years older than his sister, and had never been as handsome. But he was not at all the person to knock into a gutter, for though not in orders, he had the air of being on the verge of them, and his features, as well as his clothes, had the clerical cut. In his presence conversation became pure and colourless and full of understatements, and—just as if he was a real clergyman—neither men nor boys ever forgot that he was there. He had observed this, and it pleased him very much. His conscience permitted him to enter the Church whenever his profession, which was the scholastic, should demand it.

"No gutter in the world's as wet as this," said Agnes, who had peeled off her brother's sock, and was now toasting it at the embers on a pair of tongs.

"Surely you know the running water by the edge of the Trumpington road? It's turned on occasionally to clear away the refuse—a most primitive idea. When I was up we had a joke about it, and called it the 'Pem.'"

"How complimentary!"

"You foolish girl,—not after me, of course. We called it the 'Pem' because it is close to Pembroke College. I remember—" He smiled a little, and twiddled his toes. Then he remembered the bedmaker, and said, "My sock is now dry. My sock, please."

"Your sock is sopping. No, you don't!" She twitched the tongs away from him. Mrs. Aberdeen, without speaking, fetched a pair of Rickie's socks and a pair of Rickie's shoes.

"Thank you; ah, thank you. I am sure Mr. Elliot would allow it."

Then he said in French to his sister, "Has there been the slightest sign of Frederick?"

"Now, do call him Rickie, and talk English. I found him here. He had forgotten about us, and was very sorry. Now he's gone to get some dinner, and I can't think why he isn't back."

Mrs. Aberdeen left them.

"He wants pulling up sharply. There is nothing original in absent-mindedness. True originality lies elsewhere. Really, the lower classes have no nous. However can I wear such deformities?" For he had been madly trying to cram a right-hand foot into a left-hand shoe.

"Don't!" said Agnes hastily. "Don't touch the poor fellow's things." The sight of the smart, stubby patent leather made her almost feel faint. She had known Rickie for many years, but it seemed so dreadful and so different now that he was a man. It was her first great contact with the abnormal, and unknown fibres of her being rose in revolt against it. She frowned when she heard his uneven tread upon the stairs.

"Agnes—before he arrives—you ought never to have left me and gone to his rooms alone. A most elementary transgression. Imagine the unpleasantness if you had found him with friends. If Gerald—"

Rickie by now had got into a fluster. At the kitchens he had lost his head, and when his turn came—he had had to wait—he had yielded his place to those behind, saying that he didn't matter. And he had wasted more precious time buying bananas, though he knew that the Pembrokes were not partial to fruit. Amid much tardy and chaotic hospitality the meal got under way. All the spoons and forks were anyhow, for Mrs. Aberdeen's virtues were not practical. The fish seemed never to have been alive, the meat had no kick, and the cork of the college claret slid forth silently, as if ashamed of the contents. Agnes was particularly pleasant. But her brother could not recover himself. He still remembered their desolate arrival, and he could feel the waters of the Pem eating into his instep.

"Rickie," cried the lady, "are you aware that you haven't congratulated me on my engagement?"

Rickie laughed nervously, and said, "Why no! No more I have."

"Say something pretty, then."

"I hope you'll be very happy," he mumbled. "But I don't know anything about marriage."

"Oh, you awful boy! Herbert, isn't he just the same? But you do know something about Gerald, so don't be so chilly and cautious. I've just realized, looking at those groups, that you must have been at school together. Did you come much across him?"

"Very little," he answered, and sounded shy. He got up hastily, and began to muddle with the coffee.

"But he was in the same house. Surely that's a house group?"

"He was a prefect." He made his coffee on the simple system. One had a brown pot, into which the boiling stuff was poured. Just before serving one put in a drop of cold water, and the idea was that the grounds fell to the bottom.

"Wasn't he a kind of athletic marvel? Couldn't he knock any boy or master down?"

"Yes."

"If he had wanted to," said Mr. Pembroke, who had not spoken for some time.

"If he had wanted to," echoed Rickie. "I do hope, Agnes, you'll be most awfully happy. I don't know anything about the army, but I should think it must be most awfully interesting."

Mr. Pembroke laughed faintly.

"Yes, Rickie. The army is a most interesting profession,—the profession of Wellington and Marlborough and Lord Roberts; a most interesting profession, as you observe. A profession that may mean death—death, rather than dishonour."

"That's nice," said Rickie, speaking to himself. "Any profession may mean dishonour, but one isn't allowed to die instead. The army's different. If a soldier makes a mess, it's thought rather decent of him, isn't it, if he blows out his brains? In the other professions it somehow seems cowardly."

"I am not competent to pronounce," said Mr. Pembroke, who was not accustomed to have his schoolroom satire commented on. "I merely know that the army is the finest profession in the world. Which reminds me, Rickie—have you been thinking about yours?"

"No."

"Not at all?"

"No."

"Now, Herbert, don't bother him. Have another meringue."

"But, Rickie, my dear boy, you're twenty. It's time you thought. The Tripos is the beginning of life, not the end. In less than two years you will have got your B.A. What are you going to do with it?"

"I don't know."

"You're M.A., aren't you?" asked Agnes; but her brother proceeded—

"I have seen so many promising, brilliant lives wrecked simply on account of this—not settling soon enough. My dear boy, you must think. Consult your tastes if possible—but think. You have not a moment to lose. The Bar, like your father?"

"Oh, I wouldn't like that at all."

"I don't mention the Church."

"Oh, Rickie, do be a clergyman!" said Miss Pembroke. "You'd be simply killing in a wide-awake."

He looked at his guests hopelessly. Their kindness and competence overwhelmed him. "I wish I could talk to them as I talk to myself," he thought. "I'm not such an ass when I talk to myself. I don't believe, for instance, that quite all I thought about the cow was rot." Aloud he said, "I've sometimes wondered about writing."

"Writing?" said Mr. Pembroke, with the tone of one who gives everything its trial. "Well, what about writing? What kind of writing?"

"I rather like,"—he suppressed something in his throat,—"I rather like trying to write little stories."

"Why, I made sure it was poetry!" said Agnes. "You're just the boy for poetry."

"I had no idea you wrote. Would you let me see something? Then I could judge."

The author shook his head. "I don't show it to any one. It isn't anything. I just try because it amuses me."

"What is it about?"

"Silly nonsense."

"Are you ever going to show it to any one?"

"I don't think so."

Mr. Pembroke did not reply, firstly, because the meringue he was eating was, after all, Rickie's; secondly, because it was gluey and stuck his jaws together. Agnes observed that the writing was really a very good idea: there was Rickie's aunt,—she could push him.

"Aunt Emily never pushes any one; she says they always rebound and crush her."

"I only had the pleasure of seeing your aunt once. I should have thought her a quite uncrushable person. But she would be sure to help you."

"I couldn't show her anything. She'd think them even sillier than they are."

"Always running yourself down! There speaks the artist!"

"I'm not modest," he said anxiously. "I just know they're bad."

Mr. Pembroke's teeth were clear of meringue, and he could refrain no longer. "My dear Rickie, your father and mother are dead, and you often say your aunt takes no interest in you. Therefore your life depends on yourself. Think it over carefully, but settle, and having once settled, stick. If you think that this writing is practicable, and that you could make your living by it—that you could, if needs be, support a wife—then by all means write. But you must work. Work and drudge. Begin at the bottom of the ladder and work upwards."

Rickie's head drooped. Any metaphor silenced him. He never thought of replying that art is not a ladder—with a curate, as it were, on the first rung, a rector on the second, and a bishop, still nearer heaven, at the top. He never retorted that the artist is not a bricklayer at all, but a horseman, whose business it is to catch Pegasus at once, not to practise for him by mounting tamer colts. This is hard, hot, and generally ungraceful work, but it is not drudgery. For drudgery is not art, and cannot lead to it.

"Of course I don't really think about writing," he said, as he poured the cold water into the coffee. "Even if my things ever were decent, I don't think the magazines would take them, and the magazines are one's only chance. I read somewhere, too, that Marie Corelli's about the only person who makes a thing out of literature. I'm certain it wouldn't pay me."

"I never mentioned the word 'pay,'" said Mr. Pembroke uneasily.

"You must not consider money. There are ideals too."

"I have no ideals."

"Rickie!" she exclaimed. "Horrible boy!"

"No, Agnes, I have no ideals." Then he got very red, for it was a phrase he had caught from Ansell, and he could not remember what came next.

"The person who has no ideals," she exclaimed, "is to be pitied."

"I think so too," said Mr. Pembroke, sipping his coffee. "Life without an ideal would be like the sky without the sun."

Rickie looked towards the night, wherein there now twinkled innumerable stars—gods and heroes, virgins and brides, to whom the Greeks have given their names.

"Life without an ideal—" repeated Mr. Pembroke, and then stopped, for his mouth was full of coffee grounds. The same affliction had overtaken Agnes. After a little jocose laughter they departed to their lodgings, and Rickie, having seen them as far as the porter's lodge, hurried, singing as he went, to Ansell's room, burst open the door, and said, "Look here! Whatever do you mean by it?"

"By what?" Ansell was sitting alone with a piece of paper in front of him. On it was a diagram—a circle inside a square, inside which was again a square.

"By being so rude. You're no gentleman, and I told her so." He slammed him on the head with a sofa cushion. "I'm certain one ought to be polite, even to people who aren't saved." ("Not saved" was a phrase they applied just then to those whom they did not like or intimately know.) "And I believe she is saved. I never knew any one so always good-tempered and kind. She's been kind to me ever since I knew her. I wish you'd heard her trying to stop her brother: you'd have certainly come round. Not but what he was only being nice as well. But she is really nice. And I thought she came into the room so beautifully. Do you know—oh, of course, you despise music—but Anderson was playing Wagner, and he'd just got to the part where they sing

'Rheingold! 'Rheingold!

and the sun strikes into the waters, and the music, which up to then has so often been in E flat—"

"Goes into D sharp. I have not understood a single word, partly because you talk as if your mouth was full of plums, partly because I don't know whom you're talking about." "Miss Pembroke—whom you saw."

"I saw no one."

"Who came in?"

"No one came in."

"You're an ass!" shrieked Rickie. "She came in. You saw her come in. She and her brother have been to dinner."

"You only think so. They were not really there."

"But they stop till Monday."

"You only think that they are stopping."

"But—oh, look here, shut up! The girl like an empress—"

"I saw no empress, nor any girl, nor have you seen them."

"Ansell, don't rag."

"Elliot, I never rag, and you know it. She was not really there."

There was a moment's silence. Then Rickie exclaimed, "I've got you. You say—or was it Tilliard?—no, YOU say that the cow's there. Well—there these people are, then. Got you. Yah!"

"Did it never strike you that phenomena may be of two kinds: ONE, those which have a real existence, such as the cow; TWO, those which are the subjective product of a diseased imagination, and which, to our destruction, we invest with the semblance of reality? If this never struck you, let it strike you now."

Rickie spoke again, but received no answer. He paced a little up and down the sombre roam. Then he sat on the edge of the table and watched his clever friend draw within the square a circle, and within the circle a square, and inside that another circle, and inside that another square.

"Why will you do that?"

No answer.

"Are they real?"

"The inside one is—the one in the middle of everything, that there's never room enough to draw."

II

A little this side of Madingley, to the left of the road, there is a secluded dell, paved with grass and planted with fir-trees. It could not have been worth a visit twenty years ago, for then it was only a scar of chalk, and it is not worth a visit at the present day, for the trees have grown too thick and choked it. But when Rickie was up, it chanced to be the brief season of its romance, a season as brief for a chalk-pit as a man—its divine interval between the bareness of boyhood and the stuffiness of age. Rickie had discovered it in his second term, when the January snows had melted and left fiords and lagoons of clearest water between the inequalities of the floor. The place looked as big as Switzerland or Norway—as indeed for the moment it was—and he came upon it at a time when his life too was beginning to expand. Accordingly the dell became for him a kind of church—a church where indeed you could do anything you liked, but where anything you did would be transfigured. Like the ancient Greeks, he could even laugh at his holy place and leave it no less holy. He chatted gaily about it, and about the pleasant thoughts with which it inspired him; he took his friends there; he even took people whom he did not like. "Procul este, profani!" exclaimed a delighted aesthete on being introduced to it. But this was never to be the attitude of Rickie. He did not love the vulgar herd, but he knew that his own vulgarity would be greater if he forbade it ingress, and that it was not by preciosity that he would attain to the intimate spirit of the dell. Indeed, if he had agreed with the aesthete, he would possibly not have introduced him. If the dell was to bear any inscription, he would have liked it to be "This way to Heaven," painted on a sign-post by the high-road, and he did not realize till later years that the number of visitors would not thereby have sensibly increased.

On the blessed Monday that the Pembrokes left, he walked out here with three friends. It was a day when the sky seemed enormous. One cloud, as large as a continent, was voyaging near the sun, whilst other clouds seemed anchored to the horizon, too lazy or too happy to move. The sky itself was of the palest blue, paling to white where it approached the earth; and the earth, brown, wet, and odorous, was engaged beneath it on its yearly duty of decay. Rickie was open to the complexities of autumn; he felt extremely tiny—extremely tiny and extremely important; and perhaps the combination is as fair as any that exists. He hoped that all his life he would never be peevish or unkind.

II

"Elliot is in a dangerous state," said Ansell. They had reached the dell, and had stood for some time in silence, each leaning against a tree. It was too wet to sit down.

"How's that?" asked Rickie, who had not known he was in any state at all. He shut up Keats, whom he thought he had been reading, and slipped him back into his coat-pocket. Scarcely ever was he without a book.

"He's trying to like people."

"Then he's done for," said Widdrington. "He's dead."

"He's trying to like Hornblower."

The others gave shrill agonized cries.

"He wants to bind the college together. He wants to link us to the beefy set."

"I do like Hornblower," he protested. "I don't try."

"And Hornblower tries to like you."

"That part doesn't matter."

"But he does try to like you. He tries not to despise you. It is altogether a most public-spirited affair."

"Tilliard started them," said Widdrington. "Tilliard thinks it such a pity the college should be split into sets."

"Oh, Tilliard!" said Ansell, with much irritation. "But what can you expect from a person who's eternally beautiful? The other night we had been discussing a long time, and suddenly the light was turned on. Every one else looked a sight, as they ought. But there was Tilliard, sitting neatly on a little chair, like an undersized god, with not a curl crooked. I should say he will get into the Foreign Office."

"Why are most of us so ugly?" laughed Rickie.

"It's merely a sign of our salvation—merely another sign that the college is split."

"The college isn't split," cried Rickie, who got excited on this subject with unfailing regularity. "The college is, and has been, and always will be, one. What you call the beefy set aren't a set at all. They're just the rowing people, and naturally they chiefly see each other; but they're always nice to me or to any one. Of course, they think us rather asses, but it's quite in a pleasant way."

"That's my whole objection," said Ansell. "What right have they to think us asses in a pleasant way? Why don't they hate us? What right has Hornblower to smack me on the back when I've been rude to him?"

"Well, what right have you to be rude to him?"

"Because I hate him. You think it is so splendid to hate no one. I tell you it is a crime. You want to love every one equally, and that's worse than impossible it's wrong. When you denounce sets, you're really trying to destroy friendship."

"I maintain," said Rickie—it was a verb he clung to, in the hope that it would lend stability to what followed—"I maintain that one can like many more people than one supposes."

"And I maintain that you hate many more people than you pretend."

"I hate no one," he exclaimed with extraordinary vehemence, and the dell re-echoed that it hated no one.

"We are obliged to believe you," said Widdrington, smiling a little "but we are sorry about it."

"Not even your father?" asked Ansell.

Rickie was silent.

"Not even your father?"

The cloud above extended a great promontory across the sun. It only lay there for a moment, yet that was enough to summon the lurking coldness from the earth.

"Does he hate his father?" said Widdrington, who had not known. "Oh, good!"

"But his father's dead. He will say it doesn't count."

"Still, it's something. Do you hate yours?"

Ansell did not reply. Rickie said: "I say, I wonder whether one ought to talk like this?"

"About hating dead people?"

"Yes—"

"Did you hate your mother?" asked Widdrington.

Rickie turned crimson.

"I don't see Hornblower's such a rotter," remarked the other man, whose name was James.

"James, you are diplomatic," said Ansell. "You are trying to tide over an awkward moment. You can go."

Widdrington was crimson too. In his wish to be sprightly he had used words without thinking of their meanings. Suddenly he realized that "father" and "mother" really meant father and mother—people whom he had himself at home. He was very uncomfortable, and thought Rickie had been rather queer. He too tried to revert to Hornblower, but Ansell would not let him. The sun came out, and struck on the white ramparts of the dell. Rickie looked straight at it. Then he said abruptly—

"I think I want to talk."

"I think you do," replied Ansell.

"Shouldn't I be rather a fool if I went through Cambridge without talking? It's said never to come so easy again. All the people are dead too. I can't see why I shouldn't tell you most things about my birth and parentage and education."

"Talk away. If you bore us, we have books."

With this invitation Rickie began to relate his history. The reader who has no book will be obliged to listen to it.

Some people spend their lives in a suburb, and not for any urgent reason. This had been the fate of Rickie. He had opened his eyes to filmy heavens, and taken his first walk on asphalt. He had seen civilization as a row of semi-detached villas, and society as a state in which men do not know the men who live next door. He had himself become part of the grey monotony that surrounds all cities. There was no necessity for this—it was only rather convenient to his father.

II

Mr. Elliot was a barrister. In appearance he resembled his son, being weakly and lame, with hollow little cheeks, a broad white band of forehead, and stiff impoverished hair. His voice, which he did not transmit, was very suave, with a fine command of cynical intonation. By altering it ever so little he could make people wince, especially if they were simple or poor. Nor did he transmit his eyes. Their peculiar flatness, as if the soul looked through dirty window-panes, the unkindness of them, the cowardice, the fear in them, were to trouble the world no longer.

He married a girl whose voice was beautiful. There was no caress in it yet all who heard it were soothed, as though the world held some unexpected blessing. She called to her dogs one night over invisible waters, and he, a tourist up on the bridge, thought "that is extraordinarily adequate." In time he discovered that her figure, face, and thoughts were adequate also, and as she was not impossible socially, he married her. "I have taken a plunge," he told his family. The family, hostile at first, had not a word to say when the woman was introduced to them; and his sister declared that the plunge had been taken from the opposite bank.

Things only went right for a little time. Though beautiful without and within, Mrs. Elliot had not the gift of making her home beautiful; and one day, when she bought a carpet for the dining-room that clashed, he laughed gently, said he "really couldn't," and departed. Departure is perhaps too strong a word. In Mrs. Elliot's mouth it became, "My husband has to sleep more in town." He often came down to see them, nearly always unexpectedly, and occasionally they went to see him. "Father's house," as Rickie called it, only had three rooms, but these were full of books and pictures and flowers; and the flowers, instead of being squashed down into the vases as they were in mummy's house, rose gracefully from frames of lead which lay coiled at the bottom, as doubtless the sea serpent has to lie, coiled at the bottom of the sea. Once he was let to lift a frame out—only once, for he dropped some water on a creton. "I think he's going to have taste," said Mr. Elliot languidly. "It is quite possible," his wife replied. She had not taken off her hat and gloves, nor even pulled up her veil. Mr. Elliot laughed, and soon afterwards another lady came in, and they—went away.

"Why does father always laugh?" asked Rickie in the evening when he and his mother were sitting in the nursery.

"It is a way of your father's."

"Why does he always laugh at me? Am I so funny?" Then after a pause, "You have no sense of humour, have you, mummy?"

Mrs. Elliot, who was raising a thread of cotton to her lips, held it suspended in amazement.

"You told him so this afternoon. But I have seen you laugh." He nodded wisely. "I have seen you laugh ever so often. One day you were laughing alone all down in the sweet peas."

"Was I?"

"Yes. Were you laughing at me?"

"I was not thinking about you. Cotton, please—a reel of No. 50 white from my chest of drawers. Left hand drawer. Now which is your left hand?"

"The side my pocket is."

"And if you had no pocket?"

"The side my bad foot is."

"I meant you to say, 'the side my heart is,'" said Mrs. Elliot, holding up the duster between them. "Most of us—I mean all of us—can feel on one side a little watch, that never stops ticking. So even if you had no bad foot you would still know which is the left. No. 50 white, please. No; I'll get it myself." For she had remembered that the dark passage frightened him.

These were the outlines. Rickie filled them in with the slowness and the accuracy of a child. He was never told anything, but he discovered for himself that his father and mother did not love each other, and that his mother was lovable. He discovered that Mr. Elliot had dubbed him Rickie because he was rickety, that he took pleasure in alluding to his son's deformity, and was sorry that it was not more serious than his own. Mr. Elliot had not one scrap of genius. He gathered the pictures and the books and the flower-supports mechanically, not in any impulse of love. He passed for a cultured man because he knew how to select, and he passed for an unconventional man because he did not select quite like other people. In reality he never did or said or thought one single thing that had the slightest beauty or value. And in time Rickie discovered this as well.

The boy grew up in great loneliness. He worshipped his mother, and she was fond of him. But she was dignified and reticent, and pathos, like tattle, was disgusting to her. She was afraid of intimacy, in case it led to confidences and tears, and so all her life she held her son at a little distance. Her kindness and unselfishness knew no limits, but if he tried to be dramatic and thank her, she told him not to be a little goose. And so the only person he came to know at all was himself. He would play Halma against himself. He would conduct solitary conversations, in which one part of him asked and another part answered. It was an exciting game, and concluded with the formula: "Good-bye. Thank you. I am glad to have met you. I hope before long we shall enjoy another chat." And then perhaps he would sob for loneliness, for he would see real people—real brothers, real friends—doing in warm life the things he had pretended. "Shall I ever have a friend?" he demanded at the age of twelve. "I don't see how. They walk too fast. And a brother I shall never have."

("No loss," interrupted Widdrington.

"But I shall never have one, and so I quite want one, even now.")

When he was thirteen Mr. Elliot entered on his illness. The pretty rooms in town would not do for an invalid, and so he came back to his home. One of the first consequences was that Rickie was sent to a public school. Mrs. Elliot did what she could, but she had no hold whatever over her husband.

"He worries me," he declared. "He's a joke of which I have got tired."

"Would it be possible to send him to a private tutor's?"

"No," said Mr. Elliot, who had all the money. "Coddling."

"I agree that boys ought to rough it; but when a boy is lame and very delicate, he roughs it sufficiently if he leaves home. Rickie can't play games. He doesn't make friends. He isn't brilliant. Thinking it over, I feel that as it's like this, we can't ever hope to give him the ordinary education. Perhaps you could think it over too." No.

"I am sure that things are best for him as they are. The day-school knocks quite as many corners off him as he can stand. He hates it, but it is good for him. A public school will not be good for him. It is too rough. Instead of getting manly and hard, he will—"

"My head, please."

Rickie departed in a state of bewildered misery, which was scarcely ever to grow clearer.

Each holiday he found his father more irritable, and a little weaker. Mrs. Elliot was quickly growing old. She had to manage the servants, to hush the neighbouring children, to answer the correspondence, to paper and re-paper the rooms—and all for the sake of a man whom she did not like, and who did not conceal his dislike for her. One day she found Rickie tearful, and said rather crossly, "Well, what is it this time?"

He replied, "Oh, mummy, I've seen your wrinkles your grey hair—I'm unhappy."

Sudden tenderness overcame her, and she cried, "My darling, what does it matter? Whatever does it matter now?"

He had never known her so emotional. Yet even better did he remember another incident. Hearing high voices from his father's room, he went upstairs in the hope that the sound of his tread might stop them. Mrs. Elliot burst open the door, and seeing him, exclaimed, "My dear! If you please, he's hit me." She tried to laugh it off, but a few hours later he saw the bruise which the stick of the invalid had raised upon his mother's hand.

God alone knows how far we are in the grip of our bodies. He alone can judge how far the cruelty of Mr. Elliot was the outcome of extenuating circumstances. But Mrs. Elliot could accurately judge of its extent.

At last he died. Rickie was now fifteen, and got off a whole week's school for the funeral. His mother was rather strange. She was much happier, she looked younger, and her mourning was as unobtrusive as convention permitted. All this he had expected. But she seemed to be watching him, and to be extremely anxious for his opinion on any, subject—more especially on his father. Why? At last he saw that she was trying to establish confidence between them. But confidence cannot be established in a moment. They were both shy. The habit of years was upon them, and they alluded to the death of Mr. Elliot as an irreparable loss.

"Now that your father has gone, things will be very different."

"Shall we be poorer, mother?" No.

"Oh!"

"But naturally things will be very different."

"Yes, naturally."

"For instance, your poor father liked being near London, but I almost think we might move. Would you like that?"

"Of course, mummy." He looked down at the ground. He was not accustomed to being consulted, and it bewildered him.

"Perhaps you might like quite a different life better?"

He giggled.

"It's a little difficult for me," said Mrs. Elliot, pacing vigorously up and down the room, and more and more did her black dress seem a mockery. "In some ways you ought to be consulted: nearly all the money is left to you, as you must hear some time or other. But in other ways you're only a boy. What am I to do?"

"I don't know," he replied, appearing more helpless and unhelpful than he really was.

"For instance, would you like me to arrange things exactly as I like?"

"Oh do!" he exclaimed, thinking this a most brilliant suggestion.

"The very nicest thing of all." And he added, in his half-pedantic, half-pleasing way, "I shall be as wax in your hands, mamma."

She smiled. "Very well, darling. You shall be." And she pressed him lovingly, as though she would mould him into something beautiful.

For the next few days great preparations were in the air. She went to see his father's sister, the gifted and vivacious Aunt Emily. They were to live in the country—somewhere right in the country, with grass and trees up to the door, and birds singing everywhere, and a tutor. For he was not to go back to school. Unbelievable! He was never to go back to school, and the head-master had written saying that he regretted the step, but that possibly it was a wise one.

It was raw weather, and Mrs. Elliot watched over him with ceaseless tenderness. It seemed as if she could not do too much to shield him and to draw him nearer to her.

"Put on your greatcoat, dearest," she said to him.

"I don't think I want it," answered Rickie, remembering that he was now fifteen.

"The wind is bitter. You ought to put it on."

"But it's so heavy."

"Do put it on, dear."

He was not very often irritable or rude, but he answered, "Oh, I shan't catch cold. I do wish you wouldn't keep on bothering." He did not catch cold, but while he was out his mother died. She only survived her husband eleven days, a coincidence which was recorded on their tombstone.

Such, in substance, was the story which Rickie told his friends as they stood together in the shelter of the dell. The green bank at the entrance hid the road and the world, and now, as in spring, they could see nothing but snow-white ramparts and the evergreen foliage of the firs. Only from time to time would a beech leaf flutter in from the woods above, to comment on the waning year, and the warmth and radiance of the sun would vanish behind a passing cloud.

About the greatcoat he did not tell them, for he could not have spoken of it without tears.

III

Mr. Ansell, a provincial draper of moderate prosperity, ought by rights to have been classed not with the cow, but with those phenomena that are not really there. But his son, with pardonable illogicality, excepted him. He never suspected that his father might be the subjective product of a diseased imagination. From his earliest years he had taken him for granted, as a most undeniable and lovable fact. To be born one thing and grow up another—Ansell had accomplished this without weakening one of the ties that bound him to his home. The rooms above the shop still seemed as comfortable, the garden behind it as gracious, as they had seemed fifteen years before, when he would sit behind Miss Appleblossom's central throne, and she, like some allegorical figure, would send the change and receipted bills spinning away from her in little boxwood balls. At first the young man had attributed these happy relations to his own tact. But in time he perceived that the tact was all on the side of his father. Mr. Ansell was not merely a man of some education; he had what no education can bring—the power of detecting what is important. Like many fathers, he had spared no expense over his boy,—he had borrowed money to start him at a rapacious and fashionable private school; he had sent him to tutors; he had sent him to Cambridge. But he knew that all this was not the important thing. The important thing was freedom. The boy must use his education as he chose, and if he paid his father back it would certainly not be in his own coin. So when Stewart said, "At Cambridge, can I read for the Moral Science Tripos?" Mr. Ansell had only replied, "This philosophy—do you say that it lies behind everything?"

"Yes, I think so. It tries to discover what is good and true."

"Then, my boy, you had better read as much of it as you can."

And a year later: "I'd like to take up this philosophy seriously, but I don't feel justified."

"Why not?"

"Because it brings in no return. I think I'm a great philosopher, but then all philosophers think that, though they don't dare to say so. But, however great I am. I shan't earn money. Perhaps I shan't ever be able to keep myself. I shan't even get a good social position. You've only to say one word, and I'll work for the Civil Service. I'm good enough to get in high."

Mr. Ansell liked money and social position. But he knew that there is a more important thing, and replied, "You must take up this philosophy seriously, I think."

"Another thing—there are the girls."

"There is enough money now to get Mary and Maud as good husbands as they deserve." And Mary and Maud took the same view. It was in this plebeian household that Rickie spent part of the Christmas vacation. His own home, such as it was, was with the Silts, needy cousins of his father's, and combined to a peculiar degree the restrictions of hospitality with the discomforts of a boarding-house. Such pleasure as he had outside Cambridge was in the homes of his friends, and it was a particular joy and honour to visit Ansell, who, though as free from social snobbishness as most of us will ever manage to be, was rather careful when he drove up to the facade of his shop.

"I like our new lettering," he said thoughtfully. The words "Stewart Ansell" were repeated again and again along the High Street—curly gold letters that seemed to float in tanks of glazed chocolate.

"Rather!" said Rickie. But he wondered whether one of the bonds that kept the Ansell family united might not be their complete absence of taste—a surer bond by far than the identity of it. And he wondered this again when he sat at tea opposite a long row of crayons—Stewart as a baby, Stewart as a small boy with large feet, Stewart as a larger boy with smaller feet, Mary reading a book whose leaves were as thick as eiderdowns. And yet again did he wonder it when he woke with a gasp in the night to find a harp in luminous paint throbbing and glowering at him from the adjacent wall. "Watch and pray" was written on the harp, and until Rickie hung a towel over it the exhortation was partially successful.

It was a very happy visit. Miss Appleblosssom—who now acted as housekeeper—had met him before, during her never-forgotten expedition to Cambridge, and her admiration of University life was as shrill and as genuine now as it had been then. The girls at first were a little aggressive, for on his arrival he had been tired, and Maud had taken it for haughtiness, and said he was looking down on them. But this passed. They did not fall in love with him, nor he with them, but a morning was spent very pleasantly in snow-balling in the back garden. Ansell was rather different to what he was in Cambridge, but to Rickie not less attractive. And there was a curious charm in the hum of the shop, which swelled into a roar if one opened the partition door on a market-day.

"Listen to your money!" said Rickie. "I wish I could hear mine. I wish my money was alive."

"I don't understand."

"Mine's dead money. It's come to me through about six dead people—silently."

"Getting a little smaller and a little more respectable each time, on account of the death-duties."

"It needed to get respectable."

"Why? Did your people, too, once keep a shop?"

III

"Oh, not as bad as that! They only swindled. About a hundred years ago an Elliot did something shady and founded the fortunes of our house."

"I never knew any one so relentless to his ancestors. You make up for your soapiness towards the living."

"You'd be relentless if you'd heard the Silts, as I have, talk about 'a fortune, small perhaps, but unsoiled by trade!' Of course Aunt Emily is rather different. Oh, goodness me! I've forgotten my aunt. She lives not so far. I shall have to call on her."

Accordingly he wrote to Mrs. Failing, and said he should like to pay his respects. He told her about the Ansells, and so worded the letter that she might reasonably have sent an invitation to his friend.

She replied that she was looking forward to their tete-a-tete.

"You mustn't go round by the trains," said Mr. Ansell. "It means changing at Salisbury. By the road it's no great way. Stewart shall drive you over Salisbury Plain, and fetch you too."

"There's too much snow," said Ansell.

"Then the girls shall take you in their sledge."

"That I will," said Maud, who was not unwilling to see the inside of Cadover. But Rickie went round by the trains.

"We have all missed you," said Ansell, when he returned. "There is a general feeling that you are no nuisance, and had better stop till the end of the vac."

This he could not do. He was bound for Christmas to the Silts—"as a REAL guest," Mrs. Silt had written, underlining the word "real" twice. And after Christmas he must go to the Pembrokes.

"These are no reasons. The only real reason for doing a thing is because you want to do it. I think the talk about 'engagements' is cant."

"I think perhaps it is," said Rickie. But he went. Never had the turkey been so athletic, or the plum-pudding tied into its cloth so tightly. Yet he knew that both these symbols of hilarity had cost money, and it went to his heart when Mr. Silt said in a hungry voice, "Have you thought at all of what you want to be? No? Well, why should you? You have no need to be anything." And at dessert: "I wonder who Cadover goes to? I expect money will follow money. It always does." It was with a guilty feeling of relief that he left for the Pembrokes'.

The Pembrokes lived in an adjacent suburb, or rather "sububurb,"—the tract called Sawston, celebrated for its public school. Their style of life, however, was not particularly suburban. Their house was small and its name was Shelthorpe, but it had an air about it which suggested a certain amount of money and a certain amount of taste. There were decent water-colours in the drawing-room. Madonnas of acknowledged merit hung upon the stairs. A replica of the Hermes of Praxiteles—of course only the bust—stood in the hall with a real palm behind it. Agnes, in her slap-dash way, was a good housekeeper, and kept the pretty things well dusted. It was she who insisted on the strip of brown holland that led diagonally from the front door to the door of Herbert's study: boys' grubby feet should not go treading on her Indian square. It was she who always cleaned the picture-frames and washed the bust and the leaves of the palm. In short, if a house could speak—and sometimes it does speak more clearly than the people who live in it—the house of the Pembrokes would have said, "I am not quite like other houses, yet I am perfectly comfortable. I contain works of art and a microscope and books. But I do not live for any of these things or suffer them to disarrange me. I live for myself and for the greater houses that shall come after me. Yet in me neither the cry of money nor the cry for money shall ever be heard."

Mr. Pembroke was at the station. He did better as a host than as a guest, and welcomed the young man with real friendliness.

"We were all coming, but Gerald has strained his ankle slightly, and wants to keep quiet, as he is playing next week in a match. And, needless to say, that explains the absence of my sister."

"Gerald Dawes?"

"Yes; he's with us. I'm so glad you'll meet again."

"So am I," said Rickie with extreme awkwardness. "Does he remember me?"

"Vividly."

Vivid also was Rickie's remembrance of him.

"A splendid fellow," asserted Mr. Pembroke.

"I hope that Agnes is well."

"Thank you, yes; she is well. And I think you're looking more like other people yourself."

"I've been having a very good time with a friend."

"Indeed. That's right. Who was that?"

Rickie had a young man's reticence. He generally spoke of "a friend," "a person I know," "a place I was at." When the book of life is opening, our readings are secret, and we are unwilling to give chapter and verse. Mr. Pembroke, who was half way through the volume, and had skipped or forgotten the earlier pages, could not understand Rickie's hesitation, nor why with such awkwardness he should pronounce the harmless dissyllable "Ansell."

"Ansell? Wasn't that the pleasant fellow who asked us to lunch?"

"No. That was Anderson, who keeps below. You didn't see Ansell. The ones who came to breakfast were Tilliard and Hornblower."

"Of course. And since then you have been with the Silts. How are they?"

"Very well, thank you. They want to be remembered to you."

The Pembrokes had formerly lived near the Elliots, and had shown great kindness to Rickie when his parents died. They were thus rather in the position of family friends.

"Please remember us when you write." He added, almost roguishly, "The Silts are kindness itself. All the same, it must be just a little—dull, we thought, and we thought that you might like a change. And of course we are delighted to have you besides. That goes without saying."

"It's very good of you," said Rickie, who had accepted the invitation because he felt he ought to.

III

"Not a bit. And you mustn't expect us to be otherwise than quiet on the holidays. There is a library of a sort, as you know, and you will find Gerald a splendid fellow."

"Will they be married soon?"

"Oh no!" whispered Mr. Pembroke, shutting his eyes, as if Rickie had made some terrible faux pas. "It will be a very long engagement. He must make his way first. I have seen such endless misery result from people marrying before they have made their way."

"Yes. That is so," said Rickie despondently, thinking of the Silts.

"It's a sad unpalatable truth," said Mr. Pembroke, thinking that the despondency might be personal, "but one must accept it. My sister and Gerald, I am thankful to say, have accepted it, though naturally it has been a little pill."

Their cab lurched round the corner as he spoke, and the two patients came in sight. Agnes was leaning over the creosoted garden-gate, and behind her there stood a young man who had the figure of a Greek athlete and the face of an English one. He was fair and cleanshaven, and his colourless hair was cut rather short. The sun was in his eyes, and they, like his mouth, seemed scarcely more than slits in his healthy skin. Just where he began to be beautiful the clothes started. Round his neck went an up-and-down collar and a mauve-and-gold tie, and the rest of his limbs were hidden by a grey lounge suit, carefully creased in the right places.

"Lovely! Lovely!" cried Agnes, banging on the gate, "Your train must have been to the minute."

"Hullo!" said the athlete, and vomited with the greeting a cloud of tobacco-smoke. It must have been imprisoned in his mouth some time, for no pipe was visible.

"Hullo!" returned Rickie, laughing violently. They shook hands.

"Where are you going, Rickie?" asked Agnes. "You aren't grubby. Why don't you stop? Gerald, get the large wicker-chair. Herbert has letters, but we can sit here till lunch. It's like spring."

The garden of Shelthorpe was nearly all in front an unusual and pleasant arrangement. The front gate and the servants' entrance were both at the side, and in the remaining space the gardener had contrived a little lawn where one could sit concealed from the road by a fence, from the neighbour by a fence, from the house by a tree, and from the path by a bush.

"This is the lovers' bower," observed Agnes, sitting down on the bench. Rickie stood by her till the chair arrived.

"Are you smoking before lunch?" asked Mr. Dawes.

"No, thank you. I hardly ever smoke."

"No vices. Aren't you at Cambridge now?"

"Yes."

"What's your college?"

Rickie told him.

"Do you know Carruthers?"

"Rather!"

"I mean A. P. Carruthers, who got his socker blue."

"Rather! He's secretary to the college musical society."

"A. P. Carruthers?"

"Yes."

Mr. Dawes seemed offended. He tapped on his teeth, and remarked that the weather bad no business to be so warm in winter. "But it was fiendish before Christmas," said Agnes.

He frowned, and asked, "Do you know a man called Gerrish?"

"No."

"Ah."

"Do you know James?"

"Never heard of him."

"He's my year too. He got a blue for hockey his second term."

"I know nothing about the 'Varsity."

Rickie winced at the abbreviation "'Varsity." It was at that time the proper thing to speak of "the University."

"I haven't the time," pursued Mr. Dawes.

"No, no," said Rickie politely.

"I had the chance of being an Undergrad, myself, and, by Jove, I'm thankful I didn't!"

"Why?" asked Agnes, for there was a pause.

"Puts you back in your profession. Men who go there first, before the Army, start hopelessly behind. The same with the Stock Exchange or Painting. I know men in both, and they've never caught up the time they lost in the 'Varsity—unless, of course, you turn parson."

"I love Cambridge," said she. "All those glorious buildings, and every one so happy and running in and out of each other's rooms all day long."

"That might make an Undergrad happy, but I beg leave to state it wouldn't me. I haven't four years to throw away for the sake of being called a 'Varsity man and hobnobbing with Lords."

Rickie was prepared to find his old schoolfellow ungrammatical and bumptious, but he was not prepared to find him peevish. Athletes, he believed, were simple, straightforward people, cruel and brutal if you like, but never petty. They knocked you down and hurt you, and then went on their way rejoicing. For this, Rickie thought, there is something to be said: he had escaped the sin of despising the physically strong—a sin against which the physically weak must guard. But here was Dawes returning again and again to the subject of the University, full of transparent jealousy and petty spite, nagging, nagging, nagging, like a maiden lady who has not been invited to a tea-party. Rickie wondered whether, after all, Ansell and the extremists might not be right, and bodily beauty and strength be signs of the soul's damnation.

He glanced at Agnes. She was writing down some orderings for the tradespeople on a piece of paper. Her handsome face was intent on the work. The bench on which she and Gerald were sitting had no back, but she sat as straight as a dart. He, though strong enough to sit straight, did not take the trouble.

"Why don't they talk to each other?" thought Rickie.

"Gerald, give this paper to the cook."

"I can give it to the other slavey, can't I?"

"She'd be dressing."

"Well, there's Herbert."

"He's busy. Oh, you know where the kitchen is. Take it to the cook."

He disappeared slowly behind the tree.

"What do you think of him?" she immediately asked. He murmured civilly.

"Has he changed since he was a schoolboy?"

"In a way."

"Do tell me all about him. Why won't you?"

She might have seen a flash of horror pass over Rickie's face. The horror disappeared, for, thank God, he was now a man, whom civilization protects. But he and Gerald had met, as it were, behind the scenes, before our decorous drama opens, and there the elder boy had done things to him—absurd things, not worth chronicling separately. An apple-pie bed is nothing; pinches, kicks, boxed ears, twisted arms, pulled hair, ghosts at night, inky books, befouled photographs, amount to very little by themselves. But let them be united and continuous, and you have a hell that no grown-up devil can devise. Between Rickie and Gerald there lay a shadow that darkens life more often than we suppose. The bully and his victim never quite forget their first relations. They meet in clubs and country houses, and clap one another on the back; but in both the memory is green of a more strenuous day, when they were boys together.

He tried to say, "He was the right kind of boy, and I was the wrong kind." But Cambridge would not let him smooth the situation over by self-belittlement. If he had been the wrong kind of boy, Gerald had been a worse kind. He murmured, "We are different, very," and Miss Pembroke, perhaps suspecting something, asked no more. But she kept to the subject of Mr. Dawes, humorously depreciating her lover and discussing him without reverence. Rickie laughed, but felt uncomfortable. When people were engaged, he felt that they should be outside criticism. Yet here he was criticizing. He could not help it. He was dragged in.

"I hope his ankle is better."

"Never was bad. He's always fussing over something."

"He plays next week in a match, I think Herbert says."

"I dare say he does."

"Shall we be going?"

"Pray go if you like. I shall stop at home. I've had enough of cold feet."

It was all very colourless and odd.

Gerald returned, saying, "I can't stand your cook. What's she want to ask me questions for? I can't stand talking to servants. I say, 'If I speak to you, well and good'—and it's another thing besides if she were pretty."

"Well, I hope our ugly cook will have lunch ready in a minute," said Agnes. "We're frightfully unpunctual this morning, and I daren't say anything, because it was the same yesterday, and if I complain again they might leave. Poor Rickie must be starved."

"Why, the Silts gave me all these sandwiches and I've never eaten them. They always stuff one."

"And you thought you'd better, eh?" said Mr. Dawes, "in case you weren't stuffed here."

Miss Pembroke, who house-kept somewhat economically, looked annoyed.

The voice of Mr. Pembroke was now heard calling from the house, "Frederick! Frederick! My dear boy, pardon me. It was an important letter about the Church Defence, otherwise—. Come in and see your room."

He was glad to quit the little lawn. He had learnt too much there. It was dreadful: they did not love each other. More dreadful even than the case of his father and mother, for they, until they married, had got on pretty well. But this man was already rude and brutal and cold: he was still the school bully who twisted up the arms of little boys, and ran pins into them at chapel, and struck them in the stomach when they were swinging on the horizontal bar. Poor Agnes; why ever had she done it? Ought not somebody to interfere?

He had forgotten his sandwiches, and went back to get them.

Gerald and Agnes were locked in each other's arms.

He only looked for a moment, but the sight burnt into his brain. The man's grip was the stronger. He had drawn the woman on to his knee, was pressing her, with all his strength, against him. Already her hands slipped off him, and she whispered, "Don't you hurt—" Her face had no expression. It stared at the intruder and never saw him. Then her lover kissed it, and immediately it shone with mysterious beauty, like some star.

Rickie limped away without the sandwiches, crimson and afraid. He thought, "Do such things actually happen?" and he seemed to be looking down coloured valleys. Brighter they glowed, till gods of pure flame were born in them, and then he was looking at pinnacles of virgin snow. While Mr. Pembroke talked, the riot of fair images increased.

They invaded his being and lit lamps at unsuspected shrines. Their orchestra commenced in that suburban house, where he had to stand aside for the maid to carry in the luncheon. Music flowed past him like a river. He stood at the springs of creation and heard the primeval monotony. Then an obscure instrument gave out a little phrase.

The river continued unheeding. The phrase was repeated and a listener might know it was a fragment of the Tune of tunes. Nobler instruments accepted it, the clarionet protected, the brass encouraged, and it rose to the surface to the whisper of violins. In full unison was Love born, flame of the flame, flushing the dark river beneath him and the virgin snows above. His wings were infinite, his youth eternal; the sun was a jewel on his finger as he passed it in benediction over the world. Creation, no longer monotonous, acclaimed him, in widening melody, in brighter radiances. Was Love a column of fire? Was he a torrent of song? Was he greater than either—the touch of a man on a woman?

It was the merest accident that Rickie had not been disgusted. But this he could not know.

Mr. Pembroke, when he called the two dawdlers into lunch, was aware of a hand on his arm and a voice that murmured, "Don't—they may be happy."

He stared, and struck the gong. To its music they approached, priest and high priestess.

"Rickie, can I give these sandwiches to the boot boy?" said the one. "He would love them."

"The gong! Be quick! The gong!"

"Are you smoking before lunch?" said the other.

But they had got into heaven, and nothing could get them out of it. Others might think them surly or prosaic. He knew. He could remember every word they spoke. He would treasure every motion, every glance of either, and so in time to come, when the gates of heaven had shut, some faint radiance, some echo of wisdom might remain with him outside.

As a matter of fact, he saw them very little during his visit. He checked himself because he was unworthy. What right had he to pry, even in the spirit, upon their bliss? It was no crime to have seen them on the lawn. It would be a crime to go to it again. He tried to keep himself and his thoughts away, not because he was ascetic, but because they would not like it if they knew. This behaviour of his suited them admirably. And when any gracious little thing occurred to them—any little thing that his sympathy had contrived and allowed—they put it down to chance or to each other.

So the lovers fall into the background. They are part of the distant sunrise, and only the mountains speak to them. Rickie talks to Mr. Pembroke, amidst the unlit valleys of our over-habitable world.

IV

Sawston School had been founded by a tradesman in the seventeenth century. It was then a tiny grammar-school in a tiny town, and the City Company who governed it had to drive half a day through the woods and heath on the occasion of their annual visit. In the twentieth century they still drove, but only from the railway station; and found themselves not in a tiny town, nor yet in a large one, but amongst innumerable residences, detached and semi-detached, which had gathered round the school. For the intentions of the founder had been altered, or at all events amplified, instead of educating the "poore of my home," he now educated the upper classes of England. The change had taken place not so very far back. Till the nineteenth century the grammar-school was still composed of day scholars from the neighbourhood. Then two things happened. Firstly, the school's property rose in value, and it became rich. Secondly, for no obvious reason, it suddenly emitted a quantity of bishops. The bishops, like the stars from a Roman candle, were all colours, and flew in all directions, some high, some low, some to distant colonies, one into the Church of Rome. But many a father traced their course in the papers; many a mother wondered whether her son, if properly ignited, might not burn as bright; many a family moved to the place where living and education were so cheap, where day-boys were not looked down upon, and where the orthodox and the up-to-date were said to be combined. The school doubled its numbers. It built new class-rooms, laboratories and a gymnasium. It dropped the prefix "Grammar." It coaxed the sons of the local tradesmen into a new foundation, the "Commercial School," built a couple of miles away. And it started boarding-houses. It had not the gracious antiquity of Eton or Winchester, nor, on the other hand, had it a conscious policy like Lancing, Wellington, and other purely modern foundations. Where tradition served, it clung to them. Where new departures seemed desirable, they were made. It aimed at producing the average Englishman, and, to a very great extent, it succeeded.

Here Mr. Pembroke passed his happy and industrious life. His technical position was that of master to a form low down on the Modern Side. But his work lay elsewhere. He organized. If no organization existed, he would create one. If one did exist, he would modify it. "An organization," he would say, "is after all not an end in itself. It must contribute to a movement." When one good custom seemed likely to corrupt the school, he was ready with another; he believed that without innumerable customs there was no safety, either for boys or men.

Perhaps he is right, and always will be right. Perhaps each of us would go to ruin if for one short hour we acted as we thought fit, and attempted the service of perfect freedom. The school caps, with their elaborate symbolism, were his; his the many-tinted bathing-drawers, that showed how far a boy could swim; his the hierarchy of jerseys and blazers. It was he who instituted Bounds, and call, and the two sorts of exercise-paper, and the three sorts of caning, and "The Sawtonian," a bi-terminal magazine. His plump finger was in every pie. The dome of his skull, mild but impressive, shone at every master's meeting. He was generally acknowledged to be the coming man.

His last achievement had been the organization of the day-boys. They had been left too much to themselves, and were weak in esprit de corps; they were apt to regard home, not school, as the most important thing in their lives. Moreover, they got out of their parents' hands; they did their preparation any time and some times anyhow. They shirked games, they were out at all hours, they ate what they should not, they smoked, they bicycled on the asphalt. Now all was over. Like boarders, they were to be in at 7:15 P.M., and were not allowed out after unless with a written order from their parent or guardian; they, too, must work at fixed hours in the evening, and before breakfast next morning from 7 to 8. Games were compulsory. They must not go to parties in term time. They must keep to bounds. Of course the reform was not complete. It was impossible to control the dieting, though, on a printed circular, day-parents were implored to provide simple food. And it is also believed that some mothers disobeyed the rule about preparation, and allowed their sons to do all the work over-night and have a longer sleep in the morning. But the gulf between day-boys and boarders was considerably lessened, and grew still narrower when the day-boys too were organized into a House with house-master and colours of their own. "Through the House," said Mr. Pembroke, "one learns patriotism for the school, just as through the school one learns patriotism for the country. Our only course, therefore, is to organize the day-boys into a House." The headmaster agreed, as he often did, and the new community was formed. Mr. Pembroke, to avoid the tongues of malice, had refused the post of house-master for himself, saying to Mr. Jackson, who taught the sixth, "You keep too much in the background. Here is a chance for you." But this was a failure. Mr. Jackson, a scholar and a student, neither felt nor conveyed any enthusiasm, and when confronted with his House, would say, "Well, I don't know what we're all here for. Now I should think you'd better go home to your mothers." He returned to his background, and next term Mr. Pembroke was to take his place.

Such were the themes on which Mr. Pembroke discoursed to Rickie's civil ear. He showed him the school, and the library, and the subterranean hall where the day-boys might leave their coats and caps, and where, on festal occasions, they supped. He showed him Mr. Jackson's pretty house, and whispered, "Were it not for his brilliant intellect, it would be a case of Quickmarch!" He showed him the racquet-court, happily completed, and the chapel, unhappily still in need of funds.

Rickie was impressed, but then he was impressed by everything. Of course a House of day-boys seemed a little shadowy after Agnes and Gerald, but he imparted some reality even to that.

"The racquet-court," said Mr. Pembroke, "is most gratifying. We never expected to manage it this year. But before the Easter holidays every boy received a subscription card, and was given to understand that he must collect thirty shillings. You will scarcely believe me, but they nearly all responded. Next term there was a dinner in the great school, and all who had collected, not thirty shillings, but as much as a pound, were invited to it—for naturally one was not precise for a few shillings, the response being the really valuable thing. Practically the whole school had to come."

"They must enjoy the court tremendously."

"Ah, it isn't used very much. Racquets, as I daresay you know, is rather an expensive game. Only the wealthier boys play—and I'm sorry to say that it is not of our wealthier boys that we are always the proudest. But the point is that no public school can be called first-class until it has one. They are building them right and left."

"And now you must finish the chapel?"

"Now we must complete the chapel." He paused reverently, and said, "And here is a fragment of the original building." Rickie at once had a rush of sympathy. He, too, looked with reverence at the morsel of Jacobean brickwork, ruddy and beautiful amidst the machine-squared stones of the modern apse. The two men, who had so little in common, were thrilled with patriotism. They rejoiced that their country was great, noble, and old.

"Thank God I'm English," said Rickie suddenly.

"Thank Him indeed," said Mr. Pembroke, laying a hand on his back.

"We've been nearly as great as the Greeks, I do believe. Greater, I'm sure, than the Italians, though they did get closer to beauty. Greater than the French, though we do take all their ideas. I can't help thinking that England is immense. English literature certainly."

Mr. Pembroke removed his hand. He found such patriotism somewhat craven. Genuine patriotism comes only from the heart. It knows no parleying with reason. English ladies will declare abroad that there are no fogs in London, and Mr. Pembroke, though he would not go to this, was only restrained by the certainty of being found out. On this occasion he remarked that the Greeks lacked spiritual insight, and had a low conception of woman.

"As to women—oh! there they were dreadful," said Rickie, leaning his hand on the chapel. "I realize that more and more. But as to spiritual insight, I don't quite like to say; and I find Plato too difficult, but I know men who don't, and I fancy they mightn't agree with you."

"Far be it from me to disparage Plato. And for philosophy as a whole I have the greatest respect. But it is the crown of a man's education, not the foundation. Myself, I read it with the utmost profit, but I have known endless trouble result from boys who attempt it too soon, before they were set."

"But if those boys had died first," cried Rickie with sudden vehemence, "without knowing what there is to know—"

"Or isn't to know!" said Mr. Pembroke sarcastically.

"Or what there isn't to know. Exactly. That's it."

"My dear Rickie, what do you mean? If an old friend may be frank, you are talking great rubbish." And, with a few well-worn formulae, he propped up the young man's orthodoxy. The props were unnecessary. Rickie had his own equilibrium. Neither the Revivalism that assails a boy at about the age of fifteen, nor the scepticism that meets him five years later, could sway him from his allegiance to the church into which he had been born. But his equilibrium was personal, and the secret of it useless to others. He desired that each man should find his own.

"What does philosophy do?" the propper continued. "Does it make a man happier in life? Does it make him die more peacefully? I fancy that in the long-run Herbert Spencer will get no further than the rest of us. Ah, Rickie! I wish you could move among the school boys, and see their healthy contempt for all they cannot touch!" Here he was going too far, and had to add, "Their spiritual capacities, of course, are another matter." Then he remembered the Greeks, and said, "Which proves my original statement."

Submissive signs, as of one propped, appeared in Rickie's face. Mr. Pembroke then questioned him about the men who found Plato not difficult. But here he kept silence, patting the school chapel gently, and presently the conversation turned to topics with which they were both more competent to deal.

"Does Agnes take much interest in the school?"

"Not as much as she did. It is the result of her engagement. If our naughty soldier had not carried her off, she might have made an ideal schoolmaster's wife. I often chaff him about it, for he a little despises the intellectual professions. Natural, perfectly natural. How can a man who faces death feel as we do towards mensa or tupto?"

"Perfectly true. Absolutely true."

Mr. Pembroke remarked to himself that Frederick was improving.

"If a man shoots straight and hits straight and speaks straight, if his heart is in the right place, if he has the instincts of a Christian and a gentleman—then I, at all events, ask no better husband for my sister."

"How could you get a better?" he cried. "Do you remember the thing in 'The Clouds'?" And he quoted, as well as he could, from the invitation of the Dikaios Logos, the description of the young Athenian, perfect in body, placid in mind, who neglects his work at the Bar and trains all day among the woods and meadows, with a garland on his head and a friend to set the pace; the scent of new leaves is upon them; they rejoice in the freshness of spring; over their heads the plane-tree whispers to the elm, perhaps the most glorious invitation to the brainless life that has ever been given.

"Yes, yes," said Mr. Pembroke, who did not want a brother-in-law out of Aristophanes. Nor had he got one, for Mr. Dawes would not have bothered over the garland or noticed the spring, and would have complained that the friend ran too slowly or too fast.

"And as for her—!" But he could think of no classical parallel for Agnes. She slipped between examples. A kindly Medea, a Cleopatra with a sense of duty—these suggested her a little. She was not born in Greece, but came overseas to it—a dark, intelligent princess. With all her splendour, there were hints of splendour still hidden—hints of an older, richer, and more mysterious land. He smiled at the idea of her being "not there." Ansell, clever as he was, had made a bad blunder. She had more reality than any other woman in the world.

Mr. Pembroke looked pleased at this boyish enthusiasm. He was fond of his sister, though he knew her to be full of faults. "Yes, I envy her," he said. "She has found a worthy helpmeet for life's journey, I do believe. And though they chafe at the long engagement, it is a blessing in disguise. They learn to know each other thoroughly before contracting more intimate ties."

Rickie did not assent. The length of the engagement seemed to him unspeakably cruel. Here were two people who loved each other, and they could not marry for years because they had no beastly money. Not all Herbert's pious skill could make this out a blessing. It was bad enough being "so rich" at the Silts; here he was more ashamed of it than ever. In a few weeks he would come of age and his money be his own. What a pity things were so crookedly arranged. He did not want money, or at all events he did not want so much.

"Suppose," he meditated, for he became much worried over this,—"suppose I had a hundred pounds a year less than I shall have. Well, I should still have enough. I don't want anything but food, lodging, clothes, and now and then a railway fare. I haven't any tastes. I don't collect anything or play games. Books are nice to have, but after all there is Mudie's, or if it comes to that, the Free Library. Oh, my profession! I forgot I shall have a profession. Well, that will leave me with more to spare than ever." And he supposed away till he lost touch with the world and with what it permits, and committed an unpardonable sin.

It happened towards the end of his visit—another airless day of that mild January. Mr. Dawes was playing against a scratch team of cads, and had to go down to the ground in the morning to settle something. Rickie proposed to come too.

Hitherto he had been no nuisance. "You will be frightfully bored," said Agnes, observing the cloud on her lover's face. "And Gerald walks like a maniac."

"I had a little thought of the Museum this morning," said Mr. Pembroke. "It is very strong in flint arrow-heads."

"Ah, that's your line, Rickie. I do envy you and Herbert the way you enjoy the past."

"I almost think I'll go with Dawes, if he'll have me. I can walk quite fast just to the ground and back. Arrowheads are wonderful, but I don't really enjoy them yet, though I hope I shall in time."

Mr. Pembroke was offended, but Rickie held firm.

In a quarter of an hour he was back at the house alone, nearly crying.

IV

"Oh, did the wretch go too fast?" called Miss Pembroke from her bedroom window.

"I went too fast for him." He spoke quite sharply, and before he had time to say he was sorry and didn't mean exactly that, the window had shut.

"They've quarrelled," she thought. "Whatever about?"

She soon heard. Gerald returned in a cold stormy temper. Rickie had offered him money.

"My dear fellow don't be so cross. The child's mad."

"If it was, I'd forgive that. But I can't stand unhealthiness."

"Now, Gerald, that's where I hate you. You don't know what it is to pity the weak."

"Woman's job. So you wish I'd taken a hundred pounds a year from him. Did you ever hear such blasted cheek? Marry us—he, you, and me—a hundred pounds down and as much annual—he, of course, to pry into all we did, and we to kowtow and eat dirt-pie to him. If that's Mr. Rickety Elliot's idea of a soldier and an Englishman, it isn't mine, and I wish I'd had a horse-whip."

She was roaring with laughter. "You're babies, a pair of you, and you're the worst. Why couldn't you let the little silly down gently? There he was puffing and sniffing under my window, and I thought he'd insulted you. Why didn't you accept?"

"Accept?" he thundered.

"It would have taken the nonsense out of him for ever. Why, he was only talking out of a book."

"More fool he."

"Well, don't be angry with a fool. He means no harm. He muddles all day with poetry and old dead people, and then tries to bring it into life. It's too funny for words."

Gerald repeated that he could not stand unhealthiness.

"I don't call that exactly unhealthy."

"I do. And why he could give the money's worse."

"What do you mean?"

He became shy. "I hadn't meant to tell you. It's not quite for a lady." For, like most men who are rather animal, he was intellectually a prude. "He says he can't ever marry, owing to his foot. It wouldn't be fair to posterity. His grandfather was crocked, his father too, and he's as bad. He thinks that it's hereditary, and may get worse next generation. He's discussed it all over with other Undergrads. A bright lot they must be. He daren't risk having any children. Hence the hundred quid."

She stopped laughing. "Oh, little beast, if he said all that!"

He was encouraged to proceed. Hitherto he had not talked about their school days. Now he told her everything,—the "barley-sugar," as he called it, the pins in chapel, and how one afternoon he had tied him head-downward on to a tree trunk and then ran away—of course only for a moment.

For this she scolded him well. But she had a thrill of joy when she thought of the weak boy in the clutches of the strong one.

V

Gerald died that afternoon. He was broken up in the football match. Rickie and Mr. Pembroke were on the ground when the accident took place. It was no good torturing him by a drive to the hospital, and he was merely carried to the little pavilion and laid upon the floor. A doctor came, and so did a clergyman, but it seemed better to leave him for the last few minutes with Agnes, who had ridden down on her bicycle.

It was a strange lamentable interview. The girl was so accustomed to health, that for a time she could not understand. It must be a joke that he chose to lie there in the dust, with a rug over him and his knees bent up towards his chin. His arms were as she knew them, and their admirable muscles showed clear and clean beneath the jersey. The face, too, though a little flushed, was uninjured: it must be some curious joke.

"Gerald, what have you been doing?"

He replied, "I can't see you. It's too dark."

"Oh, I'll soon alter that," she said in her old brisk way. She opened the pavilion door. The people who were standing by it moved aside. She saw a deserted meadow, steaming and grey, and beyond it slateroofed cottages, row beside row, climbing a shapeless hill. Towards London the sky was yellow. "There. That's better." She sat down by him again, and drew his hand into her own. "Now we are all right, aren't we?"

"Where are you?"

This time she could not reply.

"What is it? Where am I going?"

"Wasn't the rector here?" said she after a silence.

"He explained heaven, and thinks that I—but—I couldn't tell a parson; but I don't seem to have any use for any of the things there."

"We are Christians," said Agnes shyly. "Dear love, we don't talk about these things, but we believe them. I think that you will get well and be as strong again as ever; but, in any case, there is a spiritual life, and we know that some day you and I—"

"I shan't do as a spirit," he interrupted, sighing pitifully. "I want you as I am, and it cannot be managed. The rector had to say so. I want—I don't want to talk. I can't see you. Shut that door."

She obeyed, and crept into his arms. Only this time her grasp was the stronger. Her heart beat louder and louder as the sound of his grew more faint. He was crying like a little frightened child, and her lips were wet with his tears. "Bear it bravely," she told him.

"I can't," he whispered. "It isn't to be done. I can't see you," and passed from her trembling with open eyes.

She rode home on her bicycle, leaving the others to follow. Some ladies who did not know what had happened bowed and smiled as she passed, and she returned their salute.

"Oh, miss, is it true?" cried the cook, her face streaming with tears.

Agnes nodded. Presumably it was true. Letters had just arrived: one was for Gerald from his mother. Life, which had given them no warning, seemed to make no comment now. The incident was outside nature, and would surely pass away like a dream. She felt slightly irritable, and the grief of the servants annoyed her.

They sobbed. "Ah, look at his marks! Ah, little he thought—little he thought!" In the brown holland strip by the front door a heavy football boot had left its impress. They had not liked Gerald, but he was a man, they were women, he had died. Their mistress ordered them to leave her.

For many minutes she sat at the foot of the stairs, rubbing her eyes. An obscure spiritual crisis was going on.

Should she weep like the servants? Or should she bear up and trust in the consoler Time? Was the death of a man so terrible after all? As she invited herself to apathy there were steps on the gravel, and Rickie Elliot burst in. He was splashed with mud, his breath was gone, and his hair fell wildly over his meagre face. She thought, "These are the people who are left alive!" From the bottom of her soul she hated him.

"I came to see what you're doing," he cried.

"Resting."

He knelt beside her, and she said, "Would you please go away?"

"Yes, dear Agnes, of course; but I must see first that you mind." Her breath caught. Her eves moved to the treads, going outwards, so firmly, so irretrievably.

He panted, "It's the worst thing that can ever happen to you in all your life, and you've got to mind it you've got to mind it. They'll come saying, 'Bear up trust to time.' No, no; they're wrong. Mind it."

Through all her misery she knew that this boy was greater than they supposed. He rose to his feet, and with intense conviction cried: "But I know—I understand. It's your death as well as his. He's gone, Agnes, and his arms will never hold you again. In God's name, mind such a thing, and don't sit fencing with your soul. Don't stop being great; that's the one crime he'll never forgive you."

She faltered, "Who—who forgives?"

"Gerald."

At the sound of his name she slid forward, and all her dishonesty left her. She acknowledged that life's meaning had vanished. Bending down, she kissed the footprint. "How can he forgive me?" she sobbed. "Where has he gone to? You could never dream such an awful thing. He couldn't see me though I opened the door—wide—plenty of light; and then he could not remember the things that should comfort him. He wasn't a—he wasn't ever a great reader, and he couldn't remember the things. The rector tried, and he couldn't—I came, and I couldn't—" She could not speak for tears. Rickie did not check her. He let her accuse herself, and fate, and Herbert, who had postponed their marriage. She might have been a wife six months; but Herbert had spoken of self-control and of all life before them. He let her kiss the footprints till their marks gave way to the marks of her lips. She moaned. "He is gone—where is he?" and then he replied quite quietly, "He is in heaven."

She begged him not to comfort her; she could not bear it.

"I did not come to comfort you. I came to see that you mind. He is in heaven, Agnes. The greatest thing is over."

Her hatred was lulled. She murmured, "Dear Rickie!" and held up her hand to him. Through her tears his meagre face showed as a seraph's who spoke the truth and forbade her to juggle with her soul. "Dear Rickie—but for the rest of my life what am I to do?"

"Anything—if you remember that the greatest thing is over."

"I don't know you," she said tremulously. "You have grown up in a moment. You never talked to us, and yet you understand it all. Tell me again—I can only trust you—where he is."

"He is in heaven."

"You are sure?"

It puzzled her that Rickie, who could scarcely tell you the time without a saving clause, should be so certain about immortality.

VI

He did not stop for the funeral. Mr. Pembroke thought that he had a bad effect on Agnes, and prevented her from acquiescing in the tragedy as rapidly as she might have done. As he expressed it, "one must not court sorrow," and he hinted to the young man that they desired to be alone.

Rickie went back to the Silts.

He was only there a few days. As soon as term opened he returned to Cambridge, for which he longed passionately. The journey thither was now familiar to him, and he took pleasure in each landmark. The fair valley of Tewin Water, the cutting into Hitchin where the train traverses the chalk, Baldock Church, Royston with its promise of downs, were nothing in themselves, but dear as stages in the pilgrimage towards the abode of peace. On the platform he met friends. They had all had pleasant vacations: it was a happy world. The atmosphere alters.

Cambridge, according to her custom, welcomed her sons with open drains. Pettycury was up, so was Trinity Street, and navvies peeped out of King's Parade. Here it was gas, there electric light, but everywhere something, and always a smell. It was also the day that the wheels fell off the station tram, and Rickie, who was naturally inside, was among the passengers who "sustained no injury but a shock, and had as hearty a laugh over the mishap afterwards as any one."

Tilliard fled into a hansom, cursing himself for having tried to do the thing cheaply. Hornblower also swept past yelling derisively, with his luggage neatly piled above his head. "Let's get out and walk," muttered Ansell. But Rickie was succouring a distressed female—Mrs. Aberdeen.

"Oh, Mrs. Aberdeen, I never saw you: I am so glad to see you—I am so very glad." Mrs. Aberdeen was cold. She did not like being spoken to outside the college, and was also distrait about her basket. Hitherto no genteel eye had even seen inside it, but in the collision its little calico veil fell off, and there was revealed—nothing. The basket was empty, and never would hold anything illegal. All the same she was distrait, and "We shall meet later, sir, I dessy," was all the greeting Rickie got from her.

"Now what kind of a life has Mrs. Aberdeen?" he exclaimed, as he and Ansell pursued the Station Road. "Here these bedders come and make us comfortable. We owe an enormous amount to them, their wages are absurd, and we know nothing about them. Off they go to Barnwell, and then their lives are hidden. I just know that Mrs. Aberdeen has a husband, but that's all. She never will talk about him. Now I do so want to fill in her life. I see one-half of it. What's the other half? She may have a real jolly house, in good taste, with a little garden and books, and pictures. Or, again, she mayn't. But in any case one ought to know. I know she'd dislike it, but she oughtn't to dislike. After all, bedders are to blame for the present lamentable state of things, just as much as gentlefolk. She ought to want me to come. She ought to introduce me to her husband."

They had reached the corner of Hills Road. Ansell spoke for the first time. He said, "Ugh!"

"Drains?"

"Yes. A spiritual cesspool."

Rickie laughed.

"I expected it from your letter."

"The one you never answered?"

"I answer none of your letters. You are quite hopeless by now. You can go to the bad. But I refuse to accompany you. I refuse to believe that every human being is a moving wonder of supreme interest and tragedy and beauty—which was what the letter in question amounted to. You'll find plenty who will believe it. It's a very popular view among people who are too idle to think; it saves them the trouble of detecting the beautiful from the ugly, the interesting from the dull, the tragic from the melodramatic. You had just come from Sawston, and were apparently carried away by the fact that Miss Pembroke had the usual amount of arms and legs."

Rickie was silent. He had told his friend how he felt, but not what had happened. Ansell could discuss love and death admirably, but somehow he would not understand lovers or a dying man, and in the letter there had been scant allusion to these concrete facts. Would Cambridge understand them either? He watched some dons who were peeping into an excavation, and throwing up their hands with humorous gestures of despair. These men would lecture next week on Catiline's conspiracy, on Luther, on Evolution, on Catullus. They dealt with so much and they had experienced so little. Was it possible he would ever come to think Cambridge narrow? In his short life Rickie had known two sudden deaths, and that is enough to disarrange any placid outlook on the world. He knew once for all that we are all of us bubbles on an extremely rough sea. Into this sea humanity has built, as it were, some little breakwaters—scientific knowledge, civilized restraint—so that the bubbles do not break so frequently or so soon. But the sea has not altered, and it was only a chance that he, Ansell, Tilliard, and Mrs. Aberdeen had not all been killed in the tram.

They waited for the other tram by the Roman Catholic Church, whose florid bulk was already receding into twilight. It is the first big building that the incoming visitor sees. "Oh, here come the colleges!" cries the Protestant parent, and then learns that it was built by a Papist who made a fortune out of movable eyes for dolls. "Built out of doll's eyes to contain idols"—that, at all events, is the legend and the joke. It watches over the apostate city, taller by many a yard than anything within, and asserting, however wildly, that here is eternity, stability, and bubbles unbreakable upon a windless sea.

A costly hymn tune announced five o'clock, and in the distance the more lovable note of St. Mary's could be heard, speaking from the heart of the town. Then the tram arrived—the slow stuffy tram that plies every twenty minutes between the unknown and the marketplace—and took them past the desecrated grounds of Downing, past Addenbrookes Hospital, girt like a Venetian palace with a mantling canal, past the Fitz William, towering upon immense substructions like any Roman temple, right up to the gates of one's own college, which looked like nothing else in the world. The porters were glad to see them, but wished it had been a hansom. "Our luggage," explained Rickie, "comes in the hotel omnibus, if you would kindly pay a shilling for mine." Ansell turned aside to some large lighted windows, the abode of a hospitable don, and from other windows there floated familiar voices and the familiar mistakes in a Beethoven sonata. The college, though small, was civilized, and proud of its civilization. It was not sufficient glory to be a Blue there, nor an additional glory to get drunk. Many a maiden lady who had read that Cambridge men were sad dogs, was surprised and perhaps a little disappointed at the reasonable life which greeted her. Miss Appleblossom in particular had had a tremendous shock. The sight of young fellows making tea and drinking water had made her wonder whether this was Cambridge College at all. "It is so," she exclaimed afterwards. "It is just as I say; and what's more, I wouldn't have it otherwise; Stewart says it's as easy as easy to get into the swim, and not at all expensive." The direction of the swim was determined a little by the genius of the place—for places have a genius, though the less we talk about it the better—and a good deal by the tutors and resident fellows, who treated with rare dexterity the products that came up yearly from the public schools. They taught the perky boy that he was not everything, and the limp boy that he might be something. They even welcomed those boys who were neither limp nor perky, but odd—those boys who had never been at a public school at all, and such do not find a welcome everywhere. And they did everything with ease—one might almost say with nonchalance, so that the boys noticed nothing, and received education, often for the first time in their lives.

But Rickie turned to none of these friends, for just then he loved his rooms better than any person. They were all he really possessed in the world, the only place he could call his own. Over the door was his name, and through the paint, like a grey ghost, he could still read the name of his predecessor. With a sigh of joy he entered the perishable home that was his for a couple of years. There was a beautiful fire, and the kettle boiled at once. He made tea on the hearth-rug and ate the biscuits which Mrs. Aberdeen had brought for him up from Anderson's. "Gentlemen," she said, "must learn to give and take." He sighed again and again, like one who had escaped from danger. With his head on the fender and all his limbs relaxed, he felt almost as safe as he felt once when his mother killed a ghost in the passage by carrying him through it in her arms. There was no ghost now; he was frightened at reality; he was frightened at the splendours and horrors of the world.

A letter from Miss Pembroke was on the table. He did not hurry to open it, for she, and all that she did, was overwhelming. She wrote like the Sibyl; her sorrowful face moved over the stars and shattered their harmonies; last night he saw her with the eyes of Blake, a virgin widow, tall, veiled, consecrated, with her hands stretched out against an everlasting wind. Why should she write? Her letters were not for the likes of him, nor to be read in rooms like his.

"We are not leaving Sawston," she wrote. "I saw how selfish it was of me to risk spoiling Herbert's career. I shall get used to any place. Now that he is gone, nothing of that sort can matter. Every one has been most kind, but you have comforted me most, though you did not mean to. I cannot think how you did it, or understood so much. I still think of you as a little boy with a lame leg,—I know you will let me say this,—and yet when it came to the point you knew more than people who have been all their lives with sorrow and death."

Rickie burnt this letter, which he ought not to have done, for it was one of the few tributes Miss Pembroke ever paid to imagination. But he felt that it did not belong to him: words so sincere should be for Gerald alone. The smoke rushed up the chimney, and he indulged in a vision. He saw it reach the outer air and beat against the low ceiling of clouds. The clouds were too strong for it; but in them was one chink, revealing one star, and through this the smoke escaped into the light of stars innumerable. Then—but then the vision failed, and the voice of science whispered that all smoke remains on earth in the form of smuts, and is troublesome to Mrs. Aberdeen.

"I am jolly unpractical," he mused. "And what is the point of it when real things are so wonderful? Who wants visions in a world that has Agnes and Gerald?" He turned on the electric light and pulled open the table-drawer. There, among spoons and corks and string, he found a fragment of a little story that he had tried to write last term. It was called "The Bay of the Fifteen Islets," and the action took place on St. John's Eve off the coast of Sicily. A party of tourists land on one of the islands. Suddenly the boatmen become uneasy, and say that the island is not generally there. It is an extra one, and they had better have tea on one of the ordinaries. "Pooh, volcanic!" says the leading tourist, and the ladies say how interesting. The island begins to rock, and so do the minds of its visitors. They start and quarrel and jabber. Fingers burst up through the sand-black fingers of sea devils. The island tilts. The tourists go mad. But just before the catastrophe one man, integer vitae scelerisque purus, sees the truth. Here are no devils. Other muscles, other minds, are pulling the island to its subterranean home. Through the advancing wall of waters he sees no grisly faces, no ghastly medieval limbs, but—But what nonsense! When real things are so wonderful, what is the point of pretending?

And so Rickie deflected his enthusiasms. Hitherto they had played on gods and heroes, on the infinite and the impossible, on virtue and beauty and strength. Now, with a steadier radiance, they transfigured a man who was dead and a woman who was still alive.

VII

Love, say orderly people, can be fallen into by two methods: (1) through the desires, (2) through the imagination. And if the orderly people are English, they add that (1) is the inferior method, and characteristic of the South. It is inferior. Yet those who pursue it at all events know what they want; they are not puzzling to themselves or ludicrous to others; they do not take the wings of the morning and fly into the uttermost parts of the sea before walking to the registry office; they cannot breed a tragedy quite like Rickie's.

He is, of course, absurdly young—not twenty-one and he will be engaged to be married at twenty-three. He has no knowledge of the world; for example, he thinks that if you do not want money you can give it to friends who do. He believes in humanity because he knows a dozen decent people. He believes in women because he has loved his mother. And his friends are as young and as ignorant as himself. They are full of the wine of life. But they have not tasted the cup—let us call it the teacup—of experience, which has made men of Mr. Pembroke's type what they are. Oh, that teacup! To be taken at prayers, at friendship, at love, till we are quite sane, efficient, quite experienced, and quite useless to God or man. We must drink it, or we shall die. But we need not drink it always. Here is our problem and our salvation. There comes a moment—God knows when—at which we can say, "I will experience no longer. I will create. I will be an experience." But to do this we must be both acute and heroic. For it is not easy, after accepting six cups of tea, to throw the seventh in the face of the hostess. And to Rickie this moment has not, as yet, been offered.

Ansell, at the end of his third year, got a first in the Moral Science Tripos. Being a scholar, he kept his rooms in college, and at once began to work for a Fellowship. Rickie got a creditable second in the Classical Tripos, Part I., and retired to sallow lodgings in Mill bane, carrying with him the degree of B.A. and a small exhibition, which was quite as much as he deserved. For Part II. he read Greek Archaeology, and got a second. All this means that Ansell was much cleverer than Rickie. As for the cow, she was still going strong, though turning a little academic as the years passed over her.

"We are bound to get narrow," sighed Rickie. He and his friend were lying in a meadow during their last summer term. In his incurable love for flowers he had plaited two garlands of buttercups and cow-parsley, and Ansell's lean Jewish face was framed in one of them. "Cambridge is wonderful, but—but it's so tiny. You have no idea—at least, I think you have no idea—how the great world looks down on it."

"I read the letters in the papers."

"It's a bad look-out."

"How?"

"Cambridge has lost touch with the times."

"Was she ever intended to touch them?"

"She satisfies," said Rickie mysteriously, "neither the professions, nor the public schools, nor the great thinking mass of men and women. There is a general feeling that her day is over, and naturally one feels pretty sick."

"Do you still write short stories?"

"Because your English has gone to the devil. You think and talk in Journalese. Define a great thinking mass."

Rickie sat up and adjusted his floral crown.

"Estimate the worth of a general feeling."

Silence.

"And thirdly, where is the great world?"

"Oh that—!"

"Yes. That," exclaimed Ansell, rising from his couch in violent excitement. "Where is it? How do you set about finding it? How long does it take to get there? What does it think? What does it do? What does it want? Oblige me with specimens of its art and literature." Silence. "Till you do, my opinions will be as follows: There is no great world at all, only a little earth, for ever isolated from the rest of the little solar system. The earth is full of tiny societies, and Cambridge is one of them. All the societies are narrow, but some are good and some are bad—just as one house is beautiful inside and another ugly. Observe the metaphor of the houses: I am coming back to it. The good societies say, `I tell you to do this because I am Cambridge.' The bad ones say, `I tell you to do that because I am the great world, not because I am 'Peckham,' or `Billingsgate,' or `Park Lane,' but `because I am the great world.' They lie. And fools like you listen to them, and believe that they are a thing which does not exist and never has existed, and confuse 'great,' which has no meaning whatever, with 'good,' which means salvation. Look at this great wreath: it'll be dead tomorrow. Look at that good flower: it'll come up again next year. Now for the other metaphor. To compare the world to Cambridge is like comparing the outsides of houses with the inside of a house. No intellectual effort is needed, no moral result is attained. You only have to say, 'Oh, what a difference!' and then come indoors again and exhibit your broadened mind."

"I never shall come indoors again," said Rickie. "That's the whole point." And his voice began to quiver. "It's well enough for those who'll get a Fellowship, but in a few weeks I shall go down. In a few years it'll be as if I've never been up. It matters very much to me what the world is like. I can't answer your questions about it; and that's no loss to you, but so much the worse for me. And then you've got a house—not a metaphorical one, but a house with father and sisters. I haven't, and never shall have. There'll never again be a home for me like Cambridge. I shall only look at the outside of homes. According to your metaphor, I shall live in the street, and it matters very much to me what I find there."

"You'll live in another house right enough," said Ansell, rather uneasily. "Only take care you pick out a decent one. I can't think why you flop about so helplessly, like a bit of seaweed. In four years you've taken as much root as any one."

"Where?"

"I should say you've been fortunate in your friends."

"Oh—that!" But he was not cynical—or cynical in a very tender way. He was thinking of the irony of friendship—so strong it is, and so fragile. We fly together, like straws in an eddy, to part in the open stream. Nature has no use for us: she has cut her stuff differently. Dutiful sons, loving husbands, responsible fathers these are what she wants, and if we are friends it must be in our spare time. Abram and Sarai were sorrowful, yet their seed became as sand of the sea, and distracts the politics of Europe at this moment. But a few verses of poetry is all that survives of David and Jonathan.

"I wish we were labelled," said Rickie. He wished that all the confidence and mutual knowledge that is born in such a place as Cambridge could be organized. People went down into the world saying, "We know and like each other; we shan't forget." But they did forget, for man is so made that he cannot remember long without a symbol; he wished there was a society, a kind of friendship office, where the marriage of true minds could be registered.

"Why labels?"

"To know each other again."

"I have taught you pessimism splendidly." He looked at his watch.

"What time?"

"Not twelve."

Rickie got up.

"Why go?" He stretched out his hand and caught hold of Rickie's ankle.

"I've got that Miss Pembroke to lunch—that girl whom you say never's there."

"Then why go? All this week you have pretended Miss Pembroke awaited you. Wednesday—Miss Pembroke to lunch. Thursday—Miss Pembroke to tea. Now again—and you didn't even invite her."

"To Cambridge, no. But the Hall man they're stopping with has so many engagements that she and her friend can often come to me, I'm glad to say. I don't think I ever told you much, but over two years ago the man she was going to marry was killed at football. She nearly died of grief. This visit to Cambridge is almost the first amusement she has felt up to taking. Oh, they go back tomorrow! Give me breakfast tomorrow."

"All right."

"But I shall see you this evening. I shall be round at your paper on Schopenhauer. Lemme go."

"Don't go," he said idly. "It's much better for you to talk to me."

"Lemme go, Stewart."

"It's amusing that you're so feeble. You—simply—can't—get—away. I wish I wanted to bully you."

Rickie laughed, and suddenly over balanced into the grass. Ansell, with unusual playfulness, held him prisoner. They lay there for few minutes, talking and ragging aimlessly. Then Rickie seized his opportunity and jerked away.

"Go, go!" yawned the other. But he was a little vexed, for he was a young man with great capacity for pleasure, and it pleased him that morning to be with his friend. The thought of two ladies waiting lunch did not deter him; stupid women, why shouldn't they wait? Why should they interfere with their betters? With his ear on the ground he listened to Rickie's departing steps, and thought, "He wastes a lot of time keeping engagements. Why will he be pleasant to fools?" And then he thought, "Why has he turned so unhappy? It isn't as it he's a philosopher, or tries to solve the riddle of existence. And he's got money of his own." Thus thinking, he fell asleep.

Meanwhile Rickie hurried away from him, and slackened and stopped, and hurried again. He was due at the Union in ten minutes, but he could not bring himself there. He dared not meet Miss Pembroke: he loved her.

The devil must have planned it. They had started so gloriously; she had been a goddess both in joy and sorrow. She was a goddess still. But he had dethroned the god whom once he had glorified equally. Slowly, slowly, the image of Gerald had faded. That was the first step. Rickie had thought, "No matter. He will be bright again. Just now all the radiance chances to be in her." And on her he had fixed his eyes. He thought of her awake. He entertained her willingly in dreams. He found her in poetry and music and in the sunset. She made him kind and strong. She made him clever. Through her he kept Cambridge in its proper place, and lived as a citizen of the great world. But one night he dreamt that she lay in his arms. This displeased him. He determined to think a little about Gerald instead. Then the fabric collapsed.

It was hard on Rickie thus to meet the devil. He did not deserve it, for he was comparatively civilized, and knew that there was nothing shameful in love. But to love this woman! If only it had been any one else! Love in return—that he could expect from no one, being too ugly and too unattractive. But the love he offered would not then have been vile. The insult to Miss Pembroke, who was consecrated, and whom he had consecrated, who could still see Gerald, and always would see him, shining on his everlasting throne this was the crime from the devil, the crime that no penance would ever purge. She knew nothing. She never would know. But the crime was registered in heaven.

He had been tempted to confide in Ansell. But to what purpose? He would say, "I love Miss Pembroke." and Stewart would reply, "You ass." And then. "I'm never going to tell her." "You ass," again. After all, it was not a practical question; Agnes would never hear of his fall. If his friend had been, as he expressed it, "labelled"; if he had been a father, or still better a brother, one might tell him of the discreditable passion. But why irritate him for no reason? Thinking "I am always angling for sympathy; I must stop myself," he hurried onward to the Union.

He found his guests half way up the stairs, reading the advertisements of coaches for the Long Vacation. He heard Mrs. Lewin say, "I wonder what he'll end by doing." A little overacting his part, he apologized nonchalantly for his lateness.

"It's always the same," cried Agnes. "Last time he forgot I was coming altogether." She wore a flowered muslin—something indescribably liquid and cool. It reminded him a little of those swift piercing streams, neither blue nor green, that gush out of the dolomites. Her face was clear and brown, like the face of a mountaineer; her hair was so plentiful that it seemed banked up above it; and her little toque, though it answered the note of the dress, was almost ludicrous, poised on so much natural glory. When she moved, the sunlight flashed on her ear-rings.

He led them up to the luncheon-room. By now he was conscious of his limitations as a host, and never attempted to entertain ladies in his lodgings. Moreover, the Union seemed less intimate. It had a faint flavour of a London club; it marked the undergraduate's nearest approach to the great world. Amid its waiters and serviettes one felt impersonal, and able to conceal the private emotions. Rickie felt that if Miss Pembroke knew one thing about him, she knew everything. During this visit he took her to no place that he greatly loved.

"Sit down, ladies. Fall to. I'm sorry. I was out towards Coton with a dreadful friend."

Mrs. Lewin pushed up her veil. She was a typical May-term chaperon, always pleasant, always hungry, and always tired. Year after year she came up to Cambridge in a tight silk dress, and year after year she nearly died of it. Her feet hurt, her limbs were cramped in a canoe, black spots danced before her eyes from eating too much mayonnaise. But still she came, if not as a mother as an aunt, if not as an aunt as a friend. Still she ascended the roof of King's, still she counted the balls of Clare, still she was on the point of grasping the organization of the May races. "And who is your friend?" she asked.

"His name is Ansell."

"Well, now, did I see him two years ago—as a bedmaker in something they did at the Foot Lights? Oh, how I roared."

"You didn't see Mr. Ansell at the Foot Lights," said Agnes, smiling.

"How do you know?" asked Rickie.

"He'd scarcely be so frivolous."

"Do you remember seeing him?"

"For a moment."

What a memory she had! And how splendidly during that moment she had behaved!

"Isn't he marvellously clever?"

"I believe so."

"Oh, give me clever people!" cried Mrs. Lewin. "They are kindness itself at the Hall, but I assure you I am depressed at times. One cannot talk bump-rowing for ever."

"I never hear about him, Rickie; but isn't he really your greatest friend?"

"I don't go in for greatest friends."

"Do you mean you like us all equally?"

"All differently, those of you I like."

"Ah, you've caught it!" cried Mrs. Lewin. "Mr. Elliot gave it you there well."

Agnes laughed, and, her elbows on the table, regarded them both through her fingers—a habit of hers. Then she said, "Can't we see the great Mr. Ansell?"

"Oh, let's. Or would he frighten me?"

"He would frighten you," said Rickie. "He's a trifle weird."

"My good Rickie, if you knew the deathly dullness of Sawston—every one saying the proper thing at the proper time, I so proper, Herbert so proper! Why, weirdness is the one thing I long for! Do arrange something."

"I'm afraid there's no opportunity. Ansell goes some vast bicycle ride this afternoon; this evening you're tied up at the Hall; and tomorrow you go."

"But there's breakfast tomorrow," said Agnes. "Look here, Rickie, bring Mr. Ansell to breakfast with us at Buoys."

Mrs. Lewin seconded the invitation.

"Bad luck again," said Rickie boldly; "I'm already fixed up for breakfast. I'll tell him of your very kind intention."

"Let's have him alone," murmured Agnes.

"My dear girl, I should die through the floor! Oh, it'll be all right about breakfast. I rather think we shall get asked this evening by that shy man who has the pretty rooms in Trinity."

"Oh, very well. Where is it you breakfast, Rickie?"

He faltered. "To Ansell's, it is—" It seemed as if he was making some great admission. So self-conscious was he, that he thought the two women exchanged glances. Had Agnes already explored that part of him that did not belong to her? Would another chance step reveal the part that did? He asked them abruptly what they would like to do after lunch.

"Anything," said Mrs. Lewin,—"anything in the world."

A walk? A boat? Ely? A drive? Some objection was raised to each. "To tell the truth," she said at last, "I do feel a wee bit tired, and what occurs to me is this. You and Agnes shall leave me here and have no more bother. I shall be perfectly happy snoozling in one of these delightful drawing-room chairs. Do what you like, and then pick me up after it."

"Alas, it's against regulations," said Rickie. "The Union won't trust lady visitors on its premises alone."

"But who's to know I'm alone? With a lot of men in the drawing-room, how's each to know that I'm not with the others?"

"That would shock Rickie," said Agnes, laughing. "He's frightfully high-principled."

"No, I'm not," said Rickie, thinking of his recent shiftiness over breakfast.

"Then come for a walk with me. I want exercise. Some connection of ours was once rector of Madingley. I shall walk out and see the church."

Mrs. Lewin was accordingly left in the Union.

"This is jolly!" Agnes exclaimed as she strode along the somewhat depressing road that leads out of Cambridge past the observatory. "Do I go too fast?"

"No, thank you. I get stronger every year. If it wasn't for the look of the thing, I should be quite happy."

"But you don't care for the look of the thing. It's only ignorant people who do that, surely."

"Perhaps. I care. I like people who are well-made and beautiful. They are of some use in the world. I understand why they are there. I cannot understand why the ugly and crippled are there, however healthy they may feel inside. Don't you know how Turner spoils his pictures by introducing a man like a bolster in the foreground? Well, in actual life every landscape is spoilt by men of worse shapes still."

"You sound like a bolster with the stuffing out." They laughed. She always blew his cobwebs away like this, with a puff of humorous mountain air. Just now the associations he attached to her were various—she reminded him of a heroine of Meredith's—but a heroine at the end of the book. All had been written about her. She had played her mighty part, and knew that it was over. He and he alone was not content, and wrote for her daily a trivial and impossible sequel.

Last time they had talked about Gerald. But that was some six months ago, when things felt easier. Today Gerald was the faintest blur. Fortunately the conversation turned to Mr. Pembroke and to education. Did women lose a lot by not knowing Greek? "A heap," said Rickie, roughly. But modern languages? Thus they got to Germany, which he had visited last Easter with Ansell; and thence to the German Emperor, and what a to-do he made; and from him to our own king (still Prince of Wales), who had lived while an undergraduate at Madingley Hall. Here it was. And all the time he thought, "It is hard on her. She has no right to be walking with me. She would be ill with disgust if she knew. It is hard on her to be loved."

They looked at the Hall, and went inside the pretty little church. Some Arundel prints hung upon the pillars, and Agnes expressed the opinion that pictures inside a place of worship were a pity. Rickie did not agree with this. He said again that nothing beautiful was ever to be regretted.

"You're cracked on beauty," she whispered—they were still inside the church. "Do hurry up and write something."

"Something beautiful?"

"I believe you can. I'm going to lecture you seriously all the way home. Take care that you don't waste your life."

They continued the conversation outside. "But I've got to hate my own writing. I believe that most people come to that stage—not so early though. What I write is too silly. It can't happen. For instance, a stupid vulgar man is engaged to a lovely young lady. He wants her to live in the towns, but she only cares for woods. She shocks him this way and that, but gradually he tames her, and makes her nearly as dull as he is. One day she has a last explosion—over the snobby wedding presents—and flies out of the drawing-room window, shouting, 'Freedom and truth!' Near the house is a little dell full of fir-trees, and she runs into it. He comes there the next moment. But she's gone."

"Awfully exciting. Where?"

"Oh Lord, she's a Dryad!" cried Rickie, in great disgust. "She's turned into a tree."

"Rickie, it's very good indeed. The kind of thing has something in it. Of course you get it all through Greek and Latin. How upset the man must be when he sees the girl turn."

"He doesn't see her. He never guesses. Such a man could never see a Dryad."

"So you describe how she turns just before he comes up?"

"No. Indeed I don't ever say that she does turn. I don't use the word 'Dryad' once."

"I think you ought to put that part plainly. Otherwise, with such an original story, people might miss the point. Have you had any luck with it?"

"Magazines? I haven't tried. I know what the stuff's worth. You see, a year or two ago I had a great idea of getting into touch with Nature, just as the Greeks were in touch; and seeing England so beautiful, I used to pretend that her trees and coppices and summer fields of parsley were alive. It's funny enough now, but it wasn't funny then, for I got in such a state that I believed, actually believed, that Fauns lived in a certain double hedgerow near the Gog Magogs, and one evening I walked a mile sooner than go through it alone."

"Good gracious!" She laid her hand on his shoulder.

He moved to the other side of the road. "It's all right now. I've changed those follies for others. But while I had them I began to write, and even now I keep on writing, though I know better. I've got quite a pile of little stories, all harping on this ridiculous idea of getting into touch with Nature."

"I wish you weren't so modest. It's simply splendid as an idea. Though—but tell me about the Dryad who was engaged to be married. What was she like?"

"I can show you the dell in which the young person disappeared. We pass it on the right in a moment."

"It does seem a pity that you don't make something of your talents. It seems such a waste to write little stories and never publish them. You must have enough for a book. Life is so full in our days that short stories are the very thing; they get read by people who'd never tackle a novel. For example, at our Dorcas we tried to read out a long affair by Henry James—Herbert saw it recommended in 'The Times.' There was no doubt it was very good, but one simply couldn't remember from one week to another what had happened. So now our aim is to get something that just lasts the hour. I take you seriously, Rickie, and that is why I am so offensive. You are too modest. People who think they can do nothing so often do nothing. I want you to plunge."

VII

It thrilled him like a trumpet-blast. She took him seriously. Could he but thank her for her divine affability! But the words would stick in his throat, or worse still would bring other words along with them. His breath came quickly, for he seldom spoke of his writing, and no one, not even Ansell, had advised him to plunge.

"But do you really think that I could take up literature?"

"Why not? You can try. Even if you fail, you can try. Of course we think you tremendously clever; and I met one of your dons at tea, and he said that your degree was not in the least a proof of your abilities: he said that you knocked up and got flurried in examinations. Oh!"—her cheek flushed,—"I wish I was a man. The whole world lies before them. They can do anything. They aren't cooped up with servants and tea parties and twaddle. But where's this dell where the Dryad disappeared?"

"We've passed it." He had meant to pass it. It was too beautiful. All he had read, all he had hoped for, all he had loved, seemed to quiver in its enchanted air. It was perilous. He dared not enter it with such a woman.

"How long ago?" She turned back. "I don't want to miss the dell. Here it must be," she added after a few moments, and sprang up the green bank that hid the entrance from the road. "Oh, what a jolly place!"

"Go right in if you want to see it," said Rickie, and did not offer to go with her. She stood for a moment looking at the view, for a few steps will increase a view in Cambridgeshire. The wind blew her dress against her. Then, like a cataract again, she vanished pure and cool into the dell.

The young man thought of her feelings no longer. His heart throbbed louder and louder, and seemed to shake him to pieces. "Rickie!"

She was calling from the dell. For an answer he sat down where he was, on the dust-bespattered margin. She could call as loud as she liked. The devil had done much, but he should not take him to her.

"Rickie!"—and it came with the tones of an angel. He drove his fingers into his ears, and invoked the name of Gerald. But there was no sign, neither angry motion in the air nor hint of January mist. June—fields of June, sky of June, songs of June. Grass of June beneath him, grass of June over the tragedy he had deemed immortal. A bird called out of the dell: "Rickie!"

A bird flew into the dell.

"Did you take me for the Dryad?" she asked. She was sitting down with his head on her lap. He had laid it there for a moment before he went out to die, and she had not let him take it away.

"I prayed you might not be a woman," he whispered.

"Darling, I am very much a woman. I do not vanish into groves and trees. I thought you would never come."

"Did you expect—?"

"I hoped. I called hoping."

Inside the dell it was neither June nor January. The chalk walls barred out the seasons, and the fir-trees did not seem to feel their passage. Only from time to time the odours of summer slipped in from the wood above, to comment on the waxing year. She bent down to touch him with her lips.

He started, and cried passionately, "Never forget that your greatest thing is over. I have forgotten: I am too weak. You shall never forget. What I said to you then is greater than what I say to you now. What he gave you then is greater than anything you will get from me."

She was frightened. Again she had the sense of something abnormal. Then she said, "What is all this nonsense?" and folded him in her arms.

VIII

Ansell stood looking at his breakfast-table, which was laid for four instead of two. His bedmaker, equally peevish, explained how it had happened. Last night, at one in the morning, the porter had been awoke with a note for the kitchens, and in that note Mr. Elliot said that all these things were to be sent to Mr. Ansell's.

"The fools have sent the original order as well. Here's the lemon-sole for two. I can't move for food."

"The note being ambiguous, the Kitchens judged best to send it all." She spoke of the kitchens in a half-respectful, half-pitying way, much as one speaks of Parliament.

"Who's to pay for it?" He peeped into the new dishes. Kidneys entombed in an omelette, hot roast chicken in watery gravy, a glazed but pallid pie.

"And who's to wash it up?" said the bedmaker to her help outside.

Ansell had disputed late last night concerning Schopenhauer, and was a little cross and tired. He bounced over to Tilliard, who kept opposite. Tilliard was eating gooseberry jam.

"Did Elliot ask you to breakfast with me?"

"No," said Tilliard mildly.

"Well, you'd better come, and bring every one you know."

So Tilliard came, bearing himself a little formally, for he was not very intimate with his neighbour. Out of the window they called to Widdrington. But he laid his hand on his stomach, thus indicating it was too late.

"Who's to pay for it?" repeated Ansell, as a man appeared from the Buttery carrying coffee on a bright tin tray.

"College coffee! How nice!" remarked Tilliard, who was cutting the pie. "But before term ends you must come and try my new machine. My sister gave it me. There is a bulb at the top, and as the water boils—"

"He might have counter-ordered the lemon-sole. That's Rickie all over. Violently economical, and then loses his head, and all the things go bad."

"Give them to the bedder while they're hot." This was done. She accepted them dispassionately, with the air of one who lives without nourishment. Tilliard continued to describe his sister's coffee machine.

"What's that?" They could hear panting and rustling on the stairs.

"It sounds like a lady," said Tilliard fearfully. He slipped the piece of pie back. It fell into position like a brick.

"Is it here? Am I right? Is it here?" The door opened and in came Mrs. Lewin. "Oh horrors! I've made a mistake."

"That's all right," said Ansell awkwardly.

"I wanted Mr. Elliot. Where are they?"

"We expect Mr. Elliot every-moment," said Tilliard.

"Don't tell me I'm right," cried Mrs. Lewin, "and that you're the terrifying Mr. Ansell." And, with obvious relief, she wrung Tilliard warmly by the hand.

"I'm Ansell," said Ansell, looking very uncouth and grim.

"How stupid of me not to know it," she gasped, and would have gone on to I know not what, but the door opened again. It was Rickie.

"Here's Miss Pembroke," he said. "I am going to marry her."

There was a profound silence.

"We oughtn't to have done things like this," said Agnes, turning to Mrs. Lewin. "We have no right to take Mr. Ansell by surprise. It is Rickie's fault. He was that obstinate. He would bring us. He ought to be horsewhipped."

"He ought, indeed," said Tilliard pleasantly, and bolted. Not till he gained his room did he realize that he had been less apt than usual. As for Ansell, the first thing he said was, "Why didn't you counter-order the lemon-sole?"

In such a situation Mrs. Lewin was of priceless value. She led the way to the table, observing, "I quite agree with Miss Pembroke. I loathe surprises. Never shall I forget my horror when the knife-boy painted the dove's cage with the dove inside. He did it as a surprise. Poor Parsival nearly died. His feathers were bright green!"

"Well, give me the lemon-soles," said Rickie. "I like them."

"The bedder's got them."

"Well, there you are! What's there to be annoyed about?"

"And while the cage was drying we put him among the bantams. They had been the greatest allies. But I suppose they took him for a parrot or a hawk, or something that bantams hate for while his cage was drying they picked out his feathers, and PICKED and PICKED out his feathers, till he was perfectly bald. 'Hugo, look,' said I. 'This is the end of Parsival. Let me have no more surprises.' He burst into tears."

Thus did Mrs. Lewin create an atmosphere. At first it seemed unreal, but gradually they got used to it, and breathed scarcely anything else throughout the meal. In such an atmosphere everything seemed of small and equal value, and the engagement of Rickie and Agnes like the feathers of Parsival, fluttered lightly to the ground. Ansell was generally silent. He was no match for these two quite clever women. Only once was there a hitch.

They had been talking gaily enough about the betrothal when Ansell suddenly interrupted with, "When is the marriage?"

"Mr. Ansell," said Agnes, blushing, "I wish you hadn't asked that. That part's dreadful. Not for years, as far as we can see."

VIII

But Rickie had not seen as far. He had not talked to her of this at all. Last night they had spoken only of love. He exclaimed, "Oh, Agnes-don't!" Mrs. Lewin laughed roguishly.

"Why this delay?" asked Ansell.

Agnes looked at Rickie, who replied, "I must get money, worse luck."

"I thought you'd got money."

He hesitated, and then said, "I must get my foot on the ladder, then."

Ansell began with, "On which ladder?" but Mrs. Lewin, using the privilege of her sex, exclaimed, "Not another word. If there's a thing I abominate, it is plans. My head goes whirling at once." What she really abominated was questions, and she saw that Ansell was turning serious. To appease him, she put on her clever manner and asked him about Germany. How had it impressed him? Were we so totally unfitted to repel invasion? Was not German scholarship overestimated? He replied discourteously, but he did reply; and if she could have stopped him thinking, her triumph would have been complete.

When they rose to go, Agnes held Ansell's hand for a moment in her own.

"Good-bye," she said. "It was very unconventional of us to come as we did, but I don't think any of us are conventional people."

He only replied, "Good-bye." The ladies started off. Rickie lingered behind to whisper, "I would have it so. I would have you begin square together. I can't talk yet—I've loved her for years—can't think what she's done it for. I'm going to write short stories. I shall start this afternoon. She declares there may be something in me."

As soon as he had left, Tilliard burst in, white with agitation, and crying, "Did you see my awful faux pas—about the horsewhip? What shall I do? I must call on Elliot. Or had I better write?"

"Miss Pembroke will not mind," said Ansell gravely. "She is unconventional." He knelt in an arm-chair and hid his face in the back.

"It was like a bomb," said Tilliard.

"It was meant to be."

"I do feel a fool. What must she think?"

"Never mind, Tilliard. You've not been as big a fool as myself. At all events, you told her he must be horsewhipped."

Tilliard hummed a little tune. He hated anything nasty, and there was nastiness in Ansell. "What did you tell her?" he asked.

"Nothing."

"What do you think of it?"

"I think: Damn those women."

"Ah, yes. One hates one's friends to get engaged. It makes one feel so old: I think that is one of the reasons. The brother just above me has lately married, and my sister was quite sick about it, though the thing was suitable in every way."

"Damn THESE women, then," said Ansell, bouncing round in the chair. "Damn these particular women."

"They looked and spoke like ladies."

"Exactly. Their diplomacy was ladylike. Their lies were ladylike. They've caught Elliot in a most ladylike way. I saw it all during the one moment we were natural. Generally we were clattering after the married one, whom—like a fool—I took for a fool. But for one moment we were natural, and during that moment Miss Pembroke told a lie, and made Rickie believe it was the truth."

"What did she say?"

"She said `we see' instead of 'I see.'"

Tilliard burst into laughter. This jaundiced young philosopher, with his kinky view of life, was too much for him.

"She said 'we see,'" repeated Ansell, "instead of 'I see,' and she made him believe that it was the truth. She caught him and makes him believe that he caught her. She came to see me and makes him think that it is his idea. That is what I mean when I say that she is a lady."

"You are too subtle for me. My dull eyes could only see two happy people."

"I never said they weren't happy."

"Then, my dear Ansell, why are you so cut up? It's beastly when a friend marries,—and I grant he's rather young,—but I should say it's the best thing for him. A decent woman—and you have proved not one thing against her—a decent woman will keep him up to the mark and stop him getting slack. She'll make him responsible and manly, for much as I like Rickie, I always find him a little effeminate. And, really,"—his voice grew sharper, for he was irritated by Ansell's conceit, "and, really, you talk as if you were mixed up in the affair. They pay a civil visit to your rooms, and you see nothing but dark plots and challenges to war."

"War!" cried Ansell, crashing his fists together. "It's war, then!"

"Oh, what a lot of tommy-rot," said Tilliard. "Can't a man and woman get engaged? My dear boy—excuse me talking like this—what on earth is it to do with us?"

"We're his friends, and I hope we always shall be, but we shan't keep his friendship by fighting. We're bound to fall into the background. Wife first, friends some way after. You may resent the order, but it is ordained by nature."

"The point is, not what's ordained by nature or any other fool, but what's right."

"You are hopelessly unpractical," said Tilliard, turning away. "And let me remind you that you've already given away your case by acknowledging that they're happy."

"She is happy because she has conquered; he is happy because he has at last hung all the world's beauty on to a single peg. He was always trying to do it. He used to call the peg humanity. Will either of these happinesses last? His can't. Hers only for a time. I fight this woman not only because she fights me, but because I foresee the most appalling catastrophe. She wants Rickie, partly to replace another man whom she lost two years ago, partly to make something out of him. He is to write. In time she will get sick of this. He won't get famous. She will only see how thin he is and how lame. She will long for a jollier husband, and I don't blame her. And, having made him thoroughly miserable and degraded, she will bolt—if she can do it like a lady."

Such were the opinions of Stewart Ansell.

IX

Seven letters written in June:—

Cambridge

Dear Rickie,

I would rather write, and you can guess what kind of letter this is when I say it is a fair copy: I have been making rough drafts all the morning. When I talk I get angry, and also at times try to be clever—two reasons why I fail to get attention paid to me. This is a letter of the prudent sort. If it makes you break off the engagement, its work is done. You are not a person who ought to marry at all. You are unfitted in body: that we once discussed. You are also unfitted in soul: you want and you need to like many people, and a man of that sort ought not to marry. "You never were attached to that great sect" who can like one person only, and if you try to enter it you will find destruction. I have read in books and I cannot afford to despise books, they are all that I have to go by—that men and women desire different things. Man wants to love mankind; woman wants to love one man. When she has him her work is over. She is the emissary of Nature, and Nature's bidding has been fulfilled. But man does not care a damn for Nature—or at least only a very little damn. He cares for a hundred things besides, and the more civilized he is the more he will care for these other hundred things, and demand not only—a wife and children, but also friends, and work, and spiritual freedom.

I believe you to be extraordinarily civilized.—Yours ever,

S.A.

Shelthorpe, 9 Sawston Park Road, Sawston

Dear Ansell,

But I'm in love—a detail you've forgotten. I can't listen to English Essays. The wretched Agnes may be an "emissary of Nature," but I only grinned when I read it. I may be extraordinarily civilized, but I don't feel so; I'm in love, and I've found a woman to love me, and I mean to have the hundred other things as well. She wants me to have them—friends and work, and spiritual freedom, and everything. You and your books miss this, because your books are too sedate. Read poetry—not only Shelley. Understand Beatrice, and Clara Middleton, and Brunhilde in the first scene of Gotterdammerung. Understand Goethe when he says "the eternal feminine leads us on," and don't write another English Essay.—Yours ever affectionately,

R.E.

Cambridge

Dear Rickie:

What am I to say? "Understand Xanthippe, and Mrs. Bennet, and Elsa in the question scene of Lohengrin"? "Understand Euripides when he says the eternal feminine leads us a pretty dance"? I shall say nothing of the sort. The allusions in this English Essay shall not be literary. My personal objections to Miss Pembroke are as follows:—(1) She is not serious. (2) She is not truthful.

Shelthorpe, 9 Sawston Park Road Sawston

My Dear Stewart,

You couldn't know. I didn't know for a moment. But this letter of yours is the most wonderful thing that has ever happened to me yet—more wonderful (I don't exaggerate) than the moment when Agnes promised to marry me. I always knew you liked me, but I never knew how much until this letter. Up to now I think we have been too much like the strong heroes in books who feel so much and say so little, and feel all the more for saying so little. Now that's over and we shall never be that kind of an ass again. We've hit—by accident—upon something permanent. You've written to me, "I hate the woman who will be your wife," and I write back, "Hate her. Can't I love you both?" She will never come between us, Stewart (She wouldn't wish to, but that's by the way), because our friendship has now passed beyond intervention. No third person could break it. We couldn't ourselves, I fancy. We may quarrel and argue till one of us dies, but the thing is registered. I only wish, dear man, you could be happier. For me, it's as if a light was suddenly held behind the world.

R.E.

Shelthorpe, 9 Sawston Park Road, Sawston

Dear Mrs. Lewin,—

The time goes flying, but I am getting to learn my wonderful boy. We speak a great deal about his work. He has just finished a curious thing called "Nemi"—about a Roman ship that is actually sunk in some lake. I cannot think how he describes the things, when he has never seen them. If, as I hope, he goes to Italy next year, he should turn out something really good. Meanwhile we are hunting for a publisher. Herbert believes that a collection of short stories is hard to get published. It is, after all, better to write one long one.

But you must not think we only talk books. What we say on other topics cannot so easily be repeated! Oh, Mrs Lewin, he is a dear, and dearer than ever now that we have him at Sawston. Herbert, in a quiet way, has been making inquiries about those Cambridge friends of his. Nothing against them, but they seem to be terribly eccentric. None of them are good at games, and they spend all their spare time thinking and discussing. They discuss what one knows and what one never will know and what one had much better not know. Herbert says it is because they have not got enough to do.—Ever your grateful and affectionate friend,

Agnes Pembroke

Shelthorpe, 9 Sawston Park Road Sawston

Dear Mr. Silt,—

Thank you for the congratulations, which I have handed over to the delighted Rickie.

(The congratulations were really addressed to Agnes—a social blunder which Mr. Pembroke deftly corrects.)

I am sorry that the rumor reached you that I was not pleased. Anything pleases me that promises my sister's happiness, and I have known your cousin nearly as long as you have. It will be a very long engagement, for he must make his way first. The dear boy is not nearly as wealthy as he supposed; having no tastes, and hardly any expenses, he used to talk as if he were a millionaire. He must at least double his income before he can dream of more intimate ties. This has been a bitter pill, but I am glad to say that they have accepted it bravely.

Hoping that you and Mrs. Silt will profit by your week at Margate.-I remain, yours very sincerely,

Herbert Pembroke

Cadover, Wilts.

Dear Miss Pembroke,—Agnes—

I hear that you are going to marry my nephew. I have no idea what he is like, and wonder whether you would bring him that I may find out. Isn't September rather a nice month? You might have to go to Stone Henge, but with that exception would be left unmolested. I do hope you will manage the visit. We met once at Mrs. Lewin's, and I have a very clear recollection of you.—Believe me, yours sincerely,

Emily Failing

X

The rain tilted a little from the south-west. For the most part it fell from a grey cloud silently, but now and then the tilt increased, and a kind of sigh passed over the country as the drops lashed the walls, trees, shepherds, and other motionless objects that stood in their slanting career. At times the cloud would descend and visibly embrace the earth, to which it had only sent messages; and the earth itself would bring forth clouds—clouds of a whiter breed—which formed in shallow valleys and followed the courses of the streams. It seemed the beginning of life. Again God said, "Shall we divide the waters from the land or not? Was not the firmament labour and glory sufficient?" At all events it was the beginning of life pastoral, behind which imagination cannot travel.

Yet complicated people were getting wet—not only the shepherds. For instance, the piano-tuner was sopping. So was the vicar's wife. So were the lieutenant and the peevish damsels in his Battleston car. Gallantry, charity, and art pursued their various missions, perspiring and muddy, while out on the slopes beyond them stood the eternal man and the eternal dog, guarding eternal sheep until the world is vegetarian.

Inside an arbour—which faced east, and thus avoided the bad weather—there sat a complicated person who was dry. She looked at the drenched world with a pleased expression, and would smile when a cloud would lay down on the village, or when the rain sighed louder than usual against her solid shelter. Ink, paperclips, and foolscap paper were on the table before her, and she could also reach an umbrella, a waterproof, a walking-stick, and an electric bell. Her age was between elderly and old, and her forehead was wrinkled with an expression of slight but perpetual pain. But the lines round her mouth indicated that she had laughed a great deal during her life, just as the clean tight skin round her eyes perhaps indicated that she had not often cried. She was dressed in brown silk. A brown silk shawl lay most becomingly over her beautiful hair.

After long thought she wrote on the paper in front of her, "The subject of this memoir first saw the light at Wolverhampton on May the 14th, 1842." She laid down her pen and said "Ugh!" A robin hopped in and she welcomed him. A sparrow followed and she stamped her foot. She watched some thick white water which was sliding like a snake down the gutter of the gravel path. It had just appeared. It must have escaped from a hollow in the chalk up behind. The earth could absorb no longer. The lady did not think of all this, for she hated questions of whence and wherefore, and the ways of the earth ("our dull stepmother") bored her unspeakably. But the water, just the snake of water, was amusing, and she flung her golosh at it to dam it up. Then she wrote feverishly, "The subject of this memoir first saw the light in the middle of the night. It was twenty to eleven. His pa was a parson, but he was not his pa's son, and never went to heaven." There was the sound of a train, and presently white smoke appeared, rising laboriously through the heavy air. It distracted her, and for about a quarter of an hour she sat perfectly still, doing nothing. At last she pushed the spoilt paper aside, took afresh piece, and was beginning to write, "On May the 14th, 1842," when there was a crunch on the gravel, and a furious voice said, "I am sorry for Flea Thompson."

"I daresay I am sorry for him too," said the lady; her voice was languid and pleasant. "Who is he?"

"Flea's a liar, and the next time we meet he'll be a football." Off slipped a sodden ulster. He hung it up angrily upon a peg: the arbour provided several.

"But who is he, and why has he that disastrous name?"

"Flea? Fleance. All the Thompsons are named out of Shakespeare. He grazes the Rings."

"Ah, I see. A pet lamb."

"Lamb! Shepherd!"

"One of my Shepherds?"

"The last time I go with his sheep. But not the last time he sees me. I am sorry for him. He dodged me today."

"Do you mean to say"—she became animated—"that you have been out in the wet keeping the sheep of Flea Thompson?"

"I had to." He blew on his fingers and took off his cap. Water trickled over his unshaven cheeks. His hair was so wet that it seemed worked upon his scalp in bronze.

"Get away, bad dog!" screamed the lady, for he had given himself a shake and spattered her dress with water. He was a powerful boy of twenty, admirably muscular, but rather too broad for his height. People called him "Podge" until they were dissuaded. Then they called him "Stephen" or "Mr. Wonham." Then he said, "You can call me Podge if you like."

"As for Flea—!" he began tempestuously. He sat down by her, and with much heavy breathing told the story,—"Flea has a girl at Wintersbridge, and I had to go with his sheep while he went to see her. Two hours. We agreed. Half an hour to go, an hour to kiss his girl, and half an hour back—and he had my bike. Four hours! Four hours and seven minutes I was on the Rings, with a fool of a dog, and sheep doing all they knew to get the turnips."

"My farm is a mystery to me," said the lady, stroking her fingers.

"Some day you must really take me to see it. It must be like a Gilbert and Sullivan opera, with a chorus of agitated employers. How is it that I have escaped? Why have I never been summoned to milk the cows, or flay the pigs, or drive the young bullocks to the pasture?"

X

He looked at her with astonishingly blue eyes—the only dry things he had about him. He could not see into her: she would have puzzled an older and clever man. He may have seen round her.

"A thing of beauty you are not. But I sometimes think you are a joy for ever."

"I beg your pardon?"

"Oh, you understand right enough," she exclaimed irritably, and then smiled, for he was conceited, and did not like being told that he was not a thing of beauty. "Large and steady feet," she continued, "have this disadvantage—you can knock down a man, but you will never knock down a woman."

"I don't know what you mean. I'm not likely—"

"Oh, never mind—never, never mind. I was being funny. I repent. Tell me about the sheep. Why did you go with them?"

"I did tell you. I had to."

"But why?"

"He had to see his girl."

"But why?"

His eyes shot past her again. It was so obvious that the man had to see his girl. For two hours though—not for four hours seven minutes.

"Did you have any lunch?"

"I don't hold with regular meals."

"Did you have a book?"

"I don't hold with books in the open. None of the older men read."

"Did you commune with yourself, or don't you hold with that?"

"Oh Lord, don't ask me!"

"You distress me. You rob the Pastoral of its lingering romance. Is there no poetry and no thought in England? Is there no one, in all these downs, who warbles with eager thought the Doric lay?"

"Chaps sing to themselves at times, if you mean that."

"I dream of Arcady. I open my eyes. Wiltshire. Of Amaryllis: Flea Thompson's girl. Of the pensive shepherd, twitching his mantle blue: you in an ulster. Aren't you sorry for me?"

"May I put in a pipe?"

"By all means put a pipe in. In return, tell me of what you were thinking for the four hours and the seven minutes."

He laughed shyly. "You do ask a man such questions."

"Did you simply waste the time?"

"I suppose so."

"I thought that Colonel Robert Ingersoll says you must be strenuous."

At the sound of this name he whisked open a little cupboard, and declaring, "I haven't a moment to spare," took out of it a pile of "Clarion" and other reprints, adorned as to their covers with bald or bearded apostles of humanity. Selecting a bald one, he began at once to read, occasionally exclaiming, "That's got them," "That's knocked Genesis," with similar ejaculations of an aspiring mind. She glanced at the pile. Reran, minus the style. Darwin, minus the modesty. A comic edition of the book of Job, by "Excelsior," Pittsburgh, Pa. "The Beginning of Life," with diagrams. "Angel or Ape?" by Mrs. Julia P. Chunk. She was amused, and wondered idly what was passing within his narrow but not uninteresting brain. Did he suppose that he was going to "find out"? She had tried once herself, but had since subsided into a sprightly orthodoxy. Why didn't he read poetry, instead of wasting his time between books like these and country like that?

The cloud parted, and the increase of light made her look up. Over the valley she saw a grave sullen down, and on its flanks a little brown smudge—her sheep, together with her shepherd, Fleance Thompson, returned to his duties at last. A trickle of water came through the arbour roof. She shrieked in dismay.

"That's all right," said her companion, moving her chair, but still keeping his place in his book.

She dried up the spot on the manuscript. Then she wrote: "Anthony Eustace Failing, the subject of this memoir, was born at Wolverhampton." But she wrote no more. She was fidgety. Another drop fell from the roof. Likewise an earwig. She wished she had not been so playful in flinging her golosh into the path. The boy who was overthrowing religion breathed somewhat heavily as he did so. Another earwig. She touched the electric bell.

"I'm going in," she observed. "It's far too wet." Again the cloud parted and caused her to add, "Weren't you rather kind to Flea?" But he was deep in the book. He read like a poor person, with lips apart and a finger that followed the print. At times he scratched his ear, or ran his tongue along a straggling blonde moustache. His face had after all a certain beauty: at all events the colouring was regal—a steady crimson from throat to forehead: the sun and the winds had worked on him daily ever since he was born. "The face of a strong man," thought the lady. "Let him thank his stars he isn't a silent strong man, or I'd turn him into the gutter." Suddenly it struck her that he was like an Irish terrier. He worried infinity as if it was a bone. Gnashing his teeth, he tried to carry the eternal subtleties by violence. As a man he often bored her, for he was always saying and doing the same things. But as a philosopher he really was a joy for ever, an inexhaustible buffoon. Taking up her pen, she began to caricature him. She drew a rabbit-warren where rabbits were at play in four dimensions. Before she had introduced the principal figure, she was interrupted by the footman. He had come up from the house to answer the bell. On seeing her he uttered a respectful cry.

"Madam! Are you here? I am very sorry. I looked for you everywhere. Mr. Elliot and Miss Pembroke arrived nearly an hour ago."

"Oh dear, oh dear!" exclaimed Mrs. Failing. "Take these papers. Where's the umbrella? Mr. Stephen will hold it over me. You hurry back and apologize. Are they happy?"

"Miss Pembroke inquired after you, madam."

"Have they had tea?"

"Yes, madam."

"Leighton!"

"Yes, sir."

"I believe you knew she was here all the time. You didn't want to wet your pretty skin."

"You must not call me 'she' to the servants," said Mrs. Failing as they walked away, she limping with a stick, he holding a great umbrella over her. "I will not have it." Then more pleasantly, "And don't tell him he lies. We all lie. I knew quite well they were coming by the four-six train. I saw it pass."

"That reminds me. Another child run over at the Roman crossing. Whish—bang—dead."

"Oh my foot! Oh my foot, my foot!" said Mrs. Failing, and paused to take breath.

"Bad?" he asked callously.

Leighton, with bowed head, passed them with the manuscript and disappeared among the laurels. The twinge of pain, which had been slight, passed away, and they proceeded, descending a green airless corridor which opened into the gravel drive.

"Isn't it odd," said Mrs. Failing, "that the Greeks should be enthusiastic about laurels—that Apollo should pursue any one who could possibly turn into such a frightful plant? What do you make of Rickie?"

"Oh, I don't know."

"Shall I lend you his story to read?"

He made no reply.

"Don't you think, Stephen, that a person in your precarious position ought to be civil to my relatives?"

"Sorry, Mrs. Failing. I meant to be civil. I only hadn't—anything to say."

She a laughed. "Are you a dear boy? I sometimes wonder; or are you a brute?"

Again he had nothing to say. Then she laughed more mischievously, and said—

"How can you be either, when you are a philosopher? Would you mind telling me—I am so anxious to learn—what happens to people when they die?"

"Don't ask ME." He knew by bitter experience that she was making fun of him.

"Oh, but I do ask you. Those paper books of yours are so up-to-date. For instance, what has happened to the child you say was killed on the line?"

The rain increased. The drops pattered hard on the leaves, and outside the corridor men and women were struggling, however stupidly, with the facts of life. Inside it they wrangled. She teased the boy, and laughed at his theories, and proved that no man can be an agnostic who has a sense of humour. Suddenly she stopped, not through any skill of his, but because she had remembered some words of Bacon: "The true atheist is he whose hands are cauterized by holy things." She thought of her distant youth. The world was not so humorous then, but it had been more important. For a moment she respected her companion, and determined to vex him no more.

They left the shelter of the laurels, crossed the broad drive, and were inside the house at last. She had got quite wet, for the weather would not let her play the simple life with impunity. As for him, he seemed a piece of the wet.

"Look here," she cried, as he hurried up to his attic, "don't shave!"

He was delighted with the permission.

"I have an idea that Miss Pembroke is of the type that pretends to be unconventional and really isn't. I want to see how she takes it. Don't shave."

In the drawing-room she could hear the guests conversing in the subdued tones of those who have not been welcomed. Having changed her dress and glanced at the poems of Milton, she went to them, with uplifted hands of apology and horror.

"But I must have tea," she announced, when they had assured her that they understood. "Otherwise I shall start by being cross. Agnes, stop me. Give me tea."

Agnes, looking pleased, moved to the table and served her hostess. Rickie followed with a pagoda of sandwiches and little cakes.

"I feel twenty-seven years younger. Rickie, you are so like your father. I feel it is twenty-seven years ago, and that he is bringing your mother to see me for the first time. It is curious—almost terrible—to see history repeating itself."

The remark was not tactful.

"I remember that visit well," she continued thoughtfully, "I suppose it was a wonderful visit, though we none of us knew it at the time. We all fell in love with your mother. I wish she would have fallen in love with us. She couldn't bear me, could she?"

"I never heard her say so, Aunt Emily."

"No; she wouldn't. I am sure your father said so, though. My dear boy, don't look so shocked. Your father and I hated each other. He said so, I said so, I say so; say so too. Then we shall start fair.—Just a cocoanut cake.—Agnes, don't you agree that it's always best to speak out?"

"Oh, rather, Mrs. Failing. But I'm shockingly straightforward."

"So am I," said the lady. "I like to get down to the bedrock.—Hullo! Slippers? Slippers in the drawingroom?"

A young man had come in silently. Agnes observed with a feeling of regret that he had not shaved. Rickie, after a moment's hesitation, remembered who it was, and shook hands with him. "You've grown since I saw you last."

He showed his teeth amiably.

"How long was that?" asked Mrs. Failing.

"Three years, wasn't it? Came over from the Ansells—friends."

"How disgraceful, Rickie! Why don't you come and see me oftener?"

He could not retort that she never asked him.

"Agnes will make you come. Oh, let me introduce Mr. Wonham—Miss Pembroke."

"I am deputy hostess," said Agnes. "May I give you some tea?"

"Thank you, but I have had a little beer."

"It is one of the shepherds," said Mrs. Failing, in low tones.

X

Agnes smiled rather wildly. Mrs. Lewin had warned her that Cadover was an extraordinary place, and that one must never be astonished at anything. A shepherd in the drawing-room! No harm. Still one ought to know whether it was a shepherd or not. At all events he was in gentleman's clothing. She was anxious not to start with a blunder, and therefore did not talk to the young fellow, but tried to gather what he was from the demeanour of Rickie.

"I am sure, Mrs. Failing, that you need not talk of 'making' people come to Cadover. There will be no difficulty, I should say."

"Thank you, my dear. Do you know who once said those exact words to me?"

"Who?"

"Rickie's mother."

"Did she really?"

"My sister-in-law was a dear. You will have heard Rickie's praises, but now you must hear mine. I never knew a woman who was so unselfish and yet had such capacities for life."

"Does one generally exclude the other?" asked Rickie.

"Unselfish people, as a rule, are deathly dull. They have no colour. They think of other people because it is easier. They give money because they are too stupid or too idle to spend it properly on themselves. That was the beauty of your mother—she gave away, but she also spent on herself, or tried to."

The light faded out of the drawing-room, in spite of it being September and only half-past six. From her low chair Agnes could see the trees by the drive, black against a blackening sky. That drive was half a mile long, and she was praising its gravelled surface when Rickie called in a voice of alarm, "I say, when did our train arrive?"

"Four-six."

"I said so."

"It arrived at four-six on the time-table," said Mr. Wonham. "I want to know when it got to the station?"

"I tell you again it was punctual. I tell you I looked at my watch. I can do no more."

Agnes was amazed. Was Rickie mad? A minute ago and they were boring each other over dogs. What had happened?

"Now, now! Quarrelling already?" asked Mrs. Failing.

The footman, bringing a lamp, lit up two angry faces.

"He says—"

"He says—"

"He says we ran over a child."

"So you did. You ran over a child in the village at four-seven by my watch. Your train was late. You couldn't have got to the station till four-ten."

"I don't believe it. We had passed the village by four-seven. Agnes, hadn't we passed the village? It must have been an express that ran over the child."

"Now is it likely"—he appealed to the practical world—"is it likely that the company would run a stopping train and then an express three minutes after it?"

"A child—" said Rickie. "I can't believe that the train killed a child." He thought of their journey. They were alone in the carriage. As the train slackened speed he had caught her for a moment in his arms. The rain beat on the windows, but they were in heaven.

"You've got to believe it," said the other, and proceeded to "rub it in." His healthy, irritable face drew close to Rickie's. "Two children were kicking and screaming on the Roman crossing. Your train, being late, came down on them. One of them was pulled off the line, but the other was caught. How will you get out of that?"

"And how will you get out of it?" cried Mrs. Failing, turning the tables on him. "Where's the child now? What has happened to its soul? You must know, Agnes, that this young gentleman is a philosopher."

"Oh, drop all that," said Mr. Wonham, suddenly collapsing.

"Drop it? Where? On my nice carpet?"

"I hate philosophy," remarked Agnes, trying to turn the subject, for she saw that it made Rickie unhappy.

"So do I. But I daren't say so before Stephen. He despises us women."

"No, I don't," said the victim, swaying to and fro on the window-sill, whither he had retreated.

"Yes, he does. He won't even trouble to answer us. Stephen! Podge! Answer me. What has happened to the child's soul?"

He flung open the window and leant from them into the dusk. They heard him mutter something about a bridge.

"What did I tell you? He won't answer my question."

The delightful moment was approaching when the boy would lose his temper: she knew it by a certain tremor in his heels.

"There wants a bridge," he exploded. "A bridge instead of all this rotten talk and the level-crossing. It wouldn't break you to build a two-arch bridge. Then the child's soul, as you call it—well, nothing would have happened to the child at all."

A gust of night air entered, accompanied by rain. The flowers in the vases rustled, and the flame of the lamp shot up and smoked the glass. Slightly irritated, she ordered him to close the window.

XI

Cadover was not a large house. But it is the largest house with which this story has dealings, and must always be thought of with respect. It was built about the year 1800, and favoured the architecture of ancient Rome—chiefly by means of five lank pilasters, which stretched from the top of it to the bottom. Between the pilasters was the glass front door, to the right of them the drawing room windows, to the left of them the windows of the dining-room, above them a triangular area, which the better-class servants knew as a "pendiment," and which had in its middle a small round hole, according to the usage of Palladio. The classical note was also sustained by eight grey steps which led from the building down into the drive, and by an attempt at a formal garden on the adjoining lawn. The lawn ended in a Ha-ha ("Ha! ha! who shall regard it?"), and thence the bare land sloped down into the village. The main garden (walled) was to the left as one faced the house, while to the right was that laurel avenue, leading up to Mrs. Failing's arbour.

It was a comfortable but not very attractive place, and, to a certain type of mind, its situation was not attractive either. From the distance it showed as a grey box, huddled against evergreens. There was no mystery about it. You saw it for miles. Its hill had none of the beetling romance of Devonshire, none of the subtle contours that prelude a cottage in Kent, but proffered its burden crudely, on a huge bare palm. "There's Cadover," visitors would say. "How small it still looks. We shall be late for lunch." And the view from the windows, though extensive, would not have been accepted by the Royal Academy. A valley, containing a stream, a road, a railway; over the valley fields of barley and wurzel, divided by no pretty hedges, and passing into a great and formless down—this was the outlook, desolate at all times, and almost terrifying beneath a cloudy sky. The down was called "Cadbury Range" ("Cocoa Squares" if you were young and funny), because high upon it—one cannot say "on the top," there being scarcely any tops in Wiltshire—because high upon it there stood a double circle of entrenchments. A bank of grass enclosed a ring of turnips, which enclosed a second bank of grass, which enclosed more turnips, and in the middle of the pattern grew one small tree. British? Roman? Saxon? Danish? The competent reader will decide. The Thompson family knew it to be far older than the Franco-German war. It was the property of Government. It was full of gold and dead soldiers who had fought with the soldiers on Castle Rings and been beaten. The road to Londinium, having forded the stream and crossed the valley road and the railway, passed up by these entrenchments. The road to London lay half a mile to the right of them.

To complete this survey one must mention the church and the farm, both of which lay over the stream in Cadford. Between them they ruled the village, one claiming the souls of the labourers, the other their bodies. If a man desired other religion or other employment he must leave. The church lay up by the railway, the farm was down by the water meadows. The vicar, a gentle charitable man scarcely realized his power, and never tried to abuse it. Mr. Wilbraham, the agent, was of another mould. He knew his place, and kept others to theirs: all society seemed spread before him like a map. The line between the county and the local, the line between the labourer and the artisan—he knew them all, and strengthened them with no uncertain touch. Everything with him was graduated—carefully graduated civility towards his superior, towards his inferiors carefully graduated incivility. So—for he was a thoughtful person—so alone, declared he, could things be kept together.

Perhaps the Comic Muse, to whom so much is now attributed, had caused his estate to be left to Mr. Failing. Mr. Failing was the author of some brilliant books on socialism,—that was why his wife married him—and for twenty-five years he reigned up at Cadover and tried to put his theories into practice. He believed that things could be kept together by accenting the similarities, not the differences of men. "We are all much more alike than we confess," was one of his favourite speeches. As a speech it sounded very well, and his wife had applauded; but when it resulted in hard work, evenings in the reading-rooms, mixed-parties, and long unobtrusive talks with dull people, she got bored. In her piquant way she declared that she was not going to love her husband, and succeeded. He took it quietly, but his brilliancy decreased. His health grew worse, and he knew that when he died there was no one to carry on his work. He felt, besides, that he had done very little. Toil as he would, he had not a practical mind, and could never dispense with Mr. Wilbraham. For all his tact, he would often stretch out the hand of brotherhood too soon, or withhold it when it would have been accepted. Most people misunderstood him, or only understood him when he was dead. In after years his reign became a golden age; but he counted a few disciples in his life-time, a few young labourers and tenant farmers, who swore tempestuously that he was not really a fool. This, he told himself, was as much as he deserved.

Cadover was inherited by his widow. She tried to sell it; she tried to let it; but she asked too much, and as it was neither a pretty place nor fertile, it was left on her hands. With many a groan she settled down to banishment. Wiltshire people, she declared, were the stupidest in England. She told them so to their faces, which made them no brighter. And their county was worthy of them: no distinction in it—no style—simply land.

But her wrath passed, or remained only as a graceful fretfulness. She made the house comfortable, and abandoned the farm to Mr. Wilbraham. With a good deal of care she selected a small circle of acquaintances, and had them to stop in the summer months. In the winter she would go to town and frequent the salons of the literary. As her lameness increased she moved about less, and at the time of her nephew's visit seldom left the place that had been forced upon her as a home. Just now she was busy. A prominent politician had quoted her husband. The young generation asked, "Who is this Mr. Failing?" and the publishers wrote, "Now is the time." She was collecting some essays and penning an introductory memoir.

Rickie admired his aunt, but did not care for her. She reminded him too much of his father. She had the same affliction, the same heartlessness, the same habit of taking life with a laugh—as if life is a pill! He also felt that she had neglected him. He would not have asked much: as for "prospects," they never entered his head, but she was his only near relative, and a little kindness and hospitality during the lonely years would have made incalculable difference. Now that he was happier and could bring her Agnes, she had asked him to stop at once. The sun as it rose next morning spoke to him of a new life. He too had a purpose and a value in the world at last. Leaning out of the window, he gazed at the earth washed clean and heard through the pure air the distant noises of the farm.

But that day nothing was to remain divine but the weather. His aunt, for reasons of her own, decreed that he should go for a ride with the Wonham boy. They were to look at Old Sarum, proceed thence to Salisbury, lunch there, see the sights, call on a certain canon for tea, and return to Cadover in the evening. The arrangement suited no one. He did not want to ride, but to be with Agnes; nor did Agnes want to be parted from him, nor Stephen to go with him. But the clearer the wishes of her guests became, the more determined was Mrs. Failing to disregard them. She smoothed away every difficulty, she converted every objection into a reason, and she ordered the horses for half-past nine.

"It is a bore," he grumbled as he sat in their little private sitting-room, breaking his finger-nails upon the coachman's gaiters. "I can't ride. I shall fall off. We should have been so happy here. It's just like Aunt Emily. Can't you imagine her saying afterwards, 'Lovers are absurd. I made a point of keeping them apart,' and then everybody laughing."

With a pretty foretaste of the future, Agnes knelt before him and did the gaiters up. "Who is this Mr. Wonham, by the bye?"

"I don't know. Some connection of Mr. Failing's, I think."

"Does he live here?"

"He used to be at school or something. He seems to have grown into a tiresome person."

"I suppose that Mrs. Failing has adopted him."

"I suppose so. I believe that she has been quite kind. I do hope she'll be kind to you this morning. I hate leaving you with her."

"Why, you say she likes me."

"Yes, but that wouldn't prevent—you see she doesn't mind what she says or what she repeats if it amuses her. If she thought it really funny, for instance, to break off our engagement, she'd try."

"Dear boy, what a frightful remark! But it would be funnier for us to see her trying. Whatever could she do?"

He kissed the hands that were still busy with the fastenings. "Nothing. I can't see one thing. We simply lie open to each other, you and I. There isn't one new corner in either of us that she could reveal. It's only that I always have in this house the most awful feeling of insecurity."

"Why?"

"If any one says or does a foolish thing it's always here. All the family breezes have started here. It's a kind of focus for aimed and aimless scandal. You know, when my father and mother had their special quarrel, my aunt was mixed up in it,—I never knew how or how much—but you may be sure she didn't calm things down, unless she found things more entertaining calm."

"Rickie! Rickie!" cried the lady from the garden, "Your riding-master's impatient."

"We really oughtn't to talk of her like this here," whispered Agnes. "It's a horrible habit."

"The habit of the country, Agnes. Ugh, this gossip!" Suddenly he flung his arms over her. "Dear—dear—let's beware of I don't know what—of nothing at all perhaps."

"Oh, buck up!" yelled the irritable Stephen. "Which am I to shorten—left stirrup or right?"

"Left!" shouted Agnes.

"How many holes?"

They hurried down. On the way she said: "I'm glad of the warning. Now I'm prepared. Your aunt will get nothing out of me."

Her betrothed tried to mount with the wrong foot according to his invariable custom. She also had to pick up his whip. At last they started, the boy showing off pretty consistently, and she was left alone with her hostess.

"Dido is quiet as a lamb," said Mrs. Failing, "and Stephen is a good fielder. What a blessing it is to have cleared out the men. What shall you and I do this heavenly morning?"

"I'm game for anything."

"Have you quite unpacked?"

"Yes."

"Any letters to write?" No.

"Then let's go to my arbour. No, we won't. It gets the morning sun, and it'll be too hot today." Already she regretted clearing out the men. On such a morning she would have liked to drive, but her third animal had gone lame. She feared, too, that Miss Pembroke was going to bore her. However, they did go to the arbour. In languid tones she pointed out the various objects of interest.

"There's the Cad, which goes into the something, which goes into the Avon. Cadbury Rings opposite, Cadchurch to the extreme left: you can't see it. You were there last night. It is famous for the drunken parson and the railway-station. Then

Cad Dauntsey. Then Cadford, that side of the stream, connected with Cadover, this. Observe the fertility of the Wiltshire mind."

"A terrible lot of Cads," said Agnes brightly.

Mrs. Failing divided her guests into those who made this joke and those who did not. The latter class was very small.

"The vicar of Cadford—not the nice drunkard—declares the name is really 'Chadford,' and he worried on till I put up a window to St. Chad in our church. His Cambridge wife pronounces it 'Hyadford.' I could smack them both. How do you like Podge? Ah! you jump; I meant you to. How do you like Podge Wonham?"

"Very nice," said Agnes, laughing.

"Nice! He is a hero."

There was a long interval of silence. Each lady looked, without much interest, at the view. Mrs. Failing's attitude towards Nature was severely aesthetic—an attitude more sterile than the severely practical. She applied the test of beauty to shadow and odour and sound; they never filled her with reverence or excitement; she never knew them as a resistless trinity that may intoxicate the worshipper with joy. If she liked a ploughed field, it was only as a spot of colour—not also as a hint of the endless strength of the earth. And today she could approve of one cloud, but object to its fellow. As for Miss Pembroke, she was not approving or objecting at all. "A hero?" she queried, when the interval had passed. Her voice was indifferent, as if she had been thinking of other things.

"A hero? Yes. Didn't you notice how heroic he was?"

"I don't think I did."

"Not at dinner? Ah, Agnes, always look out for heroism at dinner. It is their great time. They live up to the stiffness of their shirt fronts. Do you mean to say that you never noticed how he set down Rickie?"

"Oh, that about poetry!" said Agnes, laughing. "Rickie would not mind it for a moment. But why do you single out that as heroic?"

"To snub people! to set them down! to be rude to them! to make them feel small! Surely that's the lifework of a hero?"

"I shouldn't have said that. And as a matter of fact Mr. Wonham was wrong over the poetry. I made Rickie look it up afterwards."

"But of course. A hero always is wrong."

"To me," she persisted, rather gently, "a hero has always been a strong wonderful being, who champions—"

"Ah, wait till you are the dragon! I have been a dragon most of my life, I think. A dragon that wants nothing but a peaceful cave. Then in comes the strong, wonderful, delightful being, and gains a princess by piercing my hide. No, seriously, my dear Agnes, the chief characteristics of a hero are infinite disregard for the feelings of others, plus general inability to understand them."

"But surely Mr. Wonham—"

"Yes; aren't we being unkind to the poor boy. Ought we to go on talking?"

Agnes waited, remembering the warnings of Rickie, and thinking that anything she said might perhaps be repeated.

"Though even if he was here he wouldn't understand what we are saying."

"Wouldn't understand?"

Mrs. Failing gave the least flicker of an eye towards her companion. "Did you take him for clever?"

"I don't think I took him for anything." She smiled. "I have been thinking of other things, and another boy."

"But do think for a moment of Stephen. I will describe how he spent yesterday. He rose at eight. From eight to eleven he sang. The song was called, 'Father's boots will soon fit Willie.' He stopped once to say to the footman, 'She'll never finish her book. She idles: 'She' being I. At eleven he went out, and stood in the rain till four, but had the luck to see a child run over at the level-crossing. By half-past four he had knocked the bottom out of Christianity."

Agnes looked bewildered.

"Aren't you impressed? I was. I told him that he was on no account to unsettle the vicar. Open that cupboard, one of those sixpenny books tells Podge that he's made of hard little black things, another that he's made of brown things, larger and squashy. There seems a discrepancy, but anything is better for a thoughtful youth than to be made in the Garden of Eden. Let us eliminate the poetic, at whatever cost to the probable." When for a moment she spoke more gravely. "Here he is at twenty, with nothing to hold on by. I don't know what's to be done. I suppose it's my fault. But I've never had any bother over the Church of England; have you?"

"Of course I go with my Church," said Miss Pembroke, who hated this style of conversation. "I don't know, I'm sure. I think you should consult a man."

"Would Rickie help me?"

"Rickie would do anything he can." And Mrs. Failing noted the half official way in which she vouched for her lover. "But of course Rickie is a little—complicated. I doubt whether Mr. Wonham would understand him. He wants—doesn't he?—some one who's a little more assertive and more accustomed to boys. Some one more like my brother."

"Agnes!" she seized her by the arm. "Do you suppose that Mr. Pembroke would undertake my Podge?"

She shook her head. "His time is so filled up. He gets a boarding-house next term. Besides—after all I don't know what Herbert would do."

"Morality. He would teach him morality. The Thirty-Nine Articles may come of themselves, but if you have no morals you come to grief. Morality is all I demand from Mr. Herbert Pembroke. He shall be excused the use of the globes. You know, of course, that Stephen's expelled from a public school? He stole."

The school was not a public one, and the expulsion, or rather request for removal, had taken place when Stephen was fourteen. A violent spasm of dishonesty—such as often heralds the approach of manhood—had overcome him. He stole everything, especially what was difficult to steal, and hid the plunder beneath a loose plank in the passage. He was betrayed by the inclusion of a ham. This was the crisis of his career. His benefactress was just then rather bored with him. He had stopped being a pretty boy, and she rather doubted whether she would see him through. But she was so raged with the letters of the schoolmaster, and so delighted with those of the criminal, that she had him back and gave him a prize.

"No," said Agnes, "I didn't know. I should be happy to speak to Herbert, but, as I said, his time will be very full. But I know he has friends who make a speciality of weakly or—or unusual boys."

"My dear, I've tried it. Stephen kicked the weakly boys and robbed apples with the unusual ones. He was expelled again."

Agnes began to find Mrs. Failing rather tiresome. Wherever you trod on her, she seemed to slip away from beneath your feet. Agnes liked to know where she was and where other people were as well. She said: "My brother thinks a great deal of home life. I daresay he'd think that Mr. Wonham is best where he is—with you. You have been so kind to him. You"—she paused—"have been to him both father and mother."

"I'm too hot," was Mrs. Failing's reply. It seemed that Miss Pembroke had at last touched a topic on which she was reticent. She rang the electric bell,—it was only to tell the footman to take the reprints to Mr. Wonham's room,—and then murmuring something about work, proceeded herself to the house.

"Mrs. Failing—" said Agnes, who had not expected such a speedy end to their chat.

"Call me Aunt Emily. My dear?"

"Aunt Emily, what did you think of that story Rickie sent you?"

"It is bad," said Mrs. Failing. "But. But. But." Then she escaped, having told the truth, and yet leaving a pleasurable impression behind her.

XII

The excursion to Salisbury was but a poor business—in fact, Rickie never got there. They were not out of the drive before Mr. Wonham began doing acrobatics. He showed Rickie how very quickly he could turn round in his saddle and sit with his face to Aeneas's tail. "I see," said Rickie coldly, and became almost cross when they arrived in this condition at the gate behind the house, for he had to open it, and was afraid of falling. As usual, he anchored just beyond the fastenings, and then had to turn Dido, who seemed as long as a battleship. To his relief a man came forward, and murmuring, "Worst gate in the parish," pushed it wide and held it respectfully. "Thank you," cried Rickie; "many thanks." But Stephen, who was riding into the world back first, said majestically, "No, no; it doesn't count. You needn't think it does. You make it worse by touching your hat. Four hours and seven minutes! You'll see me again." The man answered nothing.

"Eh, but I'll hurt him," he chanted, as he swung into position. "That was Flea. Eh, but he's forgotten my fists; eh, but I'll hurt him."

"Why?" ventured Rickie. Last night, over cigarettes, he had been bored to death by the story of Flea. The boy had a little reminded him of Gerald—the Gerald of history, not the Gerald of romance. He was more genial, but there was the same brutality, the same peevish insistence on the pound of flesh.

"Hurt him till he learns."

"Learns what?"

"Learns, of course," retorted Stephen. Neither of them was very civil. They did not dislike each other, but they each wanted to be somewhere else—exactly the situation that Mrs. Failing had expected.

"He behaved badly," said Rickie, "because he is poorer than we are, and more ignorant. Less money has been spent on teaching him to behave."

"Well, I'll teach him for nothing."

"Perhaps his fists are stronger than yours!"

"They aren't. I looked."

After this conversation flagged. Rickie glanced back at Cadover, and thought of the insipid day that lay before him. Generally he was attracted by fresh people, and Stephen was almost fresh: they had been to him symbols of the unknown, and all that they did was interesting. But now he cared for the unknown no longer. He knew.

XII

Mr. Wilbraham passed them in his dog-cart, and lifted his hat to his employer's nephew. Stephen he ignored: he could not find him on the map.

"Good morning," said Rickie. "What a lovely morning!"

"I say," called the other, "another child dead!" Mr. Wilbraham, who had seemed inclined to chat, whipped up his horse and left them.

"There goes an out and outer," said Stephen; and then, as if introducing an entirely new subject—"Don't you think Flea Thompson treated me disgracefully?"

"I suppose he did. But I'm scarcely the person to sympathize." The allusion fell flat, and he had to explain it. "I should have done the same myself,—promised to be away two hours, and stopped four."

"Stopped-oh—oh, I understand. You being in love, you mean?"

He smiled and nodded.

"Oh, I've no objection to Flea loving. He says he can't help it. But as long as my fists are stronger, he's got to keep it in line."

"In line?"

"A man like that, when he's got a girl, thinks the rest can go to the devil. He goes cutting his work and breaking his word. Wilbraham ought to sack him. I promise you when I've a girl I'll keep her in line, and if she turns nasty, I'll get another."

Rickie smiled and said no more. But he was sorry that any one should start life with such a creed—all the more sorry because the creed caricatured his own. He too believed that life should be in a line—a line of enormous length, full of countless interests and countless figures, all well beloved. But woman was not to be "kept" to this line. Rather did she advance it continually, like some triumphant general, making each unit still more interesting, still more lovable, than it had been before. He loved Agnes, not only for herself, but because she was lighting up the human world. But he could scarcely explain this to an inexperienced animal, nor did he make the attempt.

For a long time they proceeded in silence. The hill behind Cadover was in harvest, and the horses moved regretfully between the sheaves. Stephen had picked a grass leaf, and was blowing catcalls upon it. He blew very well, and this morning all his soul went into the wail. For he was ill. He was tortured with the feeling that he could not get away and do—do something, instead of being civil to this anaemic prig. Four hours in the rain was better than this: he had not wanted to fidget in the rain. But now the air was like wine, and the stubble was smelling of wet, and over his head white clouds trundled more slowly and more seldom through broadening tracts of blue. There never had been such a morning, and he shut up his eyes and called to it. And whenever he called, Rickie shut up his eyes and winced.

At last the blade broke. "We don't go quick, do we" he remarked, and looked on the weedy track for another.

"I wish you wouldn't let me keep you. If you were alone you would be galloping or something of that sort."

"I was told I must go your pace," he said mournfully. "And you promised Miss Pembroke not to hurry."

"Well, I'll disobey." But he could not rise above a gentle trot, and even that nearly jerked him out of the saddle.

"Sit like this," said Stephen. "Can't you see like this?" Rickie lurched forward, and broke his thumb nail on the horse's neck. It bled a little, and had to be bound up.

"Thank you—awfully kind—no tighter, please—I'm simply spoiling your day."

"I can't think how a man can help riding. You've only to leave it to the horse so!—so!—just as you leave it to water in swimming."

Rickie left it to Dido, who stopped immediately.

"I said LEAVE it." His voice rose irritably. "I didn't say 'die.' Of course she stops if you die. First you sit her as if you're Sandow exercising, and then you sit like a corpse. Can't you tell her you're alive? That's all she wants."

In trying to convey the information, Rickie dropped his whip. Stephen picked it up and rammed it into the belt of his own Norfolk jacket. He was scarcely a fashionable horseman. He was not even graceful. But he rode as a living man, though Rickie was too much bored to notice it. Not a muscle in him was idle, not a muscle working hard. When he returned from the gallop his limbs were still unsatisfied and his manners still irritable. He did not know that he was ill: he knew nothing about himself at all.

"Like a howdah in the Zoo," he grumbled. "Mother Failing will buy elephants." And he proceeded to criticize his benefactress. Rickie, keenly alive to bad taste, tried to stop him, and gained instead a criticism of religion. Stephen overthrew the Mosaic cosmogony. He pointed out the discrepancies in the Gospels. He levelled his wit against the most beautiful spire in the world, now rising against the southern sky. Between whiles he went for a gallop. After a time Rickie stopped listening, and simply went his way. For Dido was a perfect mount, and as indifferent to the motions of Aeneas as if she was strolling in the Elysian fields. He had had a bad night, and the strong air made him sleepy. The wind blew from the Plain. Cadover and its valley had disappeared, and though they had not climbed much and could not see far, there was a sense of infinite space. The fields were enormous, like fields on the Continent, and the brilliant sun showed up their colours well. The green of the turnips, the gold of the harvest, and the brown of the newly turned clods, were each contrasted with morsels of grey down. But the general effect was pale, or rather silvery, for Wiltshire is not a county of heavy tints. Beneath these colours lurked the unconquerable chalk, and wherever the soil was poor it emerged. The grassy track, so gay with scabious and bedstraw, was snow-white at the bottom of its ruts. A dazzling amphitheatre gleamed in the flank of a distant hill, cut for some Olympian audience. And here and there, whatever the surface crop, the earth broke into little embankments, little ditches, little mounds: there had been no lack of drama to solace the gods.

XII

In Cadover, the perilous house, Agnes had already parted from Mrs. Failing. His thoughts returned to her. Was she, the soul of truth, in safety? Was her purity vexed by the lies and selfishness? Would she elude the caprice which had, he vaguely knew, caused suffering before? Ah, the frailty of joy! Ah, the myriads of longings that pass without fruition, and the turf grows over them! Better men, women as noble—they had died up here and their dust had been mingled, but only their dust. These are morbid thoughts, but who dare contradict them? There is much good luck in the world, but it is luck. We are none of us safe. We are children, playing or quarreling on the line, and some of us have Rickie's temperament, or his experiences, and admit it.

So he mused, that anxious little speck, and all the land seemed to comment on his fears and on his love.

Their path lay upward, over a great bald skull, half grass, half stubble. It seemed each moment there would be a splendid view. The view never came, for none of the inclines were sharp enough, and they moved over the skull for many minutes, scarcely shifting a landmark or altering the blue fringe of the distance. The spire of Salisbury did alter, but very slightly, rising and falling like the mercury in a thermometer. At the most it would be half hidden; at the least the tip would show behind the swelling barrier of earth. They passed two elder-trees—a great event. The bare patch, said Stephen, was owing to the gallows. Rickie nodded. He had lost all sense of incident. In this great solitude—more solitary than any Alpine range—he and Agnes were floating alone and for ever, between the shapeless earth and the shapeless clouds. An immense silence seemed to move towards them. A lark stopped singing, and they were glad of it. They were approaching the Throne of God. The silence touched them; the earth and all danger dissolved, but ere they quite vanished Rickie heard himself saying, "Is it exactly what we intended?"

"Yes," said a man's voice; "it's the old plan." They were in another valley. Its sides were thick with trees. Down it ran another stream and another road: it, too, sheltered a string of villages. But all was richer, larger, and more beautiful—the valley of the Avon below Amesbury.

"I've been asleep!" said Rickie, in awestruck tones.

"Never!" said the other facetiously. "Pleasant dreams?"

"Perhaps—I'm really tired of apologizing to you. How long have you been holding me on?"

"All in the day's work." He gave him back the reins.

"Where's that round hill?"

"Gone where the good niggers go. I want a drink."

This is Nature's joke in Wiltshire—her one joke. You toil on windy slopes, and feel very primeval. You are miles from your fellows, and lo! a little valley full of elms and cottages. Before Rickie had waked up to it, they had stopped by a thatched public-house, and Stephen was yelling like a maniac for beer.

There was no occasion to yell. He was not very thirsty, and they were quite ready to serve him. Nor need he have drunk in the saddle, with the air of a warrior who carries important dispatches and has not the time to dismount. A real soldier, bound on a similar errand, rode up to the inn, and Stephen feared that he would yell louder, and was hostile. But they made friends and treated each other, and slanged the proprietor and ragged the pretty girls; while Rickie, as each wave of vulgarity burst over him, sunk his head lower and lower, and wished that the earth would swallow him up. He was only used to Cambridge, and to a very small corner of that. He and his friends there believed in free speech. But they spoke freely about generalities. They were scientific and philosophic. They would have shrunk from the empirical freedom that results from a little beer.

That was what annoyed him as he rode down the new valley with two chattering companions. He was more skilled than they were in the principles of human existence, but he was not so indecently familiar with the examples. A sordid village scandal—such as Stephen described as a huge joke—sprang from certain defects in human nature, with which he was theoretically acquainted. But the example! He blushed at it like a maiden lady, in spite of its having a parallel in a beautiful idyll of Theocritus. Was experience going to be such a splendid thing after all? Were the outside of houses so very beautiful?

"That's spicy!" the soldier was saying. "Got any more like that?"

"I'se got a pome," said Stephen, and drew a piece of paper from his pocket. The valley had broadened. Old Sarum rose before them, ugly and majestic.

"Write this yourself?" he asked, chuckling.

"Rather," said Stephen, lowering his head and kissing Aeneas between the ears.

"But who's old Em'ly?" Rickie winced and frowned.

"Now you're asking.

"Old Em'ly she limps, And as—"

"I am so tired," said Rickie. Why should he stand it any longer?

He would go home to the woman he loved. "Do you mind if I give up Salisbury?"

"But we've seen nothing!" cried Stephen.

"I shouldn't enjoy anything, I am so absurdly tired."

"Left turn, then—all in the day's work." He bit at his moustache angrily.

"Good gracious me, man!—of course I'm going back alone. I'm not going to spoil your day. How could you think it of me?"

Stephen gave a loud sigh of relief. "If you do want to go home, here's your whip. Don't fall off. Say to her you wanted it, or there might be ructions."

"Certainly. Thank you for your kind care of me."

"'Old Em'ly she limps, And as—'"

Soon he was out of earshot. Soon they were lost to view. Soon they were out of his thoughts. He forgot the coarseness and the drinking and the ingratitude. A few months ago he would not have forgotten so quickly, and he might also have detected something else. But a lover is dogmatic. To him the world shall be beautiful and pure. When it is not, he ignores it.

"He's not tired," said Stephen to the soldier; "he wants his girl." And they winked at each other, and cracked jokes over the eternal comedy of love. They asked each other if they'd let a girl spoil a morning's ride. They both exhibited a profound cynicism. Stephen, who was quite without ballast, described the household at Cadover: he should say that Rickie would find Miss Pembroke kissing the footman.

"I say the footman's kissing old Em'ly."

"Jolly day," said Stephen. His voice was suddenly constrained. He was not sure whether he liked the soldier after all, nor whether he had been wise in showing him his compositions.

"'Old Em'ly she limps, And as—'"

"All right, Thomas. That'll do."

"Old Em'ly—'"

"I wish you'd dry up, like a good fellow. This is the lady's horse, you know, hang it, after all."

"In-deed!"

"Don't you see—when a fellow's on a horse, he can't let another fellow—kind of—don't you know?"

The man did know. "There's sense in that." he said approvingly. Peace was restored, and they would have reached Salisbury if they had not had some more beer. It unloosed the soldier's fancies, and again he spoke of old Em'ly, and recited the poem, with Aristophanic variations.

"Jolly day," repeated Stephen, with a straightening of the eyebrows and a quick glance at the other's body. He then warned him against the variations. In consequence he was accused of being a member of the Y.M.C.A. His blood boiled at this. He refuted the charge, and became great friends with the soldier, for the third time.

"Any objection to 'Saucy Mr. and Mrs. Tackleton'?"

"Rather not."

The soldier sang "Saucy Mr. and Mrs. Tackleton." It is really a work for two voices, most of the sauciness disappearing when taken as a solo. Nor is Mrs. Tackleton's name Em'ly.

"I call it a jolly rotten song," said Stephen crossly. "I won't stand being got at."

> *"P'r'aps y'like therold song. Lishen. "'Of all the gulls that arsshmart,*
> *There's none line pretty—Em'ly;*
> *For she's the darling of merart'"*

"Now, that's wrong." He rode up close to the singer.

"Shright."

"'Tisn't."

"It's as my mother taught me."

"I don't care."

"I'll not alter from mother's way."

Stephen was baffled. Then he said, "How does your mother make it rhyme?"

"Wot?"

"Squat. You're an ass, and I'm not. Poems want rhymes. 'Alley' comes next line."

He said "alley" was—welcome to come if it liked.

"It can't. You want Sally. Sally—alley. Em'ly-alley doesn't do."

"Emily-femily!" cried the soldier, with an inspiration that was not his when sober. "My mother taught me femily.

"'For she's the darling of merart, And she lives in my femily.'"

"Well, you'd best be careful, Thomas, and your mother too."

"Your mother's no better than she should be," said Thomas vaguely.

"Do you think I haven't heard that before?" retorted the boy. The other concluded he might now say anything. So he might—the name of old Emily excepted. Stephen cared little about his benefactress's honour, but a great deal about his own. He had made Mrs. Failing into a test. For the moment he would die for her, as a knight would die for a glove. He is not to be distinguished from a hero.

Old Sarum was passed. They approached the most beautiful spire in the world. "Lord! another of these large churches!" said the soldier. Unfriendly to Gothic, he lifted both hands to his nose, and declared that old Em'ly was buried there. He lay in the mud. His horse trotted back towards Amesbury, Stephen had twisted him out of the saddle.

"I've done him!" he yelled, though no one was there to hear. He rose up in his stirrups and shouted with joy. He flung his arms round Aeneas's neck. The elderly horse understood, capered, and bolted. It was a centaur that dashed into Salisbury and scattered the people. In the stable he would not dismount. "I've done him!" he yelled to the ostlers—apathetic men. Stretching upwards, he clung to a beam. Aeneas moved on and he was left hanging. Greatly did he incommode them by his exercises. He pulled up, he circled, he kicked the other customers. At last he fell to the earth, deliciously fatigued. His body worried him no longer.

He went, like the baby he was, to buy a white linen hat. There were soldiers about, and he thought it would disguise him. Then he had a little lunch to steady the beer. This day had turned out admirably. All the money that should have fed Rickie he could spend on himself. Instead of toiling over the Cathedral and seeing the stuffed penguins, he could stop the whole thing in the cattle market. There he met and made some friends. He watched the cheap-jacks, and saw how necessary it was to have a confident manner. He spoke confidently himself about lambs, and people listened. He spoke confidently about pigs, and they roared with laughter. He must learn more about pigs. He witnessed a performance—not too namby-pamby—of Punch and Judy. "Hullo, Podge!" cried a naughty little girl. He tried to catch her, and failed. She was one of the Cadford children. For Salisbury on market day, though it is not picturesque, is certainly representative, and you read the names of half the Wiltshire villages upon the carriers' carts. He found, in Penny Farthing Street, the cart from Wintersbridge. It would not start for several hours, but the passengers always used it as a club, and sat in it every now and then during the day. No less than three ladies were these now, staring at the shafts. One of them was Flea Thompson's girl. He asked her, quite politely, why her lover had broken faith with him in the rain. She was silent. He warned her of approaching vengeance. She was still silent, but another woman hoped that a gentleman would not be hard on a poor person. Something in this annoyed him; it wasn't a question of gentility and poverty—it was a question of two men. He determined to go back by Cadbury Rings where the shepherd would now be.

He did. But this part must be treated lightly. He rode up to the culprit with the air of a Saint George, spoke a few stern words from the saddle, tethered his steed to a hurdle, and took off his coat. "Are you ready?" he asked.

"Yes, sir," said Flea, and flung him on his back.

"That's not fair," he protested.

The other did not reply, but flung him on his head.

"How on earth did you learn that?"

"By trying often," said Flea.

Stephen sat on the ground, picking mud out of his forehead. "I meant it to be fists," he said gloomily.

"I know, sir."

"It's jolly smart though, and—and I beg your pardon all round." It cost him a great deal to say this, but he was sure that it was the right thing to say. He must acknowledge the better man. Whereas most people, if they provoke a fight and are flung, say, "You cannot rob me of my moral victory."

There was nothing further to be done. He mounted again, not exactly depressed, but feeling that this delightful world is extraordinarily unreliable. He had never expected to fling the soldier, or to be flung by Flea. "One nips or is nipped," he thought, "and never knows beforehand. I should not be surprised if many people had more in them than I suppose, while others were just the other way round. I haven't seen that sort of thing in Ingersoll, but it's quite important." Then his thoughts turned to a curious incident of long ago, when he had been "nipped"—as a little boy. He was trespassing in those woods, when he met in a narrow glade a flock of sheep. They had neither dog nor shepherd, and advanced towards him silently. He was accustomed to sheep, but had never happened to meet them in a wood before, and disliked it. He retired, slowly at first, then fast; and the flock, in a dense mass, pressed after him. His terror increased. He turned and screamed at their long white faces; and still they came on, all stuck together, like some horrible jell—. If once he got into them! Bellowing and screeching, he rushed into the undergrowth, tore himself all over, and reached home in convulsions. Mr. Failing, his only grown-up friend, was sympathetic, but quite stupid. "Pan ovium custos," he sympathetic, as he pulled out the thorns. "Why not?" "Pan ovium custos." Stephen learnt the meaning of the phrase at school, "A pan of eggs for custard." He still remembered how the other boys looked as he peeped at them between his legs, awaiting the descending cane.

So he returned, full of pleasant disconnected thoughts. He had had a rare good time. He liked every one—even that poor little Elliot—and yet no one mattered. They were all out. On the landing he saw the housemaid. He felt skittish and irresistible. Should he slip his arm round her waist? Perhaps better not; she might box his ears. And he wanted to smoke on the roof before dinner. So he only said, "Please will you stop the boy blacking my brown boots," and she with downcast eyes, answered, "Yes, sir; I will indeed."

His room was in the pediment. Classical architecture, like all things in this world that attempt serenity, is bound to have its lapses into the undignified, and Cadover lapsed hopelessly when it came to Stephen's room. It gave him one round window, to see through which he must lie upon his stomach, one trapdoor opening upon the leads, three iron girders, three beams, six buttresses, no circling, unless you count the walls, no walls unless you count the ceiling and in its embarrassment presented him with the gurgly cistern that supplied the bath water. Here he lived, absolutely happy, and unaware that Mrs. Failing had poked him up here on purpose, to prevent him from growing too bumptious. Here he worked and sang and practised on the ocharoon. Here, in the crannies, he had constructed shelves and cupboards and useless little drawers. He had only one picture—the Demeter of Onidos—and she hung straight from the roof like a joint of meat. Once she was in the drawing-room; but Mrs. Failing had got tired of her, and decreed her removal and this degradation. Now she faced the sunrise; and when the moon rose its light also fell on her, and trembled, like light upon the sea. For she was never still, and if the draught increased she would twist on her string, and would sway and tap upon the rafters until Stephen woke up and said what he thought of her. "Want your nose?" he would murmur. "Don't you wish you may get it" Then he drew the clothes over his ears, while above him, in the wind and the darkness, the goddess continued her motions.

Today, as he entered, he trod on the pile of sixpenny reprints. Leighton had brought them up. He looked at the portraits in their covers, and began to think that these people were not everything. What a fate, to look like Colonel Ingersoll, or to marry Mrs. Julia P. Chunk! The Demeter turned towards him as he bathed, and in the cold water he sang—

"They aren't beautiful, they aren't modest;
I'd just as soon follow an old stone goddess,"

and sprang upward through the skylight on to the roof. Years ago, when a nurse was washing him, he had slipped from her soapy hands and got up here. She implored him to remember that he was a little gentleman; but he forgot the fact—if it was a fact—and not even the butler could get him down. Mr. Failing, who was sitting alone in the garden too ill to read, heard a shout, "Am I an acroterium?" He looked up and saw a naked child poised on the summit of Cadover. "Yes," he replied; "but they are unfashionable. Go in," and the vision had remained with him as something peculiarly gracious. He felt that nonsense and beauty have close connections,—closer connections than Art will allow,—and that both would remain when his own heaviness and his own ugliness had perished. Mrs. Failing found in his remains a sentence that puzzled her. "I see the respectable mansion. I see the smug fortress of culture. The doors are shut. The windows are shut. But on the roof the children go dancing for ever."

XII

Stephen was a child no longer. He never stood on the pediment now, except for a bet. He never, or scarcely ever, poured water down the chimneys. When he caught the cat, he seldom dropped her into the housekeeper's bedroom. But still, when the weather was fair, he liked to come up after bathing, and get dry in the sun. Today he brought with him a towel, a pipe of tobacco, and Rickie's story. He must get it done some time, and he was tired of the six-penny reprints. The sloping gable was warm, and he lay back on it with closed eyes, gasping for pleasure. Starlings criticized him, snots fell on his clean body, and over him a little cloud was tinged with the colours of evening. "Good! good!" he whispered. "Good, oh good!" and opened the manuscript reluctantly.

What a production! Who was this girl? Where did she go to? Why so much talk about trees? "I take it he wrote it when feeling bad," he murmured, and let it fall into the gutter. It fell face downwards, and on the back he saw a neat little resume in Miss Pembroke's handwriting, intended for such as him. "Allegory. Man = modern civilization (in bad sense). Girl = getting into touch with Nature."

In touch with Nature! The girl was a tree! He lit his pipe and gazed at the radiant earth. The foreground was hidden, but there was the village with its elms, and the Roman Road, and Cadbury Rings. There, too, were those woods, and little beech copses, crowning a waste of down. Not to mention the air, or the sun, or water. Good, oh good!

In touch with Nature! What cant would the books think of next? His eyes closed. He was sleepy. Good, oh good! Sighing into his pipe, he fell asleep.

XIII

Glad as Agnes was when her lover returned for lunch, she was at the same time rather dismayed: she knew that Mrs. Failing would not like her plans altered. And her dismay was justified. Their hostess was a little stiff, and asked whether Stephen had been obnoxious.

"Indeed he hasn't. He spent the whole time looking after me."

"From which I conclude he was more obnoxious than usual." Rickie praised him diligently. But his candid nature showed everything through. His aunt soon saw that they had not got on. She had expected this—almost planned it. Nevertheless she resented it, and her resentment was to fall on him.

The storm gathered slowly, and many other things went to swell it. Weakly people, if they are not careful, hate one another, and when the weakness is hereditary the temptation increases. Elliots had never got on among themselves. They talked of "The Family," but they always turned outwards to the health and beauty that lie so promiscuously about the world. Rickie's father had turned, for a time at all events, to his mother. Rickie himself was turning to Agnes. And Mrs. Failing now was irritable, and unfair to the nephew who was lame like her horrible brother and like herself. She thought him invertebrate and conventional. She was envious of his happiness. She did not trouble to understand his art. She longed to shatter him, but knowing as she did that the human thunderbolt often rebounds and strikes the wielder, she held her hand.

Agnes watched the approaching clouds. Rickie had warned her; now she began to warn him. As the visit wore away she urged him to be pleasant to his aunt, and so convert it into a success.

He replied, "Why need it be a success?"—a reply in the manner of Ansell.

She laughed. "Oh, that's so like you men—all theory! What about your great theory of hating no one? As soon as it comes in useful you drop it."

"I don't hate Aunt Emily. Honestly. But certainly I don't want to be near her or think about her. Don't you think there are two great things in life that we ought to aim at—truth and kindness? Let's have both if we can, but let's be sure of having one or the other. My aunt gives up both for the sake of being funny."

"And Stephen Wonham," pursued Agnes. "There's another person you hate—or don't think about, if you prefer it put like that."

XIII

"The truth is, I'm changing. I'm beginning to see that the world has many people in it who don't matter. I had time for them once. Not now." There was only one gate to the kingdom of heaven now.

Agnes surprised him by saying, "But the Wonham boy is evidently a part of your aunt's life. She laughs at him, but she is fond of him."

"What's that to do with it?"

"You ought to be pleasant to him on account of it."

"Why on earth?"

She flushed a little. "I'm old-fashioned. One ought to consider one's hostess, and fall in with her life. After we leave it's another thing. But while we take her hospitality I think it's our duty."

Her good sense triumphed. Henceforth he tried to fall in with Aunt Emily's life. Aunt Emily watched him trying. The storm broke, as storms sometimes do, on Sunday.

Sunday church was a function at Cadover, though a strange one. The pompous landau rolled up to the house at a quarter to eleven. Then Mrs. Failing said, "Why am I being hurried?" and after an interval descended the steps in her ordinary clothes. She regarded the church as a sort of sitting-room, and refused even to wear a bonnet there. The village was shocked, but at the same time a little proud; it would point out the carriage to strangers and gossip about the pale smiling lady who sat in it, always alone, always late, her hair always draped in an expensive shawl.

This Sunday, though late as usual, she was not alone. Miss Pembroke, en grande toilette, sat by her side. Rickie, looking plain and devout, perched opposite. And Stephen actually came too, murmuring that it would be the Benedicite, which he had never minded. There was also the Litany, which drove him into the air again, much to Mrs. Failing's delight. She enjoyed this sort of thing. It amused her when her Protege left the pew, looking bored, athletic, and dishevelled, and groping most obviously for his pipe. She liked to keep a thoroughbred pagan to shock people. "He's gone to worship Nature," she whispered. Rickie did not look up. "Don't you think he's charming?" He made no reply.

"Charming," whispered Agnes over his head.

During the sermon she analysed her guests. Miss Pembroke—undistinguished, unimaginative, tolerable. Rickie—intolerable. "And how pedantic!" she mused. "He smells of the University library. If he was stupid in the right way he would be a don." She looked round the tiny church; at the whitewashed pillars, the humble pavement, the window full of magenta saints. There was the vicar's wife. And Mrs. Wilbraham's bonnet. Ugh! The rest of the congregation were poor women, with flat, hopeless faces—she saw them Sunday after Sunday, but did not know their names—diversified with a few reluctant plough-boys, and the vile little school children row upon row. "Ugh! what a hole," thought Mrs. Failing, whose Christianity was the type best described as "cathedral." "What a hole for a cultured woman! I don't think it has blunted my sensations, though; I still see its squalor as clearly as ever. And my nephew pretends he is worshipping. Pah! the hypocrite." Above her the vicar spoke of the danger of hurrying from one dissipation to another. She treasured his words, and continued: "I cannot stand smugness. It is the one, the unpardonable sin. Fresh air! The fresh air that has made Stephen Wonham fresh and companionable and strong. Even if it kills, I will let in the fresh air."

Thus reasoned Mrs. Failing, in the facile vein of Ibsenism. She imagined herself to be a cold-eyed Scandinavian heroine. Really she was an English old lady, who did not mind giving other people a chill provided it was not infectious.

Agnes, on the way back, noted that her hostess was a little snappish. But one is so hungry after morning service, and either so hot or so cold, that he would be a saint indeed who becomes a saint at once. Mrs. Failing, after asserting vindictively that it was impossible to make a living out of literature, was courteously left alone. Roast-beef and moselle might yet work miracles, and Agnes still hoped for the introductions—the introductions to certain editors and publishers—on which her whole diplomacy was bent. Rickie would not push himself. It was his besetting sin. Well for him that he would have a wife, and a loving wife, who knew the value of enterprise.

Unfortunately lunch was a quarter of an hour late, and during that quarter of an hour the aunt and the nephew quarrelled. She had been inveighing against the morning service, and he quietly and deliberately replied, "If organized religion is anything—and it is something to me—it will not be wrecked by a harmonium and a dull sermon."

Mrs. Failing frowned. "I envy you. It is a great thing to have no sense of beauty."

"I think I have a sense of beauty, which leads me astray if I am not careful."

"But this is a great relief to me. I thought the present day young man was an agnostic! Isn't agnosticism all the thing at Cambridge?"

"Nothing is the 'thing' at Cambridge. If a few men are agnostic there, it is for some grave reason, not because they are irritated with the way the parson says his vowels."

Agnes intervened. "Well, I side with Aunt Emily. I believe in ritual."

"Don't, my dear, side with me. He will only say you have no sense of religion either."

"Excuse me," said Rickie, perhaps he too was a little hungry,—"I never suggested such a thing. I never would suggest such a thing. Why cannot you understand my position? I almost feel it is that you won't."

"I try to understand your position night and day dear—what you mean, what you like, why you came to Cadover, and why you stop here when my presence is so obviously unpleasing to you."

"Luncheon is served," said Leighton, but he said it too late. They discussed the beef and the moselle in silence. The air was heavy and ominous. Even the Wonham boy was affected by it, shivered at times, choked once, and hastened anew into the sun. He could not understand clever people.

XIII

Agnes, in a brief anxious interview, advised the culprit to take a solitary walk. She would stop near Aunt Emily, and pave the way for an apology.

"Don't worry too much. It doesn't really matter."

"I suppose not, dear. But it seems a pity, considering we are so near the end of our visit."

"Rudeness and Grossness matter, and I've shown both, and already I'm sorry, and I hope she'll let me apologize. But from the selfish point of view it doesn't matter a straw. She's no more to us than the Wonham boy or the boot boy."

"Which way will you walk?"

"I think to that entrenchment. Look at it." They were sitting on the steps. He stretched out his hand to Cadsbury Rings, and then let it rest for a moment on her shoulder. "You're changing me," he said gently. "God bless you for it."

He enjoyed his walk. Cadford was a charming village and for a time he hung over the bridge by the mill. So clear was the stream that it seemed not water at all, but some invisible quintessence in which the happy minnows and the weeds were vibrating. And he paused again at the Roman crossing, and thought for a moment of the unknown child. The line curved suddenly: certainly it was dangerous. Then he lifted his eyes to the down. The entrenchment showed like the rim of a saucer, and over its narrow line peeped the summit of the central tree. It looked interesting. He hurried forward, with the wind behind him.

The Rings were curious rather than impressive. Neither embankment was over twelve feet high, and the grass on them had not the exquisite green of Old Sarum, but was grey and wiry. But Nature (if she arranges anything) had arranged that from them, at all events, there should be a view. The whole system of the country lay spread before Rickie, and he gained an idea of it that he never got in his elaborate ride. He saw how all the water converges at Salisbury; how Salisbury lies in a shallow basin, just at the change of the soil. He saw to the north the Plain, and the stream of the Cad flowing down from it, with a tributary that broke out suddenly, as the chalk streams do: one village had clustered round the source and clothed itself with trees. He saw Old Sarum, and hints of the Avon valley, and the land above Stone Henge. And behind him he saw the great wood beginning unobtrusively, as if the down too needed shaving; and into it the road to London slipped, covering the bushes with white dust. Chalk made the dust white, chalk made the water clear, chalk made the clean rolling outlines of the land, and favoured the grass and the distant coronals of trees. Here is the heart of our island: the Chilterns, the North Downs, the South Downs radiate hence. The fibres of England unite in Wiltshire, and did we condescend to worship her, here we should erect our national shrine.

People at that time were trying to think imperially, Rickie wondered how they did it, for he could not imagine a place larger than England. And other people talked of Italy, the spiritual fatherland of us all. Perhaps Italy would prove marvellous. But at present he conceived it as something exotic, to be admired and reverenced, but not to be loved like these unostentatious fields. He drew out a book, it was natural for him to read when he was happy, and to read out loud,—

and for a little time his voice disturbed the silence of that glorious afternoon. The book was Shelley, and it opened at a passage that he had cherished greatly two years before, and marked as "very good."

"I never was attached to that great sect Whose doctrine is that each one should select Out of the world a mistress or a friend, And all the rest, though fair and wise, commend To cold oblivion,—though it is the code Of modern morals, and the beaten road Which those poor slaves with weary footsteps tread Who travel to their home among the dead By the broad highway of the world,—and so With one sad friend, perhaps a jealous foe, The dreariest and the longest journey go."

It was "very good"—fine poetry, and, in a sense, true. Yet he was surprised that he had ever selected it so vehemently. This afternoon it seemed a little inhuman. Half a mile off two lovers were keeping company where all the villagers could see them. They cared for no one else; they felt only the pressure of each other, and so progressed, silent and oblivious, across the land. He felt them to be nearer the truth than Shelley. Even if they suffered or quarrelled, they would have been nearer the truth. He wondered whether they were Henry Adams and Jessica Thompson, both of this parish, whose banns had been asked for the second time in the church this morning. Why could he not marry on fifteen shillings a-week? And be looked at them with respect, and wished that he was not a cumbersome gentleman.

Presently he saw something less pleasant—his aunt's pony carriage. It had crossed the railway, and was advancing up the Roman road along by the straw sacks. His impulse was to retreat, but someone waved to him. It was Agnes. She waved continually, as much as to say, "Wait for us." Mrs. Failing herself raised the whip in a nonchalant way. Stephen Wonham was following on foot, some way behind. He put the Shelley back into his pocket and waited for them. When the carriage stopped by some hurdles he went down from the embankment and helped them to dismount. He felt rather nervous.

His aunt gave him one of her disquieting smiles, but said pleasantly enough, "Aren't the Rings a little immense? Agnes and I came here because we wanted an antidote to the morning service."

"Pang!" said the church bell suddenly; "pang! pang!" It sounded petty and ludicrous. They all laughed. Rickie blushed, and Agnes, with a glance that said "apologize," darted away to the entrenchment, as though unable to restrain her curiosity.

"The pony won't move," said Mrs. Failing. "Leave him for Stephen to tie up. Will you walk me to the tree in the middle? Booh! I'm tired. Give me your arm—unless you're tired as well."

"No. I came out partly in the hope of helping you."

"How sweet of you." She contrasted his blatant unselfishness with the hardness of Stephen. Stephen never came out to help you. But if you got hold of him he was some good. He didn't wobble and bend at the critical moment. Her fancy compared Rickie to the cracked church bell sending forth its message of "Pang!

pang!" to the countryside, and Stephen to the young pagans who were said to lie under this field guarding their pagan gold.

"This place is full of ghosties," she remarked; "have you seen any yet?"

"I've kept on the outer rim so far."

"Let's go to the tree in the centre."

"Here's the path." The bank of grass where he had sat was broken by a gap, through which chariots had entered, and farm carts entered now. The track, following the ancient track, led straight through turnips to a similar gap in the second circle, and thence continued, through more turnips, to the central tree.

"Pang!" said the bell, as they paused at the entrance.

"You needn't unharness," shouted Mrs. Failing, for Stephen was approaching the carriage.

"Yes, I will," he retorted.

"You will, will you?" she murmured with a smile. "I wish your brother wasn't quite so uppish. Let's get on. Doesn't that church distract you?"

"It's so faint here," said Rickie. And it sounded fainter inside, though the earthwork was neither thick nor tall; and the view, though not hidden, was greatly diminished. He was reminded for a minute of that chalk pit near Madingley, whose ramparts excluded the familiar world. Agnes was here, as she had once been there. She stood on the farther barrier, waiting to receive them when they had traversed the heart of the camp.

"Admire my mangel-wurzels," said Mrs. Failing. "They are said to grow so splendidly on account of the dead soldiers. Isn't it a sweet thought? Need I say it is your brother's?"

"Wonham's?" he suggested. It was the second time that she had made the little slip. She nodded, and he asked her what kind of ghosties haunted this curious field.

"The D.," was her prompt reply. "He leans against the tree in the middle, especially on Sunday afternoons and all the worshippers rise through the turnips and dance round him."

"Oh, these were decent people," he replied, looking downwards—"soldiers and shepherds. They have no ghosts. They worshipped Mars or Pan-Erda perhaps; not the devil."

"Pang!" went the church, and was silent, for the afternoon service had begun. They entered the second entrenchment, which was in height, breadth, and composition, similar to the first, and excluded still more of the view. His aunt continued friendly. Agnes stood watching them.

"Soldiers may seem decent in the past," she continued, "but wait till they turn into Tommies from Bulford Camp, who rob the chickens."

"I don't mind Bulford Camp," said Rickie, looking, though in vain, for signs of its snowy tents. "The men there are the sons of the men here, and have come back to the old country. War's horrible, yet one loves all continuity. And no one could mind a shepherd."

"Indeed! What about your brother—a shepherd if ever there was? Look how he bores you! Don't be so sentimental."

"But—oh, you mean—"

"Your brother Stephen."

He glanced at her nervously. He had never known her so queer before. Perhaps it was some literary allusion that he had not caught; but her face did not at that moment suggest literature. In the differential tones that one uses to an old and infirm person he said "Stephen Wonham isn't my brother, Aunt Emily."

"My dear, you're that precise. One can't say 'half-brother' every time."

They approached the central tree.

"How you do puzzle me," he said, dropping her arm and beginning to laugh. "How could I have a half-brother?"

She made no answer.

Then a horror leapt straight at him, and he beat it back and said, "I will not be frightened." The tree in the centre revolved, the tree disappeared, and he saw a room—the room where his father had lived in town. "Gently," he told himself, "gently." Still laughing, he said, "I, with a brother-younger it's not possible." The horror leapt again, and he exclaimed, "It's a foul lie!"

"My dear, my dear!"

"It's a foul lie! He wasn't—I won't stand—"

"My dear, before you say several noble things, remember that it's worse for him than for you—worse for your brother, for your half-brother, for your younger brother."

But he heard her no longer. He was gazing at the past, which he had praised so recently, which gaped ever wider, like an unhallowed grave. Turn where he would, it encircled him. It took visible form: it was this double entrenchment of the Rings. His mouth went cold, and he knew that he was going to faint among the dead. He started running, missed the exit, stumbled on the inner barrier, fell into darkness—

"Get his head down," said a voice. "Get the blood back into him. That's all he wants. Leave him to me. Elliot!"—the blood was returning—"Elliot, wake up!"

He woke up. The earth he had dreaded lay close to his eyes, and seemed beautiful. He saw the structure of the clods. A tiny beetle swung on the grass blade. On his own neck a human hand pressed, guiding the blood back to his brain.

There broke from him a cry, not of horror but of acceptance. For one short moment he understood. "Stephen—" he began, and then he heard his own name called: "Rickie! Rickie!" Agnes hurried from her post on the margin, and, as if understanding also, caught him to her breast.

Stephen offered to help them further, but finding that he made things worse, he stepped aside to let them pass and then sauntered inwards. The whole field, with concentric circles, was visible, and the broad leaves of the turnips rustled in the gathering wind. Miss Pembroke and Elliot were moving towards the Cadover entrance. Mrs. Failing stood watching in her turn on the opposite bank. He was not an inquisitive boy; but as he leant against the tree he wondered what it was all about, and whether he would ever know.

XIV

On the way back—at that very level-crossing where he had paused on his upward route—Rickie stopped suddenly and told the girl why he had fainted. Hitherto she had asked him in vain. His tone had gone from him, and he told her harshly and brutally, so that she started away with a horrified cry. Then his manner altered, and he exclaimed: "Will you mind? Are you going to mind?"

"Of course I mind," she whispered. She turned from him, and saw up on the sky-line two figures that seemed to be of enormous size.

"They're watching us. They stand on the edge watching us. This country's so open—you—you can't they watch us wherever we go. Of course you mind."

They heard the rumble of the train, and she pulled herself together. "Come, dearest, we shall be run over next. We're saying things that have no sense." But on the way back he repeated: "They can still see us. They can see every inch of this road. They watch us for ever." And when they arrived at the steps there, sure enough, were still the two figures gazing from the outer circle of the Rings.

She made him go to his room at once: he was almost hysterical. Leighton brought out some tea for her, and she sat drinking it on the little terrace. Of course she minded.

Again she was menaced by the abnormal. All had seemed so fair and so simple, so in accordance with her ideas; and then, like a corpse, this horror rose up to the surface. She saw the two figures descend and pause while one of them harnessed the pony; she saw them drive downward, and knew that before long she must face them and the world. She glanced at her engagement ring.

When the carriage drove up Mrs. Failing dismounted, but did not speak. It was Stephen who inquired after Rickie. She, scarcely knowing the sound of her own voice, replied that he was a little tired.

"Go and put up the pony," said Mrs. Failing rather sharply.

"Agnes, give me some tea."

"It is rather strong," said Agnes as the carriage drove off and left them alone. Then she noticed that Mrs. Failing herself was agitated. Her lips were trembling, and she saw the boy depart with manifest relief.

"Do you know," she said hurriedly, as if talking against time—"Do you know what upset Rickie?"

"I do indeed know."

"Has he told any one else?"

"I believe not."

"Agnes—have I been a fool?"

"You have been very unkind," said the girl, and her eyes filled with tears.

For a moment Mrs. Failing was annoyed. "Unkind? I do not see that at all. I believe in looking facts in the face. Rickie must know his ghosts some time. Why not this afternoon?"

She rose with quiet dignity, but her tears came faster. "That is not so. You told him to hurt him. I cannot think what you did it for. I suppose because he was rude to you after church. It is a mean, cowardly revenge.

"What—what if it's a lie?"

"Then, Mrs. Failing, it is sickening of you. There is no other word. Sickening. I am sorry—a nobody like myself—to speak like this. How COULD you, oh, how could you demean yourself? Why, not even a poor person—Her indignation was fine and genuine. But her tears fell no longer. Nothing menaced her if they were not really brothers.

"It is not a lie, my clear; sit down. I will swear so much solemnly. It is not a lie, but—"

Agnes waited.

"—we can call it a lie if we choose."

"I am not so childish. You have said it, and we must all suffer. You have had your fun: I conclude you did it for fun. You cannot go back. He—" She pointed towards the stables, and could not finish her sentence.

"I have not been a fool twice."

Agnes did not understand.

"My dense lady, can't you follow? I have not told Stephen one single word, neither before nor now."

There was a long silence.

Indeed, Mrs. Failing was in an awkward position.

Rickie had irritated her, and, in her desire to shock him, she had imperilled her own peace. She had felt so unconventional upon the hillside, when she loosed the horror against him; but now it was darting at her as well. Suppose the scandal came out. Stephen, who was absolutely without delicacy, would tell it to the people as soon as tell them the time. His paganism would be too assertive; it might even be in bad taste. After all, she had a prominent position in the neighbourhood; she was talked about, respected, looked up to. After all, she was growing old. And therefore, though she had no true regard for Rickie, nor for Agnes, nor for Stephen, nor for Stephen's parents, in whose tragedy she had assisted, yet she did feel that if the scandal revived it would disturb the harmony of Cadover, and therefore tried to retrace her steps. It is easy to say shocking things: it is so different to be connected with anything shocking. Life and death were not involved, but comfort and discomfort were.

The silence was broken by the sound of feet on the gravel. Agnes said hastily, "Is that really true—that he knows nothing?"

"You, Rickie, and I are the only people alive that know. He realizes what he is—with a precision that is sometimes alarming. Who he is, he doesn't know and doesn't care. I suppose he would know when I'm dead. There are papers."

"Aunt Emily, before he comes, may I say to you I'm sorry I was so rude?"

Mrs. Failing had not disliked her courage. "My dear, you may. We're all off our hinges this Sunday. Sit down by me again."

Agnes obeyed, and they awaited the arrival of Stephen. They were clever enough to understand each other. The thing must be hushed up. The matron must repair the consequences of her petulance. The girl must hide the stain in her future husband's family. Why not? Who was injured? What does a grown-up man want with a grown brother? Rickie upstairs, how grateful he would be to them for saving him.

"Stephen!"

"Yes."

"I'm tired of you. Go and bathe in the sea."

"All right."

And the whole thing was settled. She liked no fuss, and so did he. He sat down on the step to tighten his bootlaces. Then he would be ready. Mrs. Failing laid two or three sovereigns on the step above him. Agnes tried to make conversation, and said, with averted eyes, that the sea was a long way off.

"The sea's downhill. That's all I know about it." He swept up the money with a word of pleasure: he was kept like a baby in such things. Then he started off, but slowly, for he meant to walk till the morning.

"He will be gone days," said Mrs. Failing. "The comedy is finished. Let us come in."

She went to her room. The storm that she had raised had shattered her. Yet, because it was stilled for a moment, she resumed her old emancipated manner, and spoke of it as a comedy.

As for Miss Pembroke, she pretended to be emancipated no longer. People like "Stephen Wonham" were social thunderbolts, to be shunned at all costs, or at almost all costs. Her joy was now unfeigned, and she hurried upstairs to impart it to Rickie.

"I don't think we are rewarded if we do right, but we are punished if we lie. It's the fashion to laugh at poetic justice, but I do believe in half of it. Cast bitter bread upon the waters, and after many days it really will come back to you." These were the words of Mr. Failing. They were also the opinions of Stewart Ansell, another unpractical person. Rickie was trying to write to him when she entered with the good news.

"Dear, we're saved! He doesn't know, and he never is to know. I can't tell you how glad I am. All the time we saw them standing together up there, she wasn't telling him at all. She was keeping him out of the way, in case you let it out. Oh, I like her! She may be unwise, but she is nice, really. She said, 'I've been a fool but I haven't been a fool twice.' You must forgive her, Rickie. I've forgiven her, and she me; for at first I was so angry with her. Oh, my darling boy, I am so glad!"

He was shivering all over, and could not reply. At last he said, "Why hasn't she told him?"

"Because she has come to her senses."

"But she can't behave to people like that. She must tell him."

"Because he must be told such a real thing."

"Such a real thing?" the girl echoed, screwing up her forehead. "But—but you don't mean you're glad about it?"

His head bowed over the letter. "My God—no! But it's a real thing. She must tell him. I nearly told him myself—up there—when he made me look at the ground, but you happened to prevent me."

How Providence had watched over them!

"She won't tell him. I know that much."

"Then, Agnes, darling"—he drew her to the table "we must talk together a little. If she won't, then we ought to."

"WE tell him?" cried the girl, white with horror. "Tell him now, when everything has been comfortably arranged?"

"You see, darling"—he took hold of her hand—"what one must do is to think the thing out and settle what's right, I'm still all trembling and stupid. I see it mixed up with other things. I want you to help me. It seems to me that here and there in life we meet with a person or incident that is symbolical. It's nothing in itself, yet for the moment it stands for some eternal principle. We accept it, at whatever costs, and we have accepted life. But if we are frightened and reject it, the moment, so to speak, passes; the symbol is never offered again. Is this nonsense? Once before a symbol was offered to me—I shall not tell you how; but I did accept it, and cherished it through much anxiety and repulsion, and in the end I am rewarded. There will be no reward this time. I think, from such a man—the son of such a man. But I want to do what is right."

"Because doing right is its own reward," said Agnes anxiously.

"I do not think that. I have seen few examples of it. Doing right is simply doing right."

"I think that all you say is wonderfully clever; but since you ask me, it IS nonsense, dear Rickie, absolutely."

"Thank you," he said humbly, and began to stroke her hand. "But all my disgust; my indignation with my father, my love for—" He broke off; he could not bear to mention the name of his mother. "I was trying to say, I oughtn't to follow these impulses too much. There are others things. Truth. Our duty to acknowledge each man accurately, however vile he is. And apart from ideals" (here she had won the battle), "and leaving ideals aside, I couldn't meet him and keep silent. It isn't in me. I should blurt it out."

"But you won't meet him!" she cried. "It's all been arranged. We've sent him to the sea. Isn't it splendid? He's gone. My own boy won't be fantastic, will he?" Then she fought the fantasy on its own ground. "And, bye the bye, what you call the 'symbolic moment' is over. You had it up by the Rings. You tried to tell him, I interrupted you. It's not your fault. You did all you could."

She thought this excellent logic, and was surprised that he looked so gloomy. "So he's gone to the sea. For the present that does settle it. Has Aunt Emily talked about him yet?"

"No. Ask her tomorrow if you wish to know. Ask her kindly. It would be so dreadful if you did not part friends, and—"

"What's that?"

It was Stephen calling up from the drive. He had come back. Agnes threw out her hand in despair.

"Elliot!" the voice called.

They were facing each other, silent and motionless. Then Rickie advanced to the window. The girl darted in front of him. He thought he had never seen her so beautiful. She was stopping his advance quite frankly, with widespread arms.

"Elliot!"

He moved forward—into what? He pretended to himself he would rather see his brother before he answered; that it was easier to acknowledge him thus. But at the back of his soul he knew that the woman had conquered, and that he was moving forward to acknowledge her. "If he calls me again—" he thought.

"Elliot!"

"Well, if he calls me once again, I will answer him, vile as he is."

He did not call again.

Stephen had really come back for some tobacco, but as he passed under the windows he thought of the poor fellow who had been "nipped" (nothing serious, said Mrs. Failing), and determined to shout good-bye to him. And once or twice, as he followed the river into the darkness, he wondered what it was like to be so weak,—not to ride, not to swim, not to care for anything but books and a girl.

They embraced passionately. The danger had brought them very near to each other. They both needed a home to confront the menacing tumultuous world. And what weary years of work, of waiting, lay between them and that home! Still holding her fast, he said, "I was writing to Ansell when you came in."

"Do you owe him a letter?"

"No." He paused. "I was writing to tell him about this. He would help us. He always picks out the important point."

"Darling, I don't like to say anything, and I know that Mr. Ansell would keep a secret, but haven't we picked out the important point for ourselves?"

He released her and tore the letter up.

XV

The sense of purity is a puzzling and at times a fearful thing. It seems so noble, and it starts as one with morality. But it is a dangerous guide, and can lead us away not only from what is gracious, but also from what is good. Agnes, in this tangle, had followed it blindly, partly because she was a woman, and it meant more to her than it can ever mean to a man; partly because, though dangerous, it is also obvious, and makes no demand upon the intellect. She could not feel that Stephen had full human rights. He was illicit, abnormal, worse than a man diseased. And Rickie remembering whose son he was, gradually adopted her opinion. He, too, came to be glad that his brother had passed from him untried, that the symbolic moment had been rejected. Stephen was the fruit of sin; therefore he was sinful, He, too, became a sexual snob.

And now he must hear the unsavoury details. That evening they sat in the walled garden. Agues, according to arrangement, left him alone with his aunt. He asked her, and was not answered.

"You are shocked," she said in a hard, mocking voice, "It is very nice of you to be shocked, and I do not wish to grieve you further. We will not allude to it again. Let us all go on just as we are. The comedy is finished."

He could not tolerate this. His nerves were shattered, and all that was good in him revolted as well. To the horror of Agnes, who was within earshot, he replied, "You used to puzzle me, Aunt Emily, but I understand you at last. You have forgotten what other people are like. Continual selfishness leads to that. I am sure of it. I see now how you look at the world. 'Nice of me to be shocked!' I want to go tomorrow, if I may."

"Certainly, dear. The morning trains are the best." And so the disastrous visit ended.

As he walked back to the house he met a certain poor woman, whose child Stephen had rescued at the level-crossing, and who had decided, after some delay, that she must thank the kind gentleman in person. "He has got some brute courage," thought Rickie, "and it was decent of him not to boast about it." But he had labelled the boy as "Bad," and it was convenient to revert to his good qualities as seldom as possible. He preferred to brood over his coarseness, his caddish ingratitude, his irreligion. Out of these he constructed a repulsive figure, forgetting how slovenly his own perceptions had been during the past week, how dogmatic and intolerant his attitude to all that was not Love.

During the packing he was obliged to go up to the attic to find the Dryad manuscript which had never been returned. Leighton came too, and for about half an hour they hunted in the flickering light of a candle. It was a strange, ghostly place, and Rickie was quite startled when a picture swung towards him, and he saw the Demeter of Cnidus, shimmering and grey. Leighton suggested the roof. Mr. Stephen sometimes left things on the roof. So they climbed out of the skylight—the night was perfectly still—and continued the search among the gables. Enormous stars hung overhead, and the roof was bounded by chasms, impenetrable and black. "It doesn't matter," said Rickie, suddenly convinced of the futility of all that he did. "Oh, let us look properly," said Leighton, a kindly, pliable man, who had tried to shirk coming, but who was genuinely sympathetic now that he had come. They were rewarded: the manuscript lay in a gutter, charred and smudged.

The rest of the year was spent by Rickie partly in bed,—he had a curious breakdown,—partly in the attempt to get his little stories published. He had written eight or nine, and hoped they would make up a book, and that the book might be called "Pan Pipes." He was very energetic over this; he liked to work, for some imperceptible bloom had passed from the world, and he no longer found such acute pleasure in people. Mrs. Failing's old publishers, to whom the book was submitted, replied that, greatly as they found themselves interested, they did not see their way to making an offer at present. They were very polite, and singled out for special praise "Andante Pastorale," which Rickie had thought too sentimental, but which Agnes had persuaded him to include. The stories were sent to another publisher, who considered them for six weeks, and then returned them. A fragment of red cotton, Placed by Agnes between the leaves, had not shifted its position.

"Can't you try something longer, Rickie?" she said; "I believe we're on the wrong track. Try an out—and—out love-story."

"My notion just now," he replied, "is to leave the passions on the fringe." She nodded, and tapped for the waiter: they had met in a London restaurant. "I can't soar; I can only indicate. That's where the musicians have the pull, for music has wings, and when she says 'Tristan' and he says 'Isolde,' you are on the heights at once. What do people mean when they call love music artificial?"

"I know what they mean, though I can't exactly explain. Or couldn't you make your stories more obvious? I don't see any harm in that. Uncle Willie floundered hopelessly. He doesn't read much, and he got muddled. I had to explain, and then he was delighted. Of course, to write down to the public would be quite another thing and horrible. You have certain ideas, and you must express them. But couldn't you express them more clearly?"

"You see—" He got no further than "you see."

"The soul and the body. The soul's what matters," said Agnes, and tapped for the waiter again. He looked at her admiringly, but felt that she was not a perfect critic. Perhaps she was too perfect to be a critic. Actual life might seem to her so real that she could not detect the union of shadow and adamant that men call poetry. He would even go further and acknowledge that she was not as clever as himself—and he was stupid enough! She did not like discussing anything or reading solid books, and she was a little angry with such women as did. It pleased him to make these concessions, for they touched nothing in her that he valued. He looked round the restaurant, which was in Soho and decided that she was incomparable.

"At half-past two I call on the editor of the 'Holborn.' He's got a stray story to look at, and he's written about it."

"Oh, Rickie! Rickie! Why didn't you put on a boiled shirt!"

He laughed, and teased her. "'The soul's what matters. We literary people don't care about dress."

"Well, you ought to care. And I believe you do. Can't you change?"

"Too far." He had rooms in South Kensington. "And I've forgot my card-case. There's for you!"

She shook her head. "Naughty, naughty boy! Whatever will you do?"

"Send in my name, or ask for a bit of paper and write it. Hullo! that's Tilliard!"

Tilliard blushed, partly on account of the faux pas he had made last June, partly on account of the restaurant. He explained how he came to be pigging in Soho: it was so frightfully convenient and so frightfully cheap.

"Just why Rickie brings me," said Miss Pembroke.

"And I suppose you're here to study life?" said Tilliard, sitting down.

"I don't know," said Rickie, gazing round at the waiters and the guests.

"Doesn't one want to see a good deal of life for writing? There's life of a sort in Soho,—Un peu de faisan, s'il vows plait."

Agnes also grabbed at the waiter, and paid. She always did the paying, Rickie muddled with his purse.

"I'm cramming," pursued Tilliard, "and so naturally I come into contact with very little at present. But later on I hope to see things." He blushed a little, for he was talking for Rickie's edification. "It is most frightfully important not to get a narrow or academic outlook, don't you think? A person like Ansell, who goes from Cambridge, home—home, Cambridge—it must tell on him in time."

"But Mr. Ansell is a philosopher."

"A very kinky one," said Tilliard abruptly. "Not my idea of a philosopher. How goes his dissertation?"

"He never answers my letters," replied Rickie. "He never would. I've heard nothing since June."

"It's a pity he sends in this year. There are so many good people in. He'd have afar better chance if he waited."

"So I said, but he wouldn't wait. He's so keen about this particular subject."

"What is it?" asked Agnes.

"About things being real, wasn't it, Tilliard?"

"That's near enough."

"Well, good luck to him!" said the girl. "And good luck to you, Mr. Tilliard! Later on, I hope, we'll meet again."

They parted. Tilliard liked her, though he did not feel that she was quite in his couche sociale. His sister, for instance, would never have been lured into a Soho restaurant—except for the experience of the thing. Tilliard's couche sociale permitted experiences. Provided his heart did not go out to the poor and the unorthodox, he might stare at them as much as he liked. It was seeing life.

Agnes put her lover safely into an omnibus at Cambridge Circus. She shouted after him that his tie was rising over his collar, but he did not hear her. For a moment she felt depressed, and pictured quite accurately the effect that his appearance would have on the editor. The editor was a tall neat man of forty, slow of speech, slow of soul, and extraordinarily kind. He and Rickie sat over a fire, with an enormous table behind them whereon stood many books waiting to be reviewed.

"I'm sorry," he said, and paused.

Rickie smiled feebly.

"Your story does not convince." He tapped it. "I have read it with very great pleasure. It convinces in parts, but it does not convince as a whole; and stories, don't you think, ought to convince as a whole?"

"They ought indeed," said Rickie, and plunged into self-depreciation. But the editor checked him.

"No—no. Please don't talk like that. I can't bear to hear any one talk against imagination. There are countless openings for imagination,—for the mysterious, for the supernatural, for all the things you are trying to do, and which, I hope, you will succeed in doing. I'm not OBJECTING to imagination; on the contrary, I'd advise you to cultivate it, to accent it. Write a really good ghost story and we'd take it at once. Or"—he suggested it as an alternative to imagination—"or you might get inside life. It's worth doing."

"Life?" echoed Rickie anxiously.

He looked round the pleasant room, as if life might be fluttering there like an imprisoned bird. Then he looked at the editor: perhaps he was sitting inside life at this very moment. "See life, Mr. Elliot, and then send us another story." He held out his hand. "I am sorry I have to say 'No, thank you'; it's so much nicer to say, 'Yes, please.'" He laid his hand on the young man's sleeve, and added, "Well, the interview's not been so alarming after all, has it?"

"I don't think that either of us is a very alarming person," was not Rickie's reply. It was what he thought out afterwards in the omnibus. His reply was "Ow," delivered with a slight giggle.

As he rumbled westward, his face was drawn, and his eyes moved quickly to the right and left, as if he would discover something in the squalid fashionable streets some bird on the wing, some radiant archway, the face of some god beneath a beaver hat. He loved, he was loved, he had seen death and other things; but the heart of all things was hidden. There was a password and he could not learn it, nor could the kind editor of the "Holborn" teach him. He sighed, and then sighed more piteously. For had he not known the password once—known it and forgotten it already? But at this point his fortunes become intimately connected with those of Mr. Pembroke.

PART 2 — SAWSTON

XVI

In three years Mr. Pembroke had done much to solidify the day-boys at Sawston School. If they were not solid, they were at all events curdling, and his activities might reasonably turn elsewhere. He had served the school for many years, and it was really time he should be entrusted with a boarding-house. The headmaster, an impulsive man who darted about like a minnow and gave his mother a great deal of trouble, agreed with him, and also agreed with Mrs. Jackson when she said that Mr. Jackson had served the school for many years and that it was really time he should be entrusted with a boarding-house. Consequently, when Dunwood House fell vacant the headmaster found himself in rather a difficult position.

Dunwood House was the largest and most lucrative of the boarding-houses. It stood almost opposite the school buildings. Originally it had been a villa residence—a red-brick villa, covered with creepers and crowned with terracotta dragons. Mr. Annison, founder of its glory, had lived here, and had had one or two boys to live with him. Times changed. The fame of the bishops blazed brighter, the school increased, the one or two boys became a dozen, and an addition was made to Dunwood House that more than doubled its size. A huge new building, replete with every convenience, was stuck on to its right flank. Dormitories, cubicles, studies, a preparation-room, a dining-room, parquet floors, hot-air pipes—no expense was spared, and the twelve boys roamed over it like princes. Baize doors communicated on every floor with Mr. Annison's part, and he, an anxious gentleman, would stroll backwards and forwards, a little depressed at the hygienic splendours, and conscious of some vanished intimacy. Somehow he had known his boys better when they had all muddled together as one family, and algebras lay strewn upon the drawing room chairs. As the house filled, his interest in it decreased. When he retired—which he did the same summer that Rickie left Cambridge—it had already passed the summit of excellence and was beginning to decline. Its numbers were still satisfactory, and for a little time it would subsist on its past reputation. But that mysterious asset the tone had lowered, and it was therefore of great importance that Mr. Annison's successor should be a first-class man. Mr. Coates, who came next in seniority, was passed over, and rightly. The choice lay between Mr. Pembroke and Mr. Jackson, the one an organizer, the other a humanist. Mr. Jackson was master of the Sixth, and—with the exception of the headmaster, who was too busy to impart knowledge—the only first-class intellect in the school. But he could not or rather would not, keep order. He told his form that if it chose to listen to him it would learn; if it didn't, it wouldn't. One half listened. The other half made paper frogs, and bored holes in the raised map of Italy with their penknives. When the penknives gritted he punished them with undue severity, and then forgot to make them show the punishments up. Yet out of this chaos two facts emerged. Half the boys got scholarships at the University, and some of them—including several of the paper-frog sort—remained friends with him throughout their lives. Moreover, he was rich, and had a competent wife. His claim to Dunwood House was stronger than one would have supposed.

The qualifications of Mr. Pembroke have already been indicated. They prevailed—but under conditions. If things went wrong, he must promise to resign.

"In the first place," said the headmaster, "you are doing so splendidly with the day-boys. Your attitude towards the parents is magnificent. I—don't know how to replace you there. Whereas, of course, the parents of a boarder—"

"Of course," said Mr. Pembroke.

The parent of a boarder, who only had to remove his son if he was discontented with the school, was naturally in a more independent position than the parent who had brought all his goods and chattels to Sawston, and was renting a house there.

"Now the parents of boarders—this is my second point—practically demand that the house-master should have a wife."

"A most unreasonable demand," said Mr. Pembroke.

"To my mind also a bright motherly matron is quite sufficient. But that is what they demand. And that is why—do you see?—we HAVE to regard your appointment as experimental. Possibly Miss Pembroke will be able to help you. Or I don't know whether if ever—" He left the sentence unfinished. Two days later Mr. Pembroke proposed to Mrs. Orr.

He had always intended to marry when he could afford it; and once he had been in love, violently in love, but had laid the passion aside, and told it to wait till a more convenient season. This was, of course, the proper thing to do, and prudence should have been rewarded. But when, after the lapse of fifteen years, he went, as it were, to his spiritual larder and took down Love from the top shelf to offer him to Mrs. Orr, he was rather dismayed. Something had happened. Perhaps the god had flown; perhaps he had been eaten by the rats. At all events, he was not there.

Mr. Pembroke was conscientious and romantic, and knew that marriage without love is intolerable. On the other hand, he could not admit that love had vanished from him. To admit this, would argue that he had deteriorated.

Whereas he knew for a fact that he had improved, year by year. Each year be grew more moral, more efficient, more learned, more genial. So how could he fail to be more loving? He did not speak to himself as follows, because he never spoke to himself; but the following notions moved in the recesses of his mind: "It is not the fire of youth. But I am not sure that I approve of the fire of youth. Look at my sister! Once she has suffered, twice she has been most imprudent, and put me to great inconvenience besides, for if she was stopping with me she would have done the housekeeping. I rather suspect that it is a nobler, riper emotion that I am laying at the feet of Mrs. Orr." It never took him long to get muddled, or to reverse cause and effect. In a short time he believed that he had been pining for years, and only waiting for this good fortune to ask the lady to share it with him.

Mrs. Orr was quiet, clever, kindly, capable, and amusing and they were old acquaintances. Altogether it was not surprising that he should ask her to be his wife, nor very surprising that she should refuse. But she refused with a violence that alarmed them both. He left her house declaring that he had been insulted, and she, as soon as he left, passed from disgust into tears.

He was much annoyed. There was a certain Miss Herriton who, though far inferior to Mrs. Orr, would have done instead of her. But now it was impossible. He could not go offering himself about Sawston. Having engaged a matron who had the reputation for being bright and motherly, he moved into Dunwood House and opened the Michaelmas term. Everything went wrong. The cook left; the boys had a disease called roseola; Agnes, who was still drunk with her engagement, was of no assistance, but kept flying up to London to push Rickie's fortunes; and, to crown everything, the matron was too bright and not motherly enough: she neglected the little boys and was overattentive to the big ones. She left abruptly, and the voice of Mrs. Jackson arose, prophesying disaster.

Should he avert it by taking orders? Parents do not demand that a house-master should be a clergyman, yet it reassures them when he is. And he would have to take orders some time, if he hoped for a school of his own. His religious convictions were ready to hand, but he spent several uncomfortable days hunting up his religious enthusiasms. It was not unlike his attempt to marry Mrs. Orr. But his piety was more genuine, and this time he never came to the point. His sense of decency forbade him hurrying into a Church that he reverenced. Moreover, he thought of another solution: Agnes must marry Rickie in the Christmas holidays, and they must come, both of them, to Sawston, she as housekeeper, he as assistant-master. The girl was a good worker when once she was settled down; and as for Rickie, he could easily be fitted in somewhere in the school. He was not a good classic, but good enough to take the Lower Fifth. He was no athlete, but boys might profitably note that he was a perfect gentleman all the same. He had no experience, but he would gain it. He had no decision, but he could simulate it. "Above all," thought Mr. Pembroke, "it will be something regular for him to do." Of course this was not "above all." Dunwood House held that position. But Mr. Pembroke soon came to think that it was, and believed that he was planning for Rickie, just as he had believed he was pining for Mrs. Orr.

Agnes, when she got back from the lunch in Soho, was told of the plan. She refused to give any opinion until she had seen her lover. A telegram was sent to him, and next morning he arrived. He was very susceptible to the weather, and perhaps it was unfortunate that the morning was foggy. His train had been stopped outside Sawston Station, and there he had sat for half an hour, listening to the unreal noises that came from the line, and watching the shadowy figures that worked there. The gas was alight in the great drawing-room, and in its depressing rays he and Agnes greeted each other, and discussed the most momentous question of their lives. They wanted to be married: there was no doubt of that. They wanted it, both of them, dreadfully. But should they marry on these terms?

"I'd never thought of such a thing, you see. When the scholastic agencies sent me circulars after the Tripos, I tore them up at once."

"There are the holidays," said Agnes. "You would have three months in the year to yourself, and you could do your writing then."

"But who'll read what I've written?" and he told her about the editor of the "Holborn."

She became extremely grave. At the bottom of her heart she had always mistrusted the little stories, and now people who knew agreed with her. How could Rickie, or any one, make a living by pretending that Greek gods were alive, or that young ladies could vanish into trees? A sparkling society tale, full of verve and pathos, would have been another thing, and the editor might have been convinced by it.

"But what does he mean?" Rickie was saying. "What does he mean by life?"

"I know what he means, but I can't exactly explain. You ought to see life, Rickie. I think he's right there. And Mr. Tilliard was right when he said one oughtn't to be academic."

He stood in the twilight that fell from the window, she in the twilight of the gas. "I wonder what Ansell would say," he murmured.

"Oh, poor Mr. Ansell!"

He was somewhat surprised. Why was Ansell poor? It was the first time the epithet had been applied to him.

"But to change the conversation," said Agnes.

"If we did marry, we might get to Italy at Easter and escape this horrible fog."

"Yes. Perhaps there—" Perhaps life would be there. He thought of Renan, who declares that on the Acropolis at Athens beauty and wisdom do exist, really exist, as external powers. He did not aspire to beauty or wisdom, but he prayed to be delivered from the shadow of unreality that had begun to darken the world. For it was as if some power had pronounced against him—as if, by some heedless action, he had offended an Olympian god. Like many another, he wondered whether the god might be appeased by work—hard uncongenial work. Perhaps he had not worked hard enough, or had enjoyed his work too much, and for that reason the shadow was falling.

"—And above all, a schoolmaster has wonderful opportunities for doing good; one mustn't forget that."

To do good! For what other reason are we here? Let us give up our refined sensations, and our comforts, and our art, if thereby we can make other people happier and better. The woman he loved had urged him to do good! With a vehemence that surprised her, he exclaimed, "I'll do it."

"Think it over," she cautioned, though she was greatly pleased.

"No; I think over things too much."

The room grew brighter. A boy's laughter floated in, and it seemed to him that people were as important and vivid as they had been six months before. Then he was at Cambridge, idling in the parsley meadows, and weaving perishable garlands out of flowers. Now he was at Sawston, preparing to work a beneficent machine. No man works for nothing, and Rickie trusted that to him also benefits might accrue; that his wound might heal as he laboured, and his eyes recapture the Holy Grail.

XVII

In practical matters Mr. Pembroke was often a generous man. He offered Rickie a good salary, and insisted on paying Agnes as well. And as he housed them for nothing, and as Rickie would also have a salary from the school, the money question disappeared—if not forever, at all events for the present.

"I can work you in," he said. "Leave all that to me, and in a few days you shall hear from the headmaster. He shall create a vacancy. And once in, we stand or fall together. I am resolved on that."

Rickie did not like the idea of being "worked in," but he was determined to raise no difficulties. It is so easy to be refined and high-minded when we have nothing to do. But the active, useful man cannot be equally particular. Rickie's programme involved a change in values as well as a change of occupation.

"Adopt a frankly intellectual attitude," Mr. Pembroke continued. "I do not advise you at present even to profess any interest in athletics or organization. When the headmaster writes, he will probably ask whether you are an all-round man. Boldly say no. A bold 'no' is at times the best. Take your stand upon classics and general culture."

Classics! A second in the Tripos. General culture. A smattering of English Literature, and less than a smattering of French.

"That is how we begin. Then we get you a little post—say that of librarian. And so on, until you are indispensable."

Rickie laughed; the headmaster wrote, the reply was satisfactory, and in due course the new life began.

Sawston was already familiar to him. But he knew it as an amateur, and under an official gaze it grouped itself afresh. The school, a bland Gothic building, now showed as a fortress of learning, whose outworks were the boarding-houses. Those straggling roads were full of the houses of the parents of the day-boys. These shops were in bounds, those out. How often had he passed Dunwood House! He had once confused it with its rival, Cedar View. Now he was to live there—perhaps for many years. On the left of the entrance a large saffron drawing-room, full of cosy corners and dumpy chairs: here the parents would be received. On the right of the entrance a study, which he shared with Herbert: here the boys would be caned—he hoped not often. In the hall a framed certificate praising the drains, the bust of Hermes, and a carved teak monkey holding out a salver. Some of the furniture had come from Shelthorpe, some had been bought from Mr. Annison, some of it was new. But throughout he recognized a certain decision of arrangement. Nothing in the house was accidental, or there merely for its own sake. He contrasted it with his room at Cambridge, which had been a jumble of things that he loved dearly and of things that he did not love at all. Now these also had come to Dunwood House, and had been distributed where each was seemly—Sir Percival to the drawing-room, the photograph of Stockholm to the passage, his chair, his inkpot, and the portrait of his mother to the study. And then he contrasted it with the Ansells' house, to which their resolute ill-taste had given unity. He was extremely sensitive to the inside of a house, holding it an organism that expressed the thoughts, conscious and subconscious, of its inmates. He was equally sensitive to places. He would compare Cambridge with Sawston, and either with a third type of existence, to which, for want of a better name, he gave the name of "Wiltshire."

It must not be thought that he is going to waste his time. These contrasts and comparisons never took him long, and he never indulged in them until the serious business of the day was over. And, as time passed, he never indulged in them at all. The school returned at the end of January, before he had been settled in a week. His health had improved, but not greatly, and he was nervous at the prospect of confronting the assembled house. All day long cabs had been driving up, full of boys in bowler hats too big for them; and Agnes had been superintending the numbering of the said hats, and the placing of them in cupboards, since they would not be wanted till the end of the term. Each boy had, or should have had, a bag, so that he need not unpack his box till the morrow, One boy had only a brown-paper parcel, tied with hairy string, and Rickie heard the firm pleasant voice say, "But you'll bring a bag next term," and the submissive, "Yes, Mrs. Elliot," of the reply. In the passage he ran against the head boy, who was alarmingly like an undergraduate. They looked at each other suspiciously, and parted. Two minutes later he ran into another boy, and then into another, and began to wonder whether they were doing it on purpose, and if so, whether he ought to mind. As the day wore on, the noises grew louder-trampings of feet, breakdowns, jolly little squawks—and the cubicles were assigned, and the bags unpacked, and the bathing arrangements posted up, and Herbert kept on saying, "All this is informal—all this is informal. We shall meet the house at eight fifteen."

And so, at eight ten, Rickie put on his cap and gown,—hitherto symbols of pupilage, now to be symbols of dignity,—the very cap and gown that Widdrington had so recently hung upon the college fountain. Herbert, similarly attired, was waiting for him in their private dining-room, where also sat Agnes, ravenously devouring scrambled eggs. "But you'll wear your hoods," she cried. Herbert considered, and them said she was quite right. He fetched his white silk, Rickie the fragment of rabbit's wool that marks the degree of B.A. Thus attired, they proceeded through the baize door. They were a little late, and the boys, who were marshalled in the preparation room, were getting uproarious. One, forgetting how far his voice carried, shouted, "Cave! Here comes the Whelk." And another young devil yelled, "The Whelk's brought a pet with him!"

"You mustn't mind," said Herbert kindly. "We masters make a point of never minding nicknames—unless, of course, they are applied openly, in which case a thousand lines is not too much." Rickie assented, and they entered the preparation room just as the prefects had established order.

Here Herbert took his seat on a high-legged chair, while Rickie, like a queen-consort, sat near him on a chair with somewhat shorter legs. Each chair had a desk attached to it, and Herbert flung up the lid of his, and then looked round the preparation room with a quick frown, as if the contents had surprised him. So impressed was Rickie that he peeped sideways, but could only see a little blotting-paper in the desk. Then he noticed that the boys were impressed too. Their chatter ceased. They attended.

The room was almost full. The prefects, instead of lolling disdainfully in the back row, were ranged like councillors beneath the central throne. This was an innovation of Mr. Pembroke's. Carruthers, the head boy, sat in the middle, with his arm round Lloyd. It was Lloyd who had made the matron too bright: he nearly lost his colours in consequence. These two were grown up. Beside them sat Tewson, a saintly child in the spectacles, who had risen to this height by reason of his immense learning. He, like the others, was a school prefect. The house prefects, an inferior brand, were beyond, and behind came the indistinguishable many. The faces all looked alike as yet—except the face of one boy, who was inclined to cry.

"School," said Mr. Pembroke, slowly closing the lid of the desk,—"school is the world in miniature." Then he paused, as a man well may who has made such a remark. It is not, however, the intention of this work to quote an opening address. Rickie, at all events, refused to be critical: Herbert's experience was far greater than his, and he must take his tone from him. Nor could any one criticize the exhortations to be patriotic, athletic, learned, and religious, that flowed like a four-part fugue from Mr. Pembroke's mouth. He was a practised speaker—that is to say, he held his audience's attention. He told them that this term, the second of his reign, was THE term for Dunwood House; that it behooved every boy to labour during it for his house's honour, and, through the house, for the honour of the school. Taking a wider range, he spoke of England, or rather of Great Britain, and of her continental foes. Portraits of empire-builders hung on the wall, and he pointed to them. He quoted imperial poets. He showed how patriotism had broadened since the days of Shakespeare, who, for all his genius, could only write of his country as—

"This fortress built by nature for herself Against infection and the hand of war, This hazy breed of men, this little world, This precious stone set in the silver sea."

And it seemed that only a short ladder lay between the preparation room and the Anglo-Saxon hegemony of the globe. Then he paused, and in the silence came "sob, sob, sob," from a little boy, who was regretting a villa in Guildford and his mother's half acre of garden.

XVII

The proceeding terminated with the broader patriotism of the school anthem, recently composed by the organist. Words and tune were still a matter for taste, and it was Mr. Pembroke (and he only because he had the music) who gave the right intonation to

"Perish each laggard!
Let it not be said
That Sawston such within her walls hath bred."

"Come, come," he said pleasantly, as they ended with harmonies in the style of Richard Strauss. "This will never do. We must grapple with the anthem this term—you're as tuneful as—as day-boys!"

Hearty laughter, and then the whole house filed past them and shook hands.

"But how did it impress you?" Herbert asked, as soon as they were back in their own part. Agnes had provided them with a tray of food: the meals were still anyhow, and she had to fly at once to see after the boys.

"I liked the look of them."

"I meant rather, how did the house impress you as a house?"

"I don't think I thought," said Rickie rather nervously. "It is not easy to catch the spirit of a thing at once. I only saw a roomful of boys."

"My dear Rickie, don't be so diffident. You are perfectly right. You only did see a roomful of boys. As yet there's nothing else to see. The house, like the school, lacks tradition. Look at Winchester. Look at the traditional rivalry between Eton and Harrow. Tradition is of incalculable importance, if a school is to have any status. Why should Sawston be without?"

"Yes. Tradition is of incalculable value. And I envy those schools that have a natural connection with the past. Of course Sawston has a past, though not of the kind that you quite want. The sons of poor tradesmen went to it at first. So wouldn't its traditions be more likely to linger in the Commercial School?" he concluded nervously.

"You have a great deal to learn—a very great deal. Listen to me. Why has Sawston no traditions?" His round, rather foolish, face assumed the expression of a conspirator. Bending over the mutton, he whispered, "I can tell you why. Owing to the day-boys. How can traditions flourish in such soil? Picture the day-boy's life—at home for meals, at home for preparation, at home for sleep, running home with every fancied wrong. There are day-boys in your class, and, mark my words, they will give you ten times as much trouble as the boarders, late, slovenly, stopping away at the slightest pretext. And then the letters from the parents! 'Why has my boy not been moved this term?' 'Why has my boy been moved this term?' 'I am a dissenter, and do not wish my boy to subscribe to the school mission.' 'Can you let my boy off early to water the garden?' Remember that I have been a day-boy house-master, and tried to infuse some esprit de corps into them. It is practically impossible. They come as units, and units they remain. Worse. They infect the boarders. Their pestilential, critical, discontented attitude is spreading over the school. If I had my own way—"

He stopped somewhat abruptly.

"Was that why you laughed at their singing?"

"Not at all. Not at all. It is not my habit to set one section of the school against the other."

After a little they went the rounds. The boys were in bed now. "Good-night!" called Herbert, standing in the corridor of the cubicles, and from behind each of the green curtains came the sound of a voice replying, "Good-night, sir!" "Good-night," he observed into each dormitory.

Then he went to the switch in the passage and plunged the whole house into darkness. Rickie lingered behind him, strangely impressed. In the morning those boys had been scattered over England, leading their own lives. Now, for three months, they must change everything—see new faces, accept new ideals. They, like himself, must enter a beneficent machine, and learn the value of esprit de corps. Good luck attend them—good luck and a happy release. For his heart would have them not in these cubicles and dormitories, but each in his own dear home, amongst faces and things that he knew.

Next morning, after chapel, he made the acquaintance of his class. Towards that he felt very differently. Esprit de corps was not expected of it. It was simply two dozen boys who were gathered together for the purpose of learning Latin. His duties and difficulties would not lie here. He was not required to provide it with an atmosphere. The scheme of work was already mapped out, and he started gaily upon familiar words—

"Pan, ovium custos, tua si tibi Maenala curae Adsis, O Tegaee, favens."

"Do you think that beautiful?" he asked, and received the honest answer, "No, sir; I don't think I do." He met Herbert in high spirits in the quadrangle during the interval. But Herbert thought his enthusiasm rather amateurish, and cautioned him.

"You must take care they don't get out of hand. I approve of a lively teacher, but discipline must be established first."

"I felt myself a learner, not a teacher. If I'm wrong over a point, or don't know, I mean to tell them at once." Herbert shook his head.

"It's different if I was really a scholar. But I can't pose as one, can I? I know much more than the boys, but I know very little. Surely the honest thing is to be myself to them. Let them accept or refuse me as that. That's the only attitude we shall any of us profit by in the end."

Mr. Pembroke was silent. Then he observed, "There is, as you say, a higher attitude and a lower attitude. Yet here, as so often, cannot we find a golden mean between them?"

"What's that?" said a dreamy voice. They turned and saw a tall, spectacled man, who greeted the newcomer kindly, and took hold of his arm. "What's that about the golden mean?"

"Mr. Jackson—Mr. Elliot: Mr. Elliot—Mr. Jackson," said Herbert, who did not seem quite pleased. "Rickie, have you a moment to spare me?"

But the humanist spoke to the young man about the golden mean and the pinchbeck mean, adding, "You know the Greeks aren't broad church clergymen.

They really aren't, in spite of much conflicting evidence. Boys will regard Sophocles as a kind of enlightened bishop, and something tells me that they are wrong."

"Mr. Jackson is a classical enthusiast," said Herbert. "He makes the past live. I want to talk to you about the humdrum present."

"And I am warning him against the humdrum past. That's another point, Mr. Elliot. Impress on your class that many Greeks and most Romans were frightfully stupid, and if they disbelieve you, read Ctesiphon with them, or Valerius Flaccus. Whatever is that noise?"

"It comes from your class-room, I think," snapped the other master.

"So it does. Ah, yes. I expect they are putting your little Tewson into the waste-paper basket."

"I always lock my class-room in the interval—"

"Yes?"

"—and carry the key in my pocket."

"Ah. But, Mr. Elliot, I am a cousin of Widdrington's. He wrote to me about you. I am so glad. Will you, first of all, come to supper next Sunday?"

"I am afraid," put in Herbert, "that we poor housemasters must deny ourselves festivities in term time."

"But mayn't he come once, just once?"

"May, my dear Jackson! My brother-in-law is not a baby. He decides for himself."

Rickie naturally refused. As soon as they were out of hearing, Herbert said, "This is a little unfortunate. Who is Mr. Widdrington?"

"I knew him at Cambridge."

"Let me explain how we stand," he continued, after a pause.

"Jackson is the worst of the reactionaries here, while I—why should I conceal it?—have thrown in my lot with the party of progress. You will see how we suffer from him at the masters' meetings. He has no talent for organization, and yet he is always inflicting his ideas on others. It was like his impertinence to dictate to you what authors you should read, and meanwhile the sixth-form room like a bear-garden, and a school prefect being put into the waste-paper basket. My good Rickie, there's nothing to smile at. How is the school to go on with a man like that? It would be a case of 'quick march,' if it was not for his brilliant intellect. That's why I say it's a little unfortunate. You will have very little in common, you and he."

Rickie did not answer. He was very fond of Widdrington, who was a quaint, sensitive person. And he could not help being attracted by Mr. Jackson, whose welcome contrasted pleasantly with the official breeziness of his other colleagues. He wondered, too, whether it is so very reactionary to contemplate the antique.

"It is true that I vote Conservative," pursued Mr. Pembroke, apparently confronting some objector. "But why? Because the Conservatives, rather than the Liberals, stand for progress. One must not be misled by catch-words."

"Didn't you want to ask me something?"

"Ah, yes. You found a boy in your form called Varden?"

"Varden? Yes; there is."

"Drop on him heavily. He has broken the statutes of the school. He is attending as a day-boy. The statutes provide that a boy must reside with his parents or guardians. He does neither. It must be stopped. You must tell the headmaster."

"Where does the boy live?"

"At a certain Mrs. Orr's, who has no connection with the school of any kind. It must be stopped. He must either enter a boarding-house or go."

"But why should I tell?" said Rickie. He remembered the boy, an unattractive person with protruding ears, "It is the business of his house-master."

"House-master—exactly. Here we come back again. Who is now the day-boys' house-master? Jackson once again—as if anything was Jackson's business! I handed the house back last term in a most flourishing condition. It has already gone to rack and ruin for the second time. To return to Varden. I have unearthed a put-up job. Mrs. Jackson and Mrs. Orr are friends. Do you see? It all works round."

"I see. It does—or might."

"The headmaster will never sanction it when it's put to him plainly."

"But why should I put it?" said Rickie, twisting the ribbons of his gown round his fingers.

"Because you're the boy's form-master."

"Is that a reason?"

"Of course it is."

"I only wondered whether—" He did not like to say that he wondered whether he need do it his first morning.

"By some means or other you must find out—of course you know already, but you must find out from the boy. I know—I have it! Where's his health certificate?"

"He had forgotten it."

"Just like them. Well, when he brings it, it will be signed by Mrs. Orr, and you must look at it and say, 'Orr—Orr—Mrs. Orr?' or something to that effect, and then the whole thing will come naturally out."

The bell rang, and they went in for the hour of school that concluded the morning. Varden brought his health certificate—a pompous document asserting that he had not suffered from roseola or kindred ailments in the holidays—and for a long time Rickie sat with it before him, spread open upon his desk. He did not quite like the job. It suggested intrigue, and he had come to Sawston not to intrigue but to labour. Doubtless Herbert was right, and Mr. Jackson and Mrs. Orr were wrong. But why could they not have it out among themselves? Then he thought, "I am a coward, and that's why I'm raising these objections," called the boy up to him, and it did all come out naturally, more or less. Hitherto Varden had lived with his mother; but she had left Sawston at Christmas, and now he would live with Mrs. Orr. "Mr. Jackson, sir, said it would be all right."

"Yes, yes," said Rickie; "quite so." He remembered Herbert's dictum: "Masters must present a united front. If they do not—the deluge." He sent the boy back to his seat, and after school took the compromising health certificate to the headmaster. The headmaster was at that time easily excited by a breach of the constitution. "Parents or guardians," he reputed—"parents or guardians," and flew with those words on his lips to Mr. Jackson. To say that Rickie was a cat's-paw is to put it too strongly. Herbert was strictly honourable, and never pushed him into an illegal or really dangerous position; but there is no doubt that on this and on many other occasions he had to do things that he would not otherwise have done. There was always some diplomatic corner that had to be turned, always something that he had to say or not to say. As the term wore on he lost his independence—almost without knowing it. He had much to learn about boys, and he learnt not by direct observation—for which he believed he was unfitted—but by sedulous imitation of the more experienced masters. Originally he had intended to be friends with his pupils, and Mr. Pembroke commended the intention highly; but you cannot be friends either with boy or man unless you give yourself away in the process, and Mr. Pembroke did not commend this. He, for "personal intercourse," substituted the safer "personal influence," and gave his junior hints on the setting of kindly traps, in which the boy does give himself away and reveals his shy delicate thoughts, while the master, intact, commends or corrects them. Originally Rickie had meant to help boys in the anxieties that they undergo when changing into men: at Cambridge he had numbered this among life's duties. But here is a subject in which we must inevitably speak as one human being to another, not as one who has authority or the shadow of authority, and for this reason the elder schoolmaster could suggest nothing but a few formulae. Formulae, like kindly traps, were not in Rickie's line, so he abandoned these subjects altogether and confined himself to working hard at what was easy. In the house he did as Herbert did, and referred all doubtful subjects to him. In his form, oddly enough, he became a martinet. It is so much simpler to be severe. He grasped the school regulations, and insisted on prompt obedience to them. He adopted the doctrine of collective responsibility. When one boy was late, he punished the whole form. "I can't help it," he would say, as if he was a power of nature. As a teacher he was rather dull. He curbed his own enthusiasms, finding that they distracted his attention, and that while he throbbed to the music of Virgil the boys in the back row were getting unruly. But on the whole he liked his form work: he knew why he was there, and Herbert did not overshadow him so completely.

What was amiss with Herbert? He had known that something was amiss, and had entered into partnership with open eyes. The man was kind and unselfish; more than that he was truly charitable, and it was a real pleasure to him to give—pleasure to others. Certainly he might talk too much about it afterwards; but it was the doing, not the talking, that he really valued, and benefactors of this sort are not too common. He was, moreover, diligent and conscientious: his heart was in his work, and his adherence to the Church of England no mere matter of form. He was capable of affection: he was usually courteous and tolerant. Then what was amiss? Why, in spite of all these qualities, should Rickie feel that there was something wrong with him—nay, that he was wrong as a whole, and that if the Spirit of Humanity should ever hold a judgment he would assuredly be classed among the goats? The answer at first sight appeared a graceless one—it was that Herbert was stupid. Not stupid in the ordinary sense—he had a business-like brain, and acquired knowledge easily—but stupid in the important sense: his whole life was coloured by a contempt of the intellect. That he had a tolerable intellect of his own was not the point: it is in what we value, not in what we have, that the test of us resides. Now, Rickie's intellect was not remarkable. He came to his worthier results rather by imagination and instinct than by logic. An argument confused him, and he could with difficulty follow it even on paper. But he saw in this no reason for satisfaction, and tried to make such use of his brain as he could, just as a weak athlete might lovingly exercise his body. Like a weak athlete, too, he loved to watch the exploits, or rather the efforts, of others—their efforts not so much to acquire knowledge as to dispel a little of the darkness by which we and all our acquisitions are surrounded. Cambridge had taught him this, and he knew, if for no other reason, that his time there had not been in vain. And Herbert's contempt for such efforts revolted him. He saw that for all his fine talk about a spiritual life he had but one test for things—success: success for the body in this life or for the soul in the life to come. And for this reason Humanity, and perhaps such other tribunals as there may be, would assuredly reject him.

XVIII

Meanwhile he was a husband. Perhaps his union should have been emphasized before. The crown of life had been attained, the vague yearnings, the misread impulses, had found accomplishment at last. Never again must he feel lonely, or as one who stands out of the broad highway of the world and fears, like poor Shelley, to undertake the longest journey. So he reasoned, and at first took the accomplishment for granted. But as the term passed he knew that behind the yearning there remained a yearning, behind the drawn veil a veil that he could not draw. His wedding had been no mighty landmark: he would often wonder whether such and such a speech or incident came after it or before. Since that meeting in the Soho restaurant there had been so much to do—clothes to buy, presents to thank for, a brief visit to a Training College, a honeymoon as brief. In such a bustle, what spiritual union could take place? Surely the dust would settle soon: in Italy, at Easter, he might perceive the infinities of love. But love had shown him its infinities already. Neither by marriage nor by any other device can men insure themselves a vision; and Rickie's had been granted him three years before, when he had seen his wife and a dead man clasped in each other's arms. She was never to be so real to him again.

She ran about the house looking handsomer than ever. Her cheerful voice gave orders to the servants. As he sat in the study correcting compositions, she would dart in and give him a kiss. "Dear girl—" he would murmur, with a glance at the rings on her hand. The tone of their marriage life was soon set. It was to be a frank good-fellowship, and before long he found it difficult to speak in a deeper key.

One evening he made the effort. There had been more beauty than was usual at Sawston. The air was pure and quiet. Tomorrow the fog might be here, but today one said, "It is like the country." Arm in arm they strolled in the side-garden, stopping at times to notice the crocuses, or to wonder when the daffodils would flower. Suddenly he tightened his pressure, and said, "Darling, why don't you still wear ear-rings?"

"Ear-rings?" She laughed. "My taste has improved, perhaps."

So after all they never mentioned Gerald's name. But he hoped it was still dear to her. He did not want her to forget the greatest moment in her life. His love desired not ownership but confidence, and to a love so pure it does not seem terrible to come second.

He valued emotion—not for itself, but because it is the only final path to intimacy. She, ever robust and practical, always discouraged him. She was not cold; she would willingly embrace him. But she hated being upset, and would laugh or thrust him off when his voice grew serious. In this she reminded him of his mother. But his mother—he had never concealed it from himself—had glories to which his wife would never attain: glories that had unfolded against a life of horror—a life even more horrible than he had guessed. He thought of her often during these earlier months. Did she bless his union, so different to her own? Did she love his wife? He tried to speak of her to Agnes, but again she was reluctant. And perhaps it was this aversion to acknowledge the dead, whose images alone have immortality, that made her own image somewhat transient, so that when he left her no mystic influence remained, and only by an effort could he realize that God had united them forever.

They conversed and differed healthily upon other topics. A rifle corps was to be formed: she hoped that the boys would have proper uniforms, instead of shooting in their old clothes, as Mr. Jackson had suggested. There was Tewson; could nothing be done about him? He would slink away from the other prefects and go with boys of his own age. There was Lloyd: he would not learn the school anthem, saying that it hurt his throat. And above all there was Varden, who, to Rickie's bewilderment, was now a member of Dunwood House.

"He had to go somewhere," said Agnes. "Lucky for his mother that we had a vacancy."

"Yes—but when I meet Mrs. Orr—I can't help feeling ashamed."

"Oh, Mrs. Orr! Who cares for her? Her teeth are drawn. If she chooses to insinuate that we planned it, let her. Hers was rank dishonesty. She attempted to set up a boarding-house."

Mrs. Orr, who was quite rich, had attempted no such thing. She had taken the boy out of charity, and without a thought of being unconstitutional. But in had come this officious "Limpet" and upset the headmaster, and she was scolded, and Mrs. Varden was scolded, and Mr. Jackson was scolded, and the boy was scolded and placed with Mr. Pembroke, whom she revered less than any man in the world. Naturally enough, she considered it a further attempt of the authorities to snub the day-boys, for whose advantage the school had been founded. She and Mrs. Jackson discussed the subject at their tea-parties, and the latter lady was sure that no good, no good of any kind, would come to Dunwood House from such ill-gotten plunder.

"We say, 'Let them talk,'" persisted Rickie, "but I never did like letting people talk. We are right and they are wrong, but I wish the thing could have been done more quietly. The headmaster does get so excited. He has given a gang of foolish people their opportunity. I don't like being branded as the day-boy's foe, when I think how much I would have given to be a day-boy myself. My father found me a nuisance, and put me through the mill, and I can never forget it particularly the evenings."

"There's very little bullying here," said Agnes.

"There was very little bullying at my school. There was simply the atmosphere of unkindness, which no discipline can dispel. It's not what people do to you, but what they mean, that hurts."

"I don't understand."

"Physical pain doesn't hurt—at least not what I call hurt—if a man hits you by accident or play. But just a little tap, when you know it comes from hatred, is too terrible. Boys do hate each other: I remember it, and see it again. They can make strong isolated friendships, but of general good-fellowship they haven't a notion."

"All I know is there's very little bullying here."

"You see, the notion of good-fellowship develops late: you can just see its beginning here among the prefects: up at Cambridge it flourishes amazingly. That's why I pity people who don't go up to Cambridge: not because a University is smart, but because those are the magic years, and—with luck—you see up there what you couldn't see before and mayn't ever see again.

"Aren't these the magic years?" the lady demanded.

He laughed and hit at her. "I'm getting somewhat involved. But hear me, O Agnes, for I am practical. I approve of our public schools. Long may they, flourish. But I do not approve of the boarding-house system. It isn't an inevitable adjunct—"

"Good gracious me!" she shrieked. "Have you gone mad?"

"Silence, madam. Don't betray me to Herbert, or I'll give us the sack. But seriously, what is the good of, throwing boys so much together? Isn't it building their lives on a wrong basis? They don't understand each other. I wish they did, but they don't. They don't realize that human beings are simply marvellous. When they do, the whole of life changes, and you get the truc thing. But don't pretend you've got it before you have. Patriotism and esprit de corps are all very well, but masters a little forget that they must grow from sentiment. They cannot create one. Cannot-cannot—cannot. I never cared a straw for England until I cared for Englishmen, and boys can't love the school when they hate each other. Ladies and gentlemen, I will now conclude my address. And most of it is copied out of Mr. Ansell."

The truth is, he was suddenly ashamed. He had been carried away on the flood of his old emotions. Cambridge and all that it meant had stood before him passionately clear, and beside it stood his mother and the sweet family life which nurses up a boy until he can salute his equals. He was ashamed, for he remembered his new resolution—to work without criticizing, to throw himself vigorously into the machine, not to mind if he was pinched now and then by the elaborate wheels.

"Mr. Ansell!" cried his wife, laughing somewhat shrilly. "Aha! Now I understand. It's just the kind of thing poor Mr. Ansell would say. Well, I'm brutal. I believe it does Varden good to have his ears pulled now and then, and I don't care whether they pull them in play or not. Boys ought to rough it, or they never grow up into men, and your mother would have agreed with me. Oh yes; and you're all wrong about patriotism. It can, can, create a sentiment."

She was unusually precise, and had followed his thoughts with an attention that was also unusual. He wondered whether she was not right, and regretted that she proceeded to say, "My dear boy, you mustn't talk these heresies inside Dunwood House! You sound just like one of that reactionary Jackson set, who want to fling the school back a hundred years and have nothing but day-boys all dressed anyhow."

"The Jackson set have their points."

"You'd better join it."

"The Dunwood House set has its points." For Rickie suffered from the Primal Curse, which is not—as the Authorized Version suggests—the knowledge of good and evil, but the knowledge of good-and-evil.

"Then stick to the Dunwood House set."

"I do, and shall." Again he was ashamed. Why would he see the other side of things? He rebuked his soul, not unsuccessfully, and then they returned to the subject of Varden.

"I'm certain he suffers," said he, for she would do nothing but laugh. "Each boy who passes pulls his ears—very funny, no doubt; but every day they stick out more and get redder, and this afternoon, when he didn't know he was being watched, he was holding his head and moaning. I hate the look about his eyes."

"I hate the whole boy. Nasty weedy thing."

"Well, I'm a nasty weedy thing, if it comes to that."

"No, you aren't," she cried, kissing him. But he led her back to the subject. Could nothing be suggested? He drew up some new rules—alterations in the times of going to bed, and so on—the effect of which would be to provide fewer opportunities for the pulling of Varden's ears. The rules were submitted to Herbert, who sympathized with weakliness more than did his sister, and gave them his careful consideration. But unfortunately they collided with other rules, and on a closer examination he found that they also ran contrary to the fundamentals on which the government of Dunwood House was based. So nothing was done. Agnes was rather pleased, and took to teasing her husband about Varden. At last he asked her to stop. He felt uneasy about the boy—almost superstitious. His first morning's work had brought sixty pounds a year to their hotel.

XIX

They did not get to Italy at Easter. Herbert had the offer of some private pupils, and needed Rickie's help. It seemed unreasonable to leave England when money was to be made in it, so they went to Ilfracombe instead. They spent three weeks among the natural advantages and unnatural disadvantages of that resort. It was out of the season, and they encamped in a huge hotel, which took them at a reduction. By a disastrous chance the Jacksons were down there too, and a good deal of constrained civility had to pass between the two families. Constrained it was not in Mr. Jackson's case. At all times he was ready to talk, and as long as they kept off the school it was pleasant enough. But he was very indiscreet, and feminine tact had often to intervene. "Go away, dear ladies," he would then observe. "You think you see life because you see the chasms in it. Yet all the chasms are full of female skeletons." The ladies smiled anxiously. To Rickie he was friendly and even intimate. They had long talks on the deserted Capstone, while their wives sat reading in the Winter Garden and Mr. Pembroke kept an eye upon the tutored youths. "Once I had tutored youths," said Mr. Jackson, "but I lost them all by letting them paddle with my nieces. It is so impossible to remember what is proper." And sooner or later their talk gravitated towards his central passion—the Fragments of Sophocles. Some day ("never," said Herbert) he would edit them. At present they were merely in his blood. With the zeal of a scholar and the imagination of a poet he reconstructed lost dramas—Niobe, Phaedra, Philoctetes against Troy, whose names, but for an accident, would have thrilled the world. "Is it worth it?" he cried. "Had we better be planting potatoes?" And then: "We had; but this is the second best."

Agnes did not approve of these colloquies. Mr. Jackson was not a buffoon, but he behaved like one, which is what matters; and from the Winter Garden she could see people laughing at him, and at her husband, who got excited too. She hinted once or twice, but no notice was taken, and at last she said rather sharply, "Now, you're not to, Rickie. I won't have it."

"He's a type that suits me. He knows people I know, or would like to have known. He was a friend of Tony Failing's. It is so hard to realize that a man connected with one was great. Uncle Tony seems to have been. He loved poetry and music and pictures, and everything tempted him to live in a kind of cultured paradise, with the door shut upon squalor. But to have more decent people in the world—he sacrificed everything to that. He would have 'smashed the whole beauty-shop' if it would help him. I really couldn't go as far as that. I don't think one need go as far—pictures might have to be smashed, but not music or poetry; surely they help—and Jackson doesn't think so either."

"Well, I won't have it, and that's enough." She laughed, for her voice had a little been that of the professional scold. "You see we must hang together. He's in the reactionary camp."

"He doesn't know it. He doesn't know that he is in any camp at all."

"His wife is, which comes to the same."

"Still, it's the holidays—" He and Mr. Jackson had drifted apart in the term, chiefly owing to the affair of Varden. "We were to have the holidays to ourselves, you know." And following some line of thought, he continued, "He cheers one up. He does believe in poetry. Smart, sentimental books do seem absolutely absurd to him, and gods and fairies far nearer to reality. He tries to express all modern life in the terms of Greek mythology, because the Greeks looked very straight at things, and Demeter or Aphrodite are thinner veils than 'The survival of the fittest', or 'A marriage has been arranged,' and other draperies of modern journalese."

"And do you know what that means?"

"It means that poetry, not prose, lies at the core."

"No. I can tell you what it means—balder-dash."

His mouth fell. She was sweeping away the cobwebs with a vengeance. "I hope you're wrong," he replied, "for those are the lines on which I've been writing, however badly, for the last two years."

"But you write stories, not poems."

He looked at his watch. "Lessons again. One never has a moment's peace."

"Poor Rickie. You shall have a real holiday in the summer." And she called after him to say, "Remember, dear, about Mr. Jackson. Don't go talking so much to him."

Rather arbitrary. Her tone had been a little arbitrary of late. But what did it matter? Mr. Jackson was not a friend, and he must risk the chance of offending Widdrington. After the lesson he wrote to Ansell, whom he had not seen since June, asking him to come down to Ilfracombe, if only for a day. On reading the letter over, its tone displeased him. It was quite pathetic: it sounded like a cry from prison. "I can't send him such nonsense," he thought, and wrote again. But phrase it as he would the letter always suggested that he was unhappy. "What's wrong?" he wondered. "I could write anything I wanted to him once." So he scrawled "Come!" on a post-card. But even this seemed too serious. The post-card followed the letters, and Agnes found them all in the waste-paper basket.

Then she said, "I've been thinking—oughtn't you to ask Mr. Ansell over? A breath of sea air would do the poor thing good."

There was no difficulty now. He wrote at once, "My dear Stewart, We both so much wish you could come over." But the invitation was refused. A little uneasy he wrote again, using the dialect of their past intimacy. The effect of this letter was not pathetic but jaunty, and he felt a keen regret as soon as it slipped into the box. It was a relief to receive no reply.

He brooded a good deal over this painful yet intangible episode. Was the pain all of his own creating? or had it been produced by something external? And he got the answer that brooding always gives—it was both. He was morbid, and had been so since his visit to Cadover—quicker to register discomfort than joy. But, none the less, Ansell was definitely brutal, and Agnes definitely jealous. Brutality he could understand, alien as it was to himself. Jealousy, equally alien, was a harder matter. Let husband and wife be as sun and moon, or as moon and sun. Shall they therefore not give greeting to the stars? He was willing to grant that the love that inspired her might be higher than his own. Yet did it not exclude them both from much that is gracious? That dream of his when he rode on the Wiltshire expanses—a curious dream: the lark silent, the earth dissolving. And he awoke from it into a valley full of men.

She was jealous in many ways—sometimes in an open humorous fashion, sometimes more subtly, never content till "we" had extended our patronage, and, if possible, our pity. She began to patronize and pity Ansell, and most sincerely trusted that he would get his fellowship. Otherwise what was the poor fellow to do? Ridiculous as it may seem, she was even jealous of Nature. One day her husband escaped from Ilfracombe to Morthoe, and came back ecstatic over its fangs of slate, piercing an oily sea. "Sounds like an hippopotamus," she said peevishly. And when they returned to Sawston through the Virgilian counties, she disliked him looking out of the windows, for all the world as if Nature was some dangerous woman.

He resumed his duties with a feeling that he had never left them. Again he confronted the assembled house. This term was again the term; school still the world in miniature. The music of the four-part fugue entered into him more deeply, and he began to hum its little phrases. The same routine, the same diplomacies, the same old sense of only half knowing boys or men—he returned to it all: and all that changed was the cloud of unreality, which ever brooded a little more densely than before. He spoke to his wife about this, he spoke to her about everything, and she was alarmed, and wanted him to see a doctor. But he explained that it was nothing of any practical importance, nothing that interfered with his work or his appetite, nothing more than a feeling that the cow was not really there. She laughed, and "how is the cow today?" soon passed into a domestic joke.

XX

Ansell was in his favourite haunt—the reading-room of the British Museum. In that book-encircled space he always could find peace. He loved to see the volumes rising tier above tier into the misty dome. He loved the chairs that glide so noiselessly, and the radiating desks, and the central area, where the catalogue shelves curve, round the superintendent's throne. There he knew that his life was not ignoble. It was worth while to grow old and dusty seeking for truth though truth is unattainable, restating questions that have been stated at the beginning of the world. Failure would await him, but not disillusionment. It was worth while reading books, and writing a book or two which few would read, and no one, perhaps, endorse. He was not a hero, and he knew it. His father and sister, by their steady goodness, had made this life possible. But, all the same, it was not the life of a spoilt child.

In the next chair to him sat Widdrington, engaged in his historical research. His desk was edged with enormous volumes, and every few moments an assistant brought him more. They rose like a wall against Ansell. Towards the end of the morning a gap was made, and through it they held the following conversation.

"I've been stopping with my cousin at Sawston."

"M'm."

"It was quite exciting. The air rang with battle. About two-thirds of the masters have lost their heads, and are trying to produce a gimcrack copy of Eton. Last term, you know, with a great deal of puffing and blowing, they fixed the numbers of the school. This term they want to create a new boarding-house."

"They are very welcome."

"But the more boarding-houses they create, the less room they leave for day-boys. The local mothers are frantic, and so is my queer cousin. I never knew him so excited over sub-Hellenic things. There was an indignation meeting at his house. He is supposed to look after the day-boys' interests, but no one thought he would—least of all the people who gave him the post. The speeches were most eloquent. They argued that the school was founded for day-boys, and that it's intolerable to handicap them. One poor lady cried, 'Here's my Harold in the school, and my Toddie coming on. As likely as not I shall be told there is no vacancy for him. Then what am I to do? If I go, what's to become of Harold; and if I stop, what's to become of Toddie?' I must say I was touched. Family life is more real than national life—at least I've ordered all these books to prove it is—and I fancy that the bust of Euripides agreed with me, and was sorry for the hot-faced mothers. Jackson will do what he can. He didn't quite like to state the naked truth-which is, that boardinghouses pay. He explained it to me afterwards: they are the only, future open to a stupid master. It's easy enough to be a beak when you're young and athletic, and can offer the latest University smattering. The difficulty is to keep your place when you get old and stiff, and younger smatterers are pushing up behind you. Crawl into a boarding-house and you're safe. A master's life is frightfully tragic. Jackson's fairly right himself, because he has got a first-class intellect. But I met a poor brute who was hired as an athlete. He has missed his shot at a boarding-house, and there's nothing in the world for him to do but to trundle down the hill."

Ansell yawned.

"I saw Rickie too. Once I dined there."

Another yawn.

"My cousin thinks Mrs. Elliot one of the most horrible women he has ever seen. He calls her 'Medusa in Arcady.' She's so pleasant, too. But certainly it was a very stony meal."

"What kind of stoniness"

"No one stopped talking for a moment."

"That's the real kind," said Ansell moodily. "The only kind."

"Well, I," he continued, "am inclined to compare her to an electric light. Click! she's on. Click! she's off. No waste. No flicker."

"I wish she'd fuse."

"She'll never fuse—unless anything was to happen at the main."

"What do you mean by the main?" said Ansell, who always pursued a metaphor relentlessly.

Widdrington did not know what he meant, and suggested that Ansell should visit Sawston to see whether one could know.

"It is no good me going. I should not find Mrs. Elliot: she has no real existence."

"Rickie has."

"I very much doubt it. I had two letters from Ilfracombe last April, and I very much doubt that the man who wrote them can exist." Bending downwards he began to adorn the manuscript of his dissertation with a square, and inside that a circle, and inside that another square. It was his second dissertation: the first had failed.

"I think he exists: he is so unhappy."

Ansell nodded. "How did you know he was unhappy?"

"Because he was always talking." After a pause he added, "What clever young men we are!"

"Aren't we? I expect we shall get asked in marriage soon. I say, Widdrington, shall we—?"

"Accept? Of course. It is not young manly to say no."

"I meant shall we ever do a more tremendous thing,—fuse Mrs. Elliot."

"No," said Widdrington promptly. "We shall never do that in all our lives." He added, "I think you might go down to Sawston, though."

"I have already refused or ignored three invitations."

"So I gathered."

"What's the good of it?" said Ansell through his teeth. "I will not put up with little things. I would rather be rude than to listen to twaddle from a man I've known.

"You might go down to Sawston, just for a night, to see him."

"I saw him last month—at least, so Tilliard informs me. He says that we all three lunched together, that Rickie paid, and that the conversation was most interesting."

"Well, I contend that he does exist, and that if you go—oh, I can't be clever any longer. You really must go, man. I'm certain he's miserable and lonely. Dunwood House reeks of commerce and snobbery and all the things he hated most. He doesn't do anything. He doesn't make any friends. He is so odd, too. In this day-boy row that has just started he's gone for my cousin. Would you believe it? Quite spitefully. It made quite a difficulty when I wanted to dine. It isn't like him either the sentiments or the behaviour. I'm sure he's not himself. Pembroke used to look after the day-boys, and so he can't very well take the lead against them, and perhaps Rickie's doing his dirty work—and has overdone it, as decent people generally do. He's even altering to talk to. Yet he's not been married a year. Pembroke and that wife simply run him. I don't see why they should, and no more do you; and that's why I want you to go to Sawston, if only for one night."

Ansell shook his head, and looked up at the dome as other men look at the sky. In it the great arc lamps sputtered and flared, for the month was again November. Then he lowered his eyes from the cold violet radiance to the books.

"No, Widdrington; no. We don't go to see people because they are happy or unhappy. We go when we can talk to them. I cannot talk to Rickie, therefore I will not waste my time at Sawston."

"I think you're right," said Widdrington softly. "But we are bloodless brutes. I wonder whether-If we were different people—something might be done to save him. That is the curse of being a little intellectual. You and our sort have always seen too clearly. We stand aside—and meanwhile he turns into stone. Two philosophic youths repining in the British Museum! What have we done? What shall we ever do? Just drift and criticize, while people who know what they want snatch it away from us and laugh."

"Perhaps you are that sort. I'm not. When the moment comes I shall hit out like any ploughboy. Don't believe those lies about intellectual people. They're only written to soothe the majority. Do you suppose, with the world as it is, that it's an easy matter to keep quiet? Do you suppose that I didn't want to rescue him from that ghastly woman? Action! Nothing's easier than action; as fools testify. But I want to act rightly."

"The superintendent is looking at us. I must get back to my work."

"You think this all nonsense," said Ansell, detaining him. "Please remember that if I do act, you are bound to help me."

Widdrington looked a little grave. He was no anarchist. A few plaintive cries against Mrs. Elliot were all that he prepared to emit.

"There's no mystery," continued Ansell. "I haven't the shadow of a plan in my head. I know not only Rickie but the whole of his history: you remember the day near Madingley. Nothing in either helps me: I'm just watching."

"But what for?"

"For the Spirit of Life."

Widdrington was surprised. It was a phrase unknown to their philosophy. They had trespassed into poetry.

"You can't fight Medusa with anything else. If you ask me what the Spirit of Life is, or to what it is attached, I can't tell you. I only tell you, watch for it. Myself I've found it in books. Some people find it out of doors or in each other. Never mind. It's the same spirit, and I trust myself to know it anywhere, and to use it rightly."

But at this point the superintendent sent a message.

Widdrington then suggested a stroll in the galleries. It was foggy: they needed fresh air. He loved and admired his friend, but today he could not grasp him. The world as Ansell saw it seemed such a fantastic place, governed by brand-new laws. What more could one do than to see Rickie as often as possible, to invite his confidence, to offer him spiritual support? And Mrs. Elliot—what power could "fuse" a respectable woman?

Ansell consented to the stroll, but, as usual, only breathed depression. The comfort of books deserted him among those marble goddesses and gods. The eye of an artist finds pleasure in texture and poise, but he could only think of the vanished incense and deserted temples beside an unfurrowed sea.

"Let us go," he said. "I do not like carved stones."

"You are too particular," said Widdrington. "You are always expecting to meet living people. One never does. I am content with the Parthenon frieze." And he moved along a few yards of it, while Ansell followed, conscious only of its pathos.

"There's Tilliard," he observed. "Shall we kill him?"

"Please," said Widdrington, and as he spoke Tilliard joined them. He brought them news. That morning he had heard from Rickie: Mrs. Elliot was expecting a child.

"A child?" said Ansell, suddenly bewildered.

"Oh, I forgot," interposed Widdrington. "My cousin did tell me."

"You forgot! Well, after all, I forgot that it might be, We are indeed young men." He leant against the pedestal of Ilissus and remembered their talk about the Spirit of Life. In his ignorance of what a child means he wondered whether the opportunity he sought lay here.

"I am very glad," said Tilliard, not without intention. "A child will draw them even closer together. I like to see young people wrapped up in their child."

"I suppose I must be getting back to my dissertation," said Ansell. He left the Parthenon to pass by the monuments of our more reticent beliefs—the temple of the Ephesian Artemis, the statue of the Cnidian Demeter. Honest, he knew that here were powers he could not cope with, nor, as yet, understand.

XXI

The mists that had gathered round Rickie seemed to be breaking. He had found light neither in work for which he was unfitted nor in a woman who had ceased to respect him, and whom he was ceasing to love. Though he called himself fickle and took all the blame of their marriage on his own shoulders, there remained in Agnes certain terrible faults of heart and head, and no self-reproach would diminish them. The glamour of wedlock had faded; indeed, he saw now that it had faded even before wedlock, and that during the final months he had shut his eyes and pretended it was still there. But now the mists were breaking.

That November the supreme event approached. He saw it with Nature's eyes. It dawned on him, as on Ansell, that personal love and marriage only cover one side of the shield, and that on the other is graven the epic of birth. In the midst of lessons he would grow dreamy, as one who spies a new symbol for the universe, a fresh circle within the square. Within the square shall be a circle, within the circle another square, until the visual eye is baffled. Here is meaning of a kind. His mother had forgotten herself in him. He would forget himself in his son.

He was at his duties when the news arrived—taking preparation. Boys are marvellous creatures. Perhaps they will sink below the brutes; perhaps they will attain to a woman's tenderness. Though they despised Rickie, and had suffered under Agnes's meanness, their one thought this term was to be gentle and to give no trouble.

"Rickie—one moment—"

His face grew ashen. He followed Herbert into the passage, closing the door of the preparation room behind him. "Oh, is she safe?" he whispered.

"Yes, yes," said Herbert; but there sounded in his answer a sombre hostile note.

"Our boy?"

"Girl—a girl, dear Rickie; a little daughter. She—she is in many ways a healthy child. She will live—oh yes." A flash of horror passed over his face. He hurried into the preparation room, lifted the lid of his desk, glanced mechanically at the boys, and came out again.

Mrs. Lewin appeared through the door that led into their own part of the house.

"Both going on well!" she cried; but her voice also was grave, exasperated.

"What is it?" he gasped. "It's something you daren't tell me."

"Only this"—stuttered Herbert. "You mustn't mind when you see—she's lame."

Mrs. Lewin disappeared. "Lame! but not as lame as I am?"

"Oh, my dear boy, worse. Don't—oh, be a man in this. Come away from the preparation room. Remember she'll live—in many ways healthy—only just this one defect."

The horror of that week never passed away from him. To the end of his life he remembered the excuses—the consolations that the child would live; suffered very little, if at all; would walk with crutches; would certainly live. God was more merciful. A window was opened too wide on a draughty day—after a short, painless illness his daughter died. But the lesson he had learnt so glibly at Cambridge should be heeded now; no child should ever be born to him again.

XXII

That same term there took place at Dunwood House another event. With their private tragedy it seemed to have no connection; but in time Rickie perceived it as a bitter comment. Its developments were unforeseen and lasting. It was perhaps the most terrible thing he had to bear.

Varden had now been a boarder for ten months. His health had broken in the previous term,—partly, it is to be feared, as the result of the indifferent food—and during the summer holidays he was attacked by a series of agonizing earaches. His mother, a feeble person, wished to keep him at home, but Herbert dissuaded her. Soon after the death of the child there arose at Dunwood House one of those waves of hostility of which no boy knows the origin nor any master can calculate the course. Varden had never been popular—there was no reason why he should be—but he had never been seriously bullied hitherto. One evening nearly the whole house set on him. The prefects absented themselves, the bigger boys stood round and the lesser boys, to whom power was delegated, flung him down, and rubbed his face under the desks, and wrenched at his ears. The noisc penetrated the baize doors, and Herbert swept through and punished the whole house, including Varden, whom it would not do to leave out. The poor man was horrified. He approved of a little healthy roughness, but this was pure brutalization. What had come over his boys? Were they not gentlemen's sons? He would not admit that if you herd together human beings before they can understand each other the great god Pan is angry, and will in the end evade your regulations and drive them mad. That night the victim was screaming with pain, and the doctor next day spoke of an operation. The suspense lasted a whole week. Comment was made in the local papers, and the reputation not only of the house but of the school was imperilled. "If only I had known," repeated Herbert—"if only I had known I would have arranged it all differently. He should have had a cubicle." The boy did not die, but he left Sawston, never to return.

The day before his departure Rickie sat with him some time, and tried to talk in a way that was not pedantic. In his own sorrow, which he could share with no one, least of all with his wife, he was still alive to the sorrows of others. He still fought against apathy, though he was losing the battle.

"Don't lose heart," he told him. "The world isn't all going to be like this. There are temptations and trials, of course, but nothing at all of the kind you have had here."

"But school is the world in miniature, is it not, sir?" asked the boy, hoping to please one master by echoing what had been told him by another. He was always on the lookout for sympathy—: it was one of the things that had contributed to his downfall.

"I never noticed that myself. I was unhappy at school, and in the world people can be very happy."

Varden sighed and rolled about his eyes. "Are the fellows sorry for what they did to me?" he asked in an affected voice. "I am sure I forgive them from the bottom of my heart. We ought to forgive our enemies, oughtn't we, sir?"

"But they aren't your enemies. If you meet in five years' time you may find each other splendid fellows."

The boy would not admit this. He had been reading some revivalistic literature. "We ought to forgive our enemies," he repeated; "and however wicked they are, we ought not to wish them evil. When I was ill, and death seemed nearest, I had many kind letters on this subject."

Rickie knew about these "many kind letters." Varden had induced the silly nurse to write to people—people of all sorts, people that he scarcely knew or did not know at all—detailing his misfortune, and asking for spiritual aid and sympathy.

"I am sorry for them," he pursued. "I would not like to be like them."

Rickie sighed. He saw that a year at Dunwood House had produced a sanctimonious prig. "Don't think about them, Varden. Think about anything beautiful—say, music. You like music. Be happy. It's your duty. You can't be good until you've had a little happiness. Then perhaps you will think less about forgiving people and more about loving them."

"I love them already, sir." And Rickie, in desperation, asked if he might look at the many kind letters.

Permission was gladly given. A neat bundle was produced, and for about twenty minutes the master perused it, while the invalid kept watch on his face. Rooks cawed out in the playing-fields, and close under the window there was the sound of delightful, good-tempered laughter. A boy is no devil, whatever boys may be. The letters were chilly productions, somewhat clerical in tone, by whomsoever written. Varden, because he was ill at the time, had been taken seriously. The writers declared that his illness was fulfilling some mysterious purpose: suffering engendered spiritual growth: he was showing signs of this already. They consented to pray for him, some majestically, others shyly. But they all consented with one exception, who worded his refusal as follows:—

Dear A.C. Varden,—

I ought to say that I never remember seeing you. I am sorry that you are ill, and hope you are wrong about it. Why did you not write before, for I could have helped you then? When they pulled your ear, you ought to have gone like this (here was a rough sketch). I could not undertake praying, but would think of you instead, if that would do. I am twenty-two in April, built rather heavy, ordinary broad face, with eyes, etc. I write all this because you have mixed me with some one else, for I am not married, and do not want to be. I cannot think of you always, but will promise a quarter of an hour daily (say 7.00-7.15 A.M.), and might come to see you when you are better—that is, if you are a kid, and you read like one. I have been otter-hunting—

Yours sincerely,
Stephen Wonham

XXIII

Riekie went straight from Varden to his wife, who lay on the sofa in her bedroom. There was now a wide gulf between them. She, like the world she had created for him, was unreal.

"Agnes, darling," he began, stroking her hand, "such an awkward little thing has happened."

"What is it, dear? Just wait till I've added up this hook."

She had got over the tragedy: she got over everything.

When she was at leisure he told her. Hitherto they had seldom mentioned Stephen. He was classed among the unprofitable dead.

She was more sympathetic than he expected. "Dear Rickie," she murmured with averted eyes. "How tiresome for you."

"I wish that Varden had stopped with Mrs. Orr."

"Well, he leaves us for good tomorrow."

"Yes, yes. And I made him answer the letter and apologize. They had never met. It was some confusion with a man in the Church Army, living at a place called Codford. I asked the nurse. It is all explained."

"There the matter ends."

"I suppose so—if matters ever end."

"If, by ill-luck, the person does call. I will just see him and say that the boy has gone."

"You, or I. I have got over all nonsense by this time. He's absolutely nothing to me now." He took up the tradesman's book and played with it idly. On its crimson cover was stamped a grotesque sheep. How stale and stupid their life had become!

"Don't talk like that, though," she said uneasily. "Think how disastrous it would be if you made a slip in speaking to him."

"Would it? It would have been disastrous once. But I expect, as a matter of fact, that Aunt Emily has made the slip already."

His wife was displeased. "You need not talk in that cynical way. I credit Aunt Emily with better feeling. When I was there she did mention the matter, but only once. She, and I, and all who have any sense of decency, know better than to make slips, or to think of making them."

Agnes kept up what she called "the family connection." She had been once alone to Cadover, and also corresponded with Mrs. Failing. She had never told

Rickie anything about her visit nor had he ever asked her. But, from this moment, the whole subject was reopened.

"Most certainly he knows nothing," she continued. "Why, he does not even realize that Varden lives in our house! We are perfectly safe—unless Aunt Emily were to die. Perhaps then—but we are perfectly safe for the present."

"When she did mention the matter, what did she say?"

"We had a long talk," said Agnes quietly. "She told me nothing new—nothing new about the past, I mean. But we had a long talk about the present. I think" and her voice grew displeased again—"that you have been both wrong and foolish in refusing to make up your quarrel with Aunt Emily."

"Wrong and wise, I should say."

"It isn't to be expected that she—so much older and so sensitive—can make the first step. But I know she'd he glad to see you."

"As far as I can remember that final scene in the garden, I accused her of 'forgetting what other people were like.' She'll never pardon me for saying that."

Agnes was silent. To her the phrase was meaningless. Yet Rickie was correct: Mrs. Failing had resented it more than anything.

"At all events," she suggested, "you might go and see her."

"No, dear. Thank you, no."

"She is, after all—" She was going to say "your father's sister," but the expression was scarcely a happy one, and she turned it into, "She is, after all, growing old and lonely."

"So are we all!" he cried, with a lapse of tone that was now characteristic in him.

"She oughtn't to be so isolated from her proper relatives."

There was a moment's silence. Still playing with the book, he remarked, "You forget, she's got her favourite nephew."

A bright red flush spread over her cheeks. "What is the matter with you this afternoon?" she asked. "I should think you'd better go for a walk."

"Before I go, tell me what is the matter with you." He also flushed. "Why do you want me to make it up with my aunt?"

"Because it's right and proper."

"So? Or because she is old?"

"I don't understand," she retorted. But her eyes dropped. His sudden suspicion was true: she was legacy hunting.

"Agnes, dear Agnes," he began with passing tenderness, "how can you think of such things? You behave like a poor person. We don't want any money from Aunt Emily, or from any one else. It isn't virtue that makes me say it: we are not tempted in that way: we have as much as we want already."

"For the present," she answered, still looking aside.

"There isn't any future," he cried in a gust of despair.

"Rickie, what do you mean?"

What did he mean? He meant that the relations between them were fixed—that there would never be an influx of interest, nor even of passion. To the end of life they would go on beating time, and this was enough for her. She was content with the daily round, the common task, performed indifferently. But he had dreamt of another helpmate, and of other things.

"We don't want money—why, we don't even spend any on travelling. I've invested all my salary and more. As far as human foresight goes, we shall never want money." And his thoughts went out to the tiny grave. "You spoke of 'right and proper,' but the right and proper thing for my aunt to do is to leave every penny she's got to Stephen."

Her lip quivered, and for one moment he thought that she was going to cry. "What am I to do with you?" she said. "You talk like a person in poetry."

"I'll put it in prose. He's lived with her for twenty years, and he ought to be paid for it."

Poor Agnes! Indeed, what was she to do? The first moment she set foot in Cadover she had thought, "Oh, here is money. We must try and get it." Being a lady, she never mentioned the thought to her husband, but she concluded that it would occur to him too. And now, though it had occurred to him at last, he would not even write his aunt a little note.

He was to try her yet further. While they argued this point he flashed out with, "I ought to have told him that day when he called up to our room. There's where I went wrong first."

"Rickie!"

"In those days I was sentimental. I minded. For two pins I'd write to him this afternoon. Why shouldn't he know he's my brother? What's all this ridiculous mystery?"

She became incoherent.

"But WHY not? A reason why he shouldn't know."

"A reason why he SHOULD know," she retorted. "I never heard such rubbish! Give me a reason why he should know."

"Because the lie we acted has ruined our lives."

She looked in bewilderment at the well-appointed room.

"It's been like a poison we won't acknowledge. How many times have you thought of my brother? I've thought of him every day—not in love; don't misunderstand; only as a medicine I shirked. Down in what they call the subconscious self he has been hurting me." His voice broke. "Oh, my darling, we acted a lie then, and this letter reminds us of it and gives us one more chance. I have to say 'we' lied. I should be lying again if I took quite all the blame. Let us ask God's forgiveness together. Then let us write, as coldly as you please, to Stephen, and tell him he is my father's son."

Her reply need not be quoted. It was the last time he attempted intimacy. And the remainder of their conversation, though long and stormy, is also best forgotten.

Thus the first effect of Varden's letter was to make them quarrel. They had not openly disagreed before. In the evening he kissed her and said, "How absurd I was to get angry about things that happened last year. I will certainly not write to the person." She returned the kiss. But he knew that they had destroyed the habit of reverence, and would quarrel again. On his rounds he looked in at Varden and asked nonchalantly for the letter. He carried it off to his room. It was unwise of him, for his nerves were already unstrung, and the man he had tried to bury was stirring ominously. In the silence he examined the handwriting till he felt that a living creature was with him, whereas he, because his child had died, was dead. He perceived more clearly the cruelty of Nature, to whom our refinement and piety are but as bubbles, hurrying downwards on the turbid waters. They break, and the stream continues. His father, as a final insult, had brought into the world a man unlike all the rest of them, a man dowered with coarse kindliness and rustic strength, a kind of cynical ploughboy, against whom their own misery and weakness might stand more vividly relieved. "Born an Elliot—born a gentleman." So the vile phrase ran. But here was an Elliot whose badness was not even gentlemanly. For that Stephen was bad inherently he never doubted for a moment and he would have children: he, not Rickie, would contribute to the stream; he, through his remote posterity, might mingled with the unknown sea.

Thus musing he lay down to sleep, feeling diseased in body and soul. It was no wonder that the night was the most terrible he had ever known. He revisited Cambridge, and his name was a grey ghost over the door. Then there recurred the voice of a gentle shadowy woman, Mrs. Aberdeen, "It doesn't seem hardly right." Those had been her words, her only complaint against the mysteries of change and death. She bowed her head and laboured to make her "gentlemen" comfortable. She was labouring still. As he lay in bed he asked God to grant him her wisdom; that he might keep sorrow within due bounds; that he might abstain from extreme hatred and envy of Stephen. It was seldom that he prayed so definitely, or ventured to obtrude his private wishes. Religion was to him a service, a mystic communion with good; not a means of getting what he wanted on the earth. But tonight, through suffering, he was humbled, and became like Mrs. Aberdeen. Hour after hour he awaited sleep and tried to endure the faces that frothed in the gloom—his aunt's, his father's, and, worst of all, the triumphant face of his brother. Once he struck at it, and awoke, having hurt his hand on the wall. Then he prayed hysterically for pardon and rest.

Yet again did he awake, and from a more mysterious dream. He heard his mother crying. She was crying quite distinctly in the darkened room. He whispered, "Never mind, my darling, never mind," and a voice echoed, "Never mind—come away—let them die out—let them die out." He lit a candle, and the room was empty. Then, hurrying to the window, he saw above mean houses the frosty glories of Orion.

Henceforward he deteriorates. Let those who censure him suggest what he should do. He has lost the work that he loved, his friends, and his child. He remained conscientious and decent, but the spiritual part of him proceeded towards ruin.

XXIV

The coming months, though full of degradation and anxiety, were to bring him nothing so terrible as that night. It was the crisis of this agony. He was an outcast and a failure. But he was not again forced to contemplate these facts so clearly. Varden left in the morning, carrying the fatal letter with him. The whole house was relieved. The good angel was with the boys again, or else (as Herbert preferred to think) they had learnt a lesson, and were more humane in consequence. At all events, the disastrous term concluded quietly.

In the Christmas holidays the two masters made an abortive attempt to visit Italy, and at Easter there was talk of a cruise in the Aegean. Herbert actually went, and enjoyed Athens and Delphi. The Elliots paid a few visits together in England. They returned to Sawston about ten days before school opened, to find that Widdrington was again stopping with the Jacksons. Intercourse was painful, for the two families were scarcely on speaking terms; nor did the triumphant scaffoldings of the new boarding-house make things easier. (The party of progress had carried the day.) Widdrington was by nature touchy, but on this occasion he refused to take offence, and often dropped in to see them. His manner was friendly but critical. They agreed he was a nuisance. Then Agnes left, very abruptly, to see Mrs. Failing, and while she was away Rickie had a little stealthy intercourse.

Her absence, convenient as it was, puzzled him. Mrs. Silt, half goose, half stormy-petrel, had recently paid a flying visit to Cadover, and thence had flown, without an invitation, to Sawston. Generally she was not a welcome guest. On this occasion Agnes had welcomed her, and—so Rickie thought—had made her promise not to tell him something that she knew. The ladies had talked mysteriously. "Mr. Silt would be one with you there," said Mrs. Silt. Could there be any connection between the two visits?

Agnes's letters told him nothing: they never did. She was too clumsy or too cautious to express herself on paper. A drive to Stonehenge; an anthem in the Cathedral; Aunt Emily's love. And when he met her at Waterloo he learnt nothing (if there was anything to learn) from her face.

"How did you enjoy yourself?"

"Thoroughly."

"Were you and she alone?"

"Sometimes. Sometimes other people."

"Will Uncle Tony's Essays be published?"

Here she was more communicative. The book was at last in proof. Aunt Emily had written a charming introduction; but she was so idle, she never finished things off.

They got into an omnibus for the Army and Navy Stores: she wanted to do some shopping before going down to Sawston.

"Did you read any of the Essays?"

"Every one. Delightful. Couldn't put them down. Now and then he spoilt them by statistics—but you should read his descriptions of Nature. He agrees with you: says the hills and trees are alive! Aunt Emily called you his spiritual heir, which I thought nice of her. We both so lamented that you have stopped writing." She quoted fragments of the Essays as they went up in the Stores' lift.

"What else did you talk about?"

"I've told you all my news. Now for yours. Let's have tea first."

They sat down in the corridor amid ladies in every stage of fatigue—haggard ladies, scarlet ladies, ladies with parcels that twisted from every finger like joints of meat. Gentlemen were scarcer, but all were of the sub-fashionable type, to which Rickie himself now belonged.

"I haven't done anything," he said feebly. "Ate, read, been rude to tradespeople, talked to Widdrington. Herbert arrived this morning. He has brought a most beautiful photograph of the Parthenon."

"Mr. Widdrington?"

"Yes."

"What did you talk about?"

She might have heard every word. It was only the feeling of pleasure that he wished to conceal. Even when we love people, we desire to keep some corner secret from them, however small: it is a human right: it is personality. She began to cross question him, but they were interrupted. A young lady at an adjacent table suddenly rose and cried, "Yes, it is you. I thought so from your walk." It was Maud Ansell.

"Oh, do come and join us!" he cried. "Let me introduce my wife." Maud bowed quite stiffly, but Agnes, taking it for ill-breeding, was not offended.

"Then I will come!" she continued in shrill, pleasant tones, adroitly poising her tea things on either hand, and transferring them to the Elliots' table. "Why haven't you ever come to us, pray?"

"I think you didn't ask me!"

"You weren't to be asked." She sprawled forward with a wagging finger. But her eyes had the honesty of her brother's. "Don't you remember the day you left us? Father said, 'Now, Mr. Elliot—' Or did he call you 'Elliot'? How one does forget. Anyhow, father said you weren't to wait for an invitation, and you said, 'No, I won't.' Ours is a fair-sized house,"—she turned somewhat haughtily to Agnes,—"and the second spare room, on account of a harp that hangs on the wall, is always reserved for Stewart's friends."

"How is Mr. Ansell, your brother?" Maud's face fell. "Hadn't you heard?" she said in awe-struck tones.

"No."

"He hasn't got his fellowship. It's the second time he's failed. That means he will never get one. He will never be a don, nor live in Cambridge and that, as we had hoped."

"Oh, poor, poor fellow!" said Mrs. Elliot with a remorse that was sincere, though her congratulations would not have been. "I am so very sorry."

But Maud turned to Rickie. "Mr. Elliot, you might know. Tell me. What is wrong with Stewart's philosophy? What ought he to put in, or to alter, so as to succeed?"

Agnes, who knew better than this, smiled.

"I don't know," said Rickie sadly. They were none of them so clever, after all.

"Hegel," she continued vindictively. "They say he's read too much Hegel. But they never tell him what to read instead. Their own stuffy books, I suppose. Look here—no, that's the 'Windsor.'" After a little groping she produced a copy of "Mind," and handed it round as if it was a geological specimen. "Inside that there's a paragraph written about something Stewart's written about before, and there it says he's read too much Hegel, and it seems now that that's been the trouble all along." Her voice trembled. "I call it most unfair, and the fellowship's gone to a man who has counted the petals on an anemone."

Rickie had no inclination to smile.

"I wish Stewart had tried Oxford instead."

"I don't wish it!"

"You say that," she continued hotly, "and then you never come to see him, though you knew you were not to wait for an invitation."

"If it comes to that, Miss Ansell," retorted Rickie, in the laughing tones that one adopts on such occasions, "Stewart won't come to me, though he has had an invitation."

"Yes," chimed in Agnes, "we ask Mr. Ansell again and again, and he will have none of us."

Maud looked at her with a flashing eye. "My brother is a very peculiar person, and we ladies can't understand him. But I know one thing, and that's that he has a reason all round for what he does. Look here, I must be getting on. Waiter! Wai-ai-aiter! Bill, please. Separately, of course. Call the Army and Navy cheap! I know better!"

"How does the drapery department compare?" said Agnes sweetly.

The girl gave a sharp choking sound, gathered up her parcels, and left them. Rickie was too much disgusted with his wife to speak.

"Appalling person!" she gasped. "It was naughty of me, but I couldn't help it. What a dreadful fate for a clever man! To fail in life completely, and then to be thrown back on a family like that!"

"Maud is a snob and a Philistine. But, in her case, something emerges."

She glanced at him, but proceeded in her suavest tones, "Do let us make one great united attempt to get Mr. Ansell to Sawston."

"No."

"What a changeable friend you are! When we were engaged you were always talking about him."

"Would you finish your tea, and then we will buy the linoleum for the cubicles."

But she returned to the subject again, not only on that day but throughout the term. Could nothing be done for poor Mr. Ansell? It seemed that she could not rest until all that he had once held dear was humiliated. In this she strayed outside her nature: she was unpractical. And those who stray outside their nature invite disaster. Rickie, goaded by her, wrote to his friend again. The letter was in all ways unlike his old self. Ansell did not answer it. But he did write to Mr. Jackson, with whom he was not acquainted.

"Dear Mr. Jackson,—

"I understand from Widdrington that you have a large house. I would like to tell you how convenient it would be for me to come and stop in it. June suits me best.—

"Yours truly,

"Stewart Ansell"

To which Mr. Jackson replied that not only in June but during the whole year his house was at the disposal of Mr. Ansell and of any one who resembled him.

But Agnes continued her life, cheerfully beating time. She, too, knew that her marriage was a failure, and in her spare moments regretted it. She wished that her husband was handsomer, more successful, more dictatorial. But she would think, "No, no; one mustn't grumble. It can't be helped." Ansell was wrong in sup-posing she might ever leave Rickie. Spiritual apathy prevented her. Nor would she ever be tempted by a jollier man. Here criticism would willingly alter its tone. For Agnes also has her tragedy. She belonged to the type—not necessarily an elevated one—that loves once and once only. Her love for Gerald had not been a noble passion: no imagination transfigured it. But such as it was, it sprang to embrace him, and he carried it away with him when he died. Les amours gui suivrent sont moins involuntaires: by an effort of the will she had warmed herself for Rickie.

She is not conscious of her tragedy, and therefore only the gods need weep at it. But it is fair to remember that hitherto she moves as one from whom the inner life has been withdrawn.

XXV

"I am afraid," said Agnes, unfolding a letter that she had received in the morning, "that things go far from satisfactorily at Cadover."

The three were alone at supper. It was the June of Rickie's second year at Sawston.

"Indeed?" said Herbert, who took a friendly interest. "In what way?

"Do you remember us talking of Stephen—Stephen Wonham, who by an odd coincidence—"

"Yes. Who wrote last year to that miserable failure Varden. I do."

"It is about him."

"I did not like the tone of his letter."

Agnes had made her first move. She waited for her husband to reply to it. But he, though full of a painful curiosity, would not speak. She moved again.

"I don't think, Herbert, that Aunt Emily, much as I like her, is the kind of person to bring a young man up. At all events the results have been disastrous this time."

"What has happened?"

"A tangle of things." She lowered her voice. "Drink."

"Dear! Really! Was Mrs. Failing fond of him?"

"She used to be. She let him live at Cadover ever since he was a little boy. Naturally that cannot continue."

Rickie never spoke.

"And now he has taken to be violent and rude," she went on.

"In short, a beggar on horseback. Who is he? Has he got relatives?"

"She has always been both father and mother to him. Now it must all come to an end. I blame her—and she blames herself—for not being severe enough. He has grown up without fixed principles. He has always followed his inclinations, and one knows the result of that."

Herbert assented. "To me Mrs. Failing's course is perfectly plain. She has a certain responsibility. She must pay the youth's passage to one of the colonies, start him handsomely in some business, and then break off all communications."

"How funny! It is exactly what she is going to do."

"I shall then consider that she has behaved in a thoroughly honourable manner." He held out his plate for gooseberries. "His letter to Varden was neither helpful nor sympathetic, and, if written at all, it ought to have been both. I am not in the least surprised to learn that he has turned out badly. When you write next, would you tell her how sorry I am?"

"Indeed I will. Two years ago, when she was already a little anxious, she did so wish you could undertake him.

"I could not alter a grown man." But in his heart he thought he could, and smiled at his sister amiably. "Terrible, isn't it?" he remarked to Rickie. Rickie, who was trying not to mind anything, assented. And an onlooker would have supposed them a dispassionate trio, who were sorry both for Mrs. Failing and for the beggar who would bestride her horses' backs no longer. A new topic was introduced by the arrival of the evening post.

Herbert took up all the letters, as he often did.

"Jackson?" he exclaimed. "What does the fellow want?" He read, and his tone was mollified, "'Dear Mr. Pembroke,—Could you, Mrs. Elliot, and Mr. Elliot come to supper with us on Saturday next? I should not merely be pleased, I should be grateful. My wife is writing formally to Mrs. Elliot'—(Here, Agnes, take your letter),—but I venture to write as well, and to add my more uncouth entreaties.'—An olive-branch. It is time! But (ridiculous person!) does he think that we can leave the House deserted and all go out pleasuring in term time?—Rickie, a letter for you."

"Mine's the formal invitation," said Agnes. "How very odd! Mr. Ansell will be there. Surely we asked him here! Did you know he knew the Jacksons?"

"This makes refusal very difficult," said Herbert, who was anxious to accept. "At all events, Rickie ought to go."

"I do not want to go," said Rickie, slowly opening his own letter. "As Agnes says, Ansell has refused to come to us. I cannot put myself out for him."

"Who's yours from?" she demanded.

"Mrs. Silt," replied Herbert, who had seen the handwriting. "I trust she does not want to pay us a visit this term, with the examinations impending and all the machinery at full pressure. Though, Rickie, you will have to accept the Jacksons' invitation."

"I cannot possibly go. I have been too rude; with Widdrington we always meet here. I'll stop with the boys—" His voice caught suddenly. He had opened Mrs. Silt's letter.

"The Silts are not ill, I hope?"

"No. But, I say,"—he looked at his wife,—"I do think this is going too far. Really, Agnes."

"What has happened?"

"It is going too far," he repeated. He was nerving himself for another battle. "I cannot stand this sort of thing. There are limits."

He laid the letter down. It was Herbert who picked it up, and read: "Aunt Emily has just written to us. We are so glad that her troubles are over, in spite of the expense. It never does to live apart from one's own relatives so much as she has done up to now. He goes next Saturday to Canada. What you told her about him just turned the scale. She has asked us—"

"No, it's too much," he interrupted. "What I told her—told her about him—no, I will have it out at last. Agnes!"

"Yes?" said his wife, raising her eyes from Mrs. Jackson's formal invitation.

"It's you—it's you. I never mentioned him to her. Why, I've never seen her or written to her since. I accuse you."

Then Herbert overbore him, and he collapsed. He was asked what he meant. Why was he so excited? Of what did he accuse his wife. Each time he spoke more feebly, and before long the brother and sister were laughing at him. He felt bewildered, like a boy who knows that he is right but cannot put his case correctly. He repeated, "I've never mentioned him to her. It's a libel. Never in my life." And they cried, "My dear Rickie, what an absurd fuss!" Then his brain cleared. His eye fell on the letter that his wife had received from his aunt, and he reopened the battle.

"Agnes, give me that letter, if you please."

"Mrs. Jackson's?"

"My aunt's."

She put her hand on it, and looked at him doubtfully. She saw that she had failed to bully him.

"My aunt's letter," he repeated, rising to his feet and bending over the table towards her.

"Why, dear?"

"Yes, why indeed?" echoed Herbert. He too had bullied Rickie, but from a purer motive: he had tried to stamp out a dissension between husband and wife. It was not the first time he had intervened.

"The letter. For this reason: it will show me what you have done. I believe you have ruined Stephen. You have worked at it for two years. You have put words into my mouth to 'turn the scale' against him. He goes to Canada—and all the world thinks it is owing to me. As I said before—I advise you to stop smiling—you have gone a little too far."

They were all on their feet now, standing round the little table. Agnes said nothing, but the fingers of her delicate hand tightened upon the letter. When her husband snatched at it she resisted, and with the effect of a harlequinade everything went on the floor—lamb, mint sauce, gooseberries, lemonade, whisky. At once they were swamped in domesticities. She rang the bell for the servant, cries arose, dusters were brought, broken crockery (a wedding present) picked up from the carpet; while he stood wrathfully at the window, regarding the obscured sun's decline.

"I MUST see her letter," he repeated, when the agitation was over. He was too angry to be diverted from his purpose. Only slight emotions are thwarted by an interlude of farce.

"I've had enough of this quarrelling," she retorted. "You know that the Silts are inaccurate. I think you might have given me the benefit of the doubt. If you will know—have you forgotten that ride you took with him?"

"I—" he was again bewildered. "The ride where I dreamt—"

"The ride where you turned back because you could not listen to a disgraceful poem?"

"I don't understand."

"The poem was Aunt Emily. He read it to you and a stray soldier. Afterwards you told me. You said, 'Really it is shocking, his ingratitude. She ought to know about it' She does know, and I should be glad of an apology."

He had said something of the sort in a fit of irritation. Mrs. Silt was right—he had helped to turn the scale.

"Whatever I said, you knew what I meant. You knew I'd sooner cut my tongue out than have it used against him. Even then." He sighed. Had he ruined his brother? A curious tenderness came over him, and passed when he remembered his own dead child. "We have ruined him, then. Have you any objection to 'we'? We have disinherited him."

"I decide against you," interposed Herbert. "I have now heard both sides of this deplorable affair. You are talking most criminal nonsense. 'Disinherit!' Sentimental twaddle. It's been clear to me from the first that Mrs. Failing has been imposed upon by the Wonham man, a person with no legal claim on her, and any one who exposes him performs a public duty—"

"—And gets money."

"Money?" He was always uneasy at the word. "Who mentioned money?"

"Just understand me, Herbert, and of what it is that I accuse my wife." Tears came into his eyes. "It is not that I like the Wonham man, or think that he isn't a drunkard and worse. He's too awful in every way. But he ought to have my aunt's money, because he's lived all his life with her, and is her nephew as much as I am. You see, my father went wrong." He stopped, amazed at himself. How easy it had been to say! He was withering up: the power to care about this stupid secret had died.

When Herbert understood, his first thought was for Dunwood House.

"Why have I never been told?" was his first remark.

"We settled to tell no one," said Agnes. "Rickie, in his anxiety to prove me a liar, has broken his promise."

"I ought to have been told," said Herbert, his anger increasing. "Had I known, I could have averted this deplorable scene."

"Let me conclude it," said Rickie, again collapsing and leaving the dining-room. His impulse was to go straight to Cadover and make a business-like statement of the position to Stephen. Then the man would be armed, and perhaps fight the two women successfully, But he resisted the impulse. Why should he help one power of evil against another? Let them go intertwined to destruction. To enrich his brother would be as bad as enriching himself. If their aunt's money ever did come to him, he would refuse to accept it. That was the easiest and most dignified course. He troubled himself no longer with justice or pity, and the next day he asked his wife's pardon for his behaviour.

In the dining-room the conversation continued. Agnes, without much difficulty, gained her brother as an ally. She acknowledged that she had been wrong in not telling him, and he then declared that she had been right on every other point. She slurred a little over the incident of her treachery, for Herbert was sometimes clearsighted over details, though easily muddled in a general survey. Mrs. Failing had had plenty of direct causes of complaint, and she dwelt on these. She dealt, too, on the very handsome way in which the young man, "though he knew nothing, had never asked to know," was being treated by his aunt.

"'Handsome' is the word," said Herbert. "I hope not indulgently. He does not deserve indulgence."

And she knew that he, like herself, could remember money, and that it lent an acknowledged halo to her cause.

"It is not a savoury subject," he continued, with sudden stiffness. "I understand why Rickie is so hysterical. My impulse"—he laid his hand on her shoulder—"is to abandon it at once. But if I am to be of any use to you, I must hear it all. There are moments when we must look facts in the face."

She did not shrink from the subject as much as he thought, as much as she herself could have wished. Two years before, it had filled her with a physical loathing. But by now she had accustomed herself to it.

"I am afraid, Bertie boy, there is nothing else to bear, I have tried to find out again and again, but Aunt Emily will not tell me. I suppose it is natural. She wants to shield the Elliot name. She only told us in a fit of temper; then we all agreed to keep it to ourselves; then Rickie again mismanaged her, and ever since she has refused to let us know any details."

"A most unsatisfactory position." "So I feel." She sat down again with a sigh. Mrs. Failing had been a great trial to her orderly mind. "She is an odd woman. She is always laughing. She actually finds it amusing that we know no more."

"They are an odd family."

"They are indeed."

Herbert, with unusual sweetness, bent down and kissed her.

She thanked him.

Their tenderness soon passed. They exchanged it with averted eyes. It embarrassed them. There are moments for all of us when we seem obliged to speak in a new unprofitable tongue. One might fancy a seraph, vexed with our normal language, who touches the pious to blasphemy, the blasphemous to piety. The seraph passes, and we proceed unaltered—conscious, however, that we have not been ourselves, and that we may fail in this function yet again. So Agnes and Herbert, as they proceeded to discuss the Jackson's supper-party, had an uneasy memory of spiritual deserts, spiritual streams.

XXVI

Poor Mr. Ansell was actually sitting in the garden of Dunwood House. It was Sunday morning. The air was full of roasting beef. The sound of a manly hymn, taken very fast, floated over the road from the school chapel. He frowned, for he was reading a book, the Essays of Anthony Eustace Failing.

He was here on account of this book—at least so he told himself. It had just been published, and the Jacksons were sure that Mr. Elliot would have a copy. For a book one may go anywhere. It would not have been logical to enter Dunwood House for the purpose of seeing Rickie, when Rickie had not come to supper yesterday to see him. He was at Sawston to assure himself of his friend's grave. With quiet eyes he had intended to view the sods, with unfaltering fingers to inscribe the epitaph. Love remained. But in high matters he was practical. He knew that it would be useless to reveal it.

"Morning!" said a voice behind him.

He saw no reason to reply to this superfluous statement, and went on with his reading.

"Morning!" said the voice again.

As for the Essays, the thought was somewhat old-fashioned, and he picked many holes in it; nor was he anything but bored by the prospect of the brotherhood of man. However, Mr. Failing stuck to his guns, such as they were, and fired from them several good remarks. Very notable was his distinction between coarseness and vulgarity (coarseness, revealing something; vulgarity, concealing something), and his avowed preference for coarseness. Vulgarity, to him, had been the primal curse, the shoddy reticence that prevents man opening his heart to man, the power that makes against equality. From it sprang all the things that he hated—class shibboleths, ladies, lidies, the game laws, the Conservative party—all the things that accent the divergencies rather than the similarities in human nature. Whereas coarseness—But at this point Herbert Pembroke had scrawled with a blue pencil: "Childish. One reads no further."

"Morning!" repeated the voice.

Ansell read further, for here was the book of a man who had tried, however unsuccessfully, to practice what he preached. Mrs. Failing, in her Introduction, described with delicate irony his difficulties as a landlord; but she did not record the love in which his name was held. Nor could her irony touch him when he cried: "Attain the practical through the unpractical. There is no other road." Ansell was inclined to think that the unpractical is its own reward, but he respected those who attempted to journey beyond it. We must all of us go over the mountains. There is certainly no other road.

"Nice morning!" said the voice.

It was not a nice morning, so Ansell felt bound to speak. He answered: "No. Why?" A clod of earth immediately struck him on the back. He turned round indignantly, for he hated physical rudeness. A square man of ruddy aspect was pacing the gravel path, his hands deep in his pockets. He was very angry. Then he saw that the clod of earth nourished a blue lobelia, and that a wound of corresponding size appeared on the pie-shaped bed. He was not so angry. "I expect they will mind it," he reflected. Last night, at the Jacksons', Agnes had displayed a brisk pity that made him wish to wring her neck. Maude had not exaggerated. Mr. Pembroke had patronized through a sorrowful voice and large round eyes. Till he met these people he had never been told that his career was a failure. Apparently it was. They would never have been civil to him if it had been a success, if they or theirs had anything to fear from him.

In many ways Ansell was a conceited man; but he was never proud of being right. He had foreseen Rickie's catastrophe from the first, but derived from this no consolation. In many ways he was pedantic; but his pedantry lay close to the vineyards of life—far closer than that fetich Experience of the innumerable teacups. He had a great many facts to learn, and before he died he learnt a suitable quantity. But he never forgot that the holiness of the heart's imagination can alone classify these facts—can alone decide which is an exception, which an example. "How unpractical it all is!" That was his comment on Dunwood House. "How unbusiness-like! They live together without love. They work without conviction. They seek money without requiring it. They die, and nothing will have happened, either for themselves or for others." It is a comment that the academic mind will often make when first confronted with the world.

But he was becoming illogical. The clod of earth had disturbed him. Brushing the dirt off his back, he returned to the book. What a curious affair was the essay on "Gaps"! Solitude, star-crowned, pacing the fields of England, has a dialogue with Seclusion. He, poor little man, lives in the choicest scenery—among rocks, forests, emerald lawns, azure lakes. To keep people out he has built round his domain a high wall, on which is graven his motto—"Procul este profani." But he cannot enjoy himself. His only pleasure is in mocking the absent Profane. They are in his mind night and day. Their blemishes and stupidities form the subject of his great poem, "In the Heart of Nature." Then Solitude tells him that so it always will be until he makes a gap in the wall, and permits his seclusion to be the sport of circumstance. He obeys. The Profane invade him; but for short intervals they wander elsewhere, and during those intervals the heart of Nature is revealed to him.

This dialogue had really been suggested to Mr. Failing by a talk with his brother-in-law. It also touched Ansell. He looked at the man who had thrown the clod, and was now pacing with obvious youth and impudence upon the lawn. "Shall I improve my soul at his expense?" he thought. "I suppose I had better." In friendly tones he remarked, "Were you waiting for Mr. Pembroke?"

"No," said the young man. "Why?"

Ansell, after a moment's admiration, flung the Essays at him. They hit him in the back. The next moment he lay on his own back in the lobelia pie.

"But it hurts!" he gasped, in the tones of a puzzled civilization. "What you do hurts!" For the young man was nicking him over the shins with the rim of the book cover. "Little brute-ee—ow!"

"Then say Pax!"

Something revolted in Ansell. Why should he say Pax? Freeing his hand, he caught the little brute under the chin, and was again knocked into the lobelias by a blow on the mouth.

"Say Pax!" he repeated, pressing the philosopher's skull into the mould; and he added, with an anxiety that was somehow not offensive, "I do advise you. You'd really better."

Ansell swallowed a little blood. He tried to move, and he could not. He looked carefully into the young man's eyes and into the palm of his right hand, which at present swung unclenched, and he said "Pax!"

"Shake hands!" said the other, helping him up. There was nothing Ansell loathed so much as the hearty Britisher; but he shook hands, and they stared at each other awkwardly. With civil murmurs they picked the little blue flowers off each other's clothes. Ansell was trying to remember why they had quarrelled, and the young man was wondering why he had not guarded his chin properly. In the distance a hymn swung off—

"Fight the good. Fight with. All thy. Might."

They would be across from the chapel soon.

"Your book, sir?"

"Thank you, sir—yes."

"Why!" cried the young man—"why, it's 'What We Want'! At least the binding's exactly the same."

"It's called 'Essays,'" said Ansell.

"Then that's it. Mrs. Failing, you see, she wouldn't call it that, because three W's, you see, in a row, she said, are vulgar, and sound like Tolstoy, if you've heard of him."

Ansell confessed to an acquaintance, and then said, "Do you think 'What We Want' vulgar?" He was not at all interested, but he desired to escape from the atmosphere of pugilistic courtesy, more painful to him than blows themselves.

"It IS the same book," said the other—"same title, same binding." He weighed it like a brick in his muddy hands.

"Open it to see if the inside corresponds," said Ansell, swallowing a laugh and a little more blood with it.

With a liberal allowance of thumb-marks, he turned the pages over and read, "'the rural silence that is not a poet's luxury but a practical need for all men.' Yes, it is the same book." Smiling pleasantly over the discovery, he handed it back to the owner.

"And is it true?"

"I beg your pardon?"

"Is it true that rural silence is a practical need?"

"Don't ask me!"

"Have you ever tried it?"

"What?"

"Rural silence."

"A field with no noise in it, I suppose you mean. I don't understand."

Ansell smiled, but a slight fire in the man's eye checked him. After all, this was a person who could knock one down. Moreover, there was no reason why he should be teased. He had it in him to retort "No. Why?" He was not stupid in essentials. He was irritable—in Ansell's eyes a frequent sign of grace. Sitting down on the upturned seat, he remarked, "I like the book in many ways. I don't think 'What We Want' would have been a vulgar title. But I don't intend to spoil myself on the chance of mending the world, which is what the creed amounts to. Nor am I keen on rural silences."

"Curse!" he said thoughtfully, sucking at an empty pipe.

"Tobacco?"

"Please."

"Rickie's is invariably—filthy."

"Who says I know Rickie?"

"Well, you know his aunt. It's a possible link. Be gentle with Rickie. Don't knock him down if he doesn't think it's a nice morning."

The other was silent.

"Do you know him well?"

"Kind of." He was not inclined to talk. The wish to smoke was very violent in him, and Ansell noticed how he gazed at the wreaths that ascended from bowl and stem, and how, when the stem was in his mouth, he bit it. He gave the idea of an animal with just enough soul to contemplate its own bliss. United with refinement, such a type was common in Greece. It is not common today, and Ansell was surprised to find it in a friend of Rickie's. Rickie, if he could even "kind of know" such a creature, must be stirring in his grave.

"Do you know his wife too?"

"Oh yes. In a way I know Agnes. But thank you for this tobacco. Last night I nearly died. I have no money."

"Take the whole pouch—do."

After a moment's hesitation he did. "Fight the good" had scarcely ended, so quickly had their intimacy grown.

"I suppose you're a friend of Rickie's?"

Ansell was tempted to reply, "I don't know him at all." But it seemed no moment for the severer truths, so he said, "I knew him well at Cambridge, but I have seen very little of him since."

"Is it true that his baby was lame?"

"I believe so."

His teeth closed on his pipe. Chapel was over. The organist was prancing through the voluntary, and the first ripple of boys had already reached Dunwood House. In a few minutes the masters would be here too, and Ansell, who was becoming interested, hurried the conversation forward.

"Have you come far?"

"From Wiltshire. Do you know Wiltshire?" And for the first time there came into his face the shadow of a sentiment, the passing tribute to some mystery. "It's a good country. I live in one of the finest valleys out of Salisbury Plain. I mean, I lived."

"Have you been dismissed from Cadover, without a penny in your pocket?"

He was alarmed at this. Such knowledge seemed simply diabolical. Ansell explained that if his boots were chalky, if his clothes had obviously been slept in, if he knew Mrs. Failing, if he knew Wiltshire, and if he could buy no tobacco—then the deduction was possible. "You do just attend," he murmured.

The house was filling with boys, and Ansell saw, to his regret, the head of Agnes over the thuyia hedge that separated the small front garden from the side lawn where he was sitting. After a few minutes it was followed by the heads of Rickie and Mr. Pembroke. All the heads were turned the other way. But they would find his card in the hall, and if the man had left any message they would find that too. "What are you?" he demanded. "Who are you—your name—I don't care about that. But it interests me to class people, and up to now I have failed with you."

"I—" He stopped. Ansell reflected that there are worse answers. "I really don't know what I am. Used to think I was something special, but strikes me now I feel much like other chaps. Used to look down on the labourers. Used to take for granted I was a gentleman, but really I don't know where I do belong."

"One belongs to the place one sleeps in and to the people one eats with."

"As often as not I sleep out of doors and eat by myself, so that doesn't get you any further."

A silence, akin to poetry, invaded Ansell. Was it only a pose to like this man, or was he really wonderful? He was not romantic, for Romance is a figure with outstretched hands, yearning for the unattainable. Certain figures of the Greeks, to whom we continually return, suggested him a little. One expected nothing of him—no purity of phrase nor swift edged thought. Yet the conviction grew that he had been back somewhere—back to some table of the gods, spread in a field where there is no noise, and that he belonged for ever to the guests with whom he had eaten. Meanwhile he was simple and frank, and what he could tell he would tell to any one. He had not the suburban reticence. Ansell asked him, "Why did Mrs. Failing turn you out of Cadover? I should like to hear that too."

"Because she was tired of me. Because, again, I couldn't keep quiet over the farm hands. I ask you, is it right?" He became incoherent. Ansell caught, "And they grow old—they don't play games—it ends they can't play." An illustration emerged. "Take a kitten—if you fool about with her, she goes on playing well into a cat."

"But Mrs. Failing minded no mice being caught."

"Mice?" said the young man blankly. "What I was going to say is, that some one was jealous of my being at Cadover. I'll mention no names, but I fancy it was Mrs. Silt. I'm sorry for her if it was. Anyhow, she set Mrs. Failing against me. It came on the top of other things—and out I went."

"What did Mrs. Silt, whose name I don't mention, say?"

He looked guilty. "I don't know. Easy enough to find something to say. The point is that she said something. You know, Mr.—I don't know your name, mine's Wonham, but I'm more grateful than I can put it over this tobacco. I mean, you ought to know there is another side to this quarrel. It's wrong, but it's there."

Ansell told him not to be uneasy: he had already guessed that there might be another side. But he could not make out why Mr. Wonham should have come straight from the aunt to the nephew. They were now sitting on the upturned seat. "What We Want," a good deal shattered, lay between them.

"On account of above-mentioned reasons, there was a row. I don't know—you can guess the style of thing. She wanted to treat me to the colonies, and had up the parson to talk soft-sawder and make out that a boundless continent was the place for a lad like me. I said, 'I can't run up to the Rings without getting tired, nor gallop a horse out of this view without tiring it, so what is the point of a boundless continent?' Then I saw that she was frightened of me, and bluffed a bit more, and in the end I was nipped. She caught me—just like her! when I had nothing on but flannels, and was coming into the house, having licked the Cadchurch team. She stood up in the doorway between those stone pilasters and said, 'No! Never again!' and behind her was Wilbraham, whom I tried to turn out, and the gardener, and poor old Leighton, who hates being hurt. She said, 'There's a hundred pounds for you at the London bank, and as much more in December. Go!' I said, 'Keep your—money, and tell me whose son I am.' I didn't care really. I only said it on the off-chance of hurting her. Sure enough, she caught on to the doorhandle (being lame) and said, 'I can't—I promised—I don't really want to,' and Wilbraham did stare. Then—she's very queer—she burst out laughing, and went for the packet after all, and we heard her laugh through the window as she got it. She rolled it at me down the steps, and she says, 'A leaf out of the eternal comedy for you, Stephen,' or something of that sort. I opened it as I walked down the drive, she laughing always and catching on to the handle of the front door. Of course it wasn't comic at all. But down in the village there were both cricket teams, already a little tight, and the mad plumber shouting 'Rights of Man!' They knew I was turned out. We did have a row, and kept it up too. They daren't touch Wilbraham's windows, but there isn't much glass left up at Cadover. When you start, it's worth going on, but in the end I had to cut. They subscribed a bob here and a bob there, and these are Flea Thompson's Sundays. I sent a line to Leighton not to forward my own things: I don't fancy them. They aren't really mine." He did not mention his great symbolic act, performed, it is to be feared, when he was rather drunk and the friendly policeman was looking the other way. He had cast all his flannels into the little millpond, and then waded himself through the dark cold water to the new clothes on the other side. Some one had flung his pipe and his packet after him. The packet had fallen short. For this reason it was wet when he handed it to Ansell, and ink that had been dry for twenty-three years had begun to run again.

"I wondered if you're right about the hundred pounds," said Ansell gravely. "It is pleasant to be proud, but it is unpleasant to die in the night through not having any tobacco."

"But I'm not proud. Look how I've taken your pouch! The hundred pounds was—well, can't you see yourself, it was quite different? It was, so to speak, inconvenient for me to take the hundred pounds. Or look again how I took a shilling from a boy who earns nine bob a-week! Proves pretty conclusively I'm not proud."

Ansell saw it was useless to argue. He perceived, beneath the slatternly use of words, the man, buttoned up in them, just as his body was buttoned up in a shoddy suit,—and he wondered more than ever that such a man should know the Elliots. He looked at the face, which was frank, proud, and beautiful, if truth is beauty. Of mercy or tact such a face knew little. It might be coarse, but it had in it nothing vulgar or wantonly cruel. "May I read these papers?" he said.

"Of course. Oh yes; didn't I say? I'm Rickie's half-brother, come here to tell him the news. He doesn't know. There it is, put shortly for you. I was saying, though, that I bolted in the dark, slept in the rifle-butts above Salisbury, the sheds where they keep the cardboard men, you know, never locked up as they ought to be. I turned the whole place upside down to teach them."

"Here is your packet again," said Ansell. "Thank you. How interesting!" He rose from the seat and turned towards Dunwood House. He looked at the bow-windows, the cheap picturesque gables, the terracotta dragons clawing a dirty sky. He listened to the clink of plates and to the voice of Mr. Pembroke taking one of his innumerable roll-calls. He looked at the bed of lobelias. How interesting! What else was there to say?

"One must be the son of some one," remarked Stephen. And that was all he had to say. To him those names on the moistened paper were mere antiquities. He was neither proud of them nor ashamed. A man must have parents, or he cannot enter the delightful world. A man, if he has a brother, may reasonably visit him, for they may have interests in common. He continued his narrative, how in the night he had heard the clocks, how at daybreak, instead of entering the city, he had struck eastward to save money,—while Ansell still looked at the house and found that all his imagination and knowledge could lead him no farther than this: how interesting!

"—And what do you think of that for a holy horror?"

"For a what?" said Ansell, his thoughts far away.

"This man I am telling you about, who gave me a lift towards Andover, who said I was a blot on God's earth."

One o'clock struck. It was strange that neither of them had had any summons from the house.

"He said I ought to be ashamed of myself. He said, 'I'll not be the means of bringing shame to an honest gentleman and lady.' I told him not to be a fool. I said I knew what I was about. Rickie and Agnes are properly educated, which leads people to look at things straight, and not go screaming about blots. A man like me, with just a little reading at odd hours—I've got so far, and Rickie has been through Cambridge."

"And Mrs. Elliot?"

"Oh, she won't mind, and I told the man so; but he kept on saying, 'I'll not be the means of bringing shame to an honest gentleman and lady,' until I got out of his rotten cart." His eye watched the man a Nonconformist, driving away over God's earth. "I caught the train by running. I got to Waterloo at—"

Here the parlour-maid fluttered towards them, Would Mr. Wonham come in? Mrs. Elliot would be glad to see him now.

"Mrs. Elliot?" cried Ansell. "Not Mr. Elliot?"

"It's all the same," said Stephen, and moved towards the house.

"You see, I only left my name. They don't know why I've come."

"Perhaps Mr. Elliot sees me meanwhile?"

The parlour-maid looked blank. Mr. Elliot had not said so. He had been with Mrs. Elliot and Mr. Pembroke in the study. Now the gentlemen had gone upstairs.

"All right, I can wait." After all, Rickie was treating him as he had treated Rickie, as one in the grave, to whom it is futile to make any loving motion. Gone upstairs—to brush his hair for dinner! The irony of the situation appealed to him strongly. It reminded him of the Greek Drama, where the actors know so little and the spectators so much.

"But, by the bye," he called after Stephen, "I think I ought to tell you—don't—"

"What is it?"

"Don't—" Then he was silent. He had been tempted to explain everything, to tell the fellow how things stood, that he must avoid this if he wanted to attain that; that he must break the news to Rickie gently; that he must have at least one battle royal with Agnes. But it was contrary to his own spirit to coach people: he held the human soul to be a very delicate thing, which can receive eternal damage from a little patronage. Stephen must go into the house simply as himself, for thus alone would he remain there.

"I ought to knock my pipe out? Was that it?" "By no means. Go in, your pipe and you."

He hesitated, torn between propriety and desire. Then he followed the parlour-maid into the house smoking. As he entered the dinner-bell rang, and there was the sound of rushing feet, which died away into shuffling and silence. Through the window of the boys' dining-hall came the colourless voice of Rickie—"'Benedictus benedicat.'"

XXVI

Ansell prepared himself to witness the second act of the drama; forgetting that all this world, and not part of it, is a stage.

XXVII

The parlour-maid took Mr. Wonham to the study. He had been in the drawing-room before, but had got bored, and so had strolled out into the garden. Now he was in better spirits, as a man ought to be who has knocked down a man. As he passed through the hall he sparred at the teak monkey, and hung his cap on the bust of Hermes. And he greeted Mrs. Elliot with a pleasant clap of laughter. "Oh, I've come with the most tremendous news!" he cried.

She bowed, but did not shake hands, which rather surprised him. But he never troubled over "details." He seldom watched people, and never thought that they were watching him. Nor could he guess how much it meant to her that he should enter her presence smoking. Had she not said once at Cadover, "Oh, please smoke; I love the smell of a pipe"?

"Would you sit down? Exactly there, please." She placed him at a large table, opposite an inkpot and a pad of blotting-paper.

"Will you tell your 'tremendous news' to me? My brother and my husband are giving the boys their dinner."

"Ah!" said Stephen, who had had neither time nor money for breakfast in London.

"I told them not to wait for me."

So he came to the point at once. He trusted this handsome woman. His strength and his youth called to hers, expecting no prudish response. "It's very odd. It is that I'm Rickie's brother. I've just found out. I've come to tell you all."

"Yes?"

He felt in his pocket for the papers. "Half-brother I ought to have said."

"Yes?"

"I'm illegitimate. Legally speaking, that is, I've been turned out of Cadover. I haven't a penny. I—"

"There is no occasion to inflict the details." Her face, which had been an even brown, began to flush slowly in the centre of the cheeks. The colour spread till all that he saw of her was suffused, and she turned away. He thought he had shocked her, and so did she. Neither knew that the body can be insincere and express not the emotions we feel but those that we should like to feel. In reality she was quite calm, and her dislike of him had nothing emotional in it as yet.

"You see—" he began. He was determined to tell the fidgety story, for the sooner it was over the sooner they would have something to eat. Delicacy he lacked, and his sympathies were limited. But such as they were, they rang true: he put no decorous phantom between him and his desires.

"I do see. I have seen for two years." She sat down at the head of the table, where there was another ink-pot. Into this she dipped a pen. "I have seen everything, Mr. Wonham—who you are, how you have behaved at Cadover, how you must have treated Mrs. Failing yesterday; and now"—her voice became very grave—"I see why you have come here, penniless. Before you speak, we know what you will say."

His mouth fell open, and he laughed so merrily that it might have given her a warning. But she was thinking how to follow up her first success. "And I thought I was bringing tremendous news!" he cried. "I only twisted it out of Mrs. Failing last night. And Rickie knows too?"

"We have known for two years."

"But come, by the bye,—if you've known for two years, how is it you didn't—" The laugh died out of his eyes. "You aren't ashamed?" he asked, half rising from his chair. "You aren't like the man towards Andover?"

"Please, please sit down," said Agnes, in the even tones she used when speaking to the servants; "let us not discuss side issues. I am a horribly direct person, Mr. Wonham. I go always straight to the point." She opened a chequebook. "I am afraid I shall shock you. For how much?"

He was not attending.

"There is the paper we suggest you shall sign." She pushed towards him a pseudo-legal document, just composed by Herbert.

"In consideration of the sum of..., I agree to perpetual silence—to restrain from libellous...never to molest the said Frederick Elliot by intruding—'"

His brain was not quick. He read the document over twice, and he could still say, "But what's that cheque for?"

"It is my husband's. He signed for you as soon as we heard you were here. We guessed you had come to be silenced. Here is his signature. But he has left the filling in for me. For how much? I will cross it, shall I? You will just have started a banking account, if I understand Mrs. Failing rightly. It is not quite accurate to say you are penniless: I heard from her just before you returned from your cricket. She allows you two hundred a-year, I think. But this additional sum—shall I date the cheque Saturday or for tomorrow?"

At last he found words. Knocking his pipe out on the table, he said slowly, "Here's a very bad mistake."

"It is quite possible," retorted Agnes. She was glad she had taken the offensive, instead of waiting till he began his blackmailing, as had been the advice of Rickie. Aunt Emily had said that very spring, "One's only hope with Stephen is to start bullying first." Here he was, quite bewildered, smearing the pipe-ashes with his thumb. He asked to read the document again. "A stamp and all!" he remarked.

They had anticipated that his claim would exceed two pounds.

"I see. All right. It takes a fool a minute. Never mind. I've made a bad mistake."

"You refuse?" she exclaimed, for he was standing at the door. "Then do your worst! We defy you!"

"That's all right, Mrs. Elliot," he said roughly. "I don't want a scene with you, nor yet with your husband. We'll say no more about it. It's all right. I mean no harm."

"But your signature then! You must sign—you—"

He pushed past her, and said as he reached for his cap, "There, that's all right. It's my mistake. I'm sorry." He spoke like a farmer who has failed to sell a sheep. His manner was utterly prosaic, and up to the last she thought he had not understood her. "But it's money we offer you," she informed him, and then darted back to the study, believing for one terrible moment that he had picked up the blank cheque. When she returned to the hall he had gone. He was walking down the road rather quickly. At the corner he cleared his throat, spat into the gutter, and disappeared.

"There's an odd finish," she thought. She was puzzled, and determined to recast the interview a little when she related it to Rickie. She had not succeeded, for the paper was still unsigned. But she had so cowed Stephen that he would probably rest content with his two hundred a-year, and never come troubling them again. Clever management, for one knew him to be rapacious: she had heard tales of him lending to the poor and exacting repayment to the uttermost farthing. He had also stolen at school. Moderately triumphant, she hurried into the side-garden: she had just remembered Ansell: she, not Rickie, had received his card.

"Oh, Mr. Ansell!" she exclaimed, awaking him from some day-dream. "Haven't either Rickie or Herbert been out to you? Now, do come into dinner, to show you aren't offended. You will find all of us assembled in the boys' dining-hall."

To her annoyance he accepted.

"That is, if the Jacksons are not expecting you."

The Jacksons did not matter. If he might brush his clothes and bathe his lip, he would like to come.

"Oh, what has happened to you? And oh, my pretty lobelias!"

He replied, "A momentary contact with reality," and she, who did not look for sense in his remarks, hurried away to the dining-hall to announce him.

The dining-hall was not unlike the preparation room. There was the same parquet floor, and dado of shiny pitchpine. On its walls also were imperial portraits, and over the harmonium to which they sang the evening hymns was spread the Union Jack. Sunday dinner, the most pompous meal of the week, was in progress. Her brother sat at the head of the high table, her husband at the head of the second. To each he gave a reassuring nod and went to her own seat, which was among the junior boys. The beef was being carried out; she stopped it. "Mr. Ansell is coming," she called. "Herbert there is more room by you; sit up straight, boys." The boys sat up straight, and a respectful hush spread over the room.

XXVII

"Here he is!" called Rickie cheerfully, taking his cue from his wife. "Oh, this is splendid!" Ansell came in. "I'm so glad you managed this. I couldn't leave these wretches last night!" The boys tittered suitably. The atmosphere seemed normal. Even Herbert, though longing to hear what had happened to the blackmailer, gave adequate greeting to their guest: "Come in, Mr. Ansell; come here. Take us as you find us!"

"I understood," said Stewart, "that I should find you all. Mrs. Elliot told me I should. On that understanding I came."

It was at once evident that something had gone wrong.

Ansell looked round the room carefully. Then clearing his throat and ruffling his hair, he began—"I cannot see the man with whom I have talked, intimately, for an hour, in your garden."

The worst of it was they were all so far from him and from each other, each at the end of a tableful of inquisitive boys. The two masters looked at Agnes for information, for her reassuring nod had not told them much. She looked hopelessly back.

"I cannot see this man," repeated Ansell, who remained by the harmonium in the midst of astonished waitresses. "Is he to be given no lunch?"

Herbert broke the silence by fresh greetings. Rickie knew that the contest was lost, and that his friend had sided with the enemy. It was the kind of thing he would do. One must face the catastrophe quietly and with dignity. Perhaps Ansell would have turned on his heel, and left behind him only vague suspicions, if Mrs. Elliot had not tried to talk him down. "Man," she cried—"what man? Oh, I know—terrible bore! Did he get hold of you?"—thus committing their first blunder, and causing Ansell to say to Rickie, "Have you seen your brother?"

"I have not."

"Have you been told he was here?"

Rickie's answer was inaudible.

"Have you been told you have a brother?"

"Let us continue this conversation later."

"Continue it? My dear man, how can we until you know what I'm talking about? You must think me mad; but I tell you solemnly that you have a brother of whom you've never heard, and that he was in this house ten minutes ago." He paused impressively. "Your wife has happened to see him first. Being neither serious nor truthful, she is keeping you apart, telling him some lie and not telling you a word."

There was a murmur of alarm. One of the prefects rose, and Ansell set his back to the wall, quite ready for a battle. For two years he had waited for his opportunity. He would hit out at Mrs. Elliot like any ploughboy now that it had come. Rickie said: "There is a slight misunderstanding. I, like my wife, have known what there is to know for two years"—a dignified rebuff, but their second blunder.

"Exactly," said Agnes. "Now I think Mr. Ansell had better go."

"Go?" exploded Ansell. "I've everything to say yet. I beg your pardon, Mrs. Elliot, I am concerned with you no longer. This man"—he turned to the avenue of faces—"this man who teaches you has a brother. He has known of him two years and been ashamed. He has—oh—oh—how it fits together! Rickie, it's you, not Mrs. Silt, who must have sent tales of him to your aunt. It's you who've turned him out of Cadover. It's you who've ordered him to be ruined today."

Now Herbert arose. "Out of my sight, sir! But have it from me first that Rickie and his aunt have both behaved most generously. No, no, Agnes, I'll not be interrupted. Garbled versions must not get about. If the Wonham man is not satisfied now, he must be insatiable. He cannot levy blackmail on us for ever. Sir, I give you two minutes; then you will be expelled by force."

"Two minutes!" sang Ansell. "I can say a great deal in that." He put one foot on a chair and held his arms over the quivering room. He seemed transfigured into a Hebrew prophet passionate for satire and the truth. "Oh, keep quiet for two minutes," he cried, "and I'll tell you something you'll be glad to hear. You're a little afraid Stephen may come back. Don't be afraid. I bring good news. You'll never see him nor any one like him again. I must speak very plainly, for you are all three fools. I don't want you to say afterwards, 'Poor Mr. Ansell tried to be clever.' Generally I don't mind, but I should mind today. Please listen. Stephen is a bully; he drinks; he knocks one down; but he would sooner die than take money from people he did not love. Perhaps he will die, for he has nothing but a few pence that the poor gave him and some tobacco which, to my eternal glory, he accepted from me. Please listen again. Why did he come here? Because he thought you would love him, and was ready to love you. But I tell you, don't be afraid. He would sooner die now than say you were his brother. Please listen again—"

"Now, Stewart, don't go on like that," said Rickie bitterly. "It's easy enough to preach when you are an outsider. You would be more charitable if such a thing had happened to yourself. Easy enough to be unconventional when you haven't suffered and know nothing of the facts. You love anything out of the way, anything queer, that doesn't often happen, and so you get excited over this. It's useless, my dear man; you have hurt me, but you will never upset me. As soon as you stop this ridiculous scene we will finish our dinner. Spread this scandal; add to it. I'm too old to mind such nonsense. I cannot help my father's disgrace, on the one hand; nor, on the other, will I have anything to do with his blackguard of a son."

So the secret was given to the world. Agnes might colour at his speech; Herbert might calculate the effect of it on the entries for Dunwood House; but he cared for none of these things. Thank God! he was withered up at last.

"Please listen again," resumed Ansell. "Please correct two slight mistakes: firstly, Stephen is one of the greatest people I have ever met; secondly, he's not your father's son. He's the son of your mother."

It was Rickie, not Ansell, who was carried from the hall, and it was Herbert who pronounced the blessing—

"Benedicto benedicatur."

XXVII

A profound stillness succeeded the storm, and the boys, slipping away from their meal, told the news to the rest of the school, or put it in the letters they were writing home.

XXVIII

The soul has her own currency. She mints her spiritual coinage and stamps it with the image of some beloved face. With it she pays her debts, with it she reckons, saying, "This man has worth, this man is worthless." And in time she forgets its origin; it seems to her to be a thing unalterable, divine. But the soul can also have her bankruptcies.

Perhaps she will be the richer in the end. In her agony she learns to reckon clearly. Fair as the coin may have been, it was not accurate; and though she knew it not, there were treasures that it could not buy. The face, however beloved, was mortal, and as liable as the soul herself to err. We do but shift responsibility by making a standard of the dead.

There is, indeed, another coinage that bears on it not man's image but God's. It is incorruptible, and the soul may trust it safely; it will serve her beyond the stars. But it cannot give us friends, or the embrace of a lover, or the touch of children, for with our fellow mortals it has no concern. It cannot even give the joys we call trivial—fine weather, the pleasures of meat and drink, bathing and the hot sand afterwards, running, dreamless sleep. Have we learnt the true discipline of a bankruptcy if we turn to such coinage as this? Will it really profit us so much if we save our souls and lose the whole world?

PART 3 — WILTSHIRE

XXIX

Robert—there is no occasion to mention his surname: he was a young farmer of some education who tried to coax the aged soil of Wiltshire scientifically—came to Cadover on business and fell in love with Mrs. Elliot. She was there on her bridal visit, and he, an obscure nobody, was received by Mrs. Failing into the house and treated as her social equal. He was good-looking in a bucolic way, and people sometimes mistook him for a gentleman until they saw his hands. He discovered this, and one of the slow, gentle jokes he played on society was to talk upon some cultured subject with his hands behind his back and then suddenly reveal them. "Do you go in for boating?" the lady would ask; and then he explained that those particular weals are made by the handles of the plough. Upon which she became extremely interested, but found an early opportunity of talking to some one else.

He played this joke on Mrs. Elliot the first evening, not knowing that she observed him as he entered the room. He walked heavily, lifting his feet as if the carpct was furrowed, and he had no evening clothes. Every one tried to put him at his ease, but she rather suspected that he was there already, and envied him. They were introduced, and spoke of Byron, who was still fashionable. Out came his hands—the only rough hands in the drawing-room, the only hands that had ever worked. She was filled with some strange approval, and liked him.

After dinner they met again, to speak not of Byron but of manure. The other people were so clever and so amusing that it relieved her to listen to a man who told her three times not to buy artificial manure ready made, but, if she would use it, to make it herself at the last moment. Because the ammonia evaporated. Here were two packets of powder. Did they smell? No. Mix them together and pour some coffee—An appalling smell at once burst forth, and every one began to cough and cry. This was good for the earth when she felt sour, for he knew when the earth was ill. He knew, too, when she was hungry he spoke of her tantrums—the strange unscientific element in her that will baffle the scientist to the end of time. "Study away, Mrs. Elliot," he told her; "read all the books you can get hold of; but when it comes to the point, stroll out with a pipe in your mouth and do a bit of guessing." As he talked, the earth became a living being—or rather a being with a living skin,—and manure no longer dirty stuff, but a symbol of regeneration and of the birth of life from life. "So it goes on for ever!" she cried excitedly.

He replied: "Not for ever. In time the fire at the centre will cool, and nothing can go on then."

He advanced into love with open eyes, slowly, heavily, just as he had advanced across the drawing room carpet. But this time the bride did not observe his tread. She was listening to her husband, and trying not to be so stupid. When he was close to her—so close that it was difficult not to take her in his arms—he spoke to Mr. Failing, and was at once turned out of Cadover.

"I'm sorry," said Mr. Failing, as he walked down the drive with his hand on his guest's shoulder. "I had no notion you were that sort. Any one who behaves like that has to stop at the farm."

"Any one?"

"Any one." He sighed heavily, not for any personal grievance, but because he saw how unruly, how barbaric, is the soul of man. After all, this man was more civilized than most.

"Are you angry with me, sir?" He called him "sir," not because he was richer or cleverer or smarter, not because he had helped to educate him and had lent him money, but for a reason more profound—for the reason that there are gradations in heaven.

"I did think you—that a man like you wouldn't risk making people unhappy. My sister-in-law—I don't say this to stop you loving her; something else must do that—my sister-in-law, as far as I know, doesn't care for you one little bit. If you had said anything, if she had guessed that a chance person was in—this fearful state, you would simply—have opened hell. A woman of her sort would have lost all—"

"I knew that."

Mr. Failing removed his hand. He was displeased.

"But something here," said Robert incoherently. "This here." He struck himself heavily on the heart. "This here, doing something so unusual, makes it not matter what she loses—I—" After a silence he asked, "Have I quite followed you, sir, in that business of the brotherhood of man?"

"How do you mean?"

"I thought love was to bring it about."

"Love of another man's wife? Sensual love? You have understood nothing—nothing." Then he was ashamed, and cried, "I understand nothing myself." For he remembered that sensual and spiritual are not easy words to use; that there are, perhaps, not two Aphrodites, but one Aphrodite with a Janus face. "I only understand that you must try to forget her."

"I will not try."

"Promise me just this, then—not to do anything crooked."

"I'm straight. No boasting, but I couldn't do a crooked thing—No, not if I tried."

And so appallingly straight was he in after years, that Mr. Failing wished that he had phrased the promise differently.

XXIX

Robert simply waited. He told himself that it was hopeless; but something deeper than himself declared that there was hope. He gave up drink, and kept himself in all ways clean, for he wanted to be worthy of her when the time came. Women seemed fond of him, and caused him to reflect with pleasure, "They do run after me. There must be something in me. Good. I'd be done for if there wasn't." For six years he turned up the earth of Wiltshire, and read books for the sake of his mind, and talked to gentlemen for the sake of their patois, and each year he rode to Cadover to take off his hat to Mrs. Elliot, and, perhaps, to speak to her about the crops. Mr. Failing was generally present, and it struck neither man that those dull little visits were so many words out of which a lonely woman might build sentences. Then Robert went to London on business. He chanced to see Mr. Elliot with a strange lady. The time had come.

He became diplomatic, and called at Mr. Elliot's rooms to find things out. For if Mrs. Elliot was happier than he could ever make her, he would withdraw, and love her in renunciation. But if he could make her happier, he would love her in fulfilment. Mr. Elliot admitted him as a friend of his brother-in-law's, and felt very broad-minded as he did so. Robert, however, was a success. The youngish men there found him interesting, and liked to shock him with tales of naughty London and naughtier Paris. They spoke of "experience" and "sensations" and "seeing life," and when a smile ploughed over his face, concluded that his prudery was vanquished. He saw that they were much less vicious than they supposed: one boy had obviously read his sensations in a book. But he could pardon vice. What he could not pardon was triviality, and he hoped that no decent woman could pardon it either. There grew up in him a cold, steady anger against these silly people who thought it advanced to be shocking, and who described, as something particularly choice and educational, things that he had understood and fought against for years. He inquired after Mrs. Elliot, and a boy tittered. It seemed that she "did not know," that she lived in a remote suburb, taking care of a skinny baby. "I shall call some time or other," said Robert. "Do," said Mr. Elliot, smiling. And next time he saw his wife he congratulated her on her rustic admirer.

She had suffered terribly. She had asked for bread, and had been given not even a stone. People talk of hungering for the ideal, but there is another hunger, quite as divine, for facts. She had asked for facts and had been given "views," "emotional standpoints," "attitudes towards life." To a woman who believed that facts are beautiful, that the living world is beautiful beyond the laws of beauty, that manure is neither gross nor ludicrous, that a fire, not eternal, glows at the heart of the earth, it was intolerable to be put off with what the Elliots called "philosophy," and, if she refused, to be told that she had no sense of humour. "Tarrying into the Elliot family." It had sounded so splendid, for she was a penniless child with nothing to offer, and the Elliots held their heads high. For what reason? What had they ever done, except say sarcastic things, and limp, and be refined? Mr. Failing suffered too, but she suffered more, inasmuch as Frederick was more impossible than Emily. He did not like her, he practically lived apart, he was not even faithful or polite. These were grave faults, but they were human ones: she could even imagine them in a man she loved. What she could never love was a dilettante.

Robert brought her an armful of sweet-peas. He laid it on the table, put his hands behind his back, and kept them there till the end of the visit. She knew quite well why he had come, and though she also knew that he would fail, she loved him too much to snub him or to stare in virtuous indignation. "Why have you come?" she asked gravely, "and why have you brought me so many flowers?"

"My garden is full of them," he answered. "Sweetpeas need picking down. And, generally speaking, flowers are plentiful in July."

She broke his present into bunches—so much for the drawing-room, so much for the nursery, so much for the kitchen and her husband's room: he would be down for the night. The most beautiful she would keep for herself. Presently he said, "Your husband is no good. I've watched him for a week. I'm thirty, and not what you call hasty, as I used to be, or thinking that nothing matters like the French. No. I'm a plain Britisher, yet—I—I've begun wrong end, Mrs. Elliot; I should have said that I've thought chiefly of you for six years, and that though I talk here so respectfully, if I once unhooked my hands—"

There was a pause. Then she said with great sweetness, "Thank you; I am glad you love me," and rang the bell.

"What have you done that for?" he cried.

"Because you must now leave the house, and never enter it again."

"I don't go alone," and he began to get furious.

Her voice was still sweet, but strength lay in it too, as she said, "You either go now with my thanks and blessing, or else you go with the police. I am Mrs. Elliot. We need not discuss Mr. Elliot. I am Mrs. Elliot, and if you make one step towards me I give you in charge."

But the maid answered the bell not of the drawing-room, but of the front door. They were joined by Mr. Elliot, who held out his hand with much urbanity. It was not taken. He looked quickly at his wife, and said, "Am I de trop?" There was a long silence. At last she said, "Frederick, turn this man out."

"My love, why?"

Robert said that he loved her.

"Then I am de trop," said Mr. Elliot, smoothing out his gloves. He would give these sodden barbarians a lesson. "My hansom is waiting at the door. Pray make use of it."

"Don't!" she cried, almost affectionately. "Dear Frederick, it isn't a play. Just tell this man to go, or send for the police."

"On the contrary; it is French comedy of the best type. Don't you agree, sir, that the police would be an inartistic error?" He was perfectly calm and collected, whereas they were in a pitiable state.

"Turn him out at once!" she cried. "He has insulted your wife. Save me, save me!" She clung to her husband and wept. "He was going I had managed him—he would never have known—" Mr. Elliot repulsed her.

"If you don't feel inclined to start at once," he said with easy civility, "Let us have a little tea. My dear sir, do forgive me for not shooting you. Nous avons change tout cela. Please don't look so nervous. Please do unclasp your hands—"

He was alone.

"That's all right," he exclaimed, and strolled to the door. The hansom was disappearing round the corner. "That's all right," he repeated in more quavering tones as he returned to the drawing-room and saw that it was littered with sweet-peas. Their colour got on his nerves—magenta, crimson; magenta, crimson. He tried to pick them up, and they escaped. He trod them underfoot, and they multiplied and danced in the triumph of summer like a thousand butterflies. The train had left when he got to the station. He followed on to London, and there he lost all traces. At midnight he began to realize that his wife could never belong to him again.

Mr. Failing had a letter from Stockholm. It was never known what impulse sent them there. "I am sorry about it all, but it was the only way." The letter censured the law of England, "which obliges us to behave like this, or else we should never get married. I shall come back to face things: she will not come back till she is my wife. He must bring an action soon, or else we shall try one against him. It seems all very unconventional, but it is not really, it is only a difficult start. We are not like you or your wife: we want to be just ordinary people, and make the farm pay, and not be noticed all our lives."

And they were capable of living as they wanted. The class difference, which so intrigued Mrs. Failing, meant very little to them. It was there, but so were other things.

They both cared for work and living in the open, and for not speaking unless they had got something to say. Their love of beauty, like their love for each other, was not dependent on detail: it grew not from the nerves but from the soul.

"I believe a leaf of grass is no less than the journey work of the stars And the pismire is equally perfect, and a grain of sand, and the egg of the wren, And the tree toad is a chef-d'oeuvre for the highest, And the running blackberry would adorn the parlours of heaven."

They had never read these lines, and would have thought them nonsense if they had. They did not dissect—indeed they could not. But she, at all events, divined that more than perfect health and perfect weather, more than personal love, had gone to the making of those seventeen days.

"Ordinary people!" cried Mrs. Failing on hearing the letter. At that time she was young and daring. "Why, they're divine! They're forces of Nature! They're as ordinary as volcanoes. We all knew my brother was disgusting, and wanted him to be blown to pieces, but we never thought it would happen. Do look at the thing bravely, and say, as I do, that they are guiltless in the sight of God."

"I think they are," replied her husband. "But they are not guiltless in the sight of man."

"You conventional!" she exclaimed in disgust. "What they have done means misery not only for themselves but for others. For your brother, though you will not think of him. For the little boy—did you think of him? And perhaps for another child, who will have the whole world against him if it knows. They have sinned against society, and you do not diminish the misery by proving that society is bad or foolish. It is the saddest truth I have yet perceived that the Beloved Republic"—here she took up a book—"of which Swinburne speaks"—she put the book down—"will not be brought about by love alone. It will approach with no flourish of trumpets, and have no declaration of independence. Self-sacrifice and—worse still—self-mutilation are the things that sometimes help it most, and that is why we should start for Stockholm this evening." He waited for her indignation to subside, and then continued. "I don't know whether it can be hushed up. I don't yet know whether it ought to be hushed up. But we ought to provide the opportunity. There is no scandal yet. If we go, it is just possible there never will be any. We must talk over the whole thing and—"

"—And lie!" interrupted Mrs. Failing, who hated travel.

"—And see how to avoid the greatest unhappiness."

There was to be no scandal. By the time they arrived Robert had been drowned. Mrs. Elliot described how they had gone swimming, and how, "since he always lived inland," the great waves had tired him. They had raced for the open sea.

"What are your plans?" he asked. "I bring you a message from Frederick."

"I heard him call," she continued, "but I thought he was laughing. When I turned, it was too late. He put his hands behind his back and sank. For he would only have drowned me with him. I should have done the same."

Mrs. Failing was thrilled, and kissed her. But Mr. Failing knew that life does not continue heroic for long, and he gave her the message from her husband: Would she come back to him?

To his intense astonishment—at first to his regret—she replied, "I will think about it. If I loved him the very least bit I should say no. If I had anything to do with my life I should say no. But it is simply a question of beating time till I die. Nothing that is coming matters. I may as well sit in his drawing-room and dust his furniture, since he has suggested it."

And Mr. Elliot, though he made certain stipulations, was positively glad to see her. People had begun to laugh at him, and to say that his wife had run away. She had not. She had been with his sister in Sweden. In a half miraculous way the matter was hushed up. Even the Silts only scented "something strange." When Stephen was born, it was abroad. When he came to England, it was as the child of a friend of Mr. Failing's. Mrs. Elliot returned unsuspected to her husband.

But though things can be hushed up, there is no such thing as beating time; and as the years passed she realized her terrible mistake. When her lover sank, eluding her last embrace, she thought, as Agnes was to think after her, that her soul had sunk with him, and that never again should she be capable of earthly love. Nothing mattered. She might as well go and be useful to her husband and to the little boy who looked exactly like him, and who, she thought, was exactly like him in disposition. Then Stephen was born, and altered her life. She could still love people passionately; she still drew strength from the heroic past. Yet, to keep to her bond, she must see this son only as a stranger. She was protected be the conventions, and must pay them their fee. And a curious thing happened. Her second child drew her towards her first. She began to love Rickie also, and to be more than useful to him. And as her love revived, so did her capacity for suffering. Life, more important, grew more bitter. She minded her husband more, not less; and when at last he died, and she saw a glorious autumn, beautiful with the voices of boys who should call her mother, the end came for her as well, before she could remember the grave in the alien north and the dust that would never return to the dear fields that had given it.

XXX

Stephen, the son of these people, had one instinct that troubled him. At night—especially out of doors—it seemed rather strange that he was alive. The dry grass pricked his cheek, the fields were invisible and mute, and here was he, throwing stones at the darkness or smoking a pipe. The stones vanished, the pipe would burn out. But he would be here in the morning when the sun rose, and he would bathe, and run in the mist. He was proud of his good circulation, and in the morning it seemed quite natural. But at night, why should there be this difference between him and the acres of land that cooled all round him until the sun returned? What lucky chance had heated him up, and sent him, warm and lovable, into a passive world? He had other instincts, but these gave him no trouble. He simply gratified each as it occurred, provided he could do so without grave injury to his fellows. But the instinct to wonder at the night was not to be thus appeased. At first he had lived under the care of Mr. Failing the only person to whom his mother spoke freely, the only person who had treated her neither as a criminal nor as a pioneer. In their rare but intimate conversations she had asked him to educate her son. "I will teach him Latin," he answered. "The rest such a boy must remember." Latin, at all events, was a failure: who could attend to Virgil when the sound of the thresher arose, and you knew that the stack was decreasing and that rats rushed more plentifully each moment to their doom? But he was fond of Mr. Failing, and cried when he died. Mrs. Elliot, a pleasant woman, died soon after.

There was something fatal in the order of these deaths. Mr. Failing had made no provision for the boy in his will: his wife had promised to see to this. Then came Mr. Elliot's death, and, before the new home was created, the sudden death of Mrs. Elliot. She also left Stephen no money: she had none to leave. Chance threw him into the power of Mrs. Failing. "Let things go on as they are," she thought. "I will take care of this pretty little boy, and the ugly little boy can live with the Silts. After my death—well, the papers will be found after my death, and they can meet then. I like the idea of their mutual ignorance. It is amusing."

He was then twelve. With a few brief intervals of school, he lived in Wiltshire until he was driven out. Life had two distinct sides—the drawing-room and the other. In the drawing-room people talked a good deal, laughing as they talked. Being clever, they did not care for animals: one man had never seen a hedgehog. In the other life people talked and laughed separately, or even did neither. On the whole, in spite of the wet and gamekeepers, this life was preferable. He knew where he was. He glanced at the boy, or later at the man, and behaved accordingly. There was no law—the policeman was negligible. Nothing bound him but his own word, and he gave that sparingly.

It is impossible to be romantic when you have your heart's desire, and such a boy disappointed Mrs. Failing greatly. His parents had met for one brief embrace, had found one little interval between the power of the rulers of this world and the power of death. He was the child of poetry and of rebellion, and poetry should run in his veins. But he lived too near the things he loved to seem poetical. Parted from them, he might yet satisfy her, and stretch out his hands with a pagan's yearning. As it was, he only rode her horses, and trespassed, and bathed, and worked, for no obvious reason, upon her fields. Affection she did not believe in, and made no attempt to mould him; and he, for his part, was very content to harden untouched into a man. His parents had given him excellent gifts—health, sturdy limbs, and a face not ugly,—gifts that his habits confirmed. They had also given him a cloudless spirit—the spirit of the seventeen days in which he was created. But they had not given him the spirit of their sit years of waiting, and love for one person was never to be the greatest thing he knew.

"Philosophy" had postponed the quarrel between them. Incurious about his personal origin, he had a certain interest in our eternal problems. The interest never became a passion: it sprang out of his physical growth, and was soon merged in it again. Or, as he put it himself, "I must get fixed up before starting." He was soon fixed up as a materialist. Then he tore up the sixpenny reprints, and never amused Mrs. Failing so much again.

About the time he fixed himself up, he took to drink. He knew of no reason against it. The instinct was in him, and it hurt nobody. Here, as elsewhere, his motions were decided, and he passed at once from roaring jollity to silence. For those who live on thc fuddled borderland, who crawl home by the railings and maunder repentance in the morning, he had a biting contempt. A man must take his tumble and his headache. He was, in fact, as little disgusting as is conceivable; and hitherto he had not strained his constitution or his will. Nor did he get drunk as often as Agnes suggested. The real quarrel gathered elsewhere.

Presentable people have run wild in their youth. But the hour comes when they turn from their boorish company to higher things. This hour never came for Stephen. Somewhat a bully by nature, he kept where his powers would tell, and continued to quarrel and play with the men he had known as boys. He prolonged their youth unduly. "They won't settle down," said Mr. Wilbraham to his wife. "They're wanting things. It's the germ of a Trades Union. I shall get rid of a few of the worst." Then Stephen rushed up to Mrs. Failing and worried her. "It wasn't fair. So-and-so was a good sort. He did his work. Keen about it? No. Why should he be? Why should he be keen about somebody else's land? But keen enough. And very keen on football." She laughed, and said a word about So-and-so to Mr. Wilbraham. Mr. Wilbraham blazed up. "How could the farm go on without discipline? How could there be discipline if Mr. Stephen interfered? Mr. Stephen liked power. He spoke to the men like one of themselves, and pretended it was all equality, but he took care to come out top. Natural, of course, that, being a gentleman, he should. But not natural for a gentleman to loiter all day with poor peo-people and learn their work, and put wrong notions into their heads, and carry their newfangled grievances to Mrs. Failing. Which partly accounted for the deficit on the past year." She rebuked Stephen. Then he lost his temper, was rude to her, and insulted Mr. Wilbraham.

The worst days of Mr. Failing's rule seemed to be returning. And Stephen had a practical experience, and also a taste for battle, that her husband had never possessed. He drew up a list of grievances, some absurd, others fundamental. No newspapers in the reading-room, you could put a plate under the Thompsons' door, no level cricket-pitch, no allotments and no time to work in them, Mrs. Wilbraham's knife-boy underpaid. "Aren't you a little unwise?" she asked coldly. "I am more bored than you think over the farm." She was wanting to correct the proofs of the book and rewrite the prefatory memoir. In her irritation she wrote to Agnes. Agnes replied sympathetically, and Mrs. Failing, clever as she was, fell into the power of the younger woman. They discussed him at first as a wretch of a boy; then he got drunk and somehow it seemed more criminal. All that she needed now was a personal grievance, which Agnes casually supplied. Though vindictive, she was determined to treat him well, and thought with satisfaction of our distant colonies. But he burst into an odd passion: he would sooner starve than leave England. "Why?" she asked. "Are you in love?" He picked up a lump of the chalk-they were by the arbour—and made no answer. The vicar murmured, "It is not like going abroad—Greater Britain—blood is thicker than water—" A lump of chalk broke her drawing-room window on the Saturday.

Thus Stephen left Wiltshire, half-blackguard, half-martyr. Do not brand him as a socialist. He had no quarrel with society, nor any particular belief in people because they are poor. He only held the creed of "here am I and there are you," and therefore class distinctions were trivial things to him, and life no decorous scheme, but a personal combat or a personal truce. For the same reason ancestry also was trivial, and a man not the dearer because the same woman was mother to them both. Yet it seemed worth while to go to Sawston with the news. Perhaps nothing would come of it; perhaps friendly intercourse, and a home while he looked around.

When they wronged him he walked quietly away. He never thought of allotting the blame, nor or appealing to Ansell, who still sat brooding in the side-garden. He only knew that educated people could be horrible, and that a clean liver must never enter Dunwood House again. The air seemed stuffy. He spat in the gutter. Was it yesterday he had lain in the rifle-butts over Salisbury? Slightly aggrieved, he wondered why he was not back there now. "I ought to have written first," he reflected. "Here is my money gone. I cannot move. The Elliots have, as it were, practically robbed me." That was the only grudge he retained against them. Their suspicions and insults were to him as the curses of a tramp whom he passed by the wayside. They were dirty people, not his sort. He summed up the complicated tragedy as a "take in."

While Rickie was being carried upstairs, and while Ansell (had he known it) was dashing about the streets for him, he lay under a railway arch trying to settle his plans. He must pay back the friends who had given him shillings and clothes. He thought of Flea, whose Sundays he was spoiling—poor Flea, who ought to be in them now, shining before his girl. "I daresay he'll be ashamed and not go to see her, and then she'll take the other man." He was also very hungry. That worm Mrs. Elliot would be through her lunch by now. Trying his braces round him, and tearing up those old wet documents, he stepped forth to make money. A villainous young brute he looked: his clothes were dirty, and he had lost the spring of the morning. Touching the walls, frowning, talking to himself at times, he slouched disconsolately northwards; no wonder that some tawdry girls screamed at him, or that matrons averted their eyes as they hurried to afternoon church. He wandered from one suburb to another, till he was among people more villainous than himself, who bought his tobacco from him and sold him food. Again the neighbourhood "went up," and families, instead of sitting on their doorsteps, would sit behind thick muslin curtains. Again it would "go down" into a more avowed despair. Far into the night he wandered, until he came to a solemn river majestic as a stream in hell. Therein were gathered the waters of Central England—those that flow off Hindhead, off the Chilterns, off Wiltshire north of the Plain. Therein they were made intolerable ere they reached the sea. But the waters he had known escaped. Their course lay southward into the Avon by forests and beautiful fields, even swift, even pure, until they mirrored the tower of Christchurch and greeted the ramparts of the Isle of Wight. Of these he thought for a moment as he crossed the black river and entered the heart of the modern world. Here he found employment. He was not hampered by genteel traditions, and, as it was near quarter-day, managed to get taken on at a furniture warehouse. He moved people from the suburbs to London, from London to the suburbs, from one suburb to another. His companions were hurried and querulous. In particular, he loathed the foreman, a pious humbug who allowed no swearing, but indulged in something far more degraded—the Cockney repartee. The London intellect, so pert and shallow, like a stream that never reaches the ocean, disgusted him almost as much as the London physique, which for all its dexterity is not permanent, and seldom continues into the third generation. His father, had he known it, had felt the same; for between Mr. Elliot and the foreman the gulf was social, not spiritual: both spent their lives in trying to be clever. And Tony Failing had once put the thing into words: "There's no such thing as a Londoner. He's only a country man on the road to sterility."

At the end of ten days he had saved scarcely anything. Once he passed the bank where a hundred pounds lay ready for him, but it was still inconvenient for him to take them. Then duty sent him to a suburb not very far from Sawston. In the evening a man who was driving a trap asked him to hold it, and by mistake tipped him a sovereign. Stephen called after him; but the man had a woman with him and wanted to show off, and though he had meant to tip a shilling, and could not afford that, he shouted back that his sovereign was as good as any one's, and that if Stephen did not think so he could do various things and go to various places. On the action of this man much depends. Stephen changed the sovereign into a postal order, and sent it off to the people at Cadford. It did not pay them back, but it paid them something, and he felt that his soul was free.

A few shillings remained in his pocket. They would have paid his fare towards Wiltshire, a good county; but what should he do there? Who would employ him? Today the journey did not seem worth while. "Tomorrow, perhaps," he thought, and determined to spend the money on pleasure of another kind. Two-pence went for a ride on an electric tram. From the top he saw the sun descend—a disc with a dark red edge. The same sun was descending over Salisbury intolerably bright. Out of the golden haze the spire would be piercing, like a purple needle; then mists arose from the Avon and the other streams. Lamps flickered, but in the outer purity the villages were already slumbering. Salisbury is only a Gothic upstart beside these. For generations they have come down to her to buy or to worship, and have found in her the reasonable crisis of their lives; but generations before she was built they were clinging to the soil, and renewing it with sheep and dogs and men, who found the crisis of their lives upon Stonehenge. The blood of these men ran in Stephen; the vigour they had won for him was as yet untarnished; out on those downs they had united with rough women to make the thing he spoke of as "himself"; the last of them has rescued a woman of a different kind from streets and houses such as these. As the sun descended he got off the tram with a smile of expectation. A public-house lay opposite, and a boy in a dirty uniform was already lighting its enormous lamp. His lips parted, and he went in.

Two hours later, when Rickie and Herbert were going the rounds, a brick came crashing at the study window. Herbert peered into the garden, and a hooligan slipped by him into the house, wrecked the hall, lurched up the stairs, fell against the banisters, balanced for a moment on his spine, and slid over. Herbert called for the police. Rickie, who was upon the landing, caught the man by the knees and saved his life.

"What is it?" cried Agnes, emerging.

"It's Stephen come back," was the answer. "Hullo, Stephen!"

XXXI

Hither had Rickie moved in ten days—from disgust to penitence, from penitence to longing from a life of horror to a new life, in which he still surprised himself by unexpected words. Hullo, Stephen! For the son of his mother had come back, to forgive him, as she would have done, to live with him, as she had planned.

"He's drunk this time," said Agnes wearily. She too had altered: the scandal was ageing her, and Ansell came to the house daily.

"Hullo, Stephen!"

But Stephen was now insensible.

"Stephen, you live here—"

"Good gracious me!" interposed Herbert. "My advice is, that we all go to bed. The less said the better while our nerves are in this state. Very well, Rickie. Of course, Wonham sleeps the night if you wish." They carried the drunken mass into the spare room. A mass of scandal it seemed to one of them, a symbol of redemption to the other. Neither acknowledged it a man, who would answer them back after a few hours' rest.

"Ansell thought he would never forgive me," said Rickie. "For once he's wrong."

"Come to bed now, I think." And as Rickie laid his hand on the sleeper's hair, he added, "You won't do anything foolish, will you? You are still in a morbid state. Your poor mother—Pardon me, dear boy; it is my turn to speak out. You thought it was your father, and minded. It is your mother. Surely you ought to mind more?"

"I have been too far back," said Rickie gently. "Ansell took me on a journey that was even new to him. We got behind right and wrong, to a place where only one thing matters—that the Beloved should rise from the dead."

"But you won't do anything rash?"

"Why should I?"

"Remember poor Agnes," he stammered. "I—I am the first to acknowledge that we might have pursued a different policy. But we are committed to it now. It makes no difference whose son he is. I mean, he is the same person. You and I and my sister stand or fall together. It was our agreement from the first. I hope—

No more of these distressing scenes with her, there's a dear fellow. I assure you they make my heart bleed."

"Things will quiet down now."

"To bed now; I insist upon that much."

"Very well," said Rickie, and when they were in the passage, locked the door from the outside. "We want no more muddles," he explained.

Mr. Pembroke was left examining the hall. The bust of Hermes was broken. So was the pot of the palm. He could not go to bed without once more sounding Rickie. "You'll do nothing rash," he called. "The notion of him living here was, of course, a passing impulse. We three have adopted a common policy."

"Now, you go away!" called a voice that was almost flippant. "I never did belong to that great sect whose doctrine is that each one should select—at least, I'm not going to belong to it any longer. Go away to bed."

"A good night's rest is what you need," threatened Herbert, and retired, not to find one for himself.

But Rickie slept. The guilt of months and the remorse of the last ten days had alike departed. He had thought that his life was poisoned, and lo! it was purified. He had cursed his mother, and Ansell had replied, "You may be right, but you stand too near to settle. Step backwards. Pretend that it happened to me. Do you want me to curse my mother? Now, step forward and see whether anything has changed." Something had changed. He had journeyed—as on rare occasions a man must—till he stood behind right and wrong. On the banks of the grey torrent of life, love is the only flower. A little way up the stream and a little way down had Rickie glanced, and he knew that she whom he loved had risen from the dead, and might rise again. "Come away—let them die out—let them die out." Surely that dream was a vision! To-night also he hurried to the window—to remember, with a smile, that Orion is not among the stars of June.

"Let me die out. She will continue," he murmured, and in making plans for Stephen's happiness, fell asleep.

Next morning after breakfast he announced that his brother must live at Dunwood House. They were awed by the very moderation of his tone. "There's nothing else to be done. Cadover's hopeless, and a boy of those tendencies can't go drifting. There is also the question of a profession for him, and his allowance."

"We have to thank Mr. Ansell for this," was all that Agnes could say; and "I foresee disaster," was the contribution of Herbert.

"There's plenty of money about," Rickie continued. "Quite a man's-worth too much. It has been one of our absurdities. Don't look so sad, Herbert. I'm sorry for you people, but he's sure to let us down easy." For his experience of drunkards and of Stephen was small.

He supposed that he had come without malice to renew the offer of ten days ago.

"It is the end of Dunwood House."

Rickie nodded, and hoped not. Agnes, who was not looking well, began to cry. "Oh, it is too bad," she complained, "when I've saved you from him all these years." But he could not pity her, nor even sympathize with her wounded delicacy. The time for such nonsense was over. He would take his share of the blame: it was cant to assume it all.

Perhaps he was over-hard. He did not realize how large his share was, nor how his very virtues were to blame for her deterioration. "If I had a girl, I'd keep her in line," is not the remark of a fool nor of a cad. Rickie had not kept his wife in line. He had shown her all the workings of his soul, mistaking this for love; and in consequence she was the worse woman after two years of marriage, and he, on this morning of freedom, was harder upon her than he need have been.

The spare room bell rang. Herbert had a painful struggle between curiosity and duty, for the bell for chapel was ringing also, and he must go through the drizzle to school. He promised to come up in the interval, Rickie, who had rapped his head that Sunday on the edge of the table, was still forbidden to work. Before him a quiet morning lay. Secure of his victory, he took the portrait of their mother in his hand and walked leisurely upstairs. The bell continued to ring.

"See about his breakfast," he called to Agnes, who replied, "Very well." The handle of the spare room door was moving slowly. "I'm coming," he cried. The handle was still. He unlocked and entered, his heart full of charity.

But within stood a man who probably owned the world.

Rickie scarcely knew him; last night he had seemed so colorless, no negligible. In a few hours he had recaptured motion and passion and the imprint of the sunlight and the wind. He stood, not consciously heroic, with arms that dangled from broad stooping shoulders, and feet that played with a hassock on the carpet. But his hair was beautiful against the grey sky, and his eyes, recalling the sky unclouded, shot past the intruder as if to some worthier vision. So intent was their gaze that Rickie himself glanced backwards, only to see the neat passage and the banisters at the top of the stairs. Then the lips beat together twice, and out burst a torrent of amazing words.

"Add it all up, and let me know how much. I'd sooner have died. It never took me that way before. I must have broken pounds' worth. If you'll not tell the police, I promise you shan't lose, Mr. Elliot, I swear. But it may be months before I send it. Everything is to be new. You've not to be a penny out of pocket, do you see? Do let me go, this once again."

"What's the trouble?" asked Rickie, as if they had been friends for years. "My dear man, we've other things to talk about. Gracious me, what a fuss! If you'd smashed the whole house I wouldn't mind, so long as you came back."

"I'd sooner have died," gulped Stephen.

"You did nearly! It was I who caught you. Never mind yesterday's rag. What can you manage for breakfast?"

The face grew more angry and more puzzled. "Yesterday wasn't a rag," he said without focusing his eyes. "I was drunk, but naturally meant it."

"Meant what?"

"To smash you. Bad liquor did what Mrs. Elliot couldn't. I've put myself in the wrong. You've got me."

It was a poor beginning.

"As I have got you," said Rickie, controlling himself, "I want to have a talk with you. There has been a ghastly mistake."

But Stephen, with a countryman's persistency, continued on his own line. He meant to be civil, but Rickie went cold round the mouth. For he had not even been angry with them. Until he was drunk, they had been dirty people—not his sort. Then the trivial injury recurred, and he had reeled to smash them as he passed. "And I will pay for everything," was his refrain, with which the sighing of raindrops mingled. "You shan't lose a penny, if only you let me free."

"You'll pay for my coffin if you talk like that any longer! Will you, one, forgive my frightful behaviour; two, live with me?" For his only hope was in a cheerful precision.

Stephen grew more agitated. He thought it was some trick.

"I was saying I made an unspeakable mistake. Ansell put me right, but it was too late to find you. Don't think I got off easily. Ansell doesn't spare one. And you've got to forgive me, to share my life, to share my money.—I've brought you this photograph—I want it to be the first thing you accept from me—you have the greater right—I know all the story now. You know who it is?"

"Oh yes; but I don't want to drag all that in."

"It is only her wish if we live together. She was planning it when she died."

"I can't follow—because—to share your life? Did you know I called here last Sunday week?"

"Yes. But then I only knew half. I thought you were my father's son."

Stephen's anger and bewilderment were increasing. He stuttered. "What—what's the odds if you did?"

"I hated my father," said Rickie. "I loved my mother." And never had the phrases seemed so destitute of meaning.

"Last Sunday week," interrupted Stephen, his voice suddenly rising, "I came to call on you. Not as this or that's son. Not to fall on your neck. Nor to live here. Nor—damn your dirty little mind! I meant to say I didn't come for money. Sorry. Sorry. I simply came as I was, and I haven't altered since."

"Yes—yet our mother—for me she has risen from the dead since then—I know I was wrong—"

"And where do I come in?" He kicked the hassock. "I haven't risen from the dead. I haven't altered since last Sunday week. I'm—" He stuttered again. He could not quite explain what he was. "The man towards Andover—after all, he was having principles. But you've—" His voice broke. "I mind it—I'm—I don't alter—blackguard one week—live here the next—I keep to one or the other—you've hurt something most badly in me that I didn't know was there."

"Don't let us talk," said Rickie. "It gets worse every minute. Simply say you forgive me; shake hands, and have done with it."

"That I won't. That I couldn't. In fact, I don't know what you mean."

Then Rickie began a new appeal—not to pity, for now he was in no mood to whimper. For all its pathos, there was something heroic in this meeting. "I warn you to stop here with me, Stephen. No one else in the world will look after you. As far as I know, you have never been really unhappy yet or suffered, as you should do, from your faults. Last night you nearly killed yourself with drink. Never mind why I'm willing to cure you. I am willing, and I warn you to give me the chance. Forgive me or not, as you choose. I care for other things more."

Stephen looked at him at last, faintly approving. The offer was ridiculous, but it did treat him as a man.

"Let me tell you of a fault of mine, and how I was punished for it," continued Rickie. "Two years ago I behaved badly to you, up at the Rings. No, even a few days before that. We went for a ride, and I thought too much of other matters, and did not try to understand you. Then came the Rings, and in the evening, when you called up to me most kindly, I never answered. But the ride was the beginning. Ever since then I have taken the world at second-hand. I have bothered less and less to look it in the face—until not only you, but every one else has turned unreal. Never Ansell: he kept away, and somehow saved himself. But every one else. Do you remember in one of Tony Failing's books, 'Cast bitter bread upon the waters, and after many days it really does come back to you'? This had been true of my life; it will be equally true of a drunkard's, and I warn you to stop with me."

"I can't stop after that cheque," said Stephen more gently. "But I do remember the ride. I was a bit bored myself."

Agnes, who had not been seeing to the breakfast, chose this moment to call from the passage. "Of course he can't stop," she exclaimed. "For better or worse, it's settled. We've none of us altered since last Sunday week."

"There you're right, Mrs. Elliot!" he shouted, starting out of the temperate past. "We haven't altered." With a rare flash of insight he turned on Rickie. "I see your game. You don't care about ME drinking, or to shake MY hand. It's some one else you want to cure—as it were, that old photograph. You talk to me, but all the time you look at the photograph." He snatched it up.

"I've my own ideas of good manners, and to look friends between the eyes is one of them; and this"—he tore the photograph across "and this"—he tore it again—"and these—" He flung the pieces at the man, who had sunk into a chair. "For my part, I'm off."

Then Rickie was heroic no longer. Turning round in his chair, he covered his face. The man was right. He did not love him, even as he had never hated him. In either passion he had degraded him to be a symbol for the vanished past. The man was right, and would have been lovable. He longed to be back riding over those windy fields, to be back in those mystic circles, beneath pure sky. Then they could have watched and helped and taught each other, until the word was a reality, and the past not a torn photograph, but Demeter the goddess rejoicing in the spring. Ah, if he had seized those high opportunities! For they led to the highest of all, the symbolic moment, which, if a man accepts, he has accepted life.

The voice of Agnes, which had lured him then ("For my sake," she had whispered), pealed over him now in triumph. Abruptly it broke into sobs that had the effect of rain. He started up. The anger had died out of Stephen's face, not for a subtle reason but because here was a woman, near him, and unhappy.

She tried to apologize, and brought on a fresh burst of tears. Something had upset her. They heard her locking the door of her room. From that moment their intercourse was changed.

"Why does she keep crying today?" mused Rickie, as if he spoke to some mutual friend.

"I can make a guess," said Stephen, and his heavy face flushed.

"Did you insult her?" he asked feebly.

"But who's Gerald?"

Rickie raised his hand to his mouth.

"She looked at me as if she knew me, and then gasps 'Gerald,' and started crying."

"Gerald is the name of some one she once knew."

"So I thought." There was a long silence, in which they could hear a piteous gulping cough. "Where is he now?" asked Stephen.

"Dead."

"And then you—?"

Rickie nodded.

"Bad, this sort of thing."

"I didn't know of this particular thing. She acted as if she had forgotten him. Perhaps she had, and you woke him up. There are queer tricks in the world. She is overstrained. She has probably been plotting ever since you burst in last night."

"Against me?"

"Yes."

Stephen stood irresolute. "I suppose you and she pulled together?" He said at last.

"Get away from us, man! I mind losing you. Yet it's as well you don't stop."

"Oh, THAT'S out of the question," said Stephen, brushing his cap.

"If you've guessed anything, I'd be obliged if you didn't mention it. I've no right to ask, but I'd be obliged."

He nodded, and walked slowly along the landing and down the stairs. Rickie accompanied him, and even opened the front door. It was as if Agnes had absorbed the passion out of both of them. The suburb was now wrapped in a cloud, not of its own making. Sigh after sigh passed along its streets to break against dripping walls. The school, the houses were hidden, and all civilization seemed in abeyance. Only the simplest sounds, the simplest desires emerged. They agreed that this weather was strange after such a sunset.

"That's a collie," said Stephen, listening.

"I wish you'd have some breakfast before starting."

"No food, thanks. But you know" He paused. "It's all been a muddle, and I've no objection to your coming along with me."

The cloud descended lower.

XXXI

"Come with me as a man," said Stephen, already out in the mist. "Not as a brother; who cares what people did years back? We're alive together, and the rest is cant. Here am I, Rickie, and there are you, a fair wreck. They've no use for you here,—never had any, if the truth was known,—and they've only made you beastly. This house, so to speak, has the rot. It's common-sense that you should come."

"Stephen, wait a minute. What do you mean?"

"Wait's what we won't do," said Stephen at the gate.

"I must ask—"

He did wait for a minute, and sobs were heard, faint, hopeless, vindictive. Then he trudged away, and Rickie soon lost his colour and his form. But a voice persisted, saying, "Come, I do mean it. Come; I will take care of you, I can manage you."

The words were kind; yet it was not for their sake that Rickie plunged into the impalpable cloud. In the voice he had found a surer guarantee. Habits and sex may change with the new generation, features may alter with the play of a private passion, but a voice is apart from these. It lies nearer to the racial essence and perhaps to the divine; it can, at all events, overleap one grave.

XXXII

Mr. Pembroke did not receive a clear account of what had happened when he returned for the interval. His sister—he told her frankly—was concealing something from him. She could make no reply. Had she gone mad, she wondered. Hitherto she had pretended to love her husband. Why choose such a moment for the truth?

"But I understand Rickie's position," he told her. "It is an unbalanced position, yet I understand it; I noted its approach while he was ill. He imagines himself his brother's keeper. Therefore we must make concessions. We must negotiate." The negotiations were still progressing in November, the month during which this story draws to its close.

"I understand his position," he then told her. "It is both weak and defiant. He is still with those Ansells. Read this letter, which thanks me for his little stories. We sent them last month, you remember—such of them as we could find. It seems that he fills up his time by writing: he has already written a book."

She only gave him half her attention, for a beautiful wreath had just arrived from the florist's. She was taking it up to the cemetery: today her child had been dead a year.

"On the other hand, he has altered his will. Fortunately, he cannot alter much. But I fear that what is not settled on you, will go. Should I read what I wrote on this point, and also my minutes of the interview with old Mr. Ansell, and the copy of my correspondence with Stephen Wonham?"

But her fly was announced. While he put the wreath in for her, she ran for a moment upstairs. A few tears had come to her eyes. A scandalous divorce would have been more bearable than this withdrawal. People asked, "Why did her husband leave her?" and the answer came, "Oh, nothing particular; he only couldn't stand her; she lied and taught him to lie; she kept him from the work that suited him, from his friends, from his brother,—in a word, she tried to run him, which a man won't pardon." A few tears; not many. To her, life never showed itself as a classic drama, in which, by trying to advance our fortunes, we shatter them. She had turned Stephen out of Wiltshire, and he fell like a thunderbolt on Sawston and on herself. In trying to gain Mrs. Failing's money she had probably lost money which would have been her own. But irony is a subtle teacher, and she was not the woman to learn from such lessons as these. Her suffering was more direct.

Three men had wronged her; therefore she hated them, and, if she could, would do them harm.

"These negotiations are quite useless," she told Herbert when she came downstairs. "We had much better bide our time. Tell me just about Stephen Wonham, though."

He drew her into the study again. "Wonham is or was in Scotland, learning to farm with connections of the Ansells: I believe the money is to go towards setting him up. Apparently he is a hard worker. He also drinks!"

She nodded and smiled. "More than he did?"

"My informant, Mr. Tilliard—oh, I ought not to have mentioned his name. He is one of the better sort of Rickie's Cambridge friends, and has been dreadfully grieved at the collapse, but he does not want to be mixed up in it. This autumn he was up in the Lowlands, close by, and very kindly made a few unobtrusive inquiries for me. The man is becoming an habitual drunkard."

She smiled again. Stephen had evoked her secret, and she hated him more for that than for anything else that he had done. The poise of his shoulders that morning—it was no more—had recalled Gerald.

If only she had not been so tired! He had reminded her of the greatest thing she had known, and to her cloudy mind this seemed degradation. She had turned to him as to her lover; with a look, which a man of his type understood, she had asked for his pity; for one terrible moment she had desired to be held in his arms. Even Herbert was surprised when she said, "I'm glad he drinks. I hope he'll kill himself. A man like that ought never to have been born."

"Perhaps the sins of the parents are visited on the children," said Herbert, taking her to the carriage. "Yet it is not for us to decide."

"I feel sure he will be punished. What right has he—" She broke off. What right had he to our common humanity? It was a hard lesson for any one to learn. For Agnes it was impossible. Stephen was illicit, abnormal, worse than a man diseased. Yet she had turned to him: he had drawn out the truth.

"My dear, don't cry," said her brother, drawing up the windows. "I have great hopes of Mr. Tilliard—the Silts have written—Mrs. Failing will do what she can—"

As she drove to the cemetery, her bitterness turned against Ansell, who had kept her husband alive in the days after Stephen's expulsion. If he had not been there, Rickie would have renounced his mother and his brother and all the outer world, troubling no one. The mystic, inherent in him, would have prevailed. So Ansell himself had told her. And Ansell, too, had sheltered the fugitives and given them money, and saved them from the ludicrous checks that so often stop young men. But when she reached the cemetery, and stood beside the tiny grave, all her bitterness, all her hatred were turned against Rickie.

"But he'll come back in the end," she thought. "A wife has only to wait. What are his friends beside me? They too will marry. I have only to wait. His book, like all that he has done, will fail. His brother is drinking himself away. Poor aimless Rickie! I have only to keep civil. He will come back in the end."

She had moved, and found herself close to the grave of Gerald. The flowers she had planted after his death were dead, and she had not liked to renew them. There lay the athlete, and his dust was as the little child's whom she had brought into the world with such hope, with such pain.

XXXIII

That same day Rickie, feeling neither poor nor aimless, left the Ansells' for a night's visit to Cadover. His aunt had invited him—why, he could not think, nor could he think why he should refuse the invitation. She could not annoy him now, and he was not vindictive. In the dell near Madingley he had cried, "I hate no one," in his ignorance. Now, with full knowledge, he hated no one again. The weather was pleasant, the county attractive, and he was ready for a little change.

Maud and Stewart saw him off. Stephen, who was down for the holiday, had been left with his chin on the luncheon table. He had wanted to come also. Rickie pointed out that you cannot visit where you have broken the windows. There was an argument—there generally was—and now the young man had turned sulky.

"Let him do what he likes," said Ansell. "He knows more than we do. He knows everything."

"Is he to get drunk?" Rickie asked.

"Most certainly."

"And to go where he isn't asked?"

Maud, though liking a little spirit in a man, declared this to be impossible.

"Well, I wish you joy!" Rickie called, as the train moved away. "He means mischief this evening. He told me piously that he felt it beating up. Good-bye!"

"But we'll wait for you to pass," they cried. For the Salisbury train always backed out of the station and then returned, and the Ansell family, including Stewart, took an incredible pleasure in seeing it do this.

The carriage was empty. Rickie settled himself down for his little journey. First he looked at the coloured photographs. Then he read the directions for obtaining luncheon-baskets, and felt the texture of the cushions. Through the windows a signal-box interested him. Then he saw the ugly little town that was now his home, and up its chief street the Ansells' memorable facade. The spirit of a genial comedy dwelt there. It was so absurd, so kindly. The house was divided against itself and yet stood. Metaphysics, commerce, social aspirations—all lived together in harmony. Mr. Ansell had done much, but one was tempted to believe in a more capricious power—the power that abstains from "nipping." "One nips or is nipped, and never knows beforehand," quoted Rickie, and opened the poems of Shelley, a man less foolish than you supposed. How pleasant it was to read! If business worried him, if Stephen was noisy or Ansell perverse, there still remained this paradise of books. It seemed as if he had read nothing for two years. Then the train stopped for the shunting, and he heard protests from minor officials who were working on the line. They complained that some one who didn't ought to, had mounted on the footboard of the carriage. Stephen's face appeared, convulsed with laughter. With the action of a swimmer he dived in through the open window, and fell comfortably on Rickie's luggage and Rickie. He declared it was the finest joke ever known. Rickie was not so sure. "You'll be run over next," he said. "What did you do that for?"

"I'm coming with you," he giggled, rolling all that he could on to the dusty floor.

"Now, Stephen, this is too bad. Get up. We went into the whole question yesterday."

"I know; and I settled we wouldn't go into it again, spoiling my holiday."

"Well, it's execrable taste."

Now he was waving to the Ansells, and showing them a piece of soap: it was all his luggage, and even that he abandoned, for he flung it at Stewart's lofty brow.

"I can't think what you've done it for. You know how strongly I felt."

Stephen replied that he should stop in the village; meet Rickie at the lodge gates; that kind of thing.

"It's execrable taste," he repeated, trying to keep grave.

"Well, you did all you could," he exclaimed with sudden sympathy. "Leaving me talking to old Ansell, you might have thought you'd got your way. I've as much taste as most chaps, but, hang it! your aunt isn't the German Emperor. She doesn't own Wiltshire."

"You ass!" sputtered Rickie, who had taken to laugh at nonsense again.

"No, she isn't," he repeated, blowing a kiss out of the window to maidens. "Why, we started for Wiltshire on the wet morning!"

"When Stewart found us at Sawston railway station?" He smiled happily. "I never thought we should pull through."

"Well, we DIDN'T. We never did what we meant. It's nonsense that I couldn't have managed you alone. I've a notion. Slip out after your dinner this evening, and we'll get thundering tight together."

"I've a notion I won't."

"It'd do you no end of good. You'll get to know people—shepherds, carters—" He waved his arms vaguely, indicating democracy. "Then you'll sing."

"And then?"

"Plop."

"Precisely."

"But I'll catch you," promised Stephen. "We shall carry you up the hill to bed. In the morning you wake, have your row with old Em'ly, she kicks you out, we meet—we'll meet at the Rings!" He danced up and down the carriage. Some one in the next carriage punched at the partition, and when this happens, all lads with mettle know that they must punch the partition back.

"Thank you. I've a notion I won't," said Rickie when the noise had subsided—subsided for a moment only, for the following conversation took place to an accompaniment of dust and bangs. "Except as regards the Rings. We will meet there."

"Then I'll get tight by myself."

"No, you won't."

"Yes, I will. I swore to do something special this evening. I feel like it."

"In that case, I get out at the next station." He was laughing, but quite determined. Stephen had grown too dictatorial of late. The Ansells spoilt him. "It's bad enough having you there at all. Having you there drunk is impossible. I'd sooner not visit my aunt than think, when I sat with her, that you're down in the village teaching her labourers to be as beastly as yourself. Go if you will. But not with me."

"Why shouldn't I have a good time while I'm young, if I don't harm any one?" said Stephen defiantly.

"Need we discuss self."

"Oh, I can stop myself any minute I choose. I just say 'I won't' to you or any other fool, and I don't."

Rickie knew that the boast was true. He continued, "There is also a thing called Morality. You may learn in the Bible, and also from the Greeks, that your body is a temple."

"So you said in your longest letter."

"Probably I wrote like a prig, for the reason that I have never been tempted in this way; but surely it is wrong that your body should escape you."

"I don't follow," he retorted, punching.

"It isn't right, even for a little time, to forget that you exist."

"I suppose you've never been tempted to go to sleep?"

Just then the train passed through a coppice in which the grey undergrowth looked no more alive than firewood. Yet every twig in it was waiting for the spring. Rickie knew that the analogy was false, but argument confused him, and he gave up this line of attack also.

"Do be more careful over life. If your body escapes you in one thing, why not in more? A man will have other temptations."

"You mean women," said Stephen quietly, pausing for a moment in this game. "But that's absolutely different. That would be harming some one else."

"Is that the only thing that keeps you straight?"

"What else should?" And he looked not into Rickie, but past him, with the wondering eyes of a child. Rickie nodded, and referred himself to the window.

He observed that the country was smoother and more plastic. The woods had gone, and under a pale-blue sky long contours of earth were flowing, and merging, rising a little to bear some coronal of beeches, parting a little to disclose some green valley, where cottages stood under elms or beside translucent waters. It was Wiltshire at last. The train had entered the chalk. At last it slackened at a wayside platform. Without speaking he opened the door.

"What's that for?"

"To go back."

Stephen had forgotten the threat. He said that this was not playing the game.

"Surely!"

"I can't have you going back."

"Promise to behave decently then."

He was seized and pulled away from the door.

"We change at Salisbury," he remarked. "There is an hour to wait. You will find me troublesome."

"It isn't fair," exploded Stephen. "It's a lowdown trick. How can I let you go back?"

"Promise, then."

"Oh, yes, yes, yes. Y.M.C.A. But for this occasion only."

"No, no. For the rest of your holiday."

"Yes, yes. Very well. I promise."

"For the rest of your life?"

Somehow it pleased him that Stephen should bang him crossly with his elbow and say, "No. Get out. You've gone too far." So had the train. The porter at the end of the wayside platform slammed the door, and they proceeded toward Salisbury through the slowly modulating downs. Rickie pretended to read. Over the book he watched his brother's face, and wondered how bad temper could be consistent with a mind so radiant. In spite of his obstinacy and conceit, Stephen was an easy person to live with. He never fidgeted or nursed hidden grievances, or indulged in a shoddy pride. Though he spent Rickie's money as slowly as he could, he asked for it without apology: "You must put it down against me," he would say. In time—it was still very vague—he would rent or purchase a farm. There is no formula in which we may sum up decent people. So Ansell had preached, and had of course proceeded to offer a formula: "They must be serious, they must be truthful." Serious not in the sense of glum; but they must be convinced that our life is a state of some importance, and our earth not a place to beat time on. Of so much Stephen was convinced: he showed it in his work, in his play, in his self-respect, and above all—though the fact is hard to face-in his sacred passion for alcohol. Drink, today, is an unlovely thing. Between us and the heights of Cithaeron the river of sin now flows. Yet the cries still call from the mountain, and granted a man has responded to them, it is better he respond with the candour of the Greek.

"I shall stop at the Thompsons' now," said the disappointed reveller. "Prayers."

Rickie did not press his triumph, but it was a happy moment, partly because of the triumph, partly because he was sure that his brother must care for him. Stephen was too selfish to give up any pleasure without grave reasons. He was certain that he had been right to disentangle himself from Sawston, and to ignore the threats and tears that still tempted him to return. Here there was real work for him to do. Moreover, though he sought no reward, it had come. His health was better, his brain sound, his life washed clean, not by the waters of sentiment, but by the efforts of a fellow-man. Stephen was man first, brother afterwards. Herein lay his brutality and also his virtue. "Look me in the face. Don't hang on me clothes that don't belong—as you did on your wife, giving her saint's robes, whereas she was simply a woman of her own sort, who needed careful watching. Tear up the photographs. Here am I, and there are you. The rest is cant." The rest was not cant, and perhaps Stephen would confess as much in time. But Rickie needed a tonic, and a man, not a brother, must hold it to his lips.

"I see the old spire," he called, and then added, "I don't mind seeing it again."

"No one does, as far as I know. People have come from the other side of the world to see it again."

"Pious people. But I don't hold with bishops." He was young enough to be uneasy. The cathedral, a fount of superstition, must find no place in his life. At the age of twenty he had settled things.

"I've got my own philosophy," he once told Ansell, "and I don't care a straw about yours." Ansell's mirth had annoyed him not a little. And it was strange that one so settled should feel his heart leap up at the sight of an old spire. "I regard it as a public building," he told Rickie, who agreed. "It's useful, too, as a landmark." His attitude today was defensive. It was part of a subtle change that Rickie had noted in him since his return from Scotland. His face gave hints of a new maturity. "You can see the old spire from the Ridgeway," he said, suddenly laying a hand on Rickie's knee, "before rain as clearly as any telegraph post."

"How far is the Ridgeway?"

"Seventeen miles."

"Which direction?"

"North, naturally. North again from that you see Devizes, the vale of Pewsey, and the other downs. Also towards Bath. It is something of a view. You ought to get on the Ridgeway."

"I shouldn't have time for that."

"Or Beacon Hill. Or let's do Stonehenge."

"If it's fine, I suggest the Rings."

"It will be fine." Then he murmured the names of villages.

"I wish you could live here," said Rickie kindly. "I believe you love these particular acres more than the whole world."

Stephen replied that this was not the case: he was only used to them. He wished they were driving out, instead of waiting for the Cadchurch train.

They had advanced into Salisbury, and the cathedral, a public building, was grey against a tender sky. Rickie suggested that, while waiting for the train, they should visit it. He spoke of the incomparable north porch. "I've never been inside it, and I never will. Sorry to shock you, Rickie, but I must tell you plainly. I'm an atheist. I don't believe in anything."

"I do," said Rickie.

"When a man dies, it's as if he's never been," he asserted. The train drew up in Salisbury station. Here a little incident took place which caused them to alter their plans.

They found outside the station a trap driven by a small boy, who had come in from Cadford to fetch some wire-netting. "That'll do us," said Stephen, and called to the boy, "If I pay your railway-ticket back, and if I give you sixpence as well, will you let us drive back in the trap?" The boy said no. "It will be all right," said Rickie. "I am Mrs. Failing's nephew." The boy shook his head. "And you know Mr. Wonham?" The boy couldn't say he didn't. "Then what's your objection? Why? What is it? Why not?" But Stephen leant against the time-tables and spoke of other matters.

Presently the boy said, "Did you say you'd pay my railway-ticket back, Mr. Wonham?"

"Yes," said a bystander. "Didn't you hear him?"

"I heard him right enough."

Now Stephen laid his hand on the splash-board, saying, "What I want, though, is this trap here of yours, see, to drive in back myself;" and as he spoke the bystander followed him in canon, "What he wants, though, is that there trap of yours, see, to drive hisself back in."

"I've no objection," said the boy, as if deeply offended. For a time he sat motionless, and then got down, remarking, "I won't rob you of your sixpence."

"Silly little fool," snapped Rickie, as they drove through the town.

Stephen looked surprised. "What's wrong with the boy? He had to think it over. No one had asked him to do such a thing before. Next time he'd let us have the trap quick enough."

"Not if he had driven in for a cabbage instead of wire-netting."

"He never would drive in for a cabbage."

Rickie shuffled his feet. But his irritation passed. He saw that the little incident had been a quiet challenge to the civilization that he had known. "Organize." "Systematize." "Fill up every moment," "Induce esprit de corps." He reviewed the watchwords of the last two years, and found that they ignored personal contest, personal truces, personal love. By following them Sawston School had lost its quiet usefulness and become a frothy sea, wherein plunged Dunwood House, that unnecessary ship. Humbled, he turned to Stephen and said, "No, you're right. Nothing is wrong with the boy. He was honestly thinking it out." But Stephen had forgotten the incident, or else he was not inclined to talk about it. His assertive fit was over.

The direct road from Salisbury to Cadover is extremely dull. The city—which God intended to keep by the river; did she not move there, being thirsty, in the reign of William Rufus?—the city had strayed out of her own plain, climbed up her slopes, and tumbled over them in ugly cataracts of brick. The cataracts are still short, and doubtless they meet or create some commercial need. But instead of looking towards the cathedral, as all the city should, they look outwards at a pagan entrenchment, as the city should not. They neglect the poise of the earth, and the sentiments she has decreed. They are the modern spirit.

Through them the road descends into an unobtrusive country where, nevertheless, the power of the earth grows stronger. Streams do divide. Distances do still exist. It is easier to know the men in your valley than those who live in the next, across a waste of down. It is easier to know men well. The country is not paradise, and can show the vices that grieve a good man everywhere. But there is room in it, and leisure.

"I suppose," said Rickie as the twilight fell, "this kind of thing is going on all over England." Perhaps he meant that towns are after all excrescences, grey fluxions, where men, hurrying to find one another, have lost themselves. But he got no response, and expected none. Turning round in his seat, he watched the winter sun slide out of a quiet sky. The horizon was primrose, and the earth against it gave momentary hints of purple. All faded: no pageant would conclude the gracious day, and when he turned eastward the night was already established.

"Those verlands—" said Stephen, scarcely above his breath.

"What are verlands?"

He pointed at the dusk, and said, "Our name for a kind of field." Then he drove his whip into its socket, and seemed to swallow something. Rickie, straining his eyes for verlands, could only see a tumbling wilderness of brown.

"Are there many local words?"

"There have been."

"I suppose they die out."

The conversation turned curiously. In the tone of one who replies, he said, "I expect that some time or other I shall marry."

"I expect you will," said Rickie, and wondered a little why the reply seemed not abrupt. "Would we see the Rings in the daytime from here?"

"(We do see them.) But Mrs. Failing once said no decent woman would have me."

"Did you agree to that?"

"Drive a little, will you?"

The horse went slowly forward into the wilderness, that turned from brown to black. Then a luminous glimmer surrounded them, and the air grew cooler: the road was descending between parapets of chalk.

"But, Rickie, mightn't I find a girl—naturally not refined—and be happy with her in my own way? I would tell her straight I was nothing much—faithful, of course, but that she should never have all my thoughts. Out of no disrespect to her, but because all one's thoughts can't belong to any single person."

While he spoke even the road vanished, and invisible water came gurgling through the wheel-spokes. The horse had chosen the ford. "You can't own people. At least a fellow can't. It may be different for a poet. (Let the horse drink.) And I want to marry some one, and don't yet know who she is, which a poet again will tell you is disgusting. Does it disgust you? Being nothing much, surely I'd better go gently. For it's something rather outside that makes one marry, if you follow me: not exactly oneself. (Don't hurry the horse.) We want to marry, and yet—I can't explain. I fancy I'll go wading: this is our stream."

Romantic love is greater than this. There are men and women—we know it from history—who have been born into the world for each other, and for no one else, who have accomplished the longest journey locked in each other's arms. But romantic love is also the code of modern morals, and, for this reason, popular. Eternal union, eternal ownership—these are tempting baits for the average man. He swallows them, will not confess his mistake, and—perhaps to cover it—cries "dirty cynic" at such a man as Stephen.

Rickie watched the black earth unite to the black sky. But the sky overhead grew clearer, and in it twinkled the Plough and the central stars. He thought of his brother's future and of his own past, and of how much truth might lie in that antithesis of Ansell's: "A man wants to love mankind, a woman wants to love one man." At all events, he and his wife had illustrated it, and perhaps the conflict, so tragic in their own case, was elsewhere the salt of the world. Meanwhile Stephen called from the water for matches: there was some trick with paper which Mr. Failing had showed him, and which he would show Rickie now, instead of talking nonsense. Bending down, he illuminated the dimpled surface of the ford. "Quite a current." he said, and his face flickered out in the darkness. "Yes, give me the loose paper, quick! Crumple it into a ball."

Rickie obeyed, though intent on the transfigured face. He believed that a new spirit dwelt there, expelling the crudities of youth. He saw steadier eyes, and the sign of manhood set like a bar of gold upon steadier lips. Some faces are knit by beauty, or by intellect, or by a great passion: had Stephen's waited for the touch of the years?

But they played as boys who continued the nonsense of the railway carriage. The paper caught fire from the match, and spread into a rose of flame. "Now gently with me," said Stephen, and they laid it flowerlike on the stream. Gravel and tremulous weeds leapt into sight, and then the flower sailed into deep water, and up leapt the two arches of a bridge. "It'll strike!" they cried; "no, it won't; it's chosen the left," and one arch became a fairy tunnel, dropping diamonds. Then it vanished for Rickie; but Stephen, who knelt in the water, declared that it was still afloat, far through the arch, burning as if it would burn forever.

XXXIV

The carriage that Mrs. Failing had sent to meet her nephew returned from Cadchurch station empty. She was preparing for a solitary dinner when he somehow arrived, full of apologies, but more sedate than she had expected. She cut his explanations short. "Never mind how you got here. You are here, and I am quite pleased to see you." He changed his clothes and they proceeded to the dining-room.

There was a bright fire, but the curtains were not drawn. Mr. Failing had believed that windows with the night behind are more beautiful than any pictures, and his widow had kept to the custom. It was brave of her to persevere, lumps of chalk having come out of the night last June. For some obscure reason—not so obscure to Rickie—she had preserved them as mementoes of an episode. Seeing them in a row on the mantelpiece, he expected that their first topic would be Stephen. But they never mentioned him, though he was latent in all that they said.

It was of Mr. Failing that they spoke. The Essays had been a success. She was really pleased. The book was brought in at her request, and between the courses she read it aloud to her nephew, in her soft yet unsympathetic voice. Then she sent for the press notices—after all no one despises them—and read their comments on her introduction. She wielded a graceful pen, was apt, adequate, suggestive, indispensable, unnecessary. So the meal passed pleasantly away, for no one could so well combine the formal with the unconventional, and it only seemed charming when papers littered her stately table.

"My man wrote very nicely," she observed. "Now, you read me something out of him that you like. Read 'The True Patriot.'"

He took the book and found: "Let us love one another. Let our children, physical and spiritual, love one another. It is all that we can do. Perhaps the earth will neglect our love. Perhaps she will confirm it, and suffer some rallying-point, spire, mound, for the new generations to cherish."

"He wrote that when he was young. Later on he doubted whether we had better love one another, or whether the earth will confirm anything. He died a most unhappy man."

He could not help saying, "Not knowing that the earth had confirmed him."

"Has she? It is quite possible. We meet so seldom in these days, she and I. Do you see much of the earth?"

"A little."

"Do you expect that she will confirm you?"

"It is quite possible."

"Beware of her, Rickie, I think."

"I think not."

"Beware of her, surely. Going back to her really is going back—throwing away the artificiality which (though you young people won't confess it) is the only good thing in life. Don't pretend you are simple. Once I pretended. Don't pretend that you care for anything but for clever talk such as this, and for books."

"The talk," said Leighton afterwards, "certainly was clever. But it meant something, all the same." He heard no more, for his mistress told him to retire.

"And my nephew, this being so, make up your quarrel with your wife." She stretched out her hand to him with real feeling. "It is easier now than it will be later. Poor lady, she has written to me foolishly and often, but, on the whole, I side with her against you. She would grant you all that you fought for—all the people, all the theories. I have it, in her writing, that she will never interfere with your life again."

"She cannot help interfering," said Rickie, with his eyes on the black windows. "She despises me. Besides, I do not love her."

"I know, my dear. Nor she you. I am not being sentimental. I say once more, beware of the earth. We are conventional people, and conventions—if you will but see it—are majestic in their way, and will claim us in the end. We do not live for great passions or for great memories, or for anything great."

He threw up his head. "We do."

"Now listen to me. I am serious and friendly tonight, as you must have observed. I have asked you here partly to amuse myself—you belong to my March Past—but also to give you good advice. There has been a volcano—a phenomenon which I too once greatly admired. The eruption is over. Let the conventions do their work now, and clear the rubbish away. My age is fifty-nine, and I tell you solemnly that the important things in life are little things, and that people are not important at all. Go back to your wife."

He looked at her, and was filled with pity. He knew that he would never be frightened of her again. Only because she was serious and friendly did he trouble himself to reply. "There is one little fact I should like to tell you, as confuting your theory. The idea of a story—a long story—had been in my head for a year. As a dream to amuse myself—the kind of amusement you would recommend for the future. I should have had time to write it, but the people round me coloured my life, and so it never seemed worth while. For the story is not likely to pay. Then came the volcano. A few days after it was over I lay in bed looking out upon a world of rubbish. Two men I know—one intellectual, the other very much the reverse—burst into the room. They said, 'What happened to your short stories? They weren't good, but where are they? Why have you stopped writing? Why haven't you been to Italy? You must write. You must go. Because to write, to go, is you.' Well, I have written, and yesterday we sent the long story out on its rounds. The men do not like it, for different reasons. But it mattered very much to them that I should write it, and so it got written. As I told you, this is only one fact; other facts, I trust, have happened in the last five months. But I mention it to prove that people are important, and therefore, however much it inconveniences my wife, I will not go back to her."

"And Italy?" asked Mrs. Failing.

This question he avoided. Italy must wait. Now that he had the time, he had not the money.

"Or what is the long story about, then?"

"About a man and a woman who meet and are happy."

"Somewhat of a tour de force, I conclude."

He frowned. "In literature we needn't intrude our own limitations. I'm not so silly as to think that all marriages turn out like mine. My character is to blame for our catastrophe, not marriage."

"My dear, I too have married; marriage is to blame."

But here again he seemed to know better.

"Well," she said, leaving the table and moving with her dessert to the mantelpiece, "so you are abandoning marriage and taking to literature. And are happy."

"Yes."

"Because, as we used to say at Cambridge, the cow is there. The world is real again. This is a room, that a window, outside is the night."

"Go on."

He pointed to the floor. "The day is straight below, shining through other windows into other rooms."

"You are very odd," she said after a pause, "and I do not like you at all. There you sit, eating my biscuits, and all the time you know that the earth is round. Who taught you? I am going to bed now, and all the night, you tell me, you and I and the biscuits go plunging eastwards, until we reach the sun. But breakfast will be at nine as usual. Good-night."

She rang the bell twice, and her maid came with her candle and her walking-stick: it was her habit of late to go to her room as soon as dinner was over, for she had no one to sit up with. Rickie was impressed by her loneliness, and also by the mixture in her of insight and obtuseness. She was so quick, so clear-headed, so imaginative even. But all the same, she had forgotten what people were like. Finding life dull, she had dropped lies into it, as a chemist drops a new element into a solution, hoping that life would thereby sparkle or turn some beautiful colour. She loved to mislead others, and in the end her private view of false and true was obscured, and she misled herself. How she must have enjoyed their errors over Stephen! But her own error had been greater, inasmuch as it was spiritual entirely.

Leighton came in with some coffee. Feeling it unnecessary to light the drawing-room lamp for one small young man, he persuaded Rickie to say he preferred the dining-room. So Rickie sat down by the fire playing with one of the lumps of chalk. His thoughts went back to the ford, from which they had scarcely wandered. Still he heard the horse in the dark drinking, still he saw the mystic rose, and the tunnel dropping diamonds. He had driven away alone, believing the earth had confirmed him. He stood behind things at last, and knew that conventions are not majestic, and that they will not claim us in the end.

As he mused, the chalk slipped from his fingers, and fell on the coffee-cup, which broke. The china, said Leighton, was expensive. He believed it was impossible to match it now. Each cup was different. It was a harlequin set. The saucer, without the cup, was therefore useless. Would Mr. Elliot please explain to Mrs. Failing how it happened.

Rickie promised he would explain.

He had left Stephen preparing to bathe, and had heard him working up-stream like an animal, splashing in the shallows, breathing heavily as he swam the pools; at times reeds snapped, or clods of earth were pulled in. By the fire he remembered it was again November. "Should you like a walk?" he asked Leighton, and told him who stopped in the village tonight. Leighton was pleased. At nine o'clock the two young men left the house, under a sky that was still only bright in the zenith. "It will rain tomorrow," Leighton said.

"My brother says, fine tomorrow."

"Fine tomorrow," Leighton echoed.

"Now which do you mean?" asked Rickie, laughing.

Since the plumes of the fir-trees touched over the drive, only a very little light penetrated. It was clearer outside the lodge gate, and bubbles of air, which Wiltshire seemed to have travelled from an immense distance, broke gently and separately on his face. They paused on the bridge. He asked whether the little fish and the bright green weeds were here now as well as in the summer. The footman had not noticed. Over the bridge they came to the cross-roads, of which one led to Salisbury and the other up through the string of villages to the railway station. The road in front was only the Roman road, the one that went on to the downs. Turning to the left, they were in Cadford.

"He will be with the Thompsons," said Rickie, looking up at dark eaves. "Perhaps he's in bed already."

"Perhaps he will be at The Antelope."

"No. Tonight he is with the Thompsons."

"With the Thompsons." After a dozen paces he said, "The Thompsons have gone away."

"Where? Why?"

"They were turned out by Mr. Wilbraham on account of our broken windows."

"Are you sure?"

"Five families were turned out."

"That's bad for Stephen," said Rickie, after a pause. "He was looking forward—oh, it's monstrous in any case!"

"But the Thompsons have gone to London," said Leighton. "Why, that family—they say it's been in the valley hundreds of years, and never got beyond shepherding. To various parts of London."

"Let us try The Antelope, then."

"Let us try The Antelope."

The inn lay up in the village. Rickie hastened his pace. This tyranny was monstrous. Some men of the age of undergraduates had broken windows, and therefore they and their families were to be ruined. The fools who govern us find it easier to be severe. It saves them trouble to say, "The innocent must suffer with the guilty." It even gives them a thrill of pride. Against all this wicked nonsense, against the Wilbrahams and Pembrokes who try to rule our world Stephen would fight till he died. Stephen was a hero. He was a law to himself, and rightly. He was great enough to despise our small moralities. He was attaining love. This evening Rickie caught Ansell's enthusiasm, and felt it worth while to sacrifice everything for such a man.

"The Antelope," said Leighton. "Those lights under the greatest elm."

"Would you please ask if he's there, and if he'd come for a turn with me. I don't think I'll go in."

Leighton opened the door. They saw a little room, blue with tobacco-smoke. Flanking the fire were deep settles hiding all but the legs of the men who lounged in them. Between the settles stood a table, covered with mugs and glasses. The scene was picturesque—fairer than the cutglass palaces of the town.

"Oh yes, he's there," he called, and after a moment's hesitation came out.

"Would he come?"

"No. I shouldn't say so," replied Leighton, with a furtive glance. He knew that Rickie was a milksop. "First night, you know, sir, among old friends."

"Yes, I know," said Rickie. "But he might like a turn down the village. It looks stuffy inside there, and poor fun probably to watch others drinking."

Leighton shut the door.

"What was that he called after you?"

"Oh, nothing. A man when he's drunk—he says the worst he's ever heard. At least, so they say."

"A man when he's drunk?"

"Yes, Sir."

"But Stephen isn't drinking?"

"No, no."

"He couldn't be. If he broke a promise—I don't pretend he's a saint. I don't want him one. But it isn't in him to break a promise."

"Yes, sir; I understand."

"In the train he promised me not to drink—nothing theatrical: just a promise for these few days."

"No, sir." "'No, sir,'" stamped Rickie. "'Yes! no! yes!' Can't you speak out? Is he drunk or isn't he?"

Leighton, justly exasperated, cried, "He can't stand, and I've told you so again and again."

"Stephen!" shouted Rickie, darting up the steps. Heat and the smell of beer awaited him, and he spoke more furiously than he had intended. "Is there any one here who's sober?" he cried. The landlord looked over the bar angrily, and asked him what he meant. He pointed to the deep settles. "Inside there he's drunk. Tell him he's broken his word, and I will not go with him to the Rings."

"Very well. You won't go with him to the Rings," said the landlord, stepping forward and slamming the door in his face.

In the room he was only angry, but out in the cool air he remembered that Stephen was a law to himself. He had chosen to break his word, and would break it again. Nothing else bound him. To yield to temptation is not fatal for most of us. But it was the end of everything for a hero.

"He's suddenly ruined!" he cried, not yet remembering himself. For a little he stood by the elm-tree, clutching the ridges of its bark. Even so would he wrestle tomorrow, and Stephen, imperturbable, reply, "My body is my own." Or worse still, he might wrestle with a pliant Stephen who promised him glibly again. While he prayed for a miracle to convert his brother, it struck him that he must pray for himself. For he, too, was ruined.

"Why, what's the matter?" asked Leighton. "Stephen's only being with friends. Mr. Elliot, sir, don't break down. Nothing's happened bad. No one's died yet, or even hurt themselves." Ever kind, he took hold of Rickie's arm, and, pitying such a nervous fellow, set out with him for home. The shoulders of Orion rose behind them over the topmost boughs of the elm. From the bridge the whole constellation was visible, and Rickie said, "May God receive me and pardon me for trusting the earth."

"But, Mr. Elliot, what have you done that's wrong?"

"Gone bankrupt, Leighton, for the second time. Pretended again that people were real. May God have mercy on me!"

Leighton dropped his arm. Though he did not understand, a chill of disgust passed over him, and he said, "I will go back to The Antelope. I will help them put Stephen to bed."

"Do. I will wait for you here." Then he leant against the parapet and prayed passionately, for he knew that the conventions would claim him soon. God was beyond them, but ah, how far beyond, and to be reached after what degradation! At the end of this childish detour his wife awaited him, not less surely because she was only his wife in name. He was too weak. Books and friends were not enough. Little by little she would claim him and corrupt him and make him what he had been; and the woman he loved would die out, in drunkenness, in debauchery, and her strength would be dissipated by a man, her beauty defiled in a man. She would not continue. That mystic rose and the face it illumined meant nothing. The stream—he was above it now—meant nothing, though it burst from the pure turf and ran for ever to the sea. The bather, the shoulders of Orion-they all meant nothing, and were going nowhere. The whole affair was a ridiculous dream.

Leighton returned, saying, "Haven't you seen Stephen? They say he followed us: he can still walk: I told you he wasn't so bad."

"I don't think he passed me. Ought one to look?" He wandered a little along the Roman road. Again nothing mattered. At the level-crossing he leant on the gate to watch a slow goods train pass. In the glare of the engine he saw that his brother had come this way, perhaps through some sodden memory of the Rings, and now lay drunk over the rails. Wearily he did a man's duty. There was time to raise him up and push him into safety. It is also a man's duty to save his own life, and therefore he tried. The train went over his knees. He died up in Cadover, whispering, "You have been right," to Mrs. Failing.

She wrote of him to Mrs. Lewin afterwards as "one who has failed in all he undertook; one of the thousands whose dust returns to the dust, accomplishing nothing in the interval. Agnes and I buried him to the sound of our cracked bell, and pretended that he had once been alive. The other, who was always honest, kept away."

XXXV

From the window they looked over a sober valley, whose sides were not too sloping to be ploughed, and whose trend was followed by a grass-grown track. It was late on Sunday afternoon, and the valley was deserted except for one labourer, who was coasting slowly downward on a rosy bicycle. The air was very quiet. A jay screamed up in the woods behind, but the ring-doves, who roost early, were already silent. Since the window opened westward, the room was flooded with light, and Stephen, finding it hot, was working in his shirtsleeves.

"You guarantee they'll sell?" he asked, with a pen between his teeth. He was tidying up a pile of manuscripts.

"I guarantee that the world will be the gainer," said Mr. Pembroke, now a clergyman, who sat beside him at the table with an expression of refined disapproval on his face.

"I'd got the idea that the long story had its points, but that these shorter things didn't—what's the word?"

"'Convince' is probably the word you want. But that type of criticism is quite a thing of the past. Have you seen the illustrated American edition?"

"I don't remember."

"Might I send you a copy? I think you ought to possess one."

"Thank you." His eye wandered. The bicycle had disappeared into some trees, and thither, through a cloudless sky, the sun was also descending.

"Is all quite plain?" said Mr. Pembroke. "Submit these ten stories to the magazines, and make your own terms with the editors. Then—I have your word for it—you will join forces with me; and the four stories in my possession, together with yours, should make up a volume, which we might well call 'Pan Pipes.'"

"Are you sure `Pan Pipes' haven't been used up already?"

Mr. Pembroke clenched his teeth. He had been bearing with this sort of thing for nearly an hour. "If that is the case, we can select another. A title is easy to come by. But that is the idea it must suggest. The stories, as I have twice explained to you, all centre round a Nature theme. Pan, being the god of—"

"I know that," said Stephen impatiently.

"—Being the god of—"

"All right. Let's get furrard. I've learnt that."

XXXV

It was years since the schoolmaster had been interrupted, and he could not stand it. "Very well," he said. "I bow to your superior knowledge of the classics. Let us proceed."

"Oh yes the introduction. There must be one. It was the introduction with all those wrong details that sold the other book."

"You overwhelm me. I never penned the memoir with that intention."

"If you won't do one, Mrs. Keynes must!"

"My sister leads a busy life. I could not ask her. I will do it myself since you insist."

"And the binding?"

"The binding," said Mr. Pembroke coldly, "must really be left to the discretion of the publisher. We cannot be concerned with such details. Our task is purely literary." His attention wandered. He began to fidget, and finally bent down and looked under the table. "What have we here?" he asked.

Stephen looked also, and for a moment they smiled at each other over the prostrate figure of a child, who was cuddling Mr. Pembroke's boots. "She's after the blacking," he explained. "If we left her there, she'd lick them brown."

"Indeed. Is that so very safe?"

"It never did me any harm. Come up! Your tongue's dirty."

"Can I—" She was understood to ask whether she could clean her tongue on a lollie.

"No, no!" said Mr. Pembroke. "Lollipops don't clean little girls' tongues."

"Yes, they do," he retorted. "But she won't get one." He lifted her on his knee, and rasped her tongue with his handkerchief.

"Dear little thing," said the visitor perfunctorily. The child began to squall, and kicked her father in the stomach. Stephen regarded her quietly. "You tried to hurt me," he said. "Hurting doesn't count. Trying to hurt counts. Go and clean your tongue yourself. Get off my knee." Tears of another sort came into her eyes, but she obeyed him. "How's the great Bertie?" he asked.

"Thank you. My nephew is perfectly well. How came you to hear of his existence?"

"Through the Silts, of course. It isn't five miles to Cadover."

Mr. Pembroke raised his eyes mournfully. "I cannot conceive how the poor Silts go on in that great house. Whatever she intended, it could not have been that. The house, the farm, the money,—everything down to the personal articles that belong to Mr. Failing, and should have reverted to his family!"

"It's legal. Interstate succession."

"I do not dispute it. But it is a lesson to one to make a will. Mrs. Keynes and myself were electrified."

"They'll do there. They offered me the agency, but—" He looked down the cultivated slopes. His manners were growing rough, for he saw few gentlemen now, and he was either incoherent or else alarmingly direct. "However, if Lawrie Silt's a Cockney like his father, and if my next is a boy and like me—" A shy beautiful look came into his eyes, and passed unnoticed. "They'll do," he repeated.

"They turned out Wilbraham and built new cottages, and bridged the railway, and made other necessary alterations." There was a moment's silence.

Mr. Pembroke took out his watch. "I wonder if I might have the trap? I mustn't miss my train, must I? It is good of you to have granted me an interview. It is all quite plain?"

"Yes."

"A case of half and half-division of profits."

"Half and half?" said the young farmer slowly. "What do you take me for? Half and half, when I provide ten of the stories and you only four?"

"I—I—" stammered Mr. Pembroke.

"I consider you did me over the long story, and I'm damned if you do me over the short ones!"

"Hush! if you please, hush!—if only for your little girl's sake."

He lifted a clerical palm.

"You did me," his voice drove, "and all the thirty-nine Articles won't stop me saying so. That long story was meant to be mine. I got it written. You've done me out of every penny it fetched. It's dedicated to me—flat out—and you even crossed out the dedication and tidied me out of the introduction. Listen to me, Pembroke. You've done people all your life—I think without knowing it, but that won't comfort us. A wretched devil at your school once wrote to me, and he'd been done. Sham food, sham religion, sham straight talks—and when he broke down, you said it was the world in miniature." He snatched at him roughly. "But I'll show you the world." He twisted him round like a baby, and through the open door they saw only the quiet valley, but in it a rivulet that would in time bring its waters to the sea. "Look even at that—and up behind where the Plain begins and you get on the solid chalk—think of us riding some night when you're ordering your hot bottle—that's the world, and there's no miniature world. There's one world, Pembroke, and you can't tidy men out of it. They answer you back do you hear?—they answer back if you do them. If you tell a man this way that four sheep equal ten, he answers back you're a liar."

Mr. Pembroke was speechless, and—such is human nature—he chiefly resented the allusion to the hot bottle; an unmanly luxury in which he never indulged; contenting himself with nightsocks. "Enough—there is no witness present—as you have doubtless observed." But there was. For a little voice cried, "Oh, mummy, they're fighting—such fun—" and feet went pattering up the stairs. "Enough. You talk of 'doing,' but what about the money out of which you 'did' my sister? What about this picture"—he pointed to a faded photograph of Stockholm—"which you caused to be filched from the walls of my house? What about—enough! Let us conclude this disheartening scene. You object to my terms. Name yours. I shall accept them. It is futile to reason with one who is the worse for drink."

Stephen was quiet at once. "Steady on!" he said gently. "Steady on in that direction. Take one-third for your four stories and the introduction, and I will keep two-thirds for myself." Then he went to harness the horse, while Mr. Pembroke, watching his broad back, desired to bury a knife in it. The desire passed, partly because it was unclerical, partly because he had no knife, and partly because he soon blurred over what had happened. To him all criticism was "rudeness": he never heeded it, for he never needed it: he was never wrong. All his life he had ordered little human beings about, and now he was equally magisterial to big ones: Stephen was a fifth-form lout whom, owing to some flaw in the regulations, he could not send up to the headmaster to be caned.

This attitude makes for tranquillity. Before long he felt merely an injured martyr. His brain cleared. He stood deep in thought before the only other picture that the bare room boasted—the Demeter of Cnidus. Outside the sun was sinking, and its last rays fell upon the immortal features and the shattered knees. Sweet-peas offered their fragrance, and with it there entered those more mysterious scents that come from no one flower or clod of earth, but from the whole bosom of evening. He tried not to be cynical. But in his heart he could not regret that tragedy, already half-forgotten, conventionalized, indistinct. Of course death is a terrible thing. Yet death is merciful when it weeds out a failure. If we look deep enough, it is all for the best. He stared at the picture and nodded.

Stephen, who had met his visitor at the station, had intended to drive him back there. But after their spurt of temper he sent him with the boy. He remained in the doorway, glad that he was going to make money, glad that he had been angry; while the glow of the clear sky deepened, and the silence was perfected, and the scents of the night grew stronger. Old vagrancies awoke, and he resolved that, dearly as he loved his house, he would not enter it again till dawn. "Goodnight!" he called, and then the child came running, and he whispered, "Quick, then! Bring me a rug." "Good-night," he repeated, and a pleasant voice called through an upper window, "Why good-night?" He did not answer until the child was wrapped up in his arms.

"It is time that she learnt to sleep out," he cried. "If you want me, we're out on the hillside, where I used to be."

The voice protested, saying this and that.

"Stewart's in the house," said the man, "and it cannot matter, and I am going anyway."

"Stephen, I wish you wouldn't. I wish you wouldn't take her. Promise you won't say foolish things to her. Don't—I wish you'd come up for a minute—"

The child, whose face was laid against his, felt the muscles in it harden.

"Don't tell her foolish things about yourself—things that aren't any longer true. Don't worry her with old dead dreadfulness. To please me—don't."

"Just tonight I won't, then."

"Stevie, dear, please me more—don't take her with you."

At this he laughed impertinently. "I suppose I'm being kept in line," she called, and, though he could not see her, she stretched her arms towards him. For a time he stood motionless, under her window, musing on his happy tangible life. Then his breath quickened, and he wondered why he was here, and why he should hold a warm child in his arms. "It's time we were starting," he whispered, and showed the sky, whose orange was already fading into green. "Wish everything good-night."

"Good-night, dear mummy," she said sleepily. "Goodnight, dear house. Good-night, you pictures—long picture—stone lady. I see you through the window—your faces are pink."

The twilight descended. He rested his lips on her hair, and carried her, without speaking, until he reached the open down. He had often slept here himself, alone, and on his wedding-night, and he knew that the turf was dry, and that if you laid your face to it you would smell the thyme. For a moment the earth aroused her, and she began to chatter. "My prayers—" she said anxiously. He gave her one hand, and she was asleep before her fingers had nestled in its palm. Their touch made him pensive, and again he marvelled why he, the accident, was here. He was alive and had created life. By whose authority? Though he could not phrase it, he believed that he guided the future of our race, and that, century after century, his thoughts and his passions would triumph in England. The dead who had evoked him, the unborn whom he would evoke he governed the paths between them. By whose authority?

Out in the west lay Cadover and the fields of his earlier youth, and over them descended the crescent moon. His eyes followed her decline, and against her final radiance he saw, or thought he saw, the outline of the Rings. He had always been grateful, as people who understood him knew. But this evening his gratitude seemed a gift of small account. The ear was deaf, and what thanks of his could reach it? The body was dust, and in what ecstasy of his could it share? The spirit had fled, in agony and loneliness, never to know that it bequeathed him salvation.

He filled his pipe, and then sat pressing the unlit tobacco with his thumb. "What am I to do?" he thought. "Can he notice the things he gave me? A parson would know. But what's a man like me to do, who works all his life out of doors?" As he wondered, the silence of the night was broken. The whistle of Mr. Pembroke's train came faintly, and a lurid spot passed over the land—passed, and the silence returned. One thing remained that a man of his sort might do. He bent down reverently and saluted the child; to whom he had given the name of their mother.

WHERE ANGELS FEAR TO TREAD

Chapter 1

They were all at Charing Cross to see Lilia off—Philip, Harriet, Irma, Mrs. Herriton herself. Even Mrs. Theobald, squired by Mr. Kingcroft, had braved the journey from Yorkshire to bid her only daughter good-bye. Miss Abbott was likewise attended by numerous relatives, and the sight of so many people talking at once and saying such different things caused Lilia to break into ungovernable peals of laughter.

"Quite an ovation," she cried, sprawling out of her first-class carriage. "They'll take us for royalty. Oh, Mr. Kingcroft, get us foot-warmers."

The good-natured young man hurried away, and Philip, taking his place, flooded her with a final stream of advice and injunctions—where to stop, how to learn Italian, when to use mosquito-nets, what pictures to look at. "Remember," he concluded, "that it is only by going off the track that you get to know the country. See the little towns—Gubbio, Pienza, Cortona, San Gemignano, Monteriano. And don't, let me beg you, go with that awful tourist idea that Italy's only a museum of antiquities and art. Love and understand the Italians, for the people are more marvellous than the land."

"How I wish you were coming, Philip," she said, flattered at the unwonted notice her brother-in-law was giving her.

"I wish I were." He could have managed it without great difficulty, for his career at the Bar was not so intense as to prevent occasional holidays. But his family disliked his continual visits to the Continent, and he himself often found pleasure in the idea that he was too busy to leave town.

"Good-bye, dear every one. What a whirl!" She caught sight of her little daughter Irma, and felt that a touch of maternal solemnity was required. "Good-bye, darling. Mind you're always good, and do what Granny tells you."

She referred not to her own mother, but to her mother-in-law, Mrs. Herriton, who hated the title of Granny.

Irma lifted a serious face to be kissed, and said cautiously, "I'll do my best."

"She is sure to be good," said Mrs. Herriton, who was standing pensively a little out of the hubbub. But Lilia was already calling to Miss Abbott, a tall, grave, rather nice-looking young lady who was conducting her adieus in a more decorous manner on the platform.

"Caroline, my Caroline! Jump in, or your chaperon will go off without you."

And Philip, whom the idea of Italy always intoxicated, had started again, telling her of the supreme moments of her coming journey—the Campanile of Airolo, which would burst on her when she emerged from the St. Gothard tunnel, presaging the future; the view of the Ticino and Lago Maggiore as the train climbed the slopes of Monte Cenere; the view of Lugano, the view of Como—Italy gathering thick around her now—the arrival at her first resting-place, when, after long driving through dark and dirty streets, she should at last behold, amid the roar of trams and the glare of arc lamps, the buttresses of the cathedral of Milan.

"Handkerchiefs and collars," screamed Harriet, "in my inlaid box! I've lent you my inlaid box."

"Good old Harry!" She kissed every one again, and there was a moment's silence. They all smiled steadily, excepting Philip, who was choking in the fog, and old Mrs. Theobald, who had begun to cry. Miss Abbott got into the carriage. The guard himself shut the door, and told Lilia that she would be all right. Then the train moved, and they all moved with it a couple of steps, and waved their handkerchiefs, and uttered cheerful little cries. At that moment Mr. Kingcroft reappeared, carrying a footwarmer by both ends, as if it was a tea-tray. He was sorry that he was too late, and called out in a quivering voice, "Good-bye, Mrs. Charles. May you enjoy yourself, and may God bless you."

Lilia smiled and nodded, and then the absurd position of the foot-warmer overcame her, and she began to laugh again.

"Oh, I am so sorry," she cried back, "but you do look so funny. Oh, you all look so funny waving! Oh, pray!" And laughing helplessly, she was carried out into the fog.

"High spirits to begin so long a journey," said Mrs. Theobald, dabbing her eyes.

Mr. Kingcroft solemnly moved his head in token of agreement. "I wish," said he, "that Mrs. Charles had gotten the footwarmer. These London porters won't take heed to a country chap."

"But you did your best," said Mrs. Herriton. "And I think it simply noble of you to have brought Mrs. Theobald all the way here on such a day as this." Then, rather hastily, she shook hands, and left him to take Mrs. Theobald all the way back.

Sawston, her own home, was within easy reach of London, and they were not late for tea. Tea was in the dining-room, with an egg for Irma, to keep up the child's spirits. The house seemed strangely quiet after a fortnight's bustle, and their conversation was spasmodic and subdued. They wondered whether the travellers had got to Folkestone, whether it would be at all rough, and if so what would happen to poor Miss Abbott.

"And, Granny, when will the old ship get to Italy?" asked Irma.

"'Grandmother,' dear; not 'Granny,'" said Mrs. Herriton, giving her a kiss. "And we say 'a boat' or 'a steamer,' not 'a ship.' Ships have sails. And mother won't go all the way by sea. You look at the map of Europe, and you'll see why. Harriet, take her. Go with Aunt Harriet, and she'll show you the map."

"Righto!" said the little girl, and dragged the reluctant Harriet into the library. Mrs. Herriton and her son were left alone. There was immediately confidence between them.

"Here beginneth the New Life," said Philip.

"Poor child, how vulgar!" murmured Mrs. Herriton. "It's surprising that she isn't worse. But she has got a look of poor Charles about her."

"And—alas, alas!—a look of old Mrs. Theobald. What appalling apparition was that! I did think the lady was bedridden as well as imbecile. Why ever did she come?"

"Mr. Kingcroft made her. I am certain of it. He wanted to see Lilia again, and this was the only way."

"I hope he is satisfied. I did not think my sister-in-law distinguished herself in her farewells."

Mrs. Herriton shuddered. "I mind nothing, so long as she has gone—and gone with Miss Abbott. It is mortifying to think that a widow of thirty-three requires a girl ten years younger to look after her."

"I pity Miss Abbott. Fortunately one admirer is chained to England. Mr. Kingcroft cannot leave the crops or the climate or something. I don't think, either, he improved his chances today. He, as well as Lilia, has the knack of being absurd in public."

Mrs. Herriton replied, "When a man is neither well bred, nor well connected, nor handsome, nor clever, nor rich, even Lilia may discard him in time."

"No. I believe she would take any one. Right up to the last, when her boxes were packed, she was 'playing' the chinless curate. Both the curates are chinless, but hers had the dampest hands. I came on them in the Park. They were speaking of the Pentateuch."

"My dear boy! If possible, she has got worse and worse. It was your idea of Italian travel that saved us!"

Philip brightened at the little compliment. "The odd part is that she was quite eager—always asking me for information; and of course I was very glad to give it. I admit she is a Philistine, appallingly ignorant, and her taste in art is false. Still, to have any taste at all is something. And I do believe that Italy really purifies and ennobles all who visit her. She is the school as well as the playground of the world. It is really to Lilia's credit that she wants to go there."

"She would go anywhere," said his mother, who had heard enough of the praises of Italy. "I and Caroline Abbott had the greatest difficulty in dissuading her from the Riviera."

"No, Mother; no. She was really keen on Italy. This travel is quite a crisis for her." He found the situation full of whimsical romance: there was something half attractive, half repellent in the thought of this vulgar woman journeying to places he loved and revered. Why should she not be transfigured? The same had happened to the Goths.

Mrs. Herriton did not believe in romance nor in transfiguration, nor in parallels from history, nor in anything else that may disturb domestic life. She adroitly changed the subject before Philip got excited. Soon Harriet returned, having given her lesson in geography. Irma went to bed early, and was tucked up by her grandmother. Then the two ladies worked and played cards. Philip read a book. And so they all settled down to their quiet, profitable existence, and continued it without interruption through the winter.

It was now nearly ten years since Charles had fallen in love with Lilia Theobald because she was pretty, and during that time Mrs. Herriton had hardly known a moment's rest. For six months she schemed to prevent the match, and when it had taken place she turned to another task—the supervision of her daughter-in-law. Lilia must be pushed through life without bringing discredit on the family into which she had married. She was aided by Charles, by her daughter Harriet, and, as soon as he was old enough, by the clever one of the family, Philip. The birth of Irma made things still more difficult. But fortunately old Mrs. Theobald, who had attempted interference, began to break up. It was an effort to her to leave Whitby, and Mrs. Herriton discouraged the effort as far as possible. That curious duel which is fought over every baby was fought and decided early. Irma belonged to her father's family, not to her mother's.

Charles died, and the struggle recommenced. Lilia tried to assert herself, and said that she should go to take care of Mrs. Theobald. It required all Mrs. Herriton's kindness to prevent her. A house was finally taken for her at Sawston, and there for three years she lived with Irma, continually subject to the refining influences of her late husband's family.

During one of her rare Yorkshire visits trouble began again. Lilia confided to a friend that she liked a Mr. Kingcroft extremely, but that she was not exactly engaged to him. The news came round to Mrs. Herriton, who at once wrote, begging for information, and pointing out that Lilia must either be engaged or not, since no intermediate state existed. It was a good letter, and flurried Lilia extremely. She left Mr. Kingcroft without even the pressure of a rescue-party. She cried a great deal on her return to Sawston, and said she was very sorry. Mrs. Herriton took the opportunity of speaking more seriously about the duties of widowhood and motherhood than she had ever done before. But somehow things never went easily after. Lilia would not settle down in her place among Sawston matrons. She was a bad housekeeper, always in the throes of some domestic crisis, which Mrs. Herriton, who kept her servants for years, had to step across and adjust. She let Irma stop away from school for insufficient reasons, and she allowed her to wear rings. She learnt to bicycle, for the purpose of waking the place up, and coasted down the High Street one Sunday evening, falling off at the turn by the church. If she had not been a relative, it would have been entertaining. But even Philip, who in theory loved outraging English conventions, rose to the occasion, and gave her a talking which she remembered to her dying day. It was just then, too, that they discovered that she still allowed Mr. Kingcroft to write to her "as a gentleman friend," and to send presents to Irma.

Philip thought of Italy, and the situation was saved. Caroline, charming, sober, Caroline Abbott, who lived two turnings away, was seeking a companion for a year's travel. Lilia gave up her house, sold half her furniture, left the other half and Irma with Mrs. Herriton, and had now departed, amid universal approval, for a change of scene.

She wrote to them frequently during the winter—more frequently than she wrote to her mother. Her letters were always prosperous. Florence she found perfectly sweet, Naples a dream, but very whiffy. In Rome one had simply to sit still and feel. Philip, however, declared that she was improving. He was particularly gratified when in the early spring she began to visit the smaller towns that he had recommended. "In a place like this," she wrote, "one really does feel in the heart of things, and off the beaten track. Looking out of a Gothic window every morning, it seems impossible that the middle ages have passed away." The letter was from Monteriano, and concluded with a not unsuccessful description of the wonderful little town.

"It is something that she is contented," said Mrs. Herriton. "But no one could live three months with Caroline Abbott and not be the better for it."

Just then Irma came in from school, and she read her mother's letter to her, carefully correcting any grammatical errors, for she was a loyal supporter of parental authority—Irma listened politely, but soon changed the subject to hockey, in which her whole being was absorbed. They were to vote for colours that afternoon—yellow and white or yellow and green. What did her grandmother think?

Of course Mrs. Herriton had an opinion, which she sedately expounded, in spite of Harriet, who said that colours were unnecessary for children, and of Philip, who said that they were ugly. She was getting proud of Irma, who had certainly greatly improved, and could no longer be called that most appalling of things—a vulgar child. She was anxious to form her before her mother returned. So she had no objection to the leisurely movements of the travellers, and even suggested that they should overstay their year if it suited them.

Lilia's next letter was also from Monteriano, and Philip grew quite enthusiastic.

"They've stopped there over a week!" he cried. "Why! I shouldn't have done as much myself. They must be really keen, for the hotel's none too comfortable."

"I cannot understand people," said Harriet. "What can they be doing all day? And there is no church there, I suppose."

"There is Santa Deodata, one of the most beautiful churches in Italy."

"Of course I mean an English church," said Harriet stiffly. "Lilia promised me that she would always be in a large town on Sundays."

"If she goes to a service at Santa Deodata's, she will find more beauty and sincerity than there is in all the Back Kitchens of Europe."

The Back Kitchen was his nickname for St. James's, a small depressing edifice much patronized by his sister. She always resented any slight on it, and Mrs. Herriton had to intervene.

"Now, dears, don't. Listen to Lilia's letter. 'We love this place, and I do not know how I shall ever thank Philip for telling me it. It is not only so quaint, but one sees the Italians unspoiled in all their simplicity and charm here. The frescoes are wonderful. Caroline, who grows sweeter every day, is very busy sketching.'"

"Every one to his taste!" said Harriet, who always delivered a platitude as if it was an epigram. She was curiously virulent about Italy, which she had never visited, her only experience of the Continent being an occasional six weeks in the Protestant parts of Switzerland.

"Oh, Harriet is a bad lot!" said Philip as soon as she left the room. His mother laughed, and told him not to be naughty; and the appearance of Irma, just off to school, prevented further discussion. Not only in Tracts is a child a peacemaker.

"One moment, Irma," said her uncle. "I'm going to the station. I'll give you the pleasure of my company."

They started together. Irma was gratified; but conversation flagged, for Philip had not the art of talking to the young. Mrs. Herriton sat a little longer at the breakfast table, re-reading Lilia's letter. Then she helped the cook to clear, ordered dinner, and started the housemaid turning out the drawing-room, Tuesday being its day. The weather was lovely, and she thought she would do a little gardening, as it was quite early. She called Harriet, who had recovered from the insult to St. James's, and together they went to the kitchen garden and began to sow some early vegetables.

"We will save the peas to the last; they are the greatest fun," said Mrs. Herriton, who had the gift of making work a treat. She and her elderly daughter always got on very well, though they had not a great deal in common. Harriet's education had been almost too successful. As Philip once said, she had "bolted all the cardinal virtues and couldn't digest them." Though pious and patriotic, and a great moral asset for the house, she lacked that pliancy and tact which her mother so much valued, and had expected her to pick up for herself. Harriet, if she had been allowed, would have driven Lilia to an open rupture, and, what was worse, she would have done the same to Philip two years before, when he returned full of passion for Italy, and ridiculing Sawston and its ways.

"It's a shame, Mother!" she had cried. "Philip laughs at everything—the Book Club, the Debating Society, the Progressive Whist, the bazaars. People won't like it. We have our reputation. A house divided against itself cannot stand."

Mrs. Herriton replied in the memorable words, "Let Philip say what he likes, and he will let us do what we like." And Harriet had acquiesced.

They sowed the duller vegetables first, and a pleasant feeling of righteous fatigue stole over them as they addressed themselves to the peas. Harriet stretched a string to guide the row straight, and Mrs. Herriton scratched a furrow with a pointed stick. At the end of it she looked at her watch.

"It's twelve! The second post's in. Run and see if there are any letters."

Harriet did not want to go. "Let's finish the peas. There won't be any letters."

"No, dear; please go. I'll sow the peas, but you shall cover them up—and mind the birds don't see 'em!"

Chapter 1

Mrs. Herriton was very careful to let those peas trickle evenly from her hand, and at the end of the row she was conscious that she had never sown better. They were expensive too.

"Actually old Mrs. Theobald!" said Harriet, returning.

"Read me the letter. My hands are dirty. How intolerable the crested paper is."

Harriet opened the envelope.

"I don't understand," she said; "it doesn't make sense."

"Her letters never did."

"But it must be sillier than usual," said Harriet, and her voice began to quaver. "Look here, read it, Mother; I can't make head or tail."

Mrs. Herriton took the letter indulgently. "What is the difficulty?" she said after a long pause. "What is it that puzzles you in this letter?"

"The meaning—" faltered Harriet. The sparrows hopped nearer and began to eye the peas.

"The meaning is quite clear—Lilia is engaged to be married. Don't cry, dear; please me by not crying—don't talk at all. It's more than I could bear. She is going to marry some one she has met in a hotel. Take the letter and read for yourself." Suddenly she broke down over what might seem a small point. "How dare she not tell me direct! How dare she write first to Yorkshire! Pray, am I to hear through Mrs. Theobald—a patronizing, insolent letter like this? Have I no claim at all? Bear witness, dear"—she choked with passion—"bear witness that for this I'll never forgive her!"

"Oh, what is to be done?" moaned Harriet. "What is to be done?"

"This first!" She tore the letter into little pieces and scattered it over the mould. "Next, a telegram for Lilia! No! a telegram for Miss Caroline Abbott. She, too, has something to explain."

"Oh, what is to be done?" repeated Harriet, as she followed her mother to the house. She was helpless before such effrontery. What awful thing—what awful person had come to Lilia? "Some one in the hotel." The letter only said that. What kind of person? A gentleman? An Englishman? The letter did not say.

"Wire reason of stay at Monteriano. Strange rumours," read Mrs. Herriton, and addressed the telegram to Abbott, Stella d'Italia, Monteriano, Italy. "If there is an office there," she added, "we might get an answer this evening. Since Philip is back at seven, and the eight-fifteen catches the midnight boat at Dover—Harriet, when you go with this, get 100 pounds in 5 pound notes at the bank."

"Go, dear, at once; do not talk. I see Irma coming back; go quickly.... Well, Irma dear, and whose team are you in this afternoon—Miss Edith's or Miss May's?"

But as soon as she had behaved as usual to her grand-daughter, she went to the library and took out the large atlas, for she wanted to know about Monteriano. The name was in the smallest print, in the midst of a woolly-brown tangle of hills which were called the "Sub-Apennines." It was not so very far from Siena, which she had learnt at school. Past it there wandered a thin black line, notched at intervals like a saw, and she knew that this was a railway. But the map left a good deal to imagination, and she had not got any. She looked up the place in "Childe Harold," but Byron had not been there. Nor did Mark Twain visit it in the "Tramp Abroad." The resources of literature were exhausted: she must wait till Philip came home. And the thought of Philip made her try Philip's room, and there she found "Central Italy," by Baedeker, and opened it for the first time in her life and read in it as follows:—

MONTERIANO (pop. 4800). Hotels: Stella d'Italia, moderate only; Globo, dirty. * Caffe Garibaldi. Post and Telegraph office in Corso Vittorio Emmanuele, next to theatre. Photographs at Seghena's (cheaper in Florence). Diligence (1 lira) meets principal trains.

Chief attractions (2-3 hours): Santa Deodata, Palazzo Pubblico, Sant' Agostino, Santa Caterina, Sant' Ambrogio, Palazzo Capocchi. Guide (2 lire) unnecessary. A walk round the Walls should on no account be omitted. The view from the Rocca (small gratuity) is finest at sunset.

History: Monteriano, the Mons Rianus of Antiquity, whose Ghibelline tendencies are noted by Dante (Purg. xx.), definitely emancipated itself from Poggibonsi in 1261. Hence the distich, "POGGIBONIZZI, FAUI IN LA, CHE MONTERIANO SI FA CITTA!" till recently enscribed over the Siena gate. It remained independent till 1530, when it was sacked by the Papal troops and became part of the Grand Duchy of Tuscany. It is now of small importance, and seat of the district prison. The inhabitants are still noted for their agreeable manners.

The traveller will proceed direct from the Siena gate to the Collegiate Church of Santa Deodata, and inspect (5th chapel on right) the charming Frescoes....

Mrs. Herriton did not proceed. She was not one to detect the hidden charms of Baedeker. Some of the information seemed to her unnecessary, all of it was dull. Whereas Philip could never read "The view from the Rocca (small gratuity) is finest at sunset" without a catching at the heart. Restoring the book to its place, she went downstairs, and looked up and down the asphalt paths for her daughter. She saw her at last, two turnings away, vainly trying to shake off Mr. Abbott, Miss Caroline Abbott's father. Harriet was always unfortunate. At last she returned, hot, agitated, crackling with bank-notes, and Irma bounced to greet her, and trod heavily on her corn.

"Your feet grow larger every day," said the agonized Harriet, and gave her niece a violent push. Then Irma cried, and Mrs. Herriton was annoyed with Harriet for betraying irritation. Lunch was nasty; and during pudding news arrived that the cook, by sheer dexterity, had broken a very vital knob off the kitchen-range. "It is too bad," said Mrs. Herriton. Irma said it was three bad, and was told not to be rude. After lunch Harriet would get out Baedeker, and read in injured tones about Monteriano, the Mons Rianus of Antiquity, till her mother stopped her.

"It's ridiculous to read, dear. She's not trying to marry any one in the place. Some tourist, obviously, who's stopping in the hotel. The place has nothing to do with it at all."

"But what a place to go to! What nice person, too, do you meet in a hotel?"

"Nice or nasty, as I have told you several times before, is not the point. Lilia has insulted our family, and she shall suffer for it. And when you speak against hotels, I think you forget that I met your father at Chamounix. You can contribute nothing, dear, at present, and I think you had better hold your tongue. I am going to the kitchen, to speak about the range."

She spoke just too much, and the cook said that if she could not give satisfaction—she had better leave. A small thing at hand is greater than a great thing remote, and Lilia, misconducting herself upon a mountain in Central Italy, was immediately hidden. Mrs. Herriton flew to a registry office, failed; flew to another, failed again; came home, was told by the housemaid that things seemed so unsettled that she had better leave as well; had tea, wrote six letters, was interrupted by cook and housemaid, both weeping, asking her pardon, and imploring to be taken back. In the flush of victory the door-bell rang, and there was the telegram: "Lilia engaged to Italian nobility. Writing. Abbott."

"No answer," said Mrs. Herriton. "Get down Mr. Philip's Gladstone from the attic."

She would not allow herself to be frightened by the unknown. Indeed she knew a little now. The man was not an Italian noble, otherwise the telegram would have said so. It must have been written by Lilia. None but she would have been guilty of the fatuous vulgarity of "Italian nobility." She recalled phrases of this morning's letter: "We love this place—Caroline is sweeter than ever, and busy sketching—Italians full of simplicity and charm." And the remark of Baedeker, "The inhabitants are still noted for their agreeable manners," had a baleful meaning now. If Mrs. Herriton had no imagination, she had intuition, a more useful quality, and the picture she made to herself of Lilia's FIANCE did not prove altogether wrong.

So Philip was received with the news that he must start in half an hour for Monteriano. He was in a painful position. For three years he had sung the praises of the Italians, but he had never contemplated having one as a relative. He tried to soften the thing down to his mother, but in his heart of hearts he agreed with her when she said, "The man may be a duke or he may be an organ-grinder. That is not the point. If Lilia marries him she insults the memory of Charles, she insults Irma, she insults us. Therefore I forbid her, and if she disobeys we have done with her for ever."

"I will do all I can," said Philip in a low voice. It was the first time he had had anything to do. He kissed his mother and sister and puzzled Irma. The hall was warm and attractive as he looked back into it from the cold March night, and he departed for Italy reluctantly, as for something commonplace and dull.

Before Mrs. Herriton went to bed she wrote to Mrs. Theobald, using plain language about Lilia's conduct, and hinting that it was a question on which every one must definitely choose sides. She added, as if it was an afterthought, that Mrs. Theobald's letter had arrived that morning.

Just as she was going upstairs she remembered that she never covered up those peas. It upset her more than anything, and again and again she struck the banisters with vexation. Late as it was, she got a lantern from the tool-shed and went down the garden to rake the earth over them. The sparrows had taken every one. But countless fragments of the letter remained, disfiguring the tidy ground.

Chapter 2

When the bewildered tourist alights at the station of Monteriano, he finds himself in the middle of the country. There are a few houses round the railway, and many more dotted over the plain and the slopes of the hills, but of a town, mediaeval or otherwise, not the slightest sign. He must take what is suitably termed a "legno"—a piece of wood—and drive up eight miles of excellent road into the middle ages. For it is impossible, as well as sacrilegious, to be as quick as Baedeker.

It was three in the afternoon when Philip left the realms of commonsense. He was so weary with travelling that he had fallen asleep in the train. His fellow-passengers had the usual Italian gift of divination, and when Monteriano came they knew he wanted to go there, and dropped him out. His feet sank into the hot asphalt of the platform, and in a dream he watched the train depart, while the porter who ought to have been carrying his bag, ran up the line playing touch-you-last with the guard. Alas! he was in no humour for Italy. Bargaining for a legno bored him unutterably. The man asked six lire; and though Philip knew that for eight miles it should scarcely be more than four, yet he was about to give what he was asked, and so make the man discontented and unhappy for the rest of the day. He was saved from this social blunder by loud shouts, and looking up the road saw one cracking his whip and waving his reins and driving two horses furiously, and behind him there appeared the swaying figure of a woman, holding star-fish fashion on to anything she could touch. It was Miss Abbott, who had just received his letter from Milan announcing the time of his arrival, and had hurried down to meet him.

He had known Miss Abbott for years, and had never had much opinion about her one way or the other. She was good, quiet, dull, and amiable, and young only because she was twenty-three: there was nothing in her appearance or manner to suggest the fire of youth. All her life had been spent at Sawston with a dull and amiable father, and her pleasant, pallid face, bent on some respectable charity, was a familiar object of the Sawston streets. Why she had ever wished to leave them was surprising; but as she truly said, "I am John Bull to the backbone, yet I do want to see Italy, just once. Everybody says it is marvellous, and that one gets no idea of it from books at all." The curate suggested that a year was a long time; and Miss Abbott, with decorous playfulness, answered him, "Oh, but you must let me have my fling! I promise to have it once, and once only. It will give me things to think about and talk about for the rest of my life." The curate had consented; so had Mr. Abbott. And here she was in a legno, solitary, dusty, frightened, with as much to answer and to answer for as the most dashing adventuress could desire.

They shook hands without speaking. She made room for Philip and his luggage amidst the loud indignation of the unsuccessful driver, whom it required the combined eloquence of the station-master and the station beggar to confute. The silence was prolonged until they started. For three days he had been considering what he should do, and still more what he should say. He had invented a dozen imaginary conversations, in all of which his logic and eloquence procured him certain victory. But how to begin? He was in the enemy's country, and everything—the hot sun, the cold air behind the heat, the endless rows of olive-trees, regular yet mysterious—seemed hostile to the placid atmosphere of Sawston in which his thoughts took birth. At the outset he made one great concession. If the match was really suitable, and Lilia were bent on it, he would give in, and trust to his influence with his mother to set things right. He would not have made the concession in England; but here in Italy, Lilia, however wilful and silly, was at all events growing to be a human being.

"Are we to talk it over now?" he asked.

"Certainly, please," said Miss Abbott, in great agitation. "If you will be so very kind."

"Then how long has she been engaged?"

Her face was that of a perfect fool—a fool in terror.

"A short time—quite a short time," she stammered, as if the shortness of the time would reassure him.

"I should like to know how long, if you can remember."

She entered into elaborate calculations on her fingers. "Exactly eleven days," she said at last.

"How long have you been here?"

More calculations, while he tapped irritably with his foot. "Close on three weeks."

"Did you know him before you came?"

"No."

"Oh! Who is he?"

"A native of the place."

The second silence took place. They had left the plain now and were climbing up the outposts of the hills, the olive-trees still accompanying. The driver, a jolly fat man, had got out to ease the horses, and was walking by the side of the carriage.

"I understood they met at the hotel."

"It was a mistake of Mrs. Theobald's."

"I also understand that he is a member of the Italian nobility."

She did not reply.

"May I be told his name?"

Miss Abbott whispered, "Carella." But the driver heard her, and a grin split over his face. The engagement must be known already.

"Carella? Conte or Marchese, or what?"

"Signor," said Miss Abbott, and looked helplessly aside.

"Perhaps I bore you with these questions. If so, I will stop."

"Oh, no, please; not at all. I am here—my own idea—to give all information which you very naturally—and to see if somehow—please ask anything you like."

"Then how old is he?"

"Oh, quite young. Twenty-one, I believe."

There burst from Philip the exclamation, "Good Lord!"

"One would never believe it," said Miss Abbott, flushing. "He looks much older."

"And is he good-looking?" he asked, with gathering sarcasm.

She became decisive. "Very good-looking. All his features are good, and he is well built—though I dare say English standards would find him too short."

Philip, whose one physical advantage was his height, felt annoyed at her implied indifference to it.

"May I conclude that you like him?"

She replied decisively again, "As far as I have seen him, I do."

At that moment the carriage entered a little wood, which lay brown and sombre across the cultivated hill. The trees of the wood were small and leafless, but noticeable for this—that their stems stood in violets as rocks stand in the summer sea. There are such violets in England, but not so many. Nor are there so many in Art, for no painter has the courage. The cart-ruts were channels, the hollow lagoons; even the dry white margin of the road was splashed, like a causeway soon to be submerged under the advancing tide of spring. Philip paid no attention at the time: he was thinking what to say next. But his eyes had registered the beauty, and next March he did not forget that the road to Monteriano must traverse innumerable flowers.

"As far as I have seen him, I do like him," repeated Miss Abbott, after a pause.

He thought she sounded a little defiant, and crushed her at once.

"What is he, please? You haven't told me that. What's his position?"

She opened her mouth to speak, and no sound came from it. Philip waited patiently. She tried to be audacious, and failed pitiably.

"No position at all. He is kicking his heels, as my father would say. You see, he has only just finished his military service."

"As a private?"

"I suppose so. There is general conscription. He was in the Bersaglieri, I think. Isn't that the crack regiment?"

"The men in it must be short and broad. They must also be able to walk six miles an hour."

She looked at him wildly, not understanding all that he said, but feeling that he was very clever. Then she continued her defence of Signor Carella.

"And now, like most young men, he is looking out for something to do."

"Meanwhile?"

"Meanwhile, like most young men, he lives with his people—father, mother, two sisters, and a tiny tot of a brother."

There was a grating sprightliness about her that drove him nearly mad. He determined to silence her at last.

"One more question, and only one more. What is his father?"

"His father," said Miss Abbott. "Well, I don't suppose you'll think it a good match. But that's not the point. I mean the point is not—I mean that social differences—love, after all—not but what—I—"

Philip ground his teeth together and said nothing.

"Gentlemen sometimes judge hardly. But I feel that you, and at all events your mother—so really good in every sense, so really unworldly—after all, love-marriages are made in heaven."

"Yes, Miss Abbott, I know. But I am anxious to hear heaven's choice. You arouse my curiosity. Is my sister-in-law to marry an angel?"

"Mr. Herriton, don't—please, Mr. Herriton—a dentist. His father's a dentist."

Philip gave a cry of personal disgust and pain. He shuddered all over, and edged away from his companion. A dentist! A dentist at Monteriano. A dentist in fairyland! False teeth and laughing gas and the tilting chair at a place which knew the Etruscan League, and the Pax Romana, and Alaric himself, and the Countess Matilda, and the Middle Ages, all fighting and holiness, and the Renaissance, all fighting and beauty! He thought of Lilia no longer. He was anxious for himself: he feared that Romance might die.

Romance only dies with life. No pair of pincers will ever pull it out of us. But there is a spurious sentiment which cannot resist the unexpected and the incongruous and the grotesque. A touch will loosen it, and the sooner it goes from us the better. It was going from Philip now, and therefore he gave the cry of pain.

"I cannot think what is in the air," he began. "If Lilia was determined to disgrace us, she might have found a less repulsive way. A boy of medium height with a pretty face, the son of a dentist at Monteriano. Have I put it correctly? May I surmise that he has not got one penny? May I also surmise that his social position is nil? Furthermore—"

"Stop! I'll tell you no more."

"Really, Miss Abbott, it is a little late for reticence. You have equipped me admirably!"

"I'll tell you not another word!" she cried, with a spasm of terror. Then she got out her handkerchief, and seemed as if she would shed tears. After a silence, which he intended to symbolize to her the dropping of a curtain on the scene, he began to talk of other subjects.

They were among olives again, and the wood with its beauty and wildness had passed away. But as they climbed higher the country opened out, and there appeared, high on a hill to the right, Monteriano. The hazy green of the olives rose up to its walls, and it seemed to float in isolation between trees and sky, like some fantastic ship city of a dream. Its colour was brown, and it revealed not a single house—nothing but the narrow circle of the walls, and behind them seventeen towers—all that was left of the fifty-two that had filled the city in her prime. Some were only stumps, some were inclining stiffly to their fall, some were still erect, piercing like masts into the blue. It was impossible to praise it as beautiful, but it was also impossible to damn it as quaint.

Meanwhile Philip talked continually, thinking this to be great evidence of resource and tact. It showed Miss Abbott that he had probed her to the bottom, but was able to conquer his disgust, and by sheer force of intellect continue to be as agreeable and amusing as ever. He did not know that he talked a good deal of nonsense, and that the sheer force of his intellect was weakened by the sight of Monteriano, and by the thought of dentistry within those walls.

The town above them swung to the left, to the right, to the left again, as the road wound upward through the trees, and the towers began to glow in the descending sun. As they drew near, Philip saw the heads of people gathering black upon the walls, and he knew well what was happening—how the news was spreading that a stranger was in sight, and the beggars were aroused from their content and bid to adjust their deformities; how the alabaster man was running for his wares, and the Authorized Guide running for his peaked cap and his two cards of recommendation—one from Miss M'Gee, Maida Vale, the other, less valuable, from an Equerry to the Queen of Peru; how some one else was running to tell the landlady of the Stella d'Italia to put on her pearl necklace and brown boots and empty the slops from the spare bedroom; and how the landlady was running to tell Lilia and her boy that their fate was at hand.

Perhaps it was a pity Philip had talked so profusely. He had driven Miss Abbott half demented, but he had given himself no time to concert a plan. The end came so suddenly. They emerged from the trees on to the terrace before the walk, with the vision of half Tuscany radiant in the sun behind them, and then they turned in through the Siena gate, and their journey was over. The Dogana men admitted them with an air of gracious welcome, and they clattered up the narrow dark street, greeted by that mixture of curiosity and kindness which makes each Italian arrival so wonderful.

He was stunned and knew not what to do. At the hotel he received no ordinary reception. The landlady wrung him by the hand; one person snatched his umbrella, another his bag; people pushed each other out of his way. The entrance seemed blocked with a crowd. Dogs were barking, bladder whistles being blown, women waving their handkerchiefs, excited children screaming on the stairs, and at the top of the stairs was Lilia herself, very radiant, with her best blouse on.

"Welcome!" she cried. "Welcome to Monteriano!" He greeted her, for he did not know what else to do, and a sympathetic murmur rose from the crowd below.

"You told me to come here," she continued, "and I don't forget it. Let me introduce Signor Carella!"

Philip discerned in the corner behind her a young man who might eventually prove handsome and well-made, but certainly did not seem so then. He was half enveloped in the drapery of a cold dirty curtain, and nervously stuck out a hand, which Philip took and found thick and damp. There were more murmurs of approval from the stairs.

"Well, din-din's nearly ready," said Lilia. "Your room's down the passage, Philip. You needn't go changing."

He stumbled away to wash his hands, utterly crushed by her effrontery.

"Dear Caroline!" whispered Lilia as soon as he had gone. "What an angel you've been to tell him! He takes it so well. But you must have had a MAUVAIS QUART D'HEURE."

Miss Abbott's long terror suddenly turned into acidity. "I've told nothing," she snapped. "It's all for you—and if it only takes a quarter of an hour you'll be lucky!"

Dinner was a nightmare. They had the smelly dining-room to themselves. Lilia, very smart and vociferous, was at the head of the table; Miss Abbott, also in her best, sat by Philip, looking, to his irritated nerves, more like the tragedy confidante every moment. That scion of the Italian nobility, Signor Carella, sat opposite. Behind him loomed a bowl of goldfish, who swam round and round, gaping at the guests.

The face of Signor Carella was twitching too much for Philip to study it. But he could see the hands, which were not particularly clean, and did not get cleaner by fidgeting amongst the shining slabs of hair. His starched cuffs were not clean either, and as for his suit, it had obviously been bought for the occasion as something really English—a gigantic check, which did not even fit. His handkerchief he had forgotten, but never missed it. Altogether, he was quite unpresentable, and very lucky to have a father who was a dentist in Monteriano. And why, even Lilia—But as soon as the meal began it furnished Philip with an explanation.

For the youth was hungry, and his lady filled his plate with spaghetti, and when those delicious slippery worms were flying down his throat, his face relaxed and became for a moment unconscious and calm. And Philip had seen that face before in Italy a hundred times—seen it and loved it, for it was not merely beautiful, but had the charm which is the rightful heritage of all who are born on that soil. But he did not want to see it opposite him at dinner. It was not the face of a gentleman.

Conversation, to give it that name, was carried on in a mixture of English and Italian. Lilia had picked up hardly any of the latter language, and Signor Carella had not yet learnt any of the former. Occasionally Miss Abbott had to act as interpreter between the lovers, and the situation became uncouth and revolting in the extreme. Yet Philip was too cowardly to break forth and denounce the engagement. He thought he should be more effective with Lilia if he had her alone, and pretended to himself that he must hear her defence before giving judgment.

Signor Carella, heartened by the spaghetti and the throat-rasping wine, attempted to talk, and, looking politely towards Philip, said, "England is a great country. The Italians love England and the English."

Philip, in no mood for international amenities, merely bowed.

"Italy too," the other continued a little resentfully, "is a great country. She has produced many famous men—for example Garibaldi and Dante. The latter wrote the 'Inferno,' the 'Purgatorio,' the 'Paradiso.' The 'Inferno' is the most beautiful." And with the complacent tone of one who has received a solid education, he quoted the opening lines—

Nel mezzo del cammin di nostra vita
Mi ritrovai per una selva oscura
Che la diritta via era smarrita—

a quotation which was more apt than he supposed.

Lilia glanced at Philip to see whether he noticed that she was marrying no ignoramus. Anxious to exhibit all the good qualities of her betrothed, she abruptly introduced the subject of pallone, in which, it appeared, he was a proficient player. He suddenly became shy and developed a conceited grin—the grin of the village yokel whose cricket score is mentioned before a stranger. Philip himself had loved to watch pallone, that entrancing combination of lawn-tennis and fives. But he did not expect to love it quite so much again.

"Oh, look!" exclaimed Lilia, "the poor wee fish!"

A starved cat had been worrying them all for pieces of the purple quivering beef they were trying to swallow. Signor Carella, with the brutality so common in Italians, had caught her by the paw and flung her away from him. Now she had climbed up to the bowl and was trying to hook out the fish. He got up, drove her off, and finding a large glass stopper by the bowl, entirely plugged up the aperture with it.

"But may not the fish die?" said Miss Abbott. "They have no air."

"Fish live on water, not on air," he replied in a knowing voice, and sat down. Apparently he was at his ease again, for he took to spitting on the floor. Philip glanced at Lilia but did not detect her wincing. She talked bravely till the end of the disgusting meal, and then got up saying, "Well, Philip, I am sure you are ready for by-bye. We shall meet at twelve o'clock lunch tomorrow, if we don't meet before. They give us caffe later in our rooms."

It was a little too impudent. Philip replied, "I should like to see you now, please, in my room, as I have come all the way on business." He heard Miss Abbott gasp. Signor Carella, who was lighting a rank cigar, had not understood.

It was as he expected. When he was alone with Lilia he lost all nervousness. The remembrance of his long intellectual supremacy strengthened him, and he began volubly—

"My dear Lilia, don't let's have a scene. Before I arrived I thought I might have to question you. It is unnecessary. I know everything. Miss Abbott has told me a certain amount, and the rest I see for myself."

"See for yourself?" she exclaimed, and he remembered afterwards that she had flushed crimson.

"That he is probably a ruffian and certainly a cad."

"There are no cads in Italy," she said quickly.

He was taken aback. It was one of his own remarks. And she further upset him by adding, "He is the son of a dentist. Why not?"

"Thank you for the information. I know everything, as I told you before. I am also aware of the social position of an Italian who pulls teeth in a minute provincial town."

He was not aware of it, but he ventured to conclude that it was pretty, low. Nor did Lilia contradict him. But she was sharp enough to say, "Indccd, Philip, you surprise me. I understood you went in for equality and so on."

"And I understood that Signor Carella was a member of the Italian nobility."

"Well, we put it like that in the telegram so as not to shock dear Mrs. Herriton. But it is true. He is a younger branch. Of course families ramify—just as in yours there is your cousin Joseph." She adroitly picked out the only undesirable member of the Herriton clan. "Gino's father is courtesy itself, and rising rapidly in his profession. This very month he leaves Monteriano, and sets up at Poggibonsi. And for my own poor part, I think what people are is what matters, but I don't suppose you'll agree. And I should like you to know that Gino's uncle is a priest—the same as a clergyman at home."

Philip was aware of the social position of an Italian priest, and said so much about it that Lilia interrupted him with, "Well, his cousin's a lawyer at Rome."

"What kind of 'lawyer'?"

"Why, a lawyer just like you are—except that he has lots to do and can never get away."

The remark hurt more than he cared to show. He changed his method, and in a gentle, conciliating tone delivered the following speech:—

"The whole thing is like a bad dream—so bad that it cannot go on. If there was one redeeming feature about the man I might be uneasy. As it is I can trust to time. For the moment, Lilia, he has taken you in, but you will find him out soon. It is not possible that you, a lady, accustomed to ladies and gentlemen, will tolerate a man whose position is—well, not equal to the son of the servants' dentist in Coronation Place. I am not blaming you now. But I blame the glamour of Italy—I have felt it myself, you know—and I greatly blame Miss Abbott."

"Caroline! Why blame her? What's all this to do with Caroline?"

"Because we expected her to—" He saw that the answer would involve him in difficulties, and, waving his hand, continued, "So I am confident, and you in your heart agree, that this engagement will not last. Think of your life at home—think of Irma! And I'll also say think of us; for you know, Lilia, that we count you more than a relation. I should feel I was losing my own sister if you did this, and my mother would lose a daughter."

She seemed touched at last, for she turned away her face and said, "I can't break it off now!"

"Poor Lilia," said he, genuinely moved. "I know it may be painful. But I have come to rescue you, and, book-worm though I may be, I am not frightened to stand up to a bully. He's merely an insolent boy. He thinks he can keep you to your word by threats. He will be different when he sees he has a man to deal with."

What follows should be prefaced with some simile—the simile of a powder-mine, a thunderbolt, an earthquake—for it blew Philip up in the air and flattened him on the ground and swallowed him up in the depths. Lilia turned on her gallant defender and said—

"For once in my life I'll thank you to leave me alone. I'll thank your mother too. For twelve years you've trained me and tortured me, and I'll stand it no more. Do you think I'm a fool? Do you think I never felt? Ah! when I came to your house a poor young bride, how you all looked me over—never a kind word—and discussed me, and thought I might just do; and your mother corrected me, and your sister snubbed me, and you said funny things about me to show how clever you were! And when Charles died I was still to run in strings for the honour of your beastly family, and I was to be cooped up at Sawston and learn to keep house, and all my chances spoilt of marrying again. No, thank you! No, thank you! 'Bully?' 'Insolent boy?' Who's that, pray, but you? But, thank goodness, I can stand up against the world now, for I've found Gino, and this time I marry for love!"

The coarseness and truth of her attack alike overwhelmed him. But her supreme insolence found him words, and he too burst forth.

"Yes! and I forbid you to do it! You despise me, perhaps, and think I'm feeble. But you're mistaken. You are ungrateful and impertinent and contemptible, but I will save you in order to save Irma and our name. There is going to be such a row in this town that you and he'll be sorry you came to it. I shall shrink from nothing, for my blood is up. It is unwise of you to laugh. I forbid you to marry Carella, and I shall tell him so now."

"Do," she cried. "Tell him so now. Have it out with him. Gino! Gino! Come in! Avanti! Fra Filippo forbids the banns!"

Gino appeared so quickly that he must have been listening outside the door.

"Fra Filippo's blood's up. He shrinks from nothing. Oh, take care he doesn't hurt you!" She swayed about in vulgar imitation of Philip's walk, and then, with a proud glance at the square shoulders of her betrothed, flounced out of the room.

Did she intend them to fight? Philip had no intention of doing so; and no more, it seemed, had Gino, who stood nervously in the middle of the room with twitching lips and eyes.

"Please sit down, Signor Carella," said Philip in Italian. "Mrs. Herriton is rather agitated, but there is no reason we should not be calm. Might I offer you a cigarette? Please sit down."

He refused the cigarette and the chair, and remained standing in the full glare of the lamp. Philip, not averse to such assistance, got his own face into shadow.

For a long time he was silent. It might impress Gino, and it also gave him time to collect himself. He would not this time fall into the error of blustering, which he had caught so unaccountably from Lilia. He would make his power felt by restraint.

Why, when he looked up to begin, was Gino convulsed with silent laughter? It vanished immediately; but he became nervous, and was even more pompous than he intended.

"Signor Carella, I will be frank with you. I have come to prevent you marrying Mrs. Herriton, because I see you will both be unhappy together. She is English, you are Italian; she is accustomed to one thing, you to another. And—pardon me if I say it—she is rich and you are poor."

"I am not marrying her because she is rich," was the sulky reply.

"I never suggested that for a moment," said Philip courteously. "You are honourable, I am sure; but are you wise? And let me remind you that we want her with us at home. Her little daughter will be motherless, our home will be broken up. If you grant my request you will earn our thanks—and you will not be without a reward for your disappointment."

"Reward—what reward?" He bent over the back of a chair and looked earnestly at Philip. They were coming to terms pretty quickly. Poor Lilia!

Philip said slowly, "What about a thousand lire?"

His soul went forth into one exclamation, and then he was silent, with gaping lips. Philip would have given double: he had expected a bargain.

"You can have them tonight."

He found words, and said, "It is too late."

"But why?"

"Because—" His voice broke. Philip watched his face,—a face without refinement perhaps, but not without expression,—watched it quiver and re-form and dissolve from emotion into emotion. There was avarice at one moment, and insolence, and politeness, and stupidity, and cunning—and let us hope that sometimes there was love. But gradually one emotion dominated, the most unexpected of all; for his chest began to heave and his eyes to wink and his mouth to twitch, and suddenly he stood erect and roared forth his whole being in one tremendous laugh.

Philip sprang up, and Gino, who had flung wide his arms to let the glorious creature go, took him by the shoulders and shook him, and said, "Because we are married—married—married as soon as I knew you were, coming. There was no time to tell you. Oh. oh! You have come all the way for nothing. Oh! And oh, your generosity!" Suddenly he became grave, and said, "Please pardon me; I am rude. I am no better than a peasant, and I—" Here he saw Philip's face, and it was too much for him. He gasped and exploded and crammed his hands into his mouth and spat them out in another explosion, and gave Philip an aimless push, which toppled him on to the bed. He uttered a horrified Oh! and then gave up, and bolted away down the passage, shrieking like a child, to tell the joke to his wife.

For a time Philip lay on the bed, pretending to himself that he was hurt grievously. He could scarcely see for temper, and in the passage he ran against Miss Abbott, who promptly burst into tears.

"I sleep at the Globo," he told her, "and start for Sawston tomorrow morning early. He has assaulted me. I could prosecute him. But shall not."

Chapter 2

"I can't stop here," she sobbed. "I daren't stop here. You will have to take me with you!"

Chapter 3

Opposite the Volterra gate of Monteriano, outside the city, is a very respectable white-washed mud wall, with a coping of red crinkled tiles to keep it from dissolution. It would suggest a gentleman's garden if there was not in its middle a large hole, which grows larger with every rain-storm. Through the hole is visible, firstly, the iron gate that is intended to close it; secondly, a square piece of ground which, though not quite, mud, is at the same time not exactly grass; and finally, another wall, stone this time, which has a wooden door in the middle and two wooden-shuttered windows each side, and apparently forms the facade of a one-storey house.

This house is bigger than it looks, for it slides for two storeys down the hill behind, and the wooden door, which is always locked, really leads into the attic. The knowing person prefers to follow the precipitous mule-track round the turn of the mud wall till he can take the edifice in the rear. Then—being now on a level with the cellars—he lifts up his head and shouts. If his voice sounds like something light—a letter, for example, or some vegetables, or a bunch of flowers—a basket is let out of the first-floor windows by a string, into which he puts his burdens and departs. But if he sounds like something heavy, such as a log of wood, or a piece of meat, or a visitor, he is interrogated, and then bidden or forbidden to ascend. The ground floor and the upper floor of that battered house are alike deserted, and the inmates keep the central portion, just as in a dying body all life retires to the heart. There is a door at the top of the first flight of stairs, and if the visitor is admitted he will find a welcome which is not necessarily cold. There are several rooms, some dark and mostly stuffy—a reception-room adorned with horsehair chairs, wool-work stools, and a stove that is never lit—German bad taste without German domesticity broods over that room; also a living-room, which insensibly glides into a bedroom when the refining influence of hospitality is absent, and real bedrooms; and last, but not least, the loggia, where you can live day and night if you feel inclined, drinking vermouth and smoking cigarettes, with leagues of olive-trees and vineyards and blue-green hills to watch you.

It was in this house that the brief and inevitable tragedy of Lilia's married life took place. She made Gino buy it for her, because it was there she had first seen him sitting on the mud wall that faced the Volterra gate. She remembered how the evening sun had struck his hair, and how he had smiled down at her, and being both sentimental and unrefined, was determined to have the man and the place together. Things in Italy are cheap for an Italian, and, though he would have preferred a house in the piazza, or better still a house at Siena, or, bliss above bliss, a house at Leghorn, he did as she asked, thinking that perhaps she showed her good taste in preferring so retired an abode.

The house was far too big for them, and there was a general concourse of his relatives to fill it up. His father wished to make it a patriarchal concern, where all the family should have their rooms and meet together for meals, and was perfectly willing to give up the new practice at Poggibonsi and preside. Gino was quite willing too, for he was an affectionate youth who liked a large home-circle, and he told it as a pleasant bit of news to Lilia, who did not attempt to conceal her horror.

At once he was horrified too; saw that the idea was monstrous; abused himself to her for having suggested it; rushed off to tell his father that it was impossible. His father complained that prosperity was already corrupting him and making him unsympathetic and hard; his mother cried; his sisters accused him of blocking their social advance. He was apologetic, and even cringing, until they turned on Lilia. Then he turned on them, saying that they could not understand, much less associate with, the English lady who was his wife; that there should be one master in that house—himself.

Lilia praised and petted him on his return, calling him brave and a hero and other endearing epithets. But he was rather blue when his clan left Monteriano in much dignity—a dignity which was not at all impaired by the acceptance of a cheque. They took the cheque not to Poggibonsi, after all, but to Empoli—a lively, dusty town some twenty miles off. There they settled down in comfort, and the sisters said they had been driven to it by Gino.

The cheque was, of course, Lilia's, who was extremely generous, and was quite willing to know anybody so long as she had not to live with them, relations-in-law being on her nerves. She liked nothing better than finding out some obscure and distant connection—there were several of them—and acting the lady bountiful, leaving behind her bewilderment, and too often discontent. Gino wondered how it was that all his people, who had formerly seemed so pleasant, had suddenly become plaintive and disagreeable. He put it down to his lady wife's magnificence, in comparison with which all seemed common. Her money flew apace, in spite of the cheap living. She was even richer than he expected; and he remembered with shame how he had once regretted his inability to accept the thousand lire that Philip Herriton offered him in exchange for her. It would have been a shortsighted bargain.

Lilia enjoyed settling into the house, with nothing to do except give orders to smiling workpeople, and a devoted husband as interpreter. She wrote a jaunty account of her happiness to Mrs. Herriton, and Harriet answered the letter, saying (1) that all future communications should be addressed to the solicitors; (2) would Lilia return an inlaid box which Harriet had lent her—but not given—to keep handkerchiefs and collars in?

"Look what I am giving up to live with you!" she said to Gino, never omitting to lay stress on her condescension. He took her to mean the inlaid box, and said that she need not give it up at all.

"Silly fellow, no! I mean the life. Those Herritons are very well connected. They lead Sawston society. But what do I care, so long as I have my silly fellow!" She always treated him as a boy, which he was, and as a fool, which he was not, thinking herself so immeasurably superior to him that she neglected opportunity after opportunity of establishing her rule. He was good-looking and indolent; therefore he must be stupid. He was poor; therefore he would never dare to criticize his benefactress. He was passionately in love with her; therefore she could do exactly as she liked.

"It mayn't be heaven below," she thought, "but it's better than Charles."

And all the time the boy was watching her, and growing up.

She was reminded of Charles by a disagreeable letter from the solicitors, bidding her disgorge a large sum of money for Irma, in accordance with her late husband's will. It was just like Charles's suspicious nature to have provided against a second marriage. Gino was equally indignant, and between them they composed a stinging reply, which had no effect. He then said that Irma had better come out and live with them. "The air is good, so is the food; she will be happy here, and we shall not have to part with the money." But Lilia had not the courage even to suggest this to the Herritons, and an unexpected terror seized her at the thought of Irma or any English child being educated at Monteriano.

Gino became terribly depressed over the solicitors' letter, more depressed than she thought necessary. There was no more to do in the house, and he spent whole days in the loggia leaning over the parapet or sitting astride it disconsolately.

"Oh, you idle boy!" she cried, pinching his muscles. "Go and play pallone."

"I am a married man," he answered, without raising his head. "I do not play games any more."

"Go and see your friends then."

"I have no friends now."

"Silly, silly, silly! You can't stop indoors all day!"

"I want to see no one but you." He spat on to an olive-tree.

"Now, Gino, don't be silly. Go and see your friends, and bring them to see me. We both of us like society."

He looked puzzled, but allowed himself to be persuaded, went out, found that he was not as friendless as he supposed, and returned after several hours in altered spirits. Lilia congratulated herself on her good management.

"I'm ready, too, for people now," she said. "I mean to wake you all up, just as I woke up Sawston. Let's have plenty of men—and make them bring their womenkind. I mean to have real English tea-parties."

"There is my aunt and her husband; but I thought you did not want to receive my relatives."

"I never said such a—"

"But you would be right," he said earnestly. "They are not for you. Many of them are in trade, and even we are little more; you should have gentlefolk and nobility for your friends."

"Poor fellow," thought Lilia. "It is sad for him to discover that his people are vulgar." She began to tell him that she loved him just for his silly self, and he flushed and began tugging at his moustache.

"But besides your relatives I must have other people here. Your friends have wives and sisters, haven't they?"

"Oh, yes; but of course I scarcely know them."

"Not know your friends' people?"

"Why, no. If they are poor and have to work for their living I may see them—but not otherwise. Except—" He stopped. The chief exception was a young lady, to whom he had once been introduced for matrimonial purposes. But the dowry had proved inadequate, and the acquaintance terminated.

"How funny! But I mean to change all that. Bring your friends to see me, and I will make them bring their people."

He looked at her rather hopelessly.

"Well, who are the principal people here? Who leads society?"

The governor of the prison, he supposed, and the officers who assisted him.

"Well, are they married?"

"Yes."

"There we are. Do you know them?"

"Yes—in a way."

"I see," she exclaimed angrily. "They look down on you, do they, poor boy? Wait!" He assented. "Wait! I'll soon stop that. Now, who else is there?"

"The marchese, sometimes, and the canons of the Collegiate Church."

"Married?"

"The canons—" he began with twinkling eyes.

"Oh, I forgot your horrid celibacy. In England they would be the centre of everything. But why shouldn't I know them? Would it make it easier if I called all round? Isn't that your foreign way?"

He did not think it would make it easier.

"But I must know some one! Who were the men you were talking to this afternoon?"

Low-class men. He could scarcely recollect their names.

"But, Gino dear, if they're low class, why did you talk to them? Don't you care about your position?"

All Gino cared about at present was idleness and pocket-money, and his way of expressing it was to exclaim, "Ouf-pouf! How hot it is in here. No air; I sweat all over. I expire. I must cool myself, or I shall never get to sleep." In his funny abrupt way he ran out on to the loggia, where he lay full length on the parapet, and began to smoke and spit under the silence of the stars.

Lilia gathered somehow from this conversation that Continental society was not the go-as-you-please thing she had expected. Indeed she could not see where

Continental society was. Italy is such a delightful place to live in if you happen to be a man. There one may enjoy that exquisite luxury of Socialism—that true Socialism which is based not on equality of income or character, but on the equality of manners. In the democracy of the caffe or the street the great question of our life has been solved, and the brotherhood of man is a reality. But is accomplished at the expense of the sisterhood of women. Why should you not make friends with your neighbour at the theatre or in the train, when you know and he knows that feminine criticism and feminine insight and feminine prejudice will never come between you? Though you become as David and Jonathan, you need never enter his home, nor he yours. All your lives you will meet under the open air, the only roof-tree of the South, under which he will spit and swear, and you will drop your h's, and nobody will think the worse of either.

Meanwhile the women—they have, of course, their house and their church, with its admirable and frequent services, to which they are escorted by the maid. Otherwise they do not go out much, for it is not genteel to walk, and you are too poor to keep a carriage. Occasionally you will take them to the caffe or theatre, and immediately all your wonted acquaintance there desert you, except those few who are expecting and expected to marry into your family. It is all very sad. But one consolation emerges—life is very pleasant in Italy if you are a man.

Hitherto Gino had not interfered with Lilia. She was so much older than he was, and so much richer, that he regarded her as a superior being who answered to other laws. He was not wholly surprised, for strange rumours were always blowing over the Alps of lands where men and women had the same amusements and interests, and he had often met that privileged maniac, the lady tourist, on her solitary walks. Lilia took solitary walks too, and only that week a tramp had grabbed at her watch—an episode which is supposed to be indigenous in Italy, though really less frequent there than in Bond Street. Now that he knew her better, he was inevitably losing his awe: no one could live with her and keep it, especially when she had been so silly as to lose a gold watch and chain. As he lay thoughtful along the parapet, he realized for the first time the responsibilities of monied life. He must save her from dangers, physical and social, for after all she was a woman. "And I," he reflected, "though I am young, am at all events a man, and know what is right."

He found her still in the living-room, combing her hair, for she had something of the slattern in her nature, and there was no need to keep up appearances.

"You must not go out alone," he said gently. "It is not safe. If you want to walk, Perfetta shall accompany you." Perfetta was a widowed cousin, too humble for social aspirations, who was living with them as factotum.

"Very well," smiled Lilia, "very well"—as if she were addressing a solicitous kitten. But for all that she never took a solitary walk again, with one exception, till the day of her death.

Days passed, and no one called except poor relatives. She began to feel dull. Didn't he know the Sindaco or the bank manager? Even the landlady of the Stella d'Italia would be better than no one. She, when she went into the town, was pleasantly received; but people naturally found a difficulty in getting on with a lady who could not learn their language. And the tea-party, under Gino's adroit management, receded ever and ever before her.

He had a good deal of anxiety over her welfare, for she did not settle down in the house at all. But he was comforted by a welcome and unexpected visitor. As he was going one afternoon for the letters—they were delivered at the door, but it took longer to get them at the office—some one humorously threw a cloak over his head, and when he disengaged himself he saw his very dear friend Spiridione Tesi of the custom-house at Chiasso, whom he had not met for two years. What joy! what salutations! so that all the passersby smiled with approval on the amiable scene. Spiridione's brother was now station-master at Bologna, and thus he himself could spend his holiday travelling over Italy at the public expense. Hearing of Gino's marriage, he had come to see him on his way to Siena, where lived his own uncle, lately monied too.

"They all do it," he exclaimed, "myself excepted." He was not quite twenty-three. "But tell me more. She is English. That is good, very good. An English wife is very good indeed. And she is rich?"

"Immensely rich."

"Blonde or dark?"

"Blonde."

"Is it possible!"

"It pleases me very much," said Gino simply. "If you remember, I always desired a blonde." Three or four men had collected, and were listening.

"We all desire one," said Spiridione. "But you, Gino, deserve your good fortune, for you are a good son, a brave man, and a true friend, and from the very first moment I saw you I wished you well."

"No compliments, I beg," said Gino, standing with his hands crossed on his chest and a smile of pleasure on his face.

Spiridione addressed the other men, none of whom he had ever seen before. "Is it not true? Does not he deserve this wealthy blonde?"

"He does deserve her," said all the men.

It is a marvellous land, where you love it or hate it.

There were no letters, and of course they sat down at the Caffe Garibaldi, by the Collegiate Church—quite a good caffe that for so small a city. There were marble-topped tables, and pillars terra-cotta below and gold above, and on the ceiling was a fresco of the battle of Solferino. One could not have desired a prettier room. They had vermouth and little cakes with sugar on the top, which they chose gravely at the counter, pinching them first to be sure they were fresh. And though vermouth is barely alcoholic, Spiridione drenched his with soda-water to be sure that it should not get into his head.

They were in high spirits, and elaborate compliments alternated curiously with gentle horseplay. But soon they put up their legs on a pair of chairs and began to smoke.

"Tell me," said Spiridione—"I forgot to ask—is she young?"

"Thirty-three."

"Ah, well, we cannot have everything."

"But you would be surprised. Had she told me twenty-eight, I should not have disbelieved her."

"Is she SIMPATICA?" (Nothing will translate that word.)

Gino dabbed at the sugar and said after a silence, "Sufficiently so."

"It is a most important thing."

"She is rich, she is generous, she is affable, she addresses her inferiors without haughtiness."

There was another silence. "It is not sufficient," said the other. "One does not define it thus." He lowered his voice to a whisper. "Last month a German was smuggling cigars. The custom-house was dark. Yet I refused because I did not like him. The gifts of such men do not bring happiness. NON ERA SIMPATICO. He paid for every one, and the fine for deception besides."

"Do you gain much beyond your pay?" asked Gino, diverted for an instant.

"I do not accept small sums now. It is not worth the risk. But the German was another matter. But listen, my Gino, for I am older than you and more full of experience. The person who understands us at first sight, who never irritates us, who never bores, to whom we can pour forth every thought and wish, not only in speech but in silence—that is what I mean by SIMPATICO."

"There are such men, I know," said Gino. "And I have heard it said of children. But where will you find such a woman?"

"That is true. Here you are wiser than I. SONO POCO SIMPATICHE LE DONNE. And the time we waste over them is much." He sighed dolefully, as if he found the nobility of his sex a burden.

"One I have seen who may be so. She spoke very little, but she was a young lady—different to most. She, too, was English, the companion of my wife here. But Fra Filippo, the brother-in-law, took her back with him. I saw them start. He was very angry."

Then he spoke of his exciting and secret marriage, and they made fun of the unfortunate Philip, who had travelled over Europe to stop it.

"I regret though," said Gino, when they had finished laughing, "that I toppled him on to the bed. A great tall man! And when I am really amused I am often impolite."

"You will never see him again," said Spiridione, who carried plenty of philosophy about him. "And by now the scene will have passed from his mind."

"It sometimes happens that such things are recollected longest. I shall never see him again, of course; but it is no benefit to me that he should wish me ill. And even if he has forgotten, I am still sorry that I toppled him on to the bed."

So their talk continued, at one moment full of childishness and tender wisdom, the next moment scandalously gross. The shadows of the terra-cotta pillars lengthened, and tourists, flying through the Palazzo Pubblico opposite, could observe how the Italians wasted time.

The sight of tourists reminded Gino of something he might say. "I want to consult you since you are so kind as to take an interest in my affairs. My wife wishes to take solitary walks."

Spiridione was shocked.

"But I have forbidden her."

"Naturally."

"She does not yet understand. She asked me to accompany her sometimes—to walk without object! You know, she would like me to be with her all day."

"I see. I see." He knitted his brows and tried to think how he could help his friend. "She needs employment. Is she a Catholic?"

"No."

"That is a pity. She must be persuaded. It will be a great solace to her when she is alone."

"I am a Catholic, but of course I never go to church."

"Of course not. Still, you might take her at first. That is what my brother has done with his wife at Bologna and he has joined the Free Thinkers. He took her once or twice himself, and now she has acquired the habit and continues to go without him."

"Most excellent advice, and I thank you for it. But she wishes to give tea-parties—men and women together whom she has never seen."

"Oh, the English! they are always thinking of tea. They carry it by the kilogramme in their trunks, and they are so clumsy that they always pack it at the top. But it is absurd!"

"What am I to do about it?"

"Do nothing. Or ask me!"

"Come!" cried Gino, springing up. "She will be quite pleased."

The dashing young fellow coloured crimson. "Of course I was only joking."

"I know. But she wants me to take my friends. Come now! Waiter!"

"If I do come," cried the other, "and take tea with you, this bill must be my affair."

"Certainly not; you are in my country!"

A long argument ensued, in which the waiter took part, suggesting various solutions. At last Gino triumphed. The bill came to eightpence-halfpenny, and a halfpenny for the waiter brought it up to ninepence. Then there was a shower of gratitude on one side and of deprecation on the other, and when courtesies were at their height they suddenly linked arms and swung down the street, tickling each other with lemonade straws as they went.

Lilia was delighted to see them, and became more animated than Gino had known her for a long time. The tea tasted of chopped hay, and they asked to be allowed to drink it out of a wine-glass, and refused milk; but, as she repeatedly observed, this was something like. Spiridione's manners were very agreeable. He kissed her hand on introduction, and as his profession had taught him a little English, conversation did not flag.

"Do you like music?" she asked.

"Passionately," he replied. "I have not studied scientific music, but the music of the heart, yes."

So she played on the humming piano very badly, and he sang, not so badly. Gino got out a guitar and sang too, sitting out on the loggia. It was a most agreeable visit.

Gino said he would just walk his friend back to his lodgings. As they went he said, without the least trace of malice or satire in his voice, "I think you are quite right. I shall not bring people to the house any more. I do not see why an English wife should be treated differently. This is Italy."

"You are very wise," exclaimed the other; "very wise indeed. The more precious a possession the more carefully it should be guarded."

They had reached the lodging, but went on as far as the Caffe Garibaldi, where they spent a long and most delightful evening.

Chapter 4

The advance of regret can be so gradual that it is impossible to say "yesterday I was happy, today I am not." At no one moment did Lilia realize that her marriage was a failure; yet during the summer and autumn she became as unhappy as it was possible for her nature to be. She had no unkind treatment, and few unkind words, from her husband. He simply left her alone. In the morning he went out to do "business," which, as far as she could discover, meant sitting in the Farmacia. He usually returned to lunch, after which he retired to another room and slept. In the evening he grew vigorous again, and took the air on the ramparts, often having his dinner out, and seldom returning till midnight or later. There were, of course, the times when he was away altogether—at Empoli, Siena, Florence, Bologna—for he delighted in travel, and seemed to pick up friends all over the country. Lilia often heard what a favorite he was.

She began to see that she must assert herself, but she could not see how. Her self-confidence, which had overthrown Philip, had gradually oozed away. If she left the strange house there was the strange little town. If she were to disobey her husband and walk in the country, that would be stranger still—vast slopes of olives and vineyards, with chalk-white farms, and in the distance other slopes, with more olives and more farms, and more little towns outlined against the cloudless sky. "I don't call this country," she would say. "Why, it's not as wild as Sawston Park!" And, indeed, there was scarcely a touch of wildness in it—some of those slopes had been under cultivation for two thousand years. But it was terrible and mysterious all the same, and its continued presence made Lilia so uncomfortable that she forgot her nature and began to reflect.

She reflected chiefly about her marriage. The ceremony had been hasty and expensive, and the rites, whatever they were, were not those of the Church of England. Lilia had no religion in her; but for hours at a time she would be seized with a vulgar fear that she was not "married properly," and that her social position in the next world might be as obscure as it was in this. It might be safer to do the thing thoroughly, and one day she took the advice of Spiridione and joined the Roman Catholic Church, or as she called it, "Santa Deodata's." Gino approved; he, too, thought it safer, and it was fun confessing, though the priest was a stupid old man, and the whole thing was a good slap in the face for the people at home.

The people at home took the slap very soberly; indeed, there were few left for her to give it to. The Herritons were out of the question; they would not even let her write to Irma, though Irma was occasionally allowed to write to her. Mrs. Theobald was rapidly subsiding into dotage, and, as far as she could be definite about anything, had definitely sided with the Herritons. And Miss Abbott did likewise. Night after night did Lilia curse this false friend, who had agreed with her that the marriage would "do," and that the Herritons would come round to it, and then, at the first hint of opposition, had fled back to England shrieking and distraught. Miss Abbott headed the long list of those who should never be written to, and who should never be forgiven. Almost the only person who was not on that list was Mr. Kingcroft, who had unexpectedly sent an affectionate and inquiring letter. He was quite sure never to cross the Channel, and Lilia drew freely on her fancy in the reply.

At first she had seen a few English people, for Monteriano was not the end of the earth. One or two inquisitive ladies, who had heard at home of her quarrel with the Herritons, came to call. She was very sprightly, and they thought her quite unconventional, and Gino a charming boy, so all that was to the good. But by May the season, such as it was, had finished, and there would be no one till next spring. As Mrs. Herriton had often observed, Lilia had no resources. She did not like music, or reading, or work. Her one qualification for life was rather blowsy high spirits, which turned querulous or boisterous according to circumstances. She was not obedient, but she was cowardly, and in the most gentle way, which Mrs. Herriton might have envied, Gino made her do what he wanted. At first it had been rather fun to let him get the upper hand. But it was galling to discover that he could not do otherwise. He had a good strong will when he chose to use it, and would not have had the least scruple in using bolts and locks to put it into effect. There was plenty of brutality deep down in him, and one day Lilia nearly touched it.

It was the old question of going out alone.

"I always do it in England."

"This is Italy."

"Yes, but I'm older than you, and I'll settle."

"I am your husband," he said, smiling. They had finished their mid-day meal, and he wanted to go and sleep. Nothing would rouse him up, until at last Lilia, getting more and more angry, said, "And I've got the money."

He looked horrified.

Now was the moment to assert herself. She made the statement again. He got up from his chair.

"And you'd better mend your manners," she continued, "for you'd find it awkward if I stopped drawing cheques."

She was no reader of character, but she quickly became alarmed. As she said to Perfetta afterwards, "None of his clothes seemed to fit—too big in one place, too small in another." His figure rather than his face altered, the shoulders falling forward till his coat wrinkled across the back and pulled away from his wrists. He seemed all arms. He edged round the table to where she was sitting, and she sprang away and held the chair between them, too frightened to speak or to move. He looked at her with round, expressionless eyes, and slowly stretched out his left hand.

Perfetta was heard coming up from the kitchen. It seemed to wake him up, and he turned away and went to his room without a word.

"What has happened?" cried Lilia, nearly fainting. "He is ill—ill."

Perfetta looked suspicious when she heard the account. "What did you say to him?" She crossed herself.

"Hardly anything," said Lilia and crossed herself also. Thus did the two women pay homage to their outraged male.

It was clear to Lilia at last that Gino had married her for money. But he had frightened her too much to leave any place for contempt. His return was terrifying, for he was frightened too, imploring her pardon, lying at her feet, embracing her, murmuring "It was not I," striving to define things which he did not understand. He stopped in the house for three days, positively ill with physical collapse. But for all his suffering he had tamed her, and she never threatened to cut off supplies again.

Perhaps he kept her even closer than convention demanded. But he was very young, and he could not bear it to be said of him that he did not know how to treat a lady—or to manage a wife. And his own social position was uncertain. Even in England a dentist is a troublesome creature, whom careful people find difficult to class. He hovers between the professions and the trades; he may be only a little lower than the doctors, or he may be down among the chemists, or even beneath them. The son of the Italian dentist felt this too. For himself nothing mattered; he made friends with the people he liked, for he was that glorious invariable creature, a man. But his wife should visit nowhere rather than visit wrongly: seclusion was both decent and safe. The social ideals of North and South had had their brief contention, and this time the South had won.

It would have been well if he had been as strict over his own behaviour as he was over hers. But the incongruity never occurred to him for a moment. His morality was that of the average Latin, and as he was suddenly placed in the position of a gentleman, he did not see why he should not behave as such. Of course, had Lilia been different—had she asserted herself and got a grip on his character—he might possibly—though not probably—have been made a better husband as well as a better man, and at all events he could have adopted the attitude of the Englishman, whose standard is higher even when his practice is the same. But had Lilia been different she might not have married him.

The discovery of his infidelity—which she made by accident—destroyed such remnants of self-satisfaction as her life might yet possess. She broke down utterly and sobbed and cried in Perfetta's arms. Perfetta was kind and even sympathetic, but cautioned her on no account to speak to Gino, who would be furious if he was suspected. And Lilia agreed, partly because she was afraid of him, partly because it was, after all, the best and most dignified thing to do. She had given up everything for him—her daughter, her relatives, her friends, all the little comforts and luxuries of a civilized life—and even if she had the courage to break away, there was no one who would receive her now. The Herritons had been almost malignant in their efforts against her, and all her friends had one by one fallen off. So it was better to live on humbly, trying not to feel, endeavouring by a cheerful demeanour to put things right. "Perhaps," she thought, "if I have a child he will be different. I know he wants a son."

Lilia had achieved pathos despite herself, for there are some situations in which vulgarity counts no longer. Not Cordelia nor Imogen more deserves our tears.

She herself cried frequently, making herself look plain and old, which distressed her husband. He was particularly kind to her when he hardly ever saw her, and she accepted his kindness without resentment, even with gratitude, so docile had she become. She did not hate him, even as she had never loved him; with her it was only when she was excited that the semblance of either passion arose. People said she was headstrong, but really her weak brain left her cold.

Suffering, however, is more independent of temperament, and the wisest of women could hardly have suffered more.

As for Gino, he was quite as boyish as ever, and carried his iniquities like a feather. A favourite speech of his was, "Ah, one ought to marry! Spiridione is wrong; I must persuade him. Not till marriage does one realize the pleasures and the possibilities of life." So saying, he would take down his felt hat, strike it in the right place as infallibly as a German strikes his in the wrong place, and leave her.

One evening, when he had gone out thus, Lilia could stand it no longer. It was September. Sawston would be just filling up after the summer holidays. People would be running in and out of each other's houses all along the road. There were bicycle gymkhanas, and on the 30th Mrs. Herriton would be holding the annual bazaar in her garden for the C.M.S. It seemed impossible that such a free, happy life could exist. She walked out on to the loggia. Moonlight and stars in a soft purple sky. The walls of Monteriano should be glorious on such a night as this. But the house faced away from them.

Perfetta was banging in the kitchen, and the stairs down led past the kitchen door. But the stairs up to the attic—the stairs no one ever used—opened out of the living-room, and by unlocking the door at the top one might slip out to the square terrace above the house, and thus for ten minutes walk in freedom and peace.

The key was in the pocket of Gino's best suit—the English check—which he never wore. The stairs creaked and the key-hole screamed; but Perfetta was growing deaf. The walls were beautiful, but as they faced west they were in shadow. To see the light upon them she must walk round the town a little, till they were caught by the beams of the rising moon. She looked anxiously at the house, and started.

It was easy walking, for a little path ran all outside the ramparts. The few people she met wished her a civil good-night, taking her, in her hatless condition, for a peasant. The walls trended round towards the moon; and presently she came into its light, and saw all the rough towers turn into pillars of silver and black, and the ramparts into cliffs of pearl. She had no great sense of beauty, but she was sentimental, and she began to cry; for here, where a great cypress interrupted the monotony of the girdle of olives, she had sat with Gino one afternoon in March, her head upon his shoulder, while Caroline was looking at the view and sketching. Round the corner was the Siena gate, from which the road to England started, and she could hear the rumble of the diligence which was going down to catch the night train to Empoli. The next moment it was upon her, for the highroad came towards her a little before it began its long zigzag down the hill.

The driver slackened, and called to her to get in. He did not know who she was. He hoped she might be coming to the station.

"Non vengo!" she cried.

He wished her good-night, and turned his horses down the corner. As the diligence came round she saw that it was empty.

"Vengo..."

Her voice was tremulous, and did not carry. The horses swung off.

"Vengo! Vengo!"

He had begun to sing, and heard nothing. She ran down the road screaming to him to stop—that she was coming; while the distance grew greater and the noise of the diligence increased. The man's back was black and square against the moon, and if he would but turn for an instant she would be saved. She tried to cut off the corner of the zigzag, stumbling over the great clods of earth, large and hard as rocks, which lay between the eternal olives. She was too late; for, just before she regained the road, the thing swept past her, thunderous, ploughing up choking clouds of moonlit dust.

She did not call any more, for she felt very ill, and fainted; and when she revived she was lying in the road, with dust in her eyes, and dust in her mouth, and dust down her ears. There is something very terrible in dust at night-time.

"What shall I do?" she moaned. "He will be so angry."

And without further effort she slowly climbed back to captivity, shaking her garments as she went.

Ill luck pursued her to the end. It was one of the nights when Gino happened to come in. He was in the kitchen, swearing and smashing plates, while Perfetta, her apron over her head, was weeping violently. At the sight of Lilia he turned upon her and poured forth a flood of miscellaneous abuse. He was far more angry but much less alarming than he had been that day when he edged after her round the table. And Lilia gained more courage from her bad conscience than she ever had from her good one, for as he spoke she was seized with indignation and feared him no longer, and saw him for a cruel, worthless, hypocritical, dissolute upstart, and spoke in return.

Perfetta screamed for she told him everything—all she knew and all she thought. He stood with open mouth, all the anger gone out of him, feeling ashamed, and an utter fool. He was fairly and rightfully cornered. When had a husband so given himself away before? She finished; and he was dumb, for she had spoken truly. Then, alas! the absurdity of his own position grew upon him, and he laughed—as he would have laughed at the same situation on the stage.

"You laugh?" stammered Lilia.

"Ah!" he cried, "who could help it? I, who thought you knew and saw nothing—I am tricked—I am conquered. I give in. Let us talk of it no more."

He touched her on the shoulder like a good comrade, half amused and half penitent, and then, murmuring and smiling to himself, ran quietly out of the room.

Perfetta burst into congratulations. "What courage you have!" she cried; "and what good fortune! He is angry no longer! He has forgiven you!"

Neither Perfetta, nor Gino, nor Lilia herself knew the true reason of all the misery that followed. To the end he thought that kindness and a little attention would be enough to set things straight. His wife was a very ordinary woman, and why should her ideas differ from his own? No one realized that more than personalities were engaged; that the struggle was national; that generations of ancestors, good, bad, or indifferent, forbad the Latin man to be chivalrous to the northern woman, the northern woman to forgive the Latin man. All this might have been foreseen: Mrs. Herriton foresaw it from the first.

Meanwhile Lilia prided herself on her high personal standard, and Gino simply wondered why she did not come round. He hated discomfort and yearned for sympathy, but shrank from mentioning his difficulties in the town in case they were put down to his own incompetence. Spiridione was told, and replied in a philosophical but not very helpful letter. His other great friend, whom he trusted more, was still serving in Eritrea or some other desolate outpost. And, besides, what was the good of letters? Friends cannot travel through the post.

Lilia, so similar to her husband in many ways, yearned for comfort and sympathy too. The night he laughed at her she wildly took up paper and pen and wrote page after page, analysing his character, enumerating his iniquities, reporting whole conversations, tracing all the causes and the growth of her misery. She was beside herself with passion, and though she could hardly think or see, she suddenly attained to magnificence and pathos which a practised stylist might have envied. It was written like a diary, and not till its conclusion did she realize for whom it was meant.

"Irma, darling Irma, this letter is for you. I almost forgot I have a daughter. It will make you unhappy, but I want you to know everything, and you cannot learn things too soon. God bless you, my dearest, and save you. God bless your miserable mother."

Fortunately Mrs. Herriton was in when the letter arrived. She seized it and opened it in her bedroom. Another moment, and Irma's placid childhood would have been destroyed for ever.

Lilia received a brief note from Harriet, again forbidding direct communication between mother and daughter, and concluding with formal condolences. It nearly drove her mad.

"Gently! gently!" said her husband. They were sitting together on the loggia when the letter arrived. He often sat with her now, watching her for hours, puzzled and anxious, but not contrite.

"It's nothing." She went in and tore it up, and then began to write—a very short letter, whose gist was "Come and save me."

It is not good to see your wife crying when she writes—especially if you are conscious that, on the whole, your treatment of her has been reasonable and kind. It is not good, when you accidentally look over her shoulder, to see that she is writing to a man. Nor should she shake her fist at you when she leaves the room, under the impression that you are engaged in lighting a cigar and cannot see her.

Lilia went to the post herself. But in Italy so many things can be arranged. The postman was a friend of Gino's, and Mr. Kingcroft never got his letter.

So she gave up hope, became ill, and all through the autumn lay in bed. Gino was distracted. She knew why; he wanted a son. He could talk and think of nothing else. His one desire was to become the father of a man like himself, and it held him with a grip he only partially understood, for it was the first great desire, the first great passion of his life. Falling in love was a mere physical triviality, like warm sun or cool water, beside this divine hope of immortality: "I continue." He gave candles to Santa Deodata, for he was always religious at a crisis, and sometimes he went to her himself and prayed the crude uncouth demands of the simple. Impetuously he summoned all his relatives back to bear him company in his time of need, and Lilia saw strange faces flitting past her in the darkened room.

"My love!" he would say, "my dearest Lilia! Be calm. I have never loved any one but you."

She, knowing everything, would only smile gently, too broken by suffering to make sarcastic repartees.

Before the child was born he gave her a kiss, and said, "I have prayed all night for a boy."

Some strangely tender impulse moved her, and she said faintly, "You are a boy yourself, Gino."

He answered, "Then we shall be brothers."

He lay outside the room with his head against the door like a dog. When they came to tell him the glad news they found him half unconscious, and his face was wet with tears.

As for Lilia, some one said to her, "It is a beautiful boy!" But she had died in giving birth to him.

Chapter 5

At the time of Lilia's death Philip Herriton was just twenty-four years of age—indeed the news reached Sawston on his birthday. He was a tall, weakly-built young man, whose clothes had to be judiciously padded on the shoulders in order to make him pass muster. His face was plain rather than not, and there was a curious mixture in it of good and bad. He had a fine forehead and a good large nose, and both observation and sympathy were in his eyes. But below the nose and eyes all was confusion, and those people who believe that destiny resides in the mouth and chin shook their heads when they looked at him.

Philip himself, as a boy, had been keenly conscious of these defects. Sometimes when he had been bullied or hustled about at school he would retire to his cubicle and examine his features in a looking-glass, and he would sigh and say, "It is a weak face. I shall never carve a place for myself in the world." But as years went on he became either less self-conscious or more self-satisfied. The world, he found, made a niche for him as it did for every one. Decision of character might come later—or he might have it without knowing. At all events he had got a sense of beauty and a sense of humour, two most desirable gifts. The sense of beauty developed first. It caused him at the age of twenty to wear particoloured ties and a squashy hat, to be late for dinner on account of the sunset, and to catch art from Burne-Jones to Praxiteles. At twenty-two he went to Italy with some cousins, and there he absorbed into one aesthetic whole olive-trees, blue sky, frescoes, country inns, saints, peasants, mosaics, statues, beggars. He came back with the air of a prophet who would either remodel Sawston or reject it. All the energies and enthusiasms of a rather friendless life had passed into the championship of beauty.

In a short time it was over. Nothing had happened either in Sawston or within himself. He had shocked half-a-dozen people, squabbled with his sister, and bickered with his mother. He concluded that nothing could happen, not knowing that human love and love of truth sometimes conquer where love of beauty fails.

A little disenchanted, a little tired, but aesthetically intact, he resumed his placid life, relying more and more on his second gift, the gift of humour. If he could not reform the world, he could at all events laugh at it, thus attaining at least an intellectual superiority. Laughter, he read and believed, was a sign of good moral health, and he laughed on contentedly, till Lilia's marriage toppled contentment down for ever. Italy, the land of beauty, was ruined for him. She had no power to change men and things who dwelt in her. She, too, could produce avarice, brutality, stupidity—and, what was worse, vulgarity. It was on her soil and through her influence that a silly woman had married a cad. He hated Gino, the betrayer of his life's ideal, and now that the sordid tragedy had come, it filled him with pangs, not of sympathy, but of final disillusion.

The disillusion was convenient for Mrs. Herriton, who saw a trying little period ahead of her, and was glad to have her family united.

"Are we to go into mourning, do you think?" She always asked her children's advice where possible.

Harriet thought that they should. She had been detestable to Lilia while she lived, but she always felt that the dead deserve attention and sympathy. "After all she has suffered. That letter kept me awake for nights. The whole thing is like one of those horrible modern plays where no one is in 'the right.' But if we have mourning, it will mean telling Irma."

"Of course we must tell Irma!" said Philip.

"Of course," said his mother. "But I think we can still not tell her about Lilia's marriage."

"I don't think that. And she must have suspected something by now."

"So one would have supposed. But she never cared for her mother, and little girls of nine don't reason clearly. She looks on it as a long visit. And it is important, most important, that she should not receive a shock. All a child's life depends on the ideal it has of its parents. Destroy that and everything goes—morals, behaviour, everything. Absolute trust in some one else is the essence of education. That is why I have been so careful about talking of poor Lilia before her."

"But you forget this wretched baby. Waters and Adamson write that there is a baby."

"Mrs. Theobald must be told. But she doesn't count. She is breaking up very quickly. She doesn't even see Mr. Kingcroft now. He, thank goodness, I hear, has at last consoled himself with someone else."

"The child must know some time," persisted Philip, who felt a little displeased, though he could not tell with what.

"The later the better. Every moment she is developing."

"I must say it seems rather hard luck, doesn't it?"

"On Irma? Why?"

"On us, perhaps. We have morals and behaviour also, and I don't think this continual secrecy improves them."

"There's no need to twist the thing round to that," said Harriet, rather disturbed.

"Of course there isn't," said her mother. "Let's keep to the main issue. This baby's quite beside the point. Mrs. Theobald will do nothing, and it's no concern of ours."

"It will make a difference in the money, surely," said he.

"No, dear; very little. Poor Charles provided for every kind of contingency in his will. The money will come to you and Harriet, as Irma's guardians."

"Good. Does the Italian get anything?"

"He will get all hers. But you know what that is."

"Good. So those are our tactics—to tell no one about the baby, not even Miss Abbott."

"Most certainly this is the proper course," said Mrs. Herriton, preferring "course" to "tactics" for Harriet's sake. "And why ever should we tell Caroline?"

"She was so mixed up in the affair."

"Poor silly creature. The less she hears about it the better she will be pleased. I have come to be very sorry for Caroline. She, if any one, has suffered and been penitent. She burst into tears when I told her a little, only a little, of that terrible letter. I never saw such genuine remorse. We must forgive her and forget. Let the dead bury their dead. We will not trouble her with them."

Philip saw that his mother was scarcely logical. But there was no advantage in saying so. "Here beginneth the New Life, then. Do you remember, mother, that was what we said when we saw Lilia off?"

"Yes, dear; but now it is really a New Life, because we are all at accord. Then you were still infatuated with Italy. It may be full of beautiful pictures and churches, but we cannot judge a country by anything but its men."

"That is quite true," he said sadly. And as the tactics were now settled, he went out and took an aimless and solitary walk.

By the time he came back two important things had happened. Irma had been told of her mother's death, and Miss Abbott, who had called for a subscription, had been told also.

Irma had wept loudly, had asked a few sensible questions and a good many silly ones, and had been content with evasive answers. Fortunately the school prize-giving was at hand, and that, together with the prospect of new black clothes, kept her from meditating on the fact that Lilia, who had been absent so long, would now be absent for ever.

"As for Caroline," said Mrs. Herriton, "I was almost frightened. She broke down utterly. She cried even when she left the house. I comforted her as best I could, and I kissed her. It is something that the breach between her and ourselves is now entirely healed."

"Did she ask no questions—as to the nature of Lilia's death, I mean?"

"She did. But she has a mind of extraordinary delicacy. She saw that I was reticent, and she did not press me. You see, Philip, I can say to you what I could not say before Harriet. Her ideas are so crude. Really we do not want it known in Sawston that there is a baby. All peace and comfort would be lost if people came inquiring after it."

His mother knew how to manage him. He agreed enthusiastically. And a few days later, when he chanced to travel up to London with Miss Abbott, he had all the time the pleasant thrill of one who is better informed. Their last journey together had been from Monteriano back across Europe. It had been a ghastly journey, and Philip, from the force of association, rather expected something ghastly now.

He was surprised. Miss Abbott, between Sawston and Charing Cross, revealed qualities which he had never guessed her to possess. Without being exactly original, she did show a commendable intelligence, and though at times she was gauche and even uncourtly, he felt that here was a person whom it might be well to cultivate.

At first she annoyed him. They were talking, of course, about Lilia, when she broke the thread of vague commiseration and said abruptly, "It is all so strange as well as so tragic. And what I did was as strange as anything."

It was the first reference she had ever made to her contemptible behaviour. "Never mind," he said. "It's all over now. Let the dead bury their dead. It's fallen out of our lives."

"But that's why I can talk about it and tell you everything I have always wanted to. You thought me stupid and sentimental and wicked and mad, but you never really knew how much I was to blame."

"Indeed I never think about it now," said Philip gently. He knew that her nature was in the main generous and upright: it was unnecessary for her to reveal her thoughts.

"The first evening we got to Monteriano," she persisted, "Lilia went out for a walk alone, saw that Italian in a picturesque position on a wall, and fell in love. He was shabbily dressed, and she did not even know he was the son of a dentist. I must tell you I was used to this sort of thing. Once or twice before I had had to send people about their business."

"Yes; we counted on you," said Philip, with sudden sharpness. After all, if she would reveal her thoughts, she must take the consequences.

"I know you did," she retorted with equal sharpness. "Lilia saw him several times again, and I knew I ought to interfere. I called her to my bedroom one night. She was very frightened, for she knew what it was about and how severe I could be. 'Do you love this man?' I asked. 'Yes or no?' She said 'Yes.' And I said, 'Why don't you marry him if you think you'll be happy?'"

"Really—really," exploded Philip, as exasperated as if the thing had happened yesterday. "You knew Lilia all your life. Apart from everything else—as if she could choose what could make her happy!"

"Had you ever let her choose?" she flashed out. "I'm afraid that's rude," she added, trying to calm herself.

"Let us rather say unhappily expressed," said Philip, who always adopted a dry satirical manner when he was puzzled.

"I want to finish. Next morning I found Signor Carella and said the same to him. He—well, he was willing. That's all."

"And the telegram?" He looked scornfully out of the window.

Hitherto her voice had been hard, possibly in self-accusation, possibly in defiance. Now it became unmistakably sad. "Ah, the telegram! That was wrong. Lilia there was more cowardly than I was. We should have told the truth. It lost me my nerve, at all events. I came to the station meaning to tell you everything then. But we had started with a lie, and I got frightened. And at the end, when you left, I got frightened again and came with you."

"Did you really mean to stop?"

"For a time, at all events."

"Would that have suited a newly married pair?"

"It would have suited them. Lilia needed me. And as for him—I can't help feeling I might have got influence over him."

"I am ignorant of these matters," said Philip; "but I should have thought that would have increased the difficulty of the situation."

The crisp remark was wasted on her. She looked hopelessly at the raw over-built country, and said, "Well, I have explained."

"But pardon me, Miss Abbott; of most of your conduct you have given a description rather than an explanation."

He had fairly caught her, and expected that she would gape and collapse. To his surprise she answered with some spirit, "An explanation may bore you, Mr. Herriton: it drags in other topics."

"Oh, never mind."

"I hated Sawston, you see."

He was delighted. "So did and do I. That's splendid. Go on."

"I hated the idleness, the stupidity, the respectability, the petty unselfishness."

"Petty selfishness," he corrected. Sawston psychology had long been his specialty.

"Petty unselfishness," she repeated. "I had got an idea that every one here spent their lives in making little sacrifices for objects they didn't care for, to please people they didn't love; that they never learnt to be sincere—and, what's as bad, never learnt how to enjoy themselves. That's what I thought—what I thought at Monteriano."

"Why, Miss Abbott," he cried, "you should have told me this before! Think it still! I agree with lots of it. Magnificent!"

"Now Lilia," she went on, "though there were things about her I didn't like, had somehow kept the power of enjoying herself with sincerity. And Gino, I thought, was splendid, and young, and strong not only in body, and sincere as the day. If they wanted to marry, why shouldn't they do so? Why shouldn't she break with the deadening life where she had got into a groove, and would go on in it, getting more and more—worse than unhappy—apathetic till she died? Of course I was wrong. She only changed one groove for another—a worse groove. And as for him—well, you know more about him than I do. I can never trust myself to judge characters again. But I still feel he cannot have been quite bad when we first met him. Lilia—that I should dare to say it!—must have been cowardly. He was only a boy—just going to turn into something fine, I thought—and she must have mismanaged him. So that is the one time I have gone against what is proper, and there are the results. You have an explanation now."

"And much of it has been most interesting, though I don't understand everything. Did you never think of the disparity of their social position?"

"We were mad—drunk with rebellion. We had no common-sense. As soon as you came, you saw and foresaw everything."

"Oh, I don't think that." He was vaguely displeased at being credited with common-sense. For a moment Miss Abbott had seemed to him more unconventional than himself.

"I hope you see," she concluded, "why I have troubled you with this long story. Women—I heard you say the other day—are never at ease till they tell their faults out loud. Lilia is dead and her husband gone to the bad—all through me. You see, Mr. Herriton, it makes me specially unhappy; it's the only time I've ever gone into what my father calls 'real life'—and look what I've made of it! All that winter I seemed to be waking up to beauty and splendour and I don't know what; and when the spring came, I wanted to fight against the things I hated—mediocrity and dulness and spitefulness and society. I actually hated society for a day or two at Monteriano. I didn't see that all these things are invincible, and that if we go against them they will break us to pieces. Thank you for listening to so much nonsense."

"Oh, I quite sympathize with what you say," said Philip encouragingly; "it isn't nonsense, and a year or two ago I should have been saying it too. But I feel differently now, and I hope that you also will change. Society is invincible—to a certain degree. But your real life is your own, and nothing can touch it. There is no power on earth that can prevent your criticizing and despising mediocrity—nothing that can stop you retreating into splendour and beauty—into the thoughts and beliefs that make the real life—the real you."

"I have never had that experience yet. Surely I and my life must be where I live."

Evidently she had the usual feminine incapacity for grasping philosophy. But she had developed quite a personality, and he must see more of her. "There is another great consolation against invincible mediocrity," he said—"the meeting a fellow-victim. I hope that this is only the first of many discussions that we shall have together."

She made a suitable reply. The train reached Charing Cross, and they parted,—he to go to a matinee, she to buy petticoats for the corpulent poor. Her thoughts wandered as she bought them: the gulf between herself and Mr. Herriton, which she had always known to be great, now seemed to her immeasurable.

These events and conversations took place at Christmas-time. The New Life initiated by them lasted some seven months. Then a little incident—a mere little vexatious incident—brought it to its close.

Irma collected picture post-cards, and Mrs. Herriton or Harriet always glanced first at all that came, lest the child should get hold of something vulgar. On this occasion the subject seemed perfectly inoffensive—a lot of ruined factory chimneys—and Harriet was about to hand it to her niece when her eye was caught by the words on the margin. She gave a shriek and flung the card into the grate. Of course no fire was alight in July, and Irma only had to run and pick it out again.

"How dare you!" screamed her aunt. "You wicked girl! Give it here!"

Unfortunately Mrs. Herriton was out of the room. Irma, who was not in awe of Harriet, danced round the table, reading as she did so, "View of the superb city of Monteriano—from your lital brother."

Stupid Harriet caught her, boxed her ears, and tore the post-card into fragments. Irma howled with pain, and began shouting indignantly, "Who is my little brother? Why have I never heard of him before? Grandmamma! Grandmamma! Who is my little brother? Who is my—"

Mrs. Herriton swept into the room, saying, "Come with me, dear, and I will tell you. Now it is time for you to know."

Irma returned from the interview sobbing, though, as a matter of fact, she had learnt very little. But that little took hold of her imagination. She had promised secrecy—she knew not why. But what harm in talking of the little brother to those who had heard of him already?

"Aunt Harriet!" she would say. "Uncle Phil! Grandmamma! What do you suppose my little brother is doing now? Has he begun to play? Do Italian babies talk sooner than us, or would he be an English baby born abroad? Oh, I do long to see him, and be the first to teach him the Ten Commandments and the Catechism."

The last remark always made Harriet look grave.

"Really," exclaimed Mrs. Herriton, "Irma is getting too tiresome. She forgot poor Lilia soon enough."

"A living brother is more to her than a dead mother," said Philip dreamily. "She can knit him socks."

"I stopped that. She is bringing him in everywhere. It is most vexatious. The other night she asked if she might include him in the people she mentions specially in her prayers."

"What did you say?"

"Of course I allowed her," she replied coldly. "She has a right to mention any one she chooses. But I was annoyed with her this morning, and I fear that I showed it."

"And what happened this morning?"

"She asked if she could pray for her 'new father'—for the Italian!"

"Did you let her?"

"I got up without saying anything."

"You must have felt just as you did when I wanted to pray for the devil."

"He is the devil," cried Harriet.

"No, Harriet; he is too vulgar."

"I will thank you not to scoff against religion!" was Harriet's retort. "Think of that poor baby. Irma is right to pray for him. What an entrance into life for an English child!"

"My dear sister, I can reassure you. Firstly, the beastly baby is Italian. Secondly, it was promptly christened at Santa Deodata's, and a powerful combination of saints watch over—"

"Don't, dear. And, Harriet, don't be so serious—I mean not so serious when you are with Irma. She will be worse than ever if she thinks we have something to hide."

Harriet's conscience could be quite as tiresome as Philip's unconventionality. Mrs. Herriton soon made it easy for her daughter to go for six weeks to the Tirol. Then she and Philip began to grapple with Irma alone.

Just as they had got things a little quiet the beastly baby sent another picture post-card—a comic one, not particularly proper. Irma received it while they were out, and all the trouble began again.

"I cannot think," said Mrs. Herriton, "what his motive is in sending them."

Two years before, Philip would have said that the motive was to give pleasure. Now he, like his mother, tried to think of something sinister and subtle.

"Do you suppose that he guesses the situation—how anxious we are to hush the scandal up?"

"That is quite possible. He knows that Irma will worry us about the baby. Perhaps he hopes that we shall adopt it to quiet her."

"Hopeful indeed."

"At the same time he has the chance of corrupting the child's morals." She unlocked a drawer, took out the post-card, and regarded it gravely. "He entreats her to send the baby one," was her next remark.

"She might do it too!"

"I told her not to; but we must watch her carefully, without, of course, appearing to be suspicious."

Philip was getting to enjoy his mother's diplomacy. He did not think of his own morals and behaviour any more.

"Who's to watch her at school, though? She may bubble out any moment."

"We can but trust to our influence," said Mrs. Herriton.

Irma did bubble out, that very day. She was proof against a single post-card, not against two. A new little brother is a valuable sentimental asset to a school-girl, and her school was then passing through an acute phase of baby-worship. Happy the girl who had her quiver full of them, who kissed them when she left home in the morning, who had the right to extricate them from mail-carts in the interval, who dangled them at tea ere they retired to rest! That one might sing the unwritten song of Miriam, blessed above all school-girls, who was allowed to hide her baby brother in a squashy place, where none but herself could find him!

How could Irma keep silent when pretentious girls spoke of baby cousins and baby visitors—she who had a baby brother, who wrote her post-cards through his dear papa? She had promised not to tell about him—she knew not why—and she told. And one girl told another, and one girl told her mother, and the thing was out.

"Yes, it is all very sad," Mrs. Herriton kept saying. "My daughter-in-law made a very unhappy marriage, as I dare say you know. I suppose that the child will be educated in Italy. Possibly his grandmother may be doing something, but I have not heard of it. I do not expect that she will have him over. She disapproves of the father. It is altogether a painful business for her."

She was careful only to scold Irma for disobedience—that eighth deadly sin, so convenient to parents and guardians. Harriet would have plunged into needless explanations and abuse. The child was ashamed, and talked about the baby less. The end of the school year was at hand, and she hoped to get another prize. But she also had put her hand to the wheel.

It was several days before they saw Miss Abbott. Mrs. Herriton had not come across her much since the kiss of reconciliation, nor Philip since the journey to London. She had, indeed, been rather a disappointment to him. Her creditable display of originality had never been repeated: he feared she was slipping back. Now she came about the Cottage Hospital—her life was devoted to dull acts of charity—and though she got money out of him and out of his mother, she still sat tight in her chair, looking graver and more wooden than ever.

"I dare say you have heard," said Mrs. Herriton, well knowing what the matter was.

"Yes, I have. I came to ask you; have any steps been taken?"

Philip was astonished. The question was impertinent in the extreme. He had a regard for Miss Abbott, and regretted that she had been guilty of it.

"About the baby?" asked Mrs. Herriton pleasantly.

"Yes."

"As far as I know, no steps. Mrs. Theobald may have decided on something, but I have not heard of it."

"I was meaning, had you decided on anything?"

"The child is no relation of ours," said Philip. "It is therefore scarcely for us to interfere."

His mother glanced at him nervously. "Poor Lilia was almost a daughter to me once. I know what Miss Abbott means. But now things have altered. Any initiative would naturally come from Mrs. Theobald."

"But does not Mrs. Theobald always take any initiative from you?" asked Miss Abbott.

Mrs. Herriton could not help colouring. "I sometimes have given her advice in the past. I should not presume to do so now."

"Then is nothing to be done for the child at all?"

"It is extraordinarily good of you to take this unexpected interest," said Philip.

"The child came into the world through my negligence," replied Miss Abbott. "It is natural I should take an interest in it."

"My dear Caroline," said Mrs. Herriton, "you must not brood over the thing. Let bygones be bygones. The child should worry you even less than it worries us. We never even mention it. It belongs to another world."

Chapter 5

Miss Abbott got up without replying and turned to go. Her extreme gravity made Mrs. Herriton uneasy. "Of course," she added, "if Mrs. Theobald decides on any plan that seems at all practicable—I must say I don't see any such—I shall ask if I may join her in it, for Irma's sake, and share in any possible expenses."

"Please would you let me know if she decides on anything. I should like to join as well."

"My dear, how you throw about your money! We would never allow it."

"And if she decides on nothing, please also let me know. Let me know in any case."

Mrs. Herriton made a point of kissing her.

"Is the young person mad?" burst out Philip as soon as she had departed. "Never in my life have I seen such colossal impertinence. She ought to be well smacked, and sent back to Sunday-school."

His mother said nothing.

"But don't you see—she is practically threatening us? You can't put her off with Mrs. Theobald; she knows as well as we do that she is a nonentity. If we don't do anything she's going to raise a scandal—that we neglect our relatives, &c., which is, of course, a lie. Still she'll say it. Oh, dear, sweet, sober Caroline Abbott has a screw loose! We knew it at Monteriano. I had my suspicions last year one day in the train; and here it is again. The young person is mad."

She still said nothing.

"Shall I go round at once and give it her well? I'd really enjoy it."

In a low, serious voice—such a voice as she had not used to him for months—Mrs. Herriton said, "Caroline has been extremely impertinent. Yet there may be something in what she says after all. Ought the child to grow up in that place—and with that father?"

Philip started and shuddered. He saw that his mother was not sincere. Her insincerity to others had amused him, but it was disheartening when used against himself.

"Let us admit frankly," she continued, "that after all we may have responsibilities."

"I don't understand you, Mother. You are turning absolutely round. What are you up to?"

In one moment an impenetrable barrier had been erected between them. They were no longer in smiling confidence. Mrs. Herriton was off on tactics of her own—tactics which might be beyond or beneath him.

His remark offended her. "Up to? I am wondering whether I ought not to adopt the child. Is that sufficiently plain?"

"And this is the result of half-a-dozen idiocies of Miss Abbott?"

"It is. I repeat, she has been extremely impertinent. None the less she is showing me my duty. If I can rescue poor Lilia's baby from that horrible man, who will bring it up either as Papist or infidel—who will certainly bring it up to be vicious—I shall do it."

"You talk like Harriet."

"And why not?" said she, flushing at what she knew to be an insult. "Say, if you choose, that I talk like Irma. That child has seen the thing more clearly than any of us. She longs for her little brother. She shall have him. I don't care if I am impulsive."

He was sure that she was not impulsive, but did not dare to say so. Her ability frightened him. All his life he had been her puppet. She let him worship Italy, and reform Sawston—just as she had let Harriet be Low Church. She had let him talk as much as he liked. But when she wanted a thing she always got it.

And though she was frightening him, she did not inspire him with reverence. Her life, he saw, was without meaning. To what purpose was her diplomacy, her insincerity, her continued repression of vigour? Did they make any one better or happier? Did they even bring happiness to herself? Harriet with her gloomy peevish creed, Lilia with her clutches after pleasure, were after all more divine than this well-ordered, active, useless machine.

Now that his mother had wounded his vanity he could criticize her thus. But he could not rebel. To the end of his days he could probably go on doing what she wanted. He watched with a cold interest the duel between her and Miss Abbott. Mrs. Herriton's policy only appeared gradually. It was to prevent Miss Abbott interfering with the child at all costs, and if possible to prevent her at a small cost. Pride was the only solid element in her disposition. She could not bear to seem less charitable than others.

"I am planning what can be done," she would tell people, "and that kind Caroline Abbott is helping me. It is no business of either of us, but we are getting to feel that the baby must not be left entirely to that horrible man. It would be unfair to little Irma; after all, he is her half-brother. No, we have come to nothing definite."

Miss Abbott was equally civil, but not to be appeased by good intentions. The child's welfare was a sacred duty to her, not a matter of pride or even of sentiment. By it alone, she felt, could she undo a little of the evil that she had permitted to come into the world. To her imagination Monteriano had become a magic city of vice, beneath whose towers no person could grow up happy or pure. Sawston, with its semi-detached houses and snobby schools, its book teas and bazaars, was certainly petty and dull; at times she found it even contemptible. But it was not a place of sin, and at Sawston, either with the Herritons or with herself, the baby should grow up.

As soon as it was inevitable, Mrs. Herriton wrote a letter for Waters and Adamson to send to Gino—the oddest letter; Philip saw a copy of it afterwards. Its ostensible purpose was to complain of the picture postcards. Right at the end, in a few nonchalant sentences, she offered to adopt the child, provided that Gino would undertake never to come near it, and would surrender some of Lilia's money for its education.

"What do you think of it?" she asked her son. "It would not do to let him know that we are anxious for it."

"Certainly he will never suppose that."

"But what effect will the letter have on him?"

"When he gets it he will do a sum. If it is less expensive in the long run to part with a little money and to be clear of the baby, he will part with it. If he would lose, he will adopt the tone of the loving father."

"Dear, you're shockingly cynical." After a pause she added, "How would the sum work out?"

"I don't know, I'm sure. But if you wanted to ensure the baby being posted by return, you should have sent a little sum to HIM. Oh, I'm not cynical—at least I only go by what I know of him. But I am weary of the whole show. Weary of Italy. Weary, weary, weary. Sawston's a kind, pitiful place, isn't it? I will go walk in it and seek comfort."

He smiled as he spoke, for the sake of not appearing serious. When he had left her she began to smile also.

It was to the Abbotts' that he walked. Mr. Abbott offered him tea, and Caroline, who was keeping up her Italian in the next room, came in to pour it out. He told them that his mother had written to Signor Carella, and they both uttered fervent wishes for her success.

"Very fine of Mrs. Herriton, very fine indeed," said Mr. Abbott, who, like every one else, knew nothing of his daughter's exasperating behaviour. "I'm afraid it will mean a lot of expense. She will get nothing out of Italy without paying."

"There are sure to be incidental expenses," said Philip cautiously. Then he turned to Miss Abbott and said, "Do you suppose we shall have difficulty with the man?"

"It depends," she replied, with equal caution.

"From what you saw of him, should you conclude that he would make an affectionate parent?"

"I don't go by what I saw of him, but by what I know of him."

"Well, what do you conclude from that?"

"That he is a thoroughly wicked man."

"Yet thoroughly wicked men have loved their children. Look at Rodrigo Borgia, for example."

"I have also seen examples of that in my district."

With this remark the admirable young woman rose, and returned to keep up her Italian. She puzzled Philip extremely. He could understand enthusiasm, but she did not seem the least enthusiastic. He could understand pure cussedness, but it did not seem to be that either. Apparently she was deriving neither amusement nor profit from the struggle. Why, then, had she undertaken it? Perhaps she was not sincere. Perhaps, on the whole, that was most likely. She must be professing one thing and aiming at another. What the other thing could be he did not stop to consider. Insincerity was becoming his stock explanation for anything unfamiliar, whether that thing was a kindly action or a high ideal.

"She fences well," he said to his mother afterwards.

"What had you to fence about?" she said suavely. Her son might know her tactics, but she refused to admit that he knew. She still pretended to him that the baby was the one thing she wanted, and had always wanted, and that Miss Abbott was her valued ally.

And when, next week, the reply came from Italy, she showed him no face of triumph. "Read the letters," she said. "We have failed."

Gino wrote in his own language, but the solicitors had sent a laborious English translation, where "Preghiatissima Signora" was rendered as "Most Praiseworthy Madam," and every delicate compliment and superlative—superlatives are delicate in Italian—would have felled an ox. For a moment Philip forgot the matter in the manner; this grotesque memorial of the land he had loved moved him almost to tears. He knew the originals of these lumbering phrases; he also had sent "sincere auguries"; he also had addressed letters—who writes at home?—from the Caffe Garibaldi. "I didn't know I was still such an ass," he thought. "Why can't I realize that it's merely tricks of expression? A bounder's a bounder, whether he lives in Sawston or Monteriano."

"Isn't it disheartening?" said his mother.

He then read that Gino could not accept the generous offer. His paternal heart would not permit him to abandon this symbol of his deplored spouse. As for the picture post-cards, it displeased him greatly that they had been obnoxious. He would send no more. Would Mrs. Herriton, with her notorious kindness, explain this to Irma, and thank her for those which Irma (courteous Miss!) had sent to him?

"The sum works out against us," said Philip. "Or perhaps he is putting up the price."

"No," said Mrs. Herriton decidedly. "It is not that. For some perverse reason he will not part with the child. I must go and tell poor Caroline. She will be equally distressed."

She returned from the visit in the most extraordinary condition. Her face was red, she panted for breath, there were dark circles round her eyes.

"The impudence!" she shouted. "The cursed impudence! Oh, I'm swearing. I don't care. That beastly woman—how dare she interfere—I'll—Philip, dear, I'm sorry. It's no good. You must go."

"Go where? Do sit down. What's happened?" This outburst of violence from his elegant ladylike mother pained him dreadfully. He had not known that it was in her.

"She won't accept—won't accept the letter as final. You must go to Monteriano!"

"I won't!" he shouted back. "I've been and I've failed. I'll never see the place again. I hate Italy."

"If you don't go, she will."

"Abbott?"

"Yes. Going alone; would start this evening. I offered to write; she said it was 'too late!' Too late! The child, if you please—Irma's brother—to live with her, to be brought up by her and her father at our very gates, to go to school like a gentleman, she paying. Oh, you're a man! It doesn't matter for you. You can laugh. But I know what people say; and that woman goes to Italy this evening."

He seemed to be inspired. "Then let her go! Let her mess with Italy by herself. She'll come to grief somehow. Italy's too dangerous, too—"

"Stop that nonsense, Philip. I will not be disgraced by her. I WILL have the child. Pay all we've got for it. I will have it."

"Let her go to Italy!" he cried. "Let her meddle with what she doesn't understand! Look at this letter! The man who wrote it will marry her, or murder her, or do for her somehow. He's a bounder, but he's not an English bounder. He's mysterious and terrible. He's got a country behind him that's upset people from the beginning of the world."

"Harriet!" exclaimed his mother. "Harriet shall go too. Harriet, now, will be invaluable!" And before Philip had stopped talking nonsense, she had planned the whole thing and was looking out the trains.

Chapter 6

Italy, Philip had always maintained, is only her true self in the height of the summer, when the tourists have left her, and her soul awakes under the beams of a vertical sun. He now had every opportunity of seeing her at her best, for it was nearly the middle of August before he went out to meet Harriet in the Tirol.

He found his sister in a dense cloud five thousand feet above the sea, chilled to the bone, overfed, bored, and not at all unwilling to be fetched away.

"It upsets one's plans terribly," she remarked, as she squeezed out her sponges, "but obviously it is my duty."

"Did mother explain it all to you?" asked Philip.

"Yes, indeed! Mother has written me a really beautiful letter. She describes how it was that she gradually got to feel that we must rescue the poor baby from its terrible surroundings, how she has tried by letter, and it is no good—nothing but insincere compliments and hypocrisy came back. Then she says, 'There is nothing like personal influence; you and Philip will succeed where I have failed.' She says, too, that Caroline Abbott has been wonderful."

Philip assented.

"Caroline feels it as keenly almost as us. That is because she knows the man. Oh, he must be loathsome! Goodness me! I've forgotten to pack the ammonia!... It has been a terrible lesson for Caroline, but I fancy it is her turning-point. I can't help liking to think that out of all this evil good will come."

Philip saw no prospect of good, nor of beauty either. But the expedition promised to be highly comic. He was not averse to it any longer; he was simply indifferent to all in it except the humours. These would be wonderful. Harriet, worked by her mother; Mrs. Herriton, worked by Miss Abbott; Gino, worked by a cheque—what better entertainment could he desire? There was nothing to distract him this time; his sentimentality had died, so had his anxiety for the family honour. He might be a puppet's puppet, but he knew exactly the disposition of the strings.

They travelled for thirteen hours down-hill, whilst the streams broadened and the mountains shrank, and the vegetation changed, and the people ceased being ugly and drinking beer, and began instead to drink wine and to be beautiful. And the train which had picked them at sunrise out of a waste of glaciers and hotels was waltzing at sunset round the walls of Verona.

Chapter 6

"Absurd nonsense they talk about the heat," said Philip, as they drove from the station. "Supposing we were here for pleasure, what could be more pleasurable than this?"

"Did you hear, though, they are remarking on the cold?" said Harriet nervously. "I should never have thought it cold."

And on the second day the heat struck them, like a hand laid over the mouth, just as they were walking to see the tomb of Juliet. From that moment everything went wrong. They fled from Verona. Harriet's sketch-book was stolen, and the bottle of ammonia in her trunk burst over her prayer-book, so that purple patches appeared on all her clothes. Then, as she was going through Mantua at four in the morning, Philip made her look out of the window because it was Virgil's birthplace, and a smut flew in her eye, and Harriet with a smut in her eye was notorious. At Bologna they stopped twenty-four hours to rest. It was a FESTA, and children blew bladder whistles night and day. "What a religion!" said Harriet. The hotel smelt, two puppies were asleep on her bed, and her bedroom window looked into a belfry, which saluted her slumbering form every quarter of an hour. Philip left his walking-stick, his socks, and the Baedeker at Bologna; she only left her sponge-bag. Next day they crossed the Apennines with a train-sick child and a hot lady, who told them that never, never before had she sweated so profusely. "Foreigners are a filthy nation," said Harriet. "I don't care if there are tunnels; open the windows." He obeyed, and she got another smut in her eye. Nor did Florence improve matters. Eating, walking, even a cross word would bathe them both in boiling water. Philip, who was slighter of build, and less conscientious, suffered less. But Harriet had never been to Florence, and between the hours of eight and eleven she crawled like a wounded creature through the streets, and swooned before various masterpieces of art. It was an irritable couple who took tickets to Monteriano.

"Singles or returns?" said he.

"A single for me," said Harriet peevishly; "I shall never get back alive."

"Sweet creature!" said her brother, suddenly breaking down. "How helpful you will be when we come to Signor Carella!"

"Do you suppose," said Harriet, standing still among a whirl of porters—"do you suppose I am going to enter that man's house?"

"Then what have you come for, pray? For ornament?"

"To see that you do your duty."

"Oh, thanks!"

"So mother told me. For goodness sake get the tickets; here comes that hot woman again! She has the impudence to bow."

"Mother told you, did she?" said Philip wrathfully, as he went to struggle for tickets at a slit so narrow that they were handed to him edgeways. Italy was beastly, and Florence station is the centre of beastly Italy. But he had a strange feeling that he was to blame for it all; that a little influx into him of virtue would make the whole land not beastly but amusing. For there was enchantment, he was sure of that; solid enchantment, which lay behind the porters and the screaming and the dust. He could see it in the terrific blue sky beneath which they travelled, in the whitened plain which gripped life tighter than a frost, in the exhausted reaches of the Arno, in the ruins of brown castles which stood quivering upon the hills. He could see it, though his head ached and his skin was twitching, though he was here as a puppet, and though his sister knew how he was here. There was nothing pleasant in that journey to Monteriano station. But nothing—not even the discomfort—was commonplace.

"But do people live inside?" asked Harriet. They had exchanged railway-carriage for the legno, and the legno had emerged from the withered trees, and had revealed to them their destination. Philip, to be annoying, answered "No."

"What do they do there?" continued Harriet, with a frown.

"There is a caffe. A prison. A theatre. A church. Walls. A view."

"Not for me, thank you," said Harriet, after a weighty pause.

"Nobody asked you, Miss, you see. Now Lilia was asked by such a nice young gentleman, with curls all over his forehead, and teeth just as white as father makes them." Then his manner changed. "But, Harriet, do you see nothing wonderful or attractive in that place—nothing at all?"

"Nothing at all. It's frightful."

"I know it is. But it's old—awfully old."

"Beauty is the only test," said Harriet. "At least so you told me when I sketched old buildings—for the sake, I suppose, of making yourself unpleasant."

"Oh, I'm perfectly right. But at the same time—I don't know—so many things have happened here—people have lived so hard and so splendidly—I can't explain."

"I shouldn't think you could. It doesn't seem the best moment to begin your Italy mania. I thought you were cured of it by now. Instead, will you kindly tell me what you are going to do when you arrive. I do beg you will not be taken unawares this time."

"First, Harriet, I shall settle you at the Stella d'Italia, in the comfort that befits your sex and disposition. Then I shall make myself some tea. After tea I shall take a book into Santa Deodata's, and read there. It is always fresh and cool."

The martyred Harriet exclaimed, "I'm not clever, Philip. I don't go in for it, as you know. But I know what's rude. And I know what's wrong."

"Meaning—?"

"You!" she shouted, bouncing on the cushions of the legno and startling all the fleas. "What's the good of cleverness if a man's murdered a woman?"

"Harriet, I am hot. To whom do you refer?"

"He. Her. If you don't look out he'll murder you. I wish he would."

"Tut tut, tutlet! You'd find a corpse extraordinarily inconvenient." Then he tried to be less aggravating. "I heartily dislike the fellow, but we know he didn't murder her. In that letter, though she said a lot, she never said he was physically cruel."

"He has murdered her. The things he did—things one can't even mention—"

"Things which one must mention if one's to talk at all. And things which one must keep in their proper place. Because he was unfaithful to his wife, it doesn't follow that in every way he's absolutely vile." He looked at the city. It seemed to approve his remark.

"It's the supreme test. The man who is unchivalrous to a woman—"

"Oh, stow it! Take it to the Back Kitchen. It's no more a supreme test than anything else. The Italians never were chivalrous from the first. If you condemn him for that, you'll condemn the whole lot."

"I condemn the whole lot."

"And the French as well?"

"And the French as well."

"Things aren't so jolly easy," said Philip, more to himself than to her.

But for Harriet things were easy, though not jolly, and she turned upon her brother yet again. "What about the baby, pray? You've said a lot of smart things and whittled away morality and religion and I don't know what; but what about the baby? You think me a fool, but I've been noticing you all today, and you haven't mentioned the baby once. You haven't thought about it, even. You don't care. Philip! I shall not speak to you. You are intolerable."

She kept her promise, and never opened her lips all the rest of the way. But her eyes glowed with anger and resolution. For she was a straight, brave woman, as well as a peevish one.

Philip acknowledged her reproof to be true. He did not care about the baby one straw. Nevertheless, he meant to do his duty, and he was fairly confident of success. If Gino would have sold his wife for a thousand lire, for how much less would he not sell his child? It was just a commercial transaction. Why should it interfere with other things? His eyes were fixed on the towers again, just as they had been fixed when he drove with Miss Abbott. But this time his thoughts were pleasanter, for he had no such grave business on his mind. It was in the spirit of the cultivated tourist that he approached his destination.

One of the towers, rough as any other, was topped by a cross—the tower of the Collegiate Church of Santa Deodata. She was a holy maiden of the Dark Ages, the city's patron saint, and sweetness and barbarity mingle strangely in her story. So holy was she that all her life she lay upon her back in the house of her mother, refusing to eat, refusing to play, refusing to work. The devil, envious of such sanctity, tempted her in various ways. He dangled grapes above her, he showed her fascinating toys, he pushed soft pillows beneath her aching head. When all proved vain he tripped up the mother and flung her downstairs before her very eyes. But so holy was the saint that she never picked her mother up, but lay upon her back through all, and thus assured her throne in Paradise. She was only fifteen when she died, which shows how much is within the reach of any school-girl. Those who think her life was unpractical need only think of the victories upon Poggibonsi, San Gemignano, Volterra, Siena itself—all gained through the invocation of her name; they need only look at the church which rose over her grave. The grand schemes for a marble facade were never carried out, and it is brown unfinished stone until this day. But for the inside Giotto was summoned to decorate the walls of the nave. Giotto came—that is to say, he did not come, German research having decisively proved—but at all events the nave is covered with frescoes, and so are two chapels in the left transept, and the arch into the choir, and there are scraps in the choir itself. There the decoration stopped, till in the full spring of the Renaissance a great painter came to pay a few weeks' visit to his friend the Lord of Monteriano. In the intervals between the banquets and the discussions on Latin etymology and the dancing, he would stroll over to the church, and there in the fifth chapel to the right he has painted two frescoes of the death and burial of Santa Deodata. That is why Baedeker gives the place a star.

Santa Deodata was better company than Harriet, and she kept Philip in a pleasant dream until the legno drew up at the hotel. Every one there was asleep, for it was still the hour when only idiots were moving. There were not even any beggars about. The cabman put their bags down in the passage—they had left heavy luggage at the station—and strolled about till he came on the landlady's room and woke her, and sent her to them.

Then Harriet pronounced the monosyllable "Go!"

"Go where?" asked Philip, bowing to the landlady, who was swimming down the stairs.

"To the Italian. Go."

"Buona sera, signora padrona. Si ritorna volontieri a Monteriano!" (Don't be a goose. I'm not going now. You're in the way, too.) "Vorrei due camere—"

"Go. This instant. Now. I'll stand it no longer. Go!"

"I'm damned if I'll go. I want my tea."

"Swear if you like!" she cried. "Blaspheme! Abuse me! But understand, I'm in earnest."

"Harriet, don't act. Or act better."

"We've come here to get the baby back, and for nothing else. I'll not have this levity and slackness, and talk about pictures and churches. Think of mother; did she send you out for THEM?"

"Think of mother and don't straddle across the stairs. Let the cabman and the landlady come down, and let me go up and choose rooms."

"I shan't."

"Harriet, are you mad?"

"If you like. But you will not come up till you have seen the Italian."

"La signorina si sente male," said Philip, "C' e il sole."

"Poveretta!" cried the landlady and the cabman.

"Leave me alone!" said Harriet, snarling round at them. "I don't care for the lot of you. I'm English, and neither you'll come down nor he up till he goes for the baby."

"La prego-piano-piano-c e un' altra signorina che dorme—"

"We shall probably be arrested for brawling, Harriet. Have you the very slightest sense of the ludicrous?"

Harriet had not; that was why she could be so powerful. She had concocted this scene in the carriage, and nothing should baulk her of it. To the abuse in front and the coaxing behind she was equally indifferent. How long she would have stood like a glorified Horatius, keeping the staircase at both ends, was never to be known. For the young lady, whose sleep they were disturbing, awoke and opened her bedroom door, and came out on to the landing. She was Miss Abbott.

Philip's first coherent feeling was one of indignation. To be run by his mother and hectored by his sister was as much as he could stand. The intervention of a third female drove him suddenly beyond politeness. He was about to say exactly what he thought about the thing from beginning to end. But before he could do so Harriet also had seen Miss Abbott. She uttered a shrill cry of joy.

"You, Caroline, here of all people!" And in spite of the heat she darted up the stairs and imprinted an affectionate kiss upon her friend.

Philip had an inspiration. "You will have a lot to tell Miss Abbott, Harriet, and she may have as much to tell you. So I'll pay my call on Signor Carella, as you suggested, and see how things stand."

Miss Abbott uttered some noise of greeting or alarm. He did not reply to it or approach nearer to her. Without even paying the cabman, he escaped into the street.

"Tear each other's eyes out!" he cried, gesticulating at the facade of the hotel. "Give it to her, Harriet! Teach her to leave us alone. Give it to her, Caroline! Teach her to be grateful to you. Go it, ladies; go it!"

Such people as observed him were interested, but did not conclude that he was mad. This aftermath of conversation is not unknown in Italy.

He tried to think how amusing it was; but it would not do—Miss Abbott's presence affected him too personally. Either she suspected him of dishonesty, or else she was being dishonest herself. He preferred to suppose the latter. Perhaps she had seen Gino, and they had prepared some elaborate mortification for the Herritons. Perhaps Gino had sold the baby cheap to her for a joke: it was just the kind of joke that would appeal to him. Philip still remembered the laughter that had greeted his fruitless journey, and the uncouth push that had toppled him on to the bed. And whatever it might mean, Miss Abbott's presence spoilt the comedy: she would do nothing funny.

During this short meditation he had walked through the city, and was out on the other side. "Where does Signor Carella live?" he asked the men at the Dogana.

"I'll show you," said a little girl, springing out of the ground as Italian children will.

"She will show you," said the Dogana men, nodding reassuringly. "Follow her always, always, and you will come to no harm. She is a trustworthy guide. She is my

daughter."
cousin."
sister."

Philip knew these relatives well: they ramify, if need be, all over the peninsula.

"Do you chance to know whether Signor Carella is in?" he asked her.

She had just seen him go in. Philip nodded. He was looking forward to the interview this time: it would be an intellectual duet with a man of no great intellect. What was Miss Abbott up to? That was one of the things he was going to discover. While she had it out with Harriet, he would have it out with Gino. He followed the Dogana's relative softly, like a diplomatist.

He did not follow her long, for this was the Volterra gate, and the house was exactly opposite to it. In half a minute they had scrambled down the mule-track and reached the only practicable entrance. Philip laughed, partly at the thought of Lilia in such a building, partly in the confidence of victory. Meanwhile the Dogana's relative lifted up her voice and gave a shout.

For an impressive interval there was no reply. Then the figure of a woman appeared high up on the loggia.

"That is Perfetta," said the girl.

"I want to see Signor Carella," cried Philip.

"Out!"

"Out," echoed the girl complacently.

"Why on earth did you say he was in?" He could have strangled her for temper. He had been just ripe for an interview—just the right combination of indignation and acuteness: blood hot, brain cool. But nothing ever did go right in Monteriano. "When will he be back?" he called to Perfetta. It really was too bad.

She did not know. He was away on business. He might be back this evening, he might not. He had gone to Poggibonsi.

At the sound of this word the little girl put her fingers to her nose and swept them at the plain. She sang as she did so, even as her foremothers had sung seven hundred years back—

> *Poggibonizzi, fatti in la,*
> *Che Monteriano si fa citta!*

Then she asked Philip for a halfpenny. A German lady, friendly to the Past, had given her one that very spring.

"I shall have to leave a message," he called.

"Now Perfetta has gone for her basket," said the little girl. "When she returns she will lower it—so. Then you will put your card into it. Then she will raise it—thus. By this means—"

When Perfetta returned, Philip remembered to ask after the baby. It took longer to find than the basket, and he stood perspiring in the evening sun, trying to avoid the smell of the drains and to prevent the little girl from singing against Poggibonsi. The olive-trees beside him were draped with the weekly—or more probably the monthly—wash. What a frightful spotty blouse! He could not think where he had seen it. Then he remembered that it was Lilia's. She had brought it "to hack about in" at Sawston, and had taken it to Italy because "in Italy anything does." He had rebuked her for the sentiment.

"Beautiful as an angel!" bellowed Perfetta, holding out something which must be Lilia's baby. "But who am I addressing?"

"Thank you—here is my card." He had written on it a civil request to Gino for an interview next morning. But before he placed it in the basket and revealed his identity, he wished to find something out. "Has a young lady happened to call here lately—a young English lady?"

Perfetta begged his pardon: she was a little deaf.

"A young lady—pale, large, tall."

She did not quite catch.

"A YOUNG LADY!"

"Perfetta is deaf when she chooses," said the Dogana's relative. At last Philip admitted the peculiarity and strode away. He paid off the detestable child at the Volterra gate. She got two nickel pieces and was not pleased, partly because it was too much, partly because he did not look pleased when he gave it to her. He caught her fathers and cousins winking at each other as he walked past them. Monteriano seemed in one conspiracy to make him look a fool. He felt tired and anxious and muddled, and not sure of anything except that his temper was lost. In this mood he returned to the Stella d'Italia, and there, as he was ascending the stairs, Miss Abbott popped out of the dining-room on the first floor and beckoned to him mysteriously.

"I was going to make myself some tea," he said, with his hand still on the banisters.

"I should be grateful—"

So he followed her into the dining-room and shut the door.

"You see," she began, "Harriet knows nothing."

"No more do I. He was out."

"But what's that to do with it?"

He presented her with an unpleasant smile. She fenced well, as he had noticed before. "He was out. You find me as ignorant as you have left Harriet."

"What do you mean? Please, please Mr. Herriton, don't be mysterious: there isn't the time. Any moment Harriet may be down, and we shan't have decided how to behave to her. Sawston was different: we had to keep up appearances. But here we must speak out, and I think I can trust you to do it. Otherwise we'll never start clear."

"Pray let us start clear," said Philip, pacing up and down the room. "Permit me to begin by asking you a question. In which capacity have you come to Monteriano—spy or traitor?"

"Spy!" she answered, without a moment's hesitation. She was standing by the little Gothic window as she spoke—the hotel had been a palace once—and with her finger she was following the curves of the moulding as if they might feel beautiful and strange. "Spy," she repeated, for Philip was bewildered at learning her guilt so easily, and could not answer a word. "Your mother has behaved dishonourably all through. She never wanted the child; no harm in that; but she is too proud to let it come to me. She has done all she could to wreck things; she did not tell you everything; she has told Harriet nothing at all; she has lied or acted lies everywhere. I cannot trust your mother. So I have come here alone—all across

Europe; no one knows it; my father thinks I am in Normandy—to spy on Mrs. Herriton. Don't let's argue!" for he had begun, almost mechanically, to rebuke her for impertinence. "If you are here to get the child, I will help you; if you are here to fail, I shall get it instead of you."

"It is hopeless to expect you to believe me," he stammered. "But I can assert that we are here to get the child, even if it costs us all we've got. My mother has fixed no money limit whatever. I am here to carry out her instructions. I think that you will approve of them, as you have practically dictated them. I do not approve of them. They are absurd."

She nodded carelessly. She did not mind what he said. All she wanted was to get the baby out of Monteriano.

"Harriet also carries out your instructions," he continued. "She, however, approves of them, and does not know that they proceed from you. I think, Miss Abbott, you had better take entire charge of the rescue party. I have asked for an interview with Signor Carella tomorrow morning. Do you acquiesce?"

She nodded again.

"Might I ask for details of your interview with him? They might be helpful to me."

He had spoken at random. To his delight she suddenly collapsed. Her hand fell from the window. Her face was red with more than the reflection of evening.

"My interview—how do you know of it?"

"From Perfetta, if it interests you."

"Who ever is Perfetta?"

"The woman who must have let you in."

"In where?"

"Into Signor Carella's house."

"Mr. Herriton!" she exclaimed. "How could you believe her? Do you suppose that I would have entered that man's house, knowing about him all that I do? I think you have very odd ideas of what is possible for a lady. I hear you wanted Harriet to go. Very properly she refused. Eighteen months ago I might have done such a thing. But I trust I have learnt how to behave by now."

Philip began to see that there were two Miss Abbotts—the Miss Abbott who could travel alone to Monteriano, and the Miss Abbott who could not enter Gino's house when she got there. It was an amusing discovery. Which of them would respond to his next move?

"I suppose I misunderstood Perfetta. Where did you have your interview, then?"

"Not an interview—an accident—I am very sorry—I meant you to have the chance of seeing him first. Though it is your fault. You are a day late. You were due here yesterday. So I came yesterday, and, not finding you, went up to the Rocca—you know that kitchen-garden where they let you in, and there is a ladder up to a broken tower, where you can stand and see all the other towers below you and the plain and all the other hills?"

"Yes, yes. I know the Rocca; I told you of it."

"So I went up in the evening for the sunset: I had nothing to do. He was in the garden: it belongs to a friend of his."

"And you talked."

"It was very awkward for me. But I had to talk: he seemed to make me. You see he thought I was here as a tourist; he thinks so still. He intended to be civil, and I judged it better to be civil also."

"And of what did you talk?"

"The weather—there will be rain, he says, by tomorrow evening—the other towns, England, myself, about you a little, and he actually mentioned Lilia. He was perfectly disgusting; he pretended he loved her; he offered to show me her grave—the grave of the woman he has murdered!"

"My dear Miss Abbott, he is not a murderer. I have just been driving that into Harriet. And when you know the Italians as well as I do, you will realize that in all that he said to you he was perfectly sincere. The Italians are essentially dramatic; they look on death and love as spectacles. I don't doubt that he persuaded himself, for the moment, that he had behaved admirably, both as husband and widower."

"You may be right," said Miss Abbott, impressed for the first time. "When I tried to pave the way, so to speak—to hint that he had not behaved as he ought—well, it was no good at all. He couldn't or wouldn't understand."

There was something very humorous in the idea of Miss Abbott approaching Gino, on the Rocca, in the spirit of a district visitor. Philip, whose temper was returning, laughed.

"Harriet would say he has no sense of sin."

"Harriet may be right, I am afraid."

"If so, perhaps he isn't sinful!"

Miss Abbott was not one to encourage levity. "I know what he has done," she said. "What he says and what he thinks is of very little importance."

Philip smiled at her crudity. "I should like to hear, though, what he said about me. Is he preparing a warm reception?"

"Oh, no, not that. I never told him that you and Harriet were coming. You could have taken him by surprise if you liked. He only asked for you, and wished he hadn't been so rude to you eighteen months ago."

"What a memory the fellow has for little things!" He turned away as he spoke, for he did not want her to see his face. It was suffused with pleasure. For an apology, which would have been intolerable eighteen months ago, was gracious and agreeable now.

She would not let this pass. "You did not think it a little thing at the time. You told me he had assaulted you."

"I lost my temper," said Philip lightly. His vanity had been appeased, and he knew it. This tiny piece of civility had changed his mood. "Did he really—what exactly did he say?"

"He said he was sorry—pleasantly, as Italians do say such things. But he never mentioned the baby once."

What did the baby matter when the world was suddenly right way up? Philip smiled, and was shocked at himself for smiling, and smiled again. For romance had come back to Italy; there were no cads in her; she was beautiful, courteous, lovable, as of old. And Miss Abbott—she, too, was beautiful in her way, for all her gaucheness and conventionality. She really cared about life, and tried to live it properly. And Harriet—even Harriet tried.

This admirable change in Philip proceeds from nothing admirable, and may therefore provoke the gibes of the cynical. But angels and other practical people will accept it reverently, and write it down as good.

"The view from the Rocca (small gratuity) is finest at sunset," he murmured, more to himself than to her.

"And he never mentioned the baby once," Miss Abbott repeated. But she had returned to the window, and again her finger pursued the delicate curves. He watched her in silence, and was more attracted to her than he had ever been before. She really was the strangest mixture.

"The view from the Rocca—wasn't it fine?"

"What isn't fine here?" she answered gently, and then added, "I wish I was Harriet," throwing an extraordinary meaning into the words.

"Because Harriet—?"

She would not go further, but he believed that she had paid homage to the complexity of life. For her, at all events, the expedition was neither easy nor jolly. Beauty, evil, charm, vulgarity, mystery—she also acknowledged this tangle, in spite of herself. And her voice thrilled him when she broke silence with "Mr. Herriton—come here—look at this!"

She removed a pile of plates from the Gothic window, and they leant out of it. Close opposite, wedged between mean houses, there rose up one of the great towers. It is your tower: you stretch a barricade between it and the hotel, and the traffic is blocked in a moment. Farther up, where the street empties out by the church, your connections, the Merli and the Capocchi, do likewise. They command the Piazza, you the Siena gate. No one can move in either but he shall be instantly slain, either by bows or by crossbows, or by Greek fire. Beware, however, of the back bedroom windows. For they are menaced by the tower of the Aldobrandeschi, and before now arrows have stuck quivering over the washstand. Guard these windows well, lest there be a repetition of the events of February 1338, when the hotel was surprised from the rear, and your dearest friend—you could just make out that it was he—was thrown at you over the stairs.

"It reaches up to heaven," said Philip, "and down to the other place." The summit of the tower was radiant in the sun, while its base was in shadow and pasted over with advertisements. "Is it to be a symbol of the town?"

She gave no hint that she understood him. But they remained together at the window because it was a little cooler and so pleasant. Philip found a certain grace and lightness in his companion which he had never noticed in England. She was appallingly narrow, but her consciousness of wider things gave to her narrowness a pathetic charm. He did not suspect that he was more graceful too. For our vanity is such that we hold our own characters immutable, and we are slow to acknowledge that they have changed, even for the better.

Citizens came out for a little stroll before dinner. Some of them stood and gazed at the advertisements on the tower.

"Surely that isn't an opera-bill?" said Miss Abbott.

Philip put on his pince-nez. "'Lucia di Lammermoor. By the Master Donizetti. Unique representation. This evening.'

"But is there an opera? Right up here?"

"Why, yes. These people know how to live. They would sooner have a thing bad than not have it at all. That is why they have got to have so much that is good. However bad the performance is tonight, it will be alive. Italians don't love music silently, like the beastly Germans. The audience takes its share—sometimes more."

"Can't we go?"

He turned on her, but not unkindly. "But we're here to rescue a child!"

He cursed himself for the remark. All the pleasure and the light went out of her face, and she became again Miss Abbott of Sawston—good, oh, most undoubtedly good, but most appallingly dull. Dull and remorseful: it is a deadly combination, and he strove against it in vain till he was interrupted by the opening of the dining-room door.

They started as guiltily as if they had been flirting. Their interview had taken such an unexpected course. Anger, cynicism, stubborn morality—all had ended in a feeling of good-will towards each other and towards the city which had received them. And now Harriet was here—acrid, indissoluble, large; the same in Italy as in England—changing her disposition never, and her atmosphere under protest.

Yet even Harriet was human, and the better for a little tea. She did not scold Philip for finding Gino out, as she might reasonably have done. She showered civilities on Miss Abbott, exclaiming again and again that Caroline's visit was one of the most fortunate coincidences in the world. Caroline did not contradict her.

"You see him tomorrow at ten, Philip. Well, don't forget the blank cheque. Say an hour for the business. No, Italians are so slow; say two. Twelve o'clock. Lunch. Well—then it's no good going till the evening train. I can manage the baby as far as Florence—"

"My dear sister, you can't run on like that. You don't buy a pair of gloves in two hours, much less a baby."

"Three hours, then, or four; or make him learn English ways. At Florence we get a nurse—"

"But, Harriet," said Miss Abbott, "what if at first he was to refuse?"

"I don't know the meaning of the word," said Harriet impressively. "I've told the landlady that Philip and I only want our rooms one night, and we shall keep to it."

"I dare say it will be all right. But, as I told you, I thought the man I met on the Rocca a strange, difficult man."

"He's insolent to ladies, we know. But my brother can be trusted to bring him to his senses. That woman, Philip, whom you saw will carry the baby to the hotel. Of course you must tip her for it. And try, if you can, to get poor Lilia's silver bangles. They were nice quiet things, and will do for Irma. And there is an inlaid box I lent her—lent, not gave—to keep her handkerchiefs in. It's of no real value; but this is our only chance. Don't ask for it; but if you see it lying about, just say—"

"No, Harriet; I'll try for the baby, but for nothing else. I promise to do that to-morrow, and to do it in the way you wish. But tonight, as we're all tired, we want a change of topic. We want relaxation. We want to go to the theatre."

"Theatres here? And at such a moment?"

"We should hardly enjoy it, with the great interview impending," said Miss Abbott, with an anxious glance at Philip.

He did not betray her, but said, "Don't you think it's better than sitting in all the evening and getting nervous?"

His sister shook her head. "Mother wouldn't like it. It would be most unsuitable—almost irreverent. Besides all that, foreign theatres are notorious. Don't you remember those letters in the 'Church Family Newspaper'?"

"But this is an opera—'Lucia di Lammermoor'—Sir Walter Scott—classical, you know."

Harriet's face grew resigned. "Certainly one has so few opportunities of hearing music. It is sure to be very bad. But it might be better than sitting idle all the evening. We have no book, and I lost my crochet at Florence."

"Good. Miss Abbott, you are coming too?"

"It is very kind of you, Mr. Herriton. In some ways I should enjoy it; but—excuse the suggestion—I don't think we ought to go to cheap seats."

"Good gracious me!" cried Harriet, "I should never have thought of that. As likely as not, we should have tried to save money and sat among the most awful people. One keeps on forgetting this is Italy."

"Unfortunately I have no evening dress; and if the seats—"

"Oh, that'll be all right," said Philip, smiling at his timorous, scrupulous women-kind. "We'll go as we are, and buy the best we can get. Monteriano is not formal."

So this strenuous day of resolutions, plans, alarms, battles, victories, defeats, truces, ended at the opera. Miss Abbott and Harriet were both a little shamefaced. They thought of their friends at Sawston, who were supposing them to be now tilting against the powers of evil. What would Mrs. Herriton, or Irma, or the curates at the Back Kitchen say if they could see the rescue party at a place of amusement on the very first day of its mission? Philip, too, marvelled at his wish to go. He began to see that he was enjoying his time in Monteriano, in spite of the tiresomeness of his companions and the occasional contrariness of himself.

He had been to this theatre many years before, on the occasion of a performance of "La Zia di Carlo." Since then it had been thoroughly done up, in the tints of the beet-root and the tomato, and was in many other ways a credit to the little town. The orchestra had been enlarged, some of the boxes had terra-cotta draperies, and over each box was now suspended an enormous tablet, neatly framed, bearing upon it the number of that box. There was also a drop-scene, representing a pink and purple landscape, wherein sported many a lady lightly clad, and two more ladies lay along the top of the proscenium to steady a large and pallid clock. So rich and so appalling was the effect, that Philip could scarcely suppress a cry. There is something majestic in the bad taste of Italy; it is not the bad taste of a country which knows no better; it has not the nervous vulgarity of England, or the blinded vulgarity of Germany. It observes beauty, and chooses to pass it by. But it attains to beauty's confidence. This tiny theatre of Monteriano spraddled and swaggered with the best of them, and these ladies with their clock would have nodded to the young men on the ceiling of the Sistine.

Philip had tried for a box, but all the best were taken: it was rather a grand performance, and he had to be content with stalls. Harriet was fretful and insular. Miss Abbott was pleasant, and insisted on praising everything: her only regret was that she had no pretty clothes with her.

"We do all right," said Philip, amused at her unwonted vanity.

"Yes, I know; but pretty things pack as easily as ugly ones. We had no need to come to Italy like guys."

This time he did not reply, "But we're here to rescue a baby." For he saw a charming picture, as charming a picture as he had seen for years—the hot red theatre; outside the theatre, towers and dark gates and mediaeval walls; beyond the walls olive-trees in the starlight and white winding roads and fireflies and untroubled dust; and here in the middle of it all, Miss Abbott, wishing she had not come looking like a guy. She had made the right remark. Most undoubtedly she had made the right remark. This stiff suburban woman was unbending before the shrine.

"Don't you like it at all?" he asked her.

"Most awfully." And by this bald interchange they convinced each other that Romance was here.

Harriet, meanwhile, had been coughing ominously at the drop-scene, which presently rose on the grounds of Ravenswood, and the chorus of Scotch retainers burst into cry. The audience accompanied with tappings and drummings, swaying in the melody like corn in the wind. Harriet, though she did not care for music, knew how to listen to it. She uttered an acid "Shish!"

"Shut it," whispered her brother.

"We must make a stand from the beginning. They're talking."

"It is tiresome," murmured Miss Abbott; "but perhaps it isn't for us to interfere."

Harriet shook her head and shished again. The people were quiet, not because it is wrong to talk during a chorus, but because it is natural to be civil to a visitor. For a little time she kept the whole house in order, and could smile at her brother complacently.

Her success annoyed him. He had grasped the principle of opera in Italy—it aims not at illusion but at entertainment—and he did not want this great evening-party to turn into a prayer-meeting. But soon the boxes began to fill, and Harriet's power was over. Families greeted each other across the auditorium. People in the pit hailed their brothers and sons in the chorus, and told them how well they were singing. When Lucia appeared by the fountain there was loud applause, and cries of "Welcome to Monteriano!"

"Ridiculous babies!" said Harriet, settling down in her stall.

"Why, it is the famous hot lady of the Apennines," cried Philip; "the one who had never, never before—"

"Ugh! Don't. She will be very vulgar. And I'm sure it's even worse here than in the tunnel. I wish we'd never—"

Lucia began to sing, and there was a moment's silence. She was stout and ugly; but her voice was still beautiful, and as she sang the theatre murmured like a hive of happy bees. All through the coloratura she was accompanied by sighs, and its top note was drowned in a shout of universal joy.

So the opera proceeded. The singers drew inspiration from the audience, and the two great sextettes were rendered not unworthily. Miss Abbott fell into the spirit of the thing. She, too, chatted and laughed and applauded and encored, and rejoiced in the existence of beauty. As for Philip, he forgot himself as well as his mission. He was not even an enthusiastic visitor. For he had been in this place always. It was his home.

Harriet, like M. Bovary on a more famous occasion, was trying to follow the plot. Occasionally she nudged her companions, and asked them what had become of Walter Scott. She looked round grimly. The audience sounded drunk, and even Caroline, who never took a drop, was swaying oddly. Violent waves of excitement, all arising from very little, went sweeping round the theatre. The climax was reached in the mad scene. Lucia, clad in white, as befitted her malady, suddenly gathered up her streaming hair and bowed her acknowledgment to the audience. Then from the back of the stage—she feigned not to see it—there advanced a kind of bamboo clothes-horse, stuck all over with bouquets. It was very ugly, and most of the flowers in it were false. Lucia knew this, and so did the audience; and they all knew that the clothes-horse was a piece of stage property, brought in to make the performance go year after year. None the less did it unloose the great deeps. With a scream of amazement and joy she embraced the animal, pulled out one or two practicable blossoms, pressed them to her lips, and flung them into her admirers. They flung them back, with loud melodious cries, and a little boy in one of the stageboxes snatched up his sister's carnations and offered them. "Che carino!" exclaimed the singer. She darted at the little boy and kissed him. Now the noise became tremendous. "Silence! silence!" shouted many old gentlemen behind. "Let the divine creature continue!" But the young men in the adjacent box were imploring Lucia to extend her civility to them. She refused, with a humorous, expressive gesture. One of them hurled a bouquet at her. She spurned it with her foot. Then, encouraged by the roars of the audience, she picked it up and tossed it to them. Harriet was always unfortunate. The bouquet struck her full in the chest, and a little billet-doux fell out of it into her lap.

"Call this classical!" she cried, rising from her seat. "It's not even respectable! Philip! take me out at once."

"Whose is it?" shouted her brother, holding up the bouquet in one hand and the billet-doux in the other. "Whose is it?"

The house exploded, and one of the boxes was violently agitated, as if some one was being hauled to the front. Harriet moved down the gangway, and compelled Miss Abbott to follow her. Philip, still laughing and calling "Whose is it?" brought up the rear. He was drunk with excitement. The heat, the fatigue, and the enjoyment had mounted into his head.

"To the left!" the people cried. "The innamorato is to the left."

He deserted his ladies and plunged towards the box. A young man was flung stomach downwards across the balustrade. Philip handed him up the bouquet and the note. Then his own hands were seized affectionately. It all seemed quite natural.

"Why have you not written?" cried the young man. "Why do you take me by surprise?"

"Oh, I've written," said Philip hilariously. "I left a note this afternoon."

"Silence! silence!" cried the audience, who were beginning to have enough. "Let the divine creature continue." Miss Abbott and Harriet had disappeared.

"No! no!" cried the young man. "You don't escape me now." For Philip was trying feebly to disengage his hands. Amiable youths bent out of the box and invited him to enter it.

"Gino's friends are ours—"

"Friends?" cried Gino. "A relative! A brother! Fra Filippo, who has come all the way from England and never written."

"I left a message."

The audience began to hiss.

"Come in to us."

"Thank you—ladies—there is not time—"

The next moment he was swinging by his arms. The moment after he shot over the balustrade into the box. Then the conductor, seeing that the incident was over, raised his baton. The house was hushed, and Lucia di Lammermoor resumed her song of madness and death.

Philip had whispered introductions to the pleasant people who had pulled him in—tradesmen's sons perhaps they were, or medical students, or solicitors' clerks, or sons of other dentists. There is no knowing who is who in Italy. The guest of the evening was a private soldier. He shared the honour now with Philip. The two had to stand side by side in the front, and exchange compliments, whilst Gino presided, courteous, but delightfully familiar. Philip would have a spasm of horror at the muddle he had made. But the spasm would pass, and again he would be enchanted by the kind, cheerful voices, the laughter that was never vapid, and the light caress of the arm across his back.

He could not get away till the play was nearly finished, and Edgardo was singing amongst the tombs of ancestors. His new friends hoped to see him at the Garibaldi tomorrow evening. He promised; then he remembered that if they kept to Harriet's plan he would have left Monteriano. "At ten o'clock, then," he said to Gino. "I want to speak to you alone. At ten."

"Certainly!" laughed the other.

Miss Abbott was sitting up for him when he got back. Harriet, it seemed, had gone straight to bed.

"That was he, wasn't it?" she asked.

"Yes, rather."

"I suppose you didn't settle anything?"

"Why, no; how could I? The fact is—well, I got taken by surprise, but after all, what does it matter? There's no earthly reason why we shouldn't do the business pleasantly. He's a perfectly charming person, and so are his friends. I'm his friend now—his long-lost brother. What's the harm? I tell you, Miss Abbott, it's one thing for England and another for Italy. There we plan and get on high moral horses. Here we find what asses we are, for things go off quite easily, all by themselves. My hat, what a night! Did you ever see a really purple sky and really silver stars before? Well, as I was saying, it's absurd to worry; he's not a porky father. He wants that baby as little as I do. He's been ragging my dear mother—just as he ragged me eighteen months ago, and I've forgiven him. Oh, but he has a sense of humour!"

Miss Abbott, too, had a wonderful evening, nor did she ever remember such stars or such a sky. Her head, too, was full of music, and that night when she opened the window her room was filled with warm, sweet air. She was bathed in beauty within and without; she could not go to bed for happiness. Had she ever been so happy before? Yes, once before, and here, a night in March, the night Gino and Lilia had told her of their love—the night whose evil she had come now to undo.

She gave a sudden cry of shame. "This time—the same place—the same thing"—and she began to beat down her happiness, knowing it to be sinful. She was here to fight against this place, to rescue a little soul—who was innocent as yet. She was here to champion morality and purity, and the holy life of an English home. In the spring she had sinned through ignorance; she was not ignorant now. "Help me!" she cried, and shut the window as if there was magic in the encircling air. But the tunes would not go out of her head, and all night long she was troubled by torrents of music, and by applause and laughter, and angry young men who shouted the distich out of Baedeker:—

Poggibonizzi fatti in la,
Che Monteriano si fa citta!

Poggibonsi was revealed to her as they sang—a joyless, straggling place, full of people who pretended. When she woke up she knew that it had been Sawston.

Chapter 7

At about nine o'clock next morning Perfetta went out on to the loggia, not to look at the view, but to throw some dirty water at it. "Scusi tanto!" she wailed, for the water spattered a tall young lady who had for some time been tapping at the lower door.

"Is Signor Carella in?" the young lady asked. It was no business of Perfetta's to be shocked, and the style of the visitor seemed to demand the reception-room. Accordingly she opened its shutters, dusted a round patch on one of the horsehair chairs, and bade the lady do herself the inconvenience of sitting down. Then she ran into Monteriano and shouted up and down its streets until such time as her young master should hear her.

The reception-room was sacred to the dead wife. Her shiny portrait hung upon the wall—similar, doubtless, in all respects to the one which would be pasted on her tombstone. A little piece of black drapery had been tacked above the frame to lend a dignity to woe. But two of the tacks had fallen out, and the effect was now rakish, as of a drunkard's bonnet. A coon song lay open on the piano, and of the two tables one supported Baedeker's "Central Italy," the other Harriet's inlaid box. And over everything there lay a deposit of heavy white dust, which was only blown off one moment to thicken on another. It is well to be remembered with love. It is not so very dreadful to be forgotten entirely. But if we shall resent anything on earth at all, we shall resent the consecration of a deserted room.

Miss Abbott did not sit down, partly because the antimacassars might harbour fleas, partly because she had suddenly felt faint, and was glad to cling on to the funnel of the stove. She struggled with herself, for she had need to be very calm; only if she was very calm might her behaviour be justified. She had broken faith with Philip and Harriet: she was going to try for the baby before they did. If she failed she could scarcely look them in the face again.

"Harriet and her brother," she reasoned, "don't realize what is before them. She would bluster and be rude; he would be pleasant and take it as a joke. Both of them—even if they offered money—would fail. But I begin to understand the man's nature; he does not love the child, but he will be touchy about it—and that is quite as bad for us. He's charming, but he's no fool; he conquered me last year; he conquered Mr. Herriton yesterday, and if I am not careful he will conquer us all today, and the baby will grow up in Monteriano. He is terribly strong; Lilia found that out, but only I remember it now."

This attempt, and this justification of it, were the results of the long and restless night. Miss Abbott had come to believe that she alone could do battle with Gino, because she alone understood him; and she had put this, as nicely as she could, in a note which she had left for Philip. It distressed her to write such a note, partly because her education inclined her to reverence the male, partly because she had got to like Philip a good deal after their last strange interview. His pettiness would be dispersed, and as for his "unconventionality," which was so much gossiped about at Sawston, she began to see that it did not differ greatly from certain familiar notions of her own. If only he would forgive her for what she was doing now, there might perhaps be before them a long and profitable friendship. But she must succeed. No one would forgive her if she did not succeed. She prepared to do battle with the powers of evil.

The voice of her adversary was heard at last, singing fearlessly from his expanded lungs, like a professional. Herein he differed from Englishmen, who always have a little feeling against music, and sing only from the throat, apologetically. He padded upstairs, and looked in at the open door of the reception-room without seeing her. Her heart leapt and her throat was dry when he turned away and passed, still singing, into the room opposite. It is alarming not to be seen.

He had left the door of this room open, and she could see into it, right across the landing. It was in a shocking mess. Food, bedclothes, patent-leather boots, dirty plates, and knives lay strewn over a large table and on the floor. But it was the mess that comes of life, not of desolation. It was preferable to the charnel-chamber in which she was standing now, and the light in it was soft and large, as from some gracious, noble opening.

He stopped singing, and cried "Where is Perfetta?"

His back was turned, and he was lighting a cigar. He was not speaking to Miss Abbott. He could not even be expecting her. The vista of the landing and the two open doors made him both remote and significant, like an actor on the stage, intimate and unapproachable at the same time. She could no more call out to him than if he was Hamlet.

"You know!" he continued, "but you will not tell me. Exactly like you." He reclined on the table and blew a fat smoke-ring. "And why won't you tell me the numbers? I have dreamt of a red hen—that is two hundred and five, and a friend unexpected—he means eighty-two. But I try for the Terno this week. So tell me another number."

Miss Abbott did not know of the Tombola. His speech terrified her. She felt those subtle restrictions which come upon us in fatigue. Had she slept well she would have greeted him as soon as she saw him. Now it was impossible. He had got into another world.

She watched his smoke-ring. The air had carried it slowly away from him, and brought it out intact upon the landing.

"Two hundred and five—eighty-two. In any case I shall put them on Bari, not on Florence. I cannot tell you why; I have a feeling this week for Bari." Again she tried to speak. But the ring mesmerized her. It had become vast and elliptical, and floated in at the reception-room door.

"Ah! you don't care if you get the profits. You won't even say 'Thank you, Gino.' Say it, or I'll drop hot, red-hot ashes on you. 'Thank you, Gino—'"

The ring had extended its pale blue coils towards her. She lost self-control. It enveloped her. As if it was a breath from the pit, she screamed.

There he was, wanting to know what had frightened her, how she had got here, why she had never spoken. He made her sit down. He brought her wine, which she refused. She had not one word to say to him.

"What is it?" he repeated. "What has frightened you?"

He, too, was frightened, and perspiration came starting through the tan. For it is a serious thing to have been watched. We all radiate something curiously intimate when we believe ourselves to be alone.

"Business—" she said at last.

"Business with me?"

"Most important business." She was lying, white and limp, in the dusty chair.

"Before business you must get well; this is the best wine."

She refused it feebly. He poured out a glass. She drank it. As she did so she became self-conscious. However important the business, it was not proper of her to have called on him, or to accept his hospitality.

"Perhaps you are engaged," she said. "And as I am not very well—"

"You are not well enough to go back. And I am not engaged."

She looked nervously at the other room.

"Ah, now I understand," he exclaimed. "Now I see what frightened you. But why did you never speak?" And taking her into the room where he lived, he pointed to—the baby.

She had thought so much about this baby, of its welfare, its soul, its morals, its probable defects. But, like most unmarried people, she had only thought of it as a word—just as the healthy man only thinks of the word death, not of death itself. The real thing, lying asleep on a dirty rug, disconcerted her. It did not stand for a principle any longer. It was so much flesh and blood, so many inches and ounces of life—a glorious, unquestionable fact, which a man and another woman had given to the world. You could talk to it; in time it would answer you; in time it would not answer you unless it chose, but would secrete, within the compass of its body, thoughts and wonderful passions of its own. And this was the machine on which she and Mrs. Herriton and Philip and Harriet had for the last month been exercising their various ideals—had determined that in time it should move this way or that way, should accomplish this and not that. It was to be Low Church, it was to be high-principled, it was to be tactful, gentlemanly, artistic—excellent things all. Yet now that she saw this baby, lying asleep on a dirty rug, she had a great disposition not to dictate one of them, and to exert no more influence than there may be in a kiss or in the vaguest of the heartfelt prayers.

But she had practised self-discipline, and her thoughts and actions were not yet to correspond. To recover her self-esteem she tried to imagine that she was in her district, and to behave accordingly.

"What a fine child, Signor Carella. And how nice of you to talk to it. Though I see that the ungrateful little fellow is asleep! Seven months? No, eight; of course eight. Still, he is a remarkably fine child for his age."

Italian is a bad medium for condescension. The patronizing words came out gracious and sincere, and he smiled with pleasure.

"You must not stand. Let us sit on the loggia, where it is cool. I am afraid the room is very untidy," he added, with the air of a hostess who apologizes for a stray thread on the drawing-room carpet. Miss Abbott picked her way to the chair. He sat near her, astride the parapet, with one foot in the loggia and the other dangling into the view. His face was in profile, and its beautiful contours drove artfully against the misty green of the opposing hills. "Posing!" said Miss Abbott to herself. "A born artist's model."

"Mr. Herriton called yesterday," she began, "but you were out."

He started an elaborate and graceful explanation. He had gone for the day to Poggibonsi. Why had the Herritons not written to him, so that he could have received them properly? Poggibonsi would have done any day; not but what his business there was fairly important. What did she suppose that it was?

Naturally she was not greatly interested. She had not come from Sawston to guess why he had been to Poggibonsi. She answered politely that she had no idea, and returned to her mission.

"But guess!" he persisted, clapping the balustrade between his hands.

She suggested, with gentle sarcasm, that perhaps he had gone to Poggibonsi to find something to do.

He intimated that it was not as important as all that. Something to do—an almost hopeless quest! "E manca questo!" He rubbed his thumb and forefinger together, to indicate that he had no money. Then he sighed, and blew another smoke-ring. Miss Abbott took heart and turned diplomatic.

"This house," she said, "is a large house."

"Exactly," was his gloomy reply. "And when my poor wife died—" He got up, went in, and walked across the landing to the reception-room door, which he closed reverently. Then he shut the door of the living-room with his foot, returned briskly to his seat, and continued his sentence. "When my poor wife died I thought of having my relatives to live here. My father wished to give up his practice at Empoli; my mother and sisters and two aunts were also willing. But it was impossible. They have their ways of doing things, and when I was younger I was content with them. But now I am a man. I have my own ways. Do you understand?"

"Yes, I do," said Miss Abbott, thinking of her own dear father, whose tricks and habits, after twenty-five years spent in their company, were beginning to get on her nerves. She remembered, though, that she was not here to sympathize with

Gino—at all events, not to show that she sympathized. She also reminded herself that he was not worthy of sympathy. "It is a large house," she repeated.

"Immense; and the taxes! But it will be better when—Ah! but you have never guessed why I went to Poggibonsi—why it was that I was out when he called."

"I cannot guess, Signor Carella. I am here on business."

"But try."

"I cannot; I hardly know you."

"But we are old friends," he said, "and your approval will be grateful to me. You gave it me once before. Will you give it now?"

"I have not come as a friend this time," she answered stiffly. "I am not likely, Signor Carella, to approve of anything you do."

"Oh, Signorina!" He laughed, as if he found her piquant and amusing. "Surely you approve of marriage?"

"Where there is love," said Miss Abbott, looking at him hard. His face had altered in the last year, but not for the worse, which was baffling.

"Where there is love," said he, politely echoing the English view. Then he smiled on her, expecting congratulations.

"Do I understand that you are proposing to marry again?"

He nodded.

"I forbid you, then!"

He looked puzzled, but took it for some foreign banter, and laughed.

"I forbid you!" repeated Miss Abbott, and all the indignation of her sex and her nationality went thrilling through the words.

"But why?" He jumped up, frowning. His voice was squeaky and petulant, like that of a child who is suddenly forbidden a toy.

"You have ruined one woman; I forbid you to ruin another. It is not a year since Lilia died. You pretended to me the other day that you loved her. It is a lie. You wanted her money. Has this woman money too?"

"Why, yes!" he said irritably. "A little."

"And I suppose you will say that you love her."

"I shall not say it. It will be untrue. Now my poor wife—" He stopped, seeing that the comparison would involve him in difficulties. And indeed he had often found Lilia as agreeable as any one else.

Miss Abbott was furious at this final insult to her dead acquaintance. She was glad that after all she could be so angry with the boy. She glowed and throbbed; her tongue moved nimbly. At the finish, if the real business of the day had been completed, she could have swept majestically from the house. But the baby still remained, asleep on a dirty rug.

Gino was thoughtful, and stood scratching his head. He respected Miss Abbott. He wished that she would respect him. "So you do not advise me?" he said dolefully. "But why should it be a failure?"

Miss Abbott tried to remember that he was really a child still—a child with the strength and the passions of a disreputable man. "How can it succeed," she said solemnly, "where there is no love?"

"But she does love me! I forgot to tell you that."

"Indeed."

"Passionately." He laid his hand upon his own heart.

"Then God help her!"

He stamped impatiently. "Whatever I say displeases you, Signorina. God help you, for you are most unfair. You say that I ill-treated my dear wife. It is not so. I have never ill-treated any one. You complain that there is no love in this marriage. I prove that there is, and you become still more angry. What do you want? Do you suppose she will not be contented? Glad enough she is to get me, and she will do her duty well."

"Her duty!" cried Miss Abbott, with all the bitterness of which she was capable.

"Why, of course. She knows why I am marrying her."

"To succeed where Lilia failed! To be your housekeeper, your slave, you—" The words she would like to have said were too violent for her.

"To look after the baby, certainly," said he.

"The baby—?" She had forgotten it.

"It is an English marriage," he said proudly. "I do not care about the money. I am having her for my son. Did you not understand that?"

"No," said Miss Abbott, utterly bewildered. Then, for a moment, she saw light. "It is not necessary, Signor Carella. Since you are tired of the baby—"

Ever after she remembered it to her credit that she saw her mistake at once. "I don't mean that," she added quickly.

"I know," was his courteous response. "Ah, in a foreign language (and how perfectly you speak Italian) one is certain to make slips."

She looked at his face. It was apparently innocent of satire.

"You meant that we could not always be together yet, he and I. You are right. What is to be done? I cannot afford a nurse, and Perfetta is too rough. When he was ill I dare not let her touch him. When he has to be washed, which happens now and then, who does it? I. I feed him, or settle what he shall have. I sleep with him and comfort him when he is unhappy in the night. No one talks, no one may sing to him but I. Do not be unfair this time; I like to do these things. But nevertheless (his voice became pathetic) they take up a great deal of time, and are not all suitable for a young man."

"Not at all suitable," said Miss Abbott, and closed her eyes wearily. Each moment her difficulties were increasing. She wished that she was not so tired, so open to contradictory impressions. She longed for Harriet's burly obtuseness or for the soulless diplomacy of Mrs. Herriton.

"A little more wine?" asked Gino kindly.

"Oh, no, thank you! But marriage, Signor Carella, is a very serious step. Could you not manage more simply? Your relative, for example—"

"Empoli! I would as soon have him in England!"

"England, then—"

He laughed.

"He has a grandmother there, you know—Mrs. Theobald."

"He has a grandmother here. No, he is troublesome, but I must have him with me. I will not even have my father and mother too. For they would separate us," he added.

"How?"

"They would separate our thoughts."

She was silent. This cruel, vicious fellow knew of strange refinements. The horrible truth, that wicked people are capable of love, stood naked before her, and her moral being was abashed. It was her duty to rescue the baby, to save it from contagion, and she still meant to do her duty. But the comfortable sense of virtue left her. She was in the presence of something greater than right or wrong.

Forgetting that this was an interview, he had strolled back into the room, driven by the instinct she had aroused in him. "Wake up!" he cried to his baby, as if it was some grown-up friend. Then he lifted his foot and trod lightly on its stomach.

Miss Abbott cried, "Oh, take care!" She was unaccustomed to this method of awakening the young.

"He is not much longer than my boot, is he? Can you believe that in time his own boots will be as large? And that he also—"

"But ought you to treat him like that?"

He stood with one foot resting on the little body, suddenly musing, filled with the desire that his son should be like him, and should have sons like him, to people the earth. It is the strongest desire that can come to a man—if it comes to him at all—stronger even than love or the desire for personal immortality. All men vaunt it, and declare that it is theirs; but the hearts of most are set elsewhere. It is the exception who comprehends that physical and spiritual life may stream out of him for ever. Miss Abbott, for all her goodness, could not comprehend it, though such a thing is more within the comprehension of women. And when Gino pointed first to himself and then to his baby and said "father-son," she still took it as a piece of nursery prattle, and smiled mechanically.

The child, the first fruits, woke up and glared at her. Gino did not greet it, but continued the exposition of his policy.

"This woman will do exactly what I tell her. She is fond of children. She is clean; she has a pleasant voice. She is not beautiful; I cannot pretend that to you for a moment. But she is what I require."

The baby gave a piercing yell.

"Oh, do take care!" begged Miss Abbott. "You are squeezing it."

"It is nothing. If he cries silently then you may be frightened. He thinks I am going to wash him, and he is quite right."

"Wash him!" she cried. "You? Here?" The homely piece of news seemed to shatter all her plans. She had spent a long half-hour in elaborate approaches, in high moral attacks; she had neither frightened her enemy nor made him angry, nor interfered with the least detail of his domestic life.

"I had gone to the Farmacia," he continued, "and was sitting there comfortably, when suddenly I remembered that Perfetta had heated water an hour ago—over there, look, covered with a cushion. I came away at once, for really he must be washed. You must excuse me. I can put it off no longer."

"I have wasted your time," she said feebly.

He walked sternly to the loggia and drew from it a large earthenware bowl. It was dirty inside; he dusted it with a tablecloth. Then he fetched the hot water, which was in a copper pot. He poured it out. He added cold. He felt in his pocket and brought out a piccc of soap. Then he took up the baby, and, holding his cigar between his teeth, began to unwrap it. Miss Abbott turned to go.

"But why are you going? Excuse me if I wash him while we talk."

"I have nothing more to say," said Miss Abbott. All she could do now was to find Philip, confess her miserable defeat, and bid him go in her stead and prosper better. She cursed her feebleness; she longed to expose it, without apologies or tears.

"Oh, but stop a moment!" he cried. "You have not seen him yet."

"I have seen as much as I want, thank you."

The last wrapping slid off. He held out to her in his two hands a little kicking image of bronze.

"Take him!"

She would not touch the child.

"I must go at once," she cried; for the tears—the wrong tears—were hurrying to her eyes.

"Who would have believed his mother was blonde? For he is brown all over—brown every inch of him. Ah, but how beautiful he is! And he is mine; mine for ever. Even if he hates me he will be mine. He cannot help it; he is made out of me; I am his father."

It was too late to go. She could not tell why, but it was too late. She turned away her head when Gino lifted his son to his lips. This was something too remote from the prettiness of the nursery. The man was majestic; he was a part of Nature; in no ordinary love scene could he ever be so great. For a wonderful physical tie binds the parents to the children; and—by some sad, strange irony—it does not bind us children to our parents. For if it did, if we could answer their love not with gratitude but with equal love, life would lose much of its pathos and much of its squalor, and we might be wonderfully happy. Gino passionately embracing, Miss Abbott reverently averting her eyes—both of them had parents whom they did not love so very much.

"May I help you to wash him?" she asked humbly.

He gave her his son without speaking, and they knelt side by side, tucking up their sleeves. The child had stopped crying, and his arms and legs were agitated by some overpowering joy. Miss Abbott had a woman's pleasure in cleaning anything—more especially when the thing was human. She understood little babies from long experience in a district, and Gino soon ceased to give her directions, and only gave her thanks.

"It is very kind of you," he murmured, "especially in your beautiful dress. He is nearly clean already. Why, I take the whole morning! There is so much more of a baby than one expects. And Perfetta washes him just as she washes clothes. Then he screams for hours. My wife is to have a light hand. Ah, how he kicks! Has he splashed you? I am very sorry."

"I am ready for a soft towel now," said Miss Abbott, who was strangely exalted by the service.

"Certainly! certainly!" He strode in a knowing way to a cupboard. But he had no idea where the soft towel was. Generally he dabbed the baby on the first dry thing he found.

"And if you had any powder."

He struck his forehead despairingly. Apparently the stock of powder was just exhausted.

She sacrificed her own clean handkerchief. He put a chair for her on the loggia, which faced westward, and was still pleasant and cool. There she sat, with twenty miles of view behind her, and he placed the dripping baby on her knee. It shone now with health and beauty: it seemed to reflect light, like a copper vessel. Just such a baby Bellini sets languid on his mother's lap, or Signorelli flings wriggling on pavements of marble, or Lorenzo di Credi, more reverent but less divine, lays carefully among flowers, with his head upon a wisp of golden straw. For a time Gino contemplated them standing. Then, to get a better view, he knelt by the side of the chair, with his hands clasped before him.

So they were when Philip entered, and saw, to all intents and purposes, the Virgin and Child, with Donor.

"Hullo!" he exclaimed; for he was glad to find things in such cheerful trim.

She did not greet him, but rose up unsteadily and handed the baby to his father.

"No, do stop!" whispered Philip. "I got your note. I'm not offended; you're quite right. I really want you; I could never have done it alone."

No words came from her, but she raised her hands to her mouth, like one who is in sudden agony.

"Signorina, do stop a little—after all your kindness."

She burst into tears.

"What is it?" said Philip kindly.

She tried to speak, and then went away weeping bitterly.

The two men stared at each other. By a common impulse they ran on to the loggia. They were just in time to see Miss Abbott disappear among the trees.

"What is it?" asked Philip again. There was no answer, and somehow he did not want an answer. Some strange thing had happened which he could not presume to understand. He would find out from Miss Abbott, if ever he found out at all.

"Well, your business," said Gino, after a puzzled sigh.

"Our business—Miss Abbott has told you of that."

"No."

"But surely—"

"She came for business. But she forgot about it; so did I."

Perfetta, who had a genius for missing people, now returned, loudly complaining of the size of Monteriano and the intricacies of its streets. Gino told her to watch the baby. Then he offered Philip a cigar, and they proceeded to the business.

Chapter 8

"Mad!" screamed Harriet,—"absolutely stark, staring, raving mad!"

Philip judged it better not to contradict her.

"What's she here for? Answer me that. What's she doing in Monteriano in August? Why isn't she in Normandy? Answer that. She won't. I can: she's come to thwart us; she's betrayed us—got hold of mother's plans. Oh, goodness, my head!"

He was unwise enough to reply, "You mustn't accuse her of that. Though she is exasperating, she hasn't come here to betray us."

"Then why has she come here? Answer me that."

He made no answer. But fortunately his sister was too much agitated to wait for one. "Bursting in on me—crying and looking a disgusting sight—and says she has been to see the Italian. Couldn't even talk properly; pretended she had changed her opinions. What are her opinions to us? I was very calm. I said: 'Miss Abbott, I think there is a little misapprehension in this matter. My mother, Mrs. Herriton—' Oh, goodness, my head! Of course you've failed—don't trouble to answer—I know you've failed. Where's the baby, pray? Of course you haven't got it. Dear sweet Caroline won't let you. Oh, yes, and we're to go away at once and trouble the father no more. Those are her commands. Commands! COMMANDS!" And Harriet also burst into tears.

Philip governed his temper. His sister was annoying, but quite reasonable in her indignation. Moreover, Miss Abbott had behaved even worse than she supposed.

"I've not got the baby, Harriet, but at the same time I haven't exactly failed. I and Signor Carella are to have another interview this afternoon, at the Caffe Garibaldi. He is perfectly reasonable and pleasant. Should you be disposed to come with me, you would find him quite willing to discuss things. He is desperately in want of money, and has no prospect of getting any. I discovered that. At the same time, he has a certain affection for the child." For Philip's insight, or perhaps his opportunities, had not been equal to Miss Abbott's.

Harriet would only sob, and accuse her brother of insulting her; how could a lady speak to such a horrible man? That, and nothing else, was enough to stamp Caroline. Oh, poor Lilia!

Philip drummed on the bedroom window-sill. He saw no escape from the deadlock. For though he spoke cheerfully about his second interview with Gino, he felt at the bottom of his heart that it would fail. Gino was too courteous: he would not break off negotiations by sharp denial; he loved this civil, half-humorous bargaining. And he loved fooling his opponent, and did it so nicely that his opponent did not mind being fooled.

"Miss Abbott has behaved extraordinarily," he said at last; "but at the same time—"

His sister would not hear him. She burst forth again on the madness, the interference, the intolerable duplicity of Caroline.

"Harriet, you must listen. My dear, you must stop crying. I have something quite important to say."

"I shall not stop crying," said she. But in time, finding that he would not speak to her, she did stop.

"Remember that Miss Abbott has done us no harm. She said nothing to him about the matter. He assumes that she is working with us: I gathered that."

"Well, she isn't."

"Yes; but if you're careful she may be. I interpret her behaviour thus: She went to see him, honestly intending to get the child away. In the note she left me she says so, and I don't believe she'd lie."

"I do."

"When she got there, there was some pretty domestic scene between him and the baby, and she has got swept off in a gush of sentimentalism. Before very long, if I know anything about psychology, there will be a reaction. She'll be swept back."

"I don't understand your long words. Say plainly—"

"When she's swept back, she'll be invaluable. For she has made quite an impression on him. He thinks her so nice with the baby. You know, she washed it for him."

"Disgusting!"

Harriet's ejaculations were more aggravating than the rest of her. But Philip was averse to losing his temper. The access of joy that had come to him yesterday in the theatre promised to be permanent. He was more anxious than heretofore to be charitable towards the world.

"If you want to carry off the baby, keep your peace with Miss Abbott. For if she chooses, she can help you better than I can."

"There can be no peace between me and her," said Harriet gloomily.

"Did you—"

"Oh, not all I wanted. She went away before I had finished speaking—just like those cowardly people!—into the church."

"Into Santa Deodata's?"

"Yes; I'm sure she needs it. Anything more unchristian—"

In time Philip went to the church also, leaving his sister a little calmer and a little disposed to think over his advice. What had come over Miss Abbott? He had always thought her both stable and sincere. That conversation he had had with her last Christmas in the train to Charing Cross—that alone furnished him with a parallel. For the second time, Monteriano must have turned her head. He was not angry with her, for he was quite indifferent to the outcome of their expedition. He was only extremely interested.

It was now nearly midday, and the streets were clearing. But the intense heat had broken, and there was a pleasant suggestion of rain. The Piazza, with its three great attractions—the Palazzo Pubblico, the Collegiate Church, and the Caffe Garibaldi: the intellect, the soul, and the body—had never looked more charming. For a moment Philip stood in its centre, much inclined to be dreamy, and thinking how wonderful it must feel to belong to a city, however mean. He was here, however, as an emissary of civilization and as a student of character, and, after a sigh, he entered Santa Deodata's to continue his mission.

There had been a FESTA two days before, and the church still smelt of incense and of garlic. The little son of the sacristan was sweeping the nave, more for amusement than for cleanliness, sending great clouds of dust over the frescoes and the scattered worshippers. The sacristan himself had propped a ladder in the centre of the Deluge—which fills one of the nave spandrels—and was freeing a column from its wealth of scarlet calico. Much scarlet calico also lay upon the floor—for the church can look as fine as any theatre—and the sacristan's little daughter was trying to fold it up. She was wearing a tinsel crown. The crown really belonged to St. Augustine. But it had been cut too big: it fell down over his cheeks like a collar: you never saw anything so absurd. One of the canons had unhooked it just before the FIESTA began, and had given it to the sacristan's daughter.

"Please," cried Philip, "is there an English lady here?"

The man's mouth was full of tin-tacks, but he nodded cheerfully towards a kneeling figure. In the midst of this confusion Miss Abbott was praying.

He was not much surprised: a spiritual breakdown was quite to be expected. For though he was growing more charitable towards mankind, he was still a little jaunty, and too apt to stake out beforehand the course that will be pursued by the wounded soul. It did not surprise him, however, that she should greet him naturally, with none of the sour self-consciousness of a person who had just risen from her knees. This was indeed the spirit of Santa Deodata's, where a prayer to God is thought none the worse of because it comes next to a pleasant word to a neighbour. "I am sure that I need it," said she; and he, who had expected her to be ashamed, became confused, and knew not what to reply.

"I've nothing to tell you," she continued. "I have simply changed straight round. If I had planned the whole thing out, I could not have treated you worse. I can talk it over now; but please believe that I have been crying."

"And please believe that I have not come to scold you," said Philip. "I know what has happened."

"What?" asked Miss Abbott. Instinctively she led the way to the famous chapel, the fifth chapel on the right, wherein Giovanni da Empoli has painted the death and burial of the saint. Here they could sit out of the dust and the noise, and proceed with a discussion which promised to be important.

"What might have happened to me—he had made you believe that he loved the child."

"Oh, yes; he has. He will never give it up."

"At present it is still unsettled."

"It will never be settled."

"Perhaps not. Well, as I said, I know what has happened, and I am not here to scold you. But I must ask you to withdraw from the thing for the present. Harriet is furious. But she will calm down when she realizes that you have done us no harm, and will do none."

"I can do no more," she said. "But I tell you plainly I have changed sides."

"If you do no more, that is all we want. You promise not to prejudice our cause by speaking to Signor Carella?"

"Oh, certainly. I don't want to speak to him again; I shan't ever see him again."

"Quite nice, wasn't he?"

"Quite."

"Well, that's all I wanted to know. I'll go and tell Harriet of your promise, and I think things'll quiet down now."

But he did not move, for it was an increasing pleasure to him to be near her, and her charm was at its strongest today. He thought less of psychology and feminine reaction. The gush of sentimentalism which had carried her away had only made her more alluring. He was content to observe her beauty and to profit by the tenderness and the wisdom that dwelt within her.

"Why aren't you angry with me?" she asked, after a pause.

"Because I understand you—all sides, I think,—Harriet, Signor Carella, even my mother."

"You do understand wonderfully. You are the only one of us who has a general view of the muddle."

He smiled with pleasure. It was the first time she had ever praised him. His eyes rested agreeably on Santa Deodata, who was dying in full sanctity, upon her back. There was a window open behind her, revealing just such a view as he had seen that morning, and on her widowed mother's dresser there stood just such another copper pot. The saint looked neither at the view nor at the pot, and at her widowed mother still less. For lo! she had a vision: the head and shoulders of St. Augustine were sliding like some miraculous enamel along the rough-cast wall. It is a gentle saint who is content with half another saint to see her die. In her death, as in her life, Santa Deodata did not accomplish much.

"So what are you going to do?" said Miss Abbott.

Philip started, not so much at the words as at the sudden change in the voice. "Do?" he echoed, rather dismayed. "This afternoon I have another interview."

"It will come to nothing. Well?"

"Then another. If that fails I shall wire home for instructions. I dare say we may fail altogether, but we shall fail honourably."

She had often been decided. But now behind her decision there was a note of passion. She struck him not as different, but as more important, and he minded it very much when she said—

"That's not doing anything! You would be doing something if you kidnapped the baby, or if you went straight away. But that! To fail honourably! To come out of the thing as well as you can! Is that all you are after?"

"Why, yes," he stammered. "Since we talk openly, that is all I am after just now. What else is there? If I can persuade Signor Carella to give in, so much the better. If he won't, I must report the failure to my mother and then go home. Why, Miss Abbott, you can't expect me to follow you through all these turns—"

"I don't! But I do expect you to settle what is right and to follow that. Do you want the child to stop with his father, who loves him and will bring him up badly, or do you want him to come to Sawston, where no one loves him, but where he will be brought up well? There is the question put dispassionately enough even for you. Settle it. Settle which side you'll fight on. But don't go talking about an 'honourable failure,' which means simply not thinking and not acting at all."

"Because I understand the position of Signor Carella and of you, it's no reason that—"

"None at all. Fight as if you think us wrong. Oh, what's the use of your fair-mindedness if you never decide for yourself? Any one gets hold of you and makes you do what they want. And you see through them and laugh at them—and do it. It's not enough to see clearly; I'm muddle-headed and stupid, and not worth a quarter of you, but I have tried to do what seemed right at the time. And you—your brain and your insight are splendid. But when you see what's right you're too idle to do it. You told me once that we shall be judged by our intentions, not by our accomplishments. I thought it a grand remark. But we must intend to accomplish—not sit intending on a chair."

"You are wonderful!" he said gravely.

"Oh, you appreciate me!" she burst out again. "I wish you didn't. You appreciate us all—see good in all of us. And all the time you are dead—dead—dead. Look, why aren't you angry?" She came up to him, and then her mood suddenly changed, and she took hold of both his hands. "You are so splendid, Mr. Herriton, that I can't bear to see you wasted. I can't bear—she has not been good to you—your mother."

"Miss Abbott, don't worry over me. Some people are born not to do things. I'm one of them; I never did anything at school or at the Bar. I came out to stop Lilia's marriage, and it was too late. I came out intending to get the baby, and I shall return an 'honourable failure.' I never expect anything to happen now, and so I am never disappointed. You would be surprised to know what my great events are. Going to the theatre yesterday, talking to you now—I don't suppose I shall ever meet anything greater. I seem fated to pass through the world without colliding with it or moving it—and I'm sure I can't tell you whether the fate's good or evil. I don't die—I don't fall in love. And if other people die or fall in love they always do it when I'm just not there. You are quite right; life to me is just a spectacle, which—thank God, and thank Italy, and thank you—is now more beautiful and heartening than it has ever been before."

She said solemnly, "I wish something would happen to you, my dear friend; I wish something would happen to you."

"But why?" he asked, smiling. "Prove to me why I don't do as I am."

She also smiled, very gravely. She could not prove it. No argument existed. Their discourse, splendid as it had been, resulted in nothing, and their respective opinions and policies were exactly the same when they left the church as when they had entered it.

Harriet was rude at lunch. She called Miss Abbott a turncoat and a coward to her face. Miss Abbott resented neither epithet, feeling that one was justified and the other not unreasonable. She tried to avoid even the suspicion of satire in her replies. But Harriet was sure that she was satirical because she was so calm. She got more and more violent, and Philip at one time feared that she would come to blows.

"Look here!" he cried, with something of the old manner, "it's too hot for this. We've been talking and interviewing each other all the morning, and I have another interview this afternoon. I do stipulate for silence. Let each lady retire to her bedroom with a book."

"I retire to pack," said Harriet. "Please remind Signor Carella, Philip, that the baby is to be here by half-past eight this evening."

"Oh, certainly, Harriet. I shall make a point of reminding him."

"And order a carriage to take us to the evening train."

"And please," said Miss Abbott, "would you order a carriage for me too?"

"You going?" he exclaimed.

"Of course," she replied, suddenly flushing. "Why not?"

"Why, of course you would be going. Two carriages, then. Two carriages for the evening train." He looked at his sister hopelessly. "Harriet, whatever are you up to? We shall never be ready."

"Order my carriage for the evening train," said Harriet, and departed.

"Well, I suppose I shall. And I shall also have my interview with Signor Carella."

Miss Abbott gave a little sigh.

"But why should you mind? Do you suppose that I shall have the slightest influence over him?"

"No. But—I can't repeat all that I said in the church. You ought never to see him again. You ought to bundle Harriet into a carriage, not this evening, but now, and drive her straight away."

"Perhaps I ought. But it isn't a very big 'ought.' Whatever Harriet and I do the issue is the same. Why, I can see the splendour of it—even the humour. Gino sitting up here on the mountain-top with his cub. We come and ask for it. He welcomes us. We ask for it again. He is equally pleasant. I'm agreeable to spend the whole week bargaining with him. But I know that at the end of it I shall descend empty-handed to the plains. It might be finer of me to make up my mind. But I'm not a fine character. And nothing hangs on it."

"Perhaps I am extreme," she said humbly. "I've been trying to run you, just like your mother. I feel you ought to fight it out with Harriet. Every little trifle, for some reason, does seem incalculably important today, and when you say of a thing that 'nothing hangs on it,' it sounds like blasphemy. There's never any knowing—(how am I to put it?)—which of our actions, which of our idlenesses won't have things hanging on it for ever."

He assented, but her remark had only an aesthetic value. He was not prepared to take it to his heart. All the afternoon he rested—worried, but not exactly despondent. The thing would jog out somehow. Probably Miss Abbott was right. The baby had better stop where it was loved. And that, probably, was what the fates had decreed. He felt little interest in the matter, and he was sure that he had no influence.

It was not surprising, therefore, that the interview at the Caffe Garibaldi came to nothing. Neither of them took it very seriously. And before long Gino had discovered how things lay, and was ragging his companion hopelessly. Philip tried to look offended, but in the end he had to laugh. "Well, you are right," he said. "This affair is being managed by the ladies."

"Ah, the ladies—the ladies!" cried the other, and then he roared like a millionaire for two cups of black coffee, and insisted on treating his friend, as a sign that their strife was over.

"Well, I have done my best," said Philip, dipping a long slice of sugar into his cup, and watching the brown liquid ascend into it. "I shall face my mother with a good conscience. Will you bear me witness that I've done my best?"

"My poor fellow, I will!" He laid a sympathetic hand on Philip's knee.

"And that I have—" The sugar was now impregnated with coffee, and he bent forward to swallow it. As he did so his eyes swept the opposite of the Piazza, and he saw there, watching them, Harriet. "Mia sorella!" he exclaimed. Gino, much amused, laid his hand upon the little table, and beat the marble humorously with his fists. Harriet turned away and began gloomily to inspect the Palazzo Pubblico.

"Poor Harriet!" said Philip, swallowing the sugar. "One more wrench and it will all be over for her; we are leaving this evening."

Gino was sorry for this. "Then you will not be here this evening as you promised us. All three leaving?"

"All three," said Philip, who had not revealed the secession of Miss Abbott; "by the night train; at least, that is my sister's plan. So I'm afraid I shan't be here."

They watched the departing figure of Harriet, and then entered upon the final civilities. They shook each other warmly by both hands. Philip was to come again next year, and to write beforehand. He was to be introduced to Gino's wife, for he was told of the marriage now. He was to be godfather to his next baby. As for Gino, he would remember some time that Philip liked vermouth. He begged him to give his love to Irma. Mrs. Herriton—should he send her his sympathetic regards? No; perhaps that would hardly do.

So the two young men parted with a good deal of genuine affection. For the barrier of language is sometimes a blessed barrier, which only lets pass what is good. Or—to put the thing less cynically—we may be better in new clean words, which have never been tainted by our pettiness or vice. Philip, at all events, lived more graciously in Italian, the very phrases of which entice one to be happy and kind. It was horrible to think of the English of Harriet, whose every word would be as hard, as distinct, and as unfinished as a lump of coal.

Harriet, however, talked little. She had seen enough to know that her brother had failed again, and with unwonted dignity she accepted the situation. She did her packing, she wrote up her diary, she made a brown paper cover for the new Baedeker. Philip, finding her so amenable, tried to discuss their future plans. But she only said that they would sleep in Florence, and told him to telegraph for rooms. They had supper alone. Miss Abbott did not come down. The landlady told them that Signor Carella had called on Miss Abbott to say good-bye, but she, though in, had not been able to see him. She also told them that it had begun to rain. Harriet sighed, but indicated to her brother that he was not responsible.

The carriages came round at a quarter past eight. It was not raining much, but the night was extraordinarily dark, and one of the drivers wanted to go slowly to the station. Miss Abbott came down and said that she was ready, and would start at once.

"Yes, do," said Philip, who was standing in the hall. "Now that we have quarrelled we scarcely want to travel in procession all the way down the hill. Well, good-bye; it's all over at last; another scene in my pageant has shifted."

"Good-bye; it's been a great pleasure to see you. I hope that won't shift, at all events." She gripped his hand.

"You sound despondent," he said, laughing. "Don't forget that you return victorious."

"I suppose I do," she replied, more despondently than ever, and got into the carriage. He concluded that she was thinking of her reception at Sawston, whither her fame would doubtless precede her. Whatever would Mrs. Herriton do? She could make things quite unpleasant when she thought it right. She might think it right to be silent, but then there was Harriet. Who would bridle Harriet's tongue? Between the two of them Miss Abbott was bound to have a bad time. Her reputation, both for consistency and for moral enthusiasm, would be lost for ever.

"It's hard luck on her," he thought. "She is a good person. I must do for her anything I can." Their intimacy had been very rapid, but he too hoped that it would not shift. He believed that he understood her, and that she, by now, had seen the worst of him. What if after a long time—if after all—he flushed like a boy as he looked after her carriage.

He went into the dining-room to look for Harriet. Harriet was not to be found. Her bedroom, too, was empty. All that was left of her was the purple prayer-book which lay open on the bed. Philip took it up aimlessly, and saw—"Blessed be the Lord my God who teacheth my hands to war and my fingers to fight." He put the book in his pocket, and began to brood over more profitable themes.

Chapter 8

Santa Deodata gave out half past eight. All the luggage was on, and still Harriet had not appeared. "Depend upon it," said the landlady, "she has gone to Signor Carella's to say good-bye to her little nephew." Philip did not think it likely. They shouted all over the house and still there was no Harriet. He began to be uneasy. He was helpless without Miss Abbott; her grave, kind face had cheered him wonderfully, even when it looked displeased. Monteriano was sad without her; the rain was thickening; the scraps of Donizetti floated tunelessly out of the wineshops, and of the great tower opposite he could only see the base, fresh papered with the advertisements of quacks.

A man came up the street with a note. Philip read, "Start at once. Pick me up outside the gate. Pay the bearer. H. H."

"Did the lady give you this note?" he cried.

The man was unintelligible.

"Speak up!" exclaimed Philip. "Who gave it you—and where?"

Nothing but horrible sighings and bubblings came out of the man.

"Be patient with him," said the driver, turning round on the box. "It is the poor idiot." And the landlady came out of the hotel and echoed "The poor idiot. He cannot speak. He takes messages for us all."

Philip then saw that the messenger was a ghastly creature, quite bald, with trickling eyes and grey twitching nose. In another country he would have been shut up; here he was accepted as a public institution, and part of Nature's scheme.

"Ugh!" shuddered the Englishman. "Signora padrona, find out from him; this note is from my sister. What does it mean? Where did he see her?"

"It is no good," said the landlady. "He understands everything but he can explain nothing."

"He has visions of the saints," said the man who drove the cab.

"But my sister—where has she gone? How has she met him?"

"She has gone for a walk," asserted the landlady. It was a nasty evening, but she was beginning to understand the English. "She has gone for a walk—perhaps to wish good-bye to her little nephew. Preferring to come back another way, she has sent you this note by the poor idiot and is waiting for you outside the Siena gate. Many of my guests do this."

There was nothing to do but to obey the message. He shook hands with the landlady, gave the messenger a nickel piece, and drove away. After a dozen yards the carriage stopped. The poor idiot was running and whimpering behind.

"Go on," cried Philip. "I have paid him plenty."

A horrible hand pushed three soldi into his lap. It was part of the idiot's malady only to receive what was just for his services. This was the change out of the nickel piece.

"Go on!" shouted Philip, and flung the money into the road. He was frightened at the episode; the whole of life had become unreal. It was a relief to be out of the Siena gate. They drew up for a moment on the terrace. But there was no sign of Harriet. The driver called to the Dogana men. But they had seen no English lady pass.

"What am I to do?" he cried; "it is not like the lady to be late. We shall miss the train."

"Let us drive slowly," said the driver, "and you shall call her by name as we go."

So they started down into the night, Philip calling "Harriet! Harriet! Harriet!" And there she was, waiting for them in the wet, at the first turn of the zigzag.

"Harriet, why don't you answer?"

"I heard you coming," said she, and got quickly in. Not till then did he see that she carried a bundle.

"What's that?"

"Hush—"

"Whatever is that?"

"Hush—sleeping."

Harriet had succeeded where Miss Abbott and Philip had failed. It was the baby.

She would not let him talk. The baby, she repeated, was asleep, and she put up an umbrella to shield it and her from the rain. He should hear all later, so he had to conjecture the course of the wonderful interview—an interview between the South pole and the North. It was quite easy to conjecture: Gino crumpling up suddenly before the intense conviction of Harriet; being told, perhaps, to his face that he was a villain; yielding his only son perhaps for money, perhaps for nothing. "Poor Gino," he thought. "He's no greater than I am, after all."

Then he thought of Miss Abbott, whose carriage must be descending the darkness some mile or two below them, and his easy self-accusation failed. She, too, had conviction; he had felt its force; he would feel it again when she knew this day's sombre and unexpected close.

"You have been pretty secret," he said; "you might tell me a little now. What do we pay for him? All we've got?"

"Hush!" answered Harriet, and dandled the bundle laboriously, like some bony prophetess—Judith, or Deborah, or Jael. He had last seen the baby sprawling on the knees of Miss Abbott, shining and naked, with twenty miles of view behind him, and his father kneeling by his feet. And that remembrance, together with Harriet, and the darkness, and the poor idiot, and the silent rain, filled him with sorrow and with the expectation of sorrow to come.

Monteriano had long disappeared, and he could see nothing but the occasional wet stem of an olive, which their lamp illumined as they passed it. They travelled quickly, for this driver did not care how fast he went to the station, and would dash down each incline and scuttle perilously round the curves.

"Look here, Harriet," he said at last, "I feel bad; I want to see the baby."

"Hush!"

"I don't mind if I do wake him up. I want to see him. I've as much right in him as you."

Harriet gave in. But it was too dark for him to see the child's face. "Wait a minute," he whispered, and before she could stop him he had lit a match under the shelter of her umbrella. "But he's awake!" he exclaimed. The match went out.

"Good ickle quiet boysey, then."

Philip winced. "His face, do you know, struck me as all wrong."

"All wrong?"

"All puckered queerly."

"Of course—with the shadows—you couldn't see him."

"Well, hold him up again." She did so. He lit another match. It went out quickly, but not before he had seen that the baby was crying.

"Nonsense," said Harriet sharply. "We should hear him if he cried."

"No, he's crying hard; I thought so before, and I'm certain now."

Harriet touched the child's face. It was bathed in tears. "Oh, the night air, I suppose," she said, "or perhaps the wet of the rain."

"I say, you haven't hurt it, or held it the wrong way, or anything; it is too uncanny—crying and no noise. Why didn't you get Perfetta to carry it to the hotel instead of muddling with the messenger? It's a marvel he understood about the note."

"Oh, he understands." And he could feel her shudder. "He tried to carry the baby—"

"But why not Gino or Perfetta?"

"Philip, don't talk. Must I say it again? Don't talk. The baby wants to sleep." She crooned harshly as they descended, and now and then she wiped up the tears which welled inexhaustibly from the little eyes. Philip looked away, winking at times himself. It was as if they were travelling with the whole world's sorrow, as if all the mystery, all the persistency of woe were gathered to a single fount. The roads were now coated with mud, and the carriage went more quietly but not less swiftly, sliding by long zigzags into the night. He knew the landmarks pretty well: here was the crossroad to Poggibonsi; and the last view of Monteriano, if they had light, would be from here. Soon they ought to come to that little wood where violets were so plentiful in spring. He wished the weather had not changed; it was not cold, but the air was extraordinarily damp. It could not be good for the child.

"I suppose he breathes, and all that sort of thing?" he said.

"Of course," said Harriet, in an angry whisper. "You've started him again. I'm certain he was asleep. I do wish you wouldn't talk; it makes me so nervous."

"I'm nervous too. I wish he'd scream. It's too uncanny. Poor Gino! I'm terribly sorry for Gino."

"Are you?"

"Because he's weak—like most of us. He doesn't know what he wants. He doesn't grip on to life. But I like that man, and I'm sorry for him."

Naturally enough she made no answer.

"You despise him, Harriet, and you despise me. But you do us no good by it. We fools want some one to set us on our feet. Suppose a really decent woman had set up Gino—I believe Caroline Abbott might have done it—mightn't he have been another man?"

"Philip," she interrupted, with an attempt at nonchalance, "do you happen to have those matches handy? We might as well look at the baby again if you have."

The first match blew out immediately. So did the second. He suggested that they should stop the carriage and borrow the lamp from the driver.

"Oh, I don't want all that bother. Try again."

They entered the little wood as he tried to strike the third match. At last it caught. Harriet poised the umbrella rightly, and for a full quarter minute they contemplated the face that trembled in the light of the trembling flame. Then there was a shout and a crash. They were lying in the mud in darkness. The carriage had overturned.

Philip was a good deal hurt. He sat up and rocked himself to and fro, holding his arm. He could just make out the outline of the carriage above him, and the outlines of the carriage cushions and of their luggage upon the grey road. The accident had taken place in the wood, where it was even darker than in the open.

"Are you all right?" he managed to say. Harriet was screaming, the horse was kicking, the driver was cursing some other man.

Harriet's screams became coherent. "The baby—the baby—it slipped—it's gone from my arms—I stole it!"

"God help me!" said Philip. A cold circle came round his mouth, and, he fainted.

When he recovered it was still the same confusion. The horse was kicking, the baby had not been found, and Harriet still screamed like a maniac, "I stole it! I stole it! I stole it! It slipped out of my arms!"

"Keep still!" he commanded the driver. "Let no one move. We may tread on it. Keep still."

For a moment they all obeyed him. He began to crawl through the mud, touching first this, then that, grasping the cushions by mistake, listening for the faintest whisper that might guide him. He tried to light a match, holding the box in his teeth and striking at it with the uninjured hand. At last he succeeded, and the light fell upon the bundle which he was seeking.

It had rolled off the road into the wood a little way, and had fallen across a great rut. So tiny it was that had it fallen lengthways it would have disappeared, and he might never have found it.

"I stole it! I and the idiot—no one was there." She burst out laughing.

He sat down and laid it on his knee. Then he tried to cleanse the face from the mud and the rain and the tears. His arm, he supposed, was broken, but he could still move it a little, and for the moment he forgot all pain. He was listening—not for a cry, but for the tick of a heart or the slightest tremor of breath.

"Where are you?" called a voice. It was Miss Abbott, against whose carriage they had collided. She had relit one of the lamps, and was picking her way towards him.

"Silence!" he called again, and again they obeyed. He shook the bundle; he breathed into it; he opened his coat and pressed it against him. Then he listened, and heard nothing but the rain and the panting horses, and Harriet, who was somewhere chuckling to herself in the dark.

Miss Abbott approached, and took it gently from him. The face was already chilly, but thanks to Philip it was no longer wet. Nor would it again be wetted by any tear.

Chapter 9

The details of Harriet's crime were never known. In her illness she spoke more of the inlaid box that she lent to Lilia—lent, not given—than of recent troubles. It was clear that she had gone prepared for an interview with Gino, and finding him out, she had yielded to a grotesque temptation. But how far this was the result of ill-temper, to what extent she had been fortified by her religion, when and how she had met the poor idiot—these questions were never answered, nor did they interest Philip greatly. Detection was certain: they would have been arrested by the police of Florence or Milan, or at the frontier. As it was, they had been stopped in a simpler manner a few miles out of the town.

As yet he could scarcely survey the thing. It was too great. Round the Italian baby who had died in the mud there centred deep passions and high hopes. People had been wicked or wrong in the matter; no one save himself had been trivial. Now the baby had gone, but there remained this vast apparatus of pride and pity and love. For the dead, who seemed to take away so much, really take with them nothing that is ours. The passion they have aroused lives after them, easy to transmute or to transfer, but well-nigh impossible to destroy. And Philip knew that he was still voyaging on the same magnificent, perilous sea, with the sun or the clouds above him, and the tides below.

The course of the moment—that, at all events, was certain. He and no one else must take the news to Gino. It was easy to talk of Harriet's crime—easy also to blame the negligent Perfetta or Mrs. Herriton at home. Every one had contributed—even Miss Abbott and Irma. If one chose, one might consider the catastrophe composite or the work of fate. But Philip did not so choose. It was his own fault, due to acknowledged weakness in his own character. Therefore he, and no one else, must take the news of it to Gino.

Nothing prevented him. Miss Abbott was engaged with Harriet, and people had sprung out of the darkness and were conducting them towards some cottage. Philip had only to get into the uninjured carriage and order the driver to return. He was back at Monteriano after a two hours' absence. Perfetta was in the house now, and greeted him cheerfully. Pain, physical and mental, had made him stupid. It was some time before he realized that she had never missed the child.

Chapter 9

Gino was still out. The woman took him to the reception-room, just as she had taken Miss Abbott in the morning, and dusted a circle for him on one of the horsehair chairs. But it was dark now, so she left the guest a little lamp.

"I will be as quick as I can," she told him. "But there are many streets in Monteriano; he is sometimes difficult to find. I could not find him this morning."

"Go first to the Caffe Garibaldi," said Philip, remembering that this was the hour appointed by his friends of yesterday.

He occupied the time he was left alone not in thinking—there was nothing to think about; he simply had to tell a few facts—but in trying to make a sling for his broken arm. The trouble was in the elbow-joint, and as long as he kept this motionless he could go on as usual. But inflammation was beginning, and the slight-slightest jar gave him agony. The sling was not fitted before Gino leapt up the stairs, crying—

"So you are back! How glad I am! We are all waiting—"

Philip had seen too much to be nervous. In low, even tones he told what had happened; and the other, also perfectly calm, heard him to the end. In the silence Perfetta called up that she had forgotten the baby's evening milk; she must fetch it. When she had gone Gino took up the lamp without a word, and they went into the other room.

"My sister is ill," said Philip, "and Miss Abbott is guiltless. I should be glad if you did not have to trouble them."

Gino had stooped down by the way, and was feeling the place where his son had lain. Now and then he frowned a little and glanced at Philip.

"It is through me," he continued. "It happened because I was cowardly and idle. I have come to know what you will do."

Gino had left the rug, and began to pat the table from the end, as if he was blind. The action was so uncanny that Philip was driven to intervene.

"Gently, man, gently; he is not here."

He went up and touched him on the shoulder.

He twitched away, and began to pass his hands over things more rapidly—over the table, the chairs, the entire floor, the walls as high as he could reach them. Philip had not presumed to comfort him. But now the tension was too great—he tried.

"Break down, Gino; you must break down. Scream and curse and give in for a little; you must break down."

There was no reply, and no cessation of the sweeping hands.

"It is time to be unhappy. Break down or you will be ill like my sister. You will go—"

The tour of the room was over. He had touched everything in it except Philip. Now he approached him. He face was that of a man who has lost his old reason for life and seeks a new one.

"Gino!"

He stopped for a moment; then he came nearer. Philip stood his ground.

"You are to do what you like with me, Gino. Your son is dead, Gino. He died in my arms, remember. It does not excuse me; but he did die in my arms."

The left hand came forward, slowly this time. It hovered before Philip like an insect. Then it descended and gripped him by his broken elbow.

Philip struck out with all the strength of his other arm. Gino fell to the blow without a cry or a word.

"You brute!" exclaimed the Englishman. "Kill me if you like! But just you leave my broken arm alone."

Then he was seized with remorse, and knelt beside his adversary and tried to revive him. He managed to raise him up, and propped his body against his own. He passed his arm round him. Again he was filled with pity and tenderness. He awaited the revival without fear, sure that both of them were safe at last.

Gino recovered suddenly. His lips moved. For one blessed moment it seemed that he was going to speak. But he scrambled up in silence, remembering everything, and he made not towards Philip, but towards the lamp.

"Do what you like; but think first—"

The lamp was tossed across the room, out through the loggia. It broke against one of the trees below. Philip began to cry out in the dark.

Gino approached from behind and gave him a sharp pinch. Philip spun round with a yell. He had only been pinched on the back, but he knew what was in store for him. He struck out, exhorting the devil to fight him, to kill him, to do anything but this. Then he stumbled to the door. It was open. He lost his head, and, instead of turning down the stairs, he ran across the landing into the room opposite. There he lay down on the floor between the stove and the skirting-board.

His senses grew sharper. He could hear Gino coming in on tiptoe. He even knew what was passing in his mind, how now he was at fault, now he was hopeful, now he was wondering whether after all the victim had not escaped down the stairs. There was a quick swoop above him, and then a low growl like a dog's. Gino had broken his finger-nails against the stove.

Physical pain is almost too terrible to bear. We can just bear it when it comes by accident or for our good—as it generally does in modern life—except at school. But when it is caused by the malignity of a man, full grown, fashioned like ourselves, all our control disappears. Philip's one thought was to get away from that room at whatever sacrifice of nobility or pride.

Gino was now at the further end of the room, groping by the little tables. Suddenly the instinct came to him. He crawled quickly to where Philip lay and had him clean by the elbow.

The whole arm seemed red-hot, and the broken bone grated in the joint, sending out shoots of the essence of pain. His other arm was pinioned against the wall, and Gino had trampled in behind the stove and was kneeling on his legs. For the space of a minute he yelled and yelled with all the force of his lungs. Then this solace was denied him. The other hand, moist and strong, began to close round his throat.

At first he was glad, for here, he thought, was death at last. But it was only a new torture; perhaps Gino inherited the skill of his ancestors—and childlike ruffians who flung each other from the towers. Just as the windpipe closed, the hand fell off, and Philip was revived by the motion of his arm. And just as he was about to faint and gain at last one moment of oblivion, the motion stopped, and he would struggle instead against the pressure on his throat.

Vivid pictures were dancing through the pain—Lilia dying some months back in this very house, Miss Abbott bending over the baby, his mother at home, now reading evening prayers to the servants. He felt that he was growing weaker; his brain wandered; the agony did not seem so great. Not all Gino's care could indefinitely postpone the end. His yells and gurgles became mechanical—functions of the tortured flesh rather than true notes of indignation and despair. He was conscious of a horrid tumbling. Then his arm was pulled a little too roughly, and everything was quiet at last.

"But your son is dead, Gino. Your son is dead, dear Gino. Your son is dead."

The room was full of light, and Miss Abbott had Gino by the shoulders, holding him down in a chair. She was exhausted with the struggle, and her arms were trembling.

"What is the good of another death? What is the good of more pain?"

He too began to tremble. Then he turned and looked curiously at Philip, whose face, covered with dust and foam, was visible by the stove. Miss Abbott allowed him to get up, though she still held him firmly. He gave a loud and curious cry—a cry of interrogation it might be called. Below there was the noise of Perfetta returning with the baby's milk.

"Go to him," said Miss Abbott, indicating Philip. "Pick him up. Treat him kindly."

She released him, and he approached Philip slowly. His eyes were filling with trouble. He bent down, as if he would gently raise him up.

"Help! help!" moaned Philip. His body had suffered too much from Gino. It could not bear to be touched by him.

Gino seemed to understand. He stopped, crouched above him. Miss Abbott herself came forward and lifted her friend in her arms.

"Oh, the foul devil!" he murmured. "Kill him! Kill him for me."

Miss Abbott laid him tenderly on the couch and wiped his face. Then she said gravely to them both, "This thing stops here."

"Latte! latte!" cried Perfetta, hilariously ascending the stairs.

"Remember," she continued, "there is to be no revenge. I will have no more intentional evil. We are not to fight with each other any more."

"I shall never forgive him," sighed Philip.

"Latte! latte freschissima! bianca come neve!" Perfetta came in with another lamp and a little jug.

Gino spoke for the first time. "Put the milk on the table," he said. "It will not be wanted in the other room." The peril was over at last. A great sob shook the whole body, another followed, and then he gave a piercing cry of woe, and stumbled towards Miss Abbott like a child and clung to her.

All through the day Miss Abbott had seemed to Philip like a goddess, and more than ever did she seem so now. Many people look younger and more intimate during great emotion. But some there are who look older, and remote, and he could not think that there was little difference in years, and none in composition, between her and the man whose head was laid upon her breast. Her eyes were open, full of infinite pity and full of majesty, as if they discerned the boundaries of sorrow, and saw unimaginable tracts beyond. Such eyes he had seen in great pictures but never in a mortal. Her hands were folded round the sufferer, stroking him lightly, for even a goddess can do no more than that. And it seemed fitting, too, that she should bend her head and touch his forehead with her lips.

Philip looked away, as he sometimes looked away from the great pictures where visible forms suddenly become inadequate for the things they have shown to us. He was happy; he was assured that there was greatness in the world. There came to him an earnest desire to be good through the example of this good woman. He would try henceforward to be worthy of the things she had revealed. Quietly, without hysterical prayers or banging of drums, he underwent conversion. He was saved.

"That milk," said she, "need not be wasted. Take it, Signor Carella, and persuade Mr. Herriton to drink."

Gino obeyed her, and carried the child's milk to Philip. And Philip obeyed also and drank.

"Is there any left?"

"A little," answered Gino.

"Then finish it." For she was determined to use such remnants as lie about the world.

"Will you not have some?"

"I do not care for milk; finish it all."

"Philip, have you had enough milk?"

"Yes, thank you, Gino; finish it all."

He drank the milk, and then, either by accident or in some spasm of pain, broke the jug to pieces. Perfetta exclaimed in bewilderment. "It does not matter," he told her. "It does not matter. It will never be wanted any more."

Chapter 10

"He will have to marry her," said Philip. "I heard from him this morning, just as we left Milan. He finds he has gone too far to back out. It would be expensive. I don't know how much he minds—not as much as we suppose, I think. At all events there's not a word of blame in the letter. I don't believe he even feels angry. I never was so completely forgiven. Ever since you stopped him killing me, it has been a vision of perfect friendship. He nursed me, he lied for me at the inquest, and at the funeral, though he was crying, you would have thought it was my son who had died. Certainly I was the only person he had to be kind to; he was so distressed not to make Harriet's acquaintance, and that he scarcely saw anything of you. In his letter he says so again."

"Thank him, please, when you write," said Miss Abbott, "and give him my kindest regards."

"Indeed I will." He was surprised that she could slide away from the man so easily. For his own part, he was bound by ties of almost alarming intimacy. Gino had the southern knack of friendship. In the intervals of business he would pull out Philip's life, turn it inside out, remodel it, and advise him how to use it for the best. The sensation was pleasant, for he was a kind as well as a skilful operator. But Philip came away feeling that he had not a secret corner left. In that very letter Gino had again implored him, as a refuge from domestic difficulties, "to marry Miss Abbott, even if her dowry is small." And how Miss Abbott herself, after such tragic intercourse, could resume the conventions and send calm messages of esteem, was more than he could understand.

"When will you see him again?" she asked. They were standing together in the corridor of the train, slowly ascending out of Italy towards the San Gothard tunnel.

"I hope next spring. Perhaps we shall paint Siena red for a day or two with some of the new wife's money. It was one of the arguments for marrying her."

"He has no heart," she said severely. "He does not really mind about the child at all."

"No; you're wrong. He does. He is unhappy, like the rest of us. But he doesn't try to keep up appearances as we do. He knows that the things that have made him happy once will probably make him happy again—"

"He said he would never be happy again."

"In his passion. Not when he was calm. We English say it when we are calm—when we do not really believe it any longer. Gino is not ashamed of inconsistency. It is one of the many things I like him for."

"Yes; I was wrong. That is so."

"He's much more honest with himself than I am," continued Philip, "and he is honest without an effort and without pride. But you, Miss Abbott, what about you? Will you be in Italy next spring?"

"No."

"I'm sorry. When will you come back, do you think?"

"I think never."

"For whatever reason?" He stared at her as if she were some monstrosity.

"Because I understand the place. There is no need."

"Understand Italy!" he exclaimed.

"Perfectly."

"Well, I don't. And I don't understand you," he murmured to himself, as he paced away from her up the corridor. By this time he loved her very much, and he could not bear to be puzzled. He had reached love by the spiritual path: her thoughts and her goodness and her nobility had moved him first, and now her whole body and all its gestures had become transfigured by them. The beauties that are called obvious—the beauties of her hair and her voice and her limbs—he had noticed these last; Gino, who never traversed any path at all, had commended them dispassionately to his friend.

Why was he so puzzling? He had known so much about her once—what she thought, how she felt, the reasons for her actions. And now he only knew that he loved her, and all the other knowledge seemed passing from him just as he needed it most. Why would she never come to Italy again? Why had she avoided himself and Gino ever since the evening that she had saved their lives? The train was nearly empty. Harriet slumbered in a compartment by herself. He must ask her these questions now, and he returned quickly to her down the corridor.

She greeted him with a question of her own. "Are your plans decided?"

"Yes. I can't live at Sawston."

"Have you told Mrs. Herriton?"

"I wrote from Monteriano. I tried to explain things; but she will never understand me. Her view will be that the affair is settled—sadly settled since the baby is dead. Still it's over; our family circle need be vexed no more. She won't even be angry with you. You see, you have done us no harm in the long run. Unless, of course, you talk about Harriet and make a scandal. So that is my plan—London and work. What is yours?"

"Poor Harriet!" said Miss Abbott. "As if I dare judge Harriet! Or anybody." And without replying to Philip's question she left him to visit the other invalid.

Philip gazed after her mournfully, and then he looked mournfully out of the window at the decreasing streams. All the excitement was over—the inquest, Harriet's short illness, his own visit to the surgeon. He was convalescent, both in body and spirit, but convalescence brought no joy. In the looking-glass at the end of the corridor he saw his face haggard, and his shoulders pulled forward by the weight of the sling. Life was greater than he had supposed, but it was even less complete. He had seen the need for strenuous work and for righteousness. And now he saw what a very little way those things would go.

"Is Harriet going to be all right?" he asked. Miss Abbott had come back to him.

"She will soon be her old self," was the reply. For Harriet, after a short paroxysm of illness and remorse, was quickly returning to her normal state. She had been "thoroughly upset" as she phrased it, but she soon ceased to realize that anything was wrong beyond the death of a poor little child. Already she spoke of "this unlucky accident," and "the mysterious frustration of one's attempts to make things better." Miss Abbott had seen that she was comfortable, and had given her a kind kiss. But she returned feeling that Harriet, like her mother, considered the affair as settled.

"I'm clear enough about Harriet's future, and about parts of my own. But I ask again, What about yours?"

"Sawston and work," said Miss Abbott.

"No."

"Why not?" she asked, smiling.

"You've seen too much. You've seen as much and done more than I have."

"But it's so different. Of course I shall go to Sawston. You forget my father; and even if he wasn't there, I've a hundred ties: my district—I'm neglecting it shamefully—my evening classes, the St. James'—"

"Silly nonsense!" he exploded, suddenly moved to have the whole thing out with her. "You're too good—about a thousand times better than I am. You can't live in that hole; you must go among people who can hope to understand you. I mind for myself. I want to see you often—again and again."

"Of course we shall meet whenever you come down; and I hope that it will mean often."

"It's not enough; it'll only be in the old horrible way, each with a dozen relatives round us. No, Miss Abbott; it's not good enough."

"We can write at all events."

"You will write?" he cried, with a flush of pleasure. At times his hopes seemed so solid.

"I will indeed."

"But I say it's not enough—you can't go back to the old life if you wanted to. Too much has happened."

"I know that," she said sadly.

"Not only pain and sorrow, but wonderful things: that tower in the sunlight—do you remember it, and all you said to me? The theatre, even. And the next day—in the church; and our times with Gino."

"All the wonderful things are over," she said. "That is just where it is."

"I don't believe it. At all events not for me. The most wonderful things may be to come—"

"The wonderful things are over," she repeated, and looked at him so mournfully that he dare not contradict her. The train was crawling up the last ascent towards the Campanile of Airolo and the entrance of the tunnel.

"Miss Abbott," he murmured, speaking quickly, as if their free intercourse might soon be ended, "what is the matter with you? I thought I understood you, and I don't. All those two great first days at Monteriano I read you as clearly as you read me still. I saw why you had come, and why you changed sides, and afterwards I saw your wonderful courage and pity. And now you're frank with me one moment, as you used to be, and the next moment you shut me up. You see I owe too much to you—my life, and I don't know what besides. I won't stand it. You've gone too far to turn mysterious. I'll quote what you said to me: 'Don't be mysterious; there isn't the time.' I'll quote something else: 'I and my life must be where I live.' You can't live at Sawston."

He had moved her at last. She whispered to herself hurriedly. "It is tempting—" And those three words threw him into a tumult of joy. What was tempting to her? After all was the greatest of things possible? Perhaps, after long estrangement, after much tragedy, the South had brought them together in the end. That laughter in the theatre, those silver stars in the purple sky, even the violets of a departed spring, all had helped, and sorrow had helped also, and so had tenderness to others.

"It is tempting," she repeated, "not to be mysterious. I've wanted often to tell you, and then been afraid. I could never tell any one else, certainly no woman, and I think you're the one man who might understand and not be disgusted."

"Are you lonely?" he whispered. "Is it anything like that?"

"Yes." The train seemed to shake him towards her. He was resolved that though a dozen people were looking, he would yet take her in his arms. "I'm terribly lonely, or I wouldn't speak. I think you must know already." Their faces were crimson, as if the same thought was surging through them both.

"Perhaps I do." He came close to her. "Perhaps I could speak instead. But if you will say the word plainly you'll never be sorry; I will thank you for it all my life."

She said plainly, "That I love him." Then she broke down. Her body was shaken with sobs, and lest there should be any doubt she cried between the sobs for Gino! Gino! Gino!

He heard himself remark "Rather! I love him too! When I can forget how he hurt me that evening. Though whenever we shake hands—" One of them must have moved a step or two, for when she spoke again she was already a little way apart.

"You've upset me." She stifled something that was perilously near hysterics. "I thought I was past all this. You're taking it wrongly. I'm in love with Gino—don't pass it off—I mean it crudely—you know what I mean. So laugh at me."

"Laugh at love?" asked Philip.

"Yes. Pull it to pieces. Tell me I'm a fool or worse—that he's a cad. Say all you said when Lilia fell in love with him. That's the help I want. I dare tell you this because I like you—and because you're without passion; you look on life as a spectacle; you don't enter it; you only find it funny or beautiful. So I can trust you to cure me. Mr. Herriton, isn't it funny?" She tried to laugh herself, but became frightened and had to stop. "He's not a gentleman, nor a Christian, nor good in any way. He's never flattered me nor honoured me. But because he's handsome, that's been enough. The son of an Italian dentist, with a pretty face." She repeated the phrase as if it was a charm against passion. "Oh, Mr. Herriton, isn't it funny!" Then, to his relief, she began to cry. "I love him, and I'm not ashamed of it. I love him, and I'm going to Sawston, and if I mayn't speak about him to you sometimes, I shall die."

In that terrible discovery Philip managed to think not of himself but of her. He did not lament. He did not even speak to her kindly, for he saw that she could not stand it. A flippant reply was what she asked and needed—something flippant and a little cynical. And indeed it was the only reply he could trust himself to make.

"Perhaps it is what the books call 'a passing fancy'?"

She shook her head. Even this question was too pathetic. For as far as she knew anything about herself, she knew that her passions, once aroused, were sure. "If I saw him often," she said, "I might remember what he is like. Or he might grow old. But I dare not risk it, so nothing can alter me now."

"Well, if the fancy does pass, let me know." After all, he could say what he wanted.

"Oh, you shall know quick enough—"

"But before you retire to Sawston—are you so mighty sure?"

"What of?" She had stopped crying. He was treating her exactly as she had hoped.

"That you and he—" He smiled bitterly at the thought of them together. Here was the cruel antique malice of the gods, such as they once sent forth against Pasiphae. Centuries of aspiration and culture—and the world could not escape it. "I was going to say—whatever have you got in common?"

"Nothing except the times we have seen each other." Again her face was crimson. He turned his own face away.

"Which—which times?"

"The time I thought you weak and heedless, and went instead of you to get the baby. That began it, as far as I know the beginning. Or it may have begun when you took us to the theatre, and I saw him mixed up with music and light. But didn't understand till the morning. Then you opened the door—and I knew why I had been so happy. Afterwards, in the church, I prayed for us all; not for anything new, but that we might just be as we were—he with the child he loved, you and I and Harriet safe out of the place—and that I might never see him or speak to him again. I could have pulled through then—the thing was only coming near, like a wreath of smoke; it hadn't wrapped me round."

"But through my fault," said Philip solemnly, "he is parted from the child he loves. And because my life was in danger you came and saw him and spoke to him again." For the thing was even greater than she imagined. Nobody but himself would ever see round it now. And to see round it he was standing at an immense distance. He could even be glad that she had once held the beloved in her arms.

"Don't talk of 'faults.' You're my friend for ever, Mr. Herriton, I think. Only don't be charitable and shift or take the blame. Get over supposing I'm refined. That's what puzzles you. Get over that."

As he spoke she seemed to be transfigured, and to have indeed no part with refinement or unrefinement any longer. Out of this wreck there was revealed to him something indestructible—something which she, who had given it, could never take away.

"I say again, don't be charitable. If he had asked me, I might have given myself body and soul. That would have been the end of my rescue party. But all through he took me for a superior being—a goddess. I who was worshipping every inch of him, and every word he spoke. And that saved me."

Philip's eyes were fixed on the Campanile of Airolo. But he saw instead the fair myth of Endymion. This woman was a goddess to the end. For her no love could be degrading: she stood outside all degradation. This episode, which she thought so sordid, and which was so tragic for him, remained supremely beautiful. To such a height was he lifted, that without regret he could now have told her that he was her worshipper too. But what was the use of telling her? For all the wonderful things had happened.

"Thank you," was all that he permitted himself. "Thank you for everything."

She looked at him with great friendliness, for he had made her life endurable. At that moment the train entered the San Gothard tunnel. They hurried back to the carriage to close the windows lest the smuts should get into Harriet's eyes.

THE CELESTIAL OMNIBUS AND OTHER STORIES

THE STORY OF A PANIC

I

Eustace's career—if career it can be called—certainly dates from that afternoon in the chestnut woods above Ravello. I confess at once that I am a plain, simple man, with no pretensions to literary style. Still, I do flatter myself that I can tell a story without exaggerating, and I have therefore decided to give an unbiassed account of the extraordinary events of eight years ago.

Ravello is a delightful place with a delightful little hotel in which we met some charming people. There were the two Miss Robinsons, who had been there for six weeks with Eustace, their nephew, then a boy of about fourteen. Mr. Sandbach had also been there some time. He had held a curacy in the north of England, which he had been compelled to resign on account of ill-health, and while he was recruiting at Ravello he had taken in hand Eustace's education—which was then sadly deficient—and was endeavouring to fit him for one of our great public schools. Then there was Mr. Leyland, a would-be artist, and, finally, there was the nice landlady, Signora Scafetti, and the nice English-speaking waiter, Emmanuele—though at the time of which I am speaking Emmanuele was away, visiting a sick father.

To this little circle, I, my wife, and my two daughters made, I venture to think, a not unwelcome addition. But though I liked most of the company well enough, there were two of them to whom I did not take at all. They were the artist, Leyland, and the Miss Robinsons' nephew, Eustace.

Leyland was simply conceited and odious, and, as those qualities will be amply illustrated in my narrative, I need not enlarge upon them here. But Eustace was something besides: he was indescribably repellent.

I am fond of boys as a rule, and was quite disposed to be friendly. I and my daughters offered to take him out—'No, walking was such a fag.' Then I asked him to come and bathe—' No, he could not swim.'

"Every English boy should be able to swim," I said, "I will teach you myself."

"There, Eustace dear," said Miss Robinson; "here is a chance for you."

But he said he was afraid of the water!—a boy afraid!—and of course I said no more.

I would not have minded so much if he had been a really studious boy, but he neither played hard nor worked hard. His favourite occupations were lounging on the terrace in an easy chair and loafing along the high road, with his feet shuffling up the dust and his shoulders stooping forward. Naturally enough, his features were pale, his chest contracted, and his muscles undeveloped. His aunts thought him delicate; what he really needed was discipline.

That memorable day we all arranged to go for a picnic up in the chestnut woods—all, that is, except Janet, who stopped behind to finish her water-colour of the Cathedral—not a very successful attempt, I am afraid.

I wander off into these irrelevant details, because in my mind I cannot separate them from an account of the day; and it is the same with the conversation during the picnic: all is imprinted on my brain together. After a couple of hours' ascent, we left the donkeys that had carried the Miss Robinsons and my wife, and all proceeded on foot to the head of the valley—Vallone Fontana Caroso is its proper name, I find.

I have visited a good deal of fine scenery before and since, but have found little that has pleased me more. The valley ended in a vast hollow, shaped like a cup, into which radiated ravines from the precipitous hills around. Both the valley and the ravines and the ribs of hill that divided the ravines were covered with leafy, chestnut, so that the general appearance was that of a many fingered green hand, palm upwards, which was clutching, convulsively to keep us in its grasp. Far down the valley we could see Ravello and the sea, but that was the only sign of another world.

"Oh, what a perfectly lovely place," said my daughter Rose. "What a picture it would make!"

"Yes," said Mr. Sandbach. "Many a famous European gallery would be proud to have a landscape a tithe as beautiful as this upon its walls."

"On the contrary," said Leyland, "it would make a very poor picture. Indeed, it is not paintable at all."

"And why is that?" said Rose, with far more deference than he deserved.

"Look, in the first place," he replied, "how intolerably straight against the sky is the line of the hill. It would need breaking up and diversifying. And where we are standing the whole thing is out of perspective. Besides, all the colouring is monotonous and crude."

"I do not know anything about pictures," I put in, "and I do not pretend to know: but I know what is beautiful when I see it, and I am thoroughly content with this."

"Indeed, who could help being contented!" said the elder Miss Robinson and Mr. Sandbach said the same.

"Ah!" said Leyland, "you all confuse the artistic view of nature with the photographic."

Poor Rose had brought her camera with her, so I thought this positively rude. I did not wish any unpleasantness; so I merely turned away and assisted my wife and Miss Mary Robinson to put out the lunch—not a very nice lunch.

"Eustace, dear," said his aunt, "come and help us here."

He was in a particularly bad temper that morning. He had, as usual, not wanted to come, and his aunts had nearly allowed him to stop at the hotel to vex Janet. But I, with their permission, spoke to him rather sharply on the subject of exercise; and the result was that he had come, but was even more taciturn and moody than usual.

Obedience was not his strong point. He invariably questioned every command, and only executed it grumbling. I should always insist on prompt and cheerful obedience, if I had a son.

"I'm—coming—Aunt—Mary," he at last replied, and dawdled to cut a piece of wood to make a whistle, taking care not to arrive till we had finished.

"Well, well, sir!" said I, "you stroll in at the end and profit by our labours." He sighed, for he could not endure being chaffed. Miss Mary, very unwisely, insisted on giving him the wing of the chicken, in spite of all my attempts to prevent her. I remember that I had a moment's vexation when I thought that, instead of enjoying the sun, and the air, and the woods, we were all engaged in wrangling over the diet of a spoilt boy.

But, after lunch, he was a little less in evidence. He withdrew to a tree trunk, and began to loosen the bark from his whistle. I was thankful to see him employed, for once in a way. We reclined, and took a *dolce far niente*.

Those sweet chestnuts of the South are puny striplings compared with our robust Northerners. But they clothed the contours of the hills and valleys in a most pleasing way, their veil being only broken by two clearings, in one of which we were sitting.

And because these few trees were cut down, Leyland burst into a petty indictment of the proprietor.

"All the poetry is going from Nature," he cried, "her lakes and marshes are drained, her seas banked up, her forests cut down. Everywhere we see the vulgarity of desolation spreading."

I have had some experience of estates, and answered that cutting was very necessary for the health of the larger trees. Besides, it was unreasonable to expect the proprietor to derive no income from his lands.

"If you take the commercial side of landscape, you may feel pleasure in the owner's activity. But to me the mere thought that a tree is convertible into cash is disgusting."

"I see no reason," I observed politely, "to despise the gifts of Nature, because they are of value."

It did not stop him. "It is no matter," he went on, "we are all hopelessly steeped in vulgarity. I do not except myself. It is through us, and to our shame, that the Nereids have left the waters and the Oreads the mountains, that the woods no longer give shelter to Pan."

"Pan!" cried Mr. Sandbach, his mellow voice filling the valley as if it had been a great green church, "Pan is dead. That is why the woods do not shelter him." And he began to tell the striking story of the mariners who were sailing near the coast at the time of the birth of Christ, and three times heard a loud voice saying: "The great God Pan is dead."

"Yes. The great God Pan is dead," said Leyland. And he abandoned himself to that mock misery in which artistic people are so fond of indulging. His cigar went out, and he had to ask me for a match.

"How very interesting," said Rose. "I do wish I knew some ancient history."

"It is not worth your notice," said Mr. Sandbach. "Eh, Eustace?"

Eustace was finishing his whistle. He looked up, with the irritable frown in which his aunts allowed him to indulge, and made no reply.

The conversation turned to various topics and then died out. It was a cloudless afternoon in May, and the pale green of the young chestnut leaves made a pretty contrast with the dark blue of the sky. We were all sitting at the edge of the small clearing for the sake of the view, and the shade of the chestnut saplings behind us was manifestly insufficient. All sounds died away—at least that is my account: Miss Robinson says that the clamour of the birds was the first sign of uneasiness that she discerned. All sounds died away, except that, far in the distance, I could hear two boughs of a great chestnut grinding together as the tree swayed. The grinds grew shorter and shorter, and finally that sound stopped also. As I looked over the green fingers of the valley, everything was absolutely motionless and still; and that feeling of suspense which one so often experiences when Nature is in repose, began to steal over me.

Suddenly, we were all electrified by the excruciating noise of Eustace's whistle. I never heard any instrument give forth so ear-splitting and discordant a sound.

"Eustace, dear," said Miss Mary Robinson, "you might have thought of your poor Aunt Julia's head."

Leyland who had apparently been asleep, sat up.

"It is astonishing how blind a boy is to anything that is elevating or beautiful," he observed. "I should not have thought he could have found the wherewithal out here to spoil our pleasure like this."

Then the terrible silence fell upon us again. I was now standing up and watching a catspaw of wind that was running down one of the ridges opposite, turning the light green to dark as it travelled. A fanciful feeling of foreboding came over me; so I turned away, to find to my amazement, that all the others were also on their feet, watching it too.

It is not possible to describe coherently what happened next: but I, for one, am not ashamed to confess that, though the fair blue sky was above me, and the green spring woods beneath me, and the kindest of friends around me, yet I became terribly frightened, more frightened than I ever wish to become again, frightened in a way I never have known either before or after. And in the eyes of the others, too, I saw blank, expressionless fear, while their mouths strove in vain to speak and their hands to gesticulate. Yet, all around us were prosperity, beauty, and peace, and all was motionless, save the catspaw of wind, now travelling up the ridge on which we stood.

Who moved first has never been settled. It is enough to say that in one second we were tearing away along the hillside. Leyland was in front, then Mr. Sandbach, then my wife. But I only saw for a brief moment; for I ran across the little clearing and through the woods and over the undergrowth and the rocks and down the dry torrent beds into the valley below. The sky might have been black as I ran, and the trees short grass, and the hillside a level road; for I saw nothing and heard nothing and felt nothing, since all the channels of sense and reason were blocked. It was not the spiritual fear that one has known at other times, but brutal overmastering physical fear, stopping up the ears, and dropping clouds before the eyes, and filling the mouth with foul tastes. And it was no ordinary humiliation that survived; for I had been afraid, not as a man, but as a beast.

II

I cannot describe our finish any better than our start; for our fear passed away as it had come, without cause. Suddenly I was able to see, and hear, and cough, and clear my mouth. Looking back, I saw that the others were stopping too; and, in a short time, we were all together, though it was long before we could speak, and longer before we dared to.

No one was seriously injured. My poor wife had sprained her ankle, Leyland had torn one of his nails on a tree trunk, and I myself had scraped and damaged my ear. I never noticed it till I had stopped.

We were all silent, searching one another's faces. Suddenly Miss Mary Robinson gave a terrible shriek. "Oh, merciful heavens! where is Eustace?" And then she would have fallen, if Mr. Sandbach had not caught her.

"We must go back, we must go back at once," said my Rose, who was quite the most collected of the party. "But I hope—I feel he is safe."

Such was the cowardice of Leyland, that he objected. But, finding himself in a minority, and being afraid of being left alone, he gave in. Rose and I supported my poor wife, Mr. Sandbach and Miss Robinson helped Miss Mary, and we returned slowly and silently, taking forty minutes to ascend the path that we had descended in ten.

Our conversation was naturally disjointed, as no one wished to offer an opinion on what had happened. Rose was the most talkative: she startled us all by saying that she had very nearly stopped where she was.

"Do you mean to say that you weren't—that you didn't feel compelled to go?" said Mr. Sandbach.

"Oh, of course, I did feel frightened"—she was the first to use the word—"but I somehow felt that if I could stop on it would be quite different, that I shouldn't be frightened at all, so to speak." Rose never did express herself clearly: still, it is greatly to her credit that she, the youngest of us, should have held on so long at that terrible time.

"I should have stopped, I do believe," she continued, "if I had not seen mamma go."

Rose's experience comforted us a little about Eustace. But a feeling of terrible foreboding was on us all, as we painfully climbed the chestnut-covered slopes and neared the little clearing. When we reached it our tongues broke loose. There, at the further side, were the remains of our lunch, and close to them, lying motionless on his back, was Eustace.

With some presence of mind I at once cried out: "Hey, you young monkey! jump up!" But he made no reply, nor did he answer when his poor aunts spoke to him. And, to my unspeakable horror, I saw one of those green lizards dart out from under his shirt-cuff as we approached.

We stood watching him as he lay there so silently, and my ears began to tingle in expectation of the outbursts of lamentations and tears.

Miss Mary fell on her knees beside him and touched his hand, which was convulsively entwined in the long grass.

As she did so, he opened his eyes and smiled.

I have often seen that peculiar smile since, both on the possessor's face and on the photographs of him that are beginning to get into the illustrated papers. But, till then, Eustace had always worn a peevish, discontented frown; and we were all unused to this disquieting smile, which always seemed to be without adequate reason.

His aunts showered kisses on him, which he did not reciprocate, and then there was an awkward pause, Eustace seemed so natural and undisturbed, yet, if he had not had astonishing experiences himself, he ought to have been all the more astonished at our extraordinary behaviour. My wife, with ready tact, endeavoured to behave as if nothing had happened.

"Well, Mr. Eustace," she said, sitting down as she spoke, to ease her foot, "how have you been amusing yourself since we have been away?"

"Thank you, Mrs. Tytler, I have been very happy."

"And where have you been?"

"Here."

"And lying down all the time, you idle boy?"

"No, not all the time."

"What were you doing before?"

"Oh; standing or sitting."

"Stood and sat doing nothing! Don't you know the poem 'Satan finds some mischief still for——'"

"Oh, my dear madam, hush! hush!" Mr. Sandbach's voice broke in; and my wife, naturally mortified by the interruption, said no more and moved away. I was surprised to see Rose immediately take her place, and, with more freedom than she generally displayed, run her fingers through the boy's tousled hair.

"Eustace! Eustace!" she said, hurriedly, "tell me everything—every single thing."

Slowly he sat up—till then he had lain on his back.

"Oh, Rose," he whispered, and, my curiosity being aroused, I moved nearer to hear what he was going to say. As I did so, I caught sight of some goats' foot-marks in the moist earth beneath the trees.

"Apparently you have had a visit from some goats," I observed. "I had no idea they fed up here."

Eustace laboriously got on to his feet and came to see; and when he saw the footmarks he lay down and rolled on them, as a dog rolls in dirt.

After that there was a grave silence, broken at length by the solemn speech of Mr. Sandbach.

"My dear friends," he said, "it is best to confess the truth bravely. I know that what I am going to say now is what you are all now feeling. The Evil One has been very near us in bodily form. Time may yet discover some injury that he has wrought among us. But, at present, for myself at all events, I wish to offer up thanks for a merciful deliverance."

With that he knelt down, and, as the others knelt, I knelt too, though I do not believe in the Devil being allowed to assail us in visible form, as I told Mr. Sandbach afterwards. Eustace came too, and knelt quietly enough between his aunts after they had beckoned to him. But when it was over he at once got up, and began hunting for something.

"Why! Someone has cut my whistle in two," he said. (I had seen Leyland with an open knife in his hand—a superstitious act which I could hardly approve.)

"Well, it doesn't matter," he continued.

"And why doesn't it matter?" said Mr. Sandbach, who has ever since tried to entrap Eustace into an account of that mysterious hour.

"Because I don't want it any more."

"Why?"

At that he smiled; and, as no one seemed to have anything more to say, I set off as fast as I could through the wood, and hauled up a donkey to carry my poor wife home. Nothing occurred in my absence, except that Rose had again asked Eustace to tell her what had happened; and he, this time, had turned away his head, and had not answered her a single word.

As soon as I returned, we all set off. Eustace walked with difficulty, almost with pain, so that, when we reached the other donkeys, his aunts wished him to mount one of them and ride all the way home. I make it a rule never to interfere between relatives, but I put my foot down at this. As it turned out, I was perfectly right, for the healthy exercise, I suppose, began to thaw Eustace's sluggish blood and loosen his stiffened muscles. He stepped out manfully, for the first time in his life, holding his head up and taking deep draughts of air into his chest. I observed with satisfaction to Miss Mary Robinson, that Eustace was at last taking some pride in his personal appearance.

Mr. Sandbach sighed, and said that Eustace must be carefully watched, for we none of us understood him yet. Miss Mary Robinson being very much—over much, I think—guided by him, sighed too.

"Come, come. Miss Robinson," I said, "there's nothing wrong with Eustace. Our experiences are mysterious, not his. He was astonished at our sudden departure, that's why he was so strange when we returned. He's right enough—improved, if anything."

"And is the worship of athletics, the cult of insensate activity, to be counted as an improvement?" put in Leyland, fixing a large, sorrowful eye on Eustace, who had stopped to scramble on to a rock to pick some cyclamen. "The passionate desire to rend from Nature the few beauties that have been still left her—that is to be counted as an improvement too?"

It is mere waste of time to reply to such remarks, especially when they come from an unsuccessful artist, suffering from a damaged finger. I changed the conversation by asking what we should say at the hotel. After some discussion, it was agreed that we should say nothing, either there or in our letters home. Importunate truth-telling, which brings only bewilderment and discomfort to the hearers, is, in my opinion, a mistake; and, after a long discussion, I managed to make Mr. Sandbach acquiesce in my view.

Eustace did not share in our conversation. He was racing about, like a real boy, in the wood to the right. A strange feeling of shame; prevented us from openly mentioning our fright to him. Indeed, it seemed almost reasonable to conclude that it had made but little impression on him. So it disconcerted us when he bounded back with an armful of flowering acanthus, calling out:

"Do you suppose Gennaro'll be there when we get back?"

Gennaro was the stop-gap waiter, a clumsy, impertinent fisher-lad, who had been had up from Minori in the absence of the nice English-speaking Emmanuele. It was to him that we owed our scrappy lunch; and I could not conceive why Eustace desired to see him, unless it was to make mock with him of our behaviour.

"Yes, of course he will be there," said Miss Robinson. "Why do you ask, dear?"

"Oh, I thought I'd like to see him."

"And why?" snapped Mr. Sandbach.

"Because, because I do, I do; because, because I do." He danced away into the darkening wood to the rhythm of his words.

"This is very extraordinary," said Mr. Sandbach. "Did he like Gennaro before?"

"Gennaro has only been here two days," said Rose, "and I know that they haven't spoken to each other a dozen times."

Each time Eustace returned from the wood his spirits were higher. Once he came whooping down on us as a wild Indian, and another time he made believe to be a dog. The last time he came back with a poor dazed hare, too frightened to move, sitting on his arm. He was getting too uproarious, I thought; and we were all glad to leave the wood, and start upon the steep staircase path that leads down into Ravello. It was late and turning dark; and we made all the speed we could, Eustace scurrying in front of us like a goat.

Just where the staircase path debouches on the white high road, the next extraordinary incident of this extraordinary day occurred. Three old women were standing by the wayside. They, like ourselves, had come down from the woods, and they were resting their heavy bundles of fuel on the low parapet of the road. Eustace stopped in front of them, and, after a moment's deliberation, stepped forward and—kissed the left-hand one on the cheek!

"My good fellow!" exclaimed Mr. Sandbach, "are you quite crazy?"

Eustace said nothing, but offered the old woman some of his flowers, and then hurried on. I looked back; and the old woman's companions seemed as much astonished at the proceeding as we were. But she herself had put the flowers in her bosom, and was murmuring blessings.

This salutation of the old lady was the first example of Eustace's strange behaviour, and we were both surprised and alarmed. It was useless talking to him, for he either made silly replies, or else bounded away without replying at all.

He made no reference on the way home to Gennaro, and I hoped that that was forgotten. But, when we came to the Piazza, in front of the Cathedral, he screamed out: "Gennaro! Gennaro!" at the top of his voice, and began running up the little alley that led to the hotel. Sure enough, there was Gennaro at the end of it, with his arms and legs sticking out of the nice little English-speaking waiter's dress suit, and a dirty fisherman's cap on his head—for, as the poor landlady truly said, however much she superintended his toilette, he always man-aged to introduce something incongruous into it before he had done.

Eustace sprang to meet him, and leapt right up into his arms, and put his own arms round his neck. And this in the presence, not only of us, but also of the landlady, the chambermaid, the facchino, and of two American ladies who were coming for a few days' visit to the little hotel.

I always make a point of behaving pleasantly to Italians, however little they may deserve it; but this habit of promiscuous intimacy was perfectly intolerable and could only lead to familiarity and mortification for all. Taking Miss Robinson aside, I asked her permission to speak seriously to Eustace on the subject of intercourse with social inferiors. She granted it; but I determined to wait till the absurd boy had calmed down a little from the excitement of the day. Meanwhile, Gennaro, instead of attending to the wants of the two new ladies, carried Eustace into the house, as if it was the most natural thing in the world.

"Ho capito," I heard him say as he passed me. 'Ho capito' is the Italian for 'I have understood'; but, as Eustace had not spoken to him, I could not see the force of the remark. It served to increase our bewilderment, and, by the time we sat down at the dinner-table, our imaginations and our tongues were alike exhausted.

I omit from this account the various comments that were made, as few of them seem worthy of being recorded. But, for three or four hours, seven of us were pouring forth our bewilderment in a stream of appropriate and inappropriate exclamations. Some traced a connection between our behaviour in the afternoon and the behaviour of Eustace now. Others saw no connexion at all. Mr. Sandbach still held to the possibility of infernal influences, and also said that he ought to have a doctor. Leyland only saw the development of "that unspeakable Philistine, the boy." Rose maintained, to my surprise, that everything was excusable; while I began to see that the young gentleman wanted a sound thrashing. The poor Miss Robinsons swayed helplessly about between these diverse opinions; inclining now to careful supervision, now to acquiescence, now to corporal chastisement, now to Eno's Fruit Salt.

Dinner passed off fairly well, though Eustace was terribly fidgety, Gennaro as usual dropping the knives and spoons, and hawking and clearing his throat. He only knew a few words of English, and we were all reduced to Italian for making known our wants. Eustace, who had picked up a little somehow, asked for some oranges. To my annoyance, Gennaro, in his answer made use of the second person singular—a form only used when addressing those who are both intimates and equals. Eustace had brought it on himself; but an impertinence of this kind was an affront to us all, and I was determined to speak, and to speak at once.

When I heard him clearing the table I went in, and, summoning up my Italian, or rather Neapolitan—the Southern dialects are execrable—I said, "Gennaro! I heard you address Signor Eustace with 'Tu.'"

"It is true."

"You are not right. You must use 'Lei' or 'Voi'—more polite forms. And remember that, though Signor Eustace is sometimes silly and foolish—this afternoon for example—yet you must always behave respectfully to him; for he is a young English gentleman, and you are a poor Italian fisher-boy."

I know that speech sounds terribly snobbish, but in Italian one can say things that one would never dream of saying in English. Besides, it is no good speaking delicately to persons of that class. Unless you put things plainly, they take a vicious pleasure in misunderstanding you.

An honest English fisherman would have landed me one in the eye in a minute for such a remark, but the wretched down-trodden Italians have no pride. Gennaro only sighed, and said: "It is true."

"Quite so," I said, and turned to go. To my indignation I heard him add: "But sometimes it is not important."

"What do you mean?" I shouted.

He came close up to me with horrid gesticulating fingers.

"Signor Tytler, I wish to say this. If Eustazio asks me to call him 'Voi,' I will call him 'Voi.' Otherwise, no."

With that he seized up a tray of dinner things, and fled from the room with them; and I heard two more wine-glasses go on the court-yard floor.

I was now fairly angry, and strode out to interview Eustace. But he had gone to bed, and the landlady, to whom I also wished to speak, was engaged. After more vague wonderings, obscurely expressed owing to the presence of Janet and the two American ladies, we all went to bed, too, after a harassing and most extraordinary day.

III

But the day was nothing to the night.

I suppose I had slept for about four hours, when I woke suddenly thinking I heard a noise in the garden. And, immediately, before my eyes were open, cold terrible fear seized me—not fear of something that was happening, like the fear in the wood, but fear of something that might happen.

Our room was on the first floor, looking out on to the garden—or terrace, it was rather: a wedge-shaped block of ground covered with roses and vines, and intersected with little asphalt paths. It was bounded on the small side by the house; round the two long sides ran a wall, only three feet above the terrace level, but with a good twenty feet drop over it into the olive yards, for the ground fell very precipitously away.

Trembling all over I stole to the window. There, pattering up and down the asphalt, paths, was something white. I was too much alarmed to see clearly; and in the uncertain light of the stars the thing took all manner of curious shapes. Now it was a great dog, now an enormous white bat, now a mass of quickly travelling cloud. It would bounce like a ball, or take short flights like a bird, or glide slowly; like a wraith. It gave no sound—save the pattering sound of what, after all, must be human feet. And at last the obvious explanation forced itself upon my disordered mind; and I realized that Eustace had got out of bed, and that we were in for something more.

I hastily dressed myself, and went down into the dining-room which opened upon the terrace. The door was already unfastened. My terror had almost entirely passed away, but for quite five minutes I struggled with a curious cowardly feeling, which bade me not interfere with the poor strange boy, but leave him to his ghostly patterings, and merely watch him from the window, to see he took no harm.

But better impulses prevailed and, opening the door, I called out:

"Eustace! what on earth are you doing? Come in at once."

He stopped his antics, and said: "I hate my bedroom. I could not stop in it, it is too small."

"Come! come! I'm tired of affectation. You've never complained of it before."

"Besides I can't see anything—no flowers, no leaves, no sky: only a stone wall." The outlook of Eustace's room certainly was limited; but, as I told him, he had never complained of it before.

"Eustace, you talk like a child. Come in! Prompt obedience, if you please."

He did not move.

"Very well: I shall carry you in by force." I added, and made a few steps towards him. But I was soon convinced of the futility of pursuing a boy through a tangle of asphalt paths, and went in instead, to call Mr. Sandbach and Leyland to my aid.

When I returned with them he was worse than ever. He would not even answer us when we spoke, but began singing and chattering to himself in a most alarming way.

"It's a case for the doctor now," said Mr. Sandbach, gravely tapping his forehead.

He had stopped his running and was singing, first low, then loud—singing five-finger exercises, scales, hymn tunes, scraps of Wagner—anything that came into his head. His voice—a very untuneful voice—grew stronger and stronger, and he ended with a tremendous shout which boomed like a gun among the mountains, and awoke everyone who was still sleeping in the hotel. My poor wife and the two girls appeared at their respective windows, and the American ladies were heard violently ringing their bell.

"Eustace," we all cried, "stop! stop, dear boy, and come into the house."

He shook his head, and started off again—talking this time. Never have I listened to such an extraordinary speech. At any other time it would have been ludicrous, for here was a boy, with no sense of beauty and a puerile command of words, attempting to tackle themes which the greatest poets have found almost beyond their power. Eustace Robinson, aged fourteen, was standing in his nightshirt saluting, praising, and blessing, the great forces and manifestations of Nature.

He spoke first of night and the stars and planets above his head, of the swarms of fire-flies below him, of the invisible sea below the fire-flies, of the great rocks covered with anemones and shells that were slumbering in the invisible sea. He spoke of the rivers and water-falls, of the ripening bunches of grapes, of the smoking cone of Vesuvius and the hidden fire-channels that made the smoke, of the myriads of lizards who were lying curled up in the crannies of the sultry earth, of the showers of white rose-leaves that were tangled in his hair. And then he spoke of the rain and the wind by which all things are changed, of the air through which all things live, and of the woods in which all things can be hidden.

Of course, it was all absurdly high fainting: yet I could have kicked Leyland for audibly observing that it was 'a diabolical caricature of all that was most holy and beautiful in life.'

"And then,"—Eustace was going on in the pitiable conversational doggerel which was his only mode of expression—"and then there are men, but I can't make them out so well." He knelt down by the parapet, and rested his head on his arms.

"Now's the time," whispered Leyland. I hate stealth, but we darted forward and endeavoured to catch hold of him from behind. He was away in a twinkling, but turned round at once to look at us. As far as I could see in the starlight, he was crying. Leyland rushed at him again, and we tried to corner him among the asphalt paths, but without the slightest approach to success.

We returned, breathless and discomfited, leaving him to his madness in the further corner of the terrace. But my Rose had an inspiration.

"Papa," she called from the window, "if you get Gennaro, he might be able to catch him for you."

I had no wish to ask a favour of Gennaro, but, as the landlady had by now appeared on the scene, I begged her to summon him from the charcoal-bin in which he slept, and make him try what he could do.

She soon returned, and was shortly followed by Gennaro, attired in a dress coat, without either waistcoat, shirt, or vest, and a ragged pair of what had been trousers, cut short above the knees for purposes of wading. The landlady, who had quite picked up English ways, rebuked him for the incongruous and even indecent appearance which he presented.

"I have a coat and I have trousers. What more do you desire?"

"Never mind, Signora Scafetti," I put in, "As there are no ladies here, it is not of the slightest consequence." Then, turning to Gennaro, I said: "The aunts of Signor Eustace wish you to fetch him into the house."

He did not answer.

"Do you hear me? He is not well. I order you to fetch him into the house."

"Fetch! fetch!" said Signora Scafetti, and shook him roughly by the arm.

"Eustazio is well where he is."

"Fetch! fetch!" Signora Scafetti screamed, and let loose a flood of Italian, most of which, I am glad to say, I could not follow. I glanced up nervously at the girls' window, but they hardly know as much as I do, and I am thankful to say that none of us caught one word of Gennaro's answer.

The two yelled and shouted at each other for quite ten minutes, at the end of which Gennaro rushed back to his charcoal-bin and Signora Scafetti burst into tears, as well she might, for she greatly valued her English guests.

"He says," she sobbed, "that Signer Eustace is well where he is, and that he will not fetch him. I can do no more."

But I could, for, in my stupid British way, I have got some insight into the Italian character. I followed Mr. Gennaro to his place of repose, and found him wriggling down on to a dirty sack.

"I wish you to fetch Signor Eustace to me," I began.

He hurled at me an unintelligible reply.

"If you fetch him, I will give you this." And out of my pocket I took a new ten lira note.

This time he did not answer.

"This note is equal to ten lire in silver," I continued, for I knew that the poor-class Italian is unable to conceive of a single large sum.

"I know it."

"That is, two hundred soldi."

"I do not desire them. Eustazio is my friend."

I put the note into my pocket.

"Besides, you would not give it me."

"I am an Englishman. The English always do what they promise."

"That is true." It is astonishing how the most dishonest of nations trust us. Indeed they often trust us more than we trust one another. Gennaro knelt up on his sack. It was too dark to see his face, but I could feel his warm garlicky breath coming out in gasps, and I knew that the eternal avarice of the South had laid hold upon him.

"I could not fetch Eustazio to the house. He might die there."

"You need not do that," I replied patiently. "You need only bring him to me; and I will stand outside in the garden." And to this, as if it were something quite different, the pitiable youth consented.

"But give me first the ten lire."

"No,"—for I knew the kind of person with whom I had to deal. Once faithless, always faithless.

We returned to the terrace, and Gennaro, without a single word, pattered off towards the pattering that could be heard at the remoter end. Mr. Sandbach, Leyland, and myself moved away a little from the house, and stood in the shadow of the white climbing roses, practically invisible.

We heard "Eustazio" called, followed by absurd cries of pleasure from the poor boy. The pattering ceased, and we heard them talking. Their voices got nearer, and presently I could discern them through the creepers, the grotesque figure of the young man, and the slim little white-robed boy. Gennaro had his arm round Eustace's neck, and Eustace was talking away in his fluent, slip-shod Italian.

"I understand almost everything," I heard him say. "The trees, hills, stars, water, I can see all. But isn't it odd! I can't make out men a bit. Do you know what I mean?"

"Ho capito," said Gennaro gravely, and took his arm off Eustace's shoulder. But I made the new note crackle in my pocket; and he heard it. He stuck his hand out with a jerk; and the unsuspecting Eustace gripped it in his own.

"It is odd!" Eustace went on—they were quite close now—"It almost seems as if—as if——"

I darted out and caught hold of his arm, and Leyland got hold of the other arm, and Mr. Sandbach hung on to his feet. He gave shrill heart-piercing screams; and the white roses, which were falling early that year, descended in showers on him as we dragged him into the house.

As soon as we entered the house he stopped shrieking; but floods of tears silently burst forth, and spread over his upturned face.

"Not to my room," he pleaded. "It is so small."

His infinitely dolorous look filled me with strange pity, but what could I do? Besides, his window was the only one that had bars to it.

"Never mind, dear boy," said kind Mr. Sandbach. "I will bear you company till the morning."

At this his convulsive struggles began again. "Oh, please, not that. Anything but that. I will promise to lie still and not to cry more than I can help, if I am left alone."

So we laid him on the bed, and drew the sheets over him, and left him sobbing bitterly, and saying: "I nearly saw everything, and now I can see nothing at all."

We informed the Miss Robinsons of all that had happened, and returned to the dining-room, where we found Signora Scafetti and Gennaro whispering together.

Mr. Sandbach got pen and paper, and began writing to the English doctor at Naples. I at once drew out the note, and flung it down on the table to Gennaro.

"Here is your pay," I said sternly, for I was thinking of the Thirty Pieces of Silver.

"Thank you very much, sir," said Gennaro, and grabbed it.

He was going off, when Leyland, whose interest and indifference were always equally misplaced, asked him what Eustace had meant by saying 'he could not make out men a bit.'

"I cannot say. Signor Eustazio—" (I was glad to observe a little deference at last) "has a subtle brain. He understands many things."

"But I heard you say you understood," Leyland persisted.

"I understand, but I cannot explain. I am a poor Italian fisher-lad. Yet, listen: I will try." I saw to my alarm that his manner was changing, and tried to stop him. But he sat down on the edge of the table and started off, with some absolutely incoherent remarks.

"It is sad," he observed at last. "What has happened is very sad. But what can I do? I am poor. It is not I."

I turned away in contempt. Leyland went on asking questions. He wanted to know who it was that Eustace had in his mind when he spoke.

"That is easy to say," Gennaro gravely answered. "It is you, it is I. It is all in this house, and many outside it. If he wishes for mirth, we discomfort him. If he asks to be alone, we disturb him. He longed for a friend, and found none for fifteen years. Then he found me, and the first night I—I who have been in the woods and understood things too—betray him to you, and send him in to die. But what could I do?"

"Gently, gently," said I.

"Oh, assuredly he will die. He will lie in the small room all night, and in the morning he will be dead. That I know for certain."

"There, that will do," said Mr. Sandbach. "I shall be sitting with him."

"Filomena Giusti sat all night with Caterina, but Caterina was dead in the morning. They would not let her out, though I begged, and prayed, and cursed, and beat the door, and climbed the wall. They were ignorant fools, and thought I wished to carry her away. And in the morning she was dead."

"What is all this?" I asked Signora Scafetti.

"All kinds of stories will get about," she replied, "and he, least of anyone, has reason to repeat them."

"And I am alive now," he went on, "because I had neither parents nor relatives nor friends, so that, when the first night came, I could run through the woods, and climb the rocks, and plunge into the water, until I had accomplished my desire!"

We heard a cry from Eustace's room—a faint but steady sound, like the sound of wind in a distant wood, heard by one standing in tranquillity.

"That," said Gennaro, "was the last noise of Caterina. I was hanging on to her window then, and it blew out past me."

And, lifting up his hand, in which my ten lira note was safely packed, he solemnly cursed Mr. Sandbach, and Leyland, and myself, and Fate, because Eustace was dying in the upstairs room. Such is the working of the Southern mind; and I verily believe that he would not have moved even then, had not Leyland, that unspeakable idiot, upset the lamp with his elbow. It was a patent self-extinguishing lamp, bought by Signora Scafetti, at my special request, to replace the dangerous thing that she was using. The result was, that it went out; and the mere physical change from light to darkness had more power over the ignorant animal nature of Gennaro than the most obvious dictates of logic and reason.

I felt, rather than saw, that he had left the room, and shouted out to Mr. Sandbach: "Have you got the key of Eustace's room in your pocket?" But Mr. Sandbach and Leyland were both on the floor, having mistaken each other for Gennaro, and some more precious time was wasted in finding a match. Mr. Sandbach had only just time to say that he had left the key in the door, in case the Miss Robinsons wished to pay Eustace a visit, when we heard a noise on the stairs, and there was Gennaro, carrying Eustace down.

We rushed out and blocked up the passage, and they lost heart and retreated to the upper landing.

"Now they are caught," cried Signora Scafetti. "There is no other way out."

We were cautiously ascending the staircase, when there was a terrific scream from my wife's room, followed by a heavy thud on the asphalt path. They had leapt out of her window.

I reached the terrace just in time to see Eustace jumping over the parapet of the garden wall. This time I knew for certain he would be killed. But he alighted in an olive tree, looking like a great white moth; and from the tree he slid on to the earth. And as soon as his bare feet touched the clods of earth he uttered a strange loud cry, such as I should not have thought the human voice could have produced, and disappeared among the trees below.

"He has understood and he is saved," cried Gennaro, who was still sitting on the asphalt path. "Now, instead of dying he will live!"

"And you, instead of keeping the ten lire, will give them up," I retorted, for at this theatrical remark I could contain myself no longer.

"The ten lire are mine," he hissed back, in a scarcely audible voice. He clasped his hand over his breast to protect his ill-gotten gains, and, as he did so, he swayed forward and fell upon his face on the path. He had not broken any limbs, and a leap like that would never have killed an Englishman, for the drop was not great. But those miserable Italians have no stamina. Something had gone wrong inside him, and he was dead.

The morning was still far off, but the morning breeze had begun, and more rose leaves fell on us as we carried him in. Signora Scafetti burst into screams at the sight of the dead body, and, far down the valley towards the sea, there still resounded the shouts and the laughter of the escaping boy.

THE OTHER SIDE OF THE HEDGE

My pedometer told me that I was twenty-five; and, though it is a shocking thing to stop walking, I was so tired that I sat down on a milestone to rest. People outstripped me, jeering as they did so, but I was too apathetic to feel resentful, and even when Miss Eliza Dimbleby, the great educationist, swept past, exhorting me to persevere, I only smiled and raised my hat.

At first I thought I was going to be like my brother, whom I had had to leave by the road-side a year or two round the corner. He had wasted his breath on singing, and his strength on helping others. But I had travelled more wisely, and now it was only the monotony of the highway that oppressed me—dust under foot and brown crackling hedges on either side, ever since I could remember.

And I had already dropped several things—indeed, the road behind was strewn with the things we all had dropped; and the white dust was settling down on them, so that already they looked no better than stones. My muscles were so weary that I could not even bear the weight of those things I still carried. I slid off the milestone into the road, and lay there prostrate, with my face to the great parched hedge, praying that I might give up.

A little puff of air revived me. It seemed to come from the hedge; and, when I opened my eyes, there was a glint of light through the tangle of boughs and dead leaves. The hedge could not be as thick as usual. In my weak, morbid state, I longed to force my way in, and see what was on the other side. No one was in sight, or I should not have dared to try. For we of the road do not admit in conversation that there is another side at all.

I yielded to the temptation, saying to myself that I would come back in a minute. The thorns scratched my face, and I had to use my arms as a shield, depending on my feet alone to push me forward. Halfway through I would have gone back, for in the passage all the things I was carrying were scraped off me, and my clothes were torn. But I was so wedged that return was impossible, and I had to wriggle blindly forward, expecting every moment that my strength would fail me, and that I should perish in the undergrowth.

Suddenly cold water closed round my head, and I seemed sinking down for ever. I had fallen out of the hedge into a deep pool. I rose to the surface at last, crying for help, and I heard someone on the opposite bank laugh and say: "Another!" And then I was twitched out and laid panting on the dry ground.

Even when the water was out of my eyes, I was still dazed, for I had never been in so large a space, nor seen such grass and sunshine. The blue sky was no longer a strip, and beneath it the earth had risen grandly into hills—clean, bare buttresses, with beech trees in their folds, and meadows and clear pools at their feet. But the hills were not high, and there was in the landscape a sense of human occupation—so that one might have called it a park, or garden, if the words did not imply a certain triviality and constraint.

As soon as I got my breath, I turned to my rescuer and said:

"Where does this place lead to?"

"Nowhere, thank the Lord!" said he, and laughed. He was a man of fifty or sixty—just the kind of age we mistrust on the road—but there was no anxiety in his manner, and his voice was that of a boy of eighteen.

"But it must lead somewhere!" I cried, too much surprised at his answer to thank him for saving my life.

"He wants to know where it leads!" he shouted to some men on the hill side, and they laughed back, and waved their caps.

I noticed then that the pool into which I had fallen was really a moat which bent round to the left and to the right, and that the hedge followed it continually. The hedge was green on this side—its roots showed through the clear water, and fish swam about in them—and it was wreathed over with dog-roses and Traveller's Joy. But it was a barrier, and in a moment I lost all pleasure in the grass, the sky, the trees, the happy men and women, and realized that the place was but a prison, for all its beauty and extent.

We moved away from the boundary, and then followed a path almost parallel to it, across the meadows. I found it difficult walking, for I was always trying to out-distance my companion, and there was no advantage in doing this if the place led nowhere. I had never kept step with anyone since I left my brother.

I amused him by stopping suddenly and saying disconsolately, "This is perfectly terrible. One cannot advance: one cannot progress. Now we of the road——"

"Yes. I know."

"I was going to say, we advance continually."

"I know."

"We are always learning, expanding, developing. Why, even in my short life I have seen a great deal of advance—the Transvaal War, the Fiscal Question, Christian Science, Radium. Here for example—"

I took out my pedometer, but it still marked twenty-five, not a degree more.

"Oh, it's stopped! I meant to show you. It should have registered all the time I was walking with you. But it makes me only twenty-five."

"Many things don't work in here," he said, "One day a man brought in a Lee-Metford, and that wouldn't work."

"The laws of science are universal in their application. It must be the water in the moat that has injured the machinery. In normal conditions everything works.

Science and the spirit of emulation—those are the forces that have made us what we are."

I had to break off and acknowledge the pleasant greetings of people whom we passed. Some of them were singing, some talking, some engaged in gardening, hay-making, or other rudimentary industries. They all seemed happy; and I might have been happy too, if I could have forgotten that the place led nowhere.

I was startled by a young man who came sprinting across our path, took a little fence in fine style, and went tearing over a ploughed field till he plunged into a lake, across which he began to swim. Here was true energy, and I exclaimed: "A cross-country race! Where are the others?"

"There are no others," my companion replied; and, later on, when we passed some long grass from which came the voice of a girl singing exquisitely to herself, he said again: "There are no others." I was bewildered at the waste in production, and murmured to myself, "What does it all mean?"

He said: "It means nothing but itself"—and he repeated the words slowly, as if I were a child.

"I understand," I said quietly, "but I do not agree. Every achievement is worthless unless it is a link in the chain of development. And I must not trespass on your kindness any longer. I must get back somehow to the road, and have my pedometer mended."

"First, you must see the gates," he replied, "for we have gates, though we never use them."

I yielded politely, and before long we reached the moat again, at a point where it was spanned by a bridge. Over the bridge was a big gate, as white as ivory, which was fitted into a gap in the boundary hedge. The gate opened outwards, and I exclaimed in amazement, for from it ran a road—just such a road as I had left—dusty under foot, with brown crackling hedges on either side as far as the eye could reach.

"That's my road!" I cried.

He shut the gate and said: "But not your part of the road. It is through this gate that humanity went out countless ages ago, when it was first seized with the desire to walk."

I denied this, observing that the part of the road I myself had left was not more than two miles off. But with the obstinacy of his years he repeated: "It is the same road. This is the beginning, and though it seems to run straight away from us, it doubles so often, that it is never far from our boundary and sometimes touches it." He stooped down by the moat, and traced on its moist margin an absurd figure like a maze. As we walked back through the meadows, I tried to convince him of his mistake.

"The road sometimes doubles, to be sure, but that is part of our discipline. Who can doubt that its general tendency is onward? To what goal we know not—it may be to some mountain where we shall touch the sky, it may be over precipices into the sea. But that it goes forward —who can doubt that? It is the thought of that that makes us strive to excel, each in his own way, and gives us an impetus which is lacking with you. Now that man who passed us—it's true that he ran well, and jumped well, and swam well; but we have men who can run better, and men who can jump better, and who can swim better. Specialization has produced results which would surprise you. Similarly, that girl——"

Here I interrupted myself to exclaim: "Good gracious me! I could have sworn it was Miss Eliza Dimbleby over there, with her feet in the fountain!"

He believed that it was.

"Impossible! I left her on the road, and she is due to lecture this evening at Tunbridge Wells. Why, her train leaves Cannon Street in—of course my watch has stopped like everything else. She is the last person to be here."

"People always are astonished at meeting each other. All kinds come through the hedge, and come at all times—when they are drawing ahead in the race, when they are lagging behind, when they are left for dead. I often stand near the boundary listening to the sounds of the road—you know what they are—and wonder if anyone will turn aside. It is my great happiness to help someone out of the moat, as I helped you. For our country fills up slowly, though it was meant for all mankind."

"Mankind have other aims," I said gently, for I thought him well-meaning; "and I must join them." I bade him good evening, for the sun was declining, and I wished to be on the road by nightfall. To my alarm, he caught hold of me, crying: "You are not to go yet!" I tried to shake him off, for we had no interests in common, and his civility was becoming irksome to me. But for all my struggles the tiresome old man would not let go; and, as wrestling is not my speciality, I was obliged to follow him.

It was true that I could have never found alone the place where I came in, and I hoped that, when I had seen the other sights about which he was worrying, he would take me back to it. But I was determined not to sleep in the country, for I mistrusted it, and the people too, for all their friendliness. Hungry though I was, I would not join them in their evening meals of milk and fruit, and, when they gave me flowers, I flung them away as soon as I could do so unobserved. Already they were lying down for the night like cattle—some out on the bare hillside, others in groups under the beeches. In the light of an orange sunset I hurried on with my unwelcome guide, dead tired, faint for want of food, but murmuring indomitably: "Give me life, with its struggles and victories, with its failures and hatreds, with its deep moral meaning and its unknown goal!"

At last we came to a place where the encircling moat was spanned by another bridge, and where another gate interrupted the line of the boundary hedge. It was different from the first gate; for it was half transparent like horn, and opened inwards. But through it, in the waning light, I saw again just such a road as I had left—monotonous, dusty, with brown crackling hedges on either side, as far as the eye could reach.

I was strangely disquieted at the sight, which seemed to deprive me of all self-control. A man was passing us, returning for the night to the hills, with a scythe over his shoulder and a can of some liquid in his hand. I forgot the destiny of our race. I forgot the road that lay before my eyes, and I sprang at him, wrenched the can out of his hand, and began to drink.

It was nothing stronger than beer, but in my exhausted state it overcame me in a moment. As in a dream, I saw the old man shut the gate, and heard him say: "This is where your road ends, and through this gate humanity—all that is left of it—will come in to us."

Though my senses were sinking into oblivion, they seemed to expand ere they reached it. They perceived the magic song of nightingales, and the odour of invisible hay, and stars piercing the fading sky. The man whose beer I had stolen lowered me down gently to sleep off its effects, and, as he did so, I saw that he was my brother.

THE CELESTIAL OMNIBUS

I

The boy who resided at Agathox Lodge, 28, Buckingham Park Road, Surbiton, had often been puzzled by the old sign-post that stood almost opposite. He asked his mother about it, and she replied that it was a joke, and not a very nice one, which had been made many years back by some naughty young men, and that the police ought to remove it. For there were two strange things about this sign-post: firstly, it pointed up a blank alley, and, secondly, it had painted on it in faded characters, the words, "To Heaven."

"What kind of young men were they?" he asked.

"I think your father told me that one of them wrote verses, and was expelled from the University and came to grief in other ways. Still, it was a long time ago. You must ask your father about it. He will say the same as I do, that it was put up as a joke."

"So it doesn't mean anything at all?"

She sent him upstairs to put on his best things, for the Bonses were coming to tea, and he was to hand the cake-stand.

It struck him, as he wrenched on his tightening trousers, that he might do worse than ask Mr. Bons about the sign-post. His father, though very kind, always laughed at him—shrieked with laughter whenever he or any other child asked a question or spoke. But Mr. Bons was serious as well as kind. He had a beautiful house and lent one books, he was a churchwarden, and a candidate for the County Council; he had donated to the Free Library enormously, he presided over the Literary Society, and had Members of Parliament to stop with him—in short, he was probably the wisest person alive.

Yet even Mr. Bons could only say that the sign-post was a joke—the joke of a person named Shelley.

"Off course!" cried the mother; "I told you so, dear. That was the name."

"Had you never heard of Shelley?" asked Mr. Bons.

"No," said the boy, and hung his head.

"But is there no Shelley in the house?"

"Why, yes!" exclaimed the lady, in much agitation. "Dear Mr. Bons, we aren't such Philistines as that. Two at the least. One a wedding present, and the other, smaller print, in one of the spare rooms."

"I believe we have seven Shelleys," said Mr. Bons, with a slow smile. Then he brushed the cake crumbs off his stomach, and, together with his daughter, rose to go.

The boy, obeying a wink from his mother, saw them all the way to the garden gate, and when they had gone he did not at once return to the house, but gazed for a little up and down Buckingham Park Road.

His parents lived at the right end of it. After No. 39 the quality of the houses dropped very suddenly, and 64 had not even a separate servants' entrance. But at the present moment the whole road looked rather pretty, for the sun had just set in splendour, and the inequalities of rent were drowned in a saffron afterglow. Small birds twittered, and the breadwinners' train shrieked musically down through the cutting—that wonderful cutting which has drawn to itself the whole beauty out of Surbiton, and clad itself, like any Alpine valley, with the glory of the fir and the silver birch and the primrose. It was this cutting that had first stirred desires within the boy—desires for something just a little different, he knew not what desires that would return whenever things were sunlit, as they were this evening, running up and down inside him, up and down, up and down, till he would feel quite unusual all over, and as likely as not would want to cry. This evening he was even sillier, for he slipped across the road towards the sign-post and began to run up the blank alley.

The alley runs between high walls—the walls of the gardens of "Ivanhoe" and "Belle Vista" respectively. It smells a little all the way, and is scarcely twenty yards long, including the turn at the end. So not unnaturally the boy soon came to a standstill. "I'd like to kick that Shelley," he exclaimed, and glanced idly at a piece of paper which was pasted on the wall. Rather an odd piece of paper, and he read it carefully before he turned back. This is what he read:

S. AND C.R.C.C.

Alteration in Service.

Owing to lack of patronage the Company are regretfully compelled to suspend the hourly service, and to retain only the

Sunrise and Sunset Omnibuses,

which will run as usual. It is to be hoped that the public will patronize an arrangement which is intended for their convenience. As an extra inducement, the Company will, for the first time, now issue

Return Tickets!

(available one day only), which may be obtained of the driver. Passengers are again reminded that *no tickets are issued at the other end*, and that no complaints in this connection will receive consideration from the Company. Nor will the

Company be responsible for any negligence or stupidity on the part of Passengers, nor for Hailstorms, Lightning, Loss of Tickets, nor for any Act of God.

For the Direction.

Now he had never seen this notice before, nor could he imagine where the omnibus went to. S. of course was for Surbiton, and R.C.C. meant Road Car Company. But what was the meaning or the other C.? Coombe and Maiden, perhaps, of possibly "City." Yet it could not hope to compete with the South-Western. The whole thing, the boy reflected, was run on hopelessly unbusiness-like lines. Why no tickets from the other end? And what an hour to start! Then he realized that unless the notice was a hoax, an omnibus must have been starting just as he was wishing the Bonses good-bye. He peered at the ground through the gathering dusk, and there he saw what might or might not be the marks of wheels. Yet nothing had come out of the alley. And he had never seen an omnibus at any time in the Buckingham Park Road. No: it must be a hoax, like the sign-posts, like the fairy tales, like the dreams upon which he would wake suddenly in the night. And with a sigh he stepped from the alley—right into the arms of his father.

Oh, how his father laughed! "Poor, poor Popsey!" he cried. "Diddums! Diddums! Diddums think he'd walky-palky up to Evvink!" And his mother, also convulsed with laughter, appeared on the steps of Agathox Lodge. "Don't, Bob!" she gasped. "Don't be so naughty! Oh, you'll kill me! Oh, leave the boy alone!"

But all that evening the joke was kept up. The father implored to be taken too. Was it a very tiring walk? Need one wipe one's shoes on the door-mat? And the boy went to bed feeling faint and sore, and thankful for only one thing—that he had not said a word about the omnibus. It was a hoax, yet through his dreams it grew more and more real, and the streets of Surbiton, through which he saw it driving, seemed instead to become hoaxes and shadows. And very early in the morning he woke with a cry, for he had had a glimpse of its destination.

He struck a match, and its light fell not only on his watch but also on his calendar, so that he knew it to be half-an-hour to sunrise. It was pitch dark, for the fog had come down from London in the night, and all Surbiton was wrapped in its embraces. Yet he sprang out and dressed himself, for he was determined to settle once for all which was real: the omnibus or the streets. "I shall be a fool one way or the other," he thought, "until I know." Soon he was shivering in the road under the gas lamp that guarded the entrance to the alley.

To enter the alley itself required some courage. Not only was it horribly dark, but he now realized that it was an impossible terminus for an omnibus. If it had not been for a policeman, whom he heard approaching through the fog, he would never have made the attempt. The next moment he had made the attempt and failed. Nothing. Nothing but a blank alley and a very silly boy gaping at its dirty floor. It *was* a hoax. "I'll tell papa and mamma," he decided. "I deserve it. I deserve that they should know. I am too silly to be alive." And he went back to the gate of Agathox Lodge.

There he remembered that his watch was fast. The sun was not risen; it would not rise for two minutes. "Give the bus every chance," he thought cynically, and returned into the alley.

But the omnibus was there.

II

It had two horses, whose sides were still smoking from their journey, and its two great lamps shone through the fog against the alley's walls, changing their cobwebs and moss into tissues of fairyland. The driver was huddled up in a cape. He faced the blank wall, and how he had managed to drive in so neatly and so silently was one of the many things that the boy never discovered. Nor could he imagine how ever he would drive out.

"Please," his voice quavered through the foul brown air, "Please, is that an omnibus?"

"Omnibus est," said the driver, without turning round. There was a moment's silence. The policeman passed, coughing, by the entrance of the alley. The boy crouched in the shadow, for he did not want to be found out. He was pretty sure, too, that it was a Pirate; nothing else, he reasoned, would go from such odd places and at such odd hours.

"About when do you start?" He tried to sound nonchalant.

"At sunrise."

"How far do you go?"

"The whole way."

"And can I have a return ticket which will bring me all the way back?"

"You can."

"Do you know, I half think I'll come." The driver made no answer. The sun must have risen, for he unhitched the brake. And scarcely had the boy jumped in before the omnibus was off.

How? Did it turn? There was no room. Did it go forward? There was a blank wall. Yet it was moving—moving at a stately pace through the fog, which had turned from brown to yellow. The thought of warm bed and warmer breakfast made the boy feel faint. He wished he had not come. His parents would not have approved. He would have gone back to them if the weather had not made it impossible. The solitude was terrible; he was the only passenger. And the omnibus, though well-built, was cold and somewhat musty. He drew his coat round him, and in so doing chanced to feel his pocket. It was empty. He had forgotten his purse.

"Stop!" he shouted. "Stop!" And then, being of a polite disposition, he glanced up at the painted notice-board so that he might call the driver by name. "Mr. Browne! stop; O, do please stop!"

Mr. Browne did not stop, but he opened a little window and looked in at the boy. His face was a surprise, so kind it was and modest.

"Mr. Browne, I've left my purse behind. I've not got a penny. I can't pay for the ticket. Will you take my watch, please? I am in the most awful hole."

"Tickets on this line," said the driver, "whether single or return, can be purchased by coinage from no terrene mint. And a chronometer, though it had solaced the vigils of Charlemagne, or measured the slumbers of Laura, can acquire by no mutation the double-cake that charms the fangless Cerberus of Heaven!" So saying, he handed in the necessary ticket, and, while the boy said "Thank you," continued: "Titular pretensions, I know it well, are vanity. Yet they merit no censure when uttered on a laughing lip, and in an homonymous world are in some sort useful, since they do serve to distinguish one Jack from his fellow. Remember me, therefore, as Sir Thomas Browne."

"Are you a Sir? Oh, sorry!" He had heard of these gentlemen drivers. "It *is* good of you about the ticket. But if you go on at this rate, however does your bus pay?"

"It does not pay. It was not intended to pay. Many are the faults of my equipage; it is compounded too curiously of foreign woods; its cushions tickle erudition rather than promote repose; and my horses are nourished not on the evergreen pastures of the moment, but on the dried bents and clovers of Latinity. But that it pays!—that error at all events was never intended and never attained."

"Sorry again," said the boy rather hopelessly. Sir Thomas looked sad, fearing that, even for a moment, he had been the cause of sadness. He invited the boy to come up and sit beside him on the box, and together they journeyed on through the fog, which was now changing from yellow to white. There were no houses by the road; so it must be either Putney Heath or Wimbledon Common.

"Have you been a driver always?"

"I was a physician once."

"But why did you stop? Weren't you good?"

"As a healer of bodies I had scant success, and several score of my patients preceded me. But as a healer of the spirit I have succeeded beyond my hopes and my deserts. For though my draughts were not better nor subtler than those of other men, yet, by reason of the cunning goblets wherein I offered them, the queasy soul was ofttimes tempted to sip and be refreshed."

"The queasy soul," he murmured; "if the sun sets with trees in front of it, and you suddenly come strange all over, is that a queasy soul?"

"Have you felt that?"

"Why yes."

After a pause he told the boy a little, a very little, about the journey's end. But they did not chatter much, for the boy, when he liked a person, would as soon sit silent in his company as speak, and this, he discovered, was also the mind of Sir Thomas Browne and of many others with whom he was to be acquainted. He heard, however, about the young man Shelley, who was now quite a famous person, with a carriage of his own, and about some of the other drivers who are in the service of the Company. Meanwhile the light grew stronger, though the fog did not disperse. It was now more like mist than fog, and at times would travel quickly across them, as if it was part of a cloud. They had been ascending, too, in a most puzzling way; for over two hours the horses had been pulling against the collar, and even if it were Richmond Hill they ought to have been at the top long ago. Perhaps it was Epsom, or even the North Downs; yet the air seemed keener than that which blows on either. And as to the name of their destination, Sir Thomas Browne was silent.

Crash!

"Thunder, by Jove!" said the boy, "and not so far off either. Listen to the echoes! It's more like mountains."

He thought, not very vividly, of his father and mother. He saw them sitting down to sausages and listening to the storm. He saw his own empty place. Then there would be questions, alarms, theories, jokes, consolations. They would expect him back at lunch. To lunch he would not come, nor to tea, but he would be in for dinner, and so his day's truancy would be over. If he had had his purse he would have bought them presents—not that he should have known what to get them.

Crash!

The peal and the lightning came together. The cloud quivered as if it were alive, and torn streamers of mist rushed past. "Are you afraid?" asked Sir Thomas Browne.

"What is there to be afraid of? Is it much farther?"

The horses of the omnibus stopped just as a ball of fire burst up and exploded with a ringing noise that was deafening but clear, like the noise of a blacksmith's forge. All the cloud was shattered.

"Oh, listen. Sir Thomas Browne! No, I mean look; we shall get a view at last. No, I mean listen; that sounds like a rainbow!"

The noise had died into the faintest murmur, beneath which another murmur grew, spreading stealthily, steadily, in a curve that widened but did not vary. And in widening curves a rainbow was spreading from the horses' feet into the dissolving mists.

"But how beautiful! What colours! Where will it stop? It is more like the rainbows you can tread on. More like dreams."

The colour and the sound grew together. The rainbow spanned an enormous gulf. Clouds rushed under it and were pierced by it, and still it grew, reaching forward, conquering the darkness, until it touched something that seemed more solid than a cloud.

The boy stood up. "What is that out there?" he called. "What does it rest on, out at that other end?"

In the morning sunshine a precipice shone forth beyond the gulf A precipice—or was it a castle? The horses moved. They set their feet upon the rainbow.

"Oh, look!" the boy shouted. "Oh, listen! Those caves—or are they gateways? Oh, look between those cliffs at those ledges. I see people! I see trees!"

"Look also below," whispered Sir Thomas. "Neglect not the diviner Acheron."

The boy looked below, past the flames of the rainbow that licked against their wheels. The gulf also had cleared, and in its depths there flowed an everlasting river. One sunbeam entered and struck a green pool, and as they passed over he saw three maidens rise to the surface of the pool, singing, and playing with something that glistened like a ring.

"You down in the water——" he called.

They answered, "You up on the bridge——" There was a burst of music. "You up on the bridge, good luck to you. Truth in the depth, truth on the height."

"You down in the water, what are you doing?"

Sir Thomas Browne replied: "They sport in the mancipiary possession of their gold"; and the omnibus arrived.

III

The boy was in disgrace. He sat locked up in the nursery of Agathox Lodge, learning poetry for a punishment. His father had said, "My boy! I can pardon anything but untruthfulness," and had caned him, saying at each stroke, "There is *no* omnibus, *no* driver, *no* bridge, *no* mountain; you are a *truant*, *guttersnipe*, a *liar*." His father could be very stern at times. His mother had begged him to say he was sorry. But he could not say that. It was the greatest day of his life, in spite of the caning, and the poetry at the end of it.

He had returned punctually at sunset—driven not by Sir Thomas Browne, but by a maiden lady who was full of quiet fun. They had talked of omnibuses and also of barouche landaus. How far away her gentle voice seemed now! Yet it was scarcely three hours since he had left her up the alley.

His mother called through the door. "Dear, you are to come down and to bring your poetry with you."

He came down, and found that Mr. Bons was in the smoking-room with his father. It had been a dinner party.

"Here is the great traveller!" said his father grimly. "Here is the young gentleman who drives in an omnibus over rainbows, while young ladies sing to him." Pleased with his wit, he laughed.

"After all," said Mr. Bons, smiling, "there is something a little like it in Wagner. It is odd how, in quite illiterate minds, you will find glimmers of Artistic Truth. The case interests me. Let me plead for the culprit. We have all romanced in our time, haven't we?"

"Hear how kind Mr. Bons is," said his mother, while his father said, "Very well. Let him say his Poem, and that will do. He is going away to my sister on Tuesday, and she will cure him of this alley-slopering." (Laughter.) "Say your Poem."

The boy began. "'Standing aloof in giant ignorance.'"

His father laughed again—roared. "One for you, my son! 'Standing aloof in giant ignorance!' I never knew these poets talked sense. Just describes you. Here, Bons, you go in for poetry. Put him through it, will you, while I fetch up the whisky?"

"Yes, give me the Keats," said Mr. Bons. "Let him say his Keats to me."

So for a few moments the wise man and the ignorant boy were left alone in the smoking-room.

"'Standing aloof in giant ignorance, of thee I dream and of the Cyclades, as one who sits ashore and longs perchance to visit——'"

"Quite right. To visit what?"

"'To visit dolphin coral in deep seas,'" said the boy, and burst into tears.

"Come, come! why do you cry?"

"Because—because all these words that only rhymed before, now that I've come back they're me."

Mr. Bons laid the Keats down. The case was more interesting than he had expected. "*You?*" he exclaimed, "This sonnet, *you*?"

"Yes—and look further on: 'Aye, on the shores of darkness there is light, and precipices show untrodden green.' It *is* so, sir. All these things are true."

"I never doubted it," said Mr. Bons, with closed eyes.

"You—then you believe me? You believe in the omnibus and the driver and the storm and that return ticket I got for nothing and——"

"Tut, tut! No more of your yarns, my boy. I meant that I never doubted the essential truth of Poetry. Some day, when you read more, you will understand what I mean."

"But Mr. Bons, it *is* so. There *is* light upon the shores of darkness. I have seen it coming. Light and a wind."

"Nonsense," said Mr. Bons.

"If I had stopped! They tempted me. They told me to give up my ticket—for you cannot come back if you lose your ticket. They called from the river for it, and indeed I was tempted, for I have never been so happy as among those precipices. But I thought of my mother and father, and that I must fetch them. Yet they will not come, though the road starts opposite our house. It has all happened as the people up there warned me, and Mr. Bons has disbelieved me like every one else. I have been caned. I shall never see that mountain again."

"What's that about me?" said Mr. Bons, sitting up in his chair very suddenly.

"I told them about you, and how clever you were, and how many books you had, and they said, 'Mr. Bons will certainly disbelieve you.'"

"Stuff and nonsense, my young friend. You grow impertinent. I—well—I will settle the matter. Not a word to your father. I will cure you. To-morrow evening I will myself call here to take you for a walk, and at sunset we will go up this alley opposite and hunt for your omnibus, you silly little boy."

His face grew serious, for the boy was not disconcerted, but leapt about the room singing, "Joy! joy! I told them you would believe me. We will drive together over the rainbow. I told them that you would come." After all, could there be anything in the story? Wagner? Keats? Shelley? Sir Thomas Browne? Certainly the case was interesting.

And on the morrow evening, though it was pouring with rain, Mr. Bons did not omit to call at Agathox Lodge.

The boy was ready, bubbling with excitement, and skipping about in a way that rather vexed the President of the Literary Society. They took a turn down Buckingham Park Road, and then—having seen that no one was watching them—

slipped up the alley. Naturally enough (for the sun was setting) they ran straight against the omnibus.

"Good heavens!" exclaimed Mr. Bons. "Good gracious heavens!"

It was not the omnibus in which the boy had driven first, nor yet that in which he had returned. There were three horses—black, gray, and white, the gray being the finest. The driver, who turned round at the mention of goodness and of heaven, was a sallow man with terrifying jaws and sunken eyes. Mr. Bons, on seeing him, gave a cry as if of recognition, and began to tremble violently.

The boy jumped in.

"Is it possible?" cried Mr. Bons. "Is the impossible possible?"

"Sir; come in, sir. It is such a fine omnibus. Oh, here is his name—Dan some one."

Mr. Bons sprang in too. A blast of wind immediately slammed the omnibus door, and the shock jerked down all the omnibus blinds, which were very weak on their springs.

"Dan.... Show me. Good gracious heavens! we're moving."

"Hooray!" said the boy.

Mr. Bons became flustered. He had not intended to be kidnapped. He could not find the door-handle, nor push up the blinds. The omnibus was quite dark, and by the time he had struck a match, night had come on outside also. They were moving rapidly.

"A strange, a memorable adventure," he said, surveying the interior of the omnibus, which was large, roomy, and constructed with extreme regularity, every part exactly answering to every other part. Over the door (the handle of which was outside) was written, "Lasciate ogni baldanza voi che entrate"—at least, that was what was written, but Mr. Bons said that it was Lashy arty something, and that baldanza was a mistake for speranza. His voice sounded as if he was in church. Meanwhile, the boy called to the cadaverous driver for two return tickets. They were handed in without a word. Mr. Bons covered his face with his hand and again trembled. "Do you know who that is!" he whispered, when the little window had shut upon them. "It is the impossible."

"Well, I don't like him as much as Sir Thomas Browne, though I shouldn't be surprised if he had even more in him."

"More in him?" He stamped irritably. "By accident you have made the greatest discovery of the century, and all you can say is that there is more in this man. Do you remember those vellum books in my library, stamped with red lilies? This—sit still, I bring you stupendous news!—*this is the man who wrote them.*"

The boy sat quite still. "I wonder if we shall see Mrs. Gamp?" he asked, after a civil pause.

"Mrs. ——?"

"Mrs. Gamp and Mrs. Harris. I like Mrs. Harris. I came upon them quite suddenly. Mrs. Gamp's bandboxes have moved over the rainbow so badly. All the bottoms have fallen out, and two of the pippins off her bedstead tumbled into the stream."

"Out there sits the man who wrote my vellum books!" thundered Mr. Bons, "and you talk to me of Dickens and of Mrs. Gamp?"

"I know Mrs. Gamp so well," he apologized. "I could not help being glad to see her. I recognized her voice. She was telling Mrs. Harris about Mrs. Prig."

"Did you spend the whole day in her elevating company?"

"Oh, no. I raced. I met a man who took me out beyond to a race-course. You run, and there are dolphins out at sea."

"Indeed. Do you remember the man's name?"

"Achilles. No; he was later. Tom Jones."

Mr. Bons sighed heavily. "Well, my lad, you have made a miserable mess of it. Think of a cultured person with your opportunities! A cultured person would have known all these characters and known what to have said to each. He would not have wasted his time with a Mrs. Gamp or a Tom Jones. The creations of Homer, of Shakespeare, and of Him who drives us now, would alone have contented him. He would not have raced. He would have asked intelligent questions."

"But, Mr. Bons," said the boy humbly, "you will be a cultured person. I told them so."

"True, true, and I beg you not to disgrace me when we arrive. No gossiping. No running. Keep close to my side, and never speak to these Immortals unless they speak to you. Yes, and give me the return tickets. You will be losing them."

The boy surrendered the tickets, but felt a little sore. After all, he had found the way to this place. It was hard first to be disbelieved and then to be lectured. Meanwhile, the rain had stopped, and moonlight crept into the omnibus through the cracks in the blinds.

"But how is there to be a rainbow?" cried the boy.

"You distract me," snapped Mr. Bons. "I wish to meditate on beauty. I wish to goodness I was with a reverent and sympathetic person."

The lad bit his lip. He made a hundred good resolutions. He would imitate Mr. Bons all the visit. He would not laugh, or run, or sing, or do any of the vulgar things that must have disgusted his new friends last time. He would be very careful to pronounce their names properly, and to remember who knew whom. Achilles did not know Tom Jones—at least, so Mr. Bons said. The Duchess of Malfi was older than Mrs. Gamp—at least, so Mr. Bons said. He would be self-conscious, reticent, and prim. He would never say he liked any one. Yet when the Wind flew up at a chance touch of his head, all these good resolutions went to the winds, for the omnibus had reached the summit of a moonlit hill, and there was the chasm, and there, across it, stood the old precipices, dreaming, with their feet in the everlasting river. He exclaimed, "The mountain! Listen to the new tune in the water! Look at the camp fires in the ravines," and Mr. Bons, after a hasty glance, retorted, "Water? Camp fires? Ridiculous rubbish. Hold your tongue. There is nothing at all."

Yet, under his eyes, a rainbow formed, compounded not of sunlight and storm, but of moonlight and the spray of the river. The three horses put their feet upon it. He thought it the finest rainbow he had seen, but did not dare to say so, since Mr.

Bons said that nothing was there. He leant out—the window had opened—and sang the tune that rose from the sleeping waters.

"The prelude to Rhinegold?" said Mr. Bons suddenly. "Who taught you these *leit motifs*?" He, too, looked out of the window. Then he behaved very oddly. He gave a choking cry, and fell back on to the omnibus floor. He writhed and kicked. His face was green.

"Does the bridge make you dizzy?" the boy asked.

"Dizzy!" gasped Mr. Bons. "I want to go back. Tell the driver."

But the driver shook his head.

"We are nearly there," said the boy, "They are asleep. Shall I call? They will be so pleased to see you, for I have prepared them."

Mr. Bons moaned. They moved over the lunar rainbow, which ever and ever broke away behind their wheels. How still the night was! Who would be sentry at the Gate?

"I am coming," he shouted, again forgetting the hundred resolutions. "I am returning—I, the boy."

"The boy is returning," cried a voice to other voices, who repeated, "The boy is returning."

"I am bringing Mr. Bons with me."

Silence.

"I should have said Mr. Bons is bringing me with him."

Profound silence.

"Who stands sentry?"

"Achilles."

And on the rocky causeway, close to the springing of the rainbow bridge, he saw a young man who carried a wonderful shield.

"Mr. Bons, it is Achilles, armed."

"I want to go back," said Mr. Bons.

The last fragment of the rainbow melted, the wheels sang upon the living rock, the door of the omnibus burst open. Out leapt the boy—he could not resist—and sprang to meet the warrior, who, stooping suddenly, caught him on his shield.

"Achilles!" he cried, "let me get down, for I am ignorant and vulgar, and I must wait for that Mr. Bons of whom I told you yesterday."

But Achilles raised him aloft. He crouched on the wonderful shield, on heroes and burning cities, on vineyards graven in gold, on every dear passion, every joy, on the entire image of the Mountain that he had discovered, encircled, like it, with an everlasting stream. "No, no," he protested, "I am not worthy. It is Mr. Bons who must be up here."

But Mr. Bons was whimpering, and Achilles trumpeted and cried, "Stand upright upon my shield!"

"Sir, I did not mean to stand! something made me stand. Sir, why do you delay? Here is only the great Achilles, whom you knew."

Mr. Bons screamed, "I see no one. I see nothing. I want to go back." Then he cried to the driver, "Save me! Let me stop in your chariot. I have honoured you. I have quoted you. I have bound you in vellum. Take me back to my world."

The driver replied, "I am the means and not the end. I am the food and not the life. Stand by yourself, as that boy has stood. I cannot save you. For poetry is a spirit; and they that would worship it must worship in spirit and in truth."

Mr. Bons—he could not resist—crawled out of the beautiful omnibus. His face appeared, gaping horribly. His hands followed, one gripping the step, the other beating the air. Now his shoulders emerged, his chest, his stomach. With a shriek of "I see London," he fell—fell against the hard, moonlit rock, fell into it as if it were water, fell through it, vanished, and was seen by the boy no more.

"Where have you fallen to, Mr. Bons? Here is a procession arriving to honour you with music and torches. Here come the men and women whose names you know. The mountain is awake, the river is awake, over the race-course the sea is awaking those dolphins, and it is all for you. They want you——"

There was the touch of fresh leaves on his forehead. Some one had crowned him.

TELOS

From the *Kingston Gazette, Surbiton Times,* and *Paynes Park Observer*.

The body of Mr. Septimus Bons has been found in a shockingly mutilated condition in the vicinity of the Bermondsey gas-works. The deceased's pockets contained a sovereign-purse, a silver cigar-case, a bijou pronouncing dictionary, and a couple of omnibus tickets. The unfortunate gentleman had apparently been hurled from a considerable height. Foul play is suspected, and a thorough investigation is pending by the authorities.

OTHER KINGDOM

I

"*Quem*, whom; *fugis*, are you avoiding; *ab demens*, you silly ass; *habitarunt di quoque*, gods too have lived in; *silvas*, the woods.' Go ahead!"

I always brighten the classics—it is part of my system—and therefore I translated *demens* by "silly ass." But Miss Beaumont need not have made a note of the translation, and Ford, who knows better, need not have echoed after me. "Whom are you avoiding, you silly ass, gods too have lived in the woods."

"Ye—es," I replied, with scholarly hesitation. "Ye—es. *Silvas*—woods, wooded spaces, the country generally. Yes. *Demens*, of course, is *de—mens*. 'Ah, witless fellow! Gods, I say, even gods have dwelt in the woods ere now.'"

"But I thought gods always lived in the sky," said Mrs. Worters, interrupting our lesson for I think the third-and-twentieth time.

"Not always," answered Miss Beaumont. As she spoke she inserted "witless fellow" as an alternative to "silly ass."

"I always thought they lived in the sky."

"Oh, no, Mrs. Worters," the girl repeated. "Not always." And finding her place in the note-book she read as follows: "Gods. Where. Chief deities—Mount Olympus. Pan—most places, as name implies. Oreads—mountains. Sirens, Tritons, Nereids—water (salt). Naiads —water (fresh). Satyrs, Fauns, etc.—woods. Dryads—trees."

"Well, dear, you have learnt a lot. And will you now tell me what good it has done you?"

"It has helped me—" faltered Miss Beaumont. She was very earnest over her classics. She wished she could have said what good they had done her.

Ford came to her rescue, "Of course it's helped you. The classics are full of tips. They teach you how to dodge things."

I begged my young friend not to dodge his Virgil lesson.

"But they do!" he cried. "Suppose that long-haired brute Apollo wants to give you a music lesson. Well, out you pop into the laurels. Or Universal Nature comes along. You aren't feeling particularly keen on Universal Nature so you turn into a reed."

"Is Jack mad?" asked Mrs. Worters.

But Miss Beaumont had caught the allusions—which were quite ingenious I must admit. "And Croesus?" she inquired. "What was it one turned into to get away from Croesus?"

I hastened to tidy up her mythology. "Midas, Miss Beaumont, not Croesus. And he turns you—you don't turn yourself: he turns you into gold."

"There's no dodging Midas," said Ford.

"Surely—" said Miss Beaumont. She had been learning Latin not quite a fortnight, but she would have corrected the Regius Professor.

He began to tease her. "Oh, there's no dodging Midas! He just comes, he touches you, and you pay him several thousand per cent, at once. You're gold—a young golden lady—if he touches you."

"I won't be touched!" she cried, relapsing into her habitual frivolity.

"Oh, but he'll touch you."

"He sha'n't!"

"He will."

"He sha'n't!"

"He will."

Miss Beaumont took up her Virgil and smacked Ford over the head with it.

"Evelyn! Evelyn!" said Mrs. Worters. "Now you are forgetting yourself. And you also forget my question. What good has Latin done you?"

"Mr. Ford—what good has Latin done you?"

"Mr. Inskip—what good has Latin done us?"

So I was let in for the classical controversy. The arguments for the study of Latin are perfectly sound, but they are difficult to remember, and the afternoon sun was hot, and I needed my tea. But I had to justify my existence as a coach, so I took off my eye-glasses and breathed on them and said, "My dear Ford, what a question!"

"It's all right for Jack," said Mrs. Worters. "Jack has to pass his entrance examination. But what's the good of it for Evelyn? None at all."

"No, Mrs. Worters," I persisted, pointing my eye-glasses at her. "I cannot agree. Miss Beaumont is—in a sense—new to our civilization. She is entering it, and Latin is one of the subjects in her entrance examination also. No one can grasp modern life without some knowledge of its origins."

"But why should she grasp modern life?" said the tiresome woman.

"Well, there you are!" I retorted, and shut up my eye-glasses with a snap.

"Mr. Inskip, I am not there. Kindly tell me what's the good of it all. Oh, I've been through it myself: Jupiter, Venus, Juno, I know the lot of them. And many of the stories not at all proper."

"Classical education," I said drily, "is not entirely confined to classical mythology. Though even the mythology has its value. Dreams if you like, but there is value in dreams."

"I too have dreams," said Mrs. Worters, "but I am not so foolish as to mention them afterwards."

Mercifully we were interrupted. A rich virile voice close behind us said, "Cherish your dreams!" We had been joined by our host, Harcourt Worters—Mrs. Worters' son, Miss Beaumont's fiance. Ford's guardian, my employer: I must speak of him as Mr. Worters.

"Let us cherish our dreams!" he repeated. "All day I've been fighting, haggling, bargaining. And to come out on to this lawn and see you all learning Latin, so happy, so passionless, so Arcadian——"

He did not finish the sentence, but sank into the chair next to Miss Beaumont, and possessed himself of her hand. As he did so she sang: "Ah yoù sílly àss góds lìve in woóds!"

"What have we here?" said Mr. Worters with a slight frown.

With the other hand she pointed to me.

"Virgil—" I stammered. "Colloquial translation——"

"Oh, I see; a colloquial translation of poetry." Then his smile returned. "Perhaps if gods live in woods, that is why woods are so dear. I have just bought Other Kingdom Copse!"

Loud exclamations of joy. Indeed, the beeches in that copse are as fine as any in Hertfordshire. Moreover, it, and the meadow by which it is approached, have always made an ugly notch in the rounded contours of the Worters estate. So we were all very glad that Mr. Worters had purchased Other Kingdom. Only Ford kept silent, stroking his head where the Virgil had hit it, and smiling a little to himself as he did so.

"Judging from the price I paid, I should say there was a god in every tree. But price, this time was no object." He glanced at Miss Beaumont.

"You admire beeches, Evelyn, do you not?"

"I forget always which they are. Like this?"

She flung her arms up above her head, close together, so that she looked like a slender column. Then her body swayed and her delicate green dress quivered over it with the suggestion of countless leaves.

"My dear child!" exclaimed her lover.

"No: that is a silver birch," said Ford,

"Oh, of course. Like this, then." And she twitched up her skirts so that for a moment they spread out in great horizontal layers, like the layers of a beech.

We glanced at the house, but none of the servants were looking. So we laughed, and said she ought to go on the variety stage.

"Ah, this is the kind I like!" she cried, and practised the beech-tree again.

"I thought so," said Mr. Worters. "I thought so. Other Kingdom Copse is yours."

"Mine——?" She had never had such a present in her life. She could not realize it.

"The purchase will be drawn up in your name. You will sign the deed. Receive the wood, with my love. It is a second engagement ring."

"But is it—is it mine? Can I—do what I like there?"

"You can," said Mr. Worters, smiling.

She rushed at him and kissed him. She kissed Mrs. Worters. She would have kissed myself and Ford if we had not extruded elbows. The joy of possession had turned her head.

"It's mine! I can walk there, work there, live there. A wood of my own! Mine for ever."

"Yours, at all events, for ninety-nine years."

"Ninety-nine years?" I regret to say there was a tinge of disappointment in her voice.

"My dear child! Do you expect to live longer?"

"I suppose I can't," she replied, and flushed a little. "I don't know."

"Ninety-nine seems long enough to most people. I have got this house, and the very lawn you are standing on, on a lease of ninety-nine years. Yet I call them my own, and I think I am justified. Am I not?"

"Oh, yes."

"Ninety-nine years is practically for ever. Isn't it?"

"Oh, yes. It must be."

Ford possesses a most inflammatory note-book. Outside it is labelled "Private," inside it is headed "Practically a book." I saw him make an entry in it now, "Eternity: practically ninety-nine years."

Mr. Worters, as if speaking to himself, now observed: "My goodness! My goodness! How land has risen! Perfectly astounding."

I saw that he was in need of a Boswell, so I said: "Has it, indeed?"

"My dear Inskip. Guess what I could have got that wood for ten years ago! But I refused. Guess why."

We could not guess why.

"Because the transaction would not have been straight." A most becoming blush spread over his face as he uttered the noble word. "Not straight. Straight legally. But not morally straight. We were to force the hands of the man who owned it. I refused. The others—decent fellows in their way—told me I was squeamish. I said, 'Yes. Perhaps I am. My name is plain Harcourt Worters—not a well-known name if you go outside the City and my own country, but a name which, where it is known, carries, I flatter myself, some weight. And I will not sign my name to this. That is all. Call me squeamish if you like. But I will not sign. It is just a fad of mine. Let us call it a fad.'" He blushed again. Ford believes that his guardian blushes all over—if you could strip him and make him talk nobly he would look like a boiled lobster. There is a picture of him in this condition in the note-book.

"So the man who owned it then didn't own it now?" said Miss Beaumont, who had followed the narrative with some interest.

"Oh, no!" said Mr. Worters.

"Why no!" said Mrs. Worters absently, as she hunted in the grass for her knitting-needle. "Of course not. It belongs to the widow."

"Tea!" cried her son, springing vivaciously to his feet. "I see tea and I want it. Come, mother. Come along, Evelyn. I can tell you it's no joke, a hard day in the battle of life. For life is practically a battle. To all intents and purposes a battle. Except for a few lucky fellows who can read books, and so avoid the realities. But I——"

His voice died away as he escorted the two ladies over the smooth lawn and up the stone steps to the terrace, on which the footman was placing tables and little chairs and a silver kettle-stand. More ladies came out of the house. We could just hear their shouts of excitement as they also were told of the purchase of Other Kingdom.

I like Ford. The boy has the makings of a scholar and—though for some reason he objects to the word—of a gentleman. It amused me now to see his lip curl with the vague cynicism of youth. He cannot understand the footman and the solid silver kettle-stand. They make him cross. For he has dreams—not exactly spiritual dreams: Mr. Worters is the man for those—but dreams of the tangible and the actual robust dreams, which take him, not to heaven, but to another earth. There are no footmen in this other earth, and the kettle-stands, I suppose, will not be made of silver, and I know that everything is to be itself, and not practically something else. But what this means, and, if it means anything, what the good of it is, I am not prepared to say. For though I have just said "there is value in dreams," I only said it to silence old Mrs. Worters.

"Go ahead, man! We can't have tea till we've got through something."

He turned his chair away from the terrace, so that he could sit looking at the meadows and at the stream that runs through the meadows, and at the beech-trees of Other Kingdom that rise beyond the stream. Then, most gravely and admirably, he began to construe the Eclogues of Virgil.

II

Other Kingdom Copse is just like any other beech copse, and I am therefore spared the fatigue of describing it. And the stream in front of it, like many other streams, is not crossed by a bridge in the right place, and you must either walk round a mile or else you must paddle. Miss Beaumont suggested that we should paddle.

Mr. Worters accepted the suggestion tumultuously. It only became evident gradually that he was not going to adopt it.

"What fun! what fun! We will paddle to your kingdom. If only—if only it wasn't for the tea-things."

"But you can carry the tea-things on your back."

"Why, yes! so I can. Or the servants could,"

"Harcourt—no servants. This is my picnic, and my wood. I'm going to settle everything. I didn't tell you: I've got all the food. I've been in the village with Mr. Ford."

"In the village——?"

"Yes, We got biscuits and oranges and half a pound of tea. That's all you'll have. He carried them up. And he'll carry them over the stream. I want you just to lend me some tea-things—not the best ones. I'll take care of them. That's all."

"Dear creature...."

"Evelyn," said Mrs. Worters, "how much did you and Jack pay for that tea?"

"For the half-pound, tenpence."

Mrs. Worters received the announcement in gloomy silence.

"Mother!" cried Mr. Worters. "Why, I forgot! How could we go paddling with mother?"

"Oh, but, Mrs. Worters, we could carry you over."

"Thank you, dearest child. I am sure you could."

"Alas! alas! Evelyn. Mother is laughing at us. She would sooner die than be carried. And alas! there are my sisters, and Mrs. Osgood: she has a cold, tiresome woman. No: we shall have to go round by the bridge."

"But some of us——" began Ford. His guardian cut him short with a quick look.

So we went round—a procession of eight. Miss Beaumont led us. She was full of fun—at least so I thought at the time, but when I reviewed her speeches afterwards I could not find in them anything amusing. It was all this kind of thing: "Single file! Pretend you're in church and don't talk. Mr. Ford, turn out your toes. Harcourt—at the bridge throw to the Naiad a pinch of tea. She has a headache. She has had a headache for nineteen hundred years." All that she said was quite stupid. I cannot think why I liked it at the time.

As we approached the copse she said, "Mr. Inskip, sing, and we'll sing after you: Ah yoù silly àss gόds lìve in wοόds." I cleared my throat and gave out the abominable phrase, and we all chanted it as if it were a litany. There was something attractive about Miss Beaumont. I was not surprised that Harcourt had picked her out of "Ireland" and had brought her home, without money, without connections, almost without antecedents, to be his bride. It was daring of him, but he knew himself to be a daring fellow. She brought him nothing; but that he could afford, he had so vast a surplus of spiritual and commercial goods. "In time," I heard him tell his mother, "in time Evelyn will repay me a thousandfold." Meanwhile there was something attractive about her. If it were my place to like people, I could have liked her very much.

"Stop singing!" she cried. We had entered the wood. "Welcome, all of you." We bowed. Ford, who had not been laughing, bowed down to the ground. "And now be seated. Mrs. Worters—will you sit there—against that tree with a green trunk? It will show up your beautiful dress."

"Very well, dear, I will," said Mrs. Worters.

"Anna—there. Mr. Inskip next to her. Then Ruth and Mrs. Osgood. Oh, Harcourt—do sit a little forward, so that you'll hide the house. I don't want to see the house at all."

"I won't!" laughed her lover, "I want my back against a tree, too."

"Miss Beaumont," asked Ford, "where shall I sit?" He was standing at attention, like a soldier.

"Oh, look at all these Worters!" she cried, "and one little Ford in the middle of them!" For she was at that state of civilization which appreciates a pun.

"Shall I stand. Miss Beaumont? Shall I hide the house from you if I stand?"

"Sit down. Jack, you baby!" cried his guardian, breaking in with needless asperity. "Sit down!"

"He may just as well stand if he will," said she. "Just pull back your soft hat, Mr. Ford. Like a halo. Now you hide even the smoke from the chimneys. And it makes you look beautiful."

"Evelyn! Evelyn! You are too hard on the boy. You'll tire him. He's one of those bookworms. He's not strong. Let him sit down."

"Aren't you strong?" she asked.

"I am strong!" he cried. It is quite true. Ford has no right to be strong, but he is. He never did his dumb-bells or played in his school fifteen. But the muscles came. He thinks they came while he was reading Pindar.

"Then you may just as well stand, if you will."

"Evelyn! Evelyn! childish, selfish maiden! If poor Jack gets tired I will take his place. Why don't you want to see the house? Eh?"

Mrs. Worters and the Miss Worters moved uneasily. They saw that their Harcourt was not quite pleased. Theirs not to question why. It was for Evelyn to remove his displeasure, and they glanced at her.

"Well, why don't you want to see your future home? I must say—though I practically planned the house myself—that it looks very well from here. I like the gables. Miss! Answer me!"

I felt for Miss Beaumont. A home-made gable is an awful thing, and Harcourt's mansion looked like a cottage with the dropsy. But what would she say?

She said nothing.

"Well?"

It was as if he had never spoken. She was as merry, as smiling, as pretty as ever, and she said nothing. She had not realized that a question requires an answer.

For us the situation was intolerable. I had to save it by making a tactful reference to the view, which, I said, reminded me a little of the country near Veii. It did not—indeed it could not, for I have never been near Veii. But it is part of my system to make classical allusions. And at all events I saved the situation.

Miss Beaumont was serious and rational at once. She asked me the date of Veii. I made a suitable answer.

"I do like the classics," she informed us. "They are so natural. Just writing down things."

"Ye—es," said I. "But the classics have their poetry as well as their prose. They're more than a record of facts."

"Just writing down things," said Miss Beaumont, and smiled as if the silly definition pleased her.

Harcourt had recovered himself. "A very just criticism," said he. "It is what I always feel about the ancient world. It takes us but a very little way. It only writes things down."

"What do you mean?" asked Evelyn.

"I mean this—though it is presumptuous to speak in the presence of Mr. Inskip. This is what I mean. The classics are not everything. We owe them an enormous debt; I am the last to undervalue it; I, too, went through them at school. They are full of elegance and beauty. But they are not everything. They were written before men began to really feel." He coloured crimson. "Hence, the chilliness of classical art—its lack of—of a something. Whereas later things—Dante—a Madonna of Raphael—some bars of Mendelssohn——" His voice tailed reverently away. We sat with our eyes on the ground, not liking to look at Miss Beaumont. It is a fairly open secret that she also lacks a something. She has not yet developed her soul.

The silence was broken by the still small voice of Mrs. Worters saying that she was faint with hunger.

The young hostess sprang up. She would let none of us help her: it was her party. She undid the basket and emptied out the biscuits and oranges from their bags, and boiled the kettle and poured out the tea, which was horrible. But we laughed and talked with the frivolity that suits the open air, and even Mrs. Worters expectorated her flies with a smile. Over us all there stood the silent, chivalrous figure of Ford, drinking tea carefully lest it should disturb his outline. His guardian, who is a wag, chaffed him and tickled his ankles and calves.

"Well, this is nice!" said Miss Beaumont. "I am happy."

"Your wood, Evelyn!" said the ladies.

"Her wood for ever!" cried Mr. Worters. "It is an unsatisfactory arrangement, a ninety-nine years' lease. There is no feeling of permanency. I reopened negotiations. I have bought her the wood for ever—all right, dear, all right: don't make a fuss."

"But I must!" she cried. "For everything's perfect! Every one so kind—and I didn't know most of you a year ago. Oh, it is so wonderful—and now a wood—a wood of my own—a wood for ever. All of you coming to tea with me here! Dear Harcourt—dear people—and just where the house would come and spoil things, there is Mr. Ford!"

"Ha! ha!" laughed Mr. Worters, and slipped his hand up round the boy's ankle. What happened I do not know, but Ford collapsed on to the ground with a sharp cry. To an outsider it might have sounded like a cry of anger or pain. We, who knew better, laughed uproariously.

"Down he goes! Down he goes!" And they struggled playfully, kicking up the mould and the dry leaves.

"Don't hurt my wood!" cried Miss Beaumont.

Ford gave another sharp cry. Mr. Worters withdrew his hand. "Victory!" he exclaimed. "Evelyn! behold the family seat!" But Miss Beaumont, in her butterfly fashion, had left us, and was strolling away into her wood.

We packed up the tea-things and then split into groups. Ford went with the ladies. Mr. Worters did me the honour to stop by me.

"Well!" he said, in accordance with his usual formula, "and how go the classics?"

"Fairly well."

"Does Miss Beaumont show any ability?"

"I should say that she does. At all events she has enthusiasm."

"You do not think it is the enthusiasm of a child? I will be frank with you, Mr. Inskip. In many ways Miss Beaumont's practically a child. She has everything to learn: she acknowledges as much herself. Her new life is so different—so strange. Our habits—our thoughts—she has to be initiated into them all."

I saw what he was driving at, but I am not a fool, and I replied: "And how can she be initiated better than through the classics?"

"Exactly, exactly," said Mr. Worters. In the distance we heard her voice. She was counting the beech-trees. "The only question is—this Latin and Greek—what will she do with it? Can she make anything of it? Can she—well, it's not as if she will ever have to teach it to others."

"That is true." And my features might have been observed to become undecided.

"Whether, since she knows so little—I grant you she has enthusiasm. But ought one not to divert her enthusiasm—say to English literature? She scarcely knows her Tennyson at all. Last night in the conservatory I read her that wonderful scene between Arthur and Guinevere. Greek and Latin are all very well, but I sometimes feel we ought to begin at the beginning."

"You feel," said I, "that for Miss Beaumont the classics are something of a luxury."

"A luxury. That is the exact word, Mr. Inskip. A luxury. A whim. It is all very well for Jack Ford. And here we come to another point. Surely she keeps Jack back? Her knowledge must be elementary."

"Well, her knowledge *is* elementary: and I must say that it's difficult to teach them together. Jack has read a good deal, one way and another, whereas Miss Beaumont, though diligent and enthusiastic——"

"So I have been feeling. The arrangement is scarcely fair on Jack?"

"Well, I must admit——"

"Quite so. I ought never to have suggested it. It must come to an end. Of course, Mr. Inskip, it shall make no difference to you, this withdrawal of a pupil."

"The lessons shall cease at once, Mr. Worters."

Here she came up to us. "Harcourt, there are seventy-eight trees. I have had such a count."

He smiled down at her. Let me remember to say that he is tall and handsome, with a strong chin and liquid brown eyes, and a high forehead and hair not at all gray. Few things are more striking than a photograph of Mr. Harcourt Worters.

"Seventy-eight trees?"

"Seventy-eight."

"Are you pleased?"

"Oh, Harcourt——!"

I began to pack up the tea-things. They both saw and heard me. It was their own fault if they did not go further.

"I'm looking forward to the bridge," said he. "A rustic bridge at the bottom, and then, perhaps, an asphalt path from the house over the meadow, so that in all weathers we can walk here dry-shod. The boys come into the wood—look at all these initials—and I thought of putting a simple fence, to prevent any one but ourselves——"

"Harcourt!"

"A simple fence," he continued, "just like what I have put round my garden and the fields. Then at the other side of the copse, away from the house, I would put a gate, and have keys—two keys, I think—one for me and one for you—not more; and I would bring the asphalt path——"

"But Harcourt——"

"But Evelyn!"

"I—I—I——"

"You—you—you——?"

"I—I don't want an asphalt path."

"No? Perhaps you are right. Cinders perhaps. Yes. Or even gravel."

"But Harcourt—I don't want a path at all. I—I—can't afford a path."

He gave a roar of triumphant laughter. "Dearest! As if you were going to be bothered? The path's part of my present."

"The wood is your present," said Miss Beaumont. "Do you know—I don't care for the path. I'd rather always come as we came to-day. And I don't want a bridge. No—nor a fence either. I don't mind the boys and their initials. They and the girls have always come up to Other Kingdom and cut their names together in the bark. It's called the Fourth Time of Asking. I don't want it to stop."

"Ugh!" He pointed to a large heart transfixed by an arrow. "Ugh! Ugh!" I suspect that he was gaining time.

"They cut their names and go away, and when the first child is born they come again and deepen the cuts. So for each child. That's how you know: the initials that go right through to the wood are the fathers and mothers of large families, and the scratches in the bark that soon close up are boys and girls who were never married at all."

"You wonderful person! I've lived here all my life and never heard a word of this. Fancy folk-lore in Hertfordshire! I must tell the Archdeacon: he will be delighted——"

"And Harcourt, I don't want this to stop."

"My dear girl, the villagers will find other trees! There's nothing particular in Other Kingdom."

"But——"

"Other Kingdom shall be for us. You and I alone. Our initials only." His voice sank to a whisper.

"I don't want it fenced, in." Her face was turned to me; I saw that it was puzzled and frightened. "I hate fences. And bridges. And all paths. It is my wood. Please: you gave me the wood."

"Why, yes!" he replied, soothing her. But I could see that he was angry. "Of course. But aha! Evelyn, the meadow's mine; I have a right to fence there—between my domain and yours!"

"Oh, fence me out if you like! Fence me out as much as you like! But never in. Oh Harcourt, never in. I must be on the outside, I must be where any one can reach me. Year by year—while the initials deepen—the only thing worth feeling—and at last they close up—but one has felt them."

"Our initials!" he murmured, seizing upon the one word which he had understood and which was useful to him. "Let us carve our initials now. You and I—a heart if you like it, and an arrow and everything. H.W.—E.B."

"H.W.," she repeated, "and E.B."

He took out his penknife and drew her away in search of an unsullied tree. "E.B., Eternal Blessing. Mine! Mine! My haven from the world! My temple of purity. Oh the spiritual exaltation—you cannot understand it, but you will! Oh, the seclusion of Paradise. Year after year alone together, all in all to each other—year after year, soul to soul, E.B., Everlasting Bliss!"

He stretched out his hand to cut the initials. As he did so she seemed to awake from a dream. "Harcourt!" she cried, "Harcourt! What's that? What's that red stuff on your finger and thumb?"

III

Oh, my goodness! Oh, all ye goddesses and gods! Here's a mess. Mr. Worters has been reading Ford's inflammatory note-book.

"This my own fault," said Ford. "I should have labelled it 'Practically Private.' How could he know he was not meant to look inside?"

I spoke out severely, as an *employé* should. "My dear boy, none of that. The label came unstuck. That was why Mr. Worters opened the book. He never suspected it was private. See—the label's off."

"Scratched off," Ford retorted grimly, and glanced at his ankle.

I affect not to understand. "The point is this. Mr. Worters is thinking the matter over for four-and-twenty hours. If you take my advice you will apologize before that time elapses."

"And if I don't?"

"You know your own affairs of course. But don't forget that you are young and practically ignorant of life, and that you have scarcely any money of your own. As far as I can see, your career practically depends on the favour of Mr. Worters. You have laughed at him. He does not like being laughed at. It seems to me that your course is obvious."

"Apology?"

"Complete."

"And if I don't?"

"Departure."

He sat down on the stone steps and rested his head on his knees. On the lawn below us was Miss Beaumont, draggling about with some croquet balls. Her lover was out in the meadow, superintending the course of the asphalt path. For the path is to be made, and so is the bridge, and the fence is to be built round Other Kingdom after all. In time Miss Beaumont saw how unreasonable were her objections. Of her own accord, one evening in the drawing-room, she gave her Harcourt permission to do what he liked. "That wood looks nearer," said Ford.

"The inside fences have gone: that brings it nearer. But my dear boy—you must settle what you're going to do."

"How much has he read?"

"Naturally he only opened the book. From what you showed me of it, one glance would be enough."

"Did he open at the poems?"

"Poems?"

"Did he speak of the poems?"

"No. Were they about him?"

"They were not about him."

"Then it wouldn't matter if he saw them."

"It is sometimes a compliment to be mentioned," said Ford, looking up at me. The remark had a stinging fragrance about it—such a fragrance as clings to the mouth after admirable wine. It did not taste like the remark of a boy. I was sorry that my pupil was likely to wreck his career; and I told him again that he had better apologize.

"I won't speak of Mr. Worters' claim for an apology. That's an aspect on which I prefer not to touch. The point is, if you don't apologize, you go—where?"

"To an aunt at Peckham."

I pointed to the pleasant, comfortable land-scape, full of cows and carriage-horses out at grass, and civil retainers. In the midst of it stood Mr. Worters, radiating energy and wealth, like a terrestrial sun. "My dear Ford—don't be heroic! Apologize."

Unfortunately I raised my voice a little, and Miss Beaumont heard me, down on the lawn.

"Apologize?" she cried. "What about?" And as she was not interested in the game, she came up the steps towards us, trailing her croquet mallet behind her. Her walk was rather listless. She was toning down at last.

"Come indoors!" I whispered. "We must get out of this."

"Not a bit of it!" said Ford.

"What is it?" she asked, standing beside him on the step.

He swallowed something as he looked up at her. Suddenly I understood. I knew the nature and the subject of his poems. I was not so sure now that he had better apologize. The sooner he was kicked out of the place the better.

In spite of my remonstrances, he told her about the book, and her first remark was: "Oh, do let me see it!" She had no "proper feeling" of any kind. Then she said: "But why do you both look so sad?"

"We are awaiting Mr. Worters' decision," said I.

"Mr. Inskip! What nonsense! Do you suppose Harcourt'll be angry?"

"Of course he is angry, and rightly so."

"But why?"

"Ford has laughed at him."

"But what's that!" And for the first time there was anger in her voice. "Do you mean to say he'll punish some one who laughs at him? Why, for what else—for whatever reason are we all here? Not to laugh at each other! I laugh at people all day. At Mr. Ford. At you. And so does Harcourt. Oh, you've misjudged him! He won't—he couldn't be angry with people who laughed."

"Mine is not nice laughter," said Ford. "He could not well forgive me."

"You're a silly boy." She sneered at him. "You don't know Harcourt. So generous in every way. Why, he'd be as furious as I should be if you apologized. Mr. Inskip, isn't that so?"

"He has every right to an apology, I think."

"Right? What's a right? You use too many new words. 'Rights'—'apologies'—'society'—'position'—I don't follow it. What are we all here for, anyhow?"

Her discourse was full of trembling lights and shadows—frivolous one moment, the next moment asking why Humanity is here. I did not take the Moral Science Tripos, so I could not tell her.

"One thing I know—and that is that Harcourt isn't as stupid as you two. He soars above conventions. He doesn't care about 'rights' and 'apologies.' He knows that all laughter is nice, and that the other nice things are money and the soul and so on."

The soul and so on! I wonder that Harcourt out in the meadows did not have an apoplectic fit.

"Why, what a poor business your life would be," she continued, "if you all kept taking offence and apologizing! Forty million people in England and all of them touchy! How one would laugh if it was true! Just imagine!" And she did laugh. "Look at Harcourt though. He knows better. He isn't petty like that. Mr. Ford! He isn't petty like that. Why, what 's wrong with your eyes?"

He rested his head on his knees again, and we could see his eyes no longer. In dispassionate tones she informed me that she thought he was crying. Then she tapped him on the hair with her mallet and said: "Cry-baby! Cry-cry-baby! Crying about nothing!" and ran laughing down the steps. "All right!" she shouted from the lawn. "Tell the cry-baby to stop. I'm going to speak to Harcourt!"

We watched her go in silence. Ford had scarcely been crying. His eyes had only become large and angry. He used such swear-words as he knew, and then got up abruptly, and went into the house. I think he could not bear to see her disillusioned. I had no such tenderness, and it was with considerable interest that I watched Miss Beaumont approach her lord.

She walked confidently across the meadow, bowing to the workmen as they raised their hats. Her languor had passed, and with it her suggestion of "tone." She was the same crude, unsophisticated person that Harcourt had picked out of Ireland—beautiful and ludicrous in the extreme, and:—if you go in for pathos—extremely pathetic.

I saw them meet, and soon she was hanging on his arm. The motion of his hand explained to her the construction of bridges. Twice she interrupted him: he had to explain everything again. Then she got in her word, and what followed was a good deal better than a play. Their two little figures parted and met and parted again, she gesticulating, he most pompous and calm. She pleaded, she argued and—if satire can carry half a mile—she tried to be satirical. To enforce one of her childish points she made two steps back. Splash! She was floundering in the little stream.

That was the *dénouement* of the comedy. Harcourt rescued her, while the workmen crowded round in an agitated chorus. She was wet quite as far as her knees, and muddy over her ankles. In this state she was conduced towards me, and in time I began to hear words; "Influenza—a slight immersion—clothes are of no consequence beside health—pray, dearest, don't worry—yes, it must have been a shock—bed! bed! I insist on bed! Promise? Good girl. Up the steps to bed then."

They parted on the lawn, and she came obediently up the steps. Her face was full of terror and bewilderment.

"So you've had a wetting, Miss Beaumont!"

"Wetting? Oh, yes. But, Mr. Inskip—I don't understand: I've failed."

I expressed surprise.

"Mr. Ford is to go—at once. I've failed."

"I'm sorry."

"I've failed with Harcourt. He's offended. He won't laugh. He won't let me do what I want. Latin and Greek began it: I wanted to know about gods and heroes and he wouldn't let me: then I wanted no fence round Other Kingdom and no bridge and no path—and look! Now I ask that Mr. Ford, who has done nothing, sha'n't be punished for it—and he is to go away for ever."

"Impertinence is not 'nothing,' Miss Beaumont." For I must keep in with Harcourt.

"Impertinence is nothing!" she cried. "It doesn't exist. It's a sham, like 'claims' and 'position' and 'rights.' It's part of the great dream."

"What 'great dream'?" I asked, trying not to smile.

"Tell Mr. Ford—here comes Harcourt; I must go to bed. Give my love to Mr. Ford, and tell him 'to guess.' I shall never see him again, and I won't stand it. Tell him to guess. I am sorry I called him a cry-baby. He was not crying like a baby. He was crying like a grown-up person, and now I have grown up too."

I judged it right to repeat this conversation to my employer.

IV

The bridge is built, the fence finished, and Other Kingdom lies tethered by a ribbon of asphalt to our front door. The seventy-eight trees therein certainly seem nearer, and during the windy nights that followed Ford's departure we could hear their branches sighing, and would find in the morning that beech-leaves had been blown right up against the house. Miss Beaumont made no attempt to go out, much to the relief of the ladies, for Harcourt had given the word that she was not to go out unattended, and the boisterous weather deranged their petticoats. She remained indoors, neither reading nor laughing, and dressing no longer in green, but in brown.

Not noticing her presence, Mr. Worters looked in one day and said with a sigh of relief: "That's all right. The circle's completed."

"Is it indeed!" she replied.

"You there, you quiet little mouse? I only meant that our lords, the British workmen, have at last condescended to complete their labours, and have rounded us off from the world. I—in the end I was a naughty, domineering tyrant, and disobeyed you. I didn't have the gate out at the further side of the copse. Will you forgive me?"

"Anything, Harcourt, that pleases you, is certain to please me."

The ladies smiled at each other, and Mr. Worters said: "That's right, and as soon as the wind goes down we'll all progress together to your wood; and take possession of it formally, for it didn't really count that last time."

"No, it didn't really count that last time," Miss Beaumont echoed.

"Evelyn says this wind never will go down," remarked Mrs. Worters. "I don't know how she knows."

"It will never go down, as long as I am in the house."

"Really?" he said gaily. "Then come out now, and send it down with me."

They took a few turns up and down the terrace. The wind lulled for a moment, but blew fiercer than ever during lunch. As we ate, it roared and whistled down the chimney at us, and the trees of Other Kingdom frothed like the sea. Leaves and twigs flew from them, and a bough, a good-sized bough, was blown on to the smooth asphalt path, and actually switchbacked over the bridge, up the meadow, and across our very lawn. (I venture to say "our," as I am now staying on as Harcourt's secretary.) Only the stone steps prevented it from reaching the terrace and perhaps breaking the dining-room window. Miss Beaumont sprang up and, napkin in hand, ran out and touched it.

"Oh, Evelyn——" the ladies cried.

"Let her go," said Mr. Worters tolerantly. "It certainly is a remarkable incident, remarkable. We must remember to tell the Archdeacon about it."

"Harcourt," she cried, with the first hint of returning colour in her cheeks, "mightn't we go up to the copse after lunch, you and I?"

Mr. Worters considered.

"Of course, not if you don't think best."

"Inskip, what's your opinion?"

I saw what his own was, and cried, "Oh, let's go!" though I detest the wind as much as any one.

"Very well. Mother, Anna, Ruth, Mrs. Osgood—we'll all go."

And go we did, a lugubrious procession; but the gods were good to us for once, for as soon as we were started, the tempest dropped, and there ensued an extraordinary calm. After all, Miss Beaumont was something of a weather prophet. Her spirits improved every minute. She tripped in front of us along the asphalt path, and ever and anon turned round to say to her lover some gracious or alluring thing. I admired her for it. I admire people who know on which side their bread's buttered.

"Evelyn, come here!"

"Come here yourself."

"Give me a kiss."

"Come and take it then."

He ran after her, and she ran away, while all our party laughed melodiously.

"Oh, I am so happy!" she cried. "I think I've everything I want in all the world. Oh dear, those last few days indoors! But oh, I am so happy now!" She had changed her brown dress for the old flowing green one, and she began to do her skirt dance in the open meadow, lit by sudden gleams of the sunshine. It was really a beautiful sight, and Mr. Worters did not correct her, glad perhaps that she should recover her spirits, even if she lost her tone. Her feet scarcely moved, but her body so swayed and her dress spread so gloriously around her, that we were transported with joy. She danced to the song of a bird that sang passionately in Other Kingdom, and the river held back its waves to watch her (one might have supposed), and the winds lay spell-bound in their cavern, and the great clouds spell-bound in the sky. She danced away from our society and our life, back, back through the centuries till houses and fences fell and the earth lay wild to the sun. Her garment was as foliage upon her, the strength of her limbs as boughs, her throat the smooth upper branch that salutes the morning or glistens to the rain. Leaves move, leaves hide it as hers was hidden by the motion of her hair. Leaves move again and it is ours, as her throat was ours again when, parting the tangle, she faced us crying, "Oh!" crying, "Oh Harcourt! I never was so happy. I have all that there is in the world."

But he, entrammelled in love's ecstasy, forgetting certain Madonnas of Raphael, forgetting, I fancy, his soul, sprang to inarm her with, "Evelyn! Eternal Bliss! Mine to eternity! Mine!" and she sprang away. Music was added and she sang, "Oh Ford! oh Ford, among all these Worters, I am coming through you to my Kingdom. Oh Ford, my lover while I was a woman, I will never forget you, never, as long as I have branches to shade you from the sun," and, singing, crossed the stream.

Why he followed her so passionately, I do not know. It was play, she was in his own domain which a fence surrounds, and she could not possibly escape him. But he dashed round by the bridge as if all their love was at stake, and pursued her with fierceness up the hill. She ran well, but the end was a foregone conclusion, and we only speculated whether he would catch her outside or inside the copse. He gained on her inch by inch; now they were in the shadow of the trees; he had practically grasped her, he had missed; she had disappeared into the trees themselves, he following.

"Harcourt is in high spirits," said Mrs. Osgood, Anna, and Ruth.

"Evelyn!" we heard him shouting within.

We proceeded up the asphalt path.

"Evelyn! Evelyn!"

"He's not caught her yet, evidently."

"Where are you, Evelyn?"

"Miss Beaumont must have hidden herself rather cleverly."

"Look here," cried Harcourt, emerging, "have you seen Evelyn?"

"Oh, no, she's certainly inside."

"So I thought."

"Evelyn must be dodging round one of the trunks. You go this way, I that. We'll soon find her."

We searched, gaily at first, and always with a feeling that Miss Beaumont was close by, that the delicate limbs were just behind this bole, the hair and the drapery quivering among those leaves. She was beside us, above us; here was her footstep on the purple-brown earth—her bosom, her neck—she was everywhere and nowhere. Gaiety turned to irritation, irritation to anger and fear. Miss Beaumont was apparently lost. "Evelyn! Evelyn!" we continued to cry. "Oh, really, it is beyond a joke."

Then the wind arose, the more violent for its lull, and we were driven into the house by a terrific storm. We said, "At all events she will come back now." But she did not come, and the rain hissed and rose up from the dry meadows like incense smoke, and smote the quivering leaves to applause. Then it lightened. Ladies screamed, and we saw Other Kingdom as one who claps the handsy and heard it as one who roars with laughter in the thunder. Not even the Archdeacon can remember such a storm. All Harcourt's seedlings were ruined, and the tiles flew off his gables right and left. He came to me presently with a white, drawn face, saying: "Inskip, can I trust you?"

"You can, indeed."

"I have long suspected it; she has eloped with Ford."

"But how——" I gasped.

"The carriage is ready—we'll talk as we drive." Then, against the rain he shouted: "No gate in the fence, I know, but what about a ladder? While I blunder, she's over the fence, and he——"

"But you were so close. There was not the time."

"There is time for anything," he said venomously, "where a treacherous woman is concerned. I found her no better than a savage, I trained her, I educated her. But I'll break them both. I can do that; I'll break them soul and body."

No one can break Ford now. The task is impossible. But I trembled for Miss Beaumont.

We missed the train. Young couples had gone by it, several young couples, and we heard of more young couples in London, as if all the world were mocking Harcourt's solitude. In desperation we sought the squalid suburb that is now Ford's home. We swept past the dirty maid and the terrified aunt, swept upstairs, to catch him if we could red-handed. He was seated at the table, reading the *Oedipus Coloneus* of Sophocles.

"That won't take in me!" shouted Harcourt. "You've got Miss Beaumont with you, and I know it."

"No such luck," said Ford.

He stammered with rage. "Inskip—you hear that? 'No such luck'! Quote the evidence against him. I can't speak."

So I quoted her song. "'Oh Ford! Oh Ford, among all these Worters, I am coming through you to my Kingdom! Oh Ford, my lover while I was a woman, I will never forget you, never, as long as I have branches to shade you from the sun.' Soon after that, we lost her."

"And—and on another occasion she sent a message of similar effect. Inskip, bear witness. He was to 'guess' something."

"I have guessed it," said Ford.

"So you practically——"

"Oh, no, Mr. Worters, you mistake me. I have not practically guessed. I have guessed. I could tell you if I chose, but it would be no good, for she has not practically escaped you. She has escaped you absolutely, for ever and ever, as long as there are branches to shade men from the sun."

THE CURATE'S FRIEND

It is uncertain how the Faun came to be in Wiltshire. Perhaps he came over with the Roman legionaries to live with his friends in camp, talking to them of Lucretius, or Garganus or of the slopes of Etna; they in the joy of their recall forgot to take him on board, and he wept in exile; but at last he found that our hills also understood his sorrows, and rejoiced when he was happy. Or, perhaps he came to be there because he had been there always. There is nothing particularly classical about a faun: it is only that the Greeks and Italians have ever had the sharpest eyes. You will find him in the "Tempest" and the "Benedicite;" and any country which has beech clumps and sloping grass and very clear streams may reasonably produce him.

How I came to see him is a more difficult question. For to see him there is required a certain quality, for which truthfulness is too cold a name and animal spirits too coarse a one, and he alone knows how this quality came to be in me. No man has the right to call himself a fool, but I may say that I then presented the perfect semblance of one. I was facetious without humour and serious without conviction. Every Sunday I would speak to my rural parishioners about the other world in the tone of one who has been behind the scenes, or I would explain to them the errors of the Pelagians, or I would warn them against hurrying from one dissipation to another. Every Tuesday I gave what I called "straight talks to my lads"—talks which led straight past anything awkward. And every Thursday I addressed the Mothers' Union on the duties of wives or widows, and gave them practical hints on the management of a family of ten.

I took myself in, and for a time I certainly took in Emily. I have never known a girl attend so carefully to my sermons, or laugh so heartily at my jokes. It is no wonder that I became engaged. She has made an excellent wife, freely correcting her husband's absurdities, but allowing no one else to breathe a word against them; able to talk about the sub-conscious self in the drawing-room, and yet have an ear for the children crying in the nursery, or the plates breaking in the scullery. An excellent wife—better than I ever imagined. But she has not married me.

Had we stopped indoors that afternoon nothing thing would have happened. It was all owing to Emily's mother, who insisted on our tea-ing out. Opposite the village, across the stream, was a small chalk down, crowned by a beech copse, and a few Roman earth-works. (I lectured very vividly on those earthworks: they have since proved to be Saxon). Hither did I drag up a tea-basket and a heavy rug for Emily's mother, while Emily and a little friend went on in front. The little friend—who has played all through a much less important part than he supposes—was a pleasant youth, full of intelligence and poetry, especially of what he called the poetry of earth. He longed to wrest earth's secret from her, and I have seen him press his face passionately into the grass, even when he has believed himself to be alone. Emily was at that time full of vague aspirations, and, though I should have preferred them all to centre in me, yet it seemed unreasonable to deny her such other opportunities for self-culture as the neighbourhood provided.

It was then my habit, on reaching the top of any eminence, to exclaim facetiously "And who will stand on either hand and keep the bridge with me?" at the same moment violently agitating my arms or casting my wide-awake eyes at an imaginary foe. Emily and the friend received my sally as usual, nor could I detect any insincerity in their mirth. Yet I was convinced that some one was present who did not think I had been funny, and any public speaker will understand my growing uneasiness.

I was somewhat cheered by Emily's mother, who puffed up exclaiming, "Kind Harry, to carry the things! What should we do without you, even now! Oh, what a view! Can you see the dear Cathedral? No. Too hazy. Now *I'm* going to sit *right* on the rug." She smiled mysteriously. "The downs in September, you know."

We gave some perfunctory admiration to the landscape, which is indeed only beautiful to those who admire land, and to them perhaps the most beautiful in England. For here is the body of the great chalk spider who straddles over our island—whose legs are the south downs and the north downs and the Chilterns, and the tips of whose toes poke out at Cromer and Dover. He is a clean creature, who grows as few trees as he can, and those few in tidy clumps, and he loves to be tickled by quickly flowing streams. He is pimpled all over with earth-works, for from the beginning of time men have fought for the privilege of standing on him, and the oldest of our temples is built upon his back.

But in those days I liked my country snug and pretty, full of gentlemen's residences and shady bowers and people who touch their hats. The great sombre expanses on which one may walk for miles and hardly shift a landmark or meet a genteel person were still intolerable to me. I turned away as soon as propriety allowed and said "And may I now prepare the cup that cheers?"

Emily's mother replied: "Kind man, to help me. I always do say that tea out is worth the extra effort. I wish we led simpler lives." We agreed with her. I spread out the food. "Won't the kettle stand? Oh, but *make* it stand." I did so. There was a little cry, faint but distinct, as of something in pain.

"How silent it all is up here!" said Emily.

I dropped a lighted match on the grass, and again I heard the little cry.

"What is that?" I asked.

"I only said it was so silent," said Emily.

"Silent, indeed," echoed the little friend.

Silent! the place was full of noises. If the match had fallen in a drawing-room it could not have been worse, and the loudest noise came from beside Emily herself. I had exactly the sensation of going to a great party, of waiting to be announced in the echoing hall, where I could hear the voices of the guests, but could not yet see their faces. It is a nervous moment for a self-conscious man, especially if all the voices should be strange to him, and he has never met his host.

"My dear Harry!" said the elder lady, "never mind about that match. That'll smoulder away and harm no one. Tea-ee-ee! I always say—and you will find Emily the same—that as the magic hour of five approaches, no matter how good a lunch, one begins to feel a sort of——"

Now the Faun is of the kind who capers upon the Neo-Attic reliefs, and if you do not notice his ears or see his tail, you take him for a man and are horrified.

"Bathing!" I cried wildly. "Such a thing for our village lads, but I quite agree—more supervision—I blame myself. Go away, bad boy, go away!"

"What will he think of next!" said Emily, while the creature beside her stood up and beckoned to me. I advanced struggling and gesticulating with tiny steps and horrified cries, exorcising the apparition with my hat. Not otherwise had I advanced the day before, when Emily's nieces showed me their guinea pigs. And by no less hearty laughter was I greeted now. Until the strange fingers closed upon me, I still thought that here was one of my parishioners and did not cease to exclaim, "Let me go, naughty boy, let go!" And Emily's mother, believing herself to have detected the joke, replied, "Well I must confess they are naughty boys and reach one even on the rug: the downs in September, as I said before."

Here I caught sight of the tail, uttered a wild shriek and fled into the beech copse behind.

"Harry would have been a born actor," said Emily's mother as I left them.

I realized that a great crisis in my life was approaching, and that if I failed in it I might permanently lose my self-esteem. Already in the wood I was troubled by a multitude of voices—the voices of the hill beneath me, of the trees over my head, of the very insects in the bark of the tree. I could even hear the stream licking little pieces out of the meadows, and the meadows dreamily protesting. Above the din—which is no louder than the flight of a bee—rose the Faun's voice saying, "Dear priest, be placid, be placid: why are you frightened?"

"I am not frightened," said I—and indeed I was not. "But I am grieved: you have disgraced me in the presence of ladies."

"No one else has seen me," he said, smiling idly. "The women have tight boots and the man has long hair. Those kinds never see. For years I have only spoken to children, and they lose sight of me as soon as they grow up. But you will not be able to lose sight of me, and until you die you will be my friend. Now I begin to make you happy: lie upon your back or run races, or climb trees, or shall I get you blackberries, or harebells, or wives——"

In a terrible voice I said to him, "Get thee behind me!" He got behind me. "Once for all," I continued, "let me tell you that it is vain to tempt one whose happiness consists in giving happiness to others."

"I cannot understand you," he said ruefully. "What is to tempt?"

"Poor woodland creature!" said I, turning round. "How could you understand? It was idle of me to chide you. It is not in your little nature to comprehend a life of self-denial. Ah! if only I could reach you!"

"You have reached him," said the hill.

"If only I could touch you!"

"You have touched him," said the hill.

"But I will never leave you," burst out the Faun. "I will sweep out your shrine for you, I will accompany you to the meetings of matrons. I will enrich you at the bazaars."

I shook my head. "For these things I care not at all. And indeed I was minded to reject your offer of service altogether. There I was wrong. You shall help me—you shall help me to make others happy."

"Dear priest, what a curious life! People whom I have never seen—people who cannot see me—why should I make them happy?"

"My poor lad—perhaps in time you will learn why. Now begone: commence. On this very hill sits a young lady for whom I have a high regard. Commence with her. Aha! your face falls. I thought as much. You *cannot* do anything. Here is the conclusion of the whole matter!"

"I can make her happy," he replied, "if you order me; and when I have done so, perhaps you will trust me more."

Emily's mother had started home, but Emily and the little friend still sat beside the tea-things—she in her white piqué dress and biscuit straw, he in his rough but well-cut summer suit. The great pagan figure of the Faun towered insolently above them.

The friend was saying, "And have you never felt the appalling loneliness of a crowd?"

"All that," replied Emily, "have I felt, and very much more—"

Then the Faun laid his hands upon them. They, who had only intended a little cultured flirtation, resisted him as long as they could, but were gradually urged into each other's arms, and embraced with passion.

"Miscreant!" I shouted, bursting from the wood. "You have betrayed me."

"I know it: I care not," cried the little friend. "Stand aside. You are in the presence of that which you do not understand. In the great solitude we have found ourselves at last."

"Remove your accursed hands!" I shrieked to the Faun.

He obeyed and the little friend continued more calmly: "It is idle to chide. What should you know, poor clerical creature, of the mystery of love of the eternal man and the eternal woman, of the self-effectuation of a soul?"

"That is true," said Emily angrily. "Harry, you would never have made me happy. I shall treat you as a friend, but how could I give myself to a man who makes such silly jokes? When you played the buffoon at tea, your hour was sealed. I must be treated seriously: I must see infinities broadening around me as I rise. You may not approve of it, but so I am. In the great solitude I have found myself at last."

"Wretched girl!" I cried. "Great solitude! O pair of helpless puppets——"

The little friend began to lead Emily away, but I heard her whisper to him: "Dear, we can't possibly leave the basket for Harry after this: and mother's rug; do you mind having that in the other hand?"

So they departed and I flung myself upon the ground with every appearance of despair.

"Does he cry?" said the Faun.

"He does not cry," answered the hill. "His eyes are as dry as pebbles."

My tormentor made me look at him. "I see happiness at the bottom of your heart," said he.

"I trust I have my secret springs," I answered stiffly. And then I prepared a scathing denunciation, but of all the words I might have said, I only said one and it began with "D."

He gave a joyful cry, "Oh, now you really belong to us. To the end of your life you will swear when you are cross and laugh when you are happy. Now laugh!"

There was a great silence. All nature stood waiting, while a curate tried to conceal his thoughts not only from nature but from himself. I thought of my injured pride, of my baffled unselfishness, of Emily, whom I was losing through no fault of her own, of the little friend, who just then slipped beneath the heavy tea basket, and that decided me, and I laughed.

That evening, for the first time, I heard the chalk downs singing to each other across the valleys, as they often do when the air is quiet and they have had a comfortable day. From my study window I could see the sunlit figure of the Faun, sitting before the beech copse as a man sits before his house. And as night came on I knew for certain that not only was he asleep, but that the hills and woods were asleep also. The stream, of course, never slept, any more than it ever freezes. Indeed, the hour of darkness is really the hour of water, which has been somewhat stifled all day by the great pulsings of the land. That is why you can feel it and hear it from a greater distance in the night, and why a bath after sundown is most wonderful.

The joy of that first evening is still clear in my memory, in spite of all the happy years that have followed. I remember it when I ascend my pulpit—I have a living now—and look down upon the best people sitting beneath me pew after pew, generous and contented, upon the worse people, crowded in the aisles, upon the whiskered tenors of the choir, and the high-browed curates and the churchwardens fingering their bags, and the supercilious vergers who turn late comers from the door. I remember it also when I sit in my comfortable bachelor reftory, amidst the carpet slippers that good young ladies have worked for me, and the oak brackets that have been carved for me by good young men; amidst my phalanx of presentation teapots and my illuminated testimonials and all the other offerings of people who believe that I have given them a helping hand, and who really have helped me out of the mire themselves. And though I try to communicate that joy to others—as I try to communicate anything else that seems good—and though I sometimes succeed, yet I can tell no one exactly how it came to me. For if I breathed one word of that, my present life, so agreeable and profitable, would come to an end, my congregation would depart, and so should I, and instead of being an asset to my parish, I might find myself an expense to the nation. Therefore in the place of the lyrical and rhetorical treatment, so suitable to the subject, so congenial to my profession, I have been forced to use the unworthy medium of a narrative, and to delude you by declaring that this is a short story, suitable for reading in the train.

THE ROAD FROM COLONUS

I

For no very intelligible reason, Mr. Lucas had hurried ahead of his party. He was perhaps reaching the age at which independence becomes valuable, because it is so soon to be lost. Tired of attention and consideration, he liked breaking away from the younger members, to ride by himself, and to dismount unassisted. Perhaps he also relished that more subtle pleasure of being kept waiting for lunch, and of telling the others on their arrival that it was of no consequence.

So, with childish impatience, he battered the animal's sides with his heels, and made the muleteer bang it with a thick stick and prick it with a sharp one, and jolted down the hill sides through clumps of flowering shrubs and stretches of anemones and asphodel, till he heard the sound of running water, and came in sight of the group of plane trees where they were to have their meal.

Even in England those trees would have been remarkable, so huge were they, so interlaced, so magnificently clothed in quivering green. And here in Greece they were unique, the one cool spot in that hard brilliant landscape, already scorched by the heat of an April sun. In their midst was hidden a tiny Khan or country inn, a frail mud building with a broad wooden balcony in which sat an old woman spinning, while a small brown pig, eating orange peel, stood beside her. On the wet earth below squatted two children, playing some primaeval game with their fingers; and their mother, none too clean either, was messing with some rice inside. As Mrs. Forman would have said, it was all very Greek, and the fastidious Mr. Lucas felt thankful that they were bringing their own food with them, and should eat it in the open air.

Still, he was glad to be there—the muleteer had helped him off—and glad that Mrs. Forman was not there to forestall his opinions—glad even that he should not see Ethel for quite half an hour. Ethel was his youngest daughter, still unmarried. She was unselfish and affectionate, and it was generally understood that she was to devote her life to her father, and be the comfort of his old age. Mrs. Forman always referred to her as Antigone, and Mr. Lucas tried to settle down to the role of Oedipus, which seemed the only one that public opinion allowed him.

He had this in common with Oedipus, that he was growing old. Even to himself it had become obvious. He had lost interest in other people's affairs, and seldom attended when they spoke to him. He was fond of talking himself but often forgot what he was going to say, and even when he succeeded, it seldom seemed worth the effort. His phrases and gestures had become stiff and set, his anecdotes, once so successful, fell flat, his silence was as meaningless as his speech. Yet he had led a healthy, active life, had worked steadily, made money, educated his children. There was nothing and no one to blame: he was simply growing old.

At the present moment, here he was in Greece, and one of the dreams of his life was realized. Forty years ago he had caught the fever of Hellenism, and all his life he had felt that could he but visit that land, he would not have lived in vain. But Athens had been dusty, Delphi wet, Thermopylae flat, and he had listened with amazement and cynicism to the rapturous exclamations of his companions. Greece was like England: it was a man who was growing old, and it made no difference whether that man looked at the Thames or the Eurotas. It was his last hope of contradicting that logic of experience, and it was failing.

Yet Greece had done something for him, though he did not know it. It had made him discontented, and there are stirrings of life in discontent. He knew that he was not the victim of continual ill-luck. Something great was wrong, and he was pitted against no mediocre or accidental enemy. For the last month a strange desire had possessed him to die fighting.

"Greece is the land for young people," he said to himself as he stood under the plane trees, "but I will enter into it, I will possess it. Leaves shall be green again, water shall be sweet, the sky shall be blue. They were so forty years ago, and I will win them back. I do mind being old, and I will pretend no longer."

He took two steps forward, and immediately cold waters were gurgling over his ankle.

"Where does the water come from?" he asked himself. "I do not even know that." He remembered that all the hill sides were dry; yet here the road was suddenly covered with flowing streams.

He stopped still in amazement, saying: "Water out of a tree—out of a hollow tree? I never saw nor thought of that before."

For the enormous plane that leant towards the Khan was hollow—it had been burnt out for charcoal—and from its living trunk there gushed an impetuous spring, coating the bark! with fern and moss, and flowing over the mule track to create fertile meadows beyond. The simple country folk had paid to beauty and mystery such tribute as they could, for in the rind of the tree a shrine was cut, holding a lamp and a little picture of the Virgin, inheritor of the Naiad's and Dryad's joint abode.

"I never saw anything so marvellous before," said Mr. Lucas. "I could even step inside the trunk and see where the water comes from."

For a moment he hesitated to violate the shrine. Then he remembered with a smile his own thought—"the place shall be mine; I will enter it and possess it"—and leapt almost aggressively on to a stone within.

The water pressed up steadily and noiselessly from the hollow roots and hidden crevices of the plane, forming a wonderful amber pool ere it spilt over the lip of bark on to the earth outside. Mr. Lucas tasted it and it was sweet, and when he looked up the black funnel of the trunk he saw sky which was blue, and some leaves which were green; and he remembered, without smiling, another of his thoughts.

Others had been before him—indeed he had a curious sense of companionship. Little votive offerings to the presiding Power were fastened on to the bark—tiny arms and legs and eyes in tin, grotesque models of the brain or the heart—all tokens of some recovery of strength or wisdom or love. There was no such thing as the solitude of nature for the sorrows and joys of humanity had pressed even into the bosom of a tree. He spread out his arms and steadied himself against the soft charred wood, and then slowly leant back, till his body was resting on the trunk behind. His eyes closed, and he had the strange feeling of one who is moving, yet at peace—the feeling of the swimmer, who, after long struggling with chopping seas, finds that after all the tide will sweep him to his goal.

So he lay motionless, conscious only of the stream below his feet, and that all things were a stream, in which he was moving.

He was aroused at last by a shock—the shock of an arrival perhaps, for when he opened his eyes, something unimagined, indefinable, had passed over all things, and made them intelligible and good.

There was meaning in the stoop of the old woman over her work, and in the quick motions of the little pig, and in her diminishing globe of wool. A young man came singing over the streams on a mule, and there was beauty in his pose and sincerity in his greeting. The sun made no accidental patterns upon the spreading roots of the trees, and there was intention in the nodding clumps of asphodel, and in the music of the water. To Mr. Lucas, who, in a brief space of time, had discovered not only Greece, but England and all the world and life, there seemed nothing ludicrous in the desire to hang within the tree another votive offering—a little model of an entire man.

"Why, here's papa, playing at being Merlin."

All unnoticed they had arrived—Ethel, Mrs. Forman, Mr. Graham, and the English-speaking dragoman. Mr. Lucas peered out at them suspiciously. They had suddenly become unfamiliar, and all that they did seemed strained and coarse.

"Allow me to give you a hand," said Mr. Graham, a young man who was always polite to his elders.

Mr. Lucas felt annoyed. "Thank you, I can manage perfectly well by myself," he replied. His foot slipped as he stepped out of the tree, and went into the spring.

"Oh papa, my papa!" said Ethel, "what are you doing? Thank goodness I have got a change for you on the mule."

She tended him carefully, giving him clean socks and dry boots, and then sat him down on the rug beside the lunch basket, while she went with the others to explore the grove.

They came back in ecstasies, in which Mr. Lucas tried to join. But he found them intolerable. Their enthusiasm was superficial, commonplace, and spasmodic. They had no perception of the coherent beauty was flowering around them. He tried at least to explain his feelings, and what he said was:

"I am altogether pleased with the appearance of this place. It impresses me very favourably. The trees are fine, remarkably fine for Greece, and there is something very poetic in the spring of clear running water. The people too seem kindly and civil. It is decidedly an attractive place."

Mrs. Forman upbraided him for his tepid praise.

"Oh, it is a place in a thousand!" she cried "I could live and die here! I really would stop if I had not to be back at Athens! It reminds me of the Colonus of Sophocles."

"Well, I must stop," said Ethel. "I positively must."

"Yes, do! You and your father! Antigone and Oedipus. Of course you must stop at Colonus!"

Mr. Lucas was almost breathless with excitement. When he stood within the tree, he had believed that his happiness would be independent of locality. But these few minutes' conversation had undeceived him. He no longer trusted himself to journey through the world, for old thoughts, old wearinesses might be waiting to rejoin him as soon as he left the shade of the planes, and the music of the virgin water. To sleep in the Khan with the gracious, kind-eyed country people, to watch the bats flit about within the globe of shade, and see the moon turn the golden patterns into silver—one such night would place him beyond relapse, and confirm him for ever in the kingdom he had regained. But all his lips could say was: "I should be willing to put in a night here."

"You mean a week, papa! It would be sacrilege to put in less."

"A week then, a week," said his lips, irritated at being corrected, while his heart was leaping with joy. All through lunch he spoke to them no more, but watched the place he should know so well, and the people who would so soon be his companions and friends. The inmates of the Khan only consisted of an old woman, a middle-aged woman, a young man and two children, and to none of them had he spoken, yet he loved them as he loved everything that moved or breathed or existed beneath the benedictory shade of the planes.

"*En route!*" said the shrill voice of Mrs. Forman. "Ethel! Mr. Graham! The best of things must end."

"To-night," thought Mr. Lucas, "they will light the little lamp by the shrine. And when we all sit together on the balcony, perhaps they will tell me which offerings they put up."

"I beg your pardon, Mr. Lucas," said Graham, "but they want to fold up the rug you are sitting on."

Mr. Lucas got up, saying to himself: "Ethel shall go to bed first, and then I will try to tell them about my offering too—for it is a thing I must do. I think they will understand if I am left with them alone."

Ethel touched him on the cheek. "Papa! I've called you three times. All the mules are here."

"Mules? What mules?"

"Our mules. We're all waiting. Oh, Mr. Graham, do help my father on."

"I don't know what you're talking about, Ethel."

"My dearest papa, we must start. You know we have to get to Olympia to-night."

Mr. Lucas in pompous, confident tones replied: "I always did wish, Ethel, that you had a better head for plans. You know perfectly well that we are putting in a week here. It is your own suggestion."

Ethel was startled into impoliteness. "What a perfectly ridiculous idea. You must have known I was joking. Of course I meant I wished we could."

"Ah! if we could only do what we wished!" sighed Mrs. Forman, already seated on her mule.

"Surely," Ethel continued in calmer tones, "you didn't think I meant it."

"Most certainly I did. I have made all my plans on the supposition that we are stopping here, and it will be extremely inconvenient, indeed, impossible for me to start."

He delivered this remark with an air of great conviction, and Mrs. Forman and Mr. Graham had to turn away to hide their smiles.

"I am sorry I spoke so carelessly; it was wrong of me. But, you know, we can't break up our party, and even one night here would make us miss the boat at Patras."

Mrs. Forman, in an aside, called Mr. Graham's attention to the excellent way in which Ethel managed her father.

"I don't mind about the Patras boat. You said that we should stop here, and we are stopping."

It seemed as if the inhabitants of the Khan had divined in some mysterious way that the altercation touched them. The old woman stopped her spinning, while the young man and the two children stood behind Mr. Lucas, as if supporting him.

Neither arguments nor entreaties moved him. He said little, but he was absolutely determined, because for the first time he saw his daily life aright. What need had he to return to England? Who would miss him? His friends were dead or cold. Ethel loved him in a way, but, as was right, she had other interests. His other children he seldom saw. He had only one other relative, his sister Julia, whom he both feared and hated. It was no effort to struggle. He would be a fool as well as a coward if he stirred from the place which brought him happiness and peace.

At last Ethel, to humour him, and not disinclined to air her modern Greek, went into the Khan with the astonished dragoman to look at the rooms. The woman inside received them with loud welcomes, and the young man, when no one was looking, began to lead Mr. Lucas' mule to the stable.

"Drop it, you brigand!" shouted Graham, who always declared that foreigners could understand English if they chose. He was right, for the man obeyed, and they all stood waiting for Ethel's return.

She emerged at last, with close-gathered skirts, followed by the dragoman bearing the little pig, which he had bought at a bargain.

"My dear papa, I will do all I can for you, but stop in that Khan—no."

"Are there—fleas?" asked Mrs. Forman.

Ethel intimated that "fleas" was not the word.

"Well, I am afraid that settles it," said Mrs. Forman, "I know how particular Mr. Lucas is."

"It does not settle it," said Mr. Lucas. "Ethel, you go on. I do not want you. I don't know why I ever consulted you. I shall stop here alone."

"That is absolute nonsense," said Ethel, losing her temper. "How can you be left alone at your age? How would you get your meals or your bath? All your letters are waiting for you at Patras. You'll miss the boat. That means missing the London operas, and upsetting all your engagements for the month. And as if you could travel by yourself!"

"They might knife you," was Mr. Graham's contribution.

The Greeks said nothing; but whenever Mr. Lucas looked their way, they beckoned him towards the Khan. The children would even have drawn him by the coat, and the old woman on the balcony stopped her almost completed spinning, and fixed him with mysterious appealing eyes. As he fought, the issue assumed gigantic proportions, and he believed that he was not merely stopping because he had regained youth or seen beauty or found happiness, but because in, that place and with those people a supreme event was awaiting him which would transfigure the face of the world. The moment was so tremendous that he abandoned words and arguments as useless, and rested on the strength of his mighty unrevealed allies: silent men, murmuring water, and whispering trees. For the whole place called with one voice, articulate to him, and his garrulous opponents became every minute more meaningless and absurd. Soon they would be tired and go chattering away into the sun, leaving him to the cool grove and the moonlight and the destiny he foresaw.

Mrs. Forman and the dragoman had indeed already started, amid the piercing screams of the little pig, and the struggle might have gone on indefinitely if Ethel had not called in Mr. Graham.

"Can you help me?" she whispered. "He is absolutely unmanageable."

"I'm no good at arguing—but if I could help you in any other way——" and he looked down complacently at his well-made figure.

Ethel hesitated. Then she said: "Help me in any way you can. After all, it is for his good that we do it."

"Then have his mule led up behind him."

So when Mr. Lucas thought he had gained the day, he suddenly felt himself lifted off the ground, and sat sideways on the saddle, and at the same time the mule started off at a trot. He said nothing, for he had nothing to say, and even his face showed little emotion as he felt the shade pass and heard the sound of the water cease. Mr. Graham was running at his side, hat in hand, apologizing.

"I know I had no business to do it, and I do beg your pardon awfully. But I do hope that some day you too will feel that I was—damn!"

A stone had caught him in the middle of the back. It was thrown by the little boy, who was pursuing them along the mule track. He was followed by his sister, also throwing stones.

Ethel screamed to the dragoman, who was some way ahead with Mrs. Forman, but before he could rejoin them, another adversary appeared. It was the young Greek, who had cut them off in front, and now dashed down at Mr. Lucas' bridle. Fortunately Graham was an expert boxer, and it did not take him a moment to beat down the youth's feeble defence, and to send him sprawling with a bleeding mouth into the asphodel. By this time the dragoman had arrived, the children, alarmed at the fate of their brother, had desisted, and the rescue party, if such it is to be considered, retired in disorder to the trees.

"Little devils!" said Graham, laughing; with triumph. "That's the modern Greek all over. Your father meant money if he stopped, and they consider we were taking it out of their pocket."

"Oh, they are terrible—simple savages! I don't know how I shall ever thank you. You've saved my father."

"I only hope you didn't think me brutal."

"No," replied Ethel with a little sigh. "I admire strength."

Meanwhile the cavalcade reformed, and Mr. Lucas, who, as Mrs. Forman said, bore his disappointment wonderfully well, was put comfortably on to his mule. They hurried up the opposite hillside, fearful of another attack, and it was not until they had left the eventful place far behind that Ethel found an opportunity to speak to her father and ask his pardon for the way she had treated him.

"You seemed so different, dear father, and you quite frightened me. Now I feel that you are your old self again."

He did not answer, and she concluded that he was not unnaturally offended at her behaviour.

By one of those curious tricks of mountain scenery, the place they had left an hour before suddenly reappeared far below them. The Khan was hidden under the green dome, but in the open there still stood three figures, and through the pure air rose up a faint cry of defiance or farewell.

Mr. Lucas stopped irresolutely, and let the reins fall from his hand.

"Come, father dear," said Ethel gently.

He obeyed, and in another moment a spur of the hill hid the dangerous scene for ever.

II

It was breakfast time, but the gas was alight, owing to the fog. Mr. Lucas was in the middle of an account of a bad night he had spent, Ethel, who was to be married in a few weeks, had her arms on the table, listening.

"First the door bell rang, then you came back from the theatre. Then the dog started, and after the dog the cat. And at three in the morning a young hooligan passed by singing. Oh yes: then there was the water gurgling in the pipe above my head."

"I think that was only the bath water running away," said Ethel, looking rather worn.

"Well, there's nothing I dislike more than running water. It's perfectly impossible to sleep in the house. I shall give it up. I shall give notice next quarter. I shall tell the landlord plainly, 'The reason I am giving up the house is this: it is perfectly impossible to sleep in it.' If he says—says—well, what has he got to say?"

"Some more toast, father?"

"Thank you, my dear." He took it, and there was an interval of peace.

But he soon recommenced. "I'm not going to submit to the practising next door as tamely as they think. I wrote and told them so—didn't I?"

"Yes," said Ethel, who had taken care that the letter should not reach. "I have seen the governess, and she has promised to arrange it differently. And Aunt Julia hates noise. It will sure to be all right."

Her aunt, being the only unattached member of the family, was coming to keep house for her father when she left him. The reference was not a happy one, and Mr. Lucas commenced a series of half articulate sighs, which was only stopped by the arrival of the post.

"Oh, what a parcel!" cried Ethel. "For me! What can it be! Greek stamps. This is most exciting!"

It proved to be some asphodel bulbs, sent by Mrs. Forman from Athens for planting in the conservatory.

"Doesn't it bring it all back! You remember the asphodels, father. And all wrapped up in Greek newspapers. I wonder if I can read them still. I used to be able to, you know."

She rattled on, hoping to conceal the laughter of the children next door—a favourite source of querulousness at breakfast time.

"Listen to me! 'A rural disaster.' Oh, I've hit on something sad. But never mind. 'Last Tuesday at Plataniste, in the province of messenia, a shocking tragedy occurred. A large tree'—aren't I getting on well?—'blew down in the night and'—wait a minute—oh, dear! 'crushed to death the five occupants of the little Khan there, who had apparently been sitting in the balcony. The bodies of Maria Rhomaides, the aged proprietress, and of her daughter, aged forty-six, were easily recognizable, whereas that of her grandson'—oh, the rest is really too horrid; I wish I had never tried it, and what's more I feel to have heard the name Plataniste before. We didn't stop there, did we, in the spring?"

"We had lunch," said Mr. Lucas, with a faint expression of trouble on his vacant face. "Perhaps it was where the dragoman bought the pig."

"Of course," said Ethel in a nervous voice. "Where the dragoman bought the little pig. How terrible!"

"Very terrible!" said her father, whose attention was wandering to the noisy children next door. Ethel suddenly started to her feet with genuine interest.

"Good gracious!" she exclaimed. "This is an old paper. It happened not lately but in April—the night of Tuesday the eighteenth—and we—we must have been there in the afternoon."

"So we were," said Mr. Lucas. She put her hand to her heart, scarcely able to speak.

"Father, dear father, I must say it: you wanted to stop there. All those people, those poor half savage people, tried, to keep you, and they're dead. The whole place, it says, is in ruins, and even the stream has changed its course. Father, dear, if it had not been for me, and if Arthur had not helped me, you must have been killed."

Mr. Lucas waved his hand irritably. "It is not a bit of good speaking to the governess, I shall write to the landlord and say, 'The reason I am giving up the house is this: the dog barks, the children next door are intolerable, and I cannot stand the noise of running water.'"

Ethel did not check his babbling. She was aghast at the narrowness of the escape, and for a long time kept silence. At last she said: "Such a marvellous deliverance does make one believe in Providence."

Mr. Lucas, who was still composing his letter to the landlord, did not reply.

Five Novels by Thomas Hardy - Far From The Madding Crowd, The Return of the Native, The Mayor of Casterbridge, Tess of the d'Urbervilles, Jude the Obscure (complete and unabridged)
Thomas Hardy
Benediction Classics, 2013
1114 pages
ISBN: 978-1-78139-356-7

Available from www.amazon.com, www.amazon.co.uk

Thomas Hardy, (1840 - 1928) was an English novelist and poet. He was highly critical of Victorian society and focussed mainly on the declining rural communities.

Wilkie Collins Collection (complete and unabridged):The Woman in White, The Moonstone, No Name, Armadale
Wilkie Collins
Benediction Classics, 2012
1136 pages
ISBN: 978-1-78139-328-4

Available from www.amazon.com, www.amazon.co.uk

Wilkie Collins (1824-1889) is best known as the innovator of the detective novel. He was a prolific writer, with 30 novels, more than 60 short stories, 14 plays, and more than 100 non-fiction pieces to his name. He was a close friend of Charles Dickens and one of the best known and loved Victorian Fiction writers. After his death, his popularity diminished as Dickens's grew. Now, Collins is once again becoming popular with most of his books in print and film, television and radio adaptations being made. There is much still to be discovered about this great author and this volume contains his four most popular novels.

Famous Works - Mrs Dalloway, To the Lighthouse, Orlando, & A Room of One's Own
Virginia Woolf
Benediction Classics, 2012
454 pages
ISBN: 978-1-78139-207-2

Available from www.amazon.com, www.amazon.co.uk

Virginia Woolf is thought to be the foremost modernist writer of the twentieth century. Her most famous writings are reproduced in full in a single volume: Mrs Dalloway (1925), - A day in the life of a woman who is preparing a party. The novel stretches forwards and backwards in time as Clarissa wonders about the choices she has made. To the Lighthouse (1927) - a novel about loss and subjectivity. The Modern Library named it as No. 15 on its list of the 100 best English-language novels of the 20th century in 1998. It was also chosen by TIME magazine as one of the one hundred best English-language novels from 1923 to present in 2005. Orlando (1928) - a semi-biographical novel based in part on her bisexual lover Vita Sackville-West, it is considered to be Woolf's most accessible work. A Room of One's Own (1929) - a long essay based on talks that Woolf gave at Cambridge. It is seen as a feminist text, with women writers needing to find a place in a tradition dominated by men.

On the Eve
Ivan Turgenev
Benediction Classics, 2011
176 pages
ISBN: 978-1-84902-310-8

Available from www.amazon.com, www.amazon.co.uk

On the Eve is the third novel written by the famous Russian writer Ivan Turgenev, best known for his novel Fathers and Sons. It is a story, set in 1853, of love during the Crimean War and at a time of social upheaval. The heroine, Elena, is a charming, serious and courageous young woman. She is concerned about justice, but this finds no outlet in her middle class world, until she is introduced Insarov, a man below her social status, but whose idealism matches her own. He becomes Elena's husband and changes her life.

Also from Benediction Books ...

Wandering Between Two Worlds: Essays on Faith and Art
Anita Mathias
Benediction Books, 2007
152 pages
ISBN: 0955373700

Available from www.amazon.com, www.amazon.co.uk

In these wide-ranging lyrical essays, Anita Mathias writes, in lush, lovely prose, of her naughty Catholic childhood in Jamshedpur, India; her large, eccentric family in Mangalore, a sea-coast town converted by the Portuguese in the sixteenth century; her rebellion and atheism as a teenager in her Himalayan boarding school, run by German missionary nuns, St. Mary's Convent, Nainital; and her abrupt religious conversion after which she entered Mother Teresa's convent in Calcutta as a novice. Later rich, elegant essays explore the dualities of her life as a writer, mother, and Christian in the United States-- Domesticity and Art, Writing and Prayer, and the experience of being "an alien and stranger" as an immigrant in America, sensing the need for roots.

About the Author

Anita Mathias is the author of *Wandering Between Two Worlds: Essays on Faith and Art*. She has a B.A. and M.A. in English from Somerville College, Oxford University, and an M.A. in Creative Writing from the Ohio State University, USA. Anita won a National Endowment of the Arts fellowship in Creative Non-fiction in 1997. She lives in Oxford, England with her husband, Roy, and her daughters, Zoe and Irene.

Anita's website:
http://www.anitamathias.com, and
Anita's blog Dreaming Beneath the Spires:
http://dreamingbeneaththespires.blogspot.com

The Church That Had Too Much
Anita Mathias
Benediction Books, 2010
52 pages
ISBN: 9781849026567

Available from www.amazon.com, www.amazon.co.uk

The Church That Had Too Much was very well-intentioned. She wanted to love God, she wanted to love people, but she was both hampered by her muchness and the abundance of her possessions, and beset by ambition, power struggles and snobbery. Read about the surprising way The Church That Had Too Much began to resolve her problems in this deceptively simple and enchanting fable.

About the Author

Anita Mathias is the author of *Wandering Between Two Worlds: Essays on Faith and Art*. She has a B.A. and M.A. in English from Somerville College, Oxford University, and an M.A. in Creative Writing from the Ohio State University, USA. Anita won a National Endowment of the Arts fellowship in Creative Non-fiction in 1997. She lives in Oxford, England with her husband, Roy, and her daughters, Zoe and Irene.

Anita's website:
http://www.anitamathias.com, and
Anita's blog Dreaming Beneath the Spires:
http://dreamingbeneaththespires.blogspot.com

www.ingramcontent.com/pod-product-compliance
Lightning Source LLC
Chambersburg PA
CBHW081128300726
48982CB00005B/890